A Marriage Worth the Earning

the

Earning

A Pride and Prejudice Sequel

Mary L. Sherwood

A Marriage Worth the Earning

the

Earning

Volume I

~~To Have and to Hold~~

ISBN-10:   1442134550
ISBN-13:   978-1442134553

Copyright © 2009 by Mary L. Sherwood

First Edition: April 2009

Cover Photo: ©NTPL/Stephen Robson

Back Cover: ©iStock

Cover design copyright © 2009 by Mary L. Sherwood

This book is dedicated to my mother, Mary Elizabeth McCarthy, who instilled in me a love for literature, and to Jane Austen, who created some of the most inspiring characters of fiction, namely, Mr. Fitzwilliam Darcy and Miss Elizabeth Bennet.

~~~*~~*~~*~~*~~*~~~

ACKNOWLEDGEMENTS

I wish to convey my heartfelt appreciation to all who have in any way assisted me in writing this book. It is with gladness that I acknowledge the service imparted by numerous JA enthusiasts, given that without their help and aptitude this book would not have been published. I wish to offer special thanks to Adam Crown for his permission in allowing me to quote directly from his site, info@classicalfencing.com, and to Mary K. Baxley for the long tireless hours she has given in the preparation of this volume. Her expertise in formatting and design has been a godsend as has her enthusiasm. My thanks would not be complete without mentioning the encouragement of family and friends. My husband, Gary, served as the best sounding board an author could have and my son-in-law, Paul, goaded me to write my vision of the Darcy marriage in the first place. Likewise, Grace, Stuart, Whitney, Mary Kathryn, and Spencer have lent their endorsement either in direct approbation or lack of complaint as the matter may be. Last, but in no means least, a sincere tribute to Nancy, Margie, Wyvone, tJean, Dorothee, and Sybil for their unstinting support.

Chapter One

Honeymoon Bliss

It is a universal truth that the course of true love never did run smooth—or so said the famous bard, William Shakespeare.

~~*****~~

The trip from London had been tedious. Rain had stalled their carriage twice, forcing the bride and groom to stay an extra night at a local inn along the road to Derbyshire. Mr. Fitzwilliam Darcy gazed upon his wife's features as she slept. Had one week already passed since their wedding? He looked upon her fondly and lifted his index finger to trace her left brow. Oh, how he dearly loved the manner in which she raised that impish brow to him in countless ways.

He leaned close to his wife's ear and whispered, "Wake up, my dearest, for we are almost here, and the sun is at last shining to provide the Mistress of Pemberley a proper welcome to her new home."

Darcy's eyes glistened with pleasure as he detected a faint smile upon his wife's lips. With this encouragement, he leaned in fully and raised Elizabeth to his chest. With one hand he supported the back of her head while the other hand cradled her chin upward. He only paused momentarily to take a brief look at her beautiful countenance before bestowing the sweetest of kisses upon those smiling lips.

Her eyes opened with a slight flutter. She gazed adoringly upon her husband and softly parted her lips. "I love you, Fitzwilliam."

He smiled knowingly and kissed the tip of her nose before he rejoined, "As I love you."

Elizabeth stroked his forehead with her fingertips and took delight in how tousled his hair had become during their journey. Slowly, she started to weave her fingers through his tufted curls in an attempt to bring some semblance of tidiness to his unruly locks. "How close are we now?"

"A little over a mile to go."

Elizabeth immediately sat upright and began to anxiously search for her hairpins which had loosened as she slept. After straightening her hair and gown and donning her bonnet in a somewhat frenzied manner, she became conscious of her husband's amused expression. He reached for her hand and gave it a reassuring squeeze.

"Everyone will love you, Elizabeth, just as I do."

She smiled, rather unsure of such an appraisal. Of her husband's love she was certain, but, as to the rest, only time would tell.

"I am looking forward to seeing the house again," Elizabeth cried. "Walking the grounds and, well... everything!"

Darcy smiled in deep gratification for her spirited expectations and took great delight that this part of their life together had commenced. He relished that their first week of marriage had been complete bliss, and he could only foresee even greater happiness with *his* Elizabeth here with him at his beloved Pemberley. His thoughts were sublime, an ecstasy he had long allowed himself to imagine in excess was finally a reality.

As the carriage slowly moved across the stone bridge, Elizabeth cried out, "Oh look! Fitzwilliam, the house is now appearing!"

He chuckled as he witnessed her eagerness. His own eyes had beheld the same sight numerous times, but now, having Elizabeth by his side and witnessing the enthusiasm through her eyes only intensified the pleasure he had always likewise experienced.

Having come to a stop in front of the central portico, they both donned their gloves in preparation to exit the carriage. As they approached the house, Elizabeth noticed the large crowd gathered round the marble wellhead and also lined up upon the courtyard steps. "Oh, Fitzwilliam, so many people... And they will all surely freeze while waiting for us."

"Yes, I suppose it is a great lot. Pemberley House employs six and seventy individuals for the maintenance of the house, stables, grounds, and many other services."

"I will never be able to remember all their names!"

"Elizabeth, it is not necessary for you to know all their names. Only the ones with whom you deal directly will be sufficient."

Darcy alighted from the carriage first and then helped his wife descend. He turned to Mrs. Reynolds, and all the chief introductions were made. Then, addressing the remainder of the eager gathering, he quickly proclaimed, "Mrs. Darcy!" Loud cheers erupted spontaneously as Fitzwilliam Darcy, Lord and Master of his Countryseat, ascended the steps of Pemberley House with his wife, and upon reaching the top, swiftly lifted a stunned Elizabeth into his arms and carried her over the threshold of their home with a smile befitting a king. This gesture ignited a new round of joyous cheers from the servants and staff.

Once they had entered the great hall, Mr. Darcy gently placed his bride upon her own two feet. Elizabeth's eyes were still wide in bewilderment at her husband's unusual public display of affection. In a flurry, beaver, bonnet, coats and gloves were discarded. Elizabeth took her husband's proffered arm and together they ascended the grand staircase in unison. Her thoughts returned to the previous July and the first time she climbed these same steps. Things were so different then. She had been filled with uneasiness at being in the home of Mr. Darcy, and at the same time, in awe of the elegance that surrounded her.

Lost in her thoughts, her reverie was interrupted as her husband paused to open the door to a bedchamber and proceeded to guide her about the room. "This is the mistress' chamber. It was my mother's and is now yours. Do not hesitate to change a thing, Lizzy. I want you to be completely happy and comfortable with your surroundings."

Elizabeth noted that the furnishings were plush, yet regal in appearance.

"This door leads to my own room," Darcy stated.

With a gentle smile, he opened the door, and Elizabeth entered without the trepidation she felt at his – their – townhouse in London. One week was sufficient to overcome the shyness she felt on that occasion. Darcy placed a hand upon her shoulder and asked if all was satisfactory, though he already knew the answer. It took very little of monetary value to please Elizabeth, but, still, he needed to hear her say the words.

"Yes, my love, it is all so wonderful. Indeed, it is a splendour I could not have imagined." Elizabeth turned and gazed upon her husband. "You are wonderful," and, with these words expressed, she slid her hands about his neck, and, upon tiptoed feet, expressed her satisfaction in a way that mere words never could.

This happy demonstration was interrupted by the sound of Mrs. Reynolds clearing her throat, and they turned to see the housekeeper standing in the doorway. "Ahem, excuse me, sir, but Mrs. Potter wanted me to enquire if dinner should be served at the usual hour."

Darcy stepped back from Elizabeth and began to straighten his cravat. "Yes, that will be fine. We shall rest here the remainder of the afternoon. You may send Clara and Chaffin in an hour before."

Again, Elizabeth's eyes opened wide with this bold declaration from her husband pertaining to a rest that would continue for the duration of *five* hours. Her face burned crimson with the thought of what Mrs. Reynolds thoughts might be, and, as soon as the dear lady had departed, private thoughts were communicated quite openly.

"Fitzwilliam Darcy, whatever were you thinking to have told her we would rest for *five* uninterrupted hours in the middle of the day. What will they think of me?"

With barely a shrug of his shoulders, he replied in an even tone, "Let them think what they may. Do not trouble yourself. I should think such concerns would be completely behind you, Lizzy, especially in consideration of the past week."

"My dear Mr. Darcy, I would remind you that we are now no longer sequestered with only a few servants about, and, besides, I do so like Mrs. Reynolds and want to make a good first impression."

"Lizzy, five hours alone in your own bedchamber after a strenuous journey on a cold, muddied road on your first day as the mistress in your new home will not lessen Mrs. Reynolds's opinion of you. Trust me. She will only think you very tired and in need of much rest."

This reasoning seemed to placate Elizabeth's fears, and a faint smile graced her lips as she sighed in relief. "When you put it in such a reasonable light, I do feel quite relieved."

Darcy smiled lovingly as he captured her in a warm embrace, gently stroking her back before saying in a flippant air, "Of course, my dear girl, since you are standing in my chamber, she just might take you for the wanton woman you are."

Elizabeth stiffened and quickly looked into her husband's face. Their eyes locked, and, after several seconds of silence, both broke into jovial laughter at the silliness of it all. Mr. Darcy was indeed becoming a true proficient with a tease.

Dinner was a scrumptious affair. No one seemed to take notice that the couple claimed fatigue, and thus retired early for the evening. Yet, as they departed, the butler seemed to walk with a quicker step, the maids hummed pleasant tunes while they cleared the dishes, and Mr. Chaffin and Clara found extra time on their hands as their services would not be required until noon the following day. And, for the whole of the evening, many a servant noticed a smile enhancing the usually stern features of Mrs. Reynolds.

~*~

Chapter Two

A Week of Idyllic Languor

Darcy and Elizabeth basked in the luxury of late mornings, long naps and early nights. Snow had fallen the night after their arrival, and the weather served as an inducement for the couple to wile away the hours of each day in the warmth of their bed. In fact, so much snow had fallen that much of Pemberley seemed lulled into silence. The servants went about their usual tasks, but at a slower pace, since only essential chores had to be done. Elizabeth loved the snow, and, even though she had experienced it in Hertfordshire and London, nothing could have prepared her for the longer winter season of Derbyshire.

Although winters at Longbourn were almost always cold and usually produced snowfall every year, the storms were of short duration. Snow would blow in one day and blow out the next. Yet presently, Elizabeth found the snowfall to be enchanting. It seemed to her as if the Heavens had deliberately bestowed it upon Pemberley as a manifestation of its sanction of their marriage. She stood silently at the balcony doors of her chamber, mesmerized by the huge flakes gently falling from the sky.

The past week had been splendid, alone with Fitzwilliam all to herself. But she was beginning to feel a little restless and a bit uneasy at only leaving their rooms for a brief period during dinner. Their other meals were sent up on trays, and she felt certain the staff would think she had influenced her husband in favour of idle and lascivious behaviour. Maybe Lady Catherine was right after all: she, Elizabeth Bennet Darcy, was indeed polluting the shades of Pemberley. Oh! she thought, this will not do! And with this inner conviction, Elizabeth slipped a shawl about her shoulders and slippers upon her feet and marched boldly over to the bed where her husband still lay, clad as nature had made him.

Gently at first, she shook his shoulder. "Fitzwilliam, my love, do get up. The snow is lovely, and I do so want you to come and enjoy it with me." No response was to be had. She expelled air and turned her lips in a sideways pout. "Please, my love, it is almost noon, and I am tired of lying about so. Let us go for a walk or do something."

Darcy pulled the covers up higher upon his chest and then drew the pillow over his head as he shifted upon his belly. By now, Elizabeth's exasperation was quite evident upon her features, but, as with most men, Darcy was unaware of just how annoyed his wife was becoming. She would make one last plea before her assault began. Lying on the bed next to him, she ran her fingers through his hair.

"My love, please get up and get dressed so you can come outside with me to enjoy the snow. It is so beautiful, and the air will feel so exhilarating." Darcy stirred a little, and she began to smile in hopeful anticipation. Seconds passed. She tilted her head and tried to discern if he had fallen asleep again, but, while so doing, her wrist was seized by her husband's left hand. She jumped slightly at the sudden action and tried to pull her hand from his grasp, but he only held her wrist tighter. Elizabeth's ire piqued, and she quickly sat up in order to have the momentum of her legs to add strength for her escape. It was of no use. With one hand only, Darcy had managed to pull her back upon the bed and pin her down with the whole of his arm. She lay upon her back in great agitation.

"Pray! Do tell me, sir, right now, if you have any intention of accompanying me to enjoy this fine winter's day."

Silenced ensued only a little longer before Darcy replied in a rather roguish voice from beneath his pillow, "I do, dear lady, want to enjoy, as you say, 'exhilaration and beauty', but at this moment I do not find them to lie with the snow."

Elizabeth gave a quick roll of her eyes, and her brows fused in consternation as she let out an audible sigh. As she lay there thinking of a means of escape, she discerned a soft snore next to her. Ever so slowly, and with much care, did she start to slide over to the side of the bed while her husband's heavy arm still lay atop her. When she had reached the edge of the mattress, she delicately swung her legs over while her upper body remained prisoner to a sleeping guard. She gingerly took hold of his forearm and raised it slightly above her as she manoeuvred herself the rest of the way off the bed. Standing now, she slowly lowered the offending limb. Glued to the spot, she quickly decided her next course of action. Slinking across the room, she went to her boudoir and put on her heavy woollen coat and scarf over her nightgown. Then, with increasing caution, she crept to the balcony doors and softly turned the knob. Once outside, she pulled the door slightly ajar, and, in wicked merriment, began to gather snow from the balustrade. Quickly forming a snowball of gargantuan proportions, she pressed the door open again with the swing of her hip and pushed it closed with the back of her foot. Eyes shining in delight, she did not once reconsider the cruel assassination that was imminent. Instead, Elizabeth smiled widely, bit down on her lower lip, and boldly approached the bed. Swiftly, she dropped the boulder of snow upon her unsuspecting husband's bare back.

"Oohooo!" Darcy's spine quivered from the bitter shock. "Why, you little minx—you had better run!"

With this declaration, Darcy bolted from the mattress and sprang onto the floor. Elizabeth's heart pounded wildly in her ears as she ran out onto the balcony. In swift pursuit, her husband ran to the open door, but, with the sudden surge of Arctic chill, stopped in remembrance of his nakedness and turned to retrieve a sheet from the bedding. If he had looked into his wife's fine eyes beforehand, he might have noticed them ignited with desire as they observed the comeliness of his form. He was indeed a dashing man!

Elizabeth had stationed herself next to the balustrade with a snowball gathered in each hand. In no hurry now, Darcy, dressed in toga fashion, approached the open door steadily. He wore an expression of confidence as his eyes narrowed upon his wife's face, and, with a tight voice, he exclaimed, "We shall have it your way, Lizzy."

Two snowballs flew in succession, one pelting his chest while the other struck directly in his face. Darcy stopped and tightened his lips with determination as he wiped the snow from his eyes. Elizabeth's face was aglow with the spectacle of her husband's appearance. She turned quickly to gather more ammunition, but, before succeeding, her activity was apprehended by a pair of strong arms. She shrieked with glee as her husband bound her to him.

"You had better say your prayers, my dear girl, because if you think you are going to get out of this one, you are sadly mistaken."

Then, securing Elizabeth with one arm while gathering snow with the other, he commenced to christen her without mercy. He began by packing snow down the nape of her neck and then unfastened the top of her coat and crammed it down the front of her nightdress. All the while, pleas from his dear lady were quite perceptible, but to no avail. Taking one last mound of snow, he began to stuff it in her mouth. Halfway between laughter and stifled sobs, Darcy realized that tears were streaming down Elizabeth's rosy cheeks. His heart was filled with contrition, and he instantly embraced his dear wife to his breast.

"Oh, Lizzy, I will stop now. I am so sorry my love. I have been too harsh. Come, look at me and tell me all is forgiven."

Elizabeth buried her face into his chest and slowly turned her head from side to side in answer. Darcy was crestfallen that he had wounded her so. He encircled her waist with his arms and began softly kissing the top of her head. He then lifted her chin up so she would look at him. Her eyes were swollen and full of tears. With a heavy heart, he gently brushed the accumulated snow from her face and hair and from around her scarf. She looked at him in calm admiration, and he felt relief. Then, from ambush, he felt the cold sting of snow on his ear as uncontrollable laughter emanated from his wife. He was incredulous.

"Why, you little minx!" He swiftly lifted his squealing wife into his arms and declared in a most ominous tone, "Enough of this! I know how to suppress such cheekiness in you!"

Elizabeth became hysterical as he carried her through the open door. Yet, her outburst did not deter him. He closed the door with a decided push of his derrière then strode across the room and plunked his howling wife upon the bed.

Aggressively, he growled, "Come, my little vixen, and we shall tame you back into the woman I married… or then again, maybe not."

Darcy looked deeply into his wife's eyes. She, in turn, continued to giggle with satisfaction, but the mockery soon ceased when her eyes swept over her husband's shoulders, down his chest and then up again along the length of his neck and across the contour of his unshaven jaw line. Her eyes ceased their wanderings when they instinctively met his mischievously twinkling, dark brown ones.

Her left brow arched as she saucily asked, "What do you plan to do to me, sir?"

"Whatever my designs will be, Lizzy, I promise you it will be *slow* torture."

No more words were spoken, for none were needed. Sweet caresses began to be exchanged and a soggy coat, scarf and gown were soon discarded. Elizabeth would have to forgo her desired walk for the present. In the meantime, she seemed not to mind that she was right back where she started.

Unbeknownst to the newlyweds, three sets of eyes had witnessed their exhibition from a clearing not thirty yards distant. Mr. Sheldon, Darcy's steward, together with two of the tenant farmer's sons, Thomas and Joseph Wilkens, had earlier removed the wheels from the wood wagon and placed sleigh bobs on the hubs. They were loading the cut wood to take to the kitchen when their attention was suddenly drawn to the master and mistress upon their balcony. Struck speechless after the performance, they eyed each other briefly before Mr. Sheldon cleared his throat and ordered the brothers to get on with the loading in case the snowfall returned. Even though no words were exchanged, all three were in complete shock that the sombre Mr. Darcy had played like a schoolboy out in the wide open, though, a little less formally attired.

~*~

When Mr. Sheldon and the Wilkens boys arrived at the cellar drop, Mrs. Potter came out and told the steward that he and the boys were to come in and have some freshly made biscuits and cocoa after they finished their chore. This invitation was a welcome one for Thomas and Joseph who had seldom partaken of the rich drink. They worked hard at the task at hand, not only for the cocoa, but for their escape into the warmth of Pemberley's kitchen. Besides, the invitation also brought a respite from their usual routine and there was always something new to be seen, tasted, or heard from within.

Before the young men entered, Mr. Sheldon reminded them to scrape the snow from their boots and shake off their hats as well. When they crossed the threshold, Thomas noticed a small group of young housemaids seated at the far end of one of the long tables. They spoke in hushed tones and then broke out into giggles. Mrs. Potter looked at the two lads and indicated for them to have a seat at the opposite end of the table. Mr. Sheldon had walked over to where some of the men were seated. They had fallen into conversation with Mr. Manning, Pemberley's overseer.

The cook called over to the maids and cried, "Sally, get these here men a plate of biscuits and some mugs of cocoa." The maid immediately arose and went straightway to the cupboard. She returned quickly and placed the biscuits and mugs on the table. She glanced down at Thomas and said she would return with a pot of chocolate. Mr. Sheldon then called over for young Joseph to join him and Mr. Manning. When Sally returned, she boldly smiled upon Thomas, or Tommy as she had always heard him called. She started to fill the mugs, and Thomas quickly spoke because he knew an opportunity like this was rare.

"What were you and the others whispering about?"

Sally cocked her head to the right as she poured and replied, "Nothin'."

"For speaking about nothing, you sure do have a way of thinking it's funny. Were you laughing at us or, more importantly, at me?"

The girl rolled her eyes and told him in no uncertain terms that it was nothing about him. It was about something they were supposed to never talk about. This information only made Tommy more curious.

"Will you tell me?"

Sally smiled and told him she would, but if it got out that they were talking about this, Mrs. Reynolds would have their hides.

She then in a very low voice stated, "It ain't really nothin' bad, it's just that the other afternoon, Mary and me was gatherin' the linens and thought the Master and Mistress was gone since the door was open. So, we start takin' off the sheets, and we hear laughter comin' from the balcony. We look on over and see Mr. Darcy stickin' out his tongue to catch snowflakes. We hurried on out of there. Mary, of course, can't stop talking 'bout it 'cause she thinks it's so funny that a grown man like him would do such a childish thing. So, you don't have to be worryin', Tommy Wilkens, if we've been laughing at you, 'cause you see it was 'bout nothin' at all except somethin' that could get us into trouble."

Intrigued by Sally's tale and by what he had earlier witnessed with his own eyes, he asked, "Sally, do you think Mr. Darcy was being childish?"

Her eyes were downcast when she softly replied, "It don't seem childish to me. It seemed...nice."

Suddenly, the conversation was interrupted by Mrs. Potter's request that the maid take some cocoa over to Mr. Sheldon. Thomas gave Sally a quick grin, and, with a nod of her head, she was gone.

Elizabeth slept soundly in her husband's arms. He sighed as he buried his face in her hair, which was still damp from the snow. Darcy smiled as he remembered the excitement in her eyes because she had managed to entice him to enjoy the snow after all. Oh, how he loved her vivaciousness! It was truly one of the things which had caught his notice of her in the first place. He reached over and pulled the bell chord. Minutes later, Clara stepped in, and, seeing her mistress asleep, addressed Mr. Darcy.

"Yes, sir?"

"Clara, prepare Mrs. Darcy's bath now, and have Chaffin prepare mine as well. We will be coming down for luncheon today."

"Very good, sir." With a curtsey, she exited the room.

Elizabeth had awakened and heard her husband's directive.

"Fitzwilliam, we are not having our meal brought to our room?"

"No, my dear, sweet wife, we are not. Shall that upset any plans of yours?"

"No, indeed," she replied happily.

Darcy chuckled and embraced her. "My lovely Lizzy, I am afraid that now is the time to relinquish my hold upon all of your company. If it were up to me, I would have us remain as bears to hibernate the whole of the winter in this cosy den. But alas, the time has come for me to share you, at least somewhat, with the world. Georgiana will be here tomorrow accompanied by Richard, so it cannot be helped. I have waited so long to have you to myself that, truthfully, it will be hard to share you again. However, I know you, Elizabeth, and you need the enjoyment of a number of diversions besides being continually impounded in your own chambers."

"Oh, Fitzwilliam, I have loved every moment we have shared. I do not feel that I have been held captive. If so, I must be a most willing prisoner."

This declaration earned a wide smile from her husband. She thought he was so much more handsome when he smiled.

"Oh yes, you have been a most complying hostage, so much so, that I will grant you a probationary sentence."

"What, for good behaviour?"

"For the best of behaviours," he growled.

"So, am I to understand that I have been pardoned?"

"No, such an act has not been granted. I said a probationary period will be granted to you. Yet, if you are found wanting, or shall I say *not* wanting, you will be enslaved at my command."

"Very well, sir. I am most thankful for such leniency and shall not escape but be most solicitous to give a frequent accounting to my sentry."

"See that you do, Lizzy, and all will be well."

She giggled in delight and kissed his cheek. They then parted ways to prepare for the day or what was left of it.

After baths and dressing, Darcy escorted his wife down the stairs. Mrs. Reynolds smiled as she approached them with the information that all was made ready. Elizabeth looked inquisitively at her husband. He led her to the back portico. Servants busily came with coat, mufflers, gloves, beaver and bonnet. Elizabeth's curiosity was high with the whirl of activity, and she petitioned her husband for their impending agenda.

"Mrs. Darcy," he stated in cheer, "your questions will soon be answered." He then offered his arm. His whole countenance beamed with pleasure as he guided Elizabeth through the doors and down the stairs. Elizabeth's concentration on the steps as she descended prevented her noticing the gleaming sleigh, which rested just beyond the courtyard corridor. When she looked up as they neared the arch, she smiled broadly at her husband who relished every second of the surprise.

"Oh, Fitzwilliam, this will be so delightful! I have only been on a sleigh ride twice."

He helped her in and bundled her up under the quilts. Warm bricks were already in place and a basket was placed on the floor of the back seat. Elizabeth suddenly realized there was no driver when Darcy took the reins in his own hands. He slapped the leather straps upon the horses' rumps, and off they dashed.

"I thought you would like to have a change of scenery with your luncheon today, Lizzy. Do you like your surprise, my love?"

"Oh, I do like it. I like it indeed, but, Fitzwilliam Darcy, whenever did you arrange all of this? Was it after our snow fight when I fell asleep?"

"No, actually it was April, yet it was not until yesterday evening that I determined there was sufficient accumulation for a rather splendid display of Pemberley covered in winter's glory."

These words touched Elizabeth as she realized this was yet another of her husband's daydreams of her before his first disastrous proposal. She snuggled close to him and whispered in his ear, "Thank you, my love, for this wonderful surprise. You amaze me with your love, and these past two weeks have been the happiest of my life. You are too good to me."

The happy couple enjoyed the outing tremendously and, after dinner, retired to the library for a reading of Shakespeare's sonnets.

That afternoon, Sally and Mary were called by Mrs. Reynolds to change the linens of the mistress' chambers. This time the girls knew the occupants had left and so worked in relative ease as they gathered the towels and sheets. Mary, however, thought it peculiar that the top sheet was missing. The girls looked under the bed, behind chairs, and in the dressing area. Yet, the article's location remained a mystery until the spring thaw revealed its resting place on the balcony floor.

~*~

Chapter Three

Responsibilities, Trials, and Vexations Commence

The early morning light streamed through the windows of the mistress' chamber. Darcy had told Clara the previous night to leave the curtains open as she prepared the room for their retiring. He had an early appointment with his steward, and Elizabeth was to meet with Mrs. Reynolds. Today she would begin to learn the everyday details involved in being the Mistress of Pemberley. The sunshine had not yet awakened Elizabeth, so Darcy took advantage of the dawn to gaze intently at his wife's features. It astonished him that he once thought her only tolerable. Her skin was milky smooth, and he loved the way her silky, dark hair showered around him as they embraced. Temptation loomed large for the Master of Pemberley. Should he allow Elizabeth to slumber or awaken her and renew the need he felt within? Any rational being would realize that rest was required after such a late night, but rationality held no sway for a man who ardently admired his wife. Fitzwilliam Darcy was, indeed, such a man. He could no longer allow the remaining minutes to tick past without at least having some time to hold his wife before the day's demands encroached upon them.

In breathless anticipation, he began to run his fingers over Elizabeth's face and lightly kissed her brow. The kisses traced a trail to her ear and along her neck.

Elizabeth yawned and then a broad smile spread across her features as she murmured her husband's name.

"Fitzwilliam, why are you still awake? Do you not feel well?"

"It is morning, my dear love, and I find that I cannot leave this bed without bidding you a fitting farewell."

Elizabeth stretched out her arms and yawned. "What time is it?"

"A quarter past six, I believe."

Sleepily, she creased her brows together and asked, "What time is your appointment with Mr. Sheldon?"

"Half past eight."

She drowsily peered at her husband in uncertainty. She then asked, "And what time will Clara and Mr. Chaffin make ready our baths?"

"I told them to come at half an hour past seven."

"So, pray sir, what do you consider a fitting farewell?"

Smiling sheepishly, Darcy gathered Elizabeth into his arms and held her close. "I just wanted to have a moment with you before we go our separate ways. This is, after all, the first day in our marriage, Mrs. Darcy, in which we will not be spending every hour together, and I fear I miss you already."

More awake now, Elizabeth smiled affectionately and hugged her dear husband in return.

"Lizzy, shall you miss me some today, do you think?"

Her brows rose as she formulated her answer. "I know at this moment, rather than feel, that I will miss you... however, I had always perceived when we were separated at the end of the day during our engagement that the reunion was much anticipated and even more so due to the separation. So you see, I shall be thinking of you as I go about this morning with eagerness of our meeting for luncheon."

Darcy, reassured by her lovely words, embraced her more tightly. Their embraces were enhanced with soft kisses, tender caresses and loving words of adoration until the unspoken language of love was rendered.

"Lizzy?"

"Yes, my love?"

"I have been a selfish being all of my life. I fear that I shall never tire of you and that you may go mad for my inability to be satiated."

She raised her brow in a teasing manner and replied, "Never! But I do feel elated to hold such power over you, my dear husband." Then an expression of gravity immediately crossed her visage as her voice slightly quivered, "In fact, it is the opposite that I fear."

Concern lined Darcy's brow as he realized that his Elizabeth feared he would ever not desire her. How were such thoughts conceivable after two weeks filled with constant expressions of love?

Nevertheless, Darcy smiled and exclaimed, "I am glad to hear it, Lizzy. If this truly is the case, then I know we will always assuage each others fears and desires. Thus, we will live in a perpetual state of bliss, utterly and completely. And I, for one, Lizzy, will confirm my desire often, so fear never need be within your breast. Only you, Elizabeth, have captured this heart and only you can bring it the prized joy and pleasures worth having."

One lingering kiss sealed the bargain, and then the conversation turned from affairs of the heart to those of the day. Elizabeth questioned whether his cousin, Colonel Fitzwilliam, and Georgiana would be delayed due to the snowfall, yet Darcy assured her that his Uncle's sleigh would be equipped with two teams of draft horses, and they only had slightly more than two hours' journey, so it was quite probable their plans remained fixed. He then informed her that, after he had breakfasted and met with his steward, he would come in search of her and see if he could be of any assistance. This was gladly agreed upon, and, with one last kiss, the happy couple parted ways to make preparations for the day.

Elizabeth bathed quickly and had Clara pin her hair up simply. Whil Clara worked, Elizabeth observed her maid's disturbed manner in mirror.

"Clara, you seem concerned about something. Is all well?" Clara stopped pinning her mistress' hair and returned Elizabeth's gaze.

"There is something, mistress, and I am concerned of what you might think since I have only been your maid for this past week. I received word yesterday that me Mum is very ill and would like me to come to her."

"Why of course, Clara you should go! I am sure Mr. Darcy can give some assistance in helping with your travel arrangements. Where does your mother live?"

"In Liverpool, ma'am."

"Oh, that is a long way, but I am sure something can be arranged."

With downcast eyes, Clara softly voiced her fears. "It is just that I don't quite know when I might be able to return, and I do so want to be your maid, Mrs. Darcy."

"Oh Clara, do not let that trouble you. I shall speak with Mrs. Reynolds this very morning about a temporary replacement. When you are finished here, you may go and pack your trunk. I will make sure all is taken care of."

Relieved, Clara expressed her thanks and pinned the last curl of Elizabeth's hair. She then curtseyed and began to clean up from the morning bath. Mr. Darcy strode through the dressing area and stood behind Elizabeth as she looked through her jewellery box for a necklace.

"May I suggest this one?"

Elizabeth startled before perceiving her husband's reflection in the mirror.

"Fitzwilliam!" she cried, "I did not realize you were there!" She then observed a slender, blue velvet box in his hand.

"Lizzy, I have been intending to give this to you for some time." He handed her the gift and waited for her to open it. She smiled up at him and then returned her attention to the case. Eagerly, she removed the ribbon and lifted the lid. Inside lay a beautiful, dainty, cross necklace with garnets enmeshed within French wire. The jewel was much like the one she currently owned but was superior in quality and expense.

"I have always noticed how you prefer to wear your cross necklace. I thought you might enjoy having one made with the finest craftsmanship and jewels to be had. May I have the honour?"

Elizabeth's face appeared pensive as she faintly answered in the affirmative and handed her husband the box. He placed the ornament about her neck and then met her eyes in the mirror. "Do you like it, Elizabeth?"

"Oh...why yes," she replied with a weak smile. "It is very elegant, indeed. When did you purchase it?"

"At the beginning of our engagement I commissioned a special jeweller in France to fashion it. The garnets within are some of the finest to be had. arrived at Pemberley while we were still in London. I had forgotten about it until this morning when I asked Chaffin concerning the delivery. It had simply slipped my mind."

Elizabeth's emotions were in conflict. The necklace was by far more exquisite than her present one, yet it had been the one she had worn throughout her youth and had been given to her by her father. Therefore, it had great sentimental value. In fact, she had a vivid memory of the precise occasion on which her father had presented all of his daughters with necklaces. Jane received a cross a little larger then hers, Mary and Kitty both were given a locket in the shape of a heart—which Kitty had since lost—and Lydia had received a pearl drop.

She was momentarily troubled about why her husband would feel the need to replace her beloved cross necklace. She noticed him intently watching her expression and immediately decided not to presume too much about the motive for his generosity. She quickly stood and kissed Darcy's cheek and proclaimed with a playful air, "You are so thoughtful, my love. But you do not have to give me such elaborate gifts. Beware, there is great risk in my becoming spoiled from such considerations."

Darcy replied resolutely, "Not even a possibility."

They descended to the dining room and enjoyed a light breakfast. Darcy kissed Elizabeth atop her head and informed her that Mrs. Reynolds would be there shortly. An uncertain smile graced Elizabeth's face as she rose to walk her husband to the door. "I shall see you in a few hours then?"

"Most definitely." She watched his elegant gait progress down the hall. After he was gone, she returned to the table to pour herself another cup of tea as she awaited the housekeeper.

Instead of sitting, she elected to stroll around the vast table. It was indeed magnificent, and she considered the many dinners and guests it had serviced. The thought loomed large that she was now the lone individual responsible for enhancing this table. She would be appraised for her ability to provide her family and their guests with complementary courses and delectable fare. Added to those responsibilities were the décor and festivities such gatherings would require. All would be under her supervision.

Elizabeth paused to consider her reflection in the great mirror above the sideboard. Her eyes fell to the foreign cross which hung about her throat, and an ache began to stir within her heart. Yet no time for contemplation was to be had for the housekeeper suddenly appeared.

"Mrs. Darcy," she cheerfully greeted, "I hope you have not been detained long. An urgent situation arose with one of the maids."

"Mrs. Reynolds, it is quite all right. Perchance, is it Clara of whom you speak?"

"Why, yes it is. She is in need of transportation due to her mother's failing health. But with the weather such as it is, I am not sure that we can arrange the connections."

"I am certain that once Mr. Darcy is informed, he will be glad to assist and can arrange everything."

Mrs. Reynolds was slightly taken aback at the mistress' presumption. The housekeeper then stated pleasantly that these concerns would be worked out as soon as possible, but should not be a matter for the mistress to be overly troubled about. Changing the subject, she asked Mrs. Darcy how she would prefer to commence their discussion of the management of the house.

Elizabeth was a little stunned at Mrs. Reynolds's easy dismissal of her interest in Clara's travel arrangements, yet, she decided to let it be for the present and proceed with the much needed instruction from the housekeeper. After all, a week had already passed, and Elizabeth felt it would not leave a favourable impression to delay her education further. Besides, she trusted that Mrs. Reynolds would indeed take care of Clara's needs.

"Where would you suggest I begin?" This question put a smile upon the elderly woman's face. She thought this a good sign that the new mistress had some modesty about her, and she was glad of it. Her mistress compared favourably to some young ladies who were forward and brash—a particular Bingley sister came to mind.

"Well, ma'am, if you don't mind me saying, we can first go over the ledgers of the household allowances, and then move onto the responsibilities of the menus. I am inclined to think this would be a good start."

Elizabeth swayed forward on her toes while raising her brows and gestured with her arm for Mrs. Reynolds to lead on. The elderly lady led her to the personal study of the late Lady Anne Darcy. Elizabeth immediately recognized the room from her visit the previous summer.

"Mr. Darcy instructed me to have your ledgers and personal effects put in this room. It was Lady Anne's favourite room. Here, in this top left drawer, are the journals of accounts. Likewise, your own personal register of funds is kept within." Mrs. Reynolds then withdrew a lovely, brown leather-bound volume and handed it to Elizabeth.

Elizabeth caressed the ledger's beautiful, embossed spine and opened it to the first page. She noticed deposits for her pin money had started promptly upon her betrothal. She smiled at her husband's customary eagerness and consideration in pleasing her.

Mrs. Reynolds continued, "At the beginning of every month, Mr. Sheldon will draft money into the accounts. You will be responsible for the method and management of the funds. This can be done personally, or authorization to someone else can be arranged. Yet, it must always be under your continuous supervision."

Elizabeth began to examine the other ledgers now. Her eyes widened as she looked over the entries with reference to the past few months and began to feel overwhelmed at the enormity of the task.

After Elizabeth had examined most of the ledgers, Mrs. Reynolds walked over to a side cabinet and retrieved a handsome bowl-shaped platter filled with an exorbitant number of posts. "This, Mrs. Darcy, is your correspondence which has arrived over the past two weeks, every morning your missives will be placed in the dining room or set on your desk here when you are inconvenienced or not at home."

"All of these have arrived in the past two weeks?" If Elizabeth thought the responsibility of the accounts seemed overwhelming, it was nothing to the obligation such correspondence would bring. She puffed her cheeks full of air and pursed her lips to the side as she looked in dismay at the mound of communications which needed her immediate attention.

Mrs. Reynolds just smiled and asked if there were anything else she desired to know or enquire.

Expelling her retained breath, Elizabeth asked, "Is it possible for me to meet with Mrs. Potter this afternoon to go over the menus and learn the favourite dishes of Mr. Darcy and Miss Georgiana?"

Delighted by such a request, Mrs. Reynolds assured her that a meeting would be secured. It was, however, the new mistress' next request that truly warmed the trusted servant's heart.

"Mrs. Reynolds, if it would not be too much trouble, I was wondering if you would mind taking me to the picture gallery upstairs before you leave for your other duties. I am certain I could eventually find it, but only after several detours of wrong turns."

The housekeeper's face beamed with approval that the mistress showed an interest in the Darcy heritage. Thus, Mrs. Reynolds was most solicitous in fulfilling her new mistress' request. She proceeded in showing Elizabeth up the stairs and gave her directions to turn to the right, walk for a distance and the picture gallery would commence after passing the first corridor in that wing.

Elizabeth walked through the passageway with much trepidation. She was not certain that she could fulfil the duties that an estate the size of Pemberley would demand. She was not as worried about having a prepared table, because her mother had been exceptionally gifted when it came to the culinary refinements for a well-dressed social gathering. To these preparations Elizabeth had been exposed all her life, although not on such a grand scale as now.

She also did not worry too much about the management of the household expenditures. She was by no means a spendthrift. Here too, her mother's example, howbeit an unfavourable one, had educated her for the ways of a productive and peaceful home. Intemperance was one thing she had sworn would never be allowed under her own roof. Lydia was a prime example of what an imprudent upbringing could produce. Yet, it was neither of these fears which niggled in the back of her mind.

Elizabeth examined each picture in turn until she reached the one she sought—the one which had filled her breast with an awakening and longing she had never known before. Here hung the portrait of her husband as a younger man.

She lost track of time while staring at the painting and began to understand that her prime concern was simply the fear of her husband's disapprobation. Would she be able to be the Mrs. Darcy he envisioned, a Mrs. Darcy reminiscent of those whose portraits graced the walls of this gallery? Their appraisals were fixed and certain while hers remained unseen and unsure. However, Elizabeth was not a woman made for unhappy thoughts. With one last loving look upon her Fitzwilliam, she bolstered her spirit with a new resolve. His ancestors and their unborn children were depending on her, and, most of all, her husband believed in her. Moreover, she would never give Lady Catherine or Caroline Bingley the satisfaction of seeing her fail.

Thus, with determination, she returned to her study to tackle the numerous posts. Name after name appeared before her eyes, yet not one brought with it any recognition. The pile of unknowns mounted until one name in particular seized Elizabeth's attention—Mrs. George Wickham.

With a sickening hesitancy, she broke the seal and unfolded the letter.

January 2, 1813

Newcastle

My Dearest Lizzy,

I suppose you are on your honeymoon now. Mamma told me that your dear Mr. Darcy kept the whereabouts all to himself. I can only imagine that he has taken you somewhere truly grand. You now know the pleasure to be had in the marital bed, I am sure, unless your husband is not as amorous as mine. It is such a shame that George and I were not able to attend the wedding, but with us being so far and so low on funds you can only realize how heartbroken we are in having missed the festivities. Oh! You can never guess what my dear George told me about your new sister. So, I will tell you!

Elizabeth's heart froze, and her hands began to tremble. She closed her eyes in complete dread at what the next lines might convey.

He said that he was once engaged to Georgiana only a year and a half ago. They met at Ramsgate and renewed their acquaintance there. They had planned to elope but were forestalled by her ominous brother. Really Lizzy,

I do have a hard time understanding how you could marry such a man. La! Back to my tale. Well, your husband prevented their marriage, so much the better for me, and he dissolved their engagement. La! So you see your new sister and I have so much in common. I daresay that she still pines for my George, and I feel some pity for her because he is indeed an exceptional husband. When I come to visit you, I expect that Georgiana and I will have so much to talk about!

One more thing Lizzy, I hope this is not too much of a bother, and it should not be with the amount of money you now have at your disposal. George wants me to ask you if you could not spare a little monthly allowance for your dear sister and brother who live on so little here. Really, Lizzy, we have only one servant and she can only come a few hours a week!

I must say that I am dying to hear from you soon and hope to visit by summer's end. George sends his sincere congratulations and the love of a most devoted brother.

Your beloved sister,

Lydia

Elizabeth's mind was full of turmoil for such a quandary. The nerve of that villain! What was to be done? Would Lydia's foolhardiness never cease to exist? Anger raced through her veins. How dare George Wickham relate the account of Georgiana's indiscretion, the source of which was his own flatteries, falsehoods and pretensions? He had taken advantage of a sweet, young, vulnerable girl with his flapdoodle and dared to relate the tale to her gossipy sister as a genuine attachment! The motivation was clear. Wickham was using it to procure favours from her. Elizabeth was incensed, and shame began to wash over her from the perverseness of a sister who had previously cost her husband uncounted disgrace, trouble and capital.

At that moment, Darcy pleasantly entered the room. He immediately noticed his wife's agitated manner and looked at the bulk of mail before her. "Elizabeth, whatever is the matter, my love?" She quickly withdrew Lydia's missive into the fabric of her dress. Darcy walked around the desk and placed his hands upon her shoulders.

"I see you have already received felicitations from many of the residents of Derbyshire and the surrounding counties. I must say you do have by far more than I." He sat on his heels beside his despondent wife and, with words of encouragement, tried to shore up the heavy load he imagined she was feeling.

"My lovely wife, all of these do not need to be answered as of yet. I will help you sort them in order of importance so you will know which should be answered first. I am certain the whole of the countryside is anxious to meet the new Mrs. Darcy. We shall hold a ball or a soirée to introduce you.

With you by her side, Georgiana might be persuaded to perform some sonatas."

Elizabeth, still silent, only nodded in agreement. Darcy lifted her from her chair and warmly encircled her in his arms. "Mrs. Reynolds told me you had gone to the picture gallery. I looked for you there, and, when I did not find you, I came straightway to your study. Do you like your room? I remember often seeking my mother and finding her sitting in this very chair. She spent many long hours here. She would have me sit in the chair yonder and tell her of my ramblings about the grounds. Often, she would read to me as well. They were usually letters from relatives. And then she would expound upon the importance of doing one's duty to family. My mother would have been fond of you, Lizzy. I know in my heart she approves."

Elizabeth turned her sombre eyes to her husband's. She adored him. "Oh Fitzwilliam, you are too good! Thank you for sharing your memories of your mother and for your kind feelings wherewith you sense her approval."

Darcy bent low, kissed his wife, and held her in his arms as she rested her head upon his chest. He looked down at the desk and noticed she had received a letter from her sister. "Elizabeth, you did not tell me you had a letter from your sister."

Alarmed, she looked up at her husband and then followed his gaze to the desk. Relief swept over her as she saw a letter from Jane. "Oh, I guess I had not yet noticed it."

"Well, shall we open it and see how she and Bingley are faring?" Not waiting for an answer, he picked up the post but Elizabeth quickly snatched it from his hand. "No, I do not want to read it just yet. I would rather pick a time when I feel more rested."

These words were indeed agreeable to Darcy, and, with a tinge of suggestion, he slyly asked, "Shall we take a nap then, my dear wife?" He looked boyish when he wiggled his brows as he awaited her reaction.

Elizabeth smiled at his antics.

"I would love to, but I have arranged a meeting with Mrs. Potter and must prepare for Georgiana and Colonel Fitzwilliam."

"Lizzy, I will inform Mrs. Reynolds to rearrange the meeting for tomorrow after breakfast, and we can easily entertain in the music room tonight." At that moment, Mrs. Reynolds gently knocked on the open door. Without waiting for his wife's thoughts about the matter, he turned to the housekeeper and began to inform her of the changed plans. Elizabeth bit her lip in frustration at her husband's officious manner. However, she remembered Lydia's letter, opened the ledger to her personal account, and placed it therein, putting it back within the drawer along with the other financial records.

She heard her husband ask her a question but being preoccupied, did not attend to his enquiry.

"Oh!" cried Elizabeth, "I am so sorry. I was not paying attention."

Darcy looked at her oddly and then repeated the question. "Would tomorrow morning after breakfast be agreeable to meet with Mrs. Potter?"

"Oh yes," she replied. "That will be fine."

Mrs. Reynolds smiled, and, with a nod of her head, acknowledged, "Very good, ma'am."

"Oh, and, Mrs. Reynolds," Elizabeth stated, "Before you go, have you been able to secure the travel arrangements for Clara? And I will also need your suggestion for a maid to fill in during her absence."

Mrs. Reynolds and Darcy eyed one another before she answered the mistress. "The plans are not yet fixed, and I will be happy to find an alternate for Clara."

"I thank you," Elizabeth replied.

The housekeeper then turned and left the master and mistress to themselves.

"Elizabeth, what is this business about Clara needing to be exchanged?"

"Her mother is very ill and has requested she come home. She is having a difficult time securing transportation due to the snowfall, and I told Clara I was sure you would not mind assisting her in her need."

Darcy looked down momentarily and remained silent. He then lifted his eyes, smiled at his wife, and offered his arm to her. She gladly accepted and they departed the study together for the staircase where they climbed the stairs arm in arm. As Elizabeth turned towards the left, her husband gently swung her in the opposite direction. He took her hand and held it in his, caressing it lovingly as they walked forward.

"Wherever are we going, Fitzwilliam?"

"I want to take you to the picture gallery if you would not mind?"

"I would like that very much, but what about our *nap*?"

Darcy smirked at her tease and continued to walk in silence until they came upon the gallery. He then looked at his wife's face as they steadily approached his portrait. Her attention was drawn to the paintings. When they were before his likeness, she looked at him and stated, "It is a very good representation of you, Fitzwilliam." Suddenly, from the corner of her eye, she noticed folded throws against the wall next to a basket.

Elizabeth raised her brows and her eyes glistened with pleasure. "You are so full of surprises. An indoor picnic is a delightful idea. Was this another of the many daydreams you formulated last April?"

After spreading the blankets, Darcy gestured for his lovely lady to take a seat. "No, Elizabeth, this was not one of my many daydreams of our future, but when I came to find you here earlier, the thought occurred that we could dine with some of my family today." He said this with an air of liveliness. "Truly, since you have shown an interest in the gallery, I thought I could enlighten you about the Darcys who grace these walls. Would that be acceptable to you?"

"Why yes, I would like that very much, not that I am tiring of only your company—" and she thought to herself, *this is just the distraction I need to put Lydia's horrid letter out of my mind*!

Darcy opened the basket and began to retrieve the food. There was quail, apples, bread, wine and cheese. As they ate, he expounded upon the paintings.

"I was nineteen years when my portrait was painted. That of my mother is when she first married. Your likeness will be taken as well. I plan to commission an artist this spring. Your portrait will hang next to mine."

"Oh," was the only reply Elizabeth made to this revelation.

"Shall you like, do you think, to have your likeness made?"

"Oh, not at all," cried Elizabeth light-heartedly. "I will be quite put out for having to pose for so long and especially in the spring. I think it will be quite difficult."

"Yes, Elizabeth, I would imagine you will be an agitation for any artist, but not for the reason of your pent-up vigour."

A provocative smirk overtook Elizabeth's countenance as she baited, "I take it, sir, that it is time to repose?"

"Yes," he replied with anticipation shining from his eyes. "You are most astute my dear. Do let me help you stand."

After helping Elizabeth to her feet, Darcy caressed her cheek and stated tenderly, "I love you so much, Lizzy. You are so beautiful. I love the feel of your soft skin." He commenced to kiss her eagerly for several minutes as his hands freely roamed her figure.

When they parted for air, Elizabeth exclaimed, "I think we need to go to our rooms, but do you feel there will be time? Are not Georgiana and Colonel Fitzwilliam due within the hour?"

"Yes they are, but Georgiana will have to learn quickly that periods of rest are frequently required in this household. And as for Fitzwilliam, I do not care what he thinks."

This revelation brought a blush to his sweet wife's cheeks, and, with a small degree of mortification, she simply replied, "Oh my."

Darcy then exclaimed with zest, "One thing is assured, Lizzy, we will be quite refreshed when we go down to greet them."

And rest they did.

~*~

Chapter Four

Misapprehensions Abound

Georgiana was full of excitement as the sleigh neared her ancestral home. "Oh, Richard, I can hardly wait to see Elizabeth again! I have so much that I desire to tell her."

Colonel Fitzwilliam smiled delightedly at his young cousin's exuberance.

"Yes, Georgie, I dare say that by now Elizabeth longs for some companionship other than your brother's. Now, do not give me that shocked expression. You know as well as I that your brother can sometimes be, what shall I say, a stiff."

"Why, Richard, whatever do you mean? Fitzwilliam is always kind and generous. How could you say such a thing?"

"Now, Georgiana Darcy, do not play coy with me. You know exactly what I mean, and remember, I said *sometimes*."

The glint in Georgiana's eyes acknowledged Richard's portrayal of her brother. "You are partly right, but not even by half. You know as well as I that Fitzwilliam has a wonderfully wicked side. If it were not true, you would have nothing to do with him, and he would surely have nothing to do with you!"

"Touché, my dear girl!" cried the colonel. "Since when have you become so adept in the art of effrontery?"

Georgiana giggled at such an insinuation.

The sleigh came to a halt. Richard helped Georgiana out and then held her tightly by the arm as they made their way slowly up the icy steps to the front door. Servants came quickly to unburden the colonel and young miss of their wraps. Georgiana looked about in great expectation, but neither Elizabeth nor her brother were there to greet them. Just when disappointment was about to seize the young girl's heart, she spied her brother hurrying down the stairs, two at a time. Georgiana's face beamed with happiness.

"Oh Fitzwilliam!" she cried, "you are here after all! I thought you might have forgotten we were to come today."

Darcy opened his arms wide, picked her off her feet and gave her a twirl. "What, I forget about you, Georgie? Never!"

Richard observed Elizabeth breathlessly descending the stairs while pinning up some loose tresses. The colonel smirked as he also noticed the

23

flush of her face, her neck and the exposed skin beneath her collarbone. Smiling broadly, she quickly came and stood by her husband.

"Georgiana!" Elizabeth exclaimed. "I am so sorry to be late in greeting you, but I am very happy you are here."

Elizabeth leaned to embrace her new sister, and her eyes widened as the girl nearly leapt into her arms.

"Oh, Elizabeth, I am so happy to be at home and especially to be with you and my brother again! I have missed you both so much."

Darcy then shook Richard's hand as he thanked him for taking such good care of his sister. He suggested they all go into the music room and visit. This was agreeable to all, and, as they walked to the room, he asked if they had had luncheon. They answered in the affirmative, but indicated some tea would be most welcome. Darcy looked towards Elizabeth as if to say that she was to do the honours.

Perceiving his meaning, she said, "Oh yes, I shall go and find Mrs. Reynolds and have the tea prepared right away." As she turned to go, her husband took her aside and quietly instructed her to find the nearest servant and have them inform the kitchen of her request. She smiled with gratitude for her husband's kind intervention, but at the same time was slightly miffed. It was not her fault that she had not completely learned the ways of a household with so many servants to beckon. She had, after all, spent the past fortnight being exclusively instructed by her husband in *other* matters.

The tea came immediately, and Elizabeth claimed the privilege of serving her new sister and cousin. Colonel Fitzwilliam entertained them all with stories about his older brother, James, or rather, Lord Hazelton, who would one day claim title as the Earl of Matlock. His stories were slightly embellished for effect, but no one seemed to care. Darcy even regaled them with tales of his own. Being reunited brought warmth to their repartee, and their laughter filled the halls of Pemberley.

"You see, Richard?" Georgiana enquired. "My brother is not a stiff. He has been quite animated this past hour." All eyes turned to the colonel. She continued in explanation, "Richard stated that Elizabeth would be glad to have our company because she would be tiring of yours, Fitzwilliam, since you are such a stiff."

Darcy's look cast daggers towards his cousin and he exclaimed, "Very funny."

A few moments of silence ensued until Richard suddenly burst out laughing, and giggles were then discerned from the feminine quarter, as well.

Darcy merely shook his head and condescendingly replied, "You would do well, Fitzwilliam, to remember which side your bread is buttered on." This only brought another round of laughter. "Well, I hate to be the spoiler of this lovely reunion, but I am to meet with my steward, and I am sure that you, Georgiana, would like to refresh yourself before dinner which will be served at the usual hour."

"Yes, I do feel a little fatigued," Georgiana stated. They all stood to go their various ways, when Darcy asked Richard to accompany him to his study.

Elizabeth went directly to her study, as well. She paused as she entered and examined it more closely. Mesmerized, she walked to the desk and glided her hand over the sleek surface.

The desk was lovely. It was crafted from mahogany wood and had a leather-lined top with an inserted reading shelf. Swan-neck, brass handles were on all of the drawers, and a long single drawer in the centre, when opened, pulled down to reveal a writing shelf with pigeon holes and small drawers within. The bookshelves were also mahogany in the same ornate fashion as the desk. She walked over to one and noticed some titles therein. Her eyes scanned the works of Shakespeare, Samuel Johnson's Dictionary, and many more of the same books which she, herself, loved. Elizabeth walked over to the desk yet again and sat down.

She looked over to the green leather tub chair and smiled as she tried to envision Fitzwilliam as a small boy sitting in the company of his mother. Her vision swept over the entire room for a second time, and she understood why Anne Darcy would spend so much time there. *I am already in love with this very room after spending only a few moments here.*

Elizabeth opened the left drawer, and her lips pressed together in a fine line with the thought of Lydia's abominable letter. Pulling the letter from the ledger, she unfolded it as she considered whether she should tell her husband. The letter was flagrant blackmail, so Darcy should know of it, yet, she reasoned that she had planned to help Lydia financially to some degree. Moments passed as she pondered her predicament. Yes, she would tell Fitzwilliam tonight.

Oh, she could not and would not think about this now. Suddenly, Elizabeth remembered Jane's letter was still upstairs within her chambers. She quickly folded Lydia's missive and placed it in the back of the drawer, positioning her account book over it.

Anxiously, Elizabeth quitted her study to rush up the stairs and read her letter from dear Jane. A letter from her cherished sister was sure to bring some warmth and consolation in comparison to the one from foolish Lydia, who left her feeling dejected and bereft.

~*~

"What do you need, Darcy?" the colonel asked.

Darcy gestured for his cousin to sit. "Would you care for a brandy?"

Richard slung himself in the chair. "Yes, that will be most agreeable after such a cold ride. In fact, I wanted one in the sleigh and thought to bring a flask, but I knew Georgiana would scold me and be in fear of my becoming a drunkard."

Darcy poured the liquor into a crystal goblet. "Has she reason to fear?"

Sarcastically, Richard replied, "Ha, ha! Very amusing, Cousin!"

Darcy smiled briefly as he handed Richard his drink, poured one for himself, and walked to the window to gaze at the snow-covered grounds.

"So," he began as he squinted at the dazzling sight before him, "I take it the trip was rather uncomfortable?"

"Most assuredly. It was cold enough to freeze the balls off a brass monkey."

Darcy continued to contemplate the frozen landscape. He sipped his brandy and then enquired of his cousin how often they had to stop and remove ice from the horses' nostrils.

"I do not know if I remember the exact number, but several would be close to accurate. We would rest for some time, and, when we started up again, the horses would start snorting and shaking their heads rather violently. Before we knew it, we would have to stop and take care of them all over again. But, all said, with conditions as they are, I think we made fairly good time."

Darcy took another sip of his drink, his only response a studied, "Hmm."

"Darcy, are you concerned about something?"

"Well, in fact, Fitzwilliam, I am trying to decide about one of the maids travelling in these frigid conditions. Her mother is extremely ill and has requested that she come to her."

"Does she live far?"

"Lancashire. Not only there, but all the way to the border of the Irish Sea. We are talking about Liverpool."

"My word Darcy, that is far in conditions such as these. The travel will be tedious, indeed! Whatever do you plan to do?"

"Well, for one thing, now that you are here with your sleigh and team I can contemplate sending her without the fear that a crisis may arise which would put any of us at peril for the absence of all the Belgians. I will have to send all of my teams. We cannot rely on the post stations having rested horses for use. I imagine in weather such as this, the demand will have lessened the supply. So, I am ready to send one team off soon to await the party the next day so that they may have fresh horses to cover more ground if possible. Yet, they will be at the mercy of finding horses in their continued journey, or, if that is not possible, they will have to stop at every inn between here and Lancashire. How long do you plan on staying, Fitzwilliam?"

"I can stay for the month if you like. I am on leave through the first part of April, so I am at your beck and call."

"I am glad to hear it. If I do send the maid, she will have to have an escort, and finding someone to volunteer to go that far will not be effortless."

"Well, anything I can do to help, you can count on me."

"Thank you. There is something else I wish to discuss."

"Fire away."

"I would like to know what your mother and father are contemplating of late in regards to my marriage. That is if there is anything to tell."

"One thing is for sure—James and Elisha are dead set against Elizabeth."

Darcy exhaled loudly as he shrugged his shoulders. "Humph! It will be a cold day in hell before I care about the sentiments of those two."

"Yes, I agree with you there, but you know as well as I that Hazel holds great sway with father."

Darcy just shook his head in disgust and downed the remainder of his brandy. "Well," he rejoined, "I guess we had better go and dress for dinner. I am glad you are here, Fitzwilliam."

~*~

Mrs. Darcy single-mindedly absorbed the happiness that coursed from every word of Jane's letter. Elizabeth's heart overflowed with profusions of joy, and knowing her dear Jane was finally allowed to have the pleasure she so rightly deserved made her own spirit soar. She read the missive three times, and each perusal brought additional jubilation which she never would have thought possible. Both sisters were indeed blessed beyond measure. Their heartfelt desires from their earliest recollections had been granted in abundance. They had married sensible men of consequence who were honourable and esteemed, but, above all, they had married for love and were likewise loved in return.

Suddenly, Darcy opened the door which connected their chambers. His wife immediately realized he was already dressed for the evening. "Elizabeth, are you not yet dressed for dinner? You had better hurry. I will not be able to escort you down. A difficulty has arisen, and I must see Mr. Manning before dinner. I will do my best to be on time, but do not delay on my account. I will come as quickly as may be. Fitzwilliam and Georgiana will understand."

"Is there anything I can do to be of assistance?"

"Oh no, it is nothing of which you need worry." He walked over to where she stood and brushed his fingers along her cheekbone. "Have I ever told you, Mrs. Darcy, that you are a most becoming woman?"

Elizabeth was charmed by his sudden attention and her answer was a lively, "Oh, I do recall your having mentioned it at one time or another, yet,

I never tire of hearing it." Her voice trailed off leaving a gentle smile in its wake.

Darcy tilted her chin upward and captured her mouth with his. Elizabeth stood upon her toes as she slipped her arms around his neck and pulled her husband closer. In response, he encircled his arms about her waist and folded her into his chest, deepening their kiss for a little longer before his lips moved first to her jaw and then the back of her ear. Breathing out on a whisper, he said, "I will be with you as soon as can be. I love you, my Lizzy." His warm breath gently brushing her ear sent shivers across her body. She smiled and nodded her head in understanding. He pulled back and tapped her nose before he turned and strode from the room.

Elizabeth walked to her dressing room and realized that her maid had prepared a steaming hot bath. Yet, due to the time she would not have the luxury of a long soak. She began to remove her slippers and stockings when Clara came in to assist by immediately helping with her mistress' dress. Elizabeth took notice that Clara's eyes were red and swollen, and, as she lowered herself in the tub, she gently asked her maid if she were well.

"Oh, ma'am, I am all right. I have just been worrying about me Mum."

"Has Mrs. Reynolds's not arranged for your travel as of yet?"

"I don't be rightly knowing, but I suppose, with the weather and all, I might not be going."

"Oh Clara, I am sure that things can be arranged. I will arrange it myself tonight. I will do my best to make sure you are able to leave first thing in the morning."

A sudden hopefulness appeared on the young maid's face but was just as quickly replaced by uncertainty. "I thank you, Mrs. Darcy, but I'm not so sure you ought to trouble yourself."

"Nonsense, who else should be more concerned than I? I will arrange it Clara. I assure you it will be done."

The firmness of Elizabeth's words did raise the young maid's hopes, and she simply responded, "I thank you ma'am."

Afterwards, the maid hastily worked with dedication in helping Elizabeth with her toilette. The warm bath had Elizabeth's hair all a-curl, yet Clara managed to arrange her mistress' hair in an alluring, fetching style rather than the simple one she usually wore. Her locks hung lower and bounced off the back of her neck with the slightest turn of her head.

"Oh Clara!" Elizabeth exclaimed as she examined her appearance, "I do like what you have done to my rebellious curls. Thank you. I shall see you later when I retire and let you know what has been worked out. Please do not distress yourself any longer. Everything will be fine."

~*~

Colonel Fitzwilliam was just leaving his chamber as Elizabeth departed hers.

"Why, Elizabeth, I must say you do look particularly stunning tonight. Is Darcy not with you?"

"No. He was called to take care of some matters with his overseer and has asked that we begin dinner without him. He has assured me he will join us as soon as possible."

"Then, may I have the honour of escorting you to the dining room?"

Elizabeth smiled and agreed most cheerfully.

Richard offered his arm and they walked in silence until they reached the dining room door where the colonel paused.

"Allow me to say, Elizabeth, that I am extremely happy for both you and my cousin—in fact, for Georgiana, as well. We are most fortunate to have secured you in our family. Georgiana is so full of excitement that she could talk of nothing else during the whole of our trip. I do not think I have seen her quite so happy since she was a little girl. And, as for my cousin, I have never before seen the contentment which I now witness in him. You are truly a godsend."

Elizabeth reddened from such praise. However, true pleasure shone with regard to his tribute.

"I thank you for your kind words, Colonel, but I assure you that I am the one who is truly blessed to have such a sweet sister as Georgiana and a husband as noble as your cousin."

Richard pulled the chair for her, and they visited a little longer before Georgiana eagerly entered the room.

"Oh, I am so happy I am not late. Wherever is Fitzwilliam?"

Elizabeth then imparted the same information she had shared with the colonel in relation to Darcy's tardiness.

The trio partook of the meal with enjoyment. They discussed topics from music to the Season in London. While they waited for the dessert to be served, Darcy entered and was seated.

"Ah, I see I made it in time for the trifle."

They all laughed, but Elizabeth wondered at Darcy's being aware of what dessert would be served. She had to meet with Mrs. Potter and become acquainted with the cookery from the kitchens of Pemberley.

Georgiana merrily enlightened Elizabeth to the fact that her brother had an enormous sweet tooth and would seldom pass any opportunity for sweets.

Darcy simply shook his head in indifference as they all chuckled over his weakness.

The desserts were being served when Elizabeth looked to her husband and asked if arrangements had been made for Clara, and before waiting to hear a reply, she told her husband in earnest that she had promised Clara she would arrange for the girl to leave by first light on the morrow.

Darcy's face darkened. His jaw tightened as he laid his fork upon the table and his hands closed tightly. Georgiana and Richard both took notice of this change, but Elizabeth was so caught up in her communication, that she failed to observe her husband's altered mien.

"Really, Fitzwilliam, I cannot believe she has not departed already. The poor girl is so worried concerning her mother. I am surprised nothing has been arranged as of yet. Mrs. Reynolds assured me that arrangements would be made—"

With a sternness which echoed with some familiarity to Elizabeth, Darcy abruptly interrupted his wife. "Elizabeth! You know not of what you speak. Cease! I will not have this discussion at the table."

Elizabeth's shock and then humiliation were quite apparent to her new sister and cousin, yet her husband did not look at her. Instead, he picked up his fork and plunged into the dessert placed before him. Georgiana was grieved at her brother's harsh words, yet she did not dare speak. Richard, on the other hand, spoke as if nothing had occurred and asked if they would separate tonight. Darcy agreed that they would for a short while and then join the ladies in the music room. Elizabeth remained too shaken to consider eating the trifle. Instead she shifted the spoon about the plate in a useless fashion. She did not suffer long when Darcy unexpectedly arose, tossed his napkin on the table, and, without a word, quit the dining room for his study.

Richard also stood, gave a quick bow to the ladies as he informed them he anticipated their continued company within the hour, and took his leave.

Elizabeth rested her spoon, took a cleansing breath and thoughtfully said, "We are finally to ourselves, Georgiana. I have been looking forward to becoming better acquainted. I was rather hoping you would accompany me in playing some duets."

Georgiana's face lit up with joy, and she swiftly agreed. They made their way, arm in arm, to the pianoforte.

~*~

When Richard entered the study, Darcy had already poured a glass of brandy and was standing next to the fire, with his one arm propped on the mantlepiece as he stared into the flames.

"Help yourself, Fitzwilliam."

The colonel walked over to the decanters and poured a glass of port. He then sat in the chair closest to where Darcy was standing. Each man sipped his drink silently. Both seemed lost in their own thoughts when Darcy commented that the intensity of the cold had worsened and snow was falling again. Richard eyed him for several seconds before responding.

"Yes, I dare say it is *freezing*." He sipped his drink and said nothing further.

Darcy raked his fingers through his hair and looked at his cousin. He started to pace between the mantlepiece and his desk and eventually, sat in his desk chair. It seemed to Richard that Darcy was uncharacteristically slumped in his seat, as opposed to his usual, erect posture.

"Darcy, was it really necessary to reprimand your wife at the dinner table?"

Initially, Darcy's heart chilled at his cousin's words, but soon irritation reigned. His lips pressed tightly together, and he barely looked at his cousin before replying, "It is no concern of yours, Fitzwilliam."

"Perhaps not—but I saw her humiliation, and you did not."

A nerve in Darcy's cheek flinched. He clasped his hands together and began to slowly twirl his thumbs around one another.

"Richard, I take it you saw nothing offensive in her behaviour."

"Nothing deliberate, no. She is concerned for her maid. That is all."

"And," Darcy continued, "I suppose these concerns are frequent topics of conversation at your father's table."

"Of course not, Darcy. But you know as well as I that Elizabeth has not dealt with legions of servants. Her upbringing has not been the same as yours or mine."

"Then she should quickly learn the boundary of her affairs."

"Good Heavens, Darcy, she is barely five years older than Georgiana."

Darcy had had enough of his cousin's judgment. In a cynical tone, he exclaimed, "I know perfectly well the age of my wife! I can manage my personal affairs without your assistance, Fitzwilliam, and will thank you not to interfere. Shall we go and join the ladies?"

Not waiting for a reply, Darcy exited the room and left Richard speechless. The colonel frowned and shook his head in disbelief. He then swallowed the rest of his port and made his way to the music room.

As Richard approached the door, he noticed that Darcy had paused before entering. He came up behind his cousin and looked past him to see Georgiana and Elizabeth playing a lively duet. Both were giggling as they stumbled through the unrehearsed piece.

Richard spoke softly. "I cannot remember the last time I saw Georgiana this happy."

Darcy silently nodded his head in agreement and then entered the room.

Both ladies turned upon their entrance and smiled, yet Richard noticed that Elizabeth's was forced.

Darcy took a seat on the sofa next to the fire. He wanted to admire his wife's figure, and this position afforded him with the best view.

Elizabeth asked her sister-in-law if she desired to play another selection, but the young girl declined, claiming fatigue, and asked to be excused for the night.

Darcy looked at his sister intently and asked if there was anything she needed. She reassured him that only rest was required, thus he stood and embraced her, placing a kiss upon her head. Georgiana then bid Elizabeth goodnight with a very affectionate embrace. Richard, on the other hand, patted his young cousin on her head and she glared at him for the insult.

"Now Georgie," Richard quipped, "do be a good girl and run up to bed, or would you like me to tuck you in and read you a story?"

This remark earned the colonel a skewed up face from his young cousin, and then she stuck out her tongue at him most decidedly. Darcy's back was turned while he stoked the fire, so he did not see the shenanigans, but Elizabeth saw it all and smiled at their playful banter. When Georgiana quit the room, Elizabeth turned her attention back to the instrument and began to glance through the sheets of music.

Richard walked over and asked if she could play one of his favourite pieces, *Rondo Alla Turca* by Mozart. She agreed, and he sat next to her in order to turn the pages.

In a playful manner, Elizabeth said, "I warn you, Colonel, that I will not do this sonata any justice. It has a fast tempo, and I play rather slowly for such compositions as these."

The colonel smiled, delighted that she was somewhat recovered from her former ordeal at dinner. "I am sure you will play just as lovely as you always do."

Darcy turned and carefully looked at his cousin and then resumed his seat.

Elizabeth played the piece well, but she had not lied. She played the lively air in a rather slow tempo. When she finished, she looked at the colonel and said with amiability, "I am at your command for another request if you dare venture one."

Darcy shifted his body and continued to watch her as she played another selection. He noticed something different about her tonight. Maybe it was a new dress. No he remembered seeing her in it once before their marriage. All of a sudden he knew. It was the style of her hair. She had worn it like that at the Netherfield ball, but then it had small rosettes entwined for adornment. He found the style very enticing because of the way the curls bounced against her neck at the slightest movement. He breathed in deeply.

Elizabeth slurred some notes and then hit a wrong chord. Richard laughed at the mishap and said something quietly to her. Darcy's face clouded with annoyance at his cousin's savvy intercourse. He observed that Elizabeth was taking great delight in his attentions and remembered all too well the same enjoyable interactions between them at Rosings. He rubbed the back of his fist against his mouth while his face began to contort into a sulk. Elizabeth had not once looked upon him after they entered the room.

He remained in this same frame of mind for some minutes before he swiftly rose and walked to the pianoforte, leaned upon it and stared directly at her. Richard looked up in surprise and quickly noticed his cousin's annoyance.

"Why Darcy, is there something you wish Elizabeth to play?"

Elizabeth finished the sonata she was playing, and then stood. Instantly, Richard arose as well, and she exclaimed, "I cannot accept any further requests. My fingers need rest." She shot a quick glance at Darcy and curtseyed to both gentlemen. "I think I shall retire now. It has been a very enlightening evening."

Richard smiled widely, bowed, and thanked her again for the performance. Darcy stood erect as well but stared at his wife with irritation. "Mrs. Darcy, let me escort you upstairs." Elizabeth gave a slight nod and began walking ahead of him to the door.

Elizabeth heard Richard say goodnight to her husband, but he did not respond in kind.

After she and Darcy were both out of the room, he took hold of her arm in a gentle manner and asked if she were feeling well. "Quite," came her terse reply. Darcy's brow creased. He then offered his arm to her as they commenced to climb the stairs. Elizabeth hesitated at first then thought better of it and lightly placed her hand upon his forearm. He placed his free hand over hers and both proceeded in silence.

As Darcy opened her chamber door and followed her in, Elizabeth turned. He opened his mouth to speak, but the wrath permeating her countenance froze his words as a cold chill overtook his senses. The torture of the next hours would rival Elizabeth's rejection of him at Hunsford.

~*~

Chapter Five

Revenge and Frustration

Elizabeth's eyes burned with indignation, incensed by her husband's complete disregard for her feelings, and though her fiery look surely indicated otherwise, she kept her voice cool and calm as she lifted her chin and informed him, "I would rather you not sleep in my chamber tonight."

Darcy's left cheek twitched. His eyes locked with his wife's, each fixed upon the other for several drawn out moments before he spoke with a frosted tone of reserved civility.

"May I enquire, Mrs. Darcy, as to why you no longer desire me in your bed?"

Elizabeth's breath tensed as she looked at the floor and stammered, "I... I...have started my monthly courses...and so...I am indisposed." Her cheeks flamed as she swiftly turned her head and bit her lower lip.

Darcy gasped aloud. Relief washed over him when he realized his wife's reluctance to be with him was due to her indisposition. Noticing her blush, he assumed that his naïve wife was merely embarrassed. He smiled in delight at her hesitancy but then became mindful that she might be in some discomfort and therefore not feeling well.

"Lizzy, how long do your courses run?"

Her eyes widened, and she twisted her mouth before replying, "Usually, no longer than four or five days." Tears of frustration welled up in Elizabeth's eyes until one solitary tear escaped, slipping down her cheek and onto her dress.

"Do you experience any pain or discomfort at this time?"

Elizabeth tilted her head and creased her brow, wavering momentarily as she looked at him, her voice quivering as she answered, "No...none at all."

Pondering his wife's irritability, emotional dishevel and unease made Darcy construe that she was anxious from modesty rather than any discomfort, and her courses were the probable cause for such irrational behaviour.

Thus, he walked over to where she stood and put one hand upon her shoulder while, he wiped her tears away with the other. Carefully studying her, he made note how her lips pursed together as she gazed at him with a look he was unfamiliar with... a look that, had he not known better, might have adduced a warning, but this was his wife, the woman whom he loved... the woman who loved him.

He drew in a deep breath, and with a tender smile, he softly uttered, "Elizabeth, do not let this trouble you. I am accustomed to blood. It does not bother me in the least." With this said, he attempted to hold her, but she turned and walked to their bed.

Shock seized her heart. She reasoned that her husband would surely know about such matters, and, therefore, she admitted it should not be a surprise. But the confession of his being familiar with blood during lovemaking made her ill, grieved, and disheartened. Loneliness enveloped her.

Darcy, puzzled by her withdrawal, pressed further. "Whatever is the matter, Elizabeth? May I get you anything? Perhaps some wine or water?"

Elizabeth looked at him and shook her head. "No, I assure you I am fine. I would like only to rest."

He crossed the room and guided her to lie on the bed and then began to massage the back of her neck. She lay still. He continued his ministrations for several minutes longer, and she drowsily closed her eyes. Elizabeth felt devoid of emotion with his touch, but, when he started to kiss her brow, cheek, ear, and lips, she opened her eyes wide and cried, "Please, I ask you once more to sleep in your own chamber tonight!"

Incredulity entered Darcy's mind as he lay by his wife, gaping at her. He then derisively declared, "I will not sleep in any bed but *this* one. It will be *you*, Elizabeth, who leaves our bed if you so desire, ***not*** I."

Before either could say another word, a knock was heard at the door. Darcy bitterly bid entry. Mr. Chaffin appeared within the doorway. "Sir, you are wanted by Mr. Manning and Mr. Sheldon downstairs. They are waiting in your study. Would you have them remain or appoint another time?"

"Blast!" he cursed, then recollected himself. "Yes, I will be there directly."

He slid off the bed and stood. Walking to the mirror to straighten his cravat, he stated, "I hope not to be detained long, and I also hope to find you in this bed when I return."

Elizabeth did not respond but continued to lie numbly upon the mattress.

Darcy bolted from the room, nearly colliding with his cousin in the hall.

"Why, Darcy, are you going down again? I would be game for some billiards."

Darcy rolled his eyes. "No, Fitzwilliam, I have some matters of import to speak of with my steward."

"It cannot wait until morning?"

In exasperation he replied, "No, I must go now. Please excuse me."

Richard shrugged his shoulders, said something about tomorrow, and continued to his room.

When the Master of Pemberley reached the bottom of the stairs, he noticed an older woman sitting on a divan in the vestibule. He acknowledged her presence with a nod as he passed.

Mr. Sheldon and Mr. Manning were seated facing his desk. Darcy entered quietly and sat in his chair. He looked at the gentlemen before him and asked what preparations had been made.

Mr. Manning responded, "I have arranged for Thomas Wilkens to drive to Liverpool. He is young but has adequate experience tending and driving horses. His parents have consented to his going. The relief team, as you are already aware, should be at the first post station, and, if they are able to procure fresh horses themselves, they will board our Belgians and carry on to the next stop."

Mr. Sheldon spoke next. "I have found an elderly lady by the name of Mrs. Watts to be a companion for the maid. She is from Lambton and desires to go to a village near Liverpool. Her daughter is to give birth within the month, and she wishes to attend her."

The master enquired, "I suppose that is the elderly woman presently seated in the entrance hall?"

"Yes, sir, we thought it best to bring her here for the night since their route would normally take them away from Lambton. If this is not acceptable, I could take her home, and they could start earlier and go to the village first."

Darcy shook his head and told his steward that would not be necessary. He then asked if Mrs. Reynolds had been informed of the overnight guest. Sheldon told him she had not.

"Very well," Darcy stated, "it seems all is in order. I am grateful for your diligence in these preparations, especially in such uncomfortable conditions. I thank you."

Both gentlemen nodded their heads in response to Mr. Darcy's words of gratitude. They all stood, and Darcy shook their hands. After they departed, he pulled the bell cord to summon Mrs. Reynolds. She came with alacrity.

"Yes, sir?"

"Mrs. Reynolds, there is a Mrs. Watts who will travel with Clara to Liverpool. She is to stay the night. Please show her to a room and attend to her needs. She waits in the hall."

"Very good, sir. Will there be anything else?"

Darcy looked pensive for a moment and asked if she would send up to the mistress' chambers some cocoa for himself and Mrs. Darcy.

The housekeeper smiled and said she would have it done right away.

Darcy watched her go as he continued to sit for a time, staring blankly into space. Rubbing his mouth with his fingers and then running his hand through his hair, he began to reflect on his wife, whom he hoped to find in their bed upon his return. What in the world had come over her? He had heard the crude jokes, jests, and comments from men about how women act when they are 'on the rag'. Yet, he had no first-hand experience of being in close contact with any woman on a regular basis to know if this is what he should expect from Elizabeth in the future. He realized he had never experienced such anger from her as he witnessed earlier in their chamber. In the few months of their engagement, she had never shown signs of such irritability. He felt hurt for her wish of not wanting to be with him. Their marriage was barely two weeks old, and his wife no longer desired him in her bed. This was a bad omen, and he felt ill at the thought of it. Yet, it suddenly occurred to him that Elizabeth might also be out of sorts because of Clara's delayed travel plans. She would surely be overjoyed to learn that all had been established concerning her maid's journey. He arose from his chair, and, with a hopeful heart, set off for his wife's bedchamber.

~*~

Immediately after her husband departed, Elizabeth began to prepare for bed. As she was removing her clothes, Clara entered from the servants' door to assist her mistress.

"Clara, you look so happy. Have you news of your mother?"

"No, ma'am, but Mrs. Reynolds has informed me that I'll be leaving at first light. I want to thank you so much for your arrangements on my behalf. I'm not sure I would be going if not for your help."

Elizabeth's face betrayed her astonishment. She marvelled that anything had been done given the reluctance her husband demonstrated with the mere mention of the subject.

"Hmm...you mean to say that Mrs. Reynolds has informed you that I was responsible for the arrangements?"

"No," the maid replied, "but I only assumed it was so because of your promise earlier that all would be made ready, and nothing had been done before. I truly be thanking you, Mrs. Darcy, from the bottom of me heart."

Elizabeth smiled at the girl and told her she was happy for her and hoped all would be well with her mother.

Clara informed her that Mrs. Reynolds had asked Sally to attend the mistress in her absence. She assured Mrs. Darcy that Sally was a hard worker but might not have as much experience with the styling of hair.

In an effort to put her maid's mind at ease, Elizabeth averred that she was not fastidious, so Sally need not worry.

"Oh, I know that, ma'am. I told her you're one of the sweetest ladies I have ever made acquaintance with."

This compliment brought an instant smile to Elizabeth's face, and she heartily thanked Clara for it.

~*~

Upon reaching his wife's door, Darcy decided that, instead of going in, he would first go to his own chamber and call for his valet to prepare for bed. Mr. Chaffin was already within as he entered. The valet was taken aback to see his master this late in the evening within his own room. He had realized quickly after the arrival of Mrs. Darcy that his master was ardently in love with his wife and there would be no separate sleeping arrangements as so many of the landed gentry chose to do.

"Ah, Chaffin, I am glad you are here. I want you to wake me a half hour before Thomas Wilkens departs with the sleigh. I would like to speak with him before he leaves."

"Yes, sir."

"Please help me with my cravat. Do you have my nightshirt?"

Chaffin hurried to his master's aid, and while removing Mr. Darcy's cravat, waistcoat, and tailcoat, he informed him that a fresh shirt had already been laid on the bed. The manservant then helped remove each boot.

Wearing only his trousers and shirt, Darcy walked into his dressing area and started to clean his teeth with cinnamon powder. He discarded his shirt and walked back to his bed to slip on the clean one. Mr. Chaffin rushed to assist in the removal of his master's trousers, but Darcy waved him away with the mere flick of his hand. The valet continued to gather the discarded clothing and then laid out the articles for the morrow.

Darcy paused in front of his mirror and attempted to smooth his hair, with little success. He then splashed cologne on his jaw, wiping the excess upon his shirt.

~*~

Elizabeth sat at her vanity removing the pins from her hair when her husband entered. He was satisfied to see her still within. Her head turned upon his entrance, and she noticed not only the exhaustion in his face but his changed attire. Advancing to where she sat, he assumed the task of removing her hairpins. Elizabeth met his gaze in the mirror but neither spoke. One by one the pins fell to the floor and her silky tresses tumbled over her shoulders. Seeing the longing in her husband's manner as he removed the pins and looked upon her hair and face, her heart began to fill with tenderness. She realized, with Clara's news, that she no longer felt anger over his prior offence at the table.

Darcy leaned down to dust feathery, light kisses upon her neck while his hand pushed back her nightgown to expose the velvety skin of her alabaster shoulder. Breathing lightly, he placed tender, tantalizing kisses along her delicate collarbone and up onto the hollow of her neck to her ear where he took her earlobe into his mouth and gently suckled it. She moaned softly with the tantalizing sensations that the soft, velvet warmth of his lips upon her flesh produced within her body.

Suddenly he stopped and whispered on a gentle breath, "Where are you sleeping tonight, my love?"

Elizabeth turned her countenance upward and caught his gaze, her eyes burning with desire. Pleased that she wanted him, his lips turned upward into a boyish smile.

Still, she did not answer, but his smile broadened in confidence and he teasingly confirmed, "You will sleep with me, then, in *our* bed... our bed where you belong."

She only nodded in answer but still did not move. Determined to have his wife in his bed, Darcy placed more kisses behind her ear rousing a melodious moan of pleasure to escape her throat.

"You're determined to have your way, are you not, Fitzwilliam Darcy?"

"I am a man with a purpose... and my purpose is to love my wife," he murmured in-between soft kisses.

She closed her eyes and sighed deeply, tilting her head to allow him full access which he gladly took. Then, remembering the good news which was sure to please her, Darcy lifted his head and exclaimed, "I have something to tell you that I think shall make you happy."

Elizabeth opened her eyes, smiled slightly, and turned her full attention towards him.

"Your maid, Clara, will leave on the morrow. Plans have been set, and, hopefully, if all goes well on their journey, she will be with her mother by the week's end." She smiled brilliantly and Darcy asked, "Does this news bring you pleasure?"

"Most certainly, I thank you for having arranged it."

He pulled her upward into his embrace. Running his fingers through her hair, and placing more kisses upon her forehead, he bent low and captured her lips. Their kiss was deep, fervent, and lingering. Finally, as they stepped back, Darcy clutched his wife's hand and attempted to lead her to their bed. Yet, she did not move. Looking inquisitively at her, he stopped and turned back.

"Pray, what is it Lizzy?"

She took in a deep breath and squared her shoulders. "It is just that I do not understand why you would not discuss Clara's travel arrangements with me. I do not see why I should be shunned and kept in the dark where my own maid is concerned?"

Darcy eyes narrowed as he pressed his lips tight in frustration. He looked down for a moment and then puffed out the breath he was holding.

"Elizabeth, I would rather not discuss this at present. *Come* to bed."

Dropping her hand, he wearily walked to the bedstead, lifted the bedclothes and crawled beneath them. With a pat of his hand on the top of the counterpane, he signalled for her to follow suit, but she was in no mood to dismiss the subject.

"Elizabeth, come here, my love."

She folded her arms across her chest and walked slowly towards him.

Darcy yawned and claimed, "I am weary. We have had a long day. Let us rest." He pulled back the mantle, inviting her to join him.

She stood near the bedside and deliberated for some seconds before deciding to enter. After settling beneath the sheets, she turned her back to her husband and bid him a good night.

Darcy breathed out with dissatisfaction, but rolled onto his side, running his hands up and down her back. He snuggled closer while his hands went from caressing her back to her upper thigh. Kisses were placed down the side of her neck as he moulded his body against hers. He pressed against her for some time but achieved no response from his lovely lady. Then, placing his hand upon her shoulder, he gently tried to turn her to face him. Elizabeth, however, was not of a mind to acquiesce and pulled her shoulder back with each attempt. *Peeved* would correctly describe the young husband's pitiful state at this injunction.

"Lizzy, turn to face me."

She did not respond.

"Elizabeth, I know you are not asleep. Please turn and face me."

Finally she turned over and looked at him in a blank fashion. Darcy smiled and started to embrace her, but she slid away from his overture.

"Elizabeth, I will not play these cat-and-mouse games with you any longer. If you do not want to love me, just say so."

"I thought you were weary?" she stated cynically.

"I am weary…weary of your rejection."

"No, Fitzwilliam, you told me you did not wish to speak of Clara at present because you are exhausted."

Contempt scorched Darcy's countenance. "And so this is why you reject me? You might consider the humiliation you cost me before you scorn me in our bed!"

Elizabeth's colour was high. Casting off the counterpane, she leapt from the bed and marched around it to face her husband. His body likewise shifted in response, and he sat upright.

Arms at her sides with hands tightened into fists, she appeared fierce and intimidating with her stance.

"You speak of *your* humiliation with no thought of my own."

Darcy responded with his usual dismissive air when something was not to his liking. Staring directly into her face, he sputtered, "*Your* humiliation, Elizabeth? I think not. Since when have I been out of the bounds of propriety?"

She raised her brows and smirked. "Oh yes, the grand Master of Pemberley is ever attentive and proper."

"You are mocking me."

Just then a distinct knock was detected.

In irritation Darcy called out, "What?"

The door opened and in stepped a maid carrying a tray with two mugs of cocoa and some crusted, sweet bread. It was apparent the young girl could feel the tension as soon as she entered the room. Nervously, she began to convey a message from the kitchen.

"Mrs. Potter asked me to relate her regrets for how long it's taken to prepare the cocoa. She was out of milk and had to have some fetched."

Exasperation was read all over the master's deportment as he waved his pointing finger to a side table near a chair for the lass to set the tray upon.

"No bother," was the only reply he gave for the apology.

The girl curtseyed and scurried to the door. Elizabeth called to her and asked her name.

"Sally, ma'am."

"Well, Sally, I take it you are my new maid in Clara's absence?"

"Yes, mistress."

Cordially, Elizabeth stated, "I look forward to getting to know you, and please thank Mrs. Potter for the bother. I love cocoa."

The maid smiled, and, with a quick bob of her head, was gone.

Darcy shook his head and rolled his eyes at his wife's obvious ridicule with reference to his words spoken to the maid.

"Elizabeth, I will not have you continue to abuse me so."

She looked at him in wonder. "Whatever do you mean? It is not I who continues to act in such a rude manner."

He blinked in disbelief. "I suppose you thought I was uncivil just now?"

"Undoubtedly."

Bewildered, he rubbed his mouth with his hand and then got out of the bed and in a single-minded posture, walked closer to where his wife stood. Within inches of her face, Darcy wore a brooding expression while he strived to use some restraint in the level of his tone.

"Madam, maybe you are unaware of the difficulties many individuals have encountered in procuring travel arrangements for your maid. My men were sent out from their homes not only in the cold of the day, but in the bitter chill of the night to enquire for a travelling companion so Clara would not ride unaccompanied. The Berlin had to be repaired and runners put upon it in order to send one sleigh ahead in hopes that they could journey farther in one day's time. Lives are at peril because *you* made a promise to your maid that she would leave by dawn tomorrow. Yet, you belittle my reserve in informing you of the particulars that resulted as a consequence of your guarantee."

Elizabeth could feel his breath as he spoke in hot anger. She felt a mixture of fear, regret, and shame, but, most of all, rage began to rule.

Without flinching, she raised her chin in defiance and boldly declared, "If it were not for your secrecy in the first place, a promise never would have been given. I had thought *'disguise of every sort'* was your abhorrence?"

He noticed a triumphant look cross her features as she hurled his own words back into his face. With a raised voice, he ordered, "Enough! I will not be spoken to in such a fashion. I am going to bed, and I expect you to come to bed as well."

In three long strides he crossed the room and heatedly lay down upon the mattress. Elizabeth folded her arms over her chest and continued to stand in place before finally addressing her husband.

"So, you will not leave and sleep in your own chamber tonight?"

"No, Elizabeth, I will ***not***." His eyes narrowed upon her.

"Very well then. You did say earlier that I could choose not to sleep in our bed, did you not?"

Wounded, he retorted, "Do as you wish, Lizzy. I will not stop you."

She nodded her head in acknowledgement to his granted permission and then simply informed him that she would be sleeping within his bedchamber.

Feeling sorry for himself, he watched her walk to the tray and take up some bread and a mug. She sipped at her drink cautiously at first until she determined it was not scalding. "I thank you for the cocoa, Fitzwilliam. It was very thoughtful."

Elizabeth then turned and walked through the dressing rooms and into his chamber. By the time she arrived, the drink threatened to spill as she quickly set it down with trembling hands.

Breathless, she stood for a moment and then stomped her foot before closing her eyes in anguish over what she had just done. Where had her courage led? After all, her pride preceded it and would, likewise, not permit her to return. Besides, she would not tolerate her husband's insensitivity to her feelings when affairs were rightly within the bounds of her influence. No, she would have to weather this storm, and weather it she would.

She crawled beneath the counterpane and drew it up around her head. An hour later, after many shed tears, Elizabeth found sleep.

In the adjoining chamber, her husband was not quite so fortunate. He tossed and turned as he fumed over his wife's pigheadedness. He pondered over the past weeks and even before the wedding, yet he could not think of one time when she had acted so obtuse. What could have made her turn on him in such a manner? Then it suddenly dawned on him. There was one time in which she acted exactly as she had tonight: *Hunsford Parsonage.* He blinked upon this discovery but did not know what to make of it. Then, her aloofness had been due to his ill-mannered proposal. Darcy began to surmise if she could have been experiencing her courses at that time as well. Well, if this were the case, he would have to try to avoid her at all costs during such bouts. He could not abide her insolent exhibition. *Four days*! He could manage to stay out of her way for four days. Even though his body demanded otherwise, he would steel himself through it. *Yes, that's the ticket!* He then turned his pillow over and, after punching it several times, sighed and fell into a vexing, fitful sleep.

~*~

Chapter Six

Devilry and Devotion

Mr. Gaylord Chaffin was an honest man. He had been Mr. George Darcy's valet since young master Fitzwilliam Darcy was but five years of age. It was the wish of the elder Mr. Darcy that Mr. Chaffin become his son's personal man servant upon his departure to Cambridge. At the time of this transition, Mr. Chaffin was very familiar with the young master's ways and considered him a replica of his father. Fitzwilliam Darcy was not carefree, akin to most young men of noble birth. The young master did not squander his time and money on the fashionable, idle pursuits of his day: namely, gambling, drinking, and frequenting the burlesque quarters found in Covent Garden. Lascivious behaviour as this led most susceptible gentlemen into unfavourable liaisons with prostitutes from the lowest sectors of society. In fact, many of these youths were instructed and even encouraged by their fathers to seek such leisure at the well-known establishments which catered exclusively to gentlemen from Mayfair and the other West-end residences of London.

Distinct from such straying young men, Mr. Chaffin's new master was responsible. He had been groomed by his parents from an early age to take family responsibilities seriously, and he was advised specifically on the vices which could endanger the family living or jeopardize a marriage. The senior Mr. Darcy warned his son clearly of the diseases to be had in brothel houses and made his disgust quite clear concerning the acceptable practice of taking a mistress. Likewise, his father impressed upon his son the significance of marrying a woman of the highest standing, not only for his own desire, but also their suitability for bearing and perpetuating the Darcy lineage.

Fitzwilliam Darcy was made aware of all matters involved in the establishment of his familial domain. His tutelage did not take in financial administration alone, though the heir was sent to Cambridge to receive instruction specifically for this purpose. Equally, he had been primed and cast while yet a lad about the everyday functions of Pemberley.

The estate raised merino sheep. Merino sheep were known to produce the some of the world's most premium and softest wool. His father had desired that Fitzwilliam gain hands-on experience with the land in order to become familiar with the very core of Pemberley's livelihood: the mainstay which numerous individuals depended upon. Thus, George Darcy had sent his son with the overseer to be instructed in abundant tasks, from fostering the horses, mending fences and repairing drains, to the erection of sheds, yet, it was soon discovered that the young master's favoured employ was in the nurture of the sheep.

Young Master Darcy would join the overseer's sons and some of the tenant's boys in the general care of the sheep: herding, pasturing, sheering, lambing and the feeding of barley during the winter months. Often, the boys would take turns flocking the sheep together for the night. Then the lad who was shepherding them would spend the long dark hours alone with only the herd for company. Fitzwilliam learned readily that sheep were social creatures, not just with each other but with humans as well. He came to notice which ones were the leaders among the flock, and that, once trust was established with the shepherd, they would respond by name when called upon. He loved their ways and how he could calm them with the mere sound of his voice.

These tasks helped to mould the future master's outlook regarding Pemberley's revenue and those who depended upon it. Conscious of the efforts of so many in the gargantuan management of an estate such as Pemberley, he was sobered to accept the lot which would one day rest exclusively upon his shoulders. Thus, from an early age, sobriety became inherent in Fitzwilliam Darcy's character, and, due to the lessons learned from the methods his father chose, he was now a master who not only accepted his responsibilities out of tradition but, moreover, embraced them with a love attained only by those personally acquainted with the burdens and rewards associated with physical labour.

Thoughts regarding Mr. Fitzwilliam Darcy filled Mr. Chaffin's mind as he took the servants' stairs to that man's chambers. He reflected on all of his master's decisions and had not yet found one wanting. It seemed to him that Mr. Darcy had indeed married prudently, and, as a result, Pemberley's proliferation was almost certain. Chaffin opened the door and noticed that the fire was nearly out. Instead of waiting for one of the other servants to rekindle it, he picked up the coal bucket himself and poured the black nuggets into the grate. On replacing the bucket in its place, he discerned the bed covers disturbed and also noted his master's dark hair peaking out from the top of the sheets.

At this unexpected occurrence, Mr. Chaffin paused and wondered for a moment at the break in Mr. Darcy's habit of sleeping in his wife's chamber. *Oh well*, the valet surmised, *this situation is more convenient because I will not have to wait for Mrs. Darcy's maid to appear in order to summon the master for his early appointment with the Wilkens boy.*

Walking to the side of the bed, he stopped and loudly cleared his throat. "Mr. Darcy, sir, you asked me to waken you before the sleigh departs."

Beneath the covers, Elizabeth's eyes opened wide with the hearing of Mr. Chaffin's voice, and with the sudden remembrance of her hasty decision to sleep in her husband's chamber, her body stiffened.

When no response was to be had, Mr. Chaffin redoubled his efforts by stating a bit louder, "Sir, you requested that I awaken you before the party's departure."

Mr. Chaffin then did something he had only done one other time in Mr. Darcy's life: he placed his hand where he thought the master's shoulder would be and gave it a firm shake.

Jumping up in a fright as she felt Mr. Chaffin's hand upon her breast, Elizabeth screamed, which in turn caused the valet's heart to startle. Mortification clearly appeared upon both of their faces. Mr. Chaffin's mouth hung wide while his eyes blinked in shock.

"I...I am...sorry...madam. I had no idea. I take it the master has already arisen and gone down?"

Closing her eyes in humiliation, Mrs. Darcy replied, "No, actually...I am not sure. I mean... Oh! I am not sure what I mean. I think you shall find him in my chamber, Mr. Chaffin, and you may rouse him if he is not yet awake."

The valet raised his brows and replied, "Very good, madam."

He then turned and proceeded to go through the dressing chambers in search of his master when he met Sally coming in from the servant's entrance carrying buckets of hot water. He quickly informed her in as few words as possible that her mistress was residing in the master's chambers.

Sally became wide-eyed and nervously asked, "Should I be going in there for her?"

The older gentleman only shrugged his shoulders helplessly. The inexperienced maid was left to her own judgment while he sought out his master and attempted to carry out his duties to him alone. Sally deliberated and then reasoned that if Mr. Chaffin was going into the mistress' chambers, she could go into the master's. However, providence was on the young girl's side because, just as she approached the door while walking through Mr. Darcy's dressing area, Mrs. Darcy appeared in only her nightgown and smiled at her. The mistress then asked the young maid's assistance in readying herself as quickly as possible so she could see Clara off.

Sally curtseyed and informed her that she already had hot water in the bath. Elizabeth smiled and walked forward. The door between the two dressing areas remained open, and, while Elizabeth proceeded towards her chamber, Mr. Darcy advanced as well with Mr. Chaffin following closely upon his heels.

Elizabeth, holding her head high, moved to the side to allow her husband and his valet to pass. Darcy strode in his usual erect manner but stopped and moved to one side while gesturing with a slight bow and a wave of his hand for his wife to have the honours. Uncomfortably, Mr. Chaffin and Sally looked to the floor until Mrs. Darcy raised her chin high and said, "I thank you," and moved forward.

She then went through the doorway and passed by her husband with a slight brush of her arm on his. He quickly walked on, only pausing, after Chaffin had passed through, to give the door a decidedly, thunderous slam. Both Elizabeth and her maid startled from the unexpected noise and looked at one another, but said nothing.

Elizabeth hurriedly discarded her gown and asked Sally to lay out a warm woollen dress, stockings and boots. She asked for her green, heavy woollen coat.

She hastily finished her bath, and she and the maid had her dressed in record time.

"I will need my gloves and scarf, as well."

Sally ran to the closet and fetched them as Elizabeth walked past into her chamber. She noticed that Fitzwilliam had not touched his cocoa and, for a brief moment, felt badly for the extra effort Mrs. Potter had made to provide the drinks. Since she could not spare the time to reflect on the pang of guilt such thoughts produced, she reached for her scarf and gloves, thanked her maid and darted from the room.

In her mad dash, she collided with her husband in the corridor, lost her balance, and fell inelegantly upon her bottom.

"Elizabeth, whatever in the world are you doing?" Darcy reached his hand down to assist her as she stood. "Are you all right?"

Feeling a bit dizzy from the fall, she mumbled that she was fine and began to walk shakily to the stairwell. Darcy caught hold of her arm and gently pulled her back and asked, "Where do you think you are going at this time of morning?"

Closing her eyes and taking a deep breath, she replied with a coolness she did not feel, "I, like you, sir, am about to see the sleigh off."

Darcy's chin tucked back and he blinked in disbelief at his wife's absurdity. Yet, he thought it not prudent to reason with her at present, considering her foul mood the previous night.

"Well, if you are resolute on going down, then I insist on your taking my arm."

Frowning for a second, she threaded her arm through his and they descended together. Neither said a word. Elizabeth thought to maintain appearances for the rest of the household staff. Though Chaffin and Sally knew of their quarrel, they surely would say nothing. When they approached the entrance, the butler hurried to open the door for his master and mistress.

On stepping out, Darcy immediately discerned the air was not as cold as yesterday and felt heartened by this discovery—perhaps all would go well with the journey of his servants. Drawing his wife close to his side so as to prevent her falling on the frozen steps, he guided them across the snowy path to the sleigh.

Hot bricks were being placed in the front boards and back. They were then covered with light quilts. Mr. Manning began helping Mrs. Watts into the carriage. Clara stood behind, and Elizabeth broke free from her husband's grasp and approached her maid. "Clara, I am so happy that you are finally on your way. I hope you find all to be well, and I do not want you worrying about your position. I will secure it for you to be sure."

The young woman smiled and heartily embraced her mistress. "Thank ye so much, ma'am, for all you have done."

"To be truthful Clara, it had nothing to do with me. I think we owe it all to Mr. Darcy."

"I know it, ma'am, but because of your encouragement, I'm sure that is why I'm going."

Elizabeth smiled brightly and embraced her maid once more. "Now you make sure you let us know when you arrive and keep us informed of your mother's condition. I shall look forward to your return, but I want you to stay for as long as you are needed. Sally and I will make do in the meantime."

Elizabeth stepped back so Mr. Manning could assist Clara into the carriage. She turned to search the crowd for her husband and found him on the other side of the sleigh talking to a young man who was apparently the driver. She guessed the youth to be around seventeen or eighteen at the most. This surprised her since she assumed he might be inexperienced for such a strenuous journey, but her husband was in all probability made aware of all the arrangements and therefore approved of the young man. Darcy handed the youth a small leather pocketbook with the name Fitzwilliam Darcy stitched along one edge and then he shook the boy's hand. Elizabeth wondered why her husband would give this servant his own pocketbook, but then she surmised that the servant must be highly esteemed.

Darcy briefly checked over the horses one time and then stepped to the side and looked to find his wife. Seeing that she was clear, he nodded his head to Thomas, and the sleigh was off. Some servants waved and called wishes of luck and then returned to the house to begin their morning routines. Darcy came to his wife's side and offered his arm to her. She readily took it and asked, "Who was the lad driving the team? He looked awfully young."

"His name is Thomas Wilkens and he is eighteen years of age."

"Do you think he is experienced enough for these conditions?"

Darcy grimaced. "Well, let us hope."

"You mean you do not know. Fitzwilliam, why ever would you have chosen him if this be the case?"

Sighing, he patiently answered his wife. "Lizzy, he is a mere lad, it is true. He has never been given a task such as this, but he has experience with the sleigh and horses, and offered his services. Therefore, due to the fact that he has proven himself a hard worker in the past and has been faithful in every undertaking, I considered him able."

"Is that why you have entrusted him with your personal pocketbook?"

"My! My! Are we not full of questions this morning? And, since you desire to know *all* the details, it is not because of my trust in him only, but it will ensure that help shall be available if needed."

Though her husband spoke in earnest, Elizabeth felt like a child granted a special privilege at his condescension of indulging her query. She remained silent to see if he would offer any further details, but, when silence ensued, she decided to let the topic rest.

They entered the house, and the servants came to take their coats. Standing still for the removal of his wife's bonnet, Darcy waited for her in order to proceed through the entrance hall together.

He held out his hand while she put forth hers freely until it was grasped by her husband. Darcy again drew Elizabeth to his side to garner some degree of intimacy. His hand began to caress her arm, and he gave her a gentle, sidelong squeeze. "You know I love you, Elizabeth." He looked at the contour of her face to establish her reaction.

Softly, she replied, "Yes."

Darcy felt this was a good start to make up for their mishap of the previous evening, yet he was reluctant to go further. "What are your plans for the day?"

"Well, I have to meet with Mrs. Potter and the kitchen staff to go over the menus. I also desire to work on some correspondence and spend some time with Georgiana."

This pleased him and he stated, "It is too early for breakfast, and I also have some estate matters that need my attention. What do you say we take care of our business and meet for breakfast at the usual hour? Would that be satisfactory, Mrs. Darcy?"

Elizabeth bit her lip. She wished it could be that simple, but she knew that a discussion regarding Lydia's letter could no longer be avoided. "I think that is a splendid idea, but would you mind if I were to speak with you about a specific matter first?"

Darcy hesitated. He wanted no more discussions similar to the one last night. However, he realized it was a new day after all, and Elizabeth seemed more like her usual self.

"I think that can easily be arranged, your study or mine?" He smiled lovingly at her.

She was a little surprised by his playful air, and it seemed to bolster her spirit for the unveiling of an unpleasant revelation which was sure to bring her husband some discontent.

"Mine," she replied pleasantly. Darcy smiled and took her hand in his as they walked to the room.

He went directly to the green, tub chair and took a seat. He crossed one leg over the other and rested his elbows upon the chair's arms while he clasped his hands together. Elizabeth stood still, trying to decide if she wished to sit or remain standing. Her husband's voice broke her trance as he asked her to come to him, and, after Elizabeth proceeded to where he sat, he pulled her down upon his lap, encircled his arms about her and asked, "What is it you wish to speak to me about?" Darcy was sorely tempted to kiss his wife. It seemed an eternity since he had held her in his arms.

Flustered with the idea of being in such close proximity to her husband as she endeavoured to relate the blackmail made Elizabeth nervous beyond measure. She envisioned she might topple to the floor as her husband rushed for refuge to the nearest corner of the room at the shock of her distasteful tale. He might even reconsider his avowal to always sleep in her bed. Oh—what a dreadful sister and brother-in-law to contend with!

"Did I mention to you that I received a letter from Lydia the other day?"

Darcy's expression darkened as his arms fell to his side. Elizabeth began to tense more than before. He replied, "No, you did not."

Stammering with her words she forged onward. "Yes...well... she...hopes to visit Pemberley by summer's end." Elizabeth glanced at her husband's features in an effort to determine how this intelligence fared before proceeding with the worse, which would likely ban Lydia from the estate forever.

She felt Darcy shift beneath her. Hence, she decided to stand with the intention of retrieving Lydia's missive. Her husband, however, rose as well and held the palm of his hand up in mid air so as to halt her progress. Knitting her brows together, she gave him her full attention.

"In all honesty, Elizabeth, I would rather not discuss your sister at present. I have many matters of business to attend to and the morning has gone well thus far. So, surely this can wait for a later time. I am in no mood to hear of your sister and her rogue of a husband. Please spare me any details of their miseries, woes, and misfortunes. I have heard them all before."

His contempt she could easily understand, for she, too, felt it. But, it was his dismissal which truly unnerved her. Was she always to be treated as a child now that she was his wife? To be told who she could and could not be concerned for and when and when not to discuss concerns. This was preposterous, and surely this could not be her lot as the Mistress of Pemberley. It seemed to Elizabeth that, with the arrival of the colonel and Georgiana, her husband was reverting to his taciturn tendencies. She folded her arms across her chest and looked at him in frustration.

Recognizing that a repeat of last night was now beginning, he rolled his eyes, breathed in deeply and tightened his jaw to brace himself for the onslaught.

Elizabeth was at a loss to know what to do. It seemed to her that no matter what she wished to discuss, her husband was unwilling.

"Fitzwilliam, would you please just hear me out before you respond?"

The mildness in her voice caught him off guard. "Elizabeth, whatever do you mean? I always give consideration to what you say. Of course, I will listen."

His statement made her brows lift in wonder. She could scarcely believe he was ignorant of his treatment of her for the past twenty-four hours. She remained calm, however, and said, "Yes my love, you are very good to me in taking care of my comforts and pleasures." She spontaneously smiled with a wicked glee when one pleasure in particular came vividly to mind. Darcy perceived her thought and became distracted with the desire of wanting to make love to his wife immediately. But his curiosity was keen, and he listened carefully to her next words.

"I am afraid, however, that you are not as solicitous of my views." All thoughts of lovemaking were suddenly shattered, and he frowned.

"Elizabeth, whatever do you mean? Please speak plainly. On one hand you admit that I am all kindness just to contradict it a moment later. Do you not know that I made all the arrangements for your maid because of your desire to have her at home with her mother? Do you not comprehend that many have sacrificed because of you? Do I not now stand here because you desired to talk with me? I am at a loss to understand your distress." With a dejected air, he sat again in the chair and began to twist his signet ring.

She was completely dumbfounded by her husband's assessment of the situation. Was this what Charlotte meant when she claimed all marriages had their trials and vexations?

"Oh dear, Fitzwilliam, I fear that I am not conveying my thoughts in an articulate fashion."

Darcy rolled his eyes and snorted softly with this admission and, in consequence, Elizabeth became indignant once more.

"I see no reason for you to mock me, Fitzwilliam. After all, we would not need this discussion if you were considerate of my feelings."

Standing quickly, he stated, "Elizabeth, you are talking in circles. Just tell me—did I or did I not consider your feelings by arranging the travel for Clara?" He raised his hand again to gesture her to stop. "Only answer the question and then we may proceed."

Elizabeth gasped at his arrogance and with energy she cried, "How dare you indicate that I am a simpleton. Yes, maybe I am not doing the best job of communicating the problem at hand, but your presumptuous attitude is at the root of the difficulty, and your resolve in not discussing it has only complicated matters.

"You silenced me at every turn when I tried to gain an understanding of why Clara's arrangements were not forthcoming," she continued with feeling. "You treat me as a child to be scolded when my behaviour is not to your satisfaction, and you sneer in derision at my attempt to openly address it."

Darcy sighed heavily. "Elizabeth, I do not think you a simpleton. I have never thought any such thing. Yet, I will speak plainly if that is what you want. I was indeed appalled at the lack of good manners you displayed last night as we ate dinner. Whatever were you thinking to have discussed your maid's situation in that manner at the table in front of Georgiana and Fitzwilliam?"

His rebuke stung Elizabeth more than the previous night as a new wave of humiliation swept over her.

"In addition, you concern yourself in matters which are not proper. There is a line, or chain of command, so to say, that takes into consideration the wants and needs of all servants and staff. There is no possible way that I can personally attend to all of the servants' concerns. Therefore, I have an Overseer, Steward, and Housekeeper and several other staff members. These individuals deal directly with me only when they, themselves, cannot resolve matters in a satisfactory manner. If this were not the case, I would be worn to a frazzle with every whim, folly, and fancy that betook each individual within the confines of the park. I cannot involve myself in every concern as I have done with Clara. Surely, you will have to consider this before you make promises which directly involve me."

Elizabeth's eyes were downcast and she remained quiet. She felt wretched and ashamed. Memories flooded her mind's eye of her family's loud banter around the table at Longbourn as they discussed any and all topics. Her only desire at that instant was to flee her husband's presence.

Darcy frowned as he looked at his wife. He hated the bluntness of his words but felt they were unavoidable. He knew Elizabeth was rational and would soon come to see that directness was necessary to resolve their dilemma.

He walked over to her and softly queried, "If you would like to read me your sister's letter, I am willing to listen. I should have listened earlier."

Elizabeth looked intently into his eyes and considered her choices. In a small voice she said, "No, as you suggested it can wait for a different time. For the moment, I am weary of discussion. It is not really that important anyway, just Lydia's usual ramblings on all her woes as you have already surmised."

She lied and she knew it. How could she tell him one more thing which would only bring more condemnation upon her head? No, she would have to deal with Lydia and Wickham on her own. She could not bear to reveal the contents of the letter now.

Darcy's heart was heavy for her, yet he knew all was for the best. He squeezed her hand and noticed it flinch as he did so. "Well...um...I shall see you for breakfast then."

"Yes."

He turned and strode from the room. After Darcy entered his study, he determined there was insufficient time to accomplish anything before breakfast. Thus, he leaned his elbows upon the desk and cradled his head in his hands. He felt miserable.

~*~

Elizabeth walked over to her desk and pulled out her bank ledger. She then proceeded to fill out a bank draft in the name of Mrs. George Wickham. She pulled down the writing shelf and wrote her sister a note conveying all her best wishes and a little something to help them through until things improved. She blotted her signature, folded the draft within her letter and then addressed the outside before sealing it.

Resolute with her rationale, in regards to her initial intentions of assisting Lydia financially when able, Elizabeth sought out the butler.

"Mr. Greene," said she, "would you please ensure this goes out with the next post?"

"Most certainly, madam."

After thanking him, Mrs. Darcy turned towards the Breakfast room. Walking along her way, she was met by Colonel Fitzwilliam and Georgiana.

"Oh Elizabeth!" cried her sister-in-law. "I am so happy to see you this morning! I was wondering what you had planned for the day and, to be truthful, was hoping to practice duets again."

Elizabeth smiled and answered, "That would be delightful, but I first have an appointment after breakfast with Mrs. Potter to become acquainted with the kitchen staff and the planning of the menus. Would you care to join me?"

Georgiana beamed. "Yes, I would love to accompany you."

Richard offered both of his arms and simultaneously escorted the ladies to breakfast. He stated, "I hope you both slept well last night."

Georgiana spoke first. "I did and I feel full of energy to face a new day and especially one with you, Elizabeth."

The colonel cried mischievously, "I am wounded, Georgie!" Do you no longer love me or desire my company?"

"Oh, do not be so absurd," replied Miss Darcy. "You know what I mean, Richard. You cannot play the pianoforte as well and are not nearly as much fun to giggle with, well...you are sometimes. It is just that you are not a girl."

"I think I understand, duck, because I would rather drink a brandy with your brother than you."

Georgiana's mouth dropped open and then her lips puckered in a pout while she swatted her cousin with her hand. "Very funny. You think you are so clever."

Elizabeth's spirits were so enlivened by their teasing that she had completely forgotten about Lydia's burdensome letter. As they entered the dining room together, they noticed Darcy already seated at the head of the table. He instinctively stood upon their entrance.

"Georgiana and Richard, good morning," he stated. "I do hope you slept well."

"Ah Darcy!" cried the colonel. "I could not help but sleep well at Pemberley. It has every comfort which I cannot afford."

Darcy smiled and shook his head at his cousin's usual grievances of being a second son.

"Yes," Darcy retorted, "but you are indeed fortunate to have so many family and friends who put up with you that you will never lack fare, raiment, or a roof over your head. There is no real fear of your becoming a pauper."

"I dare say you are right, Cousin. I am a favourite wherever I go, except perhaps with my brother, Hazel, and his wife. They do not look fondly upon me at all."

Georgiana observed Richard closely to try to determine if he was seriously wounded or expressing his typical amusement with sarcasm. She feared the former and, with true feeling, exclaimed, "Richard, you need not care what James and Elisha think of you because we care for you far more than the whole of the family put together! And, they can all go to *Bedlam* for all I care!"

Elizabeth, Darcy and Richard were more than shocked at her outburst. Darcy was exceedingly annoyed, but Richard and Elizabeth, after a few seconds, were enormously diverted at the girl's unusual boldness.

Richard quickly reassured her. "Do not distress yourself over me, my dear Georgie. I know I am loved by you and your brother beyond measure, and I would not give two shillings for what *my* brother thinks of me."

Richard's assurance relieved Georgiana's concerns for his welfare, and, as an afterthought, she piped up, "And do not forget Elizabeth—she loves you now as much as we do."

This statement made Colonel Fitzwilliam smile at his young cousin's exuberance and caused Elizabeth to blush brightly. Darcy frowned and spoke gravely. "Yes, well...now that we have promised Pemberley's doors will always be open to you, Fitzwilliam, perhaps we can commence with breakfast."

They grinned freely at Darcy's comment, placed their napkins upon their laps, and began to enjoy the meal.

Between bites, Richard asked Darcy about his plans for the day. His cousin informed him that, after meeting with his steward in the morning, he had no fixed engagements.

"Do you have something in mind, Fitzwilliam?" Darcy asked. "Do you still want to play billiards?"

"Oh, why yes, you know I love the game, but, if the temperature is a little warmer, I thought a short ride would be in order if you are up to it."

Darcy nodded in agreement while settling his tea cup. "That would be most enjoyable."

He then looked towards his wife and asked, "Elizabeth, what do you have on your agenda today?"

She gazed at him and simply stated, "I have a meeting with Mrs. Potter immediately after breakfast, and Georgiana has agreed to join me. After which, I believe we shall to go to the music room and practice more duets." She said this last while looking towards her sister-in-law who nodded her head vigorously.

"Very good, then shall we convene at luncheon, say around two o'clock?"

"Yes," replied she, "that would be most satisfactory." All smiled in confirmation of the set plans, and Richard and Georgiana excused themselves from the table—the colonel to write a letter to his parents and Georgiana to retrieve a shawl before going to the kitchen.

Darcy remained seated, silently staring at his discarded napkin. Elizabeth sipped her tea and wondered what occupied her husband's thoughts.

Her speculation was brief as Darcy softly cleared his throat. "Eliz...," more clearing, "Elizabeth...I would ask that you not encourage Georgiana in her outbursts. She displayed an unacceptable attitude towards her family, and to be rewarded with your smiles will only encourage such an exhibition in the future."

Elizabeth could not believe her ears and felt a chill run through her body. Was he insinuating that she was unfit as an example for his sister? This was too much!

"Sir, please excuse me, but I believe Georgiana to be a steady girl who undoubtedly will mature and blossom with our guidance but not with our censure. I see nothing wrong with the concern she expressed for her cousin. It is not as though she forgot herself in front of servants, strangers, or other relatives. She was among those dearest to her. Where else should one feel free to express their opinions and feelings?"

Elizabeth sat straighter and cast a satirical stare towards her husband. "At least you refrained from upbraiding her in front of me and the colonel, for which we can all be grateful!"

Rising quickly, she pushed back from the table. Darcy was more than astonished at his wife's reproach, and resentment filled his senses. It was at this moment that Georgiana retuned. Noticing the scowls on their faces, she perceived her timing ill—something was afoot between her brother and Elizabeth.

Darcy stood immediately upon his sister's entrance and, in a commanding tone, asked that she wait in the hall for a time. Georgiana was stunned and, with a pitying look towards her new sister, retreated in silence. Pulling the bell chord, the master summoned Mrs. Reynolds.

The elderly lady entered. "Yes sir?"

"Mrs. Reynolds, would you please inform Mrs. Potter that Mrs. Darcy has been detained but will be with her shortly."

"Yes, sir, right away."

As the housekeeper departed, kitchen maids arrived with trays to gather the breakfast dishes and remaining food.

Darcy, in no mood to leave the room, sternly dismissed them. "Leave at once, and close the door behind you."

The young girls nearly tripped over each other in their frantic attempt to clear the room. In their haste, they forgot about the door, so Penny, the younger of the two, closed her eyes in despair and hurried back to secure it.

Elizabeth marvelled over the pandemonium that had just played out before her eyes. Darcy scrutinized her expression and saw defiance written all over her face.

"Madam, you exhaust my patience. I realize that it is the time of your courses, yet I think it best that we come to terms with the hostility which continues to stand between us."

"My courses?" Elizabeth questioned in complete bafflement. She then rolled her eyes and laughed.

The humour subsided abruptly when her brows arched and she defied her husband further by saying, "Hostility indeed, and of your making." She then spoke with a swiftness which her husband thought impossible.

"Fitzwilliam Darcy! How dare you inform Mrs. Reynolds that my meeting with Mrs. Potter would be delayed without consulting me? How dare you be so presumptuous as to command all around you with every whim to your inclination? I shall not stand for it another minute. I will no longer be treated as a child or scolded as one at the table. You cannot bend and shape me into something you think I should be, and, if this is your design, you will soon discover that you are seriously mistaken. I will not be moulded or owned by you. I will not have you make me over with new crosses, dresses, or directives concerning my comportment. Just because you are the Master of Pemberley, does not mean you are the master of me!"

Darcy's eyes remained fixed as his wife hurled her words at him, yet they flinched at her last sentence. "Madam, I would like to inform you..."

He was stopped in mid-sentence when Elizabeth raised the palm of her hand to him and declared, "You will have to inform me some other time and at my convenience. I have an appointment which already has been rearranged twice. I am taking my leave."

She then briskly crossed the room and left the door open with her exit.

Darcy was thunderstruck. Events could not continue in this fashion. With every attempted remedy, the situation worsened. He ran his hand through his hair and then rubbed his chin. And what could jewellery and clothes possibly have to do with the problem? There was nothing to do but leave it alone for the present and hope that time would take care of the muddle. With these thoughts, he went to his study to discuss estate business with his steward, Mr. Sheldon.

~*~

Georgiana saw Elizabeth enter the vestibule and ran up to greet her. She took in her countenance and asked timidly, "Are you all right, Elizabeth?"

Elizabeth reached for her hand and gave it a squeeze. "Why, of course. Do not worry yourself. Your brother and I are only having a difference of opinion. That is all."

"Well," Georgiana timidly offered, "if you ever need to talk about it, I am a good listener."

"Thank you, Georgiana, or may I call you Georgie? Do you mind?"

"Oh no, I do not mind in the least. In fact, the only ones who call me that are Richard and Fitzwilliam. I would so like it if you would, and do you mind if I refer to you as Lizzy, like your sisters do?"

"No, not at all," Elizabeth assured. "I have been called Lizzy by all of my kin. In fact, there really is not any appellation that I mind unless it is Eliza. Yet, even that variation does not bother me except when said by certain persons." Elizabeth wiggled her brows to her new sister and the young girl giggled in delight with the understood reference to Caroline Bingley.

They made their way to the kitchen arm-in-arm to meet with the cook. Mrs. Potter was dressed in a freshly starched apron. She curtseyed to Mrs. Darcy and the mistress did likewise. She then proudly showed Elizabeth about the kitchen, the root cellars and meat larder. Elizabeth expressed her appreciation with the size of the hearth and the brick baking ovens. The cook told her mistress that she could turn out loaves of bread by the droves, because Pemberley's kitchen was stocked with all the necessary items and modern facilities for the greatest culinary enthusiast. The cook showed great delight in telling Mrs. Darcy all of the master's favourite dishes and desserts. Georgiana also added in her favourite foods, and they enjoyed a delightful hour together.

Mrs. Potter had prepared hot cocoa and offered it to them. They readily agreed and sat at one of the long tables with several servants. Elizabeth noticed the two maids who had scurried early from her husband's outburst.

She laughed to herself with the thought that Fitzwilliam had displayed more bad humour than Georgiana's idle wish of sending her relatives to Bedlam. She suddenly felt grieved, and a long sigh was audible to those nearby.

Georgiana asked if she were fatigued. Elizabeth replied, "Oh no, I am quite well. I just think I have been indoors far too long."

Smiling widely and with eyes sparkling, Georgiana pronounced her sister-in-law's pet name in a whisper. "Lizzy," it felt wonderful to address her new sister in this intimate, family way, "would you like to go for a walk in the snow instead of playing duets? We can practice another time, and, with the sun out this morning, the weather might not be too extreme."

Elizabeth looked at the girl in wonderment and appreciation. "Oh, Georgie, I would like that very much if you are certain and will not become too chilled."

"Oh no, I love the snow and have not been able to enjoy it this year, unless you count the tedious sleigh ride from Matlock."

They finished their cocoa, thanked Mrs. Potter for her hospitality and hurried up the stairs. Elizabeth suddenly had an idea. Stopping in her advance, she enthusiastically related it to her sister-in-law.

"Georgie, have you ever made snow-people before? Since I was a little girl, whenever there was enough snow to be had, my sisters and I would make snow-people to represent everyone in our family."

"Oh!" Miss Darcy cried, "How delightful. Is it difficult?"

"Not at all, but it may be somewhat time-consuming, so, if you are not up to it, we could pass."

"No, I would like to learn how to make them. It is a wonderful idea and should be enjoyable."

"Very well. I do not think we will have time to make all of us, but I could do your brother and you could make the colonel. We will need to get their clothes in order to stuff the snow into them. Let's dress them entirely with boots, hats, gloves and all. Is that satisfactory?"

"Yes! Oh Lizzy, this is going to be such fun."

Elizabeth enquired, "Do you think you can obtain some of Richard's clothes without his knowledge? It would be splendid to surprise them with our creations."

"Oh, I am certain I can."

"Good, then meet me in the courtyard in a quarter of an hour with all that you desire to dress your 'snow-Richard' and make sure to bundle up well before coming out. I would not want you to catch a cold."

Georgiana beamed from the excitement of doing something new. She ran upstairs, retrieved a scarf and an extra set of gloves, and asked her maid to meet her at the back entrance to help her wrap up warmly for the outdoors. Gingerly, she slipped from her room and walked to Richard's door.

Knocking lightly, she held her breath and waited. When no reply came, she warily opened the door and peeked in. The bed was made already, so there would be no fear of detection by a maid. Thus, she hurried about the room in search of baggage. Confused and not knowing exactly what to bring to dress her snow-person, she faltered. As she turned towards the closet, she bumped her foot on a slender elongated, black trunk. Pondering whether it was large enough to contain clothes, she placed it on the bed. The chest revealed a red military uniform with sword and scabbard. Georgiana smiled wickedly and shut the lid. She then wrapped her shawl around the case and departed.

Elizabeth went into her dressing-chamber and then cautiously entered the master's closet. She was thankful that Mr. Chaffin was nowhere to be seen. She feared the poor valet could not bear to witness her rummaging through her husband's belongings, especially after the shock he had received that morning on finding her, instead of Mr. Darcy, in the master's bed. She flushed anew at the bright recollection of Mr. Chaffin shaking her upon her breast.

Looking over her husband's boots, she first felt alarm. They all gleamed, and none showed signs of wear. Yet, after gathering his waistcoat, cravat, trousers, tailcoat, and beaver, she espied a pair of old, well-worn boots in a back corner off to themselves. Elizabeth reasoned that these would be the best choice, since they seemed rather ancient and shabby in appearance.

Finding a satchel, she placed the clothing within. She, too, grabbed an extra pair of gloves and scarf. Then, excitedly, she left to meet Georgiana and the winter splendour that awaited them.

Georgiana was already enfolded in layers of wool when Elizabeth arrived breathlessly at the courtyard's egress. Sally ran up with her mistress' outdoor attire and began to prepare her for the activity.

Giggling, Elizabeth exclaimed, "Oh Georgie, I think we are stiff as boards! We will have a rough go of it. Are you ready?"

The young miss nodded in anticipation and both ladies, carrying their cases, slowly manoeuvred down the steps.

Elizabeth suggested they make their snow-people in the very centre of the courtyard. She put the satchel upon the ground and, in a matter-of-fact air, said to her sister-in-law as she removed her husband's clothing, "I thought it best to bring the oldest pair of Fitzwilliam's boots. That way I need not worry that the snow may harm them."

Georgiana's eyes widened for a moment, yet she said not a word, but only nodded in response. She then expressed pleasure in her own choice of garments for her cousin's snowman. Elizabeth's eyes were as large as saucers when the young girl lugged Richard's regimentals of an ensign from the case. The red colour loomed large and Elizabeth swallowed hard.

"Ah, Georgiana, your cousin's uniform. Oh, my, do you think it is wise to use this? I mean, he may not want it disturbed."

"Oh Lizzy, I think it perfect, the red will be such a bright contrast against the snow. It will be the very picture of Richard. Besides, it is the only thing I could find. I do not think he will mind in the least."

Elizabeth's eyes were still opened wide and her brows arched high as her mouth hung open. She did not want to disappoint the girl but felt truly uneasy about dressing a snowman in such a fashion. In fact, she felt a queasiness start to grow in the pit of her stomach.

"Georgie, maybe I could run back up with you and find something else. I am sure there is something that has high colour and would look just as grand."

Georgiana looked sad and frowned with the suggestion. "You do not like my choice, Elizabeth? It will take forever to get all of our wraps off, and, besides, I was most fortunate in not encountering a servant or for that matter, Richard. Please let us continue. I will take full responsibility, and I am most certain that Richard will not mind. In fact, I think he will rather like it."

Elizabeth's cheeks were ballooned out, and it looked as if her eyes were about to pop out of their sockets. She exhaled loudly and then twisted her mouth in her usual off centre pout. Thinking for a few moments, she finally relented to Georgiana's plea.

"Very well, but I must say I am not as certain as you seem to be."

Georgiana jumped up and down and then hugged her around the neck. After this display of appreciation, Elizabeth began giving instructions on how to stuff snow into the clothes and then stacking and supporting the weight of each snow person with additional snow in the needed areas.

Their cheeks and noses were all aglow from the chill, but their eyes shone just as brightly when their work was completed. Both were thrilled with their accomplishments.

When the women stepped back to admire their craftsmanship, before their eyes stood two very distinguished gentlemen.

"Oh Lizzy!" exclaimed Georgiana, "they look marvellous, and I am still of the opinion that the uniform defines Richard."

Elizabeth smiled openly. "Well, I will have to admit that the red shows quite brightly against the contrast of the landscape. I think, Georgie, that our men are quite handsome, even if they are only made from pressed flakes." Both ladies giggled aloud and were quite pleased and anxious to surprise the genuine gentleman whom the charlatans represented.

~*~

After Darcy had finished his business with Mr. Sheldon, he found Richard in the Billiard Room. He enquired of his cousin if he were ready for their ride. Richard agreed readily, quickly placing the cue within its frame. Both gentlemen went to their separate chambers to change into their riding attire. They also wanted to don their blanket shirts for extra warmth.

Richard waited in the hallway for sometime before Darcy emerged from his room. "Why, Darcy, I was about to give up on you altogether."

"I am sorry, Fitzwilliam. It is just that Chaffin had a devil of a time trying to locate my Randolph's, the boots my father gave me when I went off to Cambridge. Oddly enough, for the first time in Chaffin's career as my valet, he could not find something. So my Telford's will have to do. I am sorry to keep you waiting."

Both gentlemen looked forward to the feel of the cool crisp air on their faces and the inexpressible freedom they would experience galloping across the pristine, snow-crowned blanket which spread over the grounds of Pemberley. The morning outing was sure to bring reminiscences of winter rides shared in their youth.

As they approached the entrance hall, they noticed several servants huddled about the windows, squealing with laughter. Their levity quickly silenced when they detected the approaching, loud thuds of their master's boots.

While the maids scurried off, Darcy and Richard eyed each other in ignorance, and Richard shrugged his shoulders. Both men stopped to don their gloves before going out of doors.

Upon stepping out on the landing, the gentlemen immediately perceived what had occasioned the maids' merriment. Before them in the centre of the yard, stood two snowmen, dressed in stately fashion, clearly visible from the eastern windows.

Darcy and Richard looked intently upon them and then at one another. The master's lips pressed into a fine line, and a small whistle blew through the colonel's lips before stating, "Well, this is certainly a bolt from the blue."

Georgiana turned about and discerned her brother and cousin descending the steps at a dangerously rapid pace, considering the inclement conditions and accumulated snowfall thereon.

In excitement, she started waving her arms above her head and called out, "Brother, Richard, come and admire our handiwork!"

With this exclamation, Elizabeth turned likewise and saw their advance. She noted the grave expression on her husband's face which, in turn, spread gloom upon her own.

Darcy halted three yards from where the ladies stood. Richard caught up and glanced at Darcy to ascertain his frame of mind. He perceived a dreadfully disgruntled man and quietly addressed his cousin by his first name, which he seldom, if ever, did. "Fitzwilliam, temperance is the order of the day here. I do not believe this to be anything over the top or beyond the pale."

Darcy's face was full of fury, and he glared at Richard for his interference.

Elizabeth took it all in and briefly closed her eyes.

Georgiana, oblivious to her brother's displeasure, gleefully asked, "What do you think of our snow-people, or as Lizzy says, snow-family. They are you and Richard. Do you like them?" Darcy stared a hole through her as she spoke.

She belatedly recognized his disapproval and fell silent as she examined the toes of her boots.

Darcy slowly scrutinized each snowman without a sound. *How could Elizabeth humiliate me with such a scheme?*

He walked up to the snowman dressed in Richard's regimentals and regarded the sword and scabbard hanging smartly at its side. After fingering the fringed epaulets, he spewed, "Whichever of you is responsible for desecrating the King's Army had best disrobe this pathetic creation in an instant."

Richard, Elizabeth, and Georgiana remained affixed to where they stood.

Darcy next trudged over to the snowman which represented him. He looked at his brown beaver atop its head and the poorly tied cravat around the neck. Glancing down, he saw the pitiful figure wearing his cherished boots, the last gift from his father before his death. He tried to calm himself by taking a deep breath, but it was futile. He snatched his riding crop from the snow-gloved hand and brandished it in the air.

He then turned to his wife and contemptuously railed, "Madam, you have exposed me to the vilest ridicule imaginable. I would have hoped that our private discord would have remained just that. Yet, I see, with this blatant retaliation, it is no longer so."

Elizabeth despaired at her husband's misunderstanding and his harsh, venomous words.

Darcy stared icily into her eyes and pivoted on one heel to hasten his return indoors. He called back to his cousin, "I no longer feel like riding today, Fitzwilliam. I offer you my apologies. And, Georgiana, remove the military dress, which is an insignia of our country and the revered men who fight for her, from that abominable snowman!"

Before entering the house, Darcy heard Georgiana's sobs. He stopped upon the landing and hesitated briefly, but then opened the door and disappeared from view.

Mrs. Reynolds watched the whole display from the conservatory's window. She frowned and shook her head in disgust.

Georgiana finally made her feet walk forward. Her hands trembled so much that she could not begin to undo the brass clasps of the uniform. Richard and Elizabeth immediately came to her side.

"Shhh! Georgie, there, there," murmured the colonel in her ear. He then turned her about in order to embrace her when she suddenly leapt into his arms, crying uncontrollably. Elizabeth felt remorseful as she stood by Georgiana's side and was striving to hold back her own sobs. She gently patted her sister-in-law's back, when suddenly the flood gates opened and she, too, burst into tears. Richard shifted Georgiana to one side of his chest as he reached for Elizabeth and encompassed her within his arms in a similar manner. Both women cried miserably upon his shoulders.

Through narrowed eyes, Darcy watched the occurrence from a first floor window. His throat constricted as he looked upon the scene below. He was not pleased.

~*~

Chapter Seven

Twigged Consciences

Richard felt terrible as he clutched the two sobbing women to his breast. *What in the world is wrong with Darcy to lash out in such a vicious way to make his sister and wife undergo such anguish?* He shook his head and held Georgiana and Elizabeth closer. He distinctly felt each tremor from their sobs as they pulsated against his chest. While gently hugging the two ladies, his left hand stroked Georgiana's back in an attempt to soothe her and his right hand intuitively performed the same appeasement for Elizabeth, but then, instead of stroking her back, he drew her firmly to his chest.

Richard's grasp caused Elizabeth to struggle for breath, and her cries became short, rhythmic sniffles. She made an effort to break the colonel's hold, but he instinctively drew her back. Elizabeth's head involuntarily tilted upwards towards his as he gazed upon her, their eyes mere inches apart. They looked intently upon one another, and Richard knew that if Elizabeth's face had not been crimson from her exposure to the elements, it would have become so from the intensity of his stare.

Elizabeth saw his lips part slightly and felt the warmth of his breath on her face. Time seemed suspended as their eyes riveted upon one another with a force that penetrated their very souls. Some moments later, Elizabeth, her heart racing, ashamedly broke away from his embrace and gasped aloud.

Richard coughed uneasily and quickly looked away whilst bringing his freed arm around Georgiana. He felt ashamed, as well. Breathing in deeply, he nervously began to jest.

"Georgiana, come now, it is not all that bad! I dare say your snowman looks rather dashing in my uniform. In fact, I fear he fairly outshines me. Why even Wellington himself would have enlisted his services in his fight against Napoleon."

Georgiana lifted her head and backed a few steps away in order to look at her cousin's face. She gave him a weak smile. Elizabeth marvelled at the colonel's ability and graciousness in diffusing an uncomfortable situation and smiled at him in delight when he peered over to where she stood. She was exceedingly grateful for his obvious success in humouring Georgiana.

"Thank you, Richard, for trying to make me feel better," his cousin replied, "but, truthfully, I know you must be angry with me as well. Only you are being nice about it for some reason because…" She hesitated and dropped her gaze. "I know what I have done…to…be…so… so horrible… Aahh!" As the fountain of tears began to flow anew, Georgiana buried her head upon the colonel's chest once more and wept.

Elizabeth came closer and brightly stated, "Come Georgie, we have made an error. Let us…"

Violently shaking her head, Georgiana blurted out, "No, Elizabeth, *you* have not made a mistake. It was I who insisted that we dress mine in the regimentals. You tried very hard to persuade me not to do so."

"Oh, Georgiana," Elizabeth said calmly, "you are too hard on yourself. Now, as I was saying, we have both made a blunder. Let us immediately undress the snowmen, and soon we shall all feel better. Perhaps a spot of tea would do us good."

The young girl recognized the reasoning of Elizabeth's words and nodded her assent against the stiffness of Richard's coat. Before turning to the snowman and leaving the comfort of her cousin's arms, she gave him a tight squeeze. The colonel walked over to her side. "Let me help you, Georgie. I am quite *adroit* with these fasteners," he said as he pulled his gloves from his hands and began the long, cold process.

Elizabeth was grateful for Richard's kindness, and thus so, with a lighter heart, she turned to her own gloomy task. But, before disassembling the chap, she turned her head slightly askew and narrowed her eyes upon the frozen creation, and, with a tilt of her head and a bemused smile, she began to whisper to the impersonator, "Well, Mr. Fitzwilliam Darcy, what do you have to say for yourself now? I should dare to hope that you would be ashamed for making your sister cry so. And as for me, well, I want you to know this was *not* a planned assassination on your character, but I think, sir, *you* are doing a rather splendid job of destroying it yourself."

She then began to untangle the miserable attempt at a knot she had made with the cravat. In frustration she cried softly, "Oh, I will never understand how men can have patience with such an aggravating thing!"

Unexpectedly, two arms came about her and gloveless hands began to tug at the knot. Pretending to speak for the snowman, Darcy rasped his voice into a deep yielding tone, "Well, Mrs. Darcy, we gentlemen find the things to be quite exasperating as well. And as for the tears of my sister—" Darcy's voice caught in his throat. After a second, he continued but it was no longer in the jest of an impostor's voice. Full of tender contrition, he pressed his lips against her scarf next to her ear, and whispered, "I feel dreadfully sorry for my sister's tears and for breaking her heart." His breathing was heavy, and his cheeks quivered against Elizabeth's in fervent emotion.

Elizabeth stood still in amazement. Her breathing quickened and she blinked back her tears as her body trembled once more. And then, as if she could not believe what she had just heard, his strained voice resumed.

"Yet, what I fear most..." here his voice faltered yet again, "is...that I have destroyed your feelings for me." Some moments of silence ensued with only the heavy breathing of both being discernable.

Darcy's voice cracked. With great exertion he pled, "Oh, my dearest Elizabeth, tell me at once that I am forgiven and that you still want and desire me as your husband!"

Elizabeth's tears flowed anew. Her heart broke and she quickly turned into her husband's waiting arms, burying her head against his broad chest.

Darcy nestled his chin upon her head as a silent tear trickled down his face. Their embrace was unyielding.

Richard detected the return of the prodigal and inwardly sneered. Then a glint appeared in his eyes. Interrupting the task of removing his uniform from the snowman, he placed his index finger to his lips to ensure Georgiana's silence and wordlessly notified her of her brother's return. With his finger still over his lips, he crouched down to scoop up some snow and compressed it into a rigid ball.

Georgiana smiled in approval. In fact, she had a mind to do the same.

The hardened ball found its mark—squarely on the side of Darcy's head. His eyes flew open in bewilderment, but, before he could lift his head and react, another snowy missile grazed his face.

Elizabeth looked up in confusion, but quickly understood that, though her husband's reputation was no longer in danger, his very person was definitely under attack. She backed away as her mate hurriedly bent to gather his own weapons and, while doing so, noticed Darcy wore no greatcoat, only his waistcoat and tailcoat.

The snowballs flew back and forth in a blur, and the combat became more aggressive with each volley. Elizabeth was stunned by the aggression between Darcy and the colonel. It seemed to her that Richard's playful retaliation had turned into something more as each assaulted the other without mercy.

She looked to Georgiana for some idea of how to stop the heated escalation fuelled by the two men. Georgiana gave her an impish grin and suddenly squatted to the ground, gathering up her own ammunition.

In every window that faced the courtyard, the servants appeared, huddled about, craning their necks in unrestrained curiosity and exhilaration. Nothing like this had ever happened at Pemberley before. Their excitement turned to concern, and they all murmured "Oh...," as they saw a small amount of blood trickle down the side of their master's mouth.

Georgiana attempted to move closer to her brother to improve her accuracy, but Richard's rapid movements kept blocking her path. In frustration, she determined to plough forward with all of her might, but, when she did, unbeknownst to the men, she was knocked to the ground.

Elizabeth had had enough. She shouted out as loud as she could, "Fitzwilliam! Colonel Fitzwilliam! Stop! Stop this very instant!" Either they did not hear or they did not care, for they were no longer bombarding each other with snow but, instead, had turned to their chosen mode of wrestling on the ground in an attempt to head lock each other.

Georgiana sat in the snow, bewildered as she looked to the sword in its scabbard. She mulled over an idea, but then thought the better of it. Her attention was drawn back to her loved ones when she saw Elizabeth kneel beside the struggling men, crying out Fitzwilliam's name and striving to take hold of his flailing arms. During the attempt, she was knocked backward—much harder than Georgiana had been. Elizabeth wailed distinctly as she was thrown against the ground. Richard and Darcy, suddenly cognizant of her plight, brought their brawl to an abrupt end as horror creased their brows. Darcy immediately rolled over, inclined his body by his wife's side and anxiously implored, "Elizabeth! Are you all right? Are you hurt?"

Elizabeth gasped for air. Darcy quickly sat on his heels and raised his wife's torso in an effort to get breath into her lungs. Richard still lying upon the ground, felt helpless while witnessing her struggle. Finally, when Elizabeth took a sharp intake of breath, wheezing loudly, the colonel shut his eyes and sighed in relief as she began to breathe again.

Elizabeth sat up the rest of the way.

Darcy asked again, "Are you hurt?"

Shaking her head, she replied, "No, I think I only had the wind knocked out of me is all."

Georgiana, in the meantime, had gathered an enormous mound of snow. Cradling it in her arms, she silently walked over to where her brother knelt and promptly dropped the loosened mass over his head.

Her face beamed in satisfaction as she bent low and gazed with smugness into her brother's stunned eyes. Darcy witnessed his sister's triumphant glow. His face in turn showed astonishment and, when accompanied by the heap of snow which graced his head, dusting his dark brows and resting upon his nose, he was, indeed, a remarkable sight.

Georgiana giggled in delight, as did Richard and Elizabeth.

Darcy was amazed at their gaiety, and then, without warning, lost his balance and fell hard upon his *derrière*. The hat of snow, which had graced his head, avalanched over his face and into his lap. Unable to suppress their mirth, Georgiana, Richard and Elizabeth released peals of laughter through the frosty air.

Darcy sat in silence, completely defeated and humiliated. Richard, Elizabeth, and Georgiana, in consideration of his wounded pride, placed their hands over their mouths to stifle their amusement and became quiet. Suddenly, Darcy's shoulders began to shake, and without warning, he toppled back on the snow-covered ground and began to laugh uncontrollably.

Richard, Georgiana, and Elizabeth's eyebrows shot up in unison. This was indeed an exceptional sight—the Master of Pemberley laughing wildly like a child, and at himself, to boot!

Witnessing such a spectacle caused the others to lose control, joining in Darcy's blissful tune until all heaved with sighs of exhaustion. Tears of happiness ran down every face. Darcy then arose and offered his hand to help Elizabeth to her feet while brushing the snowy powder from her backside. Then, he did the unthinkable. Trudging to where his cousin lay, he likewise extended a hand of assistance. Richard looked intently into his cousin's eyes for a second, and then nodded slightly as he grasped the offered hand. Darcy helped to pull him up, and, when he finally stood, they both looked nervously at one another. Awkwardly, they started to cough, clear their throats, and dust off their red, swollen hands.

Elizabeth spoke first. "My love, we must go inside now or you will catch your death for being out here without your coat."

He looked into his wife's fine eyes and nodded. Thus, they all ascended the steps and entered the house.

Darcy pulled at his pocket fob for his watch and stated, "It is almost time for luncheon. But, I, for one, am inclined to have mine brought up on a tray and then take a long hot bath."

They all smiled and nodded in agreement.

Darcy then exclaimed, "We shall have dinner at the usual hour. Well, until then." He offered his arm to his wife, and they left the hall.

Richard looked at Georgiana and asked, "Do you want to have your meal in your rooms also?"

With eyes weary from the morning exercise, she yawned and answered in the affirmative.

The colonel kissed her forehead and told her to go along, and that he would be up a little later. She smiled and departed for her room.

After she left, Richard returned outdoors and removed his uniform and sword from the snowman. He smiled to himself as he pondered the recent bout of fun they had shared. However, his smile soon dissipated when thoughts of Elizabeth's sparkling eyes encroached upon his reflections. He closed his eyes in an effort to banish the image, but, in spite of his efforts, he felt warmth spread throughout his being.

~*~

When Darcy and Elizabeth entered the chamber, Sally had just finished changing the sheets on the bed. The young maid was surprised to see her mistress back so early in the day and with her husband in tow.

"I will be almost through here, ma'am," she stated nervously, "and then I can help ye change yer things." She hurriedly pulled the counterpane up and smoothed it.

In haste, Sally walked over to Elizabeth and reached out to take off her mistress' coat. Elizabeth had removed her gloves. Yet, as Darcy was in the current employment of unwrapping her scarf from her head and neck, he, without looking directly at the maid, volunteered in a low tone, "That will not be necessary. Umm...what is your name?"

"Sally."

"Ah, yes Sally, your services will not be required for some time. Send up Mrs. Darcy's luncheon and mine on trays in about an hour's time, no...almost two hours time from now, and at that time, have hot water prepared for our baths." As an afterthought, he looked in Elizabeth's eyes and asked, "That is, if this is agreeable to you, Mrs. Darcy?"

A smile spread across Elizabeth's lips. "Yes, I think that will be most satisfactory."

The maid bobbed her head and swiftly left the chamber.

Darcy took his wife's hand and caringly led her over by the fire. "I believe this will be a better location for the removal of your wet things." He then removed her coat and the shawl underneath.

"It is you, Fitzwilliam, who needs to shed your clothes. Whatever were you thinking of coming back out in the cold with no coat and gloves?"

Darcy's breathing became heavy with emotion. "I was not thinking then, nor was I thinking before."

He put his arms about her waist and looked deeply into her eyes while she in turn searched his. "My only thought when returning was of what I had just done, how my behaviour was more inappropriate than that of which I had just accused you. How..." his voice shakily choked out, "how...I had reduced you to tears...and publicly humiliated you. By the Heavens, Elizabeth, I need to know that you forgive me! I need to hear you say you do. I cannot live with myself for the pain inflicted which, I am fully aware, came from my own scorn and censure." A strangled groan escaped his throat as he closed his misty eyes and bent his head to rest it on her forehead.

Elizabeth's throat also constricted, rendering her unable to speak for some minutes. The silence accentuated Darcy's pain all the more. His chin quivered as his fingertips slowly caressed his wife's back in small circular patterns.

Tears slowly trickled down Elizabeth's cheeks as she vividly recalled the dreadful scene. She struggled with what to say to her husband at this moment that would not cause any further breech between them. One thing she knew for sure was that she wanted to plainly make him understand that she had never meant to ridicule him in front of his household, and that the dressing of the snowmen was by no means an attempt to do so.

In barely a whisper, she spoke, "Fitzwilliam, I am not sure what is happening between us, but one thing is certain, and please believe me when I say it was never my design to humiliate you in any form or fashion by making a snowman and dressing him in your clothing. It has always been a pastime from my earliest recollection, which my sisters and I indulged in whenever enough snow was to be had in Hertfordshire. I only suggested the pursuit to your sister as a means of passing the morning away outdoors." Her lips trembled as she spoke the next words. "I fear you are ashamed of me...that you feel I am not a worthy influence for your sister. I am distraught that you are upset over the regimentals, as in all honesty am I."

Her tears became earnest, and she sobbed harder as her husband tightened his embrace.

Darcy shook his head and replied in a husky voice, "Oh, no! You are the best exemplar for my sister. And, furthermore," here his voice broke completely, and he wept freely, "you are my salvation as well. You have brought meaning into my life which was before, hitherto unknown. Oh, my loveliest Elizabeth, I beg of you to tell me you still desire and need me, because I do not think I can live another day with this division between us."

Lifting her head, she gazed devotedly into her husband's tearful eyes and wiped his tear-stained cheeks with her fingertips. "There is nothing to forgive for I am as much to blame as you. I do love you so, Fitzwilliam."

Swiftly lifting her in the air, he securely enfolded her in his arms, his mouth seeking hers.

Their kiss was pointed and unrelenting. After several moments, when they finally parted, he placed her back upon her feet, but then proceeded to slowly kiss her cheeks, her eyes, her brows, her forehead, and along her jaw, neck, and behind her ears. His kisses began to quicken as he advanced down her neck, and, when he reached the curve thereof, she leaned against him in the manner he so treasured.

"Elizabeth," Darcy whispered hoarsely "I want you."

She opened her dazed eyes and looked into his dark ones filled with longing. Drawing in a shallow breath, she nodded.

He removed her dress, and let it fall to the floor, then began the same process with her corset, but suddenly stopped, and confusion shown on Elizabeth's face as Darcy rapidly crossed the room and entered her dressing chamber. However, he hastily returned carrying an armful of towels. Setting them on the floor by the fire, he returned to unfastening the corset. Next, Darcy knelt to unlace her field boots and remove the rosy, flesh toned stockings. Afterward, he stooped to retrieve a towel. Rising to his feet, he delicately dabbed her face and then her hair. Moist ringlets fell against her milky skin as he removed the scattered pins, and, rubbing ever so softly with the cloth, he attended to her arms, chest, back, and legs, until he again bent low, taking the towel to dry her feet.

She now wore only her damp chemise which clung about her shapely form most provocatively. Subsequent the freshening of her feet, his lips tenderly kissed each foot while he gazed upward. His eyes slowly swept over her figure while travelling in search of her face, drinking and delighting in her glorious bounty.

As she watched him lovingly bestow his ministrations to her, she was in awe. When their eyes met, she reached out both of her hands for him. He laid the towel aside, and taking her hands in his, he arose.

He claimed her mouth once more. Their kiss was restrained at first, but then each began to take in the ampleness of the other's lips. Darcy began to lift his wife up into his arms when she abruptly broke the kiss.

He enquired, "What is it, my love?"

Instead of a verbal answer, Elizabeth gazed into his eyes and boldly began to unbutton his waistcoat. As she did so, exhilaration immediately filled Darcy with a rush of heat, for it was the first time in their marriage that his wife had been so daring.

With his jacket and waistcoat discarded, she looked steadily into his eyes, arched one brow, and saucily smiled as she tackled the knot of his cravat. His face showed pure pleasure and his breathing quicken.

It took some moments before the neck cloth could be disposed of, but once completed, the contour of her husband's neck came into full view, and it was indeed striking to behold. A familiar stirring from deep within coursed through Elizabeth's body as she felt a warm flush.

Darcy hastily attempted to lift her for a second time, yet she placed her palms firmly upon his chest indicating a further delay. He instinctively stood still as she continued in her endeavour of removing his shirt. When that task was complete, she likewise picked up a warmed towel and started to buff his skin dry.

Darcy closed his eyes in great humility, the feeling nearly overwhelming him. His hands compassionately seized her wrists in order to stop her attention. Gutturally, he spoke, "No, Elizabeth...I will not have you serve me in this manner."

She quickly detected his loss of composure and reasoned, "Why ever not? You just performed the same labour for me. Can I not do likewise for my husband? Is the mistress greater than the master?"

Darcy shook his head. "I have never had any person perform these tasks except servants. It is out of place for you to do so."

She smiled radiantly at her husband's reservations and stood on her tiptoes to first kiss his chin and then his Adam's apple. "But I desire to dry your skin the way you have concerned yourself for mine. Let me serve you, Fitzwilliam, because I seldom have the chance of doing so."

Observing the sincerity in her face, a fleeting smile graced his own, and he nodded in submission as he breathed deeply and watched her delicate hands in their labours, relishing the soothing balm they imparted to his sore body. When her efforts were completed, she announced, "I am afraid I shall not be able to remove your boots alone, but I will be most happy to assist you."

A small chuckle escaped Darcy's lips, and his face lit up at the thought of his dear, sweet wife tugging and pulling at his boots. "There is no need, Lizzy, for I am well accustomed to the task when I have been in want of Chaffin. But, if you keep spoiling me as you have done, I may no longer be in need of a valet, and poor Chaffin might be in want of employment elsewhere."

He then bent over and picked up the remainder of the dry towels, and, before Elizabeth knew what was happening, he swiftly scooped her up into his arms and carried her to their bed. He sat and yanked off his boots. A loud thud boomed as each, in succession, dropped heavily upon the floor.

Elizabeth looked intently at the freshly made bed and timidly stated, "I feel badly for ruining this clean bed and am mortified at the state in which Sally will find it, especially in the middle of the day."

Darcy understood clearly her concern, but smiled in delight at her modesty. "Elizabeth, Sally is a woman as are you. She will think nothing of it. Yet, if you are truly troubled then we may content ourselves in reading a book if you so desire." He carefully watched her expression. Her brows creased briefly, and then she exclaimed, "You know very well, Fitzwilliam, at this moment I do not want to read a book. It is only that I am conscious of the delicacy of the situation and the ramifications there from."

He crawled beneath the covers and pulled them back in an invitation for her to do the same. Once by his side, she snuggled close and put her head upon his shoulder.

He shifted and commenced to embrace her tenderly. "I love you, Elizabeth. You are so beautiful," he murmured softly as they held each other tightly. Their embraces strengthened in fervency, each anxiously desiring to assure and be reassured by the other as they basked in the glow they shared.

"Fitzwilliam?"

"Mmm?"

"I was wondering, last night when you said that lifeblood does not bother you, why does it not?"

Confidently, he stated, "I have had many encounters where blood was present, and I do not recall ever having been appalled by it, not once."

He raised her chin with his fingers and looked squarely into her eyes. "Why do you ask?"

Elizabeth feared to continue their discussion. She did not know if she could at present handle a revelation with regard to her husband's associations with other women. She was not even sure if he would reveal such things, and if so, did she truly want to know? Yet, her curiosity heightened.

"I only wondered at your knowing so much about women and such things." Schooling her face to appear serene, she implied nonchalantly, "I suppose that all men know of such issues, and it is a common occurrence for them. Women are kept in the dark regarding such matters, and society dictates standards which in appearance apply to both sexes, but in reality, only have direct consequences on women."

Darcy's brows furrowed. He was not sure what his wife was implying. "Umm...ah...I am not sure what it is you are signifying, Lizzy. Pray, explain."

"I mean only that men are allowed to live in a way which society merely blinks at whereas a woman is marked and scorned the rest of her days for doing the very same thing."

"Pray, what are men doing which women are not?"

She looked astonished that he was not following her reasoning. "I am saying that men may have relationships outside of the bonds of marriage and society turns a blind eye, and yet, a woman who may do the very same thing is found guilty of sin and therefore shunned. Thus, she pays the penalties for her transgression all the days of her life while a man is only praised for his prowess. It is not fair."

He was truly baffled. "However did the inequalities and injustices of the sexes end up as the current topic of discussion?"

She raised her brows and bit her lip. "Oh, I'm not sure why I rattled on so about that. It is, as you say, of no consequence at the moment." She laid her head upon his chest and closed her eyes tightly in disbelief. *What on earth am I doing? No wonder curiosity killed the cat. 'Let sleeping dogs lie' would be good standing advice for my propensity to know of his former relationships. What must he be thinking*? She sighed and shook her head.

"I love you, Fitzwilliam."

He hugged her tightly in answer.

Darcy knew his wife well enough to know that she never rambled on in conversation unless there was an issue at the heart of it. Their conversations at the Netherfield Ball, Hunsford, and Rosings had taught him that difficult lesson. At the time, he had thought her views to be mere flirtations. He soon learned, however, that, in fact, they were confrontations concerning his character based on decided opinions she had previously formed.

Elizabeth pulled Darcy closer and began to lightly kiss his chest.

In his mind, he went back over their recent dialogue: *Sally, bedding, lifeblood, men's knowledge, relationships, marriage and inequalities? Men's knowledge! His knowledge of such things! Outside the bonds of marriage...his knowledge being in common with most men's about such issues outside the bonds of marriage!*

Darcy wondered at the possibility of this being the core of Elizabeth's concern.

"You know, Lizzy—that is I think you know—Pemberley's industry is chiefly from sheep farming."

Elizabeth was surprised by this sudden change of topic, but was also grateful at the same time for an avenue of escape.

"When I was a boy, my father educated me the same way in which his father had him."

Elizabeth looked up and quickly said, "You attended Eton and then Cambridge."

He smiled and nodded before continuing. "Yes, all Darcy men attend those schools for our formal education, but my father considered hard physical labour to be the best education."

Elizabeth's attention was now fully directed at her husband, and she propped herself up on her elbow and listened intently as he spoke.

"I think I was about eight years of age when my father instructed Mr. Manning to take me daily, for many hours at a time, to be tutored and made familiar with the activities and laborious tasks of the estate." He gave her a pointed look and smiled.

She quickly sat up in fascination and gazed upon her husband with this tale of his boyhood.

"Well," he grinned, "as I said, my father wished for me to have a comprehensive education. Not only was I to be shown these responsibilities, but I was to actively participate in the necessary work of caring for the estate as well. I learned from a very early age how to dig trenches until my back ached, and I was taught how to brush down horses until they gleamed. I did not mind these labours in the least. Well, there were times when it was unpleasant to be sure, but I was of the inclination and disposition for industriousness."

"What things did you find unpleasant?" Elizabeth enquired.

"It was not so much with the things, as it was regarding certain persons with whom I would have to work."

"Oh!" was the only reply Elizabeth made from this fact. She sensed that he was referring to Wickham.

He realized Elizabeth understood his inference and gravely said, "Well, yes, as I was saying, one of the chores I remember loving the most was tending our sheep. We would sheer them every spring, and I often helped with the lambing."

"The lambing?" she enquired.

"When the ewes give birth to their young," he replied.

"Yes," Elizabeth questioned further, "but you would have to assist them in giving birth?"

"Sometimes that was necessary. But mostly, we would tend them, and it was important that we remain aware of their condition in order to prepare them for the birthing process."

Elizabeth was truly fascinated that her husband had had dealings with the birthing of lambs or any animal as that was something she had assumed would be left to a field hand. Curiosity abounding, she eagerly enquired, "What are the symptoms you would look for in order to know when the ewes were ready for their lying in?"

Darcy chuckled softly. His face beamed at his wife's enthrallment with his narrative. He smiled at her openly, then sat up and reclined his back against the headboard. Reaching out his hand, he indicated for Elizabeth to come and sit beside him, which she willingly did. He put his arms around her as she snuggled close to his side.

"During the last month, the ewe usually shows signs of slowing down. Her belly has grown large, and her udder will drip with some of the first milk. She also has less energy and has difficulty in moving about. As her time approaches, a few days before her offspring is born, she will swell and change colour in and around her birthing area. The udder will become tight and full. Then, right before the birth, the ewe's hip muscles relax and, at the onset, she will become quite restless and wander away from the rest of the flock."

Elizabeth thought about the process and said, "It is quite entailed. I have never seen an actual birth of any animal. I have only seen young after it has been newly born. I imagine it is quite fascinating."

"Yes, I found it to be so. To me, it was like nothing I had ever experienced before, and I never tired of it. It was the greatest compensation for all of our labours."

She tilted her head. "When were you needed to assist?"

He drew her tighter, his fingers twirling in her hair. "Mostly, we would take notice of the ewe's time and herd her into the lambing pen where we would let nature run its course but remain nearby, if needed. And there were many times through the years that we were, indeed, needed. The feet appear first, but if they are pointing upward, problems may occur. This signifies a breech position of the lamb, and if the birth does not progress rapidly, we would have to intervene, and in a situation such as this, it is always necessary after such a birth, to hold the lamb up by the back legs and rub down his sides in order to eliminate fluid from the lungs."

Darcy paused, trying to determine his choice of words. "In births such as these, I would always be covered in blood. Yet, I did not once feel nauseous from its sight or smell. So, you see, Lizzy, lifeblood has never bothered me in the least. I consider it a natural occurrence of life. Much like when we shall bring a child into this world, there will be blood."

Elizabeth quickly lifted her head and met Darcy's eyes. She studied his gaze only for a second before comprehension dawned in her mind.

Looking intently upon her, he whispered ardently, "Have I ever told you that you are the only woman whom I have ever loved?"

This revelation was all-embracing. Elizabeth stared in wonder at her husband, marvelling at his ability in perceiving her misgivings and misconceptions. Relief washed over her, and she was elated at having her petty concerns laid to rest. Shortly, however, the elation turned to distress at her fearful implication.

Her gaze turned downward and she weakly whispered, "Fitzwilliam, whatever must you think of me?"

"I thought my sentiments were just made quite plain. What do you not understand about my not loving any woman before you? 'Tis true, Lizzy. My heart belongs only to you, and you are the only woman whom I have ever known."

Tears pooled in her eyes, and her lip quivered in contrition. "Fitzwilliam, I am ashamed for my jealousy concerning a time of your life which has no bearing on our present union. How you must think ill of me."

"Not in the least, Elizabeth. I am happy to tell you this. I have waited for so long to find a woman of your calibre and spirit. I had almost lost hope entirely and had begun to despair that women, such as you, were utter fabrications of my imagination."

With a mischievous air, she teased through her tears, "So I am your idea of a truly accomplished woman?"

Darcy smiled dazzlingly for her wittiness in quoting his very words from Netherfield. "Yes, in fact, you are, and I have to admit, compared to you, my wife, I know neither a dozen, nor even half, who truly meet my estimation of an accomplished woman."

They smiled adoringly at each other when a loud knock was heard from the chamber door. Darcy's voice beckoned them to enter as Elizabeth hurriedly yanked the covers up to her chin. Darcy grinned at her and pulled them to his chest.

Sally and Mary entered with trays for the master and mistress. Darcy instructed the maids to set them down by the fire, which they did without delay. Mary's eyes went wide in observing Mr. Darcy in bed with his wife, but Sally kept her eyes focused on nothing in particular and enquired, "Will there be anything else, sir?"

"No," he answered, "only the hot water for our baths. Thank you, Sally."

The young woman curtseyed and replied, "Very good, sir." Then she and Mary left the room. As soon as they were out of hearing, Mary giggled and excitedly remarked, "Sally, did you see that Mr. Darcy wasn't wearing a stitch, but his chest was naked. I can't believe it, right in the middle of the day! It's true what they have been saying downstairs..."

Sally interrupted her and firmly stated, "Mary, keep such thoughts to yourself and don't be going and wagging your tongue, if ye be knowing what's good for ya."

The young girl rolled her eyes at Sally's reproof. She was not worried about such things because everyone talked about how their high and mighty master was smitten with Mrs. Darcy.

~*~

After his bath, Darcy dressed in haste and made his way downstairs. He carried a shiny pair of boots in his right hand. Mrs. Reynolds spotted him before he went out into the courtyard.

"Master Fitzwilliam," the elderly woman called in an aggravated tone, "there has been an express come from the relief party." Unbeknownst to him, his housekeeper was still somewhat displeased at his unjust behaviour earlier displayed in the courtyard.

Darcy acknowledged this intelligence with a nod and asked her to have it sent up to his chamber with Chaffin. For a moment, he wondered at Mrs. Reynolds calling him by name, much like she had done when he was younger. Yet he shrugged it off and went outdoors to retrieve his boots and exchange them with the new pair. Walking up to the snow people, he instantly saw that the military uniform had been removed and replaced by either Colonel Fitzwilliam or Georgiana, or maybe both. Whoever had done so, had donned the fellow in some of Richard's other clothing. Darcy shook his head at the absurdity, yet smiled. For the next several minutes he toiled at putting the exchanged pair of boots in place, and then, in vain, he attempted to extract the packed snow from his Randolphs. After several attempts, he gave up his efforts and carried the stiff, heavy boots back to his chamber.

Upon entering his room, he caught sight of Chaffin heading for the dressing area and called after him. The valet turned and came at his master's summons.

"Yes, sir?"

"Here," Darcy indicated as he held his boots up for the valet. "Take these and see what you can do for them."

Mr. Chaffin grimaced and said somewhat disdainfully, "Very good, sir."

The manservant collected them from his master's hands and looked into each one with complete exasperation.

~*~

Mrs. Darcy sat at her vanity in front of the mirror, inspecting her reflection. Her hair had just been pinned and Sally had fastened her corset before departing to the kitchen to fetch the tea her mistress had requested. Twitching her lips from side to side, and then blowing her cheeks full of air, Elizabeth sat there in idleness as she stared at herself. Continuing in this pastime, she raised her eyebrows for further effect, coupled with the odd expressions she was creating. Exhaling loudly while relaxing her facial muscles, she looked at herself in a dumbfounded way and quietly said aloud, "I cannot imagine whatever it is he considers in thinking me truly accomplished." She then sighed, skewed her lips, and looking down into the jewellery box, began searching for her new cross. Suddenly a smile graced her face as she heard a familiar voice.

"I find a woman who has a certain something altogether in her air when she talks. Could it be called vigour? Likewise, in the way she walks, especially with a petticoat nearly six inches deep in mud, which, in and of itself, is a major feat that only a truly proficient woman would be so bold as to undertake. One might call such a woman as this, daring. Yet, when these qualities are combined with eyes that sparkle every time they look upon a beloved sister or friend, and especially a husband, and when concern is expressed for every person within her acquaintance and influence, then one might say that this is beyond a doubt, a truly accomplished woman, a woman capable of being my wife, of being Mistress of Pemberley, and the mother of my children. Nonetheless, besides these qualities, she must further her mind by extensive reading."

After the initial shock of hearing Darcy's voice from behind her, Elizabeth's face glowed from his playful repartee. He met her gaze in the reflection of her bevelled mirror, and then instinctively, his eyes roamed her figure as she sat in her chemise and corset. Darcy's breath caught in his throat. "Elizabeth, you are stunning."

She shook her head in amused disbelief. "I am not yet dressed for dinner, but you think me stunning? My, but how easily you are pleased, Mr. Darcy."

Growling softly, he brushed his lips upon her ear, "Oh, no, I am not easily pleased at all and am, therefore, as you are well aware, in a state of perpetual want." The feeling of his warm breath against her skin enticed her, and coupled with the desire she witnessed in his eyes, awakened her own senses once more.

He bent low and began to lightly kiss her neck while whispering words of his adoration. "I love you, Lizzy. Your skin is like silk, and I love to feel it." His hands slid down her bare arms and fell upon her sides where he began to stroke her waist. She reached up and wrapped her arms around his neck as he continued to extol her virtues in-between kisses while his hands freely roamed her figure.

It was at this moment that, unaware of Mr. Darcy's presence, Sally walked into the room carrying the cup of tea. But when witnessing the loving exchange between the master and mistress, she stopped cold in her tracks. She could not seem, however, to muster the strength to turn and leave. Instead, she was transfixed on the spot where she stood.

The young maid was indeed mesmerized by the caresses, kisses, sighs, and murmurings of the couple. She had never beheld a scene such as this in her entire life. Her breath caught, and her heart began to race.

Suddenly, Mr. Darcy started to undo his wife's corset, and the maid heard her mistress' voice ask if there would be time before dinner. Sally immediately felt the impropriety of being there, and her face burned with embarrassment. Fear seized her limbs as she quietly backed out of the room. Once past the dressing chamber door, she quickly turned to lean against the wall and closed her eyes tightly. She had never seen nor experienced such expressions of tenderness and devotion. Tears trickled down the young maid's cheeks as her heart was touched, thereby.

~*~

Chapter Eight

Deliberation and Fortitude

Richard and Georgiana did not seem to mind waiting for dinner to be served. In fact, their wait was no more than a quarter of an hour. They sat at the great table in an agreeable manner discussing various topics of interest—that is, until Richard brought up one topic in particular.

"So, Georgie, are you ready to be presented to society? I dare say there will be many Bond Street chaps standing in line for the chance of dancing with you."

Georgiana detested the subject. She lowered her head and wrung her hands before resting them in her lap. "You know very well, Richard, that I would be happy to never be introduced into society or become part of the *ton*. I think we have had this discussion far too often for you not to know my sentiments. So, I ask, why do you delight in pestering me about a subject you realize gives me great displeasure?"

Richard grinned, yet calmly replied, "It is not that I wish to bring you distress. It is just that the time is at hand where there can be no more avoidance of the matter. I am sure, however, with Elizabeth by your side you will be more at ease." He gave her a quick glance as if perhaps to gauge her reaction.

Georgiana twisted her mouth to the left and then to the right as she considered her sister-in-law's involvement in the whole ordeal. Resigned to the fact that the event would come about, no matter her opinion, she stated, "I suppose that having Lizzy by my side will be the best part about the whole revolting affair. So yes, it does help quite a bit to consider her being there for support and guidance during such an overwhelming time. And I certainly appreciate that I now have a sister, especially Lizzy, who cares for me."

He nodded in acknowledgment and said politely, "I think she may also be in need of your assistance, duck, with her own introduction to London society."

Georgiana's eyes opened wide in amazement at the preposterous thought.

"I do not see how I can lend Elizabeth any boost of confidence. She already is so self-assured. Why, she is one of the most confident women I know. She says things to my brother that are sometimes truly daring. I only wish to be more like her, but I know my efforts will always be paltry compared to her abilities."

Richard put his arm around her shoulders. "I am not so sure about that, Georgie. I have witnessed some things of late that have proven you are not always the green girl. In fact, you know how to give your opinions to *me* most decidedly. Let Elizabeth be your guide in the presentation of them. She is quite an original to be sure, but I think you, too, can be an original in your own right. However, I am serious about your being there for Elizabeth. She will need your encouragement to face the old tabbies, takes and vultures that never seem to get over the success of someone not immediately in their circle. It is rather ruthless out there, and, even though Elizabeth is a woman of eminence, they will not consider her their social equal. Many will give her a direct cut at every turn. Having you there will bring comfort and cheer to her when such difficult encounters occur—and occur they will. I have no doubt about it. Do you understand what it is I am saying?"

Richard's words struck a chord with Georgiana. The same reasons he gave for Elizabeth's future dilemma with the ton were similar to her own. She hated the insincerity of so many of the society women, yet she had not thought Elizabeth would have to face it with her.

She nodded at her cousin and sympathetically said, "Yes, Richard, I do see what you mean. I had not considered Elizabeth having to be introduced to them as well. In fact, I am already familiar with many of the circles wherewith we will frequent and can therefore be of some assistance to her. I suppose that I can, to some extent, give her guidance."

"Most assuredly...your confidence will be of great import to your sister, and she will trust your judgment, Georgie, and take comfort in your concern." He squeezed her hand and smiled warmly.

Suddenly, Darcy and Elizabeth appeared. Richard quickly stood and stepped aside. Darcy greeted his sister and cousin enthusiastically and apologized for their lateness while pulling out the chair for his wife. After she was comfortably seated, he quickly bestowed an affectionate kiss upon her cheek. Although Elizabeth was somewhat stunned at this show of affection, it pleased her.

Darcy sat and unfolded his napkin, placing it on his lap. The others followed suit. He picked up his spoon and commenced to eat the soup. "Well what have we tonight? It smells a little...unusual."

Georgiana resolutely volunteered, "It is Richard's favourite, coddle. I told Elizabeth his favourites as well as ours. She asked if Mrs. Potter could prepare it for him."

Darcy sipped the soup from off his spoon and eyed his cousin.

"Oh," Colonel Fitzwilliam intoned hesitantly, "I am delighted, truly. It is a dish which is not often prepared at Pemberley. Thank you Georgie and

Mary Sherwood

Elizabeth for the thought." He then looked down at his bowl and began to delve in, seriously concentrating on the consumption of his soup. He fully knew why the dish was never prepared at Pemberley. Darcy detested it.

The whole dinner party savoured their broth in silence until every drop was gone. The servants quickly gathered the bowls and then ladled the Irish meal onto their plates. Darcy simply stared at the sausage clumped unreservedly over all of the vegetables on his dish. He had disliked sausage since his childhood. Although he was not sure why, he thought it might be the texture which he found so unpalatable.

He took his fork and scraped the offending meat as well as he could from each potato. A shadow of gloom registered on his façade as he ate his meal in relative calm.

Georgiana spoke up frankly, "I wish we could have this dish more often. I like it, as well. Did you ever have it at Longbourn, Elizabeth?"

Elizabeth was unsure why the table was engulfed in silence, yet she did not feel uneasy, assuming everyone to be famished. When all eyes turned to her at Georgiana's query, she began to rethink her assumption. "Ah...why no, Georgie, this is my very first time to have coddle."

Her sister-in-law then asked, "Do you like it?"

Elizabeth noticed that everyone again paused to await her response.

"Ah...I do love potatoes and bacon." She looked intermittently at each expectant face and wondered at their continued silence. Raising her brows fully she exclaimed, "My family is not much for sausage except occasionally at breakfast. However, it is always pleasant to try new dishes."

Darcy smiled broadly, devoured the remaining potatoes from his plate and then gulped a mouthful of wine.

Georgiana casually stated, "Coddle is not one of my brother's favourites at all. He dislikes sausage, and, therefore, we never have this dish. It is a rare treat tonight."

Elizabeth was speechless as she eyed her sister-in-law in perplexity. What could Georgiana mean by having her request a dish from Mrs. Potter which she knew full well was one her brother detested? Richard still said nothing but stared at his plate and ate the favoured fare most diligently as if in a stupor.

Having her wits promptly about her, Elizabeth declared while looking directly at her husband, "Well, even if the main course has not been entirely to everyone's satisfaction, I will guarantee the dessert to be so. We are having Black Forest with cherries and spiced pecans."

Darcy caught her gaze and smiled widely, not for the appraisal of the dessert, which was, in fact, one of his favourites, but more for the fact that his dear wife had made a point of knowing his favourites and had acknowledged it openly. Moreover, he appreciated her communication because it knowingly revealed her to be ignorant of his loathing for the Irish meal upon which they now feasted.

After desserts were served and enjoyed, Darcy enquired, "Well, my dear wife and sister, Fitzwilliam and I are going to take our leave and have our accustomed refreshment. I propose that you dear ladies choose any form of entertainment to pass away the evening. Nothing will be banned—that is, if you are in agreement, Fitzwilliam?"

His cousin held a bemused expression at Darcy's attempt to repair the damage he had inflicted earlier in the day. "No, Darcy, I am not at all ill-favoured towards such a plan. I do hope, however, that they shall have mercy on us."

Georgiana was enchanted with the idea and said most assuredly, "Oh, I am sure Elizabeth and I can conjure up something we shall all enjoy."

Darcy stood and gave his sister a loving smile. He then placed his napkin on the table, walked over to his wife, and again bent low to place another kiss on her cheek. This time she smiled radiantly and quietly thanked him.

Georgiana beamed at her brother's open display of affection for his wife. She wondered if she would ever be so fortunate as to find a person whom she could love and by whom she could be loved in return.

"Well, Fitzwilliam, since we are not needed for this part of their design, let us be off to our brandies."

As soon as they left the room, Georgiana leaned across the table and asked her sister if she had any ideas for entertainment. Elizabeth bit her lip and good-humouredly narrowed her eyes upon the young lady.

"No, Georgie, none come to mind at this precise moment, and I find that I cannot even begin to contemplate such ideas until you tell me why you neglected to inform me that coddle was not a favoured dish of your brother's."

Georgiana appeared guilty as she looked at the empty dish before her. But, before she had time to think of what to say, Elizabeth arose and came around to her side where she gently placed her hand on the young woman's shoulder. "Come, Georgie, do not let this distress you. Let us go to the music room where we may speak freely."

They walked arm in arm to the room, and Georgiana seemed more at ease by her sister-in-law's preference for humour over severity. Elizabeth guided them to sit on a divan, and then, lovingly, she grasped one of Georgiana's hands and held it.

Raising one brow earnestly while looking into her sister-in-law's eyes, Elizabeth affectionately enquired, "Now, Georgie, what have you to say for yourself?"

Georgiana took in a deep breath.

"Well, it is true when I suggested this morning that we have coddle tonight, that I knew I should tell you it was not Fitzwilliam's favourite dish, but I was purely motivated on Richard's behalf. This morning at breakfast, if you will remember, he seemed a bit morose about always having to go about as a guest to all of the family instead of having a home of his own." Georgiana tightened her hand around Elizabeth's as she readily confessed, "Believe me, Elizabeth, when I say I had only thought to please Richard and assure him that he is cared for, I in no way meant to gratify Richard at your expense. I did not think it through. I hope my brother is not upset. I believe the dessert seemed to make up for it."

Georgiana's head tilted as her innocent, yet saddened eyes beseeched a response from her new sister.

Elizabeth meditated on the girl's words and then said, "I believe you, Georgie, but, in the future, I want you to simply tell me your feelings. That way we can avoid misunderstandings. I appreciate your concern for your cousin, and I do not think a cardinal sin has been broken because we served coddle. However, in all honesty, I dislike the dish, too, though I do not mind having it served. But, next time, I will have the kitchen prepare another dish, as well, and one that will be to your brother's liking."

Georgiana's face shone in relief. "Thank you, Elizabeth, for not being angry with me."

"I do have one more thing I wish to ask you," Elizabeth ventured. "Today, during the snow fight between Richard and Fitzwilliam—do they always become that aggressive with each other?"

Georgiana blinked and appeared pensive. "Well, they were always furiously competitive while growing up. They would try to out-hunt each other, outrace their horses, and, in almost everything, each would try to win. So yes, I would say they are very assertive with each other, but they enjoy it so, and neither has ever felt resentment for the other's particular successes or triumphs. They care for each other keenly."

Elizabeth smiled and cheerfully encouraged, "Now, no more talk of coddle or rivalry, but instead, let's put our heads together and come up with something truly wonderful to pass away our evening. It is not often that we are given such leeway to devise an activity they are already obliged to accept."

Both ladies happily mentioned several card games, yet neither felt like playing. They briefly considered and dismissed the pianoforte as it was always at their disposal. Then, from out of the blue, they thought of dancing and began to contemplate the idea.

Georgiana offered that they could go to the ballroom. Although it would be somewhat chilly, they reasoned that the exercise would quickly warm them. Elizabeth thought about this proposal for a moment, but then a most glorious idea popped into her head, and she excitedly expressed it to her new sister.

"Georgiana, I remember your brother informing me while in London of how he spends his free time there. He mentioned that he loves to fence. Have you ever had the opportunity of seeing him exhibit this sport?"

With true interest, the younger woman replied, "No, never, yet I have always wondered about it. Fitzwilliam does have a sword case here. That much I am sure of because he and Richard both fence. I have seen him carry the equipment to the ballroom numerous times, but they never invited me to join them as they have with billiards, so I felt it was something to which young ladies were not intended to be exposed."

Elizabeth chewed her lip and then expelled a short breath. "Humph! Do you wish to see the sport?"

"Most assuredly."

"Then, do you think we can prevail upon them to comply?"

"Well, my brother did say 'nothing will be banned,' and Richard agreed."

Elizabeth nodded and beamed with the thought of witnessing her husband's fine figure as he demonstrated his abilities with the execution of such activity, and then, without warning, she also felt thrilled within due to the conjured images of her husband's physical exertions. Her body tingled with anticipation.

~*~

Darcy asked Richard what he desired to drink to which he replied it would be port again and Darcy did likewise. They sat in relative silence, sipping their drinks, when the younger cousin spoke first.

"I received an express from the Pratt party stating they are safe and the horses in excellent condition. They mentioned that the weather was not as severe to the west. They will more than likely be making their way home on the morrow. I hope that the Wilkens lad can manage it the rest of the way."

"I imagine if the weather holds up, all will be well with him."

As the conversation lulled, they fell back into a companionable silence, each lost in their own thoughts while they sipped their wine.

Richard glanced at his cousin and downed his drink. Hastily rising to his feet, he walked over to the decanter to refill his glass with a splash more. Eyeing his cousin with a sideways glance, he decided to remain standing, and, when Darcy looked up in question, the colonel began, "Darcy is there anything wrong? I mean...is something worrying you?"

Darcy took another sip of his port and dropped his gaze.

"Why do you ask, Fitzwilliam? Should there be something worrying me?"

"Well, Darcy, I do not rightly know. I am only enquiring out of concern. You seem out of sorts compared to your recent happy mien."

"You think me unhappy?"

"No," the colonel replied patiently, "of course not. You simply seem more...tense."

"What," Darcy replied sharply, "more than my ordinary, *stiff* self?"

In frustration, Richard shook his head and exhaled loudly. "You know very well I was only chaffing with Georgiana."

Darcy uncrossed his legs and placed his empty glass on the side table. He lifted his head and caught his cousin's stare. "Were you, Richard? I am glad to know you delight my sister with such rousing accounts of how bored my wife must be with only my company."

"Why Darcy, surely this is not what has you bothered? I know you, Cousin, and something is not right with you. You are on edge more than usual. I cannot, for the life of me, Darcy, understand why the snow people made you so cross. I do understand the impropriety of Georgiana using my uniform, but for you to blow the way you did alerts me to a larger concern. You are irritable at times, to be sure. However, this past day you have revealed an exceptional display of peevishness."

Darcy's expression soured. With a scathing remark, he quickly answered his cousin, "Thank you, Richard, for a further reckoning of my faults. I wonder that you can bear to associate with me at all."

"Oh-ho...Cousin, you are sometimes as maddening as Aunt Cath—" He stopped himself midway, but it was too late.

Darcy glared at him coldly. "Go on, Fitzwilliam. I am sure there is more."

Richard looked at him resolutely. "Think about it, Darcy. You know how father is at times. You know how fastidious he can be. And then there is James. He is more so. In fact, I feel he cavils on almost everything and my *dear* sister-in-law, Elisha, unites with him in all opinions, especially in their beloved divulgences. There is truly no balance to their marriage. They only support each other in their weaknesses, and I am much taxed when in their company for too long. They disgust me."

Darcy had his head down, yet he was listening closely to Richard's feelings about his father, brother and sister-in-law. He realized he was in complete agreement with his cousin's judgment. He heaved a dejected sigh. "So, Richard, what do they have to do with me? I am sure your critique is incomplete without me on your list—only after Lady Catherine, of course. That was your judgment, was it not?"

Grimacing slightly, Richard shook his head yet bravely continued. "No, Darcy, I do not mean to insinuate that you are just like Aunt Catherine, my father, or Hazel, for that matter. Yet, it is the damnable Fitzwilliam *pride* which seems to interfere with their finding true contentment in life, and at times, it blinds you as well."

Darcy looked at his cousin again, his jaw firmly set. "Go on, Fitzwilliam—finish your point."

As the colonel resumed, Darcy quickly looked down, crossed his legs, and instinctively covered his mouth with the back of one hand while his other formed a fist by his side.

"Elizabeth is a peerless woman."

Darcy's head shot up—his eyes aflame, his mouth a fine line. But before he could say a word, Richard begged his cousin to hear him out. Darcy resumed his former attitude, except the hand that had covered his mouth was now rubbing apprehensively over his lips.

"Now, as I was saying, Cousin, your wife is indeed peerless. She, in fact, has an eminence, which, as you and I well know, many ladies of society lack, and she will likely never be accepted by the throng as such. Yet, Cousin, you know why you married her, and you knew that certain persons in our family might never accept her. However..."

Darcy shifted his position and leaning forward to rest one elbow on his leg as his hand moved from his mouth to cover his eyes, nervously massaging his brow. He remained motionless and never attempted to speak.

Inhaling deeply, Richard continued, "Do not let inconsequential matters interfere with your happiness and Elizabeth's. In time, and through trial and error, she will find her way and become a noble Mistress of Pemberley. Yet, if you continue in this vein of temper, you may botch the very bond which is the most vital. And, Cousin, any more inept handling of situations which you deem improper, like harsh reprimands at the table and brandishing crops in the air..."

Darcy's hand no longer rubbed at his temples but pinched his brows together in anguish as his cousin's sobering words hit their desired mark and pierced his heart.

"...will most assuredly in time and with frequent repetition, cause an irreparable breach between you and your wife. Do not let the Fitzwilliam obsession of what is proper dominate your sense of reason and consideration. Darcy, what you have with Elizabeth is what less than one man in a hundred may ever attain. The irrelevant things will work themselves out. Choose your battles wisely, Cousin, and refuse to let society dictate its petty expectations on your household."

No more words were spoken. Richard finally took his seat and gulped down the remaining liquid in his glass. He looked over to see how Darcy fared. His lips remained in a tight line while his jaw muscles twitched. It seemed to him that his cousin would never alter his pose, and it was, indeed, several minutes before Darcy spoke.

Breathing in deeply and sitting straight, Darcy attempted to speak, his voice strained. Several efforts were required to clear his throat before he could commence.

"Well Richard...uh...umm...if you have concluded your matrimonial counsel, we should be off. I imagine Georgiana and Elizabeth are wondering what has become of us."

Relieved that Darcy did not appear angry, the colonel stood immediately and replied affably, "Why, of course, Darcy. They may fear we have become inebriated in an attempt to renege on our promise for tonight's amusement."

Darcy merely rolled his eyes and shrugged his shoulders at his cousin's ridiculous comment. He wondered how at one moment Richard could be so astute and in the next become so outlandish.

~*~

The heads of both ladies turned as the gentlemen walked into the room. Darcy made immediate eye contact with his wife and smiled broadly. "So, ladies," he enquired, "what is the decree to be?"

His sister and wife seemed at once excited and yet reserved. Elizabeth and Georgiana eyed one another and began to speak but, unsure, suddenly stopped.

Richard smiled at their apparent secret and wondered what they had concocted.

Darcy looked from his wife to his sister. Yet, neither lady seemed to have the courage to elaborate on their decision. "May I enquire as to why you are not forthcoming with your proposal, which, I can determine from your excitement to be greatly desired? Did we not agree beforehand that nothing should be banned?"

Georgiana giggled in delight. "Well, we did consider dancing would be a most pleasant way to pass the evening."

Richard and Darcy shot alarmed looks at one another.

In trepidation, Darcy asked his sister, "And...is this still your desire?"

His sister shook her head and giggled the more. "No, Elizabeth has thought of something much better, and I am in total agreement."

Darcy's brows shot up. He looked at his wife for an explanation. Her eyes sparkled with amusement, and his breath caught. Oh, how he loved her!

Coyly, Elizabeth lured their curiosity further. "Yes, I did think of an alternative to dancing, as that activity would involve the active participation of us all, and Georgie and I are of a mind to be mere spectators."

Richard chuckled softly at the drawn-out drama in which the ladies indulged.

Pleasantly, Darcy entreated, "And...?"

Elizabeth rose and stood close to her husband's face as she bewitchingly raised one brow and vibrantly announced, "Georgiana and I desire to witness the sport of fencing. We trust you will make good on your promise and gratify our fancy."

Richard and Darcy's faces revealed surprise at first, but then both appeared compliant. Gallantly, Darcy bowed with a noble mien and stated, "Your wishes are our commands. We shall meet you fine ladies in five minutes' time in the ballroom. Make sure you come prepared with coats and gloves."

His sister quickly spoke up. "We have them already," she said as she displayed the items for all to see.

The colonel and Darcy chuckled and informed them they would make haste and return for the chosen exhibition.

~*~

All was in readiness. A table, flanked by several chairs, contained a pitcher of water, glasses and a stack of towels.

Georgiana was giddy with anticipation. "Elizabeth, I do not know what has gotten into my brother, but he certainly never would have agreed to such a thing before marrying you. You have charmed him to be sure."

Elizabeth smiled crookedly at her sister's comment and warily reminded herself that the lustre of that charm seemed to lose its allure on occasion.

The gentlemen walked in casually dressed, each wearing beige pants and black shoes, and carrying a sword. Richard wore a cream jacket over his white shirt with only one full length arm in it. Yet, Darcy wore his white shirt alone sans cravat. Elizabeth noticed that the top button of his shirt was unfastened, revealing his neck. She loved gazing at his neck and found herself momentarily dwelling on the irony that men's necks were hidden from view beneath cinched up cravats while corsets hoisted women's breasts up high for the whole world to see and admire. She smiled at the thought and then noticed that her husband also wore a black sash tied over his left hip.

Both men laid their foils on the table, and Darcy suggested that they stretch first, but, before doing so, he decided to educate the ladies about the art of fencing.

"Well, Elizabeth and Georgiana, since you have expressed an interest in this subject, let me first say that fencing is not just a sport or hobby but, more so, is considered an art of specialized skills with exact aesthetic standards. Likewise, it is a science, in that it concerns itself with a systematized body of knowledge demonstrating the operation of general laws. In fact, if fencing were only a sport, it would be the only one in which your opponent determines your score. Therefore, fencers must be honour bound. The object of fencing is to make a hit without being hit, thus, inflicting a wound on your opponent without receiving one in return. My personal feelings concerning fencing is that it develops character and lets the individual understand the true essence of warfare. Vegetius said it best with, 'They are the most enthusiastic about war who are least familiar with it.' Do you have any questions?"

Elizabeth nodded. "Why is Richard wearing a jacket and you are not?"

Darcy chuckled softly and smiled before mischievously answering her question. "One reason, I suppose, is Fitzwilliam's inferiority with speed."

Colonel Fitzwilliam snorted aloud and chuckled as well.

"So," Elizabeth continued, "is it dangerous to be hit? I mean, the points of the blades are protected, are they not?"

Darcy observed the concern on his wife's face, and, in all seriousness, strived to relieve her anxiety. "Yes, Elizabeth, foils have no sharp edges, and the point is blunted with a nail head. A button is attached to spread out the force of impact." He held up his weapon so she could inspect it closely, and he specifically had her notice the rabbit blunt fastened at the end of the point so that she would not worry.

Not completely satisfied by her examination, she questioned further, "Then why, Fitzwilliam, does Richard wear a jacket, and I assume he plans on wearing that head mask also?"

Darcy replied, "Yes...yes he does. It is just each person's personal preference. I suppose that the jacket lessens welts and minor abrasions to some degree. Yet, I would rather endure some bodily injury instead of the confinement which the jacket imposes."

Still uneasy, Elizabeth posed two more questions. "What about the helmet? Why do you not use one?"

"For the same reason," Darcy answered. "The mask protects your face and most importantly your eyes. However, experienced fencers are not to make contact with the face, and thus, I prefer to be free of its visual obstruction." He walked over to her and whispered in her ear, "We have done this many times. We shall be fine." He then leaned low, kissed her lightly against her ear, and gave her a faint smile when he arose.

She returned a tremulous smile, but nodded to him all the same.

Darcy then joined his cousin and began stretching his limbs. The women looked amused, and Georgiana attempted to stifle her laughter by covering her mouth with her hands.

After flexing his muscles, Richard walked over to the table and donned his mask and glove. Elizabeth watched as he did so and noticed his glove had a long cuff, which covered the sleeve opening of his jacket and travelled mid-way up his forearm. The other hand was bare. She saw him closely inspect the rabbit blunt over the tip of his foil. After scrutinizing the attachment, he also regarded the guard and ran his index finger lightly over its surface as a final measure of assurance.

Elizabeth unconsciously sighed aloud, drawing the colonel's attention to her.

"Is anything the matter, Elizabeth?"

"Oh, no, I was in a haze, that is all."

He then spoke softly. "Do not worry too much. Darcy is an expert in the field, and I seldom get the upper hand, yet, I do offer him a good challenge. So, let none of this trouble you."

Through the wire mesh, the colonel's eyes continued to linger on her face a little longer than they should until she twisted her lips and glanced towards her husband who was still stretching his limbs. Richard abruptly emerged from his reverie and turned around, whipping his *epée* about in an effort to accustom his grasp to the weight of the weapon.

Darcy walked in the direction of the table to retrieve his foil. First, he inspected the attached blunt in the same manner the colonel had done. Next, he pulled the glove onto his strong, right hand and grasped the sword. Squeezing the handle several times, he, too, whipped the blade in every direction to familiarize himself with its mass. The quick movements reverberated in the air creating a swishing sound.

Colonel Fitzwilliam stood in place some yards away from the ladies and waited for Darcy to begin.

Georgiana called out to her cousin from across the room, "Good luck, Richard."

He acknowledged her with a slight grin, and Darcy turned back and said to her good-naturedly, yet with confidence, "Georgiana, luck has nothing to do with it."

Elizabeth amusedly raised an eyebrow at her husband's reply. He caught her eye and gave her a dashing smile as he turned once more to join Richard in the middle of the floor.

Both men poised their bodies to commence. Each lunged forward with their right legs while wielding their foils erect with their left arms lifted in a half square. Richard led out and cried aloud, *"En garde!"*

At the start, they both accomplished quick movements. Darcy advanced towards Richard in an attack stance. Elizabeth noticed how elegantly his wrist moved the weapon about. He was in complete control, and she was amazed at how the cadence of their bodies' movements compared to a ballet. She was also awestruck by her husband's physical exertions as he lunged again and again. Richard's voice cried, "A hit!"

They broke combat briefly, and this time, Richard advanced. Their foils rapped, clinked, and glided upon the other. The men parried in circular patterns, and, just when she thought Richard was about to strike his cousin, Darcy would skilfully deflect the blow. Realizing that speed and endurance were the true aptitudes of the duel, Elizabeth was aware that her husband's long legs gave him a slight advantage, enabling him to have a longer reach with his foil. Yet, she also discerned that the contest took much concentration for calculating strategy during the heat of battle.

Freely, Richard yelled, *"Touché!"* but Darcy loudly exclaimed, "Not a touch!"

Suddenly, Darcy's blade slid over Richard's and plunged forward on his chest. Richard unreservedly called out, "An acknowledged hit!" By this time both men were perspiring profusely and Darcy tapped his right foot twice to let his cousin know he wanted to rest. The colonel pulled the mask from his head and advanced towards the table.

Elizabeth hastily poured water for both as they approached. Georgiana offered her cousin and brother towels, which they automatically took and began to wipe the perspiration from their faces. They then received the glasses of water and guzzled the cool liquid in a moment's time.

Darcy wiped the water from his mouth with the back of his hand and breathlessly asked, "How do you like fencing thus far?"

Georgiana passionately replied, "It is so fast-paced and exciting. I wish we could go and freely view it as we go to the opera house."

Richard and Darcy threw their heads back and burst out laughing.

"What?" Georgiana begged to know. "I fail to understand what is so funny."

Richard cheerfully responded to his young cousin's plea, "Oh, Georgie, the things you do come up with."

Elizabeth then came to her sister-in-law's defence and cried heatedly, "It may seem that way to you, colonel, since men are not barred from any activity which society has to offer! They are free to go to races, gambling houses, boxing matches, and countless other pursuits which many feel are not fit places for a lady to frequent!"

Richard blinked in admiration at Elizabeth's spunk and kindly remarked, "I suppose you are right. I, too, truly feel it is a load of dung for women to subsist by a double standard. Please excuse my French."

Darcy grimaced. He could not believe his cousin's occasional coarseness, especially in front of Georgiana.

Richard continued supportively, "No, Georgie, you are right. We should allow women to be spectators of this sport. In fact, they should be allowed to participate in it, if they so desire. I dare say the day will come, howbeit sometime in the distant future, when your great-great-granddaughters may be the recipients of such equality."

Both ladies were astonished at the colonel's admission but, nonetheless, were greatly gratified by it.

Darcy merely eyed the trio and placed his emptied glass upon the table. He declined to enter the conversation any further. Instead, he raised a brow and looked at his cousin, "Shall we continue?"

The men began anew. This time, it seemed to Elizabeth that Richard was more energetic and was taking the lead by progressively moving forward and forcing her husband to retreat. Then, without warning, Darcy made a rear lunge in an effort to gain the upper hand. The foils clinked in rapid succession and suddenly Darcy yelled, "Hit acknowledged!"

Just as suddenly, the others' faces registered horror as Darcy's white shirt became scarlet before their eyes. Richard instantly perceived that his sword had broken. Their screams rang out concurrently as Darcy similarly looked down and noticed the blood oozing from his chest. He instantly felt light-headed and fell unconscious to the floor.

Richard dropped his foil in an attempt to catch him but was too late. His cousin hit the hard floor with a loud thud. Without delay, the colonel ripped off his glove and helmet and knelt beside Darcy in the spreading pool of blood. As he did so, he commanded Georgiana and Elizabeth to bring the towels quickly and send for a doctor.

Georgiana stood frozen in fear, but Elizabeth swiftly came and handed Colonel Fitzwilliam the towels. She then sprinted from the ballroom whilst screaming at the top of her lungs for the first servant she could find.

Mr. Greene was walking down the corridor, and she franticly ran to him, boldly took hold of his arms and exclaimed, "Send for the doctor immediately! There has been an accident, and Mr. Darcy is bleeding badly!" The butler was horror-stricken and hastily left his mistress' side to obey her command.

Elizabeth's heart beat wildly as she raced back to the ballroom with an energy that surprised her. Dread filled her mind. What would she do if she lost him?

~*~

Chapter Nine

Panic, Introductions, Revelations, and Unease

Elizabeth re-entered the ballroom with great anxiety swelling in her breast as she ran to the colonel who knelt by his injured cousin. The vibrancy of her husband's blood, mingled with the black and white marbled floor, disturbed her senses, gripping her with fear. She filled with instant revulsion at the sight of Darcy's blood pooling by his side. She inwardly cried as she breathed deeply in an effort to keep some semblance of composure about her.

Blinking back her tears, she gazed at the sight before her. Richard had torn her husband's shirt completely open, exposing his bare abdomen while the rest of his torso was covered with saturated towels.

The colonel had both hands atop the towels pressing down hard upon his cousin's chest. He looked up to Elizabeth and firmly instructed, "Elizabeth, in Heaven's name, I need some blankets, hot water, more clean towels and rags. *Hurry!*"

Elizabeth nodded and turned. Again the young wife rushed from the room. She ran as fast as she could, travelling for what seemed like forever until finally meeting Mrs. Reynolds.

The elderly woman cried, "Mrs. Darcy, what do you need?"

Panting hard and her speech laboured, she attempted to speak quickly "Towels...hot water...and...some blankets. **PLEASE HURRY!**"

The house keeper said not a word as she departed in a flash, moving as fast as she was able.

Elizabeth again rushed back to be by her husband's side. While she ran, tears streamed from her eyes as she chewed on her forefinger with anxiety. Her mind reeled with images of Darcy placed in a casket in the very room where he was now lying, and in her mind's eye, she saw throngs of people coming to Pemberley to pay homage to the last of the Darcy linage... the last male heir of the Derbyshire dynasty. She briefly closed her eyes tightly and shook her head in an effort to dispel the terrible image from her mind. The vision did indeed vanish, but the foreboding never left her breast.

Once more, she entered the stately room to behold the horrific scene, and, before she could say a single word to the colonel, she doubled over, gasping for air.

The colonel was alarmed by Elizabeth's struggle but was helpless to assist her. He looked to Georgiana who leaned against the wall by the table, quietly crying, her hands covering her face.

Finally, taking in deep breaths, Elizabeth knelt by her husband's head and checked to see if he were still breathing. She also communicated to Richard that Mrs. Reynolds was gathering the needed items and that the butler was locating someone to dispatch for the doctor.

Sweat poured down Colonel Fitzwilliam's face as he nodded his head to her in acknowledgement. He observed Elizabeth as she looked intently upon her husband's features and realized how terrified she was. He glanced away. He, being a soldier, knew the full implications of his cousin's injury and felt just as fearful. How could he continue to live if his cousin were to die? He closed his eyes and silently groaned from within.

Upon opening them, Colonel Fitzwilliam detected Elizabeth's trembling hand as it brushed back his cousin's hair from his forehead. She then placed a gentle kiss on Darcy's left temple and whispered brokenheartedly, "My love, can you hear me? I love you, Fitzwilliam. Please…please, come back to me. Please, please, do not leave me."

A lump caught in the colonel's throat. He had witnessed carnage and destruction countless times. He had heard men moan, cry out and whimper in anguish for their mother's company as they lay upon foreign soil dying, their life's blood ebbing out of them. He had been greatly moved by it, but witnessing Elizabeth's anxious grief crystallized the men's pleas all the more in his mind. At this moment, he fully understood why they longed for their mother's care. Was there any greater comforting love on this earthly plane than that of an honourable woman? He realized at this precise moment it was the thing he desired most in his life, and he would not settle for anything less. Even if he would have to make ends meet on a colonel's pay, he would not compromise. It had cost him far too much already.

Hurriedly, Elizabeth arose and removed her coat. Next she folded it and placed it gently underneath her husband's head. Kneeling by Darcy's right side, she took the sword which lay near him and placed it several feet away and then came back to remove the glove from his hand. After completing her task, she sat upon the cold floor and lifted his limp arm into her lap. Holding his hand within both of hers, she inspected it closely. She marvelled at how large his hand was compared to the two of her own. Gazing upon his open hand, she took her index finger to trace the lines upon his palm, and instinctively, she raised his hand to her lips and kissed it lovingly. She lowered it once more to caress each finger separately. Her brow furrowed and tears silently trickled down her face as she massaged it further.

Richard was aware of each caress, whisper and kiss Elizabeth bestowed upon her unconscious husband as he himself still soundlessly applied pressure to Darcy's wound. Excruciating torment coursed through his consciousness at each expressed word of adoration from his cousin's wife, and he wondered at his ability to stay a moment longer before coming undone. He would ultimately be responsible for Darcy's death and Elizabeth's woe.

The wretched passion both Richard and Elizabeth were experiencing soon became restrained with the entrance of servants bearing blankets, linens and pails of water. Under the colonel's direction, throws were carefully placed above and beneath Darcy's legs, but none were placed under his chest. Richard was reluctant to move his cousin's torso for fear that it could cause the wound to bleed more profusely.

Mrs. Reynolds's heart filled with despair on beholding her master, her beloved boy, lying upon the floor, stone still and soaked in blood. The sight almost rendered her incapacitated. He was at death's door! And she knew it. Inhaling deeply, the old housekeeper squared her shoulders and immediately informed the colonel and Mrs. Darcy that the overseer had departed to fetch the doctor. While relating this message, she saw how Elizabeth's gown was saturated with the master's blood. The housekeeper was heartbroken and distressed that such a thing had happened to the couple when they were barely married. She shook her head in dismay to offset the gloom from swallowing her entirely. But then she took rags and began mopping up the blood from the floor. One of the younger maids gently came forward in an effort to take over the task, but Mrs. Reynolds would not allow it, asking her instead to go and get more towels and hot water.

Elizabeth became conscious of Richard by her side again and looked imploringly into his eyes. "Do you think he is no longer bleeding? Do you know how bad the wound is?"

The colonel's eyes glistened with tears, his lips trembled as he tried to answer her. "I am not sure, Elizabeth. When I tried to inspect the wound, the blood flowed excessively, and I thought it wise to apply pressure without delay."

Wearily, Elizabeth nodded and pressed her husband's hand to her cheek.

Peering over at his young cousin, Richard observed that Georgiana no longer stood but crouched against the wall, cradling her head in her hands. He thought to ask Elizabeth to go to her but decided it would be best if Mrs. Reynolds assisted her.

So, calling to her, he stated in a low voice.

"Mrs. Reynolds?"

The housekeeper stopped her unpleasant task and looked over to Colonel Fitzwilliam.

"Yes, Colonel?"

In a whisper that the elderly lady truly had to struggle to hear, Richard beseeched, "Mrs. Reynolds, do you think you could help Georgiana to her room? I am very concerned about her. I am fearful that this may prove overwhelming for her."

Elizabeth immediately searched for her sister-in-law and felt ashamed for having forgotten her. Gently, she placed her husband's arm back by his side and attempted to stand, but Mrs. Reynolds placed her hand on Elizabeth's shoulder and spoke decisively.

"No, mistress, you stay by the master's side. He will want you when he comes to. I will take care of Miss Georgiana. Leave her to my care."

The elderly lady swiftly stood erect, dipped her hands in the pail of water to clean them, and went straightway to Miss Darcy. Cautiously she knelt by the girl and spoke in a quiet voice.

A weakened smile mingled with understanding and sorrow appeared on Elizabeth's face as her eyes spoke appreciation to the colonel for remembering to take care of Georgiana. He shook his head slightly in an effort to deflect her gratitude. They both watched Mrs. Reynolds guide Miss Darcy out of the ballroom, but, before they walked through the door, Georgiana turned and called anxiously to her cousin. "Richard, will you come and let me know how my brother is... no matter the hour?"

From the same position he had been in for some time, Richard nodded and answered unfalteringly, "Yes, you can depend upon it, Georgie."

With her red, swollen face, she stared at both Richard and Elizabeth for a few seconds more, then nodded and turned, guided from the room by Mrs. Reynolds.

Elizabeth felt as if the doctor would never come, and she noticed that the muscles twitching on the colonel's face and neck. She knew he must be fatigued from being in the same posture for so long. He shifted his legs beneath him somewhat but his hand and arms remained securely over the wound on Darcy's chest.

They were alone within the room save for a few servants lingering at the open doorway.

"Richard," Elizabeth whispered, "will Fitzwilliam be able to be moved from this area? I mean, could that not start the bleeding again? It is so cold in here."

Colonel Fitzwilliam swallowed hard against the lump in his throat. He did not know what to tell her. He had seen it far too often go both ways, so he answered as best he could, "I cannot really say. The doctor will have to make that judgment. I will not lie and tell you not to worry. It depends on how deep the wound is and if the bleeding is under control, but even then..." He shook his head not knowing what more to say.

Elizabeth knelt close to Darcy's head. She again studied his pale face and noticed that small beads of perspiration entirely covered it. Taking a towel, she dabbed the moisture away. Slowly she sat back down and lifted her husband's hand yet again. She instantly noticed it was clammy. Holding it firmly between her hands, she began to sway methodically back and forth.

Richard became aware that Elizabeth's slow rhythm was beginning to quicken. He looked at his cousin's face. He was so white and ashen looking. Apprehensively, the colonel leaned his head near Darcy's to listen for the regularity of his breathing.

It was shallow. He glanced over to Elizabeth and was about to ask her to check for his cousin's pulse when he realized that she was becoming overly anxious.

Insistently, Elizabeth rocked. Richard softy called her name aloud, but she did not respond. The colonel breathed in deeply as his eyes tightened shut in misery. In exasperation he cried out, "Where in the **bloody hell** is the doctor?"

Momentarily, due to the colonel's outburst, Elizabeth stopped moving, but after a few seconds passed, she proceeded to rock at a more rapid pace than before. The servants were watching her from the hall, and Richard decided he must try to calm her.

Gently, he called her name, "Elizabeth? Elizabeth do you hear me?"

She closed her eyes and shook her head.

Richard was glad she reacted even if it was in the negative. He tried again. "Elizabeth, answer me."

She violently turned her head from side to side as she rocked inconsolably.

The colonel closed his eyes in agony and was ready to swear again when Darcy raised his head and in an unsteady voice enquired, "Where am I?"

Elizabeth swiftly twisted around to look at him. He was staring at Richard, and she heard the colonel say, "You have been hurt and are in the ballroom."

Darcy squinted at his cousin as though trying to focus. His head dropped back onto the folded coat, as he closed his eyes and enquired, "What happened?"

"My foil broke and you have sustained a wound to your chest."

Leaning near Darcy's face, Elizabeth attempted to speak calmly but was not quite successful. "Oh Fitzwilliam, what would you have me do for you?"

Darcy turned his head slightly to the side and peered at her through half-closed lids. "What? Where am I?"

Elizabeth's brow creased. "You are at Pemberley in the ballroom. I love you, Fitzwilliam."

Darcy's brow furrowed at her reply and he then posed, "Why are you here?"

Astonished, Elizabeth cried out, "I am here with you. You were fencing and there has been an accident and the doctor is coming to take care of you."

"Why are you here?"

Richard breathed in deeply. He now realized that his cousin, in all probability, had a concussion. He turned to Elizabeth and whispered, "The fall has caused him to temporarily lose his memory. Do not be distressed. He will likely keep asking the same questions over and over again for some time."

When Elizabeth tried to talk to her husband again, Darcy said nothing. After several more attempts, Elizabeth, disheartened, took his hand and resumed rocking. She wondered if he remembered her at all. Had he forgotten they were married? What would happen if he never remembered? She now had a new worry to add to her fear of his dying. With these thoughts, her deep rapid breathing testified to the new difficulty and set the pace for her assiduous sway.

Finally, the doctor, accompanied by Mr. Manning and Mr. Chaffin, entered the room, coming straightway to where Darcy lay.

The physician was a young man no more than Darcy's own age. He was new to the neighbourhood due to the passing of one of the county's revered, yet elderly physicians, Dr. Prince. As the doctor quickly pulled off his jacket, Richard noted that his shirt sleeves were already rolled mid-way up his arms. Richard glanced up as he then heard Mr. Chaffin performing the honours of introduction.

"Dr. Lowry, this is Mr. Darcy's cousin, Colonel Fitzwilliam, and this is his wife, Mrs. Darcy."

Dr. Lowry nodded, knelt next to the colonel, and, as he lifted Darcy's wrist, mechanically asked, "What has happened here, and how long has it been?"

Richard answered, "The blade on my foil broke, and he was wounded in the chest. It has been a little longer than half an hour ago."

"How long did Mr. Darcy remain conscious before he passed out?

Again, the colonel made answer, "He immediately buckled when he perceived he was bleeding. I am afraid he hit the floor hard. However, he just came to a moment ago and has asked the same questions repeatedly."

The doctor nodded as he put Darcy's wrist down by his side, quickly looked over to a distraught wife, and then back to the colonel. "I want Mrs. Darcy to quit the room this instant."

Richard's brows shot up as he enlightened the doctor. "I am not so sure she should go." But, what the colonel really thought to say was, he was almost certain she would not go.

Dr. Lowry spoke aloud but did not look at Elizabeth, "Mrs. Darcy, please leave. You are not needed at present. We will care for Mr. Darcy and inform you presently about his wellbeing."

Elizabeth shook her head and ceased rocking as she continued to clasp her husband's hand. "No, Doctor, I will not leave! I also will not get in your way."

Bitingly, Dr. Lowry barked, "Madam, you are already in my way. Leave this instant!"

Elizabeth gently put her husband's hand down, then hastily arose and walked a few feet away where she came to a stop and defiantly crossed her arms over her chest.

The doctor gestured with his head for Richard to move his hands and then he took over the occupation of compressing the patient's chest. "Take Mrs. Darcy out of this room this instant!"

Mr. Chaffin went over and offered his hand to her, but Elizabeth shunned him with a slight turn of her shoulder. Richard swiftly stood and went to her side. "Come Elizabeth," he softly entreated, "you must allow the doctor to examine Darcy."

Her breathing was harder than before as Richard took her by the arm and forcefully began to pull her along. She strived with all her strength and resisted his effort.

Breathlessly, she yelled, "I will not go!"

Darcy's head turned back and forth while his forehead creased in confusion. He weakly mumbled over and over, "Fitzwilliam...Fitzwilliam...Fitzwilliam, where am I?"

Firmly, Richard reached behind her back to take hold of her other arm which enabled him to rush her forward. She struggled, but it was to no avail. The colonel had her past the servants and into the hall in a matter of seconds. Elizabeth, however, managed to break free from his grasp. She turned to run back into the room when he grabbed hold of her yet again. Instantly she spun around and began beating her fists on his chest, screaming and crying. He pulled her tightly against his body while backing her against the wall.

Emotionally, he pleaded, "Elizabeth...in Heaven's name...you must calm yourself!"

Heatedly, she shook her head and demanded for him to release her. As Richard continued to try to reason with her, she began pinching his arm with all of her might. The servants gawked openly at the unseemly exchange between the colonel and their mistress.

Resolutely, he turned her about and lugged her down the length of the corridor. Panting hard, Elizabeth struggled for breath, but Richard was unaware of her plight as he propelled her forward. Then, halfway down the corridor, she collapsed to the floor.

Colonel Fitzwilliam immediately picked her up and tried to determine in which direction to carry her. His decision made, he strode to Darcy's study.

The colonel manoeuvred the door open with his elbow and knee and placed Elizabeth on the chaise lounge. He walked back to close the door but then decided, instead of shutting it completely, he would leave it ajar.

After situating the door, Richard looked over at Elizabeth and perceived that she was breathing easier. Walking over to the decanters, he took a glass and poured it half full of wine. He then returned to her side and placed the glass on the side table.

Sitting on the edge of the chaise beside her, he indulgently studied her features. The colonel noticed that most of her hair had fallen down around her face, and it almost made her appear cherubic had it not been for the blood-smeared blush upon her cheeks. In fact, he observed that she had blood splotched from head to toe. Suddenly wrought with an acute awareness of the pain he had cost her, his heart filled with regret for an action which was by no means premeditated and another which was.

Elizabeth began to stir and Colonel Fitzwilliam softly spoke to her. "Elizabeth, I have some wine for you. I request you drink it."

Opening her eyes widely, she stared at him. Seeing his bloodstained clothes brought the events vividly to her mind. Quickly, she covered her face with her hands and appealed to the colonel in shame, "I beg your forgiveness, Richard. I know not what I was thinking or what came over me. I am truly horrified at the thought of my behaviour towards you. Please believe me when I say that I have never in my life caused bodily injury to another soul."

"Here," Richard soothingly entreated, "drink this wine for me, and I will forgive you most readily."

She allowed him to help raise her head and took a sip. When he implored her to drink it all, she obeyed his directive without wavering.

Setting the glass back on the table, Richard looked down upon her. She met his gaze, and they stared at one another for several moments before he spoke.

"Elizabeth, there is nothing to forgive. You are distraught over your husband's welfare, and I forced you to leave his side. There is nothing to forgive. In fact, I, for once, cannot humour myself out of this one. I am the direct cause of it all. So, you see...it is," he inhaled and exhaled deeply, "I who begs the forgiveness of all concerned. I would gladly be on that floor now instead of my cousin. I am truly ill." He ran his fingers through his hair and then cradled his head into his hands.

Elizabeth gazed at his hands as they supported his head. She sat upright and placed her hand on the colonel's forearm and gave it a gentle squeeze. Richard welcomed the gesture but, at the same time, was pained by it.

She spoke unequivocally, "Richard, it is not your fault anymore than anyone else's. I am the one who suggested the demonstration in the first place. I am beside myself for bringing this about and...I feel inadequate as Mistress of Pemberley when I think of what I just now did to you in front of the servants and how I acted in the ballroom, and when...when I think of how I have acted these past two days, I feel unworthy of my husband and feel that he truly deserves better." She began to weep softly. Richard took her hand in both of his while shaking his head.

"No, Elizabeth, you are truly the best woman my cousin has ever known. He loves you dearly. I can assure you that no matter what you do, he will *always* love you. I have not seen him this happy in a long time, especially since the death of his father. He has never cared for a woman the way he cares for you." All of a sudden Richard chuckled to himself as he cheerfully recollected his cousin's foul mood after Elizabeth's rejection of him at Hunsford.

Quizzically, Elizabeth looked at the colonel's sudden mirth and raised her brows in expectation.

Smiling openly, he began to disclose Darcy's actions after that fateful event. "I do not know how much my cousin has told you about our Aunt Catherine."

She shook her head questioningly and said, "We have discussed her only once, just after we became engaged, but nothing further has been said."

While still holding Elizabeth's hand in his, he began to explicate Darcy's unusual behaviour at that time.

"When my cousin proposed to you that evening at Hunsford, he came back to Rosings in great agitation. Lady Catherine was, as you can easily imagine, greatly put out at his leaving in the first place without properly informing us of his impending absence. She therefore sent me with the errand of finding him, demanding that he be in attendance. I had just walked out of the drawing room when in came Darcy, wearing the most despicable scowl which I had ever witnessed. I asked if something were wrong, and he answered while rapidly ascending the stairs that he had urgent business to attend to and asked for me to offer his apologies to our Aunt. Well, Lady Catherine was not easily gainsaid. Yet, I returned and related Darcy's message to her. The next morning, Darcy again did not join us for breakfast, and I did not have the foggiest idea of what had become of him. Aunt Catherine was beside herself with indignation, and we all had to endure her strictures on decorum once more. In all of our annual visits to Rosings, my cousin had never quelled on etiquette before." He then paused as if to reflect on his words.

At first Elizabeth was a little disturbed by the colonel's chosen topic. However, she was intrigued by a desire to know more about a subject of which her husband was reluctant to speak, except to voice his abhorrence concerning his behaviour towards her. By giving the colonel a faint smile, Elizabeth indicated her desire to hear more.

He inhaled deeply and resumed his narrative. "As I was saying, Darcy has always been the epitome of propriety, and his behaviour at that time was truly unfathomable. I had no idea why he was behaving so differently and tried to tease it out of him, but he only became more withdrawn. Of course, I had no way on knowing at that instant that you had refused his offer of marriage. Suffice it to say, I was totally baffled. Darcy is not a man to have his feathers easily ruffled. It takes a lot to push him over the edge."

Looking down at her hand within Richard's, Elizabeth pressed her lips together and derisively thought to herself, *Such as uniforms on a snowman and the impropriety of discussing the welfare of a lady's maid at the dinner table.*

Richard apparently discerned the change in her expression and tried to quickly come to his point.

"What I am alluding to, Elizabeth, in a most unintelligible manner is this: before you, Darcy had been hounded by scores of pedigreed women with their mamas, to boot. Women would fawn and drool all over him. Hang on to his every word and mollycoddle his every want, real or imaginary. They all appeared charming, but were chameleons hiding their true natures and motives. Substantial energy was spent in the attendance of balls, assemblies, soirées, dinner arrangements, theatre engagements and months in the country all in the pursuit of a suitable wife. He became tired from the swirl of activities and all the years of obsequiousness found therein. Therefore, he became hopeless of ever marrying. We both saw too many marriages from our circles which were only procured in the name of fortune and connections, and, since there was no other adhesive for such unions, the marriages were pure shams, full of drudgery and quite frankly hell. Thus, until recently, we remained bachelors, but, then you came along and changed all of that." He said the last sentence with a twinkle in his eyes.

Elizabeth raised her eyes to him with a small degree of unease in her look, yet her countenance also encouraged him to go on.

"You see, you were a long-awaited fresh spring breeze after a cold winter's chill. Darcy was enchanted by you. When he first told me about his trip with Bingley to Hertfordshire, with all the shooting parties, dinner engagements and all, he mentioned your name in particular. When he spoke of you to Georgiana and myself, we both felt quite curious from his glowing praises of you that he might have developed some affection for you because he seldom if ever mentioned any female in our conversations."

Elizabeth's smile grew.

In earnest, Richard fixed his eyes on Elizabeth's and said, "Your open and playful, yet clever ways caught him off guard and challenged him like no other. You truly know how to drive a coach and horses through, and Darcy could not help but be captivated by your natural knack of doing so. You kowtow to no man! You are the only one capable of claiming him…the only one worthy of him. Only you have the ability to knock him off of the high horse which he tends to ride from time to time."

Elizabeth's eyes grew large, and the colonel saw the look of surprise on her face and chuckled. "My cousin has had many responsibilities placed solely upon his shoulders, especially when his father became ill. He has been groomed for these tasks since childhood. Thus, he is insipid at times to be sure, due to the heaviness of the load. However, now with you, Elizabeth, by his side, he will have a liveliness which will bring zest and flavour to the bland existence he knew before. So you see, Mrs. Darcy, never underestimate your worth to your husband. You are indeed, priceless to him! Of that, I am sure."

Elizabeth gazed at Richard as he stared at her openly with true affection. The colonel's correct portrayal of her husband's tendency to haughtiness and her own impertinence was completely accurate. She realized that Richard knew her husband well, and his choice of the word liveliness rang a bell in Elizabeth's head, as she quickly recalled her Aunt Gardiner saying to her in a letter the very same thing concerning Darcy before her engagement, 'that he only needed a little more liveliness in his life and if he married prudently, his wife may teach him.'

Elizabeth's outward show of gratitude diffused over her as tears flowed freely down her cheeks. She slowly pulled her hand from Richard's and quickly leaned forward to embrace him. This course of action appeared to put him in a state of shock, and, while holding him close, she whispered, "You are too good!" The embrace ended just as quickly as it had begun. Elizabeth leaned back and stared at the stunned man. "Thank you, Richard, for helping to quiet my fear and for caring so much for Fitzwilliam. You are truly one of the best of men."

Before standing, the colonel reached for her hand one last time. He squeezed it tightly and then, lifting it to his lips, he bestowed a kiss thereon. Afterward, he smiled at her with unabashed adoration and arose.

Breathing in deeply, he related, "I would like to go now to enquire after Darcy's welfare. Do you think you will be all right alone for awhile? I promise to return promptly and give you a full report."

Biting her lower lip, Elizabeth hesitated but then said forthrightly, "Richard, I know you have every reason to doubt me, but I desire to go with you. I promise to do whatever you ask of me. I will not disobey or be in anyone's way, no matter the circumstances we may find."

She imploringly gazed up at him, and he could deny her nothing. "Are you sure, Elizabeth? I mean, I do trust you, but I cannot guarantee that you may enter the ballroom. And, maybe you should change first. Darcy may be distressed to see you covered in his blood." His last remark temporarily diverted her as she thought of her husband's boast of his ability to stomach the sight of blood and how tonight's quirk of fate, when seeing his own, served as a refutation for such conceit. She smiled dryly then frowned.

Rising from the chaise lounge, Elizabeth looked directly into Richard's eyes. "You have my solemn promise that I will not attempt to enter, but I shall wait for your return in the hall."

Silently he nodded and then offered his arm to her.

Unbeknownst to the couple, a pair of probing eyes had taken in all of their interactions.

~*~

Richard and Elizabeth were surprised as they walked to the ballroom, to see no servants standing worriedly about the door. Elizabeth was true to her word and leaned against the wall as Richard entered without her. He returned immediately with a confused look and exclaimed, "No one is anywhere to be seen."

Elizabeth anxiously enquired, "Is Fitzwilliam gone as well?"

"Yes."

The colonel took hold of her hand, pulling her along as he walked quickly towards the vestibule of the house. He told her not to worry, that they would soon find out the whereabouts of Darcy. Inwardly, he felt it was a good sign that he had been removed so soon.

As they hurried along, Elizabeth clung to the colonel's words of encouragement while quickening her step to keep pace with him. When they entered, they were met by Mrs. Darcy's maid, Sally. She told them that a room had been prepared near the kitchen according to the doctor's directives and that Mr. Darcy was awake and calling for her.

Elizabeth sprinted away, leaving her maid and Richard several feet behind. She had to pause, however, as she came near the entrance of the kitchen, because she realized she had no idea which direction to go.

Sally came from behind to lead her mistress down a narrow hallway to a large walnut door. Elizabeth stepped forward to open the latch when Richard's hand stopped her. Her head turned while her eyes locked on his.

"Let me go first and make sure it is all right to enter."

Elizabeth acquiesced to the colonel's instruction by swiftly moving aside. He knocked, turned the handle, and stepped a little way into the room. Dr. Lowry and Mr. Chaffin promptly looked over to where he stood and bid him enter.

Richard asked pointedly, "Mrs. Darcy wishes to see her husband. May she also come?"

Dr. Lowry was drying his hands on a towel. With a quick nod, he indicated his approval.

The colonel then opened the door wide, stepped aside, and gestured with his arm for Elizabeth to proceed first.

The gentlemen within the room moved away from the narrow bed in order to give Mrs. Darcy access to her husband's side. Mr. Chaffin had cleaned his master's body to where there was no sign of blood and had dressed him in a night shirt. Elizabeth felt a sense of disappointment at seeing her husband not fully conscious since she had anticipated from Sally's report his desire of asking for her. But instead, he appeared restless, turning his head occasionally from side to side.

As she gazed upon her husband, she heard Mr. Chaffin offer to stay with Mr. Darcy throughout the night, but, when Elizabeth told him that she would stay, he excused himself for the evening and again offered his assistance if needed at anytime throughout the remainder of the night. He bowed and exited the room.

Richard spoke to the doctor first to enquire about Darcy's condition. Dr. Lowry answered him while he arranged items within his black bag. "Mr. Darcy has sustained a wound that severed a small artery in his chest wall. The wound itself is no more than an inch in length. These arteries bleed profusely but when pressure is applied and sustained, they quickly clot. That is why there was so much loss of blood, but, fortunately, no major organs were harmed, and, with a few days of rest and no strenuous physical exertion, he should mend nicely. But, I will tell you, Colonel Fitzwilliam, if you had not applied pressure to the wound when you did, he would not be with us now."

Sighing heavily with relief from the doctor's words, Elizabeth anxiously asked, "Dr. Lowry, does my husband remember now? I was told by my maid that he was calling for me earlier."

For the first time, Dr. Lowry looked squarely into her face, and in a matter-of-fact air said, "Yes he was calling for you before I prescribed him a dose of laudanum which seems to be taking effect now. He was mindful while I sutured the wound. I gave him the medicine before leaving the ballroom. He walked the whole way with my and Mr. Manning's assistance. I am pleased that the wound was not reopened by the exercise."

All eyes turned towards the patient as Darcy mumbled whilst tossing his head erratically. Elizabeth, Colonel Fitzwilliam, and Dr. Lowry all assembled close on each side of the bed straining to hear his words. After several attempts at opening his eyes, Darcy looked at the doctor to his right and then the colonel by his side. He turned his head slightly towards Elizabeth who smiled at him brightly, but his eyes quickly darted back to rest on Richard's face. Darcy's eyes glowered menacingly as he exclaimed to his cousin, "You want my wife!" Their eyes locked for a brief moment before the colonel's face turned bright red and a cold chill spread over his entire body. He inhaled deeply and began to shake his head slightly.

Alarmed by her husband's accusation, Elizabeth snatched up his hand to gain his attention. Darcy turned to look at her, but his eyes seemed not to focus on her face. The laudanum was taking effect, and, with heavy lids, he closed his eyes and began to snore faintly.

Coughing lightly, Dr. Lowry attempted to disperse the awkwardness hanging in the air from such a harrowing accusation. While rolling down his shirt sleeves and shifting his gaze from the colonel to Elizabeth, he objectively informed them, "Laudanum can cloud a person's reason and make them imagine all sorts of things. If taken for too long, it can bring on delirium."

Elizabeth eyed him suspiciously, for she realized that her husband had been given only one dose. In dread she enquired, "How much laudanum will my husband need to take?"

Dr. Lowry pressed his lips together and shrugged. "That all depends on Mr. Darcy's tolerance for pain and discomfort. He will most definitely have extreme soreness in his ribcage for a week or so, and his head may ache for a few days more. It is paramount that he rest, and, if he cannot do so on his own, the powder must be administered every evening and once more before dawn. But I do not anticipate there being a problem with this. He seems to have handled the pain quite well so far.

Elizabeth had only one more question for the doctor. She desired to know when her husband could be moved to his own chamber. Dr. Lowry indicated that if all went well with the sutures staying in place during the course of the night, he did not see any reason why Mr. Darcy could not attempt the stairs tomorrow evening if he felt up to it.

After answering her question, he asked for a room to sleep for the night due to the lateness of the hour and that he wanted to check on his patient first thing in the morning. Additionally, he desired to be close by if needed before then. Elizabeth hastily ushered him out of the small room and walked to the kitchen where she found Sally waiting for her. She informed the maid to take the doctor to the closest guest room and see to his needs. The maid curtseyed and escorted the doctor to a room and had Mrs. Potter's son come at once to start a fire while she hurriedly brought the unforeseen guest a pitcher of fresh water and towels for the washstand.

When Elizabeth returned to the sick room, she saw that Richard remained therein. He stood as she came in and nervously offered to stay with Darcy throughout the night in order for Elizabeth to bathe and get some rest. Elizabeth would not look him in the eye. She only stared off to the corner of the room and thanked him for his offer, but she informed him that she alone would stay. She added that, if his assistance was needed, she would not hesitate to call for his help.

He nodded and quietly said, "Very well. I know I cannot change your mind, and I must be off because I promised to inform Georgie." Silence ensued for a little longer before he affirmed, "Elizabeth, Darcy and Georgiana mean the world to me. I would never do anything to wilfully hurt or deceive them. I hope you believe that."

Involuntarily, her head shot up to make certain of his claim. "I know that Richard. I am deeply aware of your love and concern. Likewise, I am aware of their love of and devotion to you. And, I thank you from the bottom of my heart for saving my husband's life and for being so patient and kind to me in spite of my cruelty. You will never know the depth of my gratitude."

Unshed tears shone in the eyes of both as the colonel smiled weakly before taking his leave. He went directly to Georgiana's room to enlighten her about Darcy's condition. She was still awake and was overjoyed when he told her of the doctor's prognosis. Her happiness was evident by the numerous hugs of thanksgiving which she bestowed upon her cousin.

Afterward, he made his way to his own chamber and washed the caked blood from his hands and forearms. He then readied for bed and lay restlessly for some time. He heard the faint chimes of the clock announce midnight, but sleep eluded him. Instead, Darcy's accusation kept creeping to the forefront of his thoughts. Thinking back over the course of a highly emotional day for them all, he pondered his feelings for his cousin's wife. He remembered how she felt in his arms while she and Georgiana cried on his chest, and the memory induced the same awakening he had felt earlier. Furthermore, he thought about the close proximity which he and Elizabeth shared while Darcy had lain upon the floor and how her attentions to his wounded cousin had tormented him. Next, he considered how her body felt next to his in her anger as he pressed her back against the wall. Once more he closed his eyes in mortification for the forcefulness of his behaviour at that time. Struggling with these thoughts caused him to question: did he truly covet Elizabeth?

~*~

Likewise, another individual lay awake for a short time before finding sleep. Dr. Harrison Lowry wondered if there was any validity to his patient's charge to Colonel Fitzwilliam. He knew from his questioning that Mr. Darcy sustained some memory loss concerning the occurrence of the accident and the hours leading up to it but, the drug surely shouldn't have caused such a vehement reaction from the man. He shook his head and decided to let the matter rest. After all, it was of no concern to him as long as it had no impediment to Mr. Darcy's healing, and then he smiled ironically to himself as he wickedly thought that if the allegation were true, it would surely serve as a ready remedy for a full recovery.

~*~

Elizabeth pulled a chair next to the narrow bed. She was still mottled in blood and, from the dishevelment of her hair, rightly looked like a woman gone mad. Then again, she did not care, given that she was determined to be there when her husband awoke which would at least be sometime before dawn according to the doctor's calculation. Folding her arms on the mattress, she rested her head upon them and closed her eyes to say a prayer of thankfulness. Her husband was alive and not mortally wounded. She was truly grateful for all that Colonel Fitzwilliam and Dr. Lowry had done to save his life. In fact, everyone involved had done so much. However, shame began to enter from the corners of her mind with the analysis of her hysterical behaviour during such a critical time. What on earth had happened? In all of her memories, she had acted worse than her mother ever had. Her mother, at least, was always most willing to go to her room! What would Fitzwilliam say when he found out about her flare-up in front of the servants and Dr. Lowry, and the conflict with Richard in the hall. Closing her eyes in disbelief, she decided that she would not allow herself to think about such things right now. It was too distressing, and she was too weary. Instead, she caressed her husband's wrist with her fingers and softly said aloud, "I love you, Fitzwilliam Darcy, and I truly want to be worthy of you. I am so sorry for my foolish whim which has cost you so dearly. Please know that I will do anything to make you proud." Nothing further was said and her husband's soft snore quickly lulled her to sleep.

~*~

Chapter Ten

Discovery and Resolution

A splitting headache awakened Darcy to unfamiliar surroundings where the only light provided was from glowing embers within the grate. He squinted several times, trying to determine where he was. Then the back of his hand brushed against something hirsute. He tensed. The peculiarity from the sensation of having something foreign in his bed caused him to immediately recoil his hand in alarm. What on earth was it?

Lifting his sore head, Darcy attempted to make out whatever it was on the bed which could produce such an uncanny feeling. As he did, the left side of his chest burned from the endeavour. Thus, he groaned aloud as his head fell back on the pillow.

His cry jolted Elizabeth from her slumber. As her heart raced, she quickly lifted her head and called out, "Fitzwilliam, are you all right? Shall I go and fetch the doctor?"

Darcy's brow furrowed at the sound of his wife's voice, yet relief soon followed the unexpected surprise of her company. He quickly realized it was *her hair* which his hand had felt and he chuckled aloud from the fright that it had given him.

Elizabeth, puzzled by his delight, again asked, "My love, do you not hear me? Fitzwilliam, it is I, Elizabeth. Are you well?"

Answering with apparent pain and a tinge of amusement in his voice he replied, "Yes, my Lizzy, I now realize it is you, but for a moment there, I thought someone had let a cat in my bed to keep me company."

If it had not been dark, her husband would have seen the confusion written all over his wife's weary brow, not to mention her wild appearance. Somewhat disorientated and struggling to understand his meaning, Elizabeth became fearful that he might be delirious from the laudanum, and so she enquired, "Fitzwilliam, whatever gave you the idea you were sleeping with a cat?"

Instantly, laughter rang out followed by deep moans of pain. Alarmed, Elizabeth mindlessly stood in order to alert Dr. Lowry of her husband's predicament, but before she went through the door, Darcy cried after her, "Lizzy, do not leave me. Where am I?"

She pivoted and dashed back to his side. Darcy required her to light a candle, which she did at once. He then gazed at her for a few seconds and enquired yet again, "Where am I, and why does my chest burn?"

Elizabeth sat down on the chair and calmly began. "You are in a small room beside the kitchen. You were hurt while fencing with Richard tonight in the ballroom. Do you need me to summon the doctor? He has been given a room down the hall."

Darcy slowly shook his head as he furrowed his brow, straining to remember the incident. "I am not sure I understand you. Did you say that I was injured while fencing?"

"Yes, Fitzwilliam, and you have lost a lot of blood."

"How on earth did that occur? Welts and bruises I can understand, but I have never received a wound in all of my years of swordplay. I find it hard to believe."

Taking in a deep breath, Elizabeth explained with the best of her ability. "Well, you did not wear any protective garments apart from your glove. Whereas, Richard wore a glove, vest and mask."

He was not following her line of explanation and asked again, "How came the wound which I have suffered?"

Blurting out from raw emotions she decried, "Due to your lack of protection, when Richard made a hit upon your chest, the blade of his foil snapped causing the blunt tip to fall and allowing the broken blade to enter your chest between your ribs which, in turn, severed an artery causing you to bleed profusely. You fainted upon seeing your blood, hitting your head hard upon the floor. I thought you were going to die, Fitzwilliam! Promise me this instant that you will never again fence without proper, protective attire!"

He could hear the strain in her voice, and, even though his head still throbbed, he soothed her tension by lovingly reaching for her hand and squeezing it reassuringly."

"Elizabeth, all is well. Please, my love, I am not angry with anyone. I cannot remember a thing. I can see that you have been through much. Come," he said as he tugged at her arm to join him on the bed, but she resisted.

"My love, the bed is too narrow. I fear that your wound may reopen, and I do not want to have the doctor walk in if I were to do so."

"Elizabeth, I do not know of what you are speaking. Come and sit by me and tell me everything again. I implore you to do so. I shall alert you if it proves too much for me."

Nodding, she delicately slid by his side. He pulled her closer with his left arm and then involuntarily flinched from the pain that shot across his chest. In concern, she offered, "Oh Fitzwilliam! I should have thought to lie on the other side. Let me do so now." He agreed and released her so she could make the change.

Once she was situated, she posed, "What do you remember? I mean, do you remember anything regarding yesterday?"

Contemplating her question, he began to tally up what he vividly recalled. "I remember seeing the Wilkens boy off and..." here he paused becoming conscious of their disagreement over Clara and his asinine behaviour out in the courtyard over the snowmen. Yet, he remembered almost simultaneously her forgiveness and their passionate reconciliation. Hoarsely, he whispered, "I keenly recall your loving kindness to a man who did not deserve it. Oh, Elizabeth, you are too good. I am sorry for my irrational behaviour to you and Georgiana over the uniform."

Shaking her head in tender emotion she placed her fingertips gently against his mouth and silenced him. "No, Fitzwilliam, no more apologies. I cannot endure it. Let us instead continue to find how exacting your memory is up to the accident."

He nodded and thought to himself over the remainder of the afternoon. He recollected retrieving his boots and smiled when remembering that they had another loving encounter, yet again, and then he tried to call to mind what happened afterward. Suddenly, he remembered the coddle and black forest cake. It was beginning to come back to him now. He excitedly asked, "We separated after dinner and you and Georgiana asked to see us fence because we promised to let you choose the activity for the evening?"

Looking to her, he saw the remorse in her eyes and gently said, "Lizzy, it is no one's fault. Do not blame yourself. It was purely an accident, and I am glad to know all is well. I will mend."

She closed her eyes in disbelief. "Oh, my love, I am not so sure. But, I am grateful that you are not dead and now remember me."

"I did not remember you before?"

"Not after the accident. You came to, but kept asking the same questions. The doctor and Richard say you have sustained a concussion from the trauma to your head when you fell."

"How did I fall again?"

In patience, Elizabeth told him the whole story in detail. She realized he truly had no memory of the fencing. In fact, the thing he last remembered was coming down the stairs with Richard, carrying their foils, but after that nothing further would come.

Hesitantly she asked, "Do you remember the doctor bringing you in here?"

Concentrating hard, he made a compilation of bits and pieces which seemed a puzzle to him. "I do recall a doctor that I do not know requiring me to remain still and having me drink something. He also helped me to walk, but I cannot tell you where and how far."

"The doctor and Mr. Manning helped you walk in here. Mr. Chaffin helped to clean and dress your wound. They gave you Dover's powder. Do you recall anything after coming here?"

He tried to remember but shook his head and asked, "Where were you?"

Her faced became grave. "I am afraid that the doctor was not happy with me because I became overwrought with worry. He asked me to leave and wait while they took care of you. I am so sorry, Fitzwilliam. I do not know what came over me, and I am sure if you were aware of my behaviour at the time you would not be pleased."

He frowned. Had his actions of late produced such fear in his sweet wife that she felt the need to be cautious of her every action...her every thought? He hoped not, but feared otherwise. Breathing hard, his face contorting in remorse. "Lizzy, do not worry about what you said or did. I am sorry for your distress. I love you. Do not be concerned about your anxiety. None of us truly knows how we will respond to unforeseen calamities."

"Yes...but, Fitzwilliam, I did and said things that were not entirely proper."

"Elizabeth, I do not want to know. Leave it be. Please, no longer torture yourself with your concern over my response to behaviour which strains the best of us in such dire circumstances. I am certain no one will remember or censure you for caring for your husband's life. I am not so sure of remaining calm myself, had I been in your place. You are everything to me, Lizzy. I do not know what I would do if I thought you might be dying." He paused and whispered with a contrite spirit, "I could very well see myself banned to Bedlam with the rest of my relatives."

Shock was evident on Elizabeth's face. Was her husband teasing her over the very same issue about which he had reprimanded her regarding her smiling encouragement of Georgiana's thoughtless remark? She did not know what to make of it. However, she did feel comfort from his avowal of not being angry with her unpardonable conduct. She sighed, releasing her pent up trepidation.

"How long did the doctor say my head will hurt? It is terrible."

"Oh, my love, let me go find him, and he will give you more medicine."

"No, Elizabeth, do not. I detest the stuff. It makes me imagine things."

She stiffened. "What kind of things?"

He held his breath and debated, but thought the better of it. "It made me think your hair was a *furry* cat!"

"What!" Elizabeth exclaimed.

He smiled in a waggish manner and tousled her tresses with his hand. "Your hair scared the wits out of me. For when I awakened, I could neither make hide nor *hair* of what it was. I thought a cat must be in my bed."

Giggling, she merrily reasoned, "So, that is why you laughed so. I thought the medication had made you go mad."

"See, I am already being condemned to Bedlam."

"Um...well..." she vaguely answered.

"Well...I may be going mad about many things here of late, but in one thing I am not mistaken, there is a cat in my bed and she is a beautiful feline. In fact, I am quite smitten with her and want to take her to bed every night. I find that I cannot resist in making her purr."

Elizabeth rolled her eyes in disbelief. "Fitzwilliam Darcy, how dare you! You truly amaze me with your nonsense. Here you lie, only hours after barely escaping death, and you still tease like a schoolboy. I would never have dreamed during our engagement that you would act as such."

Feigning offence, he declared, "I promise you, dear lady, I never teased like this while at Eton nor Cambridge. Only you bring out my boyish ways. You are not happy with your husband I take it? You no longer find me pleasing unless I remain distant?"

She smirked and rolled her eyes. "There is no way, my love, in which you could ever remain such. And thus, I am sure you will find the doctor's orders quite hard to bear."

Gravity overtook his features. "Whatever do you mean?"

Giggling softly, Elizabeth made an attempt of forming a sober expression but failed when she related the doctor's words. "He said you must rest for the next week and there is to be *no* strenuous, physical exertion."

Darcy perceived his wife's meaning and pressed his lips firmly together and creased his brows.

"Lizzy, I do not think that *that* is considered strenuous."

"Oh...I am not so sure. Afterwards, you look completely exhausted to me." She bit her lip as her eyes sparkled naughtily.

"Why you little minx! I have been sadly mistaken."

In all seriousness, she enquired, "Sadly mistaken about what, Fitzwilliam?"

"About there being a tamed feline in my bed. Instead, I find a lioness!"

She rolled her eyes and then stared at him in pure amazement.

In a roguish voice, he continued, his fingers stroking beneath her jawbone. "And Lizzy, lions are the liveliest of cats, and furthermore..."

A hard knock interrupted his frolicsome jousting, causing Elizabeth to leap from the bed. Darcy smiled widely as the door crept open. "See how fast you bound." He could not resist taunting her one last time.

Seething, she whispered, "Fitzwilliam, really! Stop this instant! You are scandalous!"

Dr. Lowry was surprised to see a candle lit with both occupants awake and apparently dallying with one another from Mrs. Darcy's last remark.

He walked further into the room "I see you are already alert. I need to depart soon and would like to inspect the sutures and dressings, if I may."

Elizabeth excused herself and went to wait in the hall. Dr. Lowry put his bag on the foot of the bed and began to lift Darcy's shirt. He asked his patient, "Any nausea, shortness of breath, or chills?"

Darcy answered in the negative as the doctor loosened the dressing and looked intently at his stitch work. "It seems to be doing nicely thus far. See that you do not do anything strenuous and that you rest. I told your wife, if you feel up to climbing the stairs this evening, you may do so as long as you do not become fatigued.

Darcy's brow creased. "Anything else?"

"No...I only wish to inform you that you are a most fortunate man. Had not your cousin known to apply pressure immediately, and for so long, you would have bled to death."

Darcy swallowed hard and slowly nodded his head.

"I am leaving the medication here with instructions on how to administer it should the headaches become too intense or if your chest bothers you too much. You must rest, Mr. Darcy."

"Um, what is your name? I am sorry, I cannot remember."

"I would not expect you to. I am Harrison Lowry. I have taken over Dr. Prince's practice."

"Oh yes, of course."

"I will be back tonight to check on you unless you need me sooner. Now rest and drink plenty of liquids and broths."

With that, the doctor bid his adieu and Elizabeth re-entered. From the light of extra candles, Darcy took in her appearance and saw the blood which covered her. Her appearance, coupled with the doctor's sobering words, made him suddenly solemn, and he felt a pang of remorse for his frivolous conduct moments before. He stretched forth his hand for Elizabeth to come to him again, and so she did. Squeezing her hand, he whispered, "I am sorry, Elizabeth. You have been through so much. I should not have teased you. Please forgive my foolish behaviour just now. I love you so much."

Nodding, she tried to hold back her tears but found that his compassionate words touched her deeply, and she could not. Therefore, she sobbed by her husband's side while he soothingly caressed her hand and placed tender kisses thereon allowing her to freely release her contained emotions. After Elizabeth's tears were spent, they lay beside each other on the narrow cot and said no more, but dozed off and on until a maid was sent to stir the fire some hours later.

~*~

After bathing and dressing, Elizabeth went to Georgiana's room to enlighten her about her brother's progress and to also relate Darcy's wish to see her after breakfast. Elizabeth then informed her sister-in-law that she would be having breakfast in the dining room and asked if she cared to join her. Georgiana excitedly agreed, relating that she would be down in thirty minutes' time.

Next, Elizabeth went to Colonel Fitzwilliam's chamber and knocked. She waited a few minutes before a sleep-deprived colonel opened the door.

He blinked his eyes in surprise to see her standing before him. Biting her lips while twisting a wisp of hair near the nape of her neck, she restlessly revealed, "Fitzwilliam is asking for you."

At this bit of intelligence, the colonel's eyes opened wide. He stammered, "Umm...you mean to say he is..." Richard took a deep breath, "he...wants me to...come immediately?"

"I am not sure. Sally, my maid, informed me that Mr. Chaffin asked her to have you summoned. She has just now informed me of Fitzwilliam's request, and I told her I would deliver his wish. I first went to relate a similar message to Georgiana. Fitzwilliam wants to see her after breakfast. However, he did not mention his desire to see you to me directly."

They eyed one another for several moments as Richard leaned against the door frame. Inhaling loudly, he dropped his gaze and raked his fingers through his matted hair. With his head down, Elizabeth was able to take in his appearance. He wore the same shirt he had fenced in the night before. It was open, revealing the hair on his chest. Darcy's blood was spattered over it and caked a little on the skin of his neck and collar bone. When her eyes lowered, they widened, for she saw his legs were bare from a tad above his knees down to his feet.

Her face turned crimson and she began to fidget with her new cross necklace.

Gulping, she twisted her head and glanced down the hall. "Well, I am sure you can first bathe and then go down. I asked Sally to immediately have hot water brought up. I do not see how anything can be so important which would require you to go this instant."

He lifted his head and quickly discerned her discomfort and at once realized his improper exposure.

Hastily, he backed up and pushed the door forward to stand behind it, only poking his head around. "I thank you, Elizabeth for the message, and I will bathe and go straightway before breaking my fast."

Elizabeth bit her lip and briefly lifted her eyes to his. Richard realized she was lost in thought, and, therefore, waited for her to say something before closing the door. Several seconds passed. She stood there in deep concentration looking down. "He remembers most of the day yesterday but does not remember fencing with you. I told him it was an accident, and he knows you saved his life."

Confusion lined the Colonel Fitzwilliam's face. What was Elizabeth saying? "I only did what anyone would do, Elizabeth."

She met his eyes and both stared at the other for what seemed like several minutes instead of the mere seconds which transpired.

Richard raised his brows.

Elizabeth pulled in her lower lip underneath her teeth as she brought her hand to her throat. "He told me this morning when he awoke that he did not want to take any more medicine because it makes him imagine things."

The colonel's brow creased as he considered her words.

"He said he is imagining things?"

Carefully, she nodded and looked pointedly at him.

"Did he say what?"

She shook her head. "He started to, but chose not to do so."

"Um...very well, I am sure there is nothing to worry about. Elizabeth?"

She paused and waited for him to continue.

Softly, Richard stated, "Thank you."

She made a quick curtsey and walked away.

Closing the door, Colonel Fitzwilliam leaned against the back of it and looked heavenward. He would have to leave first thing that morning even if the relief team was not back. He could stay no longer. He had tossed and turned all night concerning his cousin's accusation, and, in all honesty, had to admit that he did or *had* wanted Elizabeth. *What man in his right mind would not?* Yet, he had let his foolish belief that he must marry for wealth interfere with the first woman who had truly captivated his heart in such a very long time. In that, there was no one to blame but himself. If he had acted sooner, things might have been different. But, he had let her slip through his hands, and things were as they were. If Darcy were to press him, he could not lie, and *that* would sever their brotherly bond forever. He closed his eyes in anguish.

~*~

Georgiana emerged from her chamber and saw Richard's fine figure turning to descend the stairs. She hastened her stride, calling after him. He turned and ascended a few steps in order to greet her.

"Good morning, Georgiana."

Her eyes sparkled. "Good morning Richard," she said with a demure smile. "Is it all right if I walk with you to breakfast?"

"I will gladly escort you, Georgie." He offered her his arm. "But, I am off to see your brother before I partake. It seems he wishes to see me straightaway. However, I will join you as soon as I can."

"That will be fine, but, after I have eaten, I too intend to visit him. He told Elizabeth that he desired to see me after breakfast. Richard, I am so relieved that his wound is not serious. You will never know how frightened I was."

Lovingly, Richard smiled down at her. Resting his free hand over hers, he gave it a firm squeeze. "I know you were frightened, duck. I was frightened as well. I think we all were."

Having reached the dining room, she nodded and then thanked him for his company as he released her arm before she entered. "I will see you later this morning, Georgie."

The colonel then turned and walked towards the kitchen. He passed maids carrying trays of food, but the aroma did not even appeal to him. Deep within his gut he was sickened, dreading the conversation which was soon to unfold with his cousin.

Knocking lightly on the door, he waited until he heard Darcy's invitation to enter.

Mr. Chaffin was plumping up some pillows behind his master's back as Richard walked into the room. With a toss of his hand, Darcy dismissed his man, and the valet punctually bowed and quitted the room.

Looking askance at Darcy, Richard muttered a good morning and a salutation of finding him in better health compared to the previous night. He noted that his cousin was shaven and wore no cravat but donned a banyan over his shirt and trousers. No waistcoat was worn, and he surmised this to be because of the need to check the dressing throughout the day. He also took in the grave expression on his cousin's face.

Darcy asked his cousin to sit down. Richard did so, but felt even more nervous and silently wished to stand.

Each cousin scrutinized the other's face for sometime before the younger started to speak.

"Richard, I understand from the doctor and my wife that you saved my life last night."

The colonel shifted his weight in his seat. Fixing his eyes upon the floor, he said nothing.

Darcy continued, "I want you to know how thankful I am to you. I cannot remember the accident at all or even fencing. But, witnessing my wife's appearance this morning made me realize what an ordeal you both have endured. Elizabeth also told me that she did not handle the situation very well. Therefore, I realize you alone carried the burden."

The colonel's head shot up with his cousin's mention of Elizabeth's distraught attitude and wondered if she had told him everything. Their eyes locked. Richard stated carefully, "She was a tremendous help in the beginning. She came straightway with the towels and then ran to find a servant to fetch the doctor. Then, she came back and went yet another time to direct someone to bring other needed supplies. She kept her head about her, but I think the lull while waiting for the doctor and witnessing the spilt blood on the floor became too much for her... and... she became understandably distressed."

Darcy's brows furrowed. Was Richard on the defensive thinking he was displeased with Elizabeth's anguish? "Yes, she did not go into so much detail, but she plainly told me that she did not handle the situation well. I assured her that, given the circumstances, not many would have."

A sigh of relief was detected by Darcy as he saw Richard's expression relax.

Suddenly, Colonel Fitzwilliam stood and began to pace the small room. He turned and faced Darcy. "I feel I must leave for Matlock. I should really spend time with father and mother before April. I do not know how long I shall be gone if my regiment is called to the Continent. I know you wanted me to wait till the Pratt party returned, but, since the weather is not as frigid, I think it best that I be on my way."

Furrowing his brow yet again, Darcy raised his hand to rub his chin. He attempted to swing his legs over the side of the bed, but abruptly stopped when a stabbing pain shot down the side of his body. His cousin came forward to offer assistance which Darcy welcomed.

Sitting on the edge of the bed now, Darcy looked up to his cousin and honestly declared, "If you feel you must go, I will not keep you. However, I wish you to stay. With winter keeping us indoors and now my convalescing, your company is greatly desired. I do not know what I would do without you, Richard. I love you very much."

Richard was shocked. In all of their years—all of their endeavours together, not once had either of them expressed verbally their love for the other. It moved him beyond words, and they each eyed the other as Darcy arose with only pressed lips, indicating the pain was excruciating. The colonel quickly came forward yet again to lend a hand, but Darcy was already standing. Thus, the proffered assistance became an embrace as the two men demonstratively displayed their deepest love and affection.

Colonel Fitzwilliam was moved to near tears. Never in his life had any member of his family openly expressed their love for him in such a manner. Both their eyes misted as they paused upon each other's shoulder. Richard inhaled deeply and broke the union. He could not find his voice to speak but stood there, silently staring into his cousin's eyes.

Darcy nodded. "I thank you, Richard."

Richard nodded in return.

Darcy slowly made his way to the hearth. Gazing into the blaze, he leaned against the mantlepiece and spoke. "I want to have a soirée for Elizabeth to start to introduce her to the *illustrious* inhabitants of Derbyshire." He said this with a small amount of sarcasm in his voice. "I would like you to be here. I thought while I am recuperating we could organize a list of the invitations, and you and Georgie, with your musical abilities, can help to make it successful. I would very much like for you to stay longer… if you could. I would deeply appreciate it, and I know the ladies would as well."

The colonel's emotions were in a quandary. He had come here expecting Darcy to throw him out of his home, and he himself was bent on leaving, yet, now, the complete reverse had happened. He was not sure what to say or do.

Turning from the mantlepiece, Darcy gave Richard an expectant look.

The colonel inhaled sharply. "When do you wish to have it?"

"A fortnight from now. I think that will give us time with the invitations and for me to recover."

Thinking a little longer, Richard conceded. "I suppose, Darcy, if you really want me to remain, I can. But, after the party, I must spend some time with my parents."

Darcy's eyes softened and a smile graced his features. Apart from seeing his mother, Darcy knew that Richard never wanted to spend too much time at Matlock. Yet, he let it pass, deciding not to enquire about his sudden desire for a change of plans. He was happy that his cousin would stay on to help make the imminent evening a success. He hated these sorts of things, and Richard always handled them with such savoir-faire and finesse that everyone seemed to enjoy themselves exceedingly while in his company. Darcy realized that he, himself, was most at home with his immediate family and a few of his few choice friends from his youth and Cambridge days whom he seldom, if ever, saw anymore.

Gratefully, Darcy looked to Richard and asked further, "Do you mind asking Georgie to meet me in my study? I do not want to stay in here a moment longer. This room has always been used as the infirmary, and I find that I have never cared for it."

Richard smiled at his cousin's remark and offered to walk with him to the study which Darcy gladly accepted his support as the two walked at a leisurely pace to the door. Then the colonel watched his cousin enter and sit on the sofa before leaving to inform Georgiana of the new location.

As Colonel Fitzwilliam departed, he felt relief and comfort, and, for the first time in what seemed like ages, had a new sense of direction regarding his life.

~*~

After having enjoyed breakfast with Elizabeth, Georgiana made her way to the study where her cousin told her she could find her brother. The door was wide open, so she paused for a moment until her eyes met Darcy's.

He bid her enter.

"Do you mind, Georgie, closing the door? I would do it, but it hurts like...well...it hurts."

"Oh, I do not mind in the least, Brother," she said as she immediately turned and pulled it to.

Darcy stretched out his hand for her to come join him on the sofa.

"Brother, I cannot tell you how relieved I am that you are all right. It was all so horrible."

"Yes...well...I am glad it is behind us now. I only have to rest a few days, and I shall be good as new."

"Oh Brother, I do not think you can imagine how frightened we all were. Elizabeth was truly amazing. She did everything Richard asked her to do. I was of no help to anyone. I just sat against the wall and covered my face. I feel so badly for my inability to have been of some assistance. In fact, Richard had Mrs. Reynolds take me to my room."

Darcy narrowed his eyes. "I am so sorry, Georgie. It was a most unfortunate occurrence. But, I will tell you as I told Elizabeth, no one knows how they will react in urgent situations. You need not worry any more concerning your behaviour. It is behind us now, and you mean so much to me—to us all. Never think you are not a help. Your caring means the world to me. I have seen many brother and sister relationships in my days, and, Georgie, the bond which you and I share is worth more than all the riches in the whole of the Empire." He paused and glanced away momentarily. "Since, we are on this very subject, I desire to speak with you about something, so hear me out, please, and do not become distressed."

He looked directly into her widened eyes. Georgiana nodded her head, realizing from his jumbled words that her brother was nervous. "Very well, I will hear you out—lock, stock and barrel—before saying another word."

Her commonplace expression made Darcy wearily realize that Richard's negligent use of jargon was having a little *too* much influence on his sister's familiarity with such idioms. However, his mind swung back to the reason he had wanted to speak with her in the first place. He reached for her hand and held it.

"Georgie, I want to apologize for my inappropriate behaviour to you and Elizabeth yesterday in the courtyard. It is unforgivable to be sure, yet I hope you will find it in your heart to forgive me. I have already apologized to Elizabeth, and I hope you shall be able to forgive my curt manner. I know you did not realize the uniform should not have been used, but that is nothing compared to my inconceivable behaviour which put a damper on your pursuit of learning a tradition which Elizabeth's family holds dear—which, in all actuality, is endearing, and I muddled it. She was trying to share that with you and me, and in return, I showed gross disrespect to both of you." He paused and released a tense breath. "I am appalled by my so doing. I care about you both greatly and desire to be both a brother and a husband on whom my family can depend and not be fearful. I will try my best to never repeat such a vile display of temper again."

Looking down at her hand within his own, he once again became silent. He caressed it with his thumb while inspecting it closely as if it was the first time he had ever looked upon it. She marvelled at his humility and the thoroughness of his admission of guilt.

Breathing deeply, Georgiana leaned to one side to give her brother a gentle hug and then acquitted him of his transgression. He winced with the gesture but she knew he was gladdened despite the pain.

"I must admit, Brother, that your behaviour since I have arrived has been quite out of the ordinary. You are always exemplary, and I have been distressed to see you so beside yourself. I fear that I am the cause of your and Elizabeth's discord. Perhaps I have come home too soon. I could go back with Richard if you would like. In spite of that, you have always been the best brother. I feel there is no need for an apology. After what I did the summer before last at Ramsgate, how can I condemn you for such a brief display of bad temper?"

Darcy no longer concerned himself with her hand but met her eyes and attempted to speak. But Georgiana stopped him.

"Brother, you at times are distant in your manner, but yesterday you were not your usual self. I do not blame you for rightfully correcting me concerning a sacred symbol of our country. I am only mortified by my own poor judgment, yet I will not dwell on it, but instead, I will learn from my mistake and be the wiser for it. I am so grateful to you, Fitzwilliam. You have done so much for me, and if you had not come when you did that horrible summer, I would have been ruined. So you see I feel I need no apology, but I am grateful for your communication and treating me like I am older just now. I do hope, however, that you will let me know if I am ever the cause of conflict. I so want to have Elizabeth as my sister and have never feared you."

He gazed at his sister approvingly. These words of wisdom were coming from a sixteen-year-old girl...no, a woman. She was a woman now, and, therefore, Darcy realized he would have to adjust his way of thinking about her. She was still naïve in so many ways, but she had truly grown in understanding this past year. He squeezed her hand tightly. "You remind me so much of our mother. I know she would be as proud as am I of the development of your nature, and Georgie, I am proud."

Georgiana glance up and smiled.

Darcy breathed softly and then added further, "Georgiana, you are not the cause of any discord between me and Elizabeth. Believe me, it is all my own doing. I hope, akin to you with the uniform, to be more the wiser due to such a calloused blunder. We all make our mistakes, but never repeating them is the essential element."

She smiled widely, and this time, she squeezed *his* hand.

"There is one more thing I wish to discuss with you."

Georgiana waited in expectation. Inwardly, she loved it when he would speak with her in such a manner. It made her feel that he was seeing her for the woman she was and not the little girl she used to be.

Darcy informed her of his desire to have a soirée for Elizabeth. He asked if he could depend upon her to play in front of such a crowd. She was apprehensive but agreed because it was for Elizabeth and for him as well. She realized the importance of the occasion and therefore, gave her hearty support. He informed her they would discuss it tonight after dinner and then make and send the invitations tomorrow. She was delighted with the plan and decided she must go and practice straightway in order to prepare.

As he watched his sister leave, the Master of Pemberley felt all would be right with the world again. His conscience was now freed from offences of his own making, and he knew he was a better person for it. If there was one single time which had ever taught him anything concerning the importance of confessions, it was his deception to Bingley. He still felt severe regret over the time which was lost to Bingley due to his presumptuous interference, and, if he dwelled on these ruminations for too long, the depth of grief formed by them would almost consume him.

~*~

The remainder of the day passed in pleasant, peaceful pursuits. They all spent many hours in the library reading various subjects of interest. Richard preferred the paper, while Darcy mainly reclined, often sleeping upon the sofa. Elizabeth read her novel and also worked on her needlepoint. Georgiana, on the other hand, was devouring her first reading of one of Ann Radcliffe's novels, *The Castles of Athlin and Dunbayne*.

That evening after dinner, Darcy felt rested and, therefore, announced that they would not go their separate ways, but rather, he asked that all gather again in the library where he desired to go over some matters of import. Elizabeth, up to this time, had not been informed about the meeting to plan for the soirée which would be their first official social engagement. So, though her husband had previously mentioned to her his desire to have such an event, it still came as something of a shock when they entered the room to find all of the correspondence which she had not yet dealt with waiting for them upon the table.

Darcy instructed everyone to take a seat and pulled the stack of letters towards him. He then asked Georgiana to take paper and pen so as to formulate a list of guests to be invited. He had Elizabeth's stationary and wax seal available so she could compose replies to the missives of importance while he and Richard read the posts and organized them for her.

In amazement, Elizabeth looked over to her husband from across the table as she contemplated his consideration and precision of helping her in the execution of an obligatory task which, in essence, as Mistress of Pemberley, fell to her alone. She had dreaded this undertaking of sorting and corresponding with people unknown to her.

She gazed adoringly at her handsome husband as he and Richard opened each letter, meticulously reading it before placing it into its designated pile. As they read each name aloud, they instructed Georgiana to write down those to be invited. Elizabeth discerned pieces of the ongoing discussion between her husband and the colonel regarding various long-standing family friends who must be included and others who were debatable. She distinctly heard Fitzwilliam tell Richard that he really did not want the gathering to become too large for their first time to entertain.

During this enterprise, he glanced up to find a penetrating look on his wife's countenance. He quickly flashed a boyish grin as they made eye contact. Her breath caught, and, at that moment, she wished to leap across the table and seize him. Suddenly, she flushed quite brightly from the stir of fervour she felt in her very being—a feeling she hoped no one in the room would notice as they gaily worked at their assigned tasks. The feeling was so strong that she thought she might need to leave the room. Wryly, she thought to herself ...My *husband is right. I am wanton, and my mother would be scandalized.*

Noticing the intensity of her stare each time he glanced up, Darcy wondered if anything was amiss. As he looked up periodically, he kept meeting her same expression. Yet, it was not until he peered over the table for the *sixth* time that he perceived the meaning of the familiar look within his wife's fine eyes. Never had Elizabeth shown an open display of ardour outside their bedchamber. His mind wandered as he no longer merely glanced towards his wife, but gazed transfixed while they openly expressed adoration for each other.

Richard completed two letters for every one of Darcy's. Likewise, the colonel found it necessary to repeat his questions and ideas more than once. Finally, Richard looked up and peered over to see what the matter was when Darcy failed to answer his question. The colonel became immediately aware of the newlyweds' unspoken passion. Serenely, he smiled to himself for the happiness of two people whom he loved dearly, and so, he no longer made comments to his cousin but continued most diligently in his own labours.

Industriously, Darcy opened, read, recommended, and sorted the missives at a fervent pace. "Wallace...no, Chalmers, um...yes..." When witnessing his cousin's rapid zeal from the corner of his eye, Richard's brows lifted in amused silence. He sneaked a peek at Elizabeth and noticed that she too was in the process of wrapping things up as she sealed her last envelope and then cupped her hand around the flame of the candle in preparation of extinguishing it. Smiling widely, Richard shook his head and returned to the several letters which still needed his perusal.

Darcy stood and began to make his excuses, "Um...umm..., I think I shall try the stairs now. I do not want to become too fatigued and then not have the energy to go up them." Elizabeth, as if on cue, immediately arose to leave also. Richard feigned surprise and then encouraged them to go, but only after standing quickly himself and mischievously offering, "Let me help you, Darce. I shall be only too glad to assist you."

Darcy deliberated and shook his head with a slight smile. "Uh...I thank you, Richard, but I think with Elizabeth I shall manage."

Georgiana made her goodnight wishes as Richard sat again to finish the three remaining letters.

A gentle rapping at the door alerted them of the butler's presence. Mr. Greene entered and informed the master that Dr. Lowry had just arrived and desired to examine him.

Darcy's expression soured. With a long breath, he informed Mr. Greene to escort the doctor to the music room. He would join him there directly.

Again, Richard shook his head in humour as he thought to himself. *...Ah, all the obstacles of love.* With that thought, he shrugged and returned to his task, but at the same time heard Darcy whisper something to his wife while she in turn said something to him. Elizabeth made her way back to the table and proceeded to light the candle and write more replies. They all worked in companionable silence.

~*~

When Darcy entered, he found the doctor admiring the portrait of Georgiana which stood on an easel next to the pianoforte. "Dr. Lowry," Darcy said as he slowly made his way into the music room.

The doctor looked to Mr. Darcy and nodded. "I suppose this woman is your sister?"

A slight crease formed between Darcy's brows. "Yes, yes she is, and it is a good likeness, I might add. She is but sixteen."

Dr. Lowry deliberately eyed Mr. Darcy concerning the appendage of his sister's age. Neither felt awkward as they openly inspected the other for several seconds. Then the doctor finally spoke, "How have you fared today?"

"Aside from being a little weary," Darcy replied, "I feel fine. I have had a dull headache the course of the day, but it has subsided."

Dr. Lowry instructed his patient to sit on the divan while he untied Darcy's robe and lifted his shirt to remove the dressing. "Um...yes, I imagine you have had a headache, but I am glad it has gone."

While the doctor looked over the injury, his patient enquired, "Where did you attend school?"

"At St. Thomas's Hospital in London, I studied under Surgeon Henry Cline, attended courses at Webb Street School of Anatomy and Medicine, and have studied in Scotland as well. I am somewhat of an unusual physician, Mr. Darcy, as I am both a physician and a surgeon, and what is more, I prefer being addressed as Dr. Lowry and *not* Mister."

The breadth of this man's credentials and the peculiar request connected with them surprised Darcy, but he nodded his head in agreement. "My father had taken my mother to St. Thomas's several times because of her frailty after my sister's birth. Dr. Lowry, if you do not mind my asking, why have you chosen to set up practice here?"

The doctor applied some ointment to Darcy's chest then began to reapply a fresh dressing while he made answer. "I do not mind at all, Mr.

Darcy. Derbyshire is the home of my maternal grandparents. I came here every summer as a boy with my mother. She is now dead, but my grandparents are still alive and in good health. They are also lonely. Having outlived all their children, they desire my company and even though they are in relatively good health, I wanted to be near them so that I might be of help to them in their old age."

"What are their names?"

"Newedgate."

Darcy's eyebrows shot up in surprise, "Sir Henry and Lady Muriel Newedgate?"

"Yes, do you know them?"

"Why yes, they were friends of my parents. In fact, when my mother was ill, I remember Mrs. Newedgate coming to visit, especially when my father was away on business. She would read to my mother."

Dr. Lowry smiled and nodded. "Yes, that sounds like my grandmother. She is most compassionate and attentive. In fact, I owe them a great deal. They helped to furnish my education. My mother married a man who, well, let us just say my father was never to be depended upon. But from the assistance of both sets of grandparents, my mother, sister and I did not go in want. In fact, I am currently staying with them until I find my own residence."

Breathing in deeply, the doctor stepped back from completing the examination and asked, "Do you feel any fever, chills, or dizziness?"

"No."

"Very good, remember to drink plenty of fluids, and I want to impress upon you the importance of no strenuous activity of any kind for at least three to four days more. And then, use caution. We do not want any internal bleeding."

Darcy appeared pensive. He stood to offer his thanks and shake the doctor's hand, but instead, he unexpectedly posed, "I imagine you could use a drink. May I offer you one? And I would like to introduce you to my wife and sister."

Dr. Lowry smiled. "I had the opportunity of meeting your wife last night, but, as for the drink and the introduction to your sister, I would be greatly obliged."

~*~

Elizabeth was in the process of blowing out the candle for the second time when her husband and the doctor entered the room. The whole party was caught unaware by Dr. Lowry's entrance and Darcy's satisfied air. Darcy addressed his family. "I have invited Dr. Lowry for a drink and to visit with us until he must leave. I believe that you have met my cousin, Colonel Richard Fitzwilliam, and my wife, Mrs. Darcy. However, my sister has not had the pleasure of an introduction. So, Dr. Lowry, this is Miss Darcy. Georgiana, Dr. Lowry has taken over Dr. Prince's practice, and, what is more, he is the grandson of Sir Henry Newedgate."

Dr. Lowry made a slight bow, and, in true cordiality, praised, "Miss Darcy, I think I must agree with your brother. Your portrait is an exceptional likeness and does you justice."

Georgiana blushed.

All cast their eyes on the shy girl and waited for her to respond to the compliment. Mustering all her courage and hoping against hopes not to stammer, she replied, "I...am glad to make your acquaintance, Dr. Lowry, and thank you for the compliment concerning my likeness."

Darcy's eyes softened with his sister's commendable effort. He asked the doctor what he could offer him to drink when Georgiana, without warning, blurted out, "And, I...want to thank you, Doctor, with all my heart for helping to save my brother's life."

Dr. Lowry's eyes were again drawn to hers. He warmly smiled and simply stated, "You are most welcome, Miss Darcy."

The colonel was diverted beyond words. The chase had already begun and Georgie was not yet out. He was certainly glad, more than ever, for Elizabeth. She would be able to help temper Darcy's nerves instead of himself. He was well aware of his cousin's vigilance when it came to Georgiana. Elizabeth would have her work cut out for her. He chuckled within but then sobered. Suddenly, he felt a pang of concern, and, in all reality, he knew that he too would worry just as much. He began to eye the doctor suspiciously.

Mrs. Darcy took inventory as well. She noticed the doctor was almost as tall as her husband, though not quite as slender. He had light brown curly hair, curlier, in fact, than Bingley's. He had a pleasant expression with fleshy cheeks when he smiled, which revealed deep dimples and showed off the bluest eyes. She looked at her sister-in-law and saw the glow upon her face as she watched her brother and Dr. Lowry converse. Elizabeth mused to herself that Georgiana could possibly be smitten the way Jane was on first seeing Charles and she sighed at the thought.

~*~

The next morning after breakfast, they narrowed down the list of names. Georgiana and Elizabeth would make and send the invitations during the course of the morning. Richard and Darcy were off to the billiards room. Richard desired to practice shots while Darcy provided him company. They would then retire to the study until luncheon. The remainder of the day seemed to be another repeat of the one before. Darcy continued to rest much of the afternoon and all enjoyed reading, and after dinner, the pleasure of playing cards passed away the hours remaining before all retired. The only other development which was out of the ordinary, besides the playing of Vingt-un, was the return of the Pratt party. Everyone was relieved by their safe arrival, Darcy in particular. The next day would bring a sleigh ride and, unbeknownst to the women, a special surprise.

The morning dawned crisp and bright with the temperature a bit below freezing, and a new snow had fallen during the night, covering the ground in a pristine blanket of white. Darcy and Richard awoke early and donned warm clothing in preparation for their scheme.

Nancy, Georgiana's maid, was asked by Mr. Darcy the night before to gather some clothing items of her mistress and then give them to Sally who was also informed to collect a complete outfit for Mrs. Darcy. The maid was to have them readied for the master first thing in the morning.

The two men ventured into the frosty landscape to return the compliment from the ladies just days earlier. Richard rolled the balls of snow so Darcy would not have to exert himself, but the master was productive with the detailing of his snow-lady by dressing her in a corset with all the trimmings and one of Elizabeth's older gowns from her Longbourn days. Bonnets were placed upon the head of each, and the gentlemen were quite satisfied with their accomplishments.

Before they returned indoors, Darcy retrieved a necklace from his coat pocket and, after chipping away some snow, placed it around the neckline of his creation. Smiling to himself, he was sure Elizabeth and Georgiana would be pleased by his and Richard's efforts.

After breakfasting, they all convened at the courtyard entrance and navigated the steps together. Georgiana and Elizabeth had their eyes downcast in order to make their way more safely. When they stepped forth upon the ground, both ladies raised their eyes to see two snow-ladies stylishly clothed in their belongings.

Elizabeth's face beamed with pleasure. She would have never dreamt of such a delightful surprise as this from her husband. Cheerfully, she exclaimed, "Oh, Fitzwilliam, they are lovely! However did your manage it without our knowing?"

Darcy then related how he and Richard had hatched the plan while in the billiards room, and he sought the assistance of their maids for the needed items. He also shared that Richard performed the burden of lifting the large mounds of snow. He did not want Elizabeth to worry about his well-being, and, knowing that she would soon enquire, averted any undue worry with the offered detail.

Richard asked Georgiana if she liked his skilful imitation of her. She replied in the affirmative, commending him on the complementary choice of bonnet and dress, although she felt that the carrot nose clashed with the colour of her bonnet. Giggling in delight, she gave Richard a hug for such a whimsical gift.

Likewise, Darcy desired to know what his wife's thoughts were concerning the artistry of his first snow-Lizzy. Elizabeth scrutinized her sculpture. Her husband's attention to detail was amazing. She saw that the contour of this snow-woman was quite shapely and only wore a light cotton dress. Breathing in deeply, she gave her critique. "Well, I see, Fitzwilliam, that you have an eye for design, but do you not think she looks somewhat cold?"

Her husband chuckled and admitted that she did at that, and he would need to remedy such an oversight straightaway. Hastily, he ascended the steps before they realized he was going. Elizabeth smiled as she saw him depart and then turned her attention back to the lovely displays. Something glistening around the neckline of her effigy made her squint to make it out and then she immediately discerned what it was: *her cross necklace from her father!* What on earth was her husband thinking? Instantly, she went to retrieve her cherished jewel. Georgiana noticed her distress. "Is anything the matter, Elizabeth?"

Her sister-in-law shook her head. But Georgiana persisted by venturing to further ask, "Is it a favourite of yours?"

"In all honesty, it is, Georgie. My father gave it to me, and I would hate to lose it. I am sure Fitzwilliam will not mind that I have removed it."

Georgiana could not resist stating, "That is so much of a coincidence. You used my brother's boots, which was the last gift given to him by our father, and he uses your necklace given to you by yours. And now, you both have retrieved them."

Elizabeth's eyes quickly veered over to the snowman she had made days before to inspect the boots. They were designed differently, and she could tell, in spite of the snowy powder sprinkled on them, that they were indeed new. Her husband must have replaced them sometime after the earlier fiasco. She realized that he was most likely distraught at seeing them along with the uniform. A new surge of guilt assailed her for her lack of judgment, yet he had said nothing to her concerning them. He was too good.

Before they departed for their outing in the sleigh, Darcy returned carrying a shawl in his hand. He went forth and wrapped it around his masterpiece. Radiating charm, he proclaimed, "There, Lizzy, she is no longer cold, and they will all grace the courtyard for some weeks to come. I like the Bennet family tradition, and, with your approval, I would like to adopt it as a Darcy one henceforth."

Softly, Elizabeth stated, "That would please me very much. I thank you, Fitzwilliam."

She adored him… not for this moment alone, but for all the moments past and yet to come. At this instant she realized he would actively assist in teaching their children this wintry ritual, something in which her father had never taken part.

The nip in the cool air renewed the spirits of all, but the tolerance which Darcy had shown her of late had warmed Elizabeth's soul.

~*~

That night, as they all visited in the music room, Georgiana excitedly interjected what had been in the back of her mind all day. "Brother, Collette Caldecott is back with her parents. I have been meaning to tell you that I ran into her in Lambton before leaving for your wedding in Hertfordshire. She was extremely surprised to find out you were marrying and asked me to send her warmest affection and felicitations for your joy. When making the invitations, I made certain to invite her along with her parents."

Richard and Darcy eyed each other instantly. The latter's face turned ashen, and Elizabeth's interest was piqued. "Who is Collette Caldecott?"

Georgiana swiftly made answer, "She is a good friend of Richard and Fitzwilliam. They always rode together on holiday, and she would join in the hunts as well."

By this time Darcy had stood and walked to the mantlepiece to watch the flames.

Richard's eyes had followed his flight, and he truly felt for his cousin. Elizabeth saw the sudden avoidance as well, and disquiet came over her.

~*~

Upon retiring in their bed, Elizabeth rested beside her husband and whispered, "Fitzwilliam?"

Sleepily he replied, "Yes, Lizzy?"

"I want to apologize for taking the particular boots which were a gift from your father. I had no way of knowing of course. However, I am truly sorry, and I hope they are not damaged too badly. I should have asked."

Darcy frowned. "Elizabeth, do not distress yourself over them. Chaffin has buffed them up rather smartly. No harm has been done. I had hoped you would have never known for this very reason."

Lifting her head while gazing into his eyes she said, "Yes, but I am sorry for my thoughtlessness, and I wanted you to know that. You are wonderful, Fitzwilliam. I am so blessed to have you as my husband."

He pulled her close and inhaled the scent of her hair. "As am I to have you, Lizzy You are my one true love."

They lay there silently for some time before Elizabeth discerned a soft snore. She knew he was now asleep and the darkness was the only witness to her restless reservations. Was she actually the only woman he had ever loved? And why, with the mere mention of Miss Caldecott's name, had he become so distant?

Chapter Eleven

Acquaintances: Old and New

As the days leading up to the soirée passed, Pemberley thrived with an overflow of activity. Elizabeth was amazed at how much preparation Mrs. Reynolds required for a mere social dinner and evening of musical entertainment. She was certain that Pemberley could not be scrubbed any cleaner, polished to a higher sheen, or more elaborately clad than it already was. Yet, each day brought subtle changes, and she noticed that the house did seem to take on a finer lustre than before. The several visits she had made to the conservatory—to determine which plants and flowers to display for the special event— brought into view with each passing the four snow-people, who magically dressed up the otherwise stark courtyard. Elizabeth smiled to herself every time she looked upon them, as did the servants, as well. Pemberley was becoming a real home again.

Word had come from Thomas Wilkens concerning the safe arrival of Clara and Mrs. Watts to their separate destinations. However, it was also reported that carriage problems would necessitate a delay in Thomas's return for some days. Then, one morning after breakfast, the unexpected happened. When Elizabeth retired to her personal study, there was a missive from her maid. She happily opened it but soon became quite disturbed by its contents. Clara had thanked her generously but then informed her mistress that she would not be returning due to her mother's continual need of her assistance. She had secured employment, which would allow her to work during the day and be at home with her mother in the evenings. The maid offered genuine regret and, once more, blessed Mrs. Darcy for her kindness and assistance in her time of need.

Elizabeth sat at her desk considering what to do regarding a lady's maid when Sally knocked upon her door. The young maid had come to inform Mrs. Darcy about the delivery of some packages from London. The mistress thanked her for the information and then asked her to come in and sit down. Sally was surprised by the invitation, yet honoured all the same. Elizabeth came straight to the point by informing the maid that Clara would not be returning.

She then stated, "Sally, I feel that you and I have gotten on rather nicely. I know that you do not feel experienced with the latest fashionable hairstyles and such, but I have never been one to worry too much about those particular aspects. However, if you are in agreement, I would like to solicit your services as my personal maid, and then we can worry about the latest craze together."

The maid was dumbfounded. Never in her wildest dreams would she have imagined this opportunity possible. Sincere gratitude showed on her face as she happily agreed to the proposal.

"I will be happy to, ma'am."

"Thank you. I think we shall perform splendidly together."

Sally's heart was full of wonderment and excitement as she left Mrs. Darcy's study. She understood that this placement would provide her with numerous occasions to visit London, Mrs. Darcy's hometown in Hertfordshire, and many other places of interest. Her wardrobe would also change. As Mrs. Darcy's personal maid, she would wear finer dresses, shoes, and coats. Additionally, she would receive her own private quarters. What is more, she would be directly under her mistress' command and no longer under the supervision of Mrs. Reynolds. It was not that Sally disliked the housekeeper—no, in fact, the reverse was true—for she had a high regard for the elderly woman's spunk, ingenuity, and loyalty.

This unexpected prospect seemed too much for the maid. She was happier than at any time in her life wherewith she could remember. Apart from one bothersome concern, which seemed to steal the pleasure of the moment—as a lady's maid, she would never be permitted to marry and have a family of her own.

The bell chord was pulled and Mrs. Reynolds came within a matter of minutes to Mrs. Darcy's study. "Yes, ma'am?"

"Oh, thank you for coming so soon, Mrs. Reynolds. I just wanted to inform you that I have received a letter from Clara stating that she will not be able to return, and therefore, has relinquished the position of lady's maid. I spoke with Sally a few moments ago and have secured her as my new maid. Consequently, she will need to move into Clara's former quarters. I hope this will not put too much strain on the availability of servants for the house."

Mrs. Reynolds informed the mistress that all would be well, and she was happy for Sally. She had always thought her to be an industrious girl with a good head on her shoulders. Before quitting the room, she thanked Mrs. Darcy for her consideration in keeping her abreast of the current situation so promptly.

Sighing in contentment over how well everything seemed to be going of late, Elizabeth decided she wanted to share with her husband the news about Clara and the latest decisions concerning the menu and musical selections for the soirée. Thus, she cleared her desk, put the folios back in the drawer, and proceeded down the hall towards Darcy's study.

Her knock was strong and rapid, and Darcy's voice gave permission to enter. Elizabeth opened the door to find that her husband was not alone, but was attended by Mr. Sheldon, Colonel Fitzwilliam, and a man and woman with whom she was unacquainted. She bit her lower lip, reluctant to enter upon seeing so many within. The gentlemen all stood at her appearance, and Darcy's eyes met hers immediately. "Ah, Mrs. Darcy, I was just about to go in search of you." He quickly came from around his desk and walked to the threshold of the door where Elizabeth stood in a state of shock. Something told her that this beautiful woman sitting off to one side of her husband's desk was no other than Collette Caldecott.

All heads turned towards Elizabeth as Darcy led her by the hand into the room. Addressing the elderly gentleman first, Darcy made the introductions. "This is Mr. McAllister Caldecott of Lockton, and Mr. Caldecott this is my wife, Mrs. Darcy." The elderly man bowed slightly, and Elizabeth curtseyed while saying how nice it was to make his acquaintance. Swiftly, Collette stood and Darcy performed the same protocol with his wife and Miss Caldecott. *Was it Elizabeth's imagination, or was her husband's hand trembling as it rested on the small of her back?*

Miss Caldecott put forth her hand, and Elizabeth took it. The former confidently exclaimed, "Why, at last I meet the woman who stole the heart of the most sought after and most illustrious man in England! I cannot believe he has become leg-shackled. Thus, I have been most anxious to see you for myself. Not in a million years would I have dreamt that Fitz would marry so young, if ever."

Elizabeth's face registered pure astonishment. *This woman was the most brazen she had ever met.* The eyes of the Mistress of Pemberley flashed as she swiftly responded, "I thank you for the compliment of my not only capturing the heart of but also *leg shackling* the most illustrious and sought after man in England. And I must say, his youth and might I add, *vigour*, only enhance the conjugal bliss we share."

Richard immediately put his hand over his mouth in an effort to squelch his mirth. This was priceless. He would not have missed it for the world. He glanced sideways to gauge his cousin's reaction, but Darcy's face was set like stone and, therefore, unreadable. The colonel was not sure if his cousin's severity was due to the rudeness of Collette or the cheek of his wife. However, knowing his cousin's stiff reserve, if was most likely both. Again, he stifled a laugh.

Colonel Fitzwilliam might have had the good manners not to chuckle out right, but Mr. Caldecott, held no such regard. He, on the other hand, burst out laughing and heartily confirmed, "Well, Mrs. Darcy, I can see why you have stolen this Derbyshire boy's heart. He has always been one to like them spirited."

Mr. Sheldon's face reddened. He never did care for the boisterous manner of Mr. Caldecott. He felt the man vulgar and could not abide his crude company for long. The steward cleared his throat and spoke up, "Mr. Darcy, I need to take my leave in order to deal with the business we discussed earlier. If you should need me, I will be back shortly before nightfall." With that, Mr. Sheldon bowed his head and quitted the room.

Darcy felt complete humiliation for the situation all were enduring, but managed to murmur a thank you to his steward on that man's going.

"Well, my lad," Mr. Caldecott said, addressing Darcy, "we need to be off. Collette could not rest until she met you, Mrs. Darcy. We are honoured for the invitation to the soirée and most anxious to enjoy the company."

Nodding her head, Elizabeth sincerely stated, "Why, yes, I thank you for your acceptance and am also happy to make your acquaintance, Mr. Caldecott. We look forward to seeing you at the soirée. And, Miss Caldecott, I shall be happy to further our association."

Collette smirked as she responded in a conspiratorial tone, "Oh, please, do call me Collette—everyone does—or just Cole. After all, that is what Rich and Fitz have called me for years. I am sure we shall become the best of friends. Perhaps, I may call you, *Liz*?"

This was said more as an affirmation than a request for permission and with such sickening sweetness, that Elizabeth rejoined with a pretentious regard of her own. "Oh, by all means, call me *Eliza*. It is what I am called by all my *dearest* friends," Elizabeth spiritedly returned as good as she was given.

Darcy swallowed hard and closed his eyes as he shook his head while Richard smiled engagingly at the ladies' verbal exchange.

The whole party walked to the foyer to say their adieus, but, before leaving, Collette turned to Darcy and Richard and flashed a brilliant smile. "I would love to ride the next time you go. It will be like old times. I shall be quite put out if I find you have gone without me!" She then turned to Elizabeth and, with great interest, enquired, "Do you ride, Eliza?"

Elizabeth grinned at the appellation and stood tall as she professed, "Oh, never. I prefer walking."

Collette seemed to drone out her next words. "How very singular. Fitz loves to ride. I am surprised you have never learnt. But we shall have to remedy that post-haste."

Darcy's cheek twitched slightly, and unexpectedly sighed as he commented, "Yes...we shall see, Miss Caldecott. I know your father is in a hurry, so let us not keep him waiting."

Laughing gaily, she coyly pouted, "Now, Fitz, we have been friends for far too long for you to be so formal with me." In boldness, she cupped her hand around his chin and gave it a quick tug as she declared, "There are only a few things more *exhilarating* than a winter's ride."

His lips tightened into a straight line, yet he said nothing.

Elizabeth's brows rose in astonished amusement. This woman was truly a work of art. She had never known any other like her, not even Miss Bingley. Although Caroline held many accomplishments, she did not hold a candle to Miss Caldecott. In fact, next to Collette, Caroline was a saint!

Finally, the Caldecotts were out the door and on their way. Elizabeth clasped her hands behind her back, smiled prettily to her husband, and then tilting her head to address the colonel, she enquired, "Tell me truly, *Rich*, do you anticipate riding with Miss Caldecott?"

Darcy rolled his eyes. Richard shrugged and smiled at the same time in response to Elizabeth's question. "Well, first off, may I call you, *Eliza*?"

Elizabeth giggled while opening her eyes wide. "Oh, please do!"

"Very well," the colonel persisted, "*Eliza*, I do like to ride, and, in all honesty, Miss Caldecott's company would not deter me from an enjoyable outing."

"So...you approve of Miss Caldecott?"

"Whether I approve or disapprove is not the issue. I find her *peculiar*." Richard's comment drew a glower from Darcy.

Elizabeth sensed something afoot between the two men. "You mean *odd*, as some use the term 'singular' to mean?"

While Elizabeth stared at Richard, Darcy's glare silently communicated a warning to his cousin as he slowly shook his head. Richard heaved a sigh and said, "No, I mean peculiar in every sense of the word and more. But that does not mean to say she is not singular, also. I think both words give an adequate description of the lady."

She then looked to her husband. "Has Miss Caldecott always been as she was this morning?"

"Um...why...yes, she has," he replied.

She waited for him to elaborate further, but he said no more.

Elizabeth was miffed. Was Collette such a good friend, after all, that neither her husband nor Richard could see she was clearly vulgar and ostentatious?

Darcy cleared his throat, and then in hope of changing the subject, asked his wife, "Were you coming to inform me about something just now, before the introductions?"

She stared at him in preoccupation, but then stated, "Ah, why, yes, I guess I was." She could not get over the fact that her husband and Richard had nothing else to offer about Collette. She knew they had to see the preposterousness in the woman. Yet, if they truly did not want to talk about it, she might as well let it rest.

"Yes, I received a missive from Clara. Do you have time to discuss it now or shall I wait till later?"

Richard excused himself, heading towards to the library to read the newspaper in order to give his cousin the privacy he needed with his wife. Darcy offered his arm to Elizabeth, told her he did have the time now and suggested they go to her study.

They entered and he sat in the tub chair while pulling her down onto his lap. "Now, what has Clara to say?"

"Fitzwilliam, my weight may prove to be too much for you. Please, allow me sit over there."

"No, you are fine where you are, Lizzy. I feel no discomfort whatsoever. In fact, I have spent almost five days with no strenuous activity," he said with that boyish grin she had grown to understand and love.

Smiling brightly at the inferred meaning, she softly replied, "I know."

He pulled her close to him, and she rested her head upon his shoulder. He then bent his head low and gave her a meaningful look. "I have missed you, Lizzy."

Nodding faintly, she whispered, "I know, and I have missed you, too."

He kissed her cheek and brought her hand up, placing slow kisses upon her palm and wrist. Then, setting her hand down gently, Darcy brushed his fingertips over her face.

"You are beautiful."

They looked intently into each other's eyes. Then, without warning, Elizabeth aggressively pressed a hand firmly on each side of her husband's face, possessively seizing his mouth with her own.

Darcy hungrily returned her overture.

Elizabeth was fuelled by her need and desire to stake her claim upon her husband. This feeling was fresh and extremely vulnerable. Before she knew what was happening, they were on the floor, their pent up longing intense. One kiss led rapidly to another. Amidst all the fervour, she returned to her senses. Trying to rein in Darcy's passion, she broke the kiss and breathlessly reminded him, "Fitzwilliam...ah...ah, would Dr. Lowry approve?"

Panting, he lifted his head, knitted his brow, and blinked in confusion. "Whatever does he have to do with anything?" He resumed their pleasurable activity, bequeathing her mouth with ardent kisses. Again, she was nearly consumed in the heat of the moment when the remembrance of their location came to the forefront of her mind. Suddenly twisting her head, she attempted, yet again, to help her husband see reason.

"Fitzwilliam, my love?"

He muttered "Hmm?" as he placed soft kisses along her neck.

Her chest heaved as she tried desperately to bring him to his right mind. "My love, we are in my study!"

He whispered in her ear, "'Tis our house, Lizzy...our house."

Fearfully, she cried, "The servants, or anyone, could walk in, **THE DOORS!**"

Instantly, he was upon his feet and with rapid strides crossed to the far side of the room. He swung the door shut, and then threw the bolt. Next, he purposefully walked in the opposite direction to hastily close and fasten the remaining door.

Intrusions were no longer a concern and, for the time being, neither were the vague uncertainties relating to Miss Caldecott. Elizabeth's last conscious thought, was Georgiana's practicing on the pianoforte in the adjoining room. The oscillating scales wafting past the barrier of locked doors served as a surging accompaniment to passions suppressed for far too long.

~*~

That evening after supper, all gathered in the music room. Georgiana and Elizabeth practiced duets in order to determine which ones would be chosen for the much—anticipated musical evening. Richard sat by their side turning pages. On occasion, he stood to lean upon the instrument in order to enjoy the view of the ladies' faces.

Darcy rested his head upon the back of the chair, his eyes closed as he listened to the melodious tunes performed by his wife and sister. He mused over Clara not returning and Sally taking her place. The girl had no experience as a lady's maid, excepting for the brief, recent past. She did not know how to style hair and such. He felt unsure. He wanted better for Elizabeth. Then his thoughts began drifting in another direction entirely.

Everything seemed to be progressing splendidly for the soirée—with the exception of Collette's recent return from a three-year stay on the Continent. Darcy wondered when he had seen her last. Thinking back, he remembered it to have been at the festivities at Almack's. She had been beautiful with flawless skin, and her sleek blonde hair was the envy of her peers. He wondered how, after that fateful day, he could still have been so attracted to her that evening in London. She knew she turned the heads of men. She also knew the power she held over them.

He placed a hand over his face as memories of her tumbled forward from the recesses of his mind. He had been seventeen, almost eighteen. She had been but sixteen at the time. However, did it come to that? What had he been thinking? How could he have allowed himself to behave as he had? How could he prevent her from influencing Elizabeth? His gut lurched with the contemplation of Collette's chronicles of their relationship, the relationships of them all. He had lied to Elizabeth about being unsullied. He had deliberately not mentioned Collette. He had wanted to forget she had ever existed.

Richard smiled at Georgiana and Elizabeth, as the two giggled and merrily enjoyed each other's company. He then looked over to Darcy sitting in the chair by the fire, his hand covering his face. The colonel could only imagine the anguish his cousin was experiencing, and he did pity him. Collette Caldecott was not a woman to gainsay.

~*~

That night, as Elizabeth lay by her husband in their bed, she could sense he was restless. She started to massage his forehead and temples, assuming another headache might be coming on. He basked in the luxury of her touch and neither spoke for some time.

After the passing of several minutes, Darcy stopped her hand's delicate undertakings with his own and brought it to his lips to kiss each finger. "Thank you, Lizzy," he murmured beneath his breath.

"Do you feel better?" Elizabeth leaned upon her elbow to take in his countenance.

He nodded in reply.

"Are you concerned about the party?"

He opened his eyes to look at her. "No."

Impishly, she started to tease, "Well, Fitz, I would like to know just how good of friends you and Cole were?"

He froze. The only reply he could make after some seconds was, "Please, Elizabeth, never call me that again."

A cold chill ran through her body by the seriousness of his words and the austere look in his eyes.

Quickly, she laid her head on her pillow and then rolled away from her husband. She felt total rejection. Why would he not discuss the woman? Why was Miss Caldecott in his study instead of the drawing room? Why did he allow her boldly to take hold of his face as she had that morning? Might he still care for her? She was, indeed, quite beautiful, and her figure just as pleasing. Had he wanted to marry her, and had she refused him? No, that could not be. He had told her that he had never loved a woman before herself.

Elizabeth wrinkled her brow. She could not make it all out and felt she would soon go mad if she continued to dwell on it. Yet, how would she ever know anything if her husband always avoided the matter?

Darcy rolled on his side, slid his body against his wife's, and placed his arm over her. "I love you, Elizabeth, so much. You are the world to me."

The silent tears that trickled down her face were her only response.

"Did you hear me, Lizzy?"

She gave a weak nod to his query. He then pressed against her body, snuggling close before drifting off to sleep.

She, on the other hand, could find no solace in his verbal and physical token. Her mind remained in a dither with thoughts of the beautiful, golden-haired woman from her husband's past. Consequently, she tossed and turned for the rest of the night...

~*~

The next morning, all met in the breakfast room as servants readied the dining parlour for the grand event, and therefore, all chairs had been removed to give the table and furnishings a thorough cleaning and polishing. The small breakfast room was bright and cheerful, painted in a yellowish hue. A silver salver was by the plates of the master, the mistress, and Colonel Fitzwilliam.

While placing his napkin upon his lap, Darcy glanced over to see who sent the missives. As he shuffled through them, he noticed one from his attorney in London, another from his Aunt Adeline, and a rather blotched one from Charles Bingley. Darcy smiled, even if Charles's name had not appeared on the front, he would have known immediately that it was from his brother-in-law due to the preponderance of ink splotches.

Richard had only one letter, and it was from his mother. Elizabeth picked up her missives from the tray and glanced through them. There was one from Kitty, one from Jane, and one from Lydia, too. *Oh, she had forgotten all about Lydia*! She put that particular letter on the bottom of the pile and placed them back on the tray. She desired to open them in her study while she was alone.

Waiting to partake of the food before him, the colonel broke the seal of his mother's missive and began reading. Georgiana kept glancing over to him in an effort to determine if it were good news or bad. The letter was long. The others were halfway through their meal by the time Richard put the now refolded post back upon the tray.

Georgiana and Elizabeth stared at him when he looked up and met their curious faces. Darcy was still drinking his coffee as he read his own letter from his attorney.

"Well?" Georgiana entreated.

Richard pretended not to know what she wanted. "What is it, duck?"

"You know what. Are you not going to let me know anything that Aunt Adeline has to say?"

"Oh, the letter?" Colonel Fitzwilliam replied in feigned ignorance. He then picked it up and offered the missive to Georgiana.

She contrived offence, "I am not asking to read it. I only want to know if there is anything of interest."

Opening the letter, Richard scanned it over to find the exact line which he knew would do the trick for his fair cousin. "Let us see, Georgie, ah, yes, here it is. 'Richard, do convince Fitzwilliam that I insist on holding the ball, and I want you boys to reply right away. The invitations need to be sent immediately.'"

Georgiana's face beamed, "She wants to have a ball? When?"

Darcy's attention was now fully transfixed upon Richard. He lowered the letter he was reading and eyed the tray for Lady Matlock's post to him. "Tell us, Fitzwilliam, straightway. Do not dangle with the information like you are so often wont to do."

Snorting lightly at Darcy's caricature of him, the colonel again scanned the letter for the desired information. "Mother says she wants to have a ball in honour of her nephew and his bride. She shall invite the whole of Derbyshire. She wants to hold it before the Season begins in April. Thus, she suggests around the first of March. She wants you to come and spend a day and night before the festivity, so she may become acquainted with Elizabeth."

"Oh! A ball at Matlock!" Georgiana cried while casting a jubilant look at her sister-in-law. "And just think, Elizabeth, it is in yours and my brother's honour!" Her vision then darted between her brother and cousin. "May I attend, and may I dance a few times? After all, I will be coming out this Season, and it is not as if we are in London where we need worry about everything we do."

Darcy and Richard could not believe their ears. Did Georgiana just declare that she was willingly going to come out for this London Season? Her brother did not comment, but only said, "We shall take your wish into consideration."

Elizabeth raised her eyebrows. Deep down, she did not see what all the fuss was about. Why should Georgiana not be allowed to dance? She would be seventeen this summer. She then recalled, however, that she did not know all the functioning of high society.

Thus, whatever her husband and the colonel decided, she would not contest it. She wanted no more disagreements between her husband and herself.

They all parted company after breakfast. Elizabeth carried her letters to her study where she decided to read Jane's first. It was not long nor did it contain the same cheerfulness as the one prior. Next, she turned to Kitty's letter. Her younger sister mentioned that there was not much to do now that all her sisters, excepting Mary, were gone. However, she also revealed that she and their mother visited Jane and Charles every day, sometimes twice. Additionally, they had to stay the night once due to rain and would often stay the following day.

Rolling her eyes at the thought of Jane's burden living so close to their mother, she opened her last letter as she thought to herself, 'Saving the worst for last.'

Lydia's letter was long and contained many lamentations of how difficult things were for her and George. However, the real thunderbolt, which took Elizabeth by complete surprise, was Lydia's announcement that she was with child and therefore needed more funds. Reading the last words made Elizabeth fume. "...*Your generosity is appreciated, but really, Lizzy, you could surely do better than that. I have the baby to think about, and we barely have any food on our table as it is. Whereas, I am sure yours is overflowing in excess. Well, La! I must be going now. I am to dine with the officers and their wives. Oh, and one more thing, was Georgiana flabbergasted to learn that we have so much in common?*"

Elizabeth tore the letter to bits. *How could her sister be so mercenary? What kind of mother would Lydia be*? Closing her eyes in disbelief, she was a little startled when opening them again to find her husband standing across her desk, looking down at her. "Is something the matter, Lizzy?"

She wanted to scream *Yes*, and then tell him that she could not stand the sight of Collette, that she had a very silly, no, *pathetic* sister and that Jane was suffering due to her mother's senselessness and lack of consideration, but instead, she merely answered, "No."

"Why then, may I ask, is there a letter torn to shreds upon your desk?"

She became alarmed and started gathering the pieces of paper, balling them up in her hand. "Oh, it is just a letter from Lydia, and I believe it has influenced my current bad temper."

"Whatever does she have to say?"

"Only that she and her husband are expecting their first child, the first Bennet grandchild."

Darcy frowned. "Elizabeth, surely you do not care that their child will be the first grandchild in your family?"

"No, in all actuality, I do not care. I only feel sorrow for the innocent babe's misfortune to have such parents." Darcy sat in his favoured chair and inhaled deeply.

"No, I would not wish the relation of George Wickham upon anybody," he replied in understanding. "I have some good news though, without reference to the Wickhams, which I hope will take away such doldrums."

Elizabeth rose quickly and joined her husband in the chair. "I could use some cheering just now, so do tell." Snuggling close, she rested her head on his shoulder.

"Well, let's see, ah, here it is," he then began to read from Bingley's missive, "*Darcy, if you do not mind, Jane, who is always the angel and never complains, would be mortified by my suggesting we come for a visit, of course, at your convenience. It is just that we never seem to have much time to ourselves. Let me know if you and Elizabeth are up for the company. I know Janey would love to see her dear sister again, and I, of course, would love to see you both as well. Give my regards to all. With affection, Charles Bingley.*"

Elizabeth's face was hidden from her husband's view, and so he asked, "Is there now a smile where there once was a dismal scowl?"

Raising her head, he was rewarded by sparkling eyes that radiated pure joy.

"Do you like my news, Lizzy?"

Coquettishly, she answered, "*Yes!*"

"Does that mean you are up for more visitors or has Richard done you in?"

"No, I think I could manage. And you? Do you wish to see Charles and Jane, again? I, too, received a letter from Jane. She did not mention or even insinuate a visit, but she is in need of one. I could tell she was not her usual, contented self, and when I read Kitty's letter I knew why. Evidently, Mama and Kitty have been going over daily, sometimes with Mary. Mama has even found reasons to stay the night and the entirety of the following day. I do feel for them both."

"Yes, I gathered from Bingley's brief account that they were having company quite often."

Rolling her eyes and puffing her cheeks full of air, Elizabeth then sighed aloud, "I fear this will continue to be a problem for them. My mother may never tire, but surely they shall."

Teasingly, he stated, "So, do you think a woman may be settled too near her family? In this case, do the circumstances warrant it to be so or not?"

She smiled at his jest, recalling their conversation at the parsonage concerning their difference of opinion about Charlotte living close to her family, even though they were fifty miles apart. Nodding her head, she agreed, "Charles and Jane are most certainly too near! I am glad we are not that close to any family, excepting your aunt and uncle."

"Yes, these are precisely my sentiments regarding the matter, and since you have opened the subject of my aunt and uncle, how do you feel, Lizzy, about a ball? Would it please you or would you rather not? We can decline the invitation, but it is imperative for us to decide because my aunt is correct, she will need to make plans immediately."

"Would you like a ball, Fitzwilliam?"

"I am not sure. Part of me considers it a favourable means for you to be introduced to the whole of Derbyshire, and my aunt's offer is most caring. As for myself, you know me, Lizzy. I detest these sorts of things. However, I imagine dancing will not be such a chore now that I have a wife. In fact, that shall be the best part—dancing with you, Lizzy."

"Then there is no reason not to accept such a generous offer from your aunt. I think a ball will be delightful. After all, I have only had the pleasure of dancing with you once, and I should like to again. You dance beautifully, Fitzwilliam. I do not understand why you dislike the entertainment so."

"I will not if I am with you." Touched by his affirmation, they embraced, and then Darcy asked, "So, it pleases you to agree to the ball?" Elizabeth nodded with composure but then cracked a grin, revealing her eagerness. Darcy rewarded her with a quick grin of his own and stated, "If this be the case, I must go and write to my aunt straightaway, albeit I would much rather stay in this chair and kiss my wife until she begs me to lock the doors."

"Why, Mr. Darcy! I have no idea of what you are speaking," She said with a mischievous grin

"Oh, ah, ah ... you do not, do you? Well, maybe I need to refresh your memory."

Mrs. Darcy sprang from off his lap and backed away. Darcy arose just as quickly and slowly started to approach his wife. She instantly took refuge behind the desk. Suddenly, her husband lunged forward, and the chase was on. Elizabeth shrieked gleefully with each attempt that her husband made to catch her. She sallied along the edge of the desk and every so often endeavoured to escape, only to quickly return to the fortification the furniture provided.

"You cannot stay behind there forever, my dear lady. I am patient and, therefore, can easily wait upon my prey."

Each stood still, sizing the other up for some moments, when in one fell swoop, Darcy hurdled the desk, causing her letters to sail to the floor. Yet, the capture was complete, and Darcy began to tickle Elizabeth unmercifully. She screamed as he strove to gain a concession from her lips. "Admit it, Lizzy!" he cried in glee, "you want me to lock the doors."

"I have no idea, sir ... oh, please, 'tis too much ... please, Fitzwilliam ... I ... cannot breathe!"

"You had better say it!"

"Say what, Brother?" A very concerned Georgiana stood in the doorway of the room.

Darcy and Elizabeth were stunned. Darcy immediately freed his wife from his grasp and then the couple started to smooth their clothing and attempted to present an appearance of composure.

Still not sure what all the commotion was about, Georgian appeared anxious. Her brother straightened his cravat and walked over to her. "There is nothing to be distressed about, Georgie. Elizabeth and I did not agree about a certain recollection when I gently reminded her of the reliability of my assertion. She became euphoric when she suddenly remembered that my perspective was, indeed correct, and therefore, expressed herself overzealously."

A thud was heard and Darcy's eyes widened in shock. He had been hit smack dab in the back of his head with what felt like a book. Without turning around, he stated, "Well, my dear ladies, I must go and make answer to our dear Aunt, Lady Matlock." He strode confidently out of the room leaving a confused expression on his sister's face as she looked down to the floor and saw a small, leather bound volume of Dante's, *The Divine Comedy*.

~*~

The morning of the soirée dawned bright and clear. The event happened to coincide with Saint Valentines' Day. All the servants were in a whirl with the last minute preparations. That morning, Darcy had decided that his family should have another outing in the sleigh, in order to have some fresh air and relaxation before the demands of the day encroached upon them all.

Mary Sherwood

While the mistress was away, a message was sent to the kitchen for Sally. It asked for the lass to come home at once due to her mother's having had a recent accident. Sally went in search of Mrs. Reynolds, since her mistress could not be reached. The housekeeper read the scrawl upon the paper and just shook her head in concern.

"Well, Sally, I suppose you need to be going. But mind you, you must be back in plenty of time to help Mrs. Darcy ready herself for the evening. Until your return, I will send Mary up in your stead. Please make sure you are back at least an hour before dinner." The maid curtseyed and assured Mrs. Reynolds that she would return in time.

Sally's parents did not live far, but Mrs. Reynolds had arranged for the wood cart, still equipped with the sleigh bobs, to transport her to her home. However, she would have to walk back to Pemberley house, and allow herself plenty of time in order to help Mrs. Darcy dress for supper. The walk would be no more than thirty minutes, possibly a little longer.

The young maid's father had been a tenant farmer for Pemberley for the past five years. He did his work, but most of the time kept mainly to himself. Sally had great anxiety as she rode along, worrying, as she frequently did, about her mother's welfare. When the wagon stopped, Mr. Manning dismounted and came around to assist the young maid from the conveyance. Sally thanked him, and then stood in front of the doorway of the very small structure, which was by no means attractive, yet was in good repair. All tenants were required to keep their dwellings in repair and as reasonably appealing as possible. Any legitimate maintenance to all structures was to be performed by the tenant, but paid for by the landlord.

As Sally lifted the door latch and entered, she felt instant relief on finding her father nowhere about, but remained cautious as she made her way through the clutter to check her parents' room, situated in the rear. She knocked lightly on the doorframe, given that there was no door, and only a blanket served in its place. No answer came, but she distinctively heard soft moans from her mother. She pulled the blanket to the side and entered. "Mum, it's me, your Sally."

Her mother did not answer, but put forth her hand, instead, to beckon her daughter to come closer. Sally did and was horrified at the discovery of her mother's face, so swollen that she was beyond recognition. Her heart broke at seeing her mother thus. The actual redness, swelling, and lacerations were not a shock to Sally, for she had seen her mother in such a way many times while growing up, but the never to this extent.

She sat gently on the bed, cradling her mother's hand, and mournfully proclaimed, "Oh, Mum, what has he done to you this time?"

Due to the severe swelling of her lips, the woman was unable to speak. Yet, her hands grasped her daughter's and squeezed, patted, and caressed it. Sally, likewise, expressed her love by bringing her mother's hands to her lips and kissing them gently. She then said, "Let me go and fetch some water. I will help to clean you up, and I'm sure you must be thirsty."

Her mother vehemently shook her head. She so desired to be able to tell her daughter to leave without delay. It would have been no use if she could have stated her wish because just as soon as she thought it, the door from the neighbouring room opened.

Sally's mother grasped hers daughter's hand in a tight hold and in great effort rose up. She embraced Sally as new tears coursed down her beet red, bludgeoned face.

"Ah, I see *Miss High and Mighty* has returned to grace us with her presence."

Sally eyes flashed towards her father, but she said nothing. Instead, she gave her mother's hand one last kiss, squeezing it firmly. Then she stood and informed no one in particular that she would go and bring back some water. Her father, however, would not move to the side to allow her to pass. "You will be cleaning up this mess, you will, and no need worrying about water right now. I'm wanting me vittles and your ma can't be getting up to make 'em. So you may just be needin' to stay for awhile."

Sally felt alarmed, but still said nothing. Her father let her pass, and she began quickly to straighten the room when he bellowed out, "Don't be concernin' yourself with that, just get me victuals!"

Straightway, she took the cast iron skillet and scraped it clean. Next, she went to the salt barrel to get a piece of pork steak. Rousing up the fire, she put the skillet directly on the brightened coals, then arranged the table and put a plate and mug of ale upon it.

Her father ate with gusto, and the slovenliness of his manner sickened his daughter. He grunted aloud as he chewed his food, and the beer drooled down the corners of his mouth with every swig. Afterward he used the back of his hand to wipe it dry.

The room was a mess, but in no time, Sally had it put in order. While her father continued to eat, she muttered that she would slip out for a second to gather some snow. The old man did not even heed what she had said. She came back with some rags filled with packed snow. She tied them up secure into two bundles, went back to her mother, and gently placed them on her eyes and lips.

Sally would not be deterred. She kept gathering new snow, and applied it to her mother's battered face. Her father slept while she tended to her mother. Gratitude filled her heart for his slumber. She prepared broth, but her mother shook her head and refused it.

The time had come for her departure. She went one last time to hold her mother's hand and whisper her goodbyes. As she arose to take her leave, her father stood in the doorway once more. "A lot of good that will be doing her, pampering her so. She only got what's her due. I hears yous are the master's wife's lady maid, ye are. I be guessing you thinks you're better than the likes of us. Look at the fancy dress you be wearing. You're thinking yer better than where ye came from? Answer me, ye disgraceful wench."

Sally swallowed hard. She knew it was best not to say a word. Walking forward, she patiently paused in front of her father in hopes that he would let her by. She knew that she must hurry in order to be back in time to help Mrs. Darcy.

"I said be answering me!" The force of his fist made a popping sound as it struck her cheek. The daughter became fearful, but tried to stay focused. Nervously, she said, "I must be going father to help the mistress. Mr. Darcy won't like my tardiness."

He slapped her one more time. "Mr. Darcy! Mr. Darcy and his new wife, all high and mighty! And now you are one of 'em too." Sally could hear the moans of her mother's anguish. The young girl felt terrible. Finally, her father stepped back, allowing her to pass. But before she was able to open the door, he grabbed her arm and shoved her hard up against the wall. "Now don't be going and letting them fine people know about poor Sally's mother or poor Sally if ye know what be best for ya. Do you be hearing me?"

She silently nodded. He shoved her forward and then said, "You're needed here, too. Make sure you come again, and soon."

In a split second, Sally was outside and her legs vigorously carried her through the snow. She held her tears as she made her way to the Great House. Once, when she was far away from her father's home, she stopped to scoop up some snow to hold it gently over her throbbing cheek.

As she approached the back of the house by the stables, Thomas Wilkens was coming around the corner. He had returned some hours earlier and had been tending to the horses and was greasing the carriage fittings. He looked up and saw a very disturbed young lady walking towards him. Then quickly, he looked about making sure no one else was around before meeting her in the path.

"Sally?" he called.

She stopped and became fearful once more. "Sally, what is wrong?"

They stood on the far side of the stable, which faced the woods and milk barn. The lass just shook her head. "It's nothin'. I must be goin' in."

He faced her now, and could see the horrible mark on her cheek. "Who did this to you, Sally?"

The young miss would not answer, but shook her head the more. "Sally, you tell me now who has done this, or I will be going straight to Mrs. Reynolds, myself."

"No, you can't be doing that!" she cried. "I can't say. Now, let me pass."

She started to go around him when his hand caught hold of her wrist, thus halting her progress. She whirled around and begged him to release her, but, before she could get the words out, she broke down and began sobbing. Thomas drew her up next to him, and in a steely voice declared, "I won't stand for anyone hurting you. You must tell me who has done this." She sobbed harder now as he gently put his arms around her, one hand holding her securely while the other caressed her back.

"If I tell you," she cried, "he will only do worse!"

"No, Sally, trust me, I will figure something out."

"It be me dad. He has always beat me and me mum, but me poor mum is so bad this time that I am frightened for her. I guess I didn't know any better before, and that's what's making it so much the worse now."

"What do you mean about not knowing before and now it is worse. How can it be worse? It is wrong, always, every time."

Shaking her head, she tried to explain while catching her breath. "Tommy, I shouldn't be telling you this, no telling what you will think of me after I do, but I can't take the guilt no more. I saw the master and mistress in her chamber in a loving way. I don't mean to say everything, but just how he looked at her and touched her. I had never seen a man look at a woman that way before. He was so gentle with her and lovin'. I finally came to my senses and left the room right away, but it has me knowin' what life can be. What it should have been for me mum." As she started crying again, he tightened his embrace and held her closer.

Whispering, he said, "Sally, I want to look at you the way Mr. Darcy looks at his wife. I want to be the one who loves you the way you deserve and the way all women deserve to be cherished."

Looking up through her tears, she saw the love in his eyes, and she cried anew, but this time the tears were not full of sorrow. "Are you sure of what you are saying, Tommy Wilkens?"

"Yes, I have wanted you for my wife for so long. I know I'm still young, and I'm not sure how I can make it for us, but I'm sure I want you for my wife." He leaned forward, and they kissed a sweet, chaste kiss. "Will you have me, Sally?"

Suddenly, a noise clamoured loudly behind the stables. Both Thomas and Sally became still. Sally began to tremble and her eyes grew wide in fear that someone had heard all of her disclosures. Thomas crept to the back of the building and saw no one, but found an empty milk bucket toppled over. Sally had noiselessly followed him, and she saw it, too.

"I must go in!" Sally became frantic. "Oh, Tommy, what will I do if someone tells about the things I told you?" She turned and ran towards the kitchen entrance without saying a word further and without giving an answer to a very besotted young man.

~*~

Dressed in coattails and wearing black, Darcy looked quite distinguished. He made his way to the dining room, anxious to see what

Elizabeth and Georgiana had decided upon for the seating arrangements. At the head of the table where he sat, she had placed on his right Mr. Pennington and then next to him the Newedgates. Dr. Lowry had also been invited with his grandparents at Darcy's request. Darcy noticed that the doctor sat across the table from his grandmother, Mrs. Newedgate, and seated on his left was Mr. Caldecott and Mrs. Caldecott was next to himself on the doctor's right. He rolled his eyes and shook his head before proceeding down the length of the table, taking note of everyone's seating. Elizabeth had placed Collette immediately to her left with Richard seated directly across the table to her right. Shrugging helplessly, he silently considered, *Could it get any worse?* Georgiana was next to Richard and the Stuarts were beside her. The Master of Pemberley contemplated for some moments, then decisively picked up Collette's card, and placed it directly to his left, where Mrs. Caldecott had been located. He then shifted Mrs. Caldecott to where Dr. Lowry was supposed to have sat. Taking up the doctor's name card, he placed it where Collette's had been. With one last look, he impulsively changed Richard's seat with the doctor's, in the hopes that Richard would keep Elizabeth occupied during the dinner without Georgiana dominating his attention. Thus, the doctor would be on Elizabeth's right and Richard on her left. Between the two men, plenty of conversation should be generated.

Straightening his waistcoat, he left the room with the intention of telling his wife about the needed changes.

~*~

When Sally hurriedly arrived through the servant's door, she found the mistress pouring buckets of water in the tub. Fear seized her and she cried out, "Oh, Mrs. Darcy, I'm so sorry how late I am! Please, let me do that while you start to undress." Elizabeth handed the pail to her maid.

"I am glad you are back, Sally. I was beginning to worry about you. Mary brought these buckets up a few minutes ago. I am running late, and when you have finished pouring, please, help me with my corset."

Sally had her mistress in the tub in a flash. As she washed, Elizabeth looked up and saw a bright bruise on the young woman's cheekbone. "Sally, how on earth has that happened to you?"

The girl looked absentmindedly and then remembered her face. "I fell."

"You fell!" What kind of fall would cause such a mark?"

At this response from her mistress, Sally became solemn and immediately Elizabeth reached out her sudsy hand and took hold of Sally's. "Tell me, Sally. You do not have to be frightened. I will not tell anyone without your consent."

The maid's face contorted with shame. "Oh, mistress, me dad has done this, but it is nothing. I am used to it. But, I must tell you something right now. I am so sorry for something I witnessed with you and your husband, and I'm so ashamed."

Squeezing the girl's hand, Elizabeth encouraged her to go on. "A few weeks ago, when you asked me to go and get you some tea while you were sitting at the vanity, I came in the room with the tea without knowing that the master had returned. I saw him being so loving to you and I ... I ...uh, I watched him kiss you before I took to my wits and left the room. I'm sorry and so ashamed. I've never seen a man be as nice as your husband was with you. I haven't told anyone about it until tonight. I told a trusted friend who saw me with the bruise, like you have now. I started crying and the guilt came too much for me. It all came tumbling out." The young maid stifled her tears while remorse and shame swept over her.

"Sally, you have no need to fear. I am not angry. You did what was right when you realized the impropriety of seeing my husband kiss me. I wish I had time to discuss this with you further, but I am so late. Please know, however, I am not angry with you in the least."

"Oh, but, ma'am, I fear someone heard me tell my friend about my father and about you and the master's tenderness."

"Do not worry. You have told me. Even if someone does say something, you came to me and confessed everything. I have the greatest confidence in you, Sally. We will talk more of this tomorrow."

"Thank you, ma'am."

The maid nodded and helped her mistress out of the tub, into her dress, and placed her hair in a simple but very becoming style.

~*~

Darcy rapped on his wife's chamber door, anxious to tell her about the changed seating arrangements when Georgiana and Richard met him in the hall. Sally opened the door and kept hidden in the shadow the best she could. Elizabeth was already walking towards her husband and the others. Once in the hall she stated, "I hope I am not too late."

Darcy became apprehensive. When would he have a chance to speak with her alone?

As they came down the stairs, they saw Mr. Greene heading towards the entrance door, and thus, Darcy, Elizabeth, Georgiana, and Richard all hurried to form a receiving line to greet the guests. Earlier, Darcy had directed that, after the majority of the guests had arrived, Richard and Georgiana would break from the line and mingle with those who waited.

The Newedgates and their grandson, Dr. Lowry, were the first to enter. Sir Henry and Lady Newedgate were very pleased to see George and Lady Anne Darcy's son, Fitzwilliam, again and to meet his pretty bride. Next the Stuarts and Mr. Pennington came. They all praised Darcy on his wife's beauty and expressed their appreciation for having been invited. Mrs.

Chalmers came unescorted, as usual. Her husband was not one for social engagements, but his wife was a true bluestocking, taking great pleasure in the arts and therefore, attended many functions without him. Richard and Georgiana joined the crowd as they all waited for the Caldecotts.

Darcy took advantage of this rare moment alone with his wife and said, "Elizabeth, I have something of which I need to inform you."

She met his gaze, and then Mr. Greene announced Mr. Caldecott, his wife, and daughter.

Mr. Caldecott boomed his greeting and tastelessly said to his wife, "This one here," referring to Elizabeth, "is a feisty one. Fitzwilliam has always liked his horses that way, and we know how he liked his women the same. I guess that is the kind raised in the country air."

Mrs. Caldecott ignored her husband's crudeness, politely shook Elizabeth's hand, and meekly said, "I am so happy to meet you, Mrs. Darcy. I am happy for you both. Pemberley will be blessed by your union."

"I thank you," Elizabeth replied, "and I am so glad you have come."

While Elizabeth conversed further with Mrs. Caldecott, Collette spoke with Darcy. Consequently, Elizabeth could not make out the whole of their conversation, yet she did hear Collette's last, very coy and sensuous remark. "I had hoped against hope that you would have a ball, it being the customary thing for a husband to do to honour his wife on Valentine's Day. I did so want to dance with you again, Fitzwilliam."

Darcy breathed in loudly and managed to say, "We preferred a soirée."

Collette then fawned over Elizabeth. "Eliza, you look so *wholesome* tonight. I am so glad to see you, again. I do want to help you learn to ride so you can come on all the hunts."

"Well, I thank you, Miss Caldecott, for the sentiment, but I am not at all sure about my desire to ride. I suppose I will have to leave all the hunts to *you*. But, since you are seated near me at dinner, we can discuss it then."

Miss Caldecott smiled with poise. A look of alarm crossed Darcy's face. How on earth would he be able to untangle this mess? He suddenly felt ill. Elizabeth would be furious with his interference now and the humiliation that it would cost her.

The party all proceeded to the dining room in the ordered manner which etiquette demanded.

Darcy pulled the chair out for his wife while whispering to her. "I love you, Elizabeth. Trust me." She became confused at his quick directive, and then she saw the obvious. Collette was seated to her husband's left. How on earth had that happened? Richard took the seat intended for her. She realized that Dr. Lowry had been changed, also. She looked to Georgiana, but could not get her attention. Her sister-in-law did not seem fazed in the least by the change, and she had been the one who had helped her in her selections.

Elizabeth's emotions ran a gamut from fear to jealousy to anger. *It must have been Fitzwilliam. He knows he has been caught, and that is why he has asked me to trust him.* She licked her dry lips and attempted to calm herself, yet it was hard to accomplish as Collette ogled her husband. More than once she cast her eyes upon him with a salacious grin before turning her gaze upon Elizabeth triumphantly. *Collette believes that Fitzwilliam prefers to sit next to her, and that I am oblivious to the changed seating.* Elizabeth's face flushed brightly.

Colonel Fitzwilliam had detected a shadow of dejection pass over Elizabeth's features as she gazed over the expanse of the table to her husband. His eyes followed hers to observe Collette monopolizing Darcy's every moment. He shook his head slowly and sighed. Wearily, Richard put forth a jovial face. Smiling engagingly at Elizabeth, he asked, "I was wondering if I may join in by singing with you tonight? One song in particular has always been a favourite of mine. I meant to ask earlier, and with your permission, I should love it if you would allow me the honour."

Elizabeth turned to the colonel and smiled sadly at him for his obvious effort to cheer her. "Which selection would that be?" she enquired.

Looking intently into her eyes, he stated, *"My Lady."*

She nodded to him and smiled anew, but the melancholy lingered. The colonel did his best to engage her in conversation. He told humorous jokes about the army and encouraged Dr. Lowry to tell stories of some of his irksome experiences he'd had while in medical school, which were, indeed, quite entertaining. Elizabeth listened to them all with politeness, but her fine eyes lacked their natural sparkle and vivaciousness.

Instead of separating, the party went directly to the music room. Georgiana commenced the recital with a selection by Mozart. Everyone was enthralled by her abilities, but Dr. Lowry was completely captivated. He had never seen one so young perform so well. Next, Elizabeth joined her sister-in-law and they performed some light-hearted duets accented by playful staccatos. Again, everyone seemed charmed.

Richard sat by them and turned the pages. He could not help but notice how Elizabeth's vision periodically veered off towards her husband and Collette. He, too, looked attentively upon them and saw that Darcy's face seemed calm as the lady chatted by his side while she periodically touched his arm, his hand, and even tugged at his cravat. He could very well imagine the drivel that Darcy was forced to endure.

Georgiana stood and curtseyed. Everyone gave Miss Darcy a standing ovation, which lasted for a full minute. This, however, left Elizabeth to perform on her own. Richard could tell she was nervous, and he knew Darcy could as well. He felt terrible.

As she began, her husband's gaze fixed intently upon her. Collette followed the path of his vision and then remarked, "I dare say I know why you married your pretty little country lass."

Without removing his eyes from his wife, he dryly stated, "I imagine not."

"Yes, yes, I can." Collette asserted. "Her figure is rather pleasing, and I do know your preferences quite well."

Darcy's face hardened, and his blood boiled. If it would not cause talk, he would have thrown the woman out of his house that instant. Instead, he decided he was finished with being polite, and, from then on, would just ignore her. She strived with all her wiles to gain his attention, but she realized it was of no use. Miss Caldecott then turned her attention towards Mrs. Darcy, scrutinizing her closely. Her lips curled into a simper as she considered, *Well, there is more than one way to skin a cat.*

When Richard arose to sing as Elizabeth played, Darcy's face registered surprise. Not once, during their rehearsals, had they practiced this melody. In fact, Richard had earlier decided that he would not sing after all, and he insisted that he would let the ladies shine instead. Yet, here his cousin stood giving a magnificent performance, his rich tenor voice entrancing the guests. He saw how Richard looked charmingly towards Elizabeth, and how she appreciated his kind-heartedness and amiability in return. These were qualities Darcy knew he lacked and did not have the propensity for, no matter how much he practiced. He sighed deeply.

Collette noticed the intentness of Darcy's gaze as it shifted between his wife and his cousin. She immediately assessed that the colonel was somewhat sweet on the new Mrs. Darcy and thought ...*My, my, how history repeats itself*. She smiled, cunningly, as she perceived the treasured Achilles' heel.

The guests all departed, enthralled with the dinner, the conversation, the music and the new Mrs. Darcy. Darcy was proud of his wife's graciousness. She performed her role as mistress marvellously, and he could not have been any prouder of her than he was tonight.

They all headed towards the stairs together when Mrs. Reynolds called after the master. He paused and looked directly into his wife's eyes, "I will be with you soon. Please wait up for me." He then departed.

Elizabeth felt an intense bereavement for an evening that had promised so much, only to be dashed by her husband's deception. If he truly abhorred disguise as he had once confessed, then he had a problem, for tonight, he demonstrated his aversion most admirably.

~*~

Mrs. Reynolds and Darcy walked into his study together.

"Yes, Mrs. Reynolds, is something wrong?"

The housekeeper did not know how to put it delicately. "Well, Master Darcy, I fear there is something that you would want brought to your attention." She hesitated.

"Please, go on."

"I don't know how to put this but bluntly. There has been conversation among the servants, which I know will anger you. I have dismissed the girl who has started it or at least repeated it with an active tongue."

"I do not understand the problem. If she has been dismissed, then there is no need to be concerned any further. These things, in the long run, work themselves out."

"Yes, I agree with you, but it's not that simple this time."

"Why ever not?"

"Because Mrs. Darcy's maid, Sally, is reported to have been the one who began the rumours in the first place, and I have no authority over the Lady's Maid. Thus, I knew I would have to inform you."

Darcy's brow furrowed, and he became pale. "What is being said? Please, do not censor it. Tell me exactly, every word."

Mrs. Reynolds inhaled and then said, "It has been said that Sally had peeped at you and the mistress during a...a private encounter, and she is speaking about it to others.

His lips tightened, as did his jaw. "Is there anything else?"

Here, the elderly lady faltered. She did not want to relate such a thing to her cherished boy. "Oh, just the usual with everyone observing your adoration for Mrs. Darcy."

His eyes widened. He knew Mrs. Reynolds, and he knew she was not telling him all.

Incredulously, he asked, "There is more, is there not?" Mrs. Reynolds scarcely nodded. He was full of dread with the thought of what could possibly make his housekeeper so reluctant.

"It is said, Master Fitzwilliam," she paused, "it is said that Sally witnessed..." she paused again as tears sprang to her eyes. Starting anew, she courageously forged onward. "It is said that Sally witnessed Mrs. Darcy and Colonel Fitzwilliam having an inappropriate conversation and then exchange a compromising embrace."

Darcy was horror-struck. When had this taken place? It was all incomprehensible. He sat down and cradled his head in his hands. The housekeeper gently patted his shoulder and then walked softly out of the room, feeling great empathy for her beloved master.

~*~

Chapter Twelve

Heartbroken Abandonment

Elizabeth sat numbly in front of the mirror, removing the hairpins one by one from her hair. Tonight she had decided to take care of herself instead of having Sally come to help her undress. The girl had been through too much already. With the removal of each pin, Elizabeth's mind was filled with thoughts and reflections as she pondered over the course of the evening. The humiliation burned anew as she reflected on Collette's delight at sitting next to Fitzwilliam, and on how she flaunted herself at him with her fearless flirtations, which were apparent for all to behold—all except... possibly... her husband.

Sighing, Elizabeth picked up her silver brush and began brushing her long, silky tresses while gazing at her reflection. *Collette is truly beautiful, ten times prettier than even Jane. She must have meant something special to Fitzwilliam at one time or he would not have rearranged the seating, especially without telling me. He had intentionally wanted to keep that audacious woman away from me. But why? What reason could there possibly be for him to be so concerned that he would make a switch at the last possible minute? Unless, he was worried that Miss Caldecott would say something—something he would not want me to know.*

She placed the brush down upon the matching tray, resting her hand on the vanity top, and while continuing to inspect her features in the glass, she rapped her nails rhythmically upon her dressing table. *I have never been a beautiful woman by any stretch of the imagination. Yet, Fitzwilliam claims that I am the first to captivate his heart. After tonight, I find this difficult to believe. It just cannot be so. His attachment to Collette must have meant more to him than mere friendship. It has been plainly evident throughout the evening that he still feels some sense of obligation to her. Why else would he sit with her all through dinner and the recital? It is too much!*

Biting her lip, she took one last hard look in the mirror. *What did Fitzwilliam see in me in the first place? I cannot ride horses...* Elizabeth quickly rolled her eyes, *I have absolutely no connections. Was I simply a challenge? No, I cannot believe that. Oh! Whatever is wrong with me?*

Suddenly, insecurity gave way to resentment. Elizabeth's chest tightened as she thought once more of Collette's eyes batting and her offensively enticing caresses. She wondered why Fitzwilliam had tolerated it and how he could allow that woman to humiliate her in such a bold manner. Then one single thought emerged considerably above all others: *Did Fitzwilliam enjoy her advances, relish in her teasing, and desire her blatant attention?* Elizabeth was not sure. She had kept her eyes fixed on Collette most of the evening and had noticed that Fitzwilliam smiled occasionally. She had no idea why he would grant such rare displays of pleasure. She thought back over their time in Hertfordshire in an effort to remember how he had acted with Caroline. Elizabeth recalled that, when he and Caroline would have their tête-à-têtes, Fitzwilliam had been mainly patient with Miss Bingley, indulging her constant prattle, and enduring her possessive fawning. Even then, she knew he had no real interest in Caroline at such times. Perhaps, he was dealing with Collette in the same way.

Exhaling loudly, she grasped her necklace and unfastened the clasp. Then she removed it from around her neck. Opening the jewellery box to place it therein, she noticed a folded piece of paper lying atop the jewels. A drawing of a heart with an arrow shot through it appeared on the outside of the fine, gilt-edged parchment. It looked like the kind of sketch a child would present to his mother, and one would think it thus if not for the beautiful handwriting appearing beneath—handwriting of which Elizabeth was quite familiar. *"On our first Valentine's Day."* Gently, Elizabeth broke the seal of her husband's missive and unfolded it. Her lips quivered in weariness from her tender, yet frayed emotions.

"On this, our first Valentine's Day as husband and wife, I want to express with the written word how much you mean to me. My Lizzy, you are my chosen dove, my lifelong companion, my virtuous bride. If not for you, I would never have known the true meaning of love. My heart belongs only to you! With all my love, Your Fitzwilliam."

Elizabeth's throat constricted. Tears began to well up and spill over her flushed cheeks. She folded the paper to look upon the drawing yet again. A faint, tremulous smile crossed her features. Once more, she opened the Valentine to read its message. *"My heart belongs only to you!"* Did he truly mean it? He had tried to tell her something. He had asked her to trust him. Surely, he did care for her sentiments, and he must have his reasons for his behaviour of late. Should she give him the benefit of the doubt?

With her fingertips, she reached up and quickly brushed back the tears, which now flowed freely from her eyes. She knew he loved her. She knew he wanted her. She would trust him no matter the pain it had cost her. Hurriedly, she slipped out of her clothes and chose to wear one of her sheer, red nightgowns, which she had never worn before—one she had been prompted to purchase by her Aunt Gardiner's suggestion and encouragement. It would be her Valentine offering to her husband.

~*~

Darcy remained in his study, pondering his housekeeper's words. *'It is said that Sally witnessed Mrs. Darcy and Colonel Fitzwilliam having an inappropriate conversation and then exchange a compromising embrace.'*

Sitting behind his desk with the back of his head resting against the chair, he allowed her words to swirl round and round in his head. *There is no denying it any longer: Richard is in love with Elizabeth and she, too, has feelings for him.* The faded lines of tears streaked his face. His hands tightened into fists as they lay by his side. Breathing deeply, he sat slowly upright while he contemplated what to do.

Sally would have to be dismissed. He could not tolerate such deception from a servant in her position. He and Elizabeth would never have an ounce of privacy with such a person about. Chaffin would have never uttered a syllable no matter what he might have heard or seen. However, Darcy realized that his valet had been groomed for his position from an early age, just as he himself had been groomed from his birth to become the Master of Pemberley. Sally, on the other hand, had been raised the daughter of a tenant farmer father. She lacked education and training, and, therefore, she was inadequate for her current role of Lady's maid. When Elizabeth had informed him that she had secured the maid to fulfil Clara's position, he was not happy. Yet he kept his opinion to himself because he desired for Elizabeth to feel that she was *indeed* the mistress of her own household. Considering all that he now knew, however, he was gladdened that he had sent an express to his solicitor in London desiring to know more about acquiring a French Lady's maid. It was all the mode, and these young maids were trained especially in their field. They were socially refined, knowledgeable in the latest fashion, skilled in needlework, and, above everything else, were instructed in the importance of being loyal and discreet. This morning, his attorney had sent him all the necessary information and legality involved in such a venture. Hiring one of these women was a complex endeavour. Such maids were few in number and, thus, were costly.

Tomorrow, he would call Sally to his study and question her. He hesitated taking this course of action. Maybe he should have Mrs. Reynolds join him while he spoke with the young woman. Yes, that would be best. The maid would feel uncomfortable speaking alone with him about such an intimate matter. However, she was the one who disclosed the information in the first place, and it was necessary to discover the underlying mischief behind such an accusation concerning his wife and cousin. He once again felt ill with the mere possibility of its being true and decided to think upon it no longer. The uncertainty had been in the back of his mind for some time now, and it was becoming harder and harder to suppress his own suspicions. Still, a part of him did not want to know.

Wearily he stood, not looking forward to Elizabeth's just wrath for his interference in the seating arrangements in relation to Collette. He closed his eyes firmly in an attempt to erase memories that would forever haunt him. He could not go there. No he would not. It was still too painful and fresh, though it had occurred more than ten years earlier. For now, he must go upstairs and give Elizabeth the explanation and apology that she so rightfully deserved. Picking up the candle, he set off for their chamber, striving to devise a rational reason for an officious act that was anything but rational.

~*~

Elizabeth had lit all the candles in the room and placed them on the night tables on each side of the bed. One candle she had left upon her vanity dresser to provide extra light for her husband as he entered the room. She had no idea if he would enter from the hall, her dressing area, or at all.

She climbed upon the large bed with the help of a stool. Strategically placing the pillows about her, she twisted around and smoothed out the airy fabric of her gown before positioning herself semi-reclined upon the fluffy mound of support.

She was giddy with anticipation, but, as each minute ticked past, her eyes began to droop. Every now and then, she would lazily open them and sneak a peek in an effort to determine the time. It was eleven-thirty. Valentine's Day was not yet over, but it was nearly so. What could be detaining her husband for so long? Striving with all her might, she willed herself to stay awake, but it was to no avail. Soon, she drifted into a cheerful slumber, dreaming visions of her husband's brilliant smile upon finding her in such a bold nightdress. It was more daring than the one she had worn on their wedding night. A pleasant smile graced her lips.

Darcy went to his own chamber first. He discarded his tailcoat, waistcoat, and cravat. Then he sat down and struggled with each boot. After their removal, he walked over to his bed, where Chaffin had placed his nightshirt. He picked it up and carried it with him as he made his way to the dressing room. Here, he placed the clean shirt down and powdered his brush to clean his teeth. Leaning over the water basin, he splashed fresh water upon his face a few times and then dabbed a towel over his brow to wipe off the droplets that clung to his skin.

He proceeded through the connecting antechamber as he unbuttoned his shirt with one hand while carrying the fresh one in the other. Pausing, he opened his wife's chamber door to be greeted by illuminations from what seemed like every candle in the house. He quickly discerned his wife resting atop the covers of their bed. Noiselessly, he moved closer.

The candles illuminated the crimson fabric of the gauzy gown she wore, lending it a flaming brilliance that was unimaginable. His breath caught and his pulse quickened as he took in her appearance. She was beautiful to behold. The ethereal splendour of his wife instantly mollified the ponderous meditations upon which he had laboured during the past hour.

As he stood gazing upon her, Elizabeth's eyelids fluttered open. She smiled dreamily at her husband and exclaimed, "Oh, Fitzwilliam, you are here! What time is it my love?"

His heart raced while glancing at the clock upon the mantlepiece. "It is a quarter to midnight."

Elizabeth's face beamed with pleasure as she stated, "Then it is not too late. I wanted to give you my Valentine token of affection in return for yours."

He marvelled at her compassion and charitable heart. She was not angry at his erroneous ways but instead, forgiving!

She looked up at him adoringly as she raised one brow and asked her silent husband, who at that precise moment spoke with his eyes alone. "Do you like my tribute for our first Valentine's Day together—the first Valentine's day of the rest of our lives?"

He was at a loss for words. He swallowed hard and could only stare upon her lovely face and form. His pulse no longer raced but, rather, tears filled his eyes as overflowing gratitude penetrated the inner chambers of his heart. This visual, verbal, and soon to be *very* tangible demonstration from his wife testified to him of her virtuous calibre and commitment.

In a hoarse whisper, he sanctioned her offering. "Oh, my Elizabeth, I simply love and adore you."

The shirt he held fell to the floor as a devoted husband and wife fell into each other's arms and worshipfully reverenced the other's true worth.

~*~

The next morning, Georgiana and Richard sat in the breakfast room enjoying their meal. Darcy had ordered his and Elizabeth's meal to be brought up on a tray. They had slept in late and, therefore, stayed within their chamber.

Placing her glass of juice down by her plate, Georgiana looked up and plucked up enough courage to ask her cousin what had been on her mind not only for most of the previous evening but still burdened her the first thing when she had awakened. "Um...hmm, Richard?'

Glancing up, he made eye contact and replied, "Yes, duck?"

Twisting the napkin in her hand, she bit her lip and looked doe-eyed at her cousin, tentatively stammering, "I...I...I...was wondering..."

He observed her uneasiness and encouraged, "What is it, duck? You know you can ask me anything. Have I ever chastised you or discouraged you in any way to make you so timid?"

"Oh no! Never! It is just that I have never before asked anything like I wish to know now."

Richard pushed his plate forward while tossing the napkin upon it and then sat upright. "Fire away, Georgie. Nothing you can say will shock me or make me reprimand you. What do you want to know? I will answer it as honestly and with as much knowledge as I am able."

Georgiana mirrored her cousin's actions and sat confident, assured by his words. Breathing in deeply, she began, "Very well, Richard, I do have something which I am certain my brother would not want me to ask or know. What I mean to say is that he would think a true lady would and should never ask questions such as these."

She shyly gauged his reaction thus far, and, as he seemed unaffected by her declaration, she continued with determination.

"I will first tell you my feelings, before I ask my question or questions." Richard never broke eye contact and nodded his understanding of her approach. Again, she inhaled deeply and then began in earnest. "When I met Miss Caldecott in Lambton back in December, before leaving for London and then on to Hertfordshire for the wedding, I was so happy to see her. She was just as beautiful as I had always remembered, in fact more so. I remembered how much fun you all had when you were younger. She would come to Pemberley with her brother, or sometimes with her father, to play games such as chess, billiards, and cards, as well as ride horses, and numerous other activities. She participated in so many things with the both of you. She was full of life, and I was fascinated by her. She seemed exciting and, well, frankly, ideal. I often wondered why her friendship with my brother seemed to wane. In all honesty, I secretively hoped that they would marry one day." Georgiana shyly glanced to gauge Richard's reaction to such a bold sentiment.

The colonel's feelings were impossible to make out, but he did not appear shocked or disturbed, so she persisted. "Last night during dinner—well even before in the vestibule—she was not the same Collette I remembered from my childhood. Even though I did not say anything at the time, I was stunned to find the name cards exchanged. Collette had been moved to sit where Elizabeth had placed Mrs. Caldecott, and Dr. Lowry had been moved to sit where you had once been assigned. I am puzzled by it. I wonder if Elizabeth had last minute reservations and decided to place Miss Caldecott next to my brother for old time's sake. Yet, that is the least of my concerns. As I have already stated, Collette is not the same as I recalled. So, my questions are these: Was I deceived in my opinion about her years ago? And, how close were she and my brother? What I mean to say is, quite bluntly, did he love her at one time, or did she love him?"

Richard's face remained impassive. He stared deeply into Georgiana's eyes before formulating his answer. "First, Georgie, I, for one, do not think your wonderings and questions to be inappropriate. In fact, the opposite is the case. You are showing wisdom in pondering thusly. How else can we make out other's characters if we are not able to analyze their actions and motives? We must use caution, of course, when we do this, or we could jump to conclusions which might prove to be false."

Georgiana piped up, "As Elizabeth did concerning Fitzwilliam's character when she first refused him?"

He chuckled. "Something like that. But remember, your brother admitted he had behaved poorly, and how else could she judge just how honourable a man he truly is? As I was saying, for you to realize that Miss Caldecott does not act the same gives credit to your insight and discernment. It is very astute of you to do so, and I might add that it is what I hope you will do when lines of young men come to call upon you. I want you to be careful. There are so many people who are deceitful and have ulterior motives for acting the way they do."

Wickham immediately tumbled to the forefront of Georgiana's mind.

Richard noticed that her face appeared glum, and he assumed it was from his mentioning the long lines of suitors. He smiled faintly at her. He hated what she would have to endure in finding someone to love her for her good self and not for her fortune of thirty thousand pounds. It was a tricky business.

"Um…let me now address your questions. From your childhood perspective, Georgie, I am sure Miss Caldecott was enchanting. I at one time found her to be so myself. However, I am afraid your assessment concerning her manner last night is the *true* Collette. I will tell you openly and not mince my words. She is a flirt of the worst kind. She is not an honourable woman."

"So, when a woman makes advances towards a man, it makes her dishonourable?"

Richard's brow creased. He did not want to give Georgiana the wrong idea about flirting. After all, some flirtations were required from the female sex to encourage some men to acquire the nerve to pursue certain ladies.

"Let me say this," the colonel replied cautiously, "flirtations are not all bad. There are times when they are even helpful in the cat and mouse game of finding a partner. However, they should be done in taste and never at the expense of embarrassing others by being too forward."

His cousin appeared not to understand, so he redoubled his efforts. "Georgiana, when you meet a young man who is unattached and you are attracted and interested in knowing more about him, you need to let him know by showing some sign of partiality. This should be done by the manner in which you smile at him and in the comments of interest that you offer. All of these things encourage a man, especially a shy suitor, to continue his advances. Flirtations at this stage should be minimal and subtle, if at all. When you are spoken for and you enter into courtship, then flirtations with your intended are quite proper and will enhance the relationship. But even then, one must use propriety. It is a balancing act. Some are more competent at it than others. Now as to Miss Caldecott's methods, she is extremely bold and puffed up in self-importance. She is not to be trusted, Georgie, and neither is her brother. The only respectable person in that household is their mother. She is a true lady."

"If this be the case, then why ever did my brother form an attachment with such a woman, and why did he let her act the way she did last night?"

Richard shook his head. He had no idea how to explain this one. Sighing, he made an attempt. "I think your brother was deceived in his opinion of Miss Caldecott in his youth. They were family friends, and she was not as forward as she is now. Yet, in hindsight, her nature is essentially the same. In spite of her impropriety, your brother is a gentleman, and being such, would never intentionally slight a woman, even were the lady not a principled one. That is all I feel I can offer you, Georgie. Do you feel you understand better?"

"I suppose a little better. I am so amazed at how people present false impressions. It makes the world a lot more difficult than it otherwise need be."

"Yes, it does. I want to say something more. Until we understand your brother's wishes, let us take our cue from him and tolerate Collette as best we can."

"Very well, I always tolerate everybody, Richard. Miss Bingley has given me much practice in this area."

He took delight in Georgiana's rejoinder. Smiling understandingly, he reached across the table for her hand. She at once responded to his intent by putting hers forward as well, allowing him to press it within his own. He then suggested, "Shall we go and play some duets together?'

"What, you are going to risk Elizabeth's knowing you play the pianoforte? Are you sure your ego could endure the blow if it were known?"

He hardily laughed as he stood and offered her his arm, which his cousin gladly accepted.

~*~

After the breakfast trays were carried away, Elizabeth decided to broach the topic of last night's fiasco. In a soft compliant voice, she began, "Fitzwilliam, I know you are anxious to go to your study to conduct some business, but I was wondering if you would now tell me why you wanted me to trust you last night. I presume it was you who changed the seating arrangements?"

His lips drew into a straight line, as he whirled his signet ring on his small finger.

Hesitantly, he replied, "Yes, yes, I did."

She waited, but soon became aware that he would not venture further. "I must admit, Fitzwilliam, I think it was inconsiderate of you to have done such a thing without consulting my feelings about the matter. Yet, you asked me to trust you, and I do. However, I will not do so blindly."

He breathed in deeply. He had fancied that she might have forgiven him with no questions asked, but he knew her too well and realized it was all wishful thinking on his part.

She waited.

"Ah...um...well...," Darcy nervously rubbed his fingers over his unshaven jaw. "Well...," he cleared his throat before proceeding. "Last night...when I came to your chamber door...if you recall...I had every intention of telling you about my interference. I admit that I took liberties in so doing, for you did not know all the particulars of why certain guests might be more comfortable seated elsewhere." Darcy hoped that this would suffice. He anxiously tried to determine her response. Yet, he could tell by the way Elizabeth contemplated what he had just told her that she, more than likely, would not be satisfied by such a paltry offering. He waited.

"My love," Elizabeth strived to state calmly. "I understand that you felt what you did was indeed for the best, but can you imagine my humiliation after having told Miss Caldecott that she was to sit by me, and then I am made to look like the fool when her seat is ... clear across the other end of the table?" She rushed through the last several words in obvious frustration.

Darcy felt hideous for the pain he had cost her. "Elizabeth, in all reality I did try to tell you. I do realize the embarrassing predicament in which I placed you. I was wholly inconsiderate and officious in making such a change without your concurrence. All I can offer is my heartfelt apology." He leaned forward, took her hand in his and said, "I am sorry, Lizzy." He then lifted her hand and kissed it.

"Very well, Fitzwilliam, I accept your apology, but I must say that Miss Caldecott is *not* a lady."

He met her eyes and truthfully stated, "I agree totally with your assessment."

She stared at him in amazement. "If this be the case, why do you put up with her?"

"She is the daughter of my mother's good friend, and, therefore, I tolerate her prattle. Much like you do with Mr. Collins."

Her brow furrowed. She understood that there was ridiculousness in so many people, if not all, that had to be taken with a grain of salt. Yet, to Elizabeth, the case of Miss Collette Caldecott did not apply here.

"Is there anything else, Elizabeth?"

Elizabeth searched his eyes and then shook her head. "I know you have much to do, I am satisfied, I suppose." She bit her lip and paused. "I...must admit...that I do not know the neighbourhood or have the understanding of the inhabitants' temperaments as you do, however, I thank you for answering my questions."

He nodded, leaned forward, kissed her forehead, and stood. "I will see you for luncheon then?"

"Yes, I am going to take a long soak in the bath. I will be down later."

With another nod of his head, Darcy turned to leave, and then halted to take one last glimpse at her fine eyes. "Lizzy," he softly stated, "thank you for your beautiful gift. I will think of it every Valentine's Day and cherish it for the rest of my life."

Meeting his gaze, she smiled warmly. "I love you, Fitzwilliam."

"I know," he replied with a tender smile.

Darcy turned to go a second time, and then spun around upon remembering that he wanted to inform his wife about his recollection. "Oh Lizzy, this morning while I lay in bed, I remembered more about the night of the accident. I remembered, of all things, your conversation with Georgiana concerning the privileges of women, and how Richard told Georgie that maybe someday, in the distant future, women would have the same liberties as men."

Her brows rose in surprise. "That is wonderful. Do you remember anything else?"

"No, only that small bit."

She watched him go and wondered if he would eventually remember everything. She then thought to herself, *I am not at all happy, my dear husband, with your explanations about last night. I realize you have a taciturn nature, and thus it is like pulling teeth in order to get you to elaborate on anything when you lack the will of doing so.*

Sighing with what she felt was a small degree of continued frustration, Elizabeth stood in anticipation of taking a long, hot soak to soothe away her reservations that roiled beneath the surface and calm mounting resentments that threatened a thunderous avalanche.

~*~

The first order of business that day was for Darcy to write and send an express to his attorney in London with the specific purpose of employing, as soon as possible, a French Lady's maid for Elizabeth. When he had completed that task, he went in search of Mrs. Reynolds.

The housekeeper smiled when seeing her master in better spirits and immediately asked what was needed. He explained that he would like to have a private conference with Sally before dismissing her. He then requested that Mrs. Reynolds be present during the conference to help the maid feel as comfortable as possible with such a delicate subject to discuss. In addition, Darcy informed his housekeeper that he wished Nancy to serve as both Mrs. Darcy's maid as well as his sister's until a new girl could be hired.

~*~

Elizabeth sat soaking in the tub when she was disturbed by a knock on the chamber door. Quickly leaving the dressing area to discover what was wanted, Sally opened the door to find Nancy standing in the hall. The one maid informed the other, "Sally, Mrs. Reynolds would like to see you right away. I have been sent to help with Mrs. Darcy for the time being."

Sally was surprised, but nodded and asked to have a moment before departing. She went straight to Elizabeth and in a small voice said, "Ma'am, I am wanted downstairs, and Nancy is here to help you."

Elizabeth looked at her maid with an odd expression on her face and asked, "Who wants you, Sally?"

"Mrs. Reynolds, ma'am."

"Oh, very well, I shall see you later. I wish to speak with you more concerning what we discussed yesterday evening."

Nodding her head in agreement, Sally curtseyed, and then departed.

~*~

Mrs. Reynolds waited for the maid in the entry hall and smiled at her as she informed her of the master's wish to speak with her.

Sally's heart beat wildly in fear. She worried that word had gotten out about what she had seen regarding the master and mistress or that her father had hit her and beat her mother.

Mr. Darcy stood as the ladies entered, and he gestured for Sally to be seated in a chair directly in front of his desk. Mrs. Reynolds stayed in the back of the room and sat on the chair near the door.

Darcy could see that the girl was nervous, and, for the first time, noticed how she appeared only a little older than Georgiana despite the heavy powder she wore on her face. He briefly considered the heavily applied cosmetic, but dismissed his reservation and began to proceed with the unpleasant business at hand.

"Sally, I wanted to speak with you this morning regarding some very disturbing rumours that have been circulating throughout the household staff. And there is no way of knowing how far they have gone. Do you know of what I am referring?"

Nervously, she nodded. Darcy continued, "Sally, do you know what the automatic consequence is for gossiping?"

"Yes, sir. Dismissal."

"Yes. Um…I have been informed that you have spoken to someone about Mrs. Darcy and me sharing a treasured moment." His face burned with embarrassment and so did the maid's. "Is this correct?" he enquired.

Tears came into view as she quietly replied, "Yes, sir."

Nodding, he thought for a minute and then added, "It is also said that you claim to have witnessed my wife and cousin, Colonel Fitzwilliam, in a compromising embrace and have said that you saw them involved in an inappropriate conversation."

Her eyes opened wide in shock. "No, sir. I never said such a thing to no one, and I never saw or heard such a thing either."

Darcy's brow creased. "You mean to say you never saw such a thing, and that it is a falsehood?"

"I don't be rightly knowing if it is a falsehood, but I never saw anything of the sort. I never said anything such as that to no one. I only mentioned to one person about witnessing you with the mistress, and I would like to say how badly I feel for it."

He was perplexed. Was she lying to him? "Sally, are you sure?"

"Yes, Mr. Darcy. I admitted to you what I'm guilty of, but I will not admit to that. I doubt it's true."

"What makes you think so?"

"Because," the maid stated out rightly, "Mrs. Darcy is in love with you."

"Yes, she is," the master replied," but that does not make such a horrid accusation go away. I will have to believe you if you say you did not initiate it. However, I still must dismiss you for your indiscretion in revealing what you witnessed in the privacy of my wife's chambers. Do you understand?"

Her lips twitched as she fought back her tears. "Yes, sir, I understand. I can't be trusted."

"Who did you tell, Sally? I also want to speak with them."

She became alarmed. "I would rather not say, sir."

He eyed her sceptically. How guilty was she? "Of course, I cannot force you to do so, but I think it would be best to make sure this person understands that their services are in jeopardy by repeating such things."

She instantly became frightened for Thomas and blurted out, "It was Tommy Wilkens, and Tommy won't be telling nobody. He is true to his word."

"I see...Sally, how on earth did you speak about such a thing to a member of the opposite sex?" Darcy immediately regretted asking such a question to this frightened girl as a vivid memory from his youth seared his own conscience. He saw the shame in her face and stood to come around the desk. He sat in the chair beside her and addressed her softly. "Sally, I am sorry for my censure. Please, if you can find it in your heart, disregard that inconsiderate remark. Who am I to judge?"

She shook her head and sniffled out her next words. "You are right in all your judgments. I know you are an honest and good man, and I am in the wrong."

He closed his eyes in despair. How could he have censured her so harshly over the very same thing he himself had done? His voice was filled with contrition, "No, Sally, I do try to be honest, but I have my failings as well. We all do. Please, forgive me."

She nodded and remained silent. "I have arranged for Mr. Manning to take you home, and I shall pay you a full month's salary. Even if I personally wanted to keep you on, Sally, I cannot. It would make an impression upon the minds of all the servants that there would be no consequences for insubordination. Do you understand?"

"Yes, sir."

"I am sorry, Sally."

"Mr. Darcy?"

"Yes?"

"May I go and speak with the mistress before I go?"

"I do not think that would be wise. I shall let her know your regret."

Her lips continued to tremble as she gave her thanks. She rose and left with Mrs. Reynolds in order to go and gather her few belongings and return to the home of her parents.

~*~

When Elizabeth arrived in the dining room, she was surprised to see only Georgiana within. "Georgie," she enquired, "have Fitzwilliam and Richard already eaten?"

The young lady's face appeared pensive as she cast her eyes down and bit first her lower lip and then the upper. Hesitantly, she made answer, "They have gone riding."

"Oh, I am glad of it," Elizabeth stated cheerfully while buttering a scone. "I know they both have been wanting to for some time."

Georgiana deliberated for a few moments before enlightening her beloved, new sister about who had accompanied her brother and cousin. "Lizzy?"

Yes, Georgie?"

Elizabeth did not wait for a reply, but took a bite of her bread and interjected, "Mmm...this jam is delicious. What kind is it?" She looked up at her sister and noted that something seemed amiss. "Georgie, what is wrong?"

"Oh, it is gooseberry, and Lizzy... Miss Caldecott and her father are riding with my brother and Richard."

Elizabeth's enjoyment of the rich jam and bread was suspended in mid-bite. She choked. Hurriedly, she reached for the water goblet to suppress her coughing, but it only became worse. Her face reddened as she strived to take in air.

Alarmed, Georgiana thumped upon her back. Elizabeth again tried to drink, but became frantic at the attempt, until her sister-in-law took the flat side of her fist and hit her squarely between her shoulders. Loud gasps of air let Georgiana know that Elizabeth was finally breathing again, but full of worry, she asked, "Lizzy, shall I call for Dr. Lowry?"

Still not able to speak as tears of distress trickled down the corner of her eyes, Elizabeth adamantly shook her head and finally croaked out, "**NO!**"

"Very well," Georgiana answered dubiously, "if you are sure."

She sat next to Elizabeth and then asked, "Would you like some wine?"

Elizabeth nodded. With eagerness, the young girl sprang to her feet and was at the sideboard filling a rather large tumbler with the rosy liquid.

"Here, this should take care of the scratchiness."

Elizabeth took the glass from her hand and gulped down every single drop. Gasping, she then stated, "I thank you, Georgie."

"Oh, you are most welcome. I can get you some fresh venison and some warm bread, if you wish."

"No," Elizabeth replied, "I think the wine will suffice for the time being."

"Very well," Georgiana stated and then folded her hands in her lap and looked pointedly at her sister-in-law.

Elizabeth was lost in a stupor, but then suddenly she stood and offered her hand to her sister-in-law. Georgiana also rose and placed her hand within Lizzy's.

"Georgie," she enquired, "shall we go to the music room?"

When they entered, Elizabeth petitioned, "I find I am in need of some solace. Would it be asking too much to request that you play something soothing for me while I rest here on the divan?"

Georgiana gladly stated, "No, not at all." Quickly shuffling through the music, she found the piece she thought might do the trick.

Elizabeth simmered inside as she tried to talk herself out of her obvious jealousy. Fitzwilliam should have come to inform her. Why ever did he not? This evidently was his mode of operation, and she resented it greatly. In an effort to stop the mounting anger, she decided to concentrate on the melody in hope of casting off thoughts of Collette's guile and her husband's lack of consideration.

After several minutes, a knock was heard from the opened door, and Elizabeth leaned forward to see what was wanted. Nancy, Georgiana's maid, stood patiently at the door. Elizabeth smiled and gestured with her hand for her to enter. Nancy walked forward, and gave a quick curtsey. "Ma'am, I was wondering if you will need my assistance earlier than mistress Georgiana or should I take care of her needs first?"

Elizabeth creased her brow. Something was amiss and she would not rest until she knew the particulars. As she calmly arose from her seat, she indicated for Nancy to follow her into her study. She shut the door and turned to the perplexed maid who seemed amazed at such a sojourn in response to her simple question.

"Nancy, why do you need to come and take care of me again? Is something the matter with Sally? Has she been called back home again?"

The maid's eyes grew large as she realized the mistress was ignorant about Sally's dismissal. Stuttering, she tried to answer, "I, I, thought…that …you, ah, th-that you knew."

"Knew what?"

"All I know, ma'am, is Sally is no longer employed here, and until another maid is obtained, I am to care for you and Miss Georgiana."

"Oh!" Mrs. Darcy exclaimed. "Who told you this?"

"Mrs. Reynolds said that it was the master's instructions, ma'am."

"I see. Thank you, Nancy. That will be all." Elizabeth dismissed the maid with a curt nod.

"But, ma'am, shall I help you first or Miss Georgiana?"

"Oh, Miss Georgiana only, I shall take care of myself this evening. Tomorrow, I will let you know how we will schedule for the future."

"Very well. Thank you, ma'am." The maid departed the room through the door that connected directly to the hall.

Elizabeth stood still with her arms folded over her chest. This was really too much. She could no longer stand by and let her husband continue in such a calloused manner. Abruptly, she turned and went back to the music room where Georgiana was still playing. Watching her sister-in-law, Elizabeth realized that she remained unaware that she had left with Nancy. Thus, she moved to her sister's side. Georgiana glanced up and immediately stopped playing.

"Elizabeth, are you unwell? You look so flushed. Are you sure you do not want the doctor?"

Inhaling deeply, she stated, "No, Georgie, but I thank you for your concern. I am going to my chamber now and may be indisposed for some time. I shall see you later this evening."

Georgiana nodded in concern, and then Elizabeth added, "Georgie, I have been made to understand that Nancy will be assisting both of us until a new maid can be found for me. Are you comfortable with this arrangement?"

"Yes, I am fine with the arrangement. You may be attended to whenever you choose. I can be last."

"Shall we discuss it tomorrow?"

"That will be agreeable."

Georgiana turned back to her music.

Elizabeth considered her course of action and began by climbing the stairs with purpose.

~*~

Some hours later, the gentlemen returned. Darcy was in a foul mood. During the morning, Collette had assaulted him constantly with suggestions and not so subtle hints, requesting to get to know Elizabeth better. She assured him that she only desired to help his wife feel more comfortable with the ladies of Derbyshire society. Repeatedly, Collette would extol his wife's virtues, saying she was charming, unaffected, and naïve, thus, Elizabeth required her guidance. She suggested a tea or maybe an afternoon gathering with Mrs. Chalmers's vast literary abilities and the topic of choice should be Lord Byron. She simply loved Byron herself and thought the ladies would find him a mouth-watering morsel for discussion.

Darcy sarcastically thought to himself that she and Lord Byron had much in common, yet in his opinion, Lord Byron was the nobler person. Every time Miss Caldecott implied such concern over Elizabeth's need of her assistance, he would tell her there was no reason to worry because Georgiana desired to have the pleasure of doing the honours. Collette laughed merrily at this response and reminded him that Georgiana was a child who had not yet come out herself, and thus, the responsibility should and would fall to her. Darcy could not comprehend the audacity of the woman, and he decided to give up and remain silent for the rest of their outing, speaking only on occasion to her father. Realizing his reticence, Collette then openly flirted with Richard as if Darcy were no longer there. Richard, as was his jovial self, seemed to take pleasure in her attentions.

Upon their return, the master went straight to his chamber and pulled the bell chord. Chaffin was there promptly and commenced to help his master discard his clothing while informing him that he had prepared a bath. Darcy was grateful and hurriedly bathed. He knew he needed to speak with Elizabeth about Sally and was quite concerned that Elizabeth would become upset concerning the tales her maid had spread.

After he dressed, he went to his wife's chamber, but she was not there. He then looked in the music room, but it was vacant. Her study was vacant as well. Walking the length of the hall, he entered the library hoping to find her there. Instead, Richard, Georgiana and Dr. Lowry were within. Darcy was a little taken aback on seeing the doctor and enquired, "Dr. Lowry, it is good to see you again. Has something in particular brought you to Pemberley?"

Georgiana piped up before Dr. Lowry had a chance to respond. "I sent for him, Brother, because Elizabeth choked on her food during luncheon. She told me that she was going to her chamber, and even though she insisted she was not in need of a doctor, I was worried and sent for him despite her refusal. But now, I cannot find her about. No one has seen her, and we have searched the house over."

Fear gripped Darcy's heart and alarm lined his features at this intelligence.

"When and where did you last see her, Georgie?"

"In the music room after luncheon. She told me she was going to her chamber. I felt she was not feeling well."

Darcy's expression darkened. "Did she seem anxious about anything? Of what were you speaking before she retired?"

"I think she might have been upset because she nearly choked to death on her bread with jam, and I believe that she was distressed more than she would say. She did mention one other thing before she went upstairs that I found a bit odd."

"What did she say? Georgiana, tell me at once?"

"Well," Georgiana tilted her head, "she was concerned about…"

"About what!"

Georgiana glanced away and then back to catch her brother's piercing gaze. "About whether I was comfortable with sharing Nancy as a maid."

Inhaling loudly, he rolled his eyes and asked bitterly, "Did you tell her about Nancy?"

"No," Georgiana stated resolutely as she looked into her brother's eyes. "I gathered that she already knew. Why?"

In great agitation, he began to give directives. "Richard, have the horses saddled. Dr. Lowry, if you could stay a while longer, I would appreciate it. I want to make sure my wife is not harmed. I fear she may have been out walking in the weather these last hours. She loves outdoor exercise and the elements seldom deter her."

Dr. Lowry nodded. "Let me come as well."

Inhaling in gratitude, Darcy nodded his head towards the physician and replied, "I thank you."

Georgiana ran to her brother's side and took hold of his arm as he strode down the hall in search of Mrs. Reynolds.

"Brother, have I done something wrong?"

He briefly stopped and looked into her eyes, "No, Georgie, I have. Now, go and wait. If Elizabeth returns, inform Mrs. Reynolds right away."

His sister nodded in understanding as he left to prepare for a prompt departure.

~*~

Elizabeth was determined to speak with her maid. As she set off from the courtyard, she saw a young man whom she asked for directions to Sally's home. The lad introduced himself as Joseph Wilkens, and he offered to take her there in the wagon, but she refused. She needed to release her pent up anger, and she knew walking would surely help. Besides, it was not too long of a walk. Oh, how she missed her rambles at Longbourn. She missed her father so much right now and even her mother…a thought that was truly daunting. She shook her head at the irony of her contemplations.

Slowly and steadily she trudged through the snow, and as Elizabeth trampled onward, her anger increased. She was furious…furious with her husband's intervention, yet *again*, and she would no longer stand by accepting superficial apologies on his part. How could he behave towards her in this unfeeling manner, as if she were not to be consulted and informed on decisions that were clearly in her area of domain—about things that affected her directly, such as her personal servant?

Was she to be seen but not heard? She realized now the foolishness she displayed in trusting him last night. What he had done both then and now was despicable. He appeared to care more for the feelings of Collette than for those of his own wife. Waves of nausea surged deep within her stomach as she remembered Collette's triumphant glare, which she had bestowed upon her, while sitting self-assuredly by her husband's side. Tears mingled with the anger. Contempt and insult caused a rush of colour to flow hotly upon her cold cheeks as she trudged ahead. She felt trifled with and used. Mr. Chaffin had better get accustomed to her occupying his masters' bed, because at this moment, she could not stand the thought of being in her husband's arms or in their shared bed ever again.

As she approached the dwelling, knowing that it must be Sally's house, she halted. What if the girl's father were in a temper? Thinking how she would respond if this were the case, she boldly walked up to the door and rapped hard. A small voice called out, asking who was there. Elizabeth recognized it to be Sally's and she cried, "Sally, it is I, Mrs. Darcy. Please, let me speak with you."

The door opened wide. Elizabeth found before her a swollen eyed, trembling young woman, who stepped aside to allow her access. "Sally whatever is the matter?"

"Oh, Mrs. Darcy, me dad has beat me mum and she has died!"

Elizabeth's mouth dropped open. "Oh Sally! Are you certain, quite certain?"

"Yes, it's been not yet an hour since she has gone."

Immediately, Elizabeth drew Sally to her. The maid sobbed uncontrollably as she spoke in words that were unintelligible.

"Shh…Sally, she no longer suffers or feels any pain."

"I know that," she sniffled, "but I cannot help it all the same."

"Yes, that is all right. Cry all you like. I am here and will not leave you."

"Oh, no, but you must go, ma'am. Me dad will not like me leaving now. He won't like finding you here either."

Mrs. Darcy thought warily to herself that her husband would not like it either, but the way she felt at this moment, she was ready to take on the whole world. Elizabeth stood there and gently rocked back and forth while rubbing Sally's back, striving to soothe the young woman. As she continued to embrace her, the young girl cried until the tears would no longer come.

"Sally, I know you feel that you cannot leave your father, but he will have to suffer the consequences of his own sins. However, you no longer need to suffer with him."

"But the master said he cannot let me stay because of the bad example it will be to the others."

Elizabeth silently bristled. *How dare that man? He may be the Master of Pemberley, but he cannot treat people who make innocent mistakes with such callousness.* Still holding her close, Elizabeth asserted, "Then you shall be my personal guest, until we can find someplace suitable for you. May I see your mother?"

Sally looked up into the mistress' eyes. They were kind and caring eyes. She nodded timidly and led the way to the dismal room, a room which reeked of stale liquor.

Standing beside the bed, Elizabeth looked upon the battered woman. Elizabeth winced and shook her head at the pitiful sight before her. The woman had the appearance of someone quite old. *What a dreadful life she must have lived.* Taking the woman's hand into her own, she first felt her forehead and then checked her pulse, reassuring herself that she was indeed dead.

Turning to Sally, she gently asked, "Sally, may I cover her now?"

Slowly, the girl nodded, but quickly bent low to bestow one last kiss upon her mother's strange, cool, and leathery brow. As she did so, Sally whispered softly, "I love ye, Mum." Tears spilling from her eyes, the daughter then stood and stepped back.

Raising the quilt high, Elizabeth pulled it over the woman's disfigured face and smoothed it out lovingly.

"Sally, we must leave quickly. Please gather whatever you need, and let us be off."

They had just walked into the adjoining room when the door blew open, bringing in a rush of frigid air and a man who appeared to be intoxicated. Elizabeth immediately understood that the man must be Sally's father. Both women stood, unmoving and quite petrified.

A small stout man with a hardened expression asked roughly, "What is going on here?"

Visibly shaken, Elisabeth stepped forward and offered her hand, and, with all the strength she could muster, looked directly in his eyes as she spoke. "I am Mrs. Darcy, and I have come to ask Sally to return home with me. I assume you are her father. She is a most helpful young lady, and I greatly care for her welfare."

He sneered, "Ah, to be noticed by the *highness* herself!"

Elizabeth directed Sally in a serious, low tone to get her things. Abruptly, her father bolted the door and hissed, "She won't be going nowheres, and neither will *you.*"

Sally pleaded, "Dad, mum is dead. I'll stay. Please, just please let Mrs. Darcy leave. She has been very kind."

Breathing heavily, he approached Elizabeth and put his face against hers. "You rich are all the same, thinking you can have what ye want. Well, not this time."

Elizabeth could feel the heat of his rank breath against her neck, and the filthiness of his appearance disgusted her.

Her pulsed raced. What was to be done? This man was truly mad. Attempting to sound brave, she stated, "My husband will be expecting us shortly. He will come for us if we are not home soon." She knew this was not true. She foolishly told no one of her intention to visit Sally. She knew that her absence would eventually bring about a search, but unless the young lad whom she had asked for directions was made aware of the hunt, all hope of discovery was lost.

He laughed violently. "Your husband doesn't know you are here. There is no team or horse. Besides, what master would let the mistress walk all this way by herself? You are a choice one—that ye are."

Coming forward, Sally attempted to push her father away from the mistress, but he caught hold of her arm instead. "Why you filthy, little slut!" he roared.

He struck her hard and then raised his hand to deliver another blow. Elizabeth stepped in-between them and intercepted his arm in an effort to allow the young girl an escape. Enraged now, he pushed Sally down to the floor while raising his free arm to backhand Mrs. Darcy. With great force, he hit her squarely on her nose and cheek. Dazed, she stumbled backward a few steps and slumped to the floor. A streak of blood trickled down her face and dripped onto the floorboards.

~*~

Darcy and Colonel Fitzwilliam, riding their mounts hard were nearing Sally's house. After learning from the younger Wilkens boy that he had given Mrs. Darcy directions to the maid's home, they had driven the horses furiously across the fields and through the woods. Dr. Lowry and Thomas Wilkens followed more slowly in the doctor's carriage.

The snow sprayed upward from the horses' hooves as they came to a skidding halt. Darcy dismounted his horse and in an instant was at the door. He began to lift the handle. It would not budge. Richard now stood by his side as Darcy pounded the door with his fists, demanding to be allowed entrance.

Sally called out to them as she quickly arose to unfasten the latch. Her father stopped her, pulling her by her hair and angrily slinging her clear across the room, her body slamming into the table. He then moved to retrieve his gun from above the chimney-piece.

Mary Sherwood

In unison, Darcy and Richard thrust against the door with their shoulders, and after several attempts, were able to break it wide open as they burst through. Darcy's attention was instantly drawn to his wife's body, slumped on the floor, her face covered in blood. In wrath, he moved forward, reaching to take hold of the worthless man's throat, but the feel of hard, cold metal stopped him. Sally's father had shoved the barrel of his gun into the master's gut.

~*~

Chapter Thirteen

Suspicion and Grief

Darcy's anxiety escalated. His breathing turned erratic and shallow. Not only was the barrel of a rifle pressed hard into his abdomen, but his wife lay on the floor, unconscious, her face swollen and bloodied. He was furious that a man would mistreat any woman, but to strike his Elizabeth was unimaginable.

"Things look a lot different at the end of a barrel, don't they, Mr. Darcy?" With a leering eye, Sally's father clearly revelled in his power to humiliate the Master of Pemberley.

Darcy stood motionless, his arms outstretched at his side, suspended in mid-air with his palms open. He looked upon the contemptuous man with abhorrence, and agonized over how, with each passing second, he would ensure everyone's safety. From the corner of his eye he saw Sally rise to her feet and advance quietly towards the fire. He instantly realized his cousin had silently gestured to the girl, understanding that she was going to try to prevent her father from doing any further evil.

Elizabeth began to stir, her soft moans discerned by all. Darcy glanced over to her and felt a moment of relief knowing she was alive. Realizing the need to keep the lunatic's attention directed on him lest the man discover his daughter's ruse, Darcy attempted to engage him in conversation.

"I am not sure what has happened here," Darcy said cautiously. "But, would you care to enlighten me as to how my wife came to be hurt?"

The weapon was shoved harder against Darcy's flesh, and he winced from the sudden spasm of pain.

"You don't need to be askin' no questions or worryin' about nothin'. Look who's havin' the power now, eh, Mr. Darcy?"

Fully alert now, Elizabeth's eyes widened in shock as she beheld the gun aimed at her husband. She quickly perceived Richard as he gave her a knowing look while he pressed his forefinger against his lips, signalling her to remain silent. While Sally nervously crept near her father, the others held their breaths. She hefted a large cast iron skillet and, without hesitation, she crashed the skillet down upon her father's skull with all of her might. The colonel lunged to grab the barrel of the gun and pull it aside as Darcy angrily seized the falling man by the lapels of his coat.

Colonel Fitzwilliam laid the gun down and placed a firm grip upon his cousin's arm, attempting to curb his fury. In a hushed voice, he advised, "Darcy, it would be akin to beating a dead horse."

Mary Sherwood

Returning to his senses, Darcy immediately let the brute slip to the floor. He then looked towards his wife. Sally, who was kneeling at the mistress' side, arose in search of a wet rag as Colonel Fitzwilliam went into the other room.

Darcy's eyes locked with Elizabeth's. Each stared at the other for several seconds, and, in those few moments, he clearly read his wife's animosity towards himself. He walked over and knelt down beside her, gently cupping her chin in his hand to better inspect the effect of the debilitating blow she had received. His fingers softly brushed over her face as Elizabeth closed her eyes and swiftly turned her head to the side, freeing her chin from her husband's hold. Darcy whispered to her, "Lizzy, will you not even look at me?" Her eyes remained clenched as she kept her head averted.

Only a moment before, her heart had beat wildly in fear for her husband's life, but now, all of her resentment had returned in full force, and she could no longer tolerate his comforting condolences.

Sally returned with a wet cloth and began washing her mistress' face. Darcy, still crouching at Elizabeth's side, watched as the former maid's gentle hands wiped the blood away. He was at a loss to know what to do. Suddenly, he was roused from his dejected thoughts when the doctor and Thomas Wilkens walked into the cold room.

Dr. Lowry joined Sally and Darcy by Elizabeth's side and enquired, "Mrs. Darcy, may I inspect your face?" She nodded weakly, and he immediately removed his gloves and took hold of her chin in the same manner that Darcy had earlier, but this time, Elizabeth allowed the inspection, an inspection which moments before she had denied her husband.

Darcy was thankful for the opportunity afforded to him by Dr. Lowry's examination. He was now able to see the exact extent of the harm done. He observed the doctor's fingers probing her features as gently as possible. Elizabeth gasped and flinched when he pressed upon the bridge of her nose, and with her shrinking, Darcy's chest tightened in anger tinged with remorse. He was enraged at Sally's father, to be sure, and irritated at Collette's insistence on their riding together that afternoon, but he reserved his harshest censure for himself at allowing it all to happen in the first place.

Richard leaned against the doorframe of the adjoining room and looked over to where they were all huddled together. He cleared his throat in an effort to gain his cousin's attention. As Darcy's eyes met his, he motioned with a jerk of his head for his cousin to join him. Darcy hesitated briefly, but then arose and walked to the colonel, leaving Dr. Lowry to continue his examination.

Looking gravely into his cousin's eyes, Colonel Fitzwilliam pointed over his shoulder with his thumb as he softly stated, "Cousin, you had better come in here with me."

The men entered the room. Richard drew back the covers, revealing Sally's dead mother. Darcy grimaced with an audible intake of air. Holding the blanket up, the colonel shook his head slowly as they gazed upon the battered corpse. "It looks as though the poor woman suffered a great deal before she passed."

Darcy could not believe his eyes. It was utterly unfathomable that a man could do such a thing to his wife.

The colonel asked as he lowered the covering, "What do you want us to do with him? He will most likely be unconscious for some time with that nasty blow from the skillet. That is, if he is not dead already."

Running his hand through his hair, Darcy stared at the floor, contemplating what was to be done. "I will go back with the women and Dr. Lowry. Could you and Thomas stay here and stand guard over him, until I send someone to relieve you? I shall send Mr. Sheldon to Lambton to obtain the law." Now, looking up and over at the corpse lying beneath the blanket, he exclaimed, "The law may not charge him for the beating of his own wife, but he will surely be charged with the beating of mine!"

"Yes," his cousin replied, "I will stay. Is there anything else you need?"

Shaking his head wearily, Darcy drew in a slow breath "No. I thank you, Richard."

Colonel Fitzwilliam perceived the strain on his cousin's face and he silently wondered how something like this could come about. What in Heaven's name was Elizabeth doing here? Yet, he decided that now was not the time to enquire. Witnessing Darcy's grief made him fully aware that there had to be some grand misunderstanding between Elizabeth and his cousin.

They returned to find Dr. Lowry examining Sally. And while the daughter was distracted with the doctor's attentions, Thomas Wilkens was bent low over her father, checking his pulse. The young man arose and walked over to the men and said, "He's still breathing."

Darcy nodded and then informed Thomas that Sally's mother, in the other room, was not. She was, in fact, dead. He asked the young man to stay with Colonel Fitzwilliam, until he could send someone in their stead.

Thomas nodded in agreement, and then quickly asked, "Mr. Darcy, sir, I want to know where Sally shall be going. I wish to come and speak with her."

Understanding dawned in Darcy's mind. This lad was in love with the girl. "She shall come to Pemberley to stay for awhile. You may call in the morning after breakfast."

"Thank you, sir."

Dr. Lowry then joined their circle and pointed to Sally while speaking to no one in particular. "I see no major damage done to the young woman. She received a large bruise when she was thrown against the table, but no bones appear to be broken." The doctor then looked directly at Darcy. "As for Mrs. Darcy, she has sustained a rather nasty blow to her nose and cheekbone. I do not feel that her nose is broken, but it will swell for some time and be extremely tender. I have compressed snow in some handkerchiefs that she shall need to hold upon her face, on and off, for the remainder of the day. It will help to numb the pain and relieve the inflammation.

Briefly, Darcy closed his eyes in pain on hearing the doctor's appraisal. "Dr. Lowry, Colonel Fitzwilliam will show you into the other room for a moment, and then I feel we must take the women back to the warmth of the house."

While the doctor went with the colonel and Thomas Wilkens joined them, Darcy walked over to Sally and Elizabeth. "Come, let us go to the carriage and get you both to the warmth of the house." Sally grabbed her threadbare shawl without saying a word. Darcy offered his hand to his wife, but she shook her head and declined to accept his support. She asked Sally if she desired to take anything with her besides her bag, which was still packed. The maid went to a rack on the wall and took down a worn, yet beautiful, quilt. Elizabeth assumed her mother had made it.

When the men came out of the room, Dr. Lowry's eyes met Darcy's, conveying his utter disgust with that to which he had been made privy.

Darcy helped Sally into the carriage, and then turned to Elizabeth. She bit her lip and deliberated but went forward unassisted. He felt a surge of wretchedness flow through his body at his wife's rebuke. Forlorn, he climbed in and sat beside the doctor for their return to Pemberley House.

As the carriage lurched forward, Sally looked back and met Tommy's eyes. She looked longingly at him as they pulled away. Thomas's trance was broken when Colonel Fitzwilliam suggested that, in order to ensure their own safety, they must tie up Sally's father until the magistrate arrived.

~*~

Georgiana was waiting at the east entrance when the party returned. She gasped aloud when catching sight of her sister-in-law's swollen face. "Oh, Elizabeth!"

Striving to appear brave, Elizabeth presented a tentative smile and jokingly replied, "Now, Georgie, it looks much worse than it is, really."

As Miss Darcy opened her mouth to ask how it happened, she caught her brother's cautious look and remained silent. "Georgie, ask Mrs. Reynolds ...um, uh."

His sister stared at him in confusion, and then he turned to Elizabeth, and, showing her the respect she was due as Mistress of Pemberley, requested her instruction. "Mrs. Darcy, where would you wish Sally to be situated for her stay?"

She spoke without glancing at her husband. "Georgie, would you please have Mrs. Reynolds prepare a room on the ground storey away from the servants' quarters for Sally."

Timidly, Georgiana nodded and went in search of the housekeeper.

"Elizabeth, may I speak with you alone?"

She bit her lower lip and kept her eyes fixed on a vase that adorned a foyer table. "I would like to speak with Sally first, if you do not mind. You may speak with me afterwards. Besides, you should offer Dr. Lowry a drink when he returns. I am sure he would appreciate something warm."

Darcy appeared pensive, but slowly nodded his head and answered, "Very well." He watched her walk off with the maid. He shook his head, and sighed heavily. There was nothing to do but wait for Dr. Lowry to enter. The physician was still speaking with Mr. Sheldon and Mr. Manning, before they departed for Lambton to acquire the services of the magistrate.

When the doctor entered, Darcy enquired if he would care for a brandy or maybe port. Dr. Lowry gratefully accepted and they went to his study. They briefly discussed the possibility of an inquest concerning the unfortunate incident and agreed that Elizabeth would more than likely be questioned. The doctor made his farewell and promised to come back to check on Mrs. Darcy in the morning. He instructed, however, to send for him if his services were needed sooner. Darcy sincerely thanked him for his assistance.

After seeing the doctor to the door, the master went in search of his sister. Georgiana was in the library attempting to concentrate on a newspaper article with little satisfaction. She arose anxiously when her brother appeared. "Oh, Fitzwilliam, I am so glad that you have taken pity on me and will no longer keep me in suspense. How in the world did Elizabeth receive such an injury?"

Darcy grimaced, and for a split second, closed his eyes. He hated to relate such a sordid tale to his sister, especially one due to his stupidity, but his sister was owed an answer to her enquiry.

Steadying himself, he replied, "She went to see her former maid at her home. Sally's father is a cruel being. It appears that he has beaten his wife to death. He…" Darcy closed his eyes tightly and Georgiana detected the pain in his voice when he stated, "He forcefully struck Elizabeth as she endeavoured to help Sally. At least that is what I assume happened, since I do not have all the details."

"Oh, Brother, that is horrible! Poor Sally, and poor Elizabeth. Is Elizabeth going to be well?"

"Yes, Dr. Lowry believes she will heal with the passage of time. Earlier, I had dismissed Sally, as you are aware but unfortunately, neglected to inform Elizabeth of my decision. She must have found out from Nancy. As I was not the one to inform her of this situation, she does not yet understand the reasons and is distraught, once again, with my interference."

Georgiana softly enquired, "Once again?"

Sighing loudly, he exclaimed, "Yes! Last night, without first speaking to her, I changed the name cards at dinner. Did Elizabeth not mention this to you?"

"Oh, Brother, you did not!"

"Yes, Georgie, I am afraid I did. I had planned to tell her before the guests arrived, but I never found the opportunity to do so. She says that she has forgiven me for that offence, but I am afraid not informing her about Sally has not set well with her. It was abominably rude of me to do so without first speaking with her. Frankly, Georgie, I am not used to having to inform another of my intentions, except perhaps, when I confer with Richard about your welfare. I am in gross error concerning Elizabeth's feelings, and I am not sure she will forgive me so willingly this time." He slumped down in the chair and slid his fingers through his hair.

Georgiana licked her lips. She felt sorry for him and wanted to comfort him, but she realized he was correct in his self- analysis. In fact, she knew exactly how Elizabeth felt. Even though she understood that she had the best of brothers, she was keenly aware of how he was accustomed to orchestrating everything for almost everyone, especially for her, without consulting her feelings on the matter beforehand. Yet, she trusted his judgment and was seldom troubled by it. Unperturbed, that is, apart from one instance, and that was when he had left her in the guardianship of Mrs. Younge.

~*~

Sally followed Mrs. Darcy to her study and, feeling that she could now speak freely by closing the door behind them, Elizabeth asked her former maid how she had come to be dismissed. After providing all the particulars of her discharge, Sally enquired whether Elizabeth had repeated the information she had shared with her to the master. Looking directly into the younger woman's eyes, Elizabeth informed her that she had not told a soul. Sally then assumed that the person eavesdropping on her and Thomas Wilkens's exchange must have revealed their conversation since Mr. Darcy had already known about her unconscionable act. The maid considered telling Mrs. Darcy about the *other* rumour she was accused of spreading, but just then Mrs. Reynolds knocked on the door to inform the mistress that a room had been prepared in the north wing, and therefore, she thought the better of it, deciding it best to say no more.

For the time being, Elizabeth similarly, felt it wise to let the matter rest. Consequently, she thanked the housekeeper, and then asked her to escort Sally to her chamber.

After their departure, Elizabeth closed her eyes and rested her elbows upon her desk, cradling her head in her hands. For some time, she sat there, silently contemplating the deplorable difficulty she found herself to be in until the throbbing of her face became intense. Hence, she decided to go upstairs to rest when a missive on the salver caught her attention. It was another letter from Lydia. Why would her sister write again so soon? Too weary to discover the reason, she placed the letter in the drawer with her ledgers, determined to attend to it on the morrow.

In exhaustion, Elizabeth made her way to her chamber and upon gazing at her reflection in the mirror, she immediately decided to undress and prepare for bed. Her face was swollen, and she presently did not feel like socializing. Hurriedly, she removed the pins from her hair and brushed and braided it. Next, she took off her dress and stockings. It was at this juncture that Elizabeth remembered that the particular corset she wore fastened from the back and, therefore, she would have to sleep in it. Walking into her dressing area to get a nightdress, her mind preoccupied with all that had taken place, she startled at finding her husband advancing towards her.

Darcy noticed her jerk in surprise. Quickly, he bowed and made an apology. "Lizzy, I did not mean to frighten you. I am sorry."

Elizabeth inhaled and continued with the task of getting a gown. She walked back to her chamber and then stopped to pull the gown over her head. Darcy rushed forward to assist her and became aware that she was still wearing her corset. "Lizzy, let me help you take this off." He had already begun untying the laces when she pulled away from him.

"I thank you all the same, but I wish to sleep in it."

"Elizabeth, do be reasonable. You will be more comfortable in just your gown."

Sparks flew from her eyes and bitterness peppered her voice. "I suppose you know everything that I *do* and *do not* need. In fact, you know what is best for everyone." She defiantly pulled the gown over her head and then went to clean her teeth.

Darcy slumped to the bed and sat miserably while he waited for her to return.

She approached the bed and began to search for the stool. He realized immediately what she was doing, and he too scrutinized the floor to find it. Yet it was not there. Rapidly, he rolled over to the other side of the bed to look as well. They looked at each other when both realized the stool was not to be had. Darcy got up off the bed and went down on his hands and knees to see if it somehow had been pushed underneath. He called out to his wife while crouched upon the floor, "It is not here either, Lizzy."

She tightened her lips, then contemplated making a full run and diving on top of the bed, but that would not do. She might injure her nose anew and cause her face to swell all the more.

Darcy stood and observed his wife gripping the counterpane tightly, using it as if it were a rope to give her the needed leverage to pull herself onto the bed, yet the coverlet slipped towards her. He suppressed a grin. Oh, how he adored her independent spirit.

After one more attempt, almost managing to gain access to the tall furnishing, Darcy quickly came around, grabbed her by her hip and upper legs, and deposited her gently on top of the mattress. His artless assistance seemed to smooth her ruffled feathers to some degree. She held her chin high and averted her vision before thanking her husband in a formal tone.

"I am glad to be of service to you," he rejoined while looking intently upon her proud expression. "And I shall find out what has happened to the stool. I take it you are retiring for the night?"

"Yes, I am."

Darcy paused, fidgeting with his ring, considering what to say or do next, when he proposed suddenly, "I will go and bring some snow and ready it for you. Dr. Lowry wants you to hold it in place for as long as you can."

"Yes, I know."

"I shall be back then."

Elizabeth called out to him in his leaving, "I am sure Nancy or some other servant could do it. So, please, do not trouble yourself. Send someone else."

With his hand on the doorknob, Darcy slowly turned around, and looking at his wife forlornly, he lovingly stated, "You are my wife. I wish to assist you. It is no trouble at all." He strode resolutely out of the room.

Elizabeth lifted the counterpane wearily and crawled beneath it. The bed felt wonderful. She had always loved to climb into bed. Ever since she had been a little girl, the sensation of being tucked in, ensconced within the covers, brought instant feelings of comfort and security. Pondering her husband's concern towards her wellbeing made her realize that she was not as angry with him as she had been in the carriage. However, Elizabeth knew that her anger was still simmering beneath the surface and things would have to change drastically for it to disappear. Fitzwilliam could not continue to treat her as if she were a child. Thus, for the time being, she no longer desired him in her bed. Would he respect her wishes?

She knew he must be upset with her for going to see Sally without informing anyone. It was a valid point, and she could understand it, especially considering what had happened: how her effrontery almost cost them all dearly. She closed her eyes in shame. These self-defeating recriminations over such improper conduct became too much for her, and she looked to the night table for something to read to help alleviate her guilty conscience.

As she reached for a book, she noticed that the Valentine token from her husband rested on its cover. She started to reach for it, but then thought again. She did not wish to consider any terms of endearment from him right now. She loved what he had written, but, until his actions conformed to his words, his poetic composition would remain just that, *mere words*.

Lying back upon her pillow, she contemplated Sally's predicament and wondered who had told Fitzwilliam that Sally had been gossiping. She knew there was no hope in keeping her on. He would never agree to such a thing because a worthy example had to be maintained at all times for the servants, or mayhem would reign. She knew this line of reasoning to be sound. However, if her husband came to understand that Sally had already confessed the misdeed to her in advance, then maybe his righteous anger could be abated.

Darcy opened her chamber door from the hall and carried the chilly bundle to her. He desired to lie by her side and place it upon her cheek himself, but he knew she would not allow it. Therefore, he handed it to her without ceremony. She whispered her gratitude and said no more.

Considering what to do next, Darcy stood there staring at his wife while involuntarily twisting the cuff of his shirtsleeve. Her eyes were closed or she would have witnessed the suffering in his deliberation. Shrugging his shoulders slightly, he quietly, yet firmly asked, "Lizzy, may I speak with you now or do you wish to rest some and converse with me later?"

She opened her eyes and looked at him. "You may speak now, if you so desire. I will listen. However, I warn you, Fitzwilliam, I only desire whole truths and nothing less from now on."

His brow knitted. What did she mean by that comment? He had always told her the truth. He shook his head and decided to leave that remark for another time.

"Elizabeth, I would like you to explain what happened at Sally's parents' home. I am not sure how all of this came about."

Somehow, she was surprised with the request. She thought he would start out with an apology.

Still holding the cold compress to her face, she began evenly. "It is simple enough, Fitzwilliam, I was furious that you had dismissed Sally without informing me of your intentions and without even considering my wishes. I am so angry with you right now, Fitzwilliam, that I could, well, let us just say I am extremely angry." She stopped and took a deep breath.

He turned and walked over to the window with his back to her.

Rolling her eyes at his customary retreat, she continued in a less frustrated tone. "I had found out from Nancy that my maid had been dismissed, and I had no idea why." She paused again because she knew that what she had just said was not quite true. Yet, she decided she would discuss that part later on. "I felt the need to speak with Sally and make sure that everything was well with her. I chose to walk because I needed to clear my mind of the resentment I was feeling!" She said the last few words hotly. Once again, she breathed deeply in an effort to gain composure. "I am sorry."

He turned about to look at her and asked, "Pray, whatever for?"

"I am sorry for losing my temper while speaking with you just now. Fitzwilliam, I do not know if you realize this yet, but when I become frustrated, I can, well, that is to say—I can become vehement with my speech."

His eyes twinkled in delight. Oh, how he wanted to kiss her right there and then. How could she forget that he knew her fervent nature all too well? Instead of a kiss testifying to the passion he felt for her at this moment, a small smile was all the demonstration he could offer. "Please, Lizzy, continue."

She peered over at him and sighed. Again, she inhaled. "I found Sally at home alone, crying. She told me straightaway that her mother had passed on. She wept, and I felt helpless not knowing what to do for her. So, I just held her. After she calmed some, she took me to see her mother... Oh, Fitzwilliam, it was horrible."

He crossed the room and sat on the bed next to her. "I know, Lizzy, I saw her myself."

She nodded, and then said, "I covered her face after Sally kissed her goodbye. I felt ill for the both of them, and I was anxious to leave. I knew if her father were to come home, he would most likely not let her depart. I could not allow her to stay there alone with him any longer."

"You did the right thing, Elizabeth."

She gazed into his eyes. *Did he really think so*? "You are not angry with me for going?"

As he sat by her side, he bent his head low and ran his hand through his hair. Then, twisting his ring as he spoke, he acknowledged, "How can I be angry with you? I grant you, Elizabeth, that going to Sally's alone, was a foolish decision on your part, but taking into consideration that it was the natural consequence of my own imprudent decision, it significantly lessens the thoughtlessness of yours. Therefore, no, I am not angry with you in the least, only at myself for not having involved you in making the decision to dismiss your maid. If I had discussed it with you in the first place, this whole sorry business could have been avoided."

"You think you should have spoken with me first?"

"Utterly and completely."

"Oh, Fitzwilliam, I am surprised to hear you say so. I mean, I did not think... I mean..."

"Go on, Lizzy, you can say it. You think I am just as proud and arrogant as you had thought me in the past."

Her eyes widened. She bit her lip and smiled impishly. "Well, I suppose I do, sometimes." She quickly bit her lip again, wondering if he would take refuge at the windowpane once more.

He narrowed his eyes upon her. Immediately, she became uneasy and wished she had not surrendered her opinion so readily. Perhaps he was more upset than he had admitted?

Soberly, Darcy stated, "Well, you still have not told me why he struck you."

"Oh, that. He hit Sally when I tried to intervene on her behalf. To try and stop him, I grabbed his arm as he attempted to strike her again. As a result, his anger turned towards me."

"Oh, Elizabeth, I feel wretched that I have allowed this to happen. I will not even ask for forgiveness. I do not deserve any."

She was dumbfounded. He was indeed sorry, but he did not entreat her pardon as he had in the past. She was not sure what to make of it.

"Fitzwilliam, there is one more thing I need to tell you." He looked at her expectantly. "Sally told me last night about having seen us kiss. I had noticed a bruise on her face and she was reluctant to tell me how she had received it. She finally confided that her father had, indeed, hit her, and shortly thereafter, she acknowledged having seen our intimate exchange. She confessed that she left the room as soon as she overcame her shock. I had not told you because I had promised her I would tell no one. Yet, I had planned to speak with her today. I wished to get her expressed permission to inform you of her father's cruelty, as well as her approval to let you know what she had confided in me."

Once more, Darcy shut his eyes and shook his head. Elizabeth had already known about Sally's admission, and he had mistakenly assumed that she would have been mortified by such a revelation. "Did she tell you to whom she had shared this information?"

"No. She did not mention a name, but said only that she had told a trusted friend."

Darcy eyed his wife closely. "Elizabeth, did Sally say if she saw anything else?"

"No, she did not. Why, is there something else?"

He gazed deeply into her eyes for a moment and then cast a vacant look to the floor. "Well, nothing of consequence."

"Fitzwilliam, who told you that Sally had been tattling?"

"Mrs. Reynolds."

"Who told her?"

Darcy realized that he did not know that particular detail, except that it was another servant. "I am not sure who told her, but she has dismissed another individual who was involved."

"She came to you, instead of me?"

"Yes, I suppose she is used to informing me of such things. She could not dismiss Sally, since she was now your Lady's maid and requested my intervention."

Elizabeth was hurt more than ever now. "Really, Fitzwilliam, I am appalled that I was not informed, and I need time to think this through. You treat me like a child, making decisions for me as if I were Georgiana! In fact, she is nearly seventeen, yet she may not even be allowed to dance at her aunt's ball."

This was too much. Darcy stood erect. "Lizzy, you are tired. I will go and let you rest."

"No, you will not go! You wanted to speak with me, and we will finish this conversation."

"No, I refuse to talk with you when you will not be reasonable."

"I am not the one who is unreasonable. Richard, I am sure, would let her dance, but you must control everything for everyone! He is gentle and caring."

Heated resentment rolled off Darcy's tongue. "Elizabeth, what is the better alternative? Raise her to scamper about the countryside and attend assemblies and balls at the age of thirteen or fourteen!"

She gasped.

Immediately Darcy regretted his unbridled words. How in the world could he have just said such a thing? "Elizabeth, I am not referring to you."

Contemptuously, she replied, "Why of course you are not. I am sure you only meant Kitty and Lydia. The rest of the Bennet girls never *scampered* about the countryside. You are right, Fitzwilliam, you should go. I do need my rest. In fact, I need to sleep soundly and not be disturbed for the entire night."

He looked at her with a wounded expression. "Very well, have it your way, Elizabeth." He shook his head and sneered as he declared, "I will not disturb your slumber or your *wilful* opinions."

He walked quickly across the room and through the dressing chambers. Pausing for a moment, he then walked over to the window in his own chamber and stretched one arm upward, the other poised on his hip as he rested the weight of his body against the frame.

Sulkily, he thought of his wife's high opinion of his cousin. She thought Richard was not as severe and, therefore, more agreeable! *Perhaps that is why she smiles at him so often?* He shook his head and sought to stop the venomous thoughts from pouring forth. He was unsuccessful, and his doubts were given free rein to roam where they would. His wife cared deeply for his cousin, of that he was certain. A moment ago, did she not admit that very thing?

Leaning his forehead upon his outstretched arm, his face contorted in anguish. He feared in his gut that there must be some truth to the purported rumour. Someone must have witnessed Elizabeth and Richard in a compromising embrace and heard an inappropriate conversation. What private words did his wife and cousin share, which could lead to an embrace, or did the embrace lead to tender words?

Looking out into the darkness, he realized he must go down to speak with his steward and overseer. They would be back soon and waiting for him. He felt miserable. Instead of changing his clothing for supper and going downstairs, he walked over to the bed and flung himself upon it. He lay outstretched across the bed, feeling completely confounded. Covering his face with his hands, a solitary tear of frustration escaped and wet his temple. Additional tears soon welled up in his eyes, threatening to spill over. With the palms of his hands, he swabbed at his eyes in an attempt to make them cease. He lay there berating himself for his unintentional remark relating to his wife's liberal upbringing. While running his hand through his hair, he heard the servant's door open into his dressing area. He knew Chaffin would soon enter, and he decided he must make himself arise. However, it was too late. Chaffin dutifully crossed the room with his vision directed on the floor before Darcy had a chance to will himself off the bed. It was the valet's customary habit each evening to place a fresh nightshirt upon the bed for his master, and upon seeing Mr. Darcy spread atop the covers, he quickly bowed and said, "Excuse me, sir. I did not realize you were within. I will come back later."

He turned to go when Darcy called after him. Thus, he turned back to do his master's bidding.

Darcy swung his long legs up and over the side of the bed, and then sat upright. He looked his valet squarely in the eye. "Chaffin, you have always been honest with me, and I expect you to be so now. Are you by chance aware of gossip circulating in the servant's quarters concerning my wife?"

Mr. Chaffin appeared glum. "Yes, sir, I have heard the tittle-tattle, and I am the one who informed Mrs. Reynolds concerning it."

With emphasis, Darcy asked, "What exactly is the tittle-tattle?"

"Sir? You want me to repeat the scullery maids' conversations to you, sir?"

"Yes, yes I do."

"All of them?"

Shock registered on the master's face. Did the servants ever work?

"Yes, Chaffin. Each and every conversation, and by the way, have you heard any of these rumours spread directly by Sally, Mrs. Darcy's maid?"

"No, sir, never directly from her lips, but I have heard a maid give her credit as the source of the information which she passed on. Are you certain that you want me to relate such idle nonsense? After all, sir, I have only heard bits and pieces."

With intensity, Darcy cried, "Yes, I do, and please, do get on with it, man!"

The valet frowned. Looking at the floor, he flatly stated, "Very well, sir. One such conversation went something along the line of: 'Mr. Darcy's hands caressed Mrs. Darcy hungrily as she tried to dress for dinner, and that after, they had been in bed for the whole of the afternoon.'" Darcy turned beet red and quickly averted his gaze as he drew the back of his fist over his mouth.

Chaffin continued, 'She was only in her...corset and chemise, and it made them...late for dinner.' Oh, yes, another bit goes something like: 'Mrs. Darcy has him acting like a child, catching snowflakes on his tongue.' "Is there something specific you wish to know sir, because such prattle is most common?"

Darcy looked up sharply and asked, "Do you know something more than these tales from young goggle-eyed maids?"

"I suppose you mean," he paused to clear his throat. Turning his head, he continued, "... about Mrs. Darcy and Colonel Fitzwilliam?"

Darcy's eyes widened as he looked at his valet in exasperation, "Precisely!"

"Well, sir, again, I am not sure if you should give credit to such accounts."

"Chaffin, just tell me all the *chitchat* you have heard."

"Very well, but do, please, remember the source, sir." Darcy looked at his valet with annoyance "Yes, sir. It is said amongst some servants...that Colonel Fitzwilliam...carried Mrs. Darcy in his arms to the master's study. Uh...they were then all alone and spoke together for a long time. Mrs. Darcy had been crying, but..." Chaffin paused and rolled his eyes before continuing, "The colonel told her his most tender feelings...and it made her smile. They were holding hands...and he kissed her hand. Umm...the mistress then put her arms around...the colonel...and they embraced."

Darcy's hand now cupped his mouth and chin tightly while his heart sank into his stomach.

Mr. Chaffin had paused, realizing the distress that was overtaking his master.

With his heart racing, Darcy tried to sound composed as he feebly asked, "Is there anything more?"

"Yes, sir, one last bit."

"Say it and be done with it."

"It is said that Mrs. Darcy looked into the Colonel Fitzwilliam's eyes and told him he was the best of men. She supposedly told him that she cared for him greatly, and then...' Well, sir, really." Darcy stared pointedly for him to finish. In a diffident manner, Chaffin sighed and concluded with, "It is rumoured that they kissed most passionately."

Silence ensued. Mr. Chaffin remained standing in place, holding the nightshirt while waiting for his master to say something.

Darcy felt like he could not get air to fill his lungs, he felt as if his heart had been ripped from his chest. His features paled and after taking several deep breaths, he stated hoarsely, "Thank you, Chaffin. I...will dress for dinner shortly. Would you be so kind as to wait for me in my dressing chamber?"

"Yes, sir." The valet, however, did not move. He hated seeing his master distraught over foolish gossip. "Sir?"

Darcy was unaware that his valet remained by the bed and looked up, confused, and said, "Yes, Chaffin, what is it?"

"Only this, sir, I would not take much stock in the prattle of young girls."

"Oh, that, well, yes. I see what you mean. Thank you."

"Yes, sir." Mr. Chaffin bowed and left his master alone. Yet, Darcy was not alone at all. His constant companion from that moment forth was the vicious, green-eyed fiend commonly known as jealousy.

~*~

Darcy dressed for dinner and descended to join the others. He made apologies for Elizabeth's absence to his sister and cousin. They ate their meal in relative silence, lost in their own thoughts and unwilling to mention their concerns out of fear that the subject would prove too nerve-racking for the others. Richard asked to speak to his cousin after the meal, but Darcy declined, claiming that he had urgent business to attend to with his overseer. Coolly, he stated that their conversation could be postponed for a later time.

Richard eyed him guardedly. He wondered if Darcy blamed himself for what had happened to his wife. He knew too well that his cousin felt personally responsible for the burdens of everyone about him. Therefore, he would most willingly carry the borrowed loads of others upon his solitary shoulders. The colonel sighed and hoped in near futility that in time Elizabeth would help to alleviate his cousin's propensity to take on the cares of the whole world.

Mr. Manning and Mr. Sheldon were waiting for their employer within his personal study. Darcy offered both men a drink before they began their discussion. The gentlemen told the master of the constable's dealings with Mr. Hibbs, Sally's father. The guilty man was now in Lambton's gaol, under lock and key. They also informed Mr. Darcy that, though common law permitted husbands to beat their wives, if he desired to press charges, their case would go to court since the man had struck Mrs. Darcy. Given Dr. Lowry's report that Mrs. Hibb's death was directly related to the brutal beating she had received at the hands of her husband, they had due cause.

The master sat and listened to the two men for a full twenty minutes before he said a word. "There is no doubt that I wish to have an indictment brought against this scoundrel, yet I must first consult Mrs. Darcy's feelings in regard to this matter. I will let you both know first thing after breakfast on the morrow, and then, Mr. Sheldon, I will have you inform the magistrate of our intended course of action. I thank you both for all that you have done today. I must admit, however, to feeling great concern that this fiend was right under our very noses. Had either of you ever heard or seen anything of this nature from him before?"

"Well, sir," said Mr. Manning stroking the rim of his hat, "I knew he kept to himself and never attended Pemberley's festivals. His wife was seldom seen, but they were known as hard workers and always did what was asked of them. I guess only the lass could tell us for sure when her father came upon such a bad temper."

"Yes, it is possible that she could." After saying these words, Darcy stood, demonstrating to the men that the interview was at a conclusion. They, in turn, stood, nodded their heads, and shook hands with him. Mr. Darcy, dismissing Sheldon, asked Manning to remain. He had some further business to attend to with him alone. Mr. Sheldon quietly quit the room. The master and overseer then discussed Mr. Darcy's additional interests for some time, until both men were satisfied with the arrangement for the impending endeavour.

When Mr. Manning left, Darcy decided to go in search of his sister. He found her with Richard in the music room, seated at the pianoforte, playing duets. Of course, the eldest cousin did not have the skill of the younger, but their simple melodies were enjoyable, nonetheless. Darcy walked up to the pianoforte and surprised them both with his presence.

Startled, Richard commented, "Why, Darcy, I thought you had retired for the night. Since you obviously did not, might this be a good time to speak?"

"Darcy shook his head. "If it is all the same to you, Richard, I would rather wait until tomorrow. I must go over some figures tonight for my overseer and check in on Elizabeth. I have just come to tell Georgie good night."

"Oh," Georgie exclaimed as she hurriedly stood and came around the bench to give her brother a hug. It seemed too long since she had last embraced him, and she was certain that after today, he would need to know how much he was loved. Opening her arms wide, she took him by surprise as she encircled the whole of his torso, his arms still by his side, and squeezed him tightly. She whispered in his ear, "I love you, Brother. You are the best brother in the world."

When she released him, he quickly brought his arms up and pulled her to his chest, holding her close with his chin upon her crown. Chokingly, he whispered in return, "Thank you, Georgie, I need your love so much!"

As she stepped away, she looked at him with wonder and concern. He was extremely emotional, and she worried that something terrible must have happened.

"Well then, until morning." He released his grasp, smiled vaguely to her and glanced at his cousin with a straight face. He then turned and walked from the room with his familiar gait of confidence.

Georgiana and Richard just stared at one another and remained silent. Then the colonel encouraged Georgiana to play again. They played a little longer, but the earlier pleasure they had derived from the activity had lost all its charm.

~*~

By the time Darcy had finished going over the accounts in his study, it was nearly midnight. He blew out the candles on his desk except for one, which he carried as he made his way up the stairs. He had looked in on his wife earlier, and found her sleeping soundly. He now wondered what to do. Should he slip into their bed beside her or sleep once more in his own chamber? He frowned upon such a thought, but Elizabeth had made it perfectly clear that she did not want him in her bed.

He turned the doorknob quietly and entered her chamber. After blowing out the candle, he waited for his eyes to adjust to the darkness. Silently, he made his way over to the bed and stood next to Elizabeth's side. His jaw tightened as he remembered her lying on the floor with blood covering her face. For the hundredth time that evening, he berated himself for letting such harm come to her. Listening closely, he could hear that her breathing was peaceful. He startled as his wife suddenly turned over on her side and reached her arm across the empty portion of the bed. Her hand began to caress the sheet, yet when not finding the desired form, she hastily pulled the spare pillow into her arms and cuddled it close to her chest.

Looking upon her back now, he knew he needed to get some rest, but he felt truly blighted. Desperately, he wanted to lie by his wife, take her in his arms, and feel for himself that she was alive and well. It almost became his downfall. But whether or not she wanted him in her bed was not the heart of the issue—he would have to put his feelings aside. He must respect her wishes, at least the ones that were rightfully her privilege, to prove her true worth to him. Sighing, Darcy slipped away and exited to the master's chamber, where he would sleep alone.

~*~

The following morning, the Master of Pemberley was up early and dressed before the rest of the household. He desired to see his wife and went, accordingly, to her chamber. He lit a candle and set it on the night table beside the bed. He brought the stool from his own chamber, for her to use until Chaffin could locate the missing one. He sat gently on the edge of the mattress and whispered, "Lizzy, are you awake?'

She was indeed awake, but at first, she did not answer. She had been awake since her husband had crept out of the room the previous night. The long hours which had followed, brought her only the fellowship of sorrow, hurt, doubt, and anger. Her feelings of resentment had worsened, and she was still in an ill temper. However, as Darcy arose to walk away, she spoke. "I am now awake, Fitzwilliam."

He turned and stood still while staring down at her form. "Did you sleep well?"

"No."

"I am sorry to hear it. Did your injury keep you awake?"

She remained motionless and replied, "I suppose it gave support to my current dilemmas."

"I shall go and get you another compress, I shall not be long."

He left before she had a chance to ask him not to worry with it.

After a few minutes, he returned and handed her the bundle full of snow. She took it and thanked him.

"Lizzy, would you like me to call for Nancy to help you this morning? I am more than willing to assist you."

"I will manage myself. After all, I have had to share a maid with four sisters, and, therefore, we had to take care of ourselves quite often. I guess it came with the territory of our *rough* and *ready* ways."

Sighing, he shook his head and realized she was still angry with him over the careless statement he had made last night. "Elizabeth, I am sorry for my unkind remark last evening. Please, forgive me."

"Fitzwilliam, I need time. I am by far the angriest I have ever been in my life. I must have time to think this all through."

"Very well, Elizabeth. Take all the time you need. I shall be most eager to speak with you when you are ready. I am sorry for my constant blunders. Now, if you could just sit up, I will unfasten your corset, and then ring for hot water for you. That way you can take care of yourself. I, however, will be happy to assist you in any way."

She leaned forward to allow him to lift her gown and untie the laces. "There now, I shall inform Chaffin to have hot water sent up for you. Please lie here a little longer to allow the compress to help alleviate the swelling. Is there anything else you need?"

"No, I thank you."

"Very well, I shall see you later on in the morning. I have business to attend to in my study should you need me, and I am having my breakfast brought there on a tray."

She nodded and closed her eyes as she held the bundle over her nose and cheek. Gazing upon her face, he was overwhelmed by misery. He wanted to place a kiss upon her brow, but was certain she no longer desired his affection. Thus, he quietly took his leave.

Elizabeth stayed in bed for another quarter of an hour until the snow began to seep through the cloth. She bathed, dressed in a simple morning dress, and went downstairs to see her former maid.

Sally, in a sombre mood, greeted her. Elizabeth asked if Mrs. Reynolds had seen to her dinner the previous night and had arranged for any of her other needs. She told the mistress that the housekeeper had indeed taken care of all her wants. Elizabeth then explained that she would visit her again later on in the course of the morning, and that they could then discuss what to do for her mother's burial. The young woman agreed that that would be fine and thanked her.

Famished, after having not eaten very much the previous day, Elizabeth made her way to the breakfast room.

Georgiana and Richard had just arrived a few moments earlier. Richard stood as Elizabeth entered and quickly pulled out the chair for her. "I thank you, Richard."

"Is Darcy not joining us?"

"No, he has urgent business and so is within his study."

Georgiana spoke next. "Lizzy, I am so sorry about what happened to you and Sally."

Richard nodded in sympathy. "Not to mention what happened to the poor girl's mother. Her father is now being held in custody, and the law will act upon it. I spoke with Mr. Manning this morning, and he informed me as much. It is a despicable thing that a man can beat his wife freely, and the law allows such cruelty, claiming that it is a husband's justifiable right to keep his wife in line. I could never fathom desiring such protection from the law."

With a tinge of anger, Georgiana spoke. "Well, Richard, it is just as we were saying a week or so ago, that men have all the civil liberties and women are their property."

Richard appeared glum as he remembered very well the strong feelings Georgiana and Elizabeth had expressed with great fervour on the night of the fencing accident.

Elizabeth asked, "But in the case of Sally's father, the law *will* take action?"

He stared at her for a second, and then said, "He will be charged for assaulting you, not his wife."

"Oh," was all the reply that Elizabeth offered to this intelligence. With nothing more to be said, they ate their breakfast in companionable silence, and then separated to go about their individual tasks.

Elizabeth went straightway to her study to read the avoided missive from Mrs. Wickham. She could not imagine what her sister might say or want now.

Mary Sherwood

She sat in her leather chair and opened the drawer. The missive was lengthy and not at all in her sister's hand. Elizabeth instantly knew that this letter must have been written in the hand of her brother-in-law. He implored his new sister for money because he had found himself to be in some sort of scrape and desperately needed her assistance. His flowing address was the usual superfluous tongue of the sweet talking rake that he was. With familiarity, he told her of how she was, indeed, more desirable than her sister. He insinuated how clever she was in ensnaring a man of so much wealth. All of this was said with elegance and confidence as if it were, in all actuality, fact. Then, before concluding, he asked her to pay his special regard to Georgiana and expressed his hope that nothing untoward would proceed Miss Darcy's distinguishing Season in London.

Feeling ill, Elizabeth folded the missive and began to calculate her options. She could go straight to her husband, but then they were already in such a bind with each other. She felt certain this would be just one more thing he could hold over her head, like the comment he had made the previous night about their unruly upbringing. In addition, it was embarrassing to have caused her husband so much mortification concerning Wickham. Thinking on the situation further, she thought of going to Colonel Fitzwilliam for counsel. However, surely this would not be wise. After all, he was not her husband and, therefore, it would be entirely improper for her to do so. She placed the letter in the back of the drawer and, arising swiftly, made her way to her husband's study.

As she advanced, she spied the colonel leaning against the wall opposite of the closed study door. Not noticing her approach, he was a little surprised to see her. "Why Elizabeth, I did not hear you coming. He laughed and then asked, "Are you joining the queue to speak with Darcy?"

"Why, I suppose I am. Do you have urgent business with him?"

"I do not consider it urgent, but I truly wish to speak with him before I leave."

"You are leaving? I so hoped you would remain awhile longer to spend time with Bingley and Jane when they arrive. I would so very much like for you to get to know my sister. She is the dearest sister in the world." Elizabeth attempted a smile but she winced while doing so.

Pained to see her shiny, swollen cheek and puffy nose, Richard returned her brief smile. He silently cursed as he thought of the brutality she had experienced. It made his blood boil, and he almost wished he had allowed Darcy to beat the man to a pulp. He, likewise, would have enjoyed participating in the thrashing.

The colonel was roused from his daydream by the sound of Elizabeth's voice, but her words had escaped him. "I am sorry, Elizabeth, I did not hear what you enquired. I fear I was lost in thought. Do you mind repeating it?"

She smiled inwardly at the colonel's candid nature. "I asked if you would reconsider, and please, stay with us a little while longer."

"Oh, I am not sure. I mean, I should spend some time with my parents."

As Richard related this message to her, the door of the study swung open. Darcy and Mr. Manning came walking out of the room, still engaged in conversation. Instantly taking note of his wife and cousin, halting their own conversation when they appeared, his jaw tightened. Mr. Manning expressed his appreciation for the information provided and Darcy nodded to him as he began to take his leave. He then looked between his wife and cousin. They all stood staring at each other for some seconds. Darcy's throat constricted in anguish as he asked, "Is there something I could do for you both?"

Elizabeth perceived his cloudy demeanour and no longer had the courage to discuss Wickham's letter. Instead, she implored, "Fitzwilliam, I have been trying to encourage Richard to stay on longer to enjoy the company of Charles and Jane. Please, do tell him you desire it as well." She smiled openly to her husband as she made the request.

Darcy held his chin high as he narrowly surveyed his cousin. He breathed deeply and scrupulously stated, "Yes, Richard, you must stay. Elizabeth desires it. I am sure that Bingley and Jane would delight in your company as well."

Instantly Richard knew something was wrong. His cousin was in a definite mood again, and he imagined it was due to yesterday's incident. Slowly shaking his head, the colonel kindly declined the offer.

Darcy would not hear of it. In fact, he insisted that he stay at least for a day or two of their planned company's visit.

Finally, Colonel Fitzwilliam agreed, and then requested a conference with him.

Darcy again declined his cousin's request, truthfully stating that he had many matters of business that needed tending during the morning and, therefore, would not be able to speak with him until later in the day.

Thanking him, Richard told him it could wait until that time. He then left his cousin and his cousin's wife to themselves.

Darcy turned and asked, "Is there anything else you desire, Elizabeth?"

Her eyes swept over his face, but then she averted her gaze. *He must be angry with me because I desired for him to sleep elsewhere. Yet, he did come to me and take care of my needs this morning. Something is not right.* "No, I see you are busy. May we talk later as well?"

"Elizabeth, I desire to hear anything you have to say." Taking in a deep breath, he continued, "In fact, I need to speak with you about pressing charges against Sally's father, Mr. Hibbs. This may be the only way in which the law can officially administer justice. However, I will not do so if you do not desire it. You will have to be questioned, and, therefore, more embarrassing situations may be involved."

"Yes, Richard informed me at breakfast that this may be the case."

Darcy's cheek twitched with the mere mention of his cousin's input concerning the matter. Eyeing her closely, he unreservedly stated, "You may think upon it and let me know."

She searched his eyes and could tell he spoke from his heart and would indeed, let her decide without his opinion. With renewed courage, she determined to raise the topic of the horrid letter.

Perceiving that she desired to say something, Darcy waited in anticipation. Just as she opened her mouth to speak, Mr. Greene came walking towards them with Thomas Wilkens. Thus, due to the interruption, Elizabeth quickly exclaimed, "Please, excuse me!"

Darcy's brow furrowed, and his heart weighed heavily in his chest as he watched her depart from his presence.

~*~

Chapter Fourteen

Disquiet and Sisterly Affection

In the course of the morning, Elizabeth had made arrangements with Sally concerning the burial of the young woman's mother. They had determined that it would take place on the morrow, and that she would be laid to rest in the local parish cemetery in Lambton. After the funeral arrangements had been settled, Dr. Lowry had arrived to check on Mrs. Darcy's injury from the previous day. He reported with certainty that her nose was not broken and advised her to rest and continue to apply cold compresses for the remainder of the day. Subsequent to the physician's visit, Elizabeth felt the urgency of dealing with the delicate situation regarding her younger sister, and so, excusing herself, she went directly to her study to pen a missive. She had no more than settled in her chair when Darcy knocked and sought permission to enter. While nodding her acquiescence, she noted that he carried a letter in his hand.

"Elizabeth, I just received an express from Bingley. He writes that he and Jane still desire to come and are planning on the trip, but there has been a change in the number of visitors to expect. Evidently, Miss Bingley has recently come to Netherfield and will accompany them during their stay here at Pemberley." Darcy lowered his eyes to meet those of his wife, instantly detecting the ire ignited therein.

"Yes...well..." he stated with a tinge of bile rising in his throat before proceeding. "In addition, he writes that your mother is strongly encouraging them to bring Kitty, insisting that she would benefit from such a visit. Bingley goes on to say that if these extra guests prove too much strain on our hospitality, then they shall understand and come at another time."

Husband and wife gazed at each other for a few moments, wordlessly communicating their shared disappointment. Darcy knew an intelligence such as this would put a damper on Elizabeth's anticipating her favoured sister's visit. While he took in the daunting expression on his wife's face, he searched for words to express his sentiments, but it was she who spoke first, stating forthrightly, "I shall not lie and pretend that the prospect of extra company is not a disappointment to me, because it is." She sighed in resignation. "However, I confess that I would rather have Jane with Kitty and Miss Bingley in tow, than to have no Jane at all."

"Yes...I suspected you would say as much. I shall send an express immediately so Bingley will know how to proceed, and will inform my aunt of the additional guests so that she may extend an invitation to the ball for them as well."

Instead of leaving, Darcy stepped closer and gazed at his wife as she sat at the desk that had once belonged to his mother. He smiled and softly enquired, "Have you given any more thought about pressing charges against Mr. Hibbs?"

"Yes, I have, but before I offer my response, I wish to know your opinion on the matter."

This surprised him a little, and he decidedly stated, "I desire to press charges, but only if you desire it also."

With certainty, she made answer. "Yes, I do, but not so much for my own suffering as for his wife's." They stared at one another for a few seconds more, both contemplating the unfortunate woman's brutal death and the horrid ordeal they had recently borne in connection to it. Each felt an extreme sense of gratitude fill their hearts for how blessed they were to still be alive and to now be gazing into the other's eyes, yet neither said a word. At length, Darcy voiced his respect for her decision and then conveyed the need to send an express in order to notify his steward on their course of action in regards to his former tenant. He quickly bowed and departed.

After he had gone, Elizabeth sighed and pulled out her personal ledger to determine how much allowance she could afford to send to the Wickhams. While staring at the figures, a sudden headache developed, and thus she put the record book away, deciding to deal with it on the morrow. Wearily, she stood, feeling completely drained. Lacking the energy to climb the stairs to her chamber, she made her way to the library. Finding the room was empty, she decided to lie down on the chaise lounge where she soon drifted off into a restful slumber. Her slumber was so soporific that she slept for several hours until awakened by a noise.

Elizabeth's eyes opened groggily, realizing that Colonel Fitzwilliam had entered the library and was now busily engaged in selecting a book. In an instant, he became aware of her presence.

"Oh, Elizabeth, please forgive me for disturbing you. I recently finished the book I had been reading, and I was trying to choose another," he said as he stood by the table, close to where she lay.

Yawning widely, Elizabeth covered her mouth, slowly sitting up. "What time is it, Colonel? I fear I have slept far too long."

He smiled and then informed her it was almost time for dinner. The colonel noted that this intelligence distressed her as she frantically began to feel for the loosened pins tangled within her hair. He leaned against the table and watched her in amusement.

"Elizabeth, do not worry so. We shall gladly wait for you."

"Oh, Richard," she stated in a downhearted fashion, "I feel…I feel so distressed…" but before she could finish her sentence, they both noticed

Darcy standing in the doorway, leaning against the casing with his arms folded over his chest, observing them closely.

With restraint, the Master of Pemberley enquired, "Why ever do you feel distressed, Elizabeth?" The displeasure in his query was easily detected by both his wife and cousin.

"I…that is…" she faltered.

Richard looked at his cousin sceptically as Darcy asked his wife again, "You were telling my cousin that you feel distressed. Why ever do you feel so?"

"Pray," she made answer. "I just discovered that I am late in dressing for supper, which is the reason for my present unease."

"Well," Darcy said in response to her reply, "as Fitzwilliam offered, we shall wait for you. There is no need for you to be anxious. I have been searching for you this past hour."

Elizabeth felt chilled by the coldness she read in his impassive look, and thus, she sincerely expressed, "I am sorry. I fell asleep on the divan and slept longer than intended."

Darcy abruptly walked to her and offered his hand, which she immediately took. "I shall accompany you upstairs."

As they made their way to her chamber, he asked, "Elizabeth, shall I have Nancy come to assist you or may I perform the service?"

"I am certain that I can manage on my own, yet I thank you," She replied as they crossed the threshold of her chamber. Upon entering, Elizabeth began to prepare for dinner.

Darcy strode over to her vanity chair and took a seat where he watched while she undressed. When he noticed her struggling with the fasteners on her dress, he sprung to his feet, quickly taking over the occupation of disengaging them. She ceased her attempts, allowing him to help. Quietly, Elizabeth said, "I thank you again, Fitzwilliam."

Sitting back down at her vanity, he ventured to ask in a subdued tone, "Why was Fitzwilliam in the library with you just now?"

Even as Elizabeth slipped on a blue, silk gown, she made answer without taking notice of her husband's fixed stare. "I suppose he came to search for a book."

"Ah," he replied and arose hastily, aiding his wife with the new dress she was donning.

"Why did you wish to nap in the library?"

"Um, I am not sure. I suppose I felt tired and did not want to climb the stairs. I considered that I would disturb no one in that room. Do you not wish for me to rest there?"

"Oh, no, you may rest there. It is only that I had been searching for you for some time and had become concerned when I could not find you."

Elizabeth turned and raised a brow, "But you did find me."

He gazed deeply into her dark, emerald eyes and merely replied, "Yes."

Thinking it best to let the topic drop for the present, Darcy stood, lifted his arm, and escorted his wife out. With little to no conversation between them, they descended the stairs and went down to dinner where everyone at the table ate with hearty appetites, except for the master who remained quiet throughout the meal. Afterward, Darcy announced they would not separate but retire to the music room. The colonel realized his cousin was avoiding, altogether, the possibility of having a conversation with him. As they entered the room, Richard at once took the chair by the pianoforte to help turn the pages for the women, while Darcy sat by the fire and watched his sister as she began to play. Poised on one of the divans, Elizabeth picked up her embroidery.

After Miss Darcy played several selections, she implored her sister-in-law to join her for some duets. Elizabeth smiled and looked up at Georgiana. "I am not inclined to do so tonight, although, I do thank you for the invitation."

The colonel applied warmly, "Oh, please, do reconsider, Elizabeth. You and Georgie play such light-hearted melodies that it cannot help but put us all in higher spirits."

Darcy caught how his wife's features lit up with Fitzwilliam's encouragement, and he watched as she came straightaway to share the bench with his sister. Their duets did create a joyful air as the three tittered gaily throughout the performances. It pained him to witness how animated his wife became when by his cousin's side. There was no doubt in his mind that she took immense pleasure in Fitzwilliam's company and admired him greatly.

While they paused to make another selection, Darcy arose and immediately informed them that he was weary and would therefore retire early. Elizabeth stood as well, ready to accompany him. "Elizabeth, I see no reason for you to go to bed prematurely. After all, you had a long rest this afternoon. So, please, stay and enjoy playing a while longer."

It was true. She did not feel weary in the least, yet she felt he expected her to come with him. Concern showed upon her brow as she contemplated the choice before her. "It is true, I am not tired, but I will accompany you nonetheless."

"No," Darcy rejoined coolly, "I would be far happier knowing you are enjoying yourself. Good night."

In an instant, he strode from the room. Richard, Georgiana, and Elizabeth looked at one another in wonder. Then the colonel shrugged and good-humouredly reached forward for a certain sheet of music, suggesting, "Georgiana, play this one again."

Elizabeth bit her lip, torn by her husband's brusque manner, but did join her sister-in-law in playing the lively tune.

When the clock struck eleven, the small party made their way to their chambers. Goodnight wishes echoed faintly in the hall as each parted company. Darcy lay awake listening to the sound of their voices drift into his chamber. Although he had encouraged Elizabeth to remain and enjoy herself, he could not help but feel hurt that she had chosen to do so, and recalling her words from the previous night, claiming that she was the angriest that she had ever been and that she would need time, only frustrated him further. Tonight, she seemed quite cheerful towards him, at least when she was not alone in his company. Her behaviour confounded him.

Darcy frowned, and then rolled his eyes as he remembered how eager she was to please his cousin. Bitterly, he decided that he would not go to her bed. If she desired him, she would have to make the first sign of reconciliation. Despite all he was guilty of, he had been willing to discuss their marital discord, but she had not. With the resolution set firmly in his mind, he swiftly turned over to lie on his stomach, putting the pillow over his head as he tried to banish images of his wife's beaming smile in response to his cousin's charismatic charm.

There was a lit candle on the vanity, which enabled Elizabeth to make her way around her room. Looking over to the bed for her husband's form, she discovered he was not there and felt a sudden pang of loneliness. Yesterday, she had been so upset with him that she had believed she would not wish to share her bed for some time. Yet, his open confession, coupled with his loving kindness towards her, had since begun to soften her heart, and she was willing to forgive him. He had so readily admitted his error and justified her gross mistake of going to Sally's home as a natural consequence of his inconsideration. However, sometime during the course of the day, he had become distant. Elizabeth considered, *in all reality, could he still truly be angry with me concerning the whole affair that unfolded yesterday, and could that be the reason for his avoidance of me? Or does he still feel slighted by my previous desire to sleep alone, and therefore, he is now too wilful to come back to our bed?* She sighed, not knowing the answer. After managing to undress in a most difficult and awkward fashion, Elizabeth slid between the cool, crisp sheets. She did not feel the usual contentment that retiring had always brought. Instead, she felt swallowed up by the massive, canopied bed and bereft by the empty space at her side, a space customarily filled by the warmth of her husband's body.

~*~

The following morning, Mr. Chaffin was uneasy to see his master sleeping in his own chamber for the second night in a row and considered, *has Mr. Darcy given credence to the gossip concerning Mrs. Darcy and the colonel?* The valet was worried that this might be the case. He awakened Mr. Darcy at the planned hour and helped him to dress. With a heavy heart, he then watched his master make his way through the dressing rooms and to the mistress' chamber.

When Darcy entered, he immediately espied his wife still in bed, sleeping beneath the covers. He walked over and stared at her. She was beautiful when asleep. Of course, she was beautiful to him at all times, but he especially took pleasure in these private moments, when he could enjoy her beauty in its dishevelled state.

He delicately sat on the bed, his eyes remaining fixed upon her. His heart broke as he regarded her bruised face. Softly, he called her name.

"Elizabeth?"

Her brow quivered, and she replied sleepily, "Hmm?"

"Elizabeth, you need to arise. I may help you, or shall I call for Nancy?"

She yawned while opening her eyes. "Oh, what time is it? I must have overslept."

"It is time for breakfast, but I could have a tray sent up if you would like."

Elizabeth gazed at him. His hair was still damp from his bath, and she could smell the familiar scent of his cologne. Pulling in her lower lip, she bit down upon it and looked intently into his eyes. "Fitzwilliam, I think we really need to speak with one another. I want you to know how sorry I am for having gone after Sally alone. It was extremely foolish of me, and, in spite of your wrong, it does not lessen mine."

She waited for a response, but he just stared at her for several moments and then enquired, "Elizabeth, why did you desire to marry me?"

Her brows rose in surprise, shocked at such an unexpected question. Frankly, she asserted, "I love you, Fitzwilliam."

Staring deeply into his wife's eyes, he took in her breathtaking beauty and queried, "Yes, but why?"

As her lips began to part to make a reply, a strong knock rapped at the chamber door. Darcy rolled his eyes and shrugged his shoulders. He arose from the bed, marched across the room and swung the door wide-open. Mr. Greene, the butler, informed his master, "Sir, the constable from Lambton is here and wishes to speak with you."

"Yes…well, tell him I shall be down directly. In the meantime, offer him some refreshment, coffee or tea, and thank you, Greene."

"Very good, sir," the servant bowed and departed.

Darcy walked back to the bed, and Elizabeth noted the frustration on his face. Gesturing with both hands pointing towards the door, he said, "I suppose you heard that I am needed downstairs. I hope it will not take too long. I shall attempt, if the constable will agree to do so, to defer any questioning of you regarding yesterday's incident for another time. That is, if you wish them to be deferred."

Hastily sitting up in the bed, she replied, "Yes, I do. I am not at all ready. Fitzwilliam, could you not have another maid come and help me, until we find a replacement?"

"No, I no longer can trust mere house maids in the privacy of our rooms. I hope you understand my position."

"Yes…I suppose I do," she responded, knowing that his reasoning was indeed sound.

"I would gladly help you myself, but since I am unable at this time, I will send Nancy straight way."

"Very well. I thank you, and I shall strive to be ready if the constable does need to speak with me."

Their eyes locked for a brief moment, and then Darcy bowed and quickly left the room.

~*~

After questioning Mr. Darcy, the constable was required to wait a quarter of an hour before Mrs. Darcy made an appearance.

When the interview was complete, Elizabeth went upstairs to dress for the committal of Sally's mother. The day before, she had given Sally an older black mourning dress that she had brought with her from Longbourn. She herself wore a dark brown frock, since she had not had a new one made. After Nancy had helped her get dressed, she made her way through the dressing areas and knocked on her husband's chamber door. She realized that it was the first time she had come to his chamber to seek him.

The valet opened the door, and Darcy turned towards his wife while fastening his cufflinks. "I am almost ready, Elizabeth." He then asked Chaffin if he had umbrellas ready for the carriage since it looked like rain. His man went straightaway to procure the needed items.

Darcy looked at his wife after he finished pulling on his overcoat. "It is a rather glum day outside, but I suppose it is fitting when considering the circumstances which will bring us to the church yard."

"Yes," was all the reply given to his observation.

They made their way to the courtyard and found Sally already seated in the carriage. Elizabeth greeted her former maid, and they were off for the small journey. The warmer weather had instigated the melting of the snow, thus the equipage forged through the sludge. The sky above was as dreary as were the roads below, with clouds hovering over, threatening a downpour upon the few who gathered.

As they exited the carriage, Elizabeth observed that Mr. Manning and both Wilkens brothers were already present. The parson, Mr. Theodore Weston, officiating over the short service, spoke briefly about the meek and afflicted. He also offered comfort by pointing out that Mrs. Hibbs was now in Heaven's glory and in the bosom of their Lord. The plain wooden box, which contained that woman's corpse, was lowered into the grave by ropes. All the men present helped with the internment, except the parson. Once the last prayer was invoked, Sally stepped forward, scooped up a handful of moist dirt and dropped it in to what seemed a dark, never-ending abyss.

Just as they entered their carriage to return to Pemberley House, the darkened clouds unshackled and a heavy shower beat hard upon its roof.

The melting snow combined with the heavy rain lengthened their return. When the horses came to a halt, Darcy quickly hopped out and a footman handed him an opened umbrella. The master assisted his wife and Sally to descend. They all entered the house under the protection of the awnings. Servants rushed forth to help discard the damp coats, hats, and bonnets while the butler informed the master that Mr. Sheldon awaited him in the study. Darcy immediately bowed to the ladies and departed. Elizabeth and Sally proceeded to the front corridor, and, when they entered therein, Mr. Greene had just allowed the admittance of Thomas Wilkens. The young man stood by the doors soaked through, water dripping off his coat onto the marble floor as the butler walked up to Mrs. Darcy and announced, "A Mr. Thomas Wilkens is here to see Miss Hibbs."

Elizabeth's eyes twinkled in delight. She realized by the intense look that Thomas directed towards Sally that he was a man deeply in love.

The mistress turned to her former maid and said, "You may go into the waiting room here and visit with your company."

Elizabeth escorted them to the room and asked them to be seated. She then expressed while standing in the open doorway, "I shall be in my study should you need me."

A half an hour later, Sally knocked on the study door. Mrs. Darcy arose and bid her to enter. The young lady's face, which had appeared only an hour ago so dismal, was now shining with an unmistakable brilliance. With her eyes reflecting the same excitement as Sally's, Elizabeth anxiously enquired, "Sally, it appears you have some good news."

"Oh yes, ma'am. It is the best news imaginable. Thomas has asked me to marry him, and I have said yes. But before yesterday, Tommy didn't know how we could manage to do so. However, that has all changed now because Mr. Manning has offered Tommy the most unbelievable prospect." The young woman had to pause to take a breath, and Elizabeth waited anxiously.

"Oh, Mrs. Darcy, it is too much!"

Elizabeth smiled, remembering Jane expressing the same words to her after Bingley's proposal. She listened intently as the young woman spoke further.

"Mr. Manning is offering an apprenticeship of overseer to Tommy, and with his help, we will be gettin' married with a special licence in three or four days' time. There is a cottage not far from the Manning's that needs some repair, and we are to start working on it this afternoon. This means I will never have to be a maid for no one again." The girl, suddenly mortified by her bold statement, flushed in embarrassment. "Oh, Mrs. Darcy, I won't have ye be thinkin' that I'm not grateful to you, for I truly am. I just can't believe that Tommy and me will be able to have our own place, a place where I will tend to my own home and my own future younglings."

An open smile revealed Elizabeth's white teeth as tears glistened in her eyes. She laughed softly in delight. "Oh, Sally, I am so happy for you both. Fitzwilliam, I mean, Mr Darcy, has a very high opinion of your young man. I am sure he will be pleased when he hears about your good news and present happiness." They embraced, and Elizabeth then suggested, "We need to find you a dress to wear. Do you have anything in mind?"

Sally smiled and simply said, "I was going to wear this black one you gave me because it is by far finer than any dress I have ever owned, and I am in mourning."

"Oh, please, Sally, allow me to give you another one I wore before marrying. It was one of my favourites and, after all, we measure the same. I do realize you are in mourning, but your circumstance is unique. Do say you will at least let me show it to you."

A huge smile appeared on the young lady's face as she nodded her head vigorously. Elizabeth took her by the hand, and they made their way up to her chamber. Searching the closet over, she finally found the dress that she had in mind and held it out for Sally's viewing.

"Oh, mistress, it is so beautiful. I could not take that dress from you. It is too fine."

"I assure you, Sally, that I think it a very fine dress, too. In fact, it was the nicest dress I owned before I married my husband. I am very fond of this dress because I wore it the first time I ever danced with Mr. Darcy. It would mean so much to me if you were to wear it as your wedding dress. I think Mr. Wilkens would very much like seeing his bride in this colour instead of black. This is a happy time, and even though your mother has passed, I am sure she too would desire you to mark your special occasion by wearing the colour of a bride. Do not let society's conventions worry you any. So, please, say you will wear it. Would you like to try it on?"

Sally briefly hesitated, but soon displayed child-like wonder as she nodded in excitement. Elizabeth helped take off the young woman's mourning dress and put on the creamy white gown. She then led her to her vanity mirror and stood behind her. Sally's eyes widened, as did her smile. "Oh, Mrs. Darcy, it is indeed lovely!"

"Yes, it is, but more so because you are a very beautiful woman, and I dare say that you will take Thomas Wilkens's breath away when he sees you in this dress. So, please, say you will allow me to give it to you?"

"No, I cannot take something this grand from you." Disappointment shown on Elizabeth's face, but then Sally quickly added, "But, if you do not mind lending it, I will gladly marry in it and then return to wearing my black dress in respect for me mum."

Elizabeth nodded in delight and then the two women embraced tightly. Additionally, she helped to find a bonnet and gloves for Sally to wear with the dress. She found some slippers to match as well, and even though they were a little tight, both women felt they would do for the brief duration of the ceremony.

Elizabeth escorted Sally back to her room. When they parted company, the mistress felt full of exhilaration and energy. She wished the weather could be finer so she could run freely and feel the air upon her face. As an alternative, however, Elizabeth climbed the stairs and went to the picture gallery. There she walked the length of the corridor and smiled at the unfamiliar faces in the long line of the Darcy lineage. She stopped in front of her husband's portrait. His dark brown eyes captivated hers and while mesmerized therein, her heart overflowed with a deep, abiding love for him as she gazed upon his youthful rendering. His facial features were very much then as they were now, but he had been nearing the end of his youth when this likeness had been painted, and therefore, his physique appeared lankier compared to his figure at present, being more muscular and broad.

While gazing up at his portrait, it suddenly occurred to her that her husband likely already knew about Sally's impending marriage and was the very source of the young couple's good fortune. *Fitzwilliam must have been not only the one to give his bond for the special licence but he provided the necessary capital for Thomas Wilkens to be apprenticed to Mr. Manning. Who else could afford such an exorbitant expense?* She blinked at the reality of this recognition, which instantly filled her heart full to overflowing in devotion and admiration for her husband. Elizabeth's breast swelled with the thought that he was *truly* the best man she had ever known.

Desiring greatly to express her gratitude to him, she hurriedly sprinted back to the stairs, taking the steps two at a time. Unbeknownst to the Mistress of Pemberley, due to her intense concentration of navigating her way, a group of men had gathered in the entrance hall. All the men immediately became silent and turned their heads towards the loud thuds which her boots created as she came barrelling down the stairway in a very unladylike fashion. Colonel Fitzwilliam grinned openly at the vigorous exuberance of his cousin's wife, as did Dr. Lowry. Others in the group, however, raised their eyebrows in disapproval, but Fitzwilliam Darcy pressed his lips tightly together and gave no other outward sign of the surprise he felt at seeing his wife breathlessly running towards the group.

Mrs. Darcy was only a few feet away when she looked up and stopped in her tracks. Her face appeared already in high colour due to the exercise, but not half so much as when she became aware of everyone's eyes fixed upon her. Elizabeth felt herself blush a deep crimson. She swallowed hard and quickly searched the crowd for her husband's face. As she hastily looked from one man to the next, she became aware of Dr. Lowry and the colonel and the mirth expressed upon their features. At the same time, she clearly read the disdain in the faces of the others, and instantly became apprehensive about the look she would find upon her husband's countenance.

Darcy read her anxiety. Hastily, he broke from the group and went to her while saying aloud, "Excuse me, gentlemen. I shall be right with you."

Elizabeth searched his face as he walked towards her, fearing he was angry. In a low voice, she made an apology. "Fitzwilliam, I am so sorry. I did not think."

He gently took her by the arm and escorted her into the music room where he closed the door. Again, she cried, "Oh, please, believe me, Fitzwilliam, when I say I am sorry to have caused you such mortification!"

She looked entreatingly into his dark eyes, and then she discerned his lips forming into a grin while his eyes twinkled in pleasure. "Elizabeth, I am not embarrassed in the least. Few men could boast at having such a delightful wife. I wish I had the time to speak with you further, but there is an urgent situation at the coalmine near Chesterfield and Alfreton. These men are here to solicit our aid to organize a relief party. I may be gone for some time."

He looked deeply into her widened eyes and with great emotion, whispered, "Know that I love you, Elizabeth." Hurriedly, he turned to quit the room and headed back to meet the men who were now at the front entrance, outside the house. Elizabeth followed, but stopped as he stepped outdoors. The men spoke only several minutes more, before they parted company. Darcy and Colonel Fitzwilliam quickly came back into the house. The master started giving commands to Mr. Greene. He required that his overseer be immediately notified to meet him at the courtyard entrance in ten minutes' time, and before Elizabeth knew it, he walked speedily away calling out for the assistance of Mrs. Reynolds.

Colonel Fitzwilliam called to his cousin, stating that he would await his arrival in the courtyard. He had begun to make his way to the stairs when Elizabeth breathlessly ran after him and exclaimed, "Colonel…please…will you tell me exactly what is going on?"

Richard paused, turned to look at her, and replied, "Oh, Elizabeth, there has been a cave-in at the mine some fifteen miles east of Lambton. There are several men trapped. We are forming a rescue party, and we are going to the mine to assist." He turned to leave, but then turned back just as quickly as he realized how frightened she was. Placing his hands on her shoulders, he looked unwaveringly into her eyes and vowed, "I will look out for Darcy and not let him do anything heroic. You have my word upon it!" He gave her shoulders a quick squeeze.

She nodded slightly as she whispered a thank you to him. When he turned once more, she watched him go up the stairs with fear in her heart. As Darcy entered from the hall, he witnessed his cousin's hands upon his wife's shoulders and the exchanged looks between them, yet he could not hear their words. He remembered the admonishment from the Book of Common Prayer: 'From envy, hatred, and malice, and all uncharitableness, Good Lord, deliver us.' He felt he had always kept these emotions in check, but he knew it was true no longer. At this exact moment, he greatly resented his cousin's considerations for his wife. He felt assured that what he had seen yesterday and what he had just witnessed, only confirmed his growing wariness and the truth to the gossip.

Elizabeth still stood on the stairs not knowing what to do when she noticed her husband rushing forward. "Oh, Fitzwilliam, can you not stop and speak with me for one moment?"

He shook his head as he passed her. She abruptly turned and began to follow at his heels, trying to keep up with his long legs as they took the stairs two at a time. However, no matter how she tried, Elizabeth lagged behind. He had already turned into his room, shutting the door behind him by the time she had reached the top of the stairs. Without hesitation, she marched down the corridor, opened his chamber door, and without knocking, boldly walked in, clearly out of breath. Mr. Chaffin had already removed his master's jacket and was in the process of unbuttoning of his waistcoat. From the corner of his eye, he saw Mrs. Darcy approach. With a wave of his hand, Darcy motioned for his wife to leave.

In a distant manner, he firmly directed, "Elizabeth, go. I have not the time to speak with you. Go and do whatever it is you are fond of doing."

Shock registered on Elizabeth's face. Why had he suddenly become so curt with her? His inflicted sting was apparent in her voice as she inhaled sharply between her words in an effort to forestall her tears. "Fitzwilliam...what have I done...to deserve...such a slight from you?" Her lips trembled, and the tears silently flowed down her cheeks.

Darcy shut his eyes tightly and let out a small groan of anguish.

Speedily, Mr. Chaffin removed his master's waistcoat and walked off in the direction of the dressing room. As soon as his valet had stepped away, Darcy reached out for his wife and pulled her close. She now sobbed openly onto his chest. In what seemed to be a frantic madness, Darcy began kissing the top of her head with quick short kisses while his arms pressed her closer. He reached for her chin and tilted her head back, so he could have access to her face. She felt the pressure of his lips as they vigorously brushed against her skin.

Elizabeth's lips trembled with joy. Breathlessly, she cried, "Fitzwilliam! Fitzwilliam! Fitzwilliam!" She tilted her head back further and looked into his eyes.

He gazed ashamedly at her. "Oh, Elizabeth!" He opened his mouth to speak further, but she raised her hand and gently pressed her fingers over his lips. A small moan escaped from his throat as he pulled her hand back and began to kiss the tip of each finger that had rested on his mouth.

Suddenly, pulling her hand away from his lips, he cupped the back of her head and hungrily covered her mouth with his.

Observing the fervent exchange between his master and Mrs. Darcy, Mr. Chaffin stopped in mid-stride. He looked down while holding the clothes that Mr. Darcy desired to wear for the chilly night ahead and hesitated. Should he leave and let his master be late, or should he somehow obtain his attention? He was happy to see the master and mistress no more at odds with one another, yet, he also knew the situation warranted great speed. Glancing up for a second, he took in their passion once more. Knowing he must do something, Mr. Chaffin quickly veered his eyes upward and noisily cleared his throat.

Oblivious to their surroundings, Darcy and Elizabeth held each other in a lover's embrace, deepening their kiss, each seeking to have their love reassured by the other.

Mr. Chaffin looked again and realized the situation would call for a more direct approach. In a loud voice, he called out, "Mr. Darcy, would you have me come back at a more convenient time, sir?"

Breathing heavily, they abruptly broke their kiss, their eyes tightly closed. Darcy sighed and rested his forehead on his wife's. While so doing, he shook his head and croaked out, "No, Chaffin, please do not go. I am ready."

The valet advanced slowly, since the husband and wife remained in an unyielding embrace. When he was but a few feet away, he halted and waited.

Inhaling loudly, Darcy gave his wife a quick hug, and then backed away. He let his valet put the warmer clothing on him as he gazed into Elizabeth's eyes. She stood motionless, silently observing the valet taking care of her husband's needs.

When Mr. Chaffin finished buttoning the last button, he handed his master a small satchel. Elizabeth internalized at that moment that her husband more than likely would not return for the night and maybe not for several nights.

Darcy muttered a thank you to his valet, and turned to his wife. Brushing back a loosened curl from off her cheek, he stated, "Elizabeth, I know we need to speak, but I do not know when I shall return. I love you. Come, walk down with me." He took her hand in his and held it firmly while they made their way downstairs.

As they neared the courtyard entrance, Darcy and Elizabeth became aware that Dr. Lowry, Mr. Manning, and Richard were waiting for him. Elizabeth also became sensitive to the fact that Sally and Thomas Wilkens were there saying their farewells. Additionally, she took note that Georgiana stood off by herself, and her eyes gave the impression that she was anxious. Thus, as Darcy spoke with Mr. Manning, she walked over to her sister-in-law and put her arm around her as she waited for the unavoidable departure.

Outside, it no longer rained, but only drizzled, and even though the days were becoming warmer, the nights were still quite cold and biting with a sharp wind that whipped through the peaks. Elizabeth saw blankets, food, and many other provisions carried out to be loaded into the carriages and wagon. As soon as Darcy finished speaking to his overseer, he came over to his sister and wife. Georgiana rushed into his arms and mumbled into his coat. "I love you, Fitzwilliam!" He told her not to worry and promised that they would all be home before she knew it.

As their embrace ended, he looked at Elizabeth and choked with repressed emotion. He pressed his lips together as he took his wife into a quick, yet tight squeeze. When he stepped back, they silently gazed at each other for a fraction of a second and then Darcy quickly turned to go. While crossing the threshold, he paused and, twisting his head around, made eye contact with his wife once more. There in the open doorway, he offered a slight bow of his head and tipped the brim of his beaver. Elizabeth smiled widely at him, and then he was gone.

~*~

Within a quarter of an hour after their departure, Mrs. Darcy's anxiety became extreme. The only way that she knew how to deal with such unease was to stay busy, and whatever she did had to be more demanding than the occupation afforded by mere needlework. Thus, as she and Georgiana ate a late luncheon, she informed her of Sally's impending marriage to Thomas Wilkens and the need to fix up the cottage.

Georgiana knew instantly what Elizabeth wanted before her sister-in-law even had a chance to get the question out of her mouth. In excitement, Georgiana volunteered, "Oh, Elizabeth, the rain is all but gone, and it would be such a surprise for Thomas to return to a home of his own, readied so that they can marry that much sooner. Do say you want to go and work on it immediately and that I might accompany you. I am sure Sally will like the idea as well."

Elizabeth's eyes sparkled at her dear sister-in-law's enthusiasm, and she laughingly stated, "Well, Georgie, I must admit that is exactly what I am hoping to do. Therefore, shall we finish our meal? Then I shall go in search of Mrs. Reynolds for the needed supplies. Of course, I shall do that after I make sure Sally is in agreement with the plan. What do you say?"

"Yes, Lizzy, it will help the time to pass so much more agreeably."

"Again, my sentiments exactly, my dear, sweet Georgie."

As the ladies walked arm and arm out of the dining room, Georgiana broke from Elizabeth and made her way to the kitchen to have Mrs. Potter pack some food to take with them while Elizabeth went to enquire of Sally what she thought of their scheme. Sally beamed when she heard of their wish and readily agreed. Hence, Elizabeth petitioned Mrs. Reynolds for cleaning supplies, materials for curtains, and some coal to light a fire.

Mrs. Reynolds arranged for Thomas's younger brother, Joseph, to drive the women to the cottage, so he could help them with any heavy work which might need to be done. The cottage was small, but not nearly as small as the tenant dwellings, for its hearth was larger, and there was a dry cupboard for dishes and food supplies. The well was in good repair and not far from the house. Elizabeth, Georgiana, and Sally worked hard airing, sweeping, and scrubbing down every nook and cranny of the three rooms. They were glad to have Joseph on hand because he was most helpful in bringing in fresh pails of water and dumping out the dirty ones. He liked being of service to them and enjoyed the chance it gave him to get to know his future sister as well. In his estimation, he thought his brother a very lucky man. Joseph's parents were just as proud of his older brother, and extremely thankful for the blessing of his having been offered the apprenticeship of overseer. Equally, they could not be any happier with his choice of a wife. Most people knew that Sally was honest, a hard worker, and a very pretty girl.

Sighing in exhaustion, Elizabeth recommended that they cease their endeavours for the night and come back on the morrow to add the finishing touches. They were all covered in grime as they climbed into the carriage, yet they giggled in delight, very pleased with their accomplishments.

All the maids in the kitchen were quite surprised to see the Mistress of Pemberley walk into the kitchen plastered with grunge. She politely informed them that she could not find Mrs. Reynolds at the moment and greatly desired a bath. Therefore, she wondered if someone could bring up hot water for her tub. Mrs. Potter nodded and informed Mrs. Darcy not to worry, that there would be hot water brought up in a jiffy. Elizabeth's teeth showed brighter than usual as she flashed the cook a thankful smile. The maids and cook simply stared at her, blinking in astonishment. In all their born days, they had never seen a mistress' face covered in soot.

Elizabeth had no idea what a spectacle she made until she entered her chamber and looked into the mirror. Aloud she exclaimed, "Oh, my! No wonder they were all staring at me as if I had escaped from a madhouse!"

A few short giggles escaped her lips as she thought of the maids' shocked faces, and then full wails of hysterical laughter rang through the halls. Mr. Chaffin was in his master's dressing area restocking supplies when he heard the mistress' cackles begin. He stopped his task as he became alarmed at the unfathomable sound that wafted loudly under the dressing doors. It came in intervals, and was a combination of a muffled cry mixed with the sound of the din of yelping hyenas. He rushed through the adjoining door into the mistress' boudoir and, suddenly, an extremely large clamour was heard. Elizabeth instinctively cupped her hands over her mouth and tried to gain composure as she giddily called out,

"Ha! Oh, I mean, who is there?"

"Mr. Chaffin, madam."

Elizabeth instantly opened the door and her hand flew to her mouth at the sight of the valet sprawled out on the carpet. "Oh, Mr. Chaffin, do let me help you!" she exclaimed as she bent low to lend him a hand. He gladly took her hand to help steady himself upward, until he stood again. Back upon his feet, he gawked openly at Mrs. Darcy.

Elizabeth wondered if the man was inebriated. Since his master was away, he did have a lot of free time on his hands and at the moment, she had never known him to be so out of kilter. "Are you all right? May I help you?" she asked.

The valet raised his brow at the irony. Here, he had rushed forward to help her, but instead, she ended up assisting him. Yet, by the look of it, he felt that she needed attention far worse than he did. "No, madam, I thank you. However, I do believe that I have just found the missing stool."

Both looked at the toppled stool which evidently been covered with clothing, and then they made eye contact, yet again. All of a sudden, Mr. Chaffin and Mrs. Darcy burst out laughing simultaneously, but the shared glee came from unrelated sources. The mistress was tickled by such a bizarre finding of the much sought after stool while the valet's jollity was due to the mistress' street urchin appearance. Their shared mirth soon dissipated as scullery maids came through the servant's door with buckets of steaming water. Mrs. Darcy bid the valet a good evening while she left for her much needed bath.

~*~

That night when it was time to retire for bed, an extremely lonely Elizabeth slipped between the sheets. Anxiety over the safety of her husband dominated her thoughts. As she tossed and turned, she shook her head and bit her lower lip. This would not do! Quickly, she pushed back the covers and leapt from her bed. She strode across the room, pausing long enough to grab her robe from the back of the chair by the fire and don it. She then crossed the room, opened the door, and marched across the hall and halted abruptly, knocking firmly upon Georgiana's door.

The young lady within jumped from the sudden pounding, but came forthwith to answer.

"Oh, Elizabeth!" Georgiana exclaimed. "What has happened? Are Richard and Fitzwilliam dead?"

Seeing the terror on her sister-in-law's countenance made Elizabeth's heart melt in compassion, and she quickly conveyed, "No, they are alive! I am so sorry, Georgie, for frightening you. Please forgive me."

"I feared it was going to be someone coming to tell me dreadful news."

Elizabeth nodded. "I too am worried. I was wondering, Georgie, if you would care to come and talk with me until we get sleepy. Jane and I would talk way into the night, especially when we were upset."

Georgiana's face lit up. "Oh, I would love to!" She hurriedly retrieved her robe and then crossed the hall with Elizabeth into the mistress' chamber. They both used the stool to gain access to the tall bed. Giggling, each cheerfully pulled the counterpane back and snuggled up underneath it.

"Oh, Lizzy, I have never done this before," Georgiana responded with lively excitement.

The two of them were lying on their sides, gazing into the other's eyes with their noses nearly touching. Georgiana relished their closeness and was extremely happy at having this opportunity to be alone with Elizabeth.

"Well, Georgie, having always been surrounded by other women, I find it difficult to imagine not ever having female companionship. You must have had many lonely times growing up," Elizabeth said in tender compassion as she grasped the young woman's hand.

"Oh, yes, Lizzy, I will admit, I have been lonely so often. As you know, Fitzwilliam is much older than I am, and even though I have had companions, there was not anyone with whom I could share my deepest feelings. Well, that is, practically no one."

"Practically no one? So there is someone with whom you confide?" Elizabeth questioned with a raised brow.

"Yes, when I am able to see them. Yet, it is not the same as having you here."

Elizabeth thought upon this someone and wondered who it could be. She then stared directly into Georgiana's eyes. "Do you feel close to Mrs. Annesley?"

The younger lady raised her brows in thought. "I do think highly of her. She is very wise and kind, and she has been most helpful to me after...well, after my imprudent endeavour almost two years ago."

The embarrassment and pain were still apparent in Georgiana's voice. Elizabeth thought to change the subject, thus, after snuggling close with their arms entwined, she enquired in a playful tone, "Tell me, Georgie, what do you think regarding our new doctor? I have no way of judging, of course, since I did not know the former doctor of the neighbourhood."

"Well, he is handsome, is he not?" Georgiana asked.

Smiling widely, Elizabeth asserted, "Well, even though I personally think no man can compare to your brother in looks or deportment, I must admit, Dr. Lowry is a handsome fellow. He has beautiful, curly hair, much like Charles Bingley's. What do you think, Georgie?"

"Yes, his hair is quite curly, and I find him to be a candid sort of man, much like Richard."

Elizabeth noticed the pensive look that crossed her sister-in-law's face and ventured to ask, "You think the colonel and the doctor are alike?"

"Oh," Georgiana's brow creased in thought, "I am not at all sure if their dispositions are similar in all aspects, but I do feel they are forthright in their opinions and communications. I also think they keep their tempers in check."

Raising her brows, Elizabeth considered the insight that Georgiana offered. "I do suppose you are correct. My dealing with Dr. Lowry the night of the accident, and then during the soirée dinner and his subsequent examination of me, leads me to be in agreement with your assessment. He is quite forthright. He also seems extremely intelligent and knowledgeable in the field of medicine. I must admit, at first I did not care for him. However, I sensed that Fitzwilliam thought highly of him, and he has proved, thus far, to be a hard working and loyal doctor. Fitzwilliam has also told me he came to this area with the express purpose of caring for his grandparents as they age. This particular point alone clearly commends his nobleness."

Nodding, Georgiana then stated, "I think Richard is just as noble. He is very intelligent and kind, sings beautifully, plays the pianoforte quite well, and knows much concerning strategy and combat. He is also a wonderful conversationalist and his humour delights me to no end. Lizzy, do you consider Richard a handsome man?"

Elizabeth's eyes widened at such an abrupt question. "Well, Georgie, I do think Richard is extremely intelligent, and I am sure he is a noble military commander. I also feel that he is a very attractive man. His looks are not necessarily the kind to strike a person's fancy when he first walks into a room, and yet, immediately upon making his acquaintance and conversing with him at Hunsford, I liked your cousin very much."

"Did you think my brother handsome when you first looked upon him?"

Biting her lower lip, Elizabeth saucily grinned. "*Yes*! I most certainly did. Yet, I did not like him at all because, at the time, his manners proved to be most disagreeable. My father has always said, 'Handsome is as handsome does.' So you see, Georgie, Richard did not appear as dashing as your brother did, but his manners were easy, considerate, and pleasant. Thus, I would concur with my father's oft-repeated maxim. First impressions can be very misleading. No matter how handsome a person is, if their manners are cold, insensitive, and selfish, then we no longer find them so attractive. Real beauty is derived from a person's individual integrity and kind-heartedness to others. Once I knew Fitzwilliam's true nature, I found him to be the handsomest man in the world." The last statement was spoken with great emotion.

Georgiana was thoughtful for a moment before replying, "I see what you mean. In the past, I have been mistaken in regards to this very issue. At one time, I thought George Wickham truly handsome, and I suppose in all reality his looks *are* quite dashing. Nevertheless, his lies and abhorrent ways only disgust me now, and I no longer think of him as such." Georgiana looked at Elizabeth and noticed the sudden sadness her face revealed. "Oh, Elizabeth, forgive me. I am so sorry to bring his name into our conversation. Let us think of something else to discuss."

Smiling to Georgiana, Elizabeth nodded, yet she realized that she must send that scoundrel money soon, for there was no way of knowing what sort of rumours he would spread concerning Georgiana. The villain's tales might do some damage with the flapping tongues of the ton, especially considering that this would be the year of Georgie's coming out. Elizabeth closed her eyes tightly and thought, *it is all so vexing*!

Georgiana reached to put her hand on Lizzy's shoulder, sensing that something was troubling her. "I love you, Lizzy. If you need to confide in me, I shall try to do my best to help you in any way I can."

Choking back her tears, Elizabeth managed a small smile, and then pulled her sister-in-law into a tight embrace. "I know you would, Georgie. I could not have hoped for a finer or truer sister than you when I married your brother. I love you, too! Georgie, I also thought George Wickham handsome and gallant. I was so wrong, and learned the hard way that it takes time to know someone. People are not always what they profess to be."

After this admission, they became silent, each lost in their own thoughts. Elizabeth speculated about Georgiana's affection for the colonel and wondered if there was a remote possibility that Richard might reciprocate it.

Georgiana's thoughts focused on the very same question, not in speculation, but with assiduousness and confidence.

The two Darcy women remained nestled close to one another as they drifted off to sleep in the companionship of peaceful contentment.

~*~

The next morning found Elizabeth, Georgiana, and Sally adding finishing touches to their efforts of the previous day. Elizabeth had brought candles and candleholders. Georgiana, who had been working on an intricate doily for the whole of the year, had finished it recently, and decided to give it to Sally as a wedding present to grace her new home. Sally thought it was the most delicate thing she had ever seen and praised it profusely as she thanked the miss for such a fine gift.

When they returned home, Elizabeth went in search of Mrs. Reynolds to enquire if there had been any word about the recovery effort at the mine.

The housekeeper informed the mistress that no word had come as of yet, but, if none came by the morning, then on the morrow, Mr. Sheldon would ride over and find out how things were progressing. Elizabeth thanked her and then made her way to her study.

As she entered, she noticed two letters upon the salver on her desk. One was from her mother and the other from Charlotte. She opened her mother's first. It was surprisingly pleasant. She informed her of Lydia's news of being with child and then let her know how happy she was that Kitty would have the opportunity to be with her two eldest sisters. Mrs. Bennet extolled the fact that, as Mistress of Pemberley, Elizabeth should help her sisters advance in society as much as possible. Elizabeth rolled her eyes as she vividly remembered her mother's exultation at the Netherfield Ball where she had embarrassed them all, exclaiming audibly enough that the whole room was left in no uncertainty as to Mrs. Bennet's desire for Jane and her girls... 'And that will throw them into the path of other rich men!' Sighing, she said aloud, "Oh, Mama!" She then read her mother's inexhaustible ramblings about how wonderfully Jane had settled, how she was certain that Netherfield held nothing compared to Pemberley, but also how it was so grand to have two daughters with such handsome, wealthy husbands.

Next, Elizabeth read Charlotte's missive. She spoke about her confinement and the great activity of the baby. She also informed Elizabeth that Lady Catherine was still in ill humour concerning their marriage, but that she, personally, paid no heed to the bitterness of her husband's patroness.

After reading the letters, Elizabeth opened her personal account book and tried to decide how much money she could scrape together to send Lydia. She shuddered as her eyes looked upon the recent letter that she had received. Swiftly lifting it, she thrust it to the back of the drawer. Hearing a knock on the opened door, her head snapped up, and she observed Mrs. Reynolds waiting for her attention.

Her heart sank. Was there bad news? "Yes, Mrs. Reynolds? Do come in. How may I help you?"

The housekeeper approached the desk with a worried expression on her face. Elizabeth's heart began to pound harder within her chest. "Has something happened to Mr. Darcy?" she asked in trepidation.

Mrs. Reynolds's face immediately softened. "Oh, no, mistress, I am so sorry. It is nothing of that nature. It is, well, it is just ... Oh, Mrs. Darcy, I really do not know what to tell you for the master has said nothing about hiring a new maid to me. Has he to you?"

"I am not sure I follow you. Mr. Darcy has indeed told me that he intends to find a new maid for me, but he has not said anything further. Why do you ask?"

"Well, because, mistress, there is a young woman with papers waiting in the entrance hall. The papers are a legal agreement which states she is your new lady's maid, and that Mr. Darcy has employed her especially for you."

"Oh, I am surprised that he forgot to tell me before he left, but he was in such a hurry that I imagine it slipped his mind. I shall come straight away to meet her." Elizabeth put her account book back in the drawer and swiftly arose.

The elderly woman stood in place, looking apprehensively. Elizabeth asked, "Mrs. Reynolds, is anything the matter?"

"Well, ma'am, can you speak French?"

Elizabeth stared at her in confusion. "No, I only know a few phrases."

"I was afraid you might say that, ma'am."

Apprehensively, Elizabeth enquired hesitantly as she stared at the housekeeper in dread, "Oh, Mrs. Reynolds, why ever do you ask? Please tell me that this woman speaks English."

The housekeeper sighed loudly. "I am afraid that this maid is a native French woman and only speaks French…no English at all. I couldn't understand a word she said, and she couldn't understand me either."

The mistress' eyes widened. "Oh my, that could prove to be a problem." She bit her lip and stated resolutely, "Nonetheless, Mrs. Reynolds, I am sure that she and I shall manage somehow."

Elizabeth walked with the housekeeper to the entry hall where the young woman waited.

Upon first glance, Elizabeth noticed the prettiness of the young maid. She was petite and had a flawless complexion. Brightly, the mistress smiled while extending her hand, saying in what little of the language she knew, "Bonjour, je suis Mrs. Darcy, et je suis ravie de faire votre connaissance."

Standing very straight for all five feet and one inch of her, the maid responded, "Bonjour, Mme. Darcy, je m'appelle, Yvette. Enchantée."

The new maid rattled away for some time, but the only thing Elizabeth felt she understood from the woman's discourse was the word hello and that her name must be Yvette. Elizabeth smiled and nodded, but had no idea what to say or do next when the young woman quit speaking. "Oh, my," was all that the mistress could mumble as she looked to Mrs. Reynolds. The older woman shrugged her shoulders and volunteered, "Miss Darcy is fluent in the language. Would you like for me to go and ask for her assistance?"

Inhaling loudly, Elizabeth made answer, "Oh, yes, please, and do tell her the situation. And ask if she can join us as soon as possible. Also, if you have not already done so, would you please have Clara's old room prepared?"

"It is ready and waiting, Mrs. Darcy."

Elizabeth could see the satisfaction in Mrs. Reynolds's eyes in reporting this fact, and then she responded to the housekeeper, "Somehow, I already knew that would be the case. You are a jewel, Mrs. Reynolds, and I thank you from the bottom of my heart."

This praise earned the mistress a rare smile from the housekeeper, who nodded, and then went in search of Miss Darcy.

Georgiana came down with alacrity and interpreted everything the maid had to say. Yvette was happy that this young lady could speak her native tongue so well, and she excitedly told her to tell Mrs. Darcy, "Ma dernière maîtresse est morte la semaine dernière et je suis venue tout droit de Londres quant Mr. Kearns a obtenu mes services pour votre mari. On m'a dit que Mr. Darcy désirait que vous ayez la meilleure assistance qui existe, et mes compétences vont dépasser toutes vos attentes."

After Yvette had finished rattling off what appeared to be gibberish to Elizabeth and Mrs. Reynolds, the two women looked to Georgiana for explanation. "She says to you, Elizabeth, 'Yes, I am so happy to be here. My name is Yvette. My last mistress died this past week, and I came right away from London when Mr. Kearns acquired my services for your husband. I was told that Mr. Darcy desires for you to have the best assistance available and my abilities will surpass all of his expectations."

Elizabeth raised her brows and looked to the housekeeper and Georgiana. They both grinned from the maid's bold declaration of self-confidence.

Elizabeth and Georgiana walked Yvette to her private chamber, then Georgiana said to her, "Voilà votre chambre. Je reviendrai une fois que vous serez installée et je vous ferai faire le tour de la maison."

Turning to Elizabeth, she interpreted what she had just said in French. "I told her, this is your room. I will come back after you are settled, and then we can give you a tour of the house."

Elizabeth thanked Georgiana, but worried that the language impediment might prove too much for them all. Time would tell.

After Elizabeth and Georgiana left, they caught each other's look and giggled. "Oh, Lizzy, I have no idea what Fitzwilliam was thinking when he hired a professional French lady's maid to work for you. It will be truly delicious to see you attempt to communicate with her."

"Why, Georgiana Darcy, you are a sly being, and here I thought you were always so compliant and good."

Georgiana's face became troubled upon hearing her sister-in-law's words. "Elizabeth, I am sorry if I have offended you."

Laughing, Elizabeth replied, "Georgie, you have not offended me. I was teasing you for being so bold just now. I do like that part of you. You hide it quite often, but I have seen you jest freely with your cousin."

Georgiana blushed brightly as a big smile spread across her face. "Yes, I think I feel the most comfortable with Richard, and I am coming to feel more and more comfortable around you, too, Elizabeth. You are a dream come true. I have always wanted a sister."

While chewing on her lip, Elizabeth worried for her sister-in-law. It appeared that the colonel was the person Georgiana had been referring to last night. It was quite evident that she felt stronger feelings for her cousin than mere familial affection. She wondered if Richard even suspected it.

~*~

That night after dinner, Elizabeth and Georgiana invited Sally to the music room. They played a variety of tunes for her. Sally sat enthralled by their performance. She enjoyed their duets, but most of all, she loved hearing Elizabeth sing. She was sure she had never heard anyone sing so well.

As the two sisters made their way up to their chambers, they agreed that they would sleep together once more. Each went their separate ways to ready for the night. Yvette was waiting for her new mistress. Elizabeth found her new maid's penchant for talkativeness amazing. The petite woman could rattle out more words in a minute than her mother and Lydia put together. Right away, the mistress became conscious of the fact that Yvette took her position very seriously. As soon as Elizabeth walked through her chamber door, the maid entered from the dressing area and started to remove her mistress' clothes with a dexterousness that Elizabeth had seldom, if ever, seen. Before she knew what had happened, the pins had been removed from her hair and then it was brushed and parted. The maid suddenly left her side while chattering a slew of words that were unintelligible to Elizabeth. Thus, she sat at her vanity, remaining stationary so that the strands of her hair would stay separated. Yvette came back carrying an exquisite satin ribbon and began intertwining it with Elizabeth's hair as she braided. The effect of such a trimming was quite fascinating. It lent such a feminine touch to Elizabeth's appearance that she truly admired the maid's ability. She smiled and said, "Merci beaucoup."

Yvette nodded in confidence and simply replied, "Oui."

When the maid left, Elizabeth stood and leaned in towards the mirror to gain a closer view. The gold threads within the ribbon shimmered against the candlelight. Raising her eyebrows, she tilted her head to the left and then to the right. She then stopped and inspected it awhile longer. She liked Yvette's creation and was grateful to have again the assistance of a maid.

Georgiana tentatively knocked on the door. Elizabeth opened it and bowed low while waving her arm to gesture for her sister-in-law to enter, and then, in playful mockery, she officially invited, "Do, please, come in."

Georgiana giggled at Elizabeth's silliness and curtseyed. "I thank you most kindly for asking."

Instantly, grabbing her by the hand, Elizabeth led her to the mirror and posed, "Do you like how Yvette has fashioned my unruly hair? And it is to sleep in!"

"Oh, Lizzy, I do like it. The ribbon is divine. So, do you think she will work out even with the language barrier?"

"Well, I must admit she is truly a wonder to behold, and, even though she talks non-stop, she is a skilled lady's maid."

Elizabeth blew out the candle on the vanity, and they both dashed over to the bed. Georgiana climbed up first and pulled back the covers. Elizabeth followed behind her and then blew out the candle on the side table.

They shifted about restlessly for a few moments in anticipation. As they calmed, Georgiana asked, "Elizabeth, are you frightened for Fitzwilliam and Richard?"

Elizabeth's brow quivered as her fingers began to delicately tug and twist the end of her braided hair. "Yes, I am. I have been praying for them and for all the others as well."

"I have been, also."

They were silent for a few moments more when Elizabeth decided a change of subject was necessary to dispel their apprehension, and thus, she enquired, "Georgie, do you look forward to coming out this Season?"

Scrunching up her nose, she shook her head, and replied, "No, I truly do not. In fact, if it were left for me to decide, I would never attend any of the endless balls and festivities. I hate society in London. But...," Elizabeth detected a glimmer appear in Georgiana's eyes when she paused. "I must confess, Lizzy, I do love the shops and the theatre, but it only takes a few visits to those establishments to keep me quite content for several months on end."

Elizabeth's brow creased. She realized that until she had married Fitzwilliam and come to Pemberley, that Georgiana had never truly experienced any enjoyable female companionship, which was a direct consequence of her aversion to society in general. She had never been given the opportunity to develop a close friendship with her own sex. "Georgiana, have I mentioned to you that my sister Kitty is coming to visit us with Jane and Charles? She is a year older than you are, but I think you two will enjoy each other's company very much. She has few close friends, and I know she is excited about furthering her acquaintance with you."

"Oh, I will be delighted to spend time with Kitty. I enjoyed speaking with her during the wedding breakfast at Netherfield."

Breathing in deeply, Elizabeth sighed as she related sardonically, "Caroline Bingley is coming, as well."

"Oh."

Silence ensued for a few seconds, until all of a sudden, they both began giggling in unison and then Elizabeth gleefully exclaimed, "Georgie, we are truly wicked!"

Happiness sounding in her voice, Georgiana concurred, "Yes, Lizzy, I do believe we are!"

They both hugged each other tightly and talked for another hour, until they yawned in sleepiness. Again, they cuddled close as they had the night before and drifted off into a soothing slumber.

~*~

In the early hours of the morning, the men returned to the stables of Pemberley. Mr. Manning and Joseph Wilkens unhitched the carriage as Darcy and Colonel Fitzwilliam took the saddles off their horses. The men had had very little rest in the past forty-eight hours. Even though Darcy had not slept in days, he felt alert, desiring only to gaze into his wife's lively eyes, caress her soft skin, and lose himself within her arms.

They entered the silent house and quietly went up the stairs. Neither said a word to the other. The colonel had had enough of Darcy's avoidance. When they had ridden to the coalmine a few days earlier, Richard had endeavoured to take the opportunity to speak with his cousin at that time, yet Darcy had eluded each attempt. Previously that evening, as they journeyed back to Pemberley, he tried anew, but Darcy barely spoke two words together. Thus, Richard decided they were both too exhausted. He determined that he would go to bed, and then, sometime later in the course of the day, bluntly insist that they speak to one another.

Darcy entered his chamber and walked across the room to pull the bell cord, but hesitated. Changing his mind, he began to disrobe as he walked to his dressing area, leaving a trail of filthy clothing behind him. Heading to his bathtub, he stood by it, and then leaned down. Reaching out with his hand to see if Chaffin had performed his customary procedure, he smiled, and then lifted out his hand dripping with water. Yes, Chaffin was as efficient as ever. His valet, when unsure of the actual time his master would return, had always had a tub of water prepared in anticipation of his arrival. Darcy imagined that Chaffin had poured the water at midnight when the now tepid water must have been steaming hot. No matter. He sat on the tub's edge, pulled off each boot, removed his trousers, and climbed within its smooth interior.

It felt luxurious to soak in a bath again, yet he did not linger long. Rather, he busily washed the filth from his body and vacated the tub in haste. Wrapping a towel around his waist, he then picked up another one to rub the dampness from his hair. After cleaning his teeth and splashing on some cologne, he trod softly into his wife's chamber swathed only in linen.

Coming closer to the bed, he could tell that Elizabeth was not alone. An additional form appeared by her side. His brow creased as he wondered who it could be. Standing at the foot of the bed, he held the candle high and instantly made out Georgiana's features. Captivated, he stepped closer to inspect the two women whom he loved the most in the world. There they were lying side by side with one of Georgiana's arms linked with one of

Mary Sherwood

Elizabeth's. A broad smiled crept over his face as he stood and watched them sleep. It was several minutes before Darcy departed the room. Yet, he only did so when he became conscious of the goose bumps spreading over his exposed skin.

Walking back through the dressing chambers, he made his way to the bed and undid the towel, letting it drop to the floor. He picked up his nightshirt from off the counterpane and slipped it over his head. Then, pulling back the covers, he climbed between the sheets. A smile still graced his features as he thought about his wife's goodness in being the sister and feminine confidante that Georgiana had always desired, yet had never had. It was something that he, obviously, could never give her. With these ponderings, his eyes began to mist. He was amazed by how much he loved his wife. Each day, it seemed he loved her more than he had the day before. Nonetheless, after seeing Elizabeth in their bed with his sister, this night, in the sisterly bond of love, his heart seemed to swell up in a fullness that had hitherto been unknown to him at any time in his remembrance. Slowly his smile melted away as his lips began to quiver and his throat became taut. Adoringly, he whispered aloud, "Oh, my Elizabeth, how I ardently love and admire you." Tears of love and gratitude dampened his pillow as his exhausted body finally yielded to the world of veiled dreams.

~*~

Chapter Fifteen

Implacable Resentment

Elizabeth and Georgiana were awakened much earlier than planned by Yvette singing merrily from the dressing room as she prepared Mrs. Darcy's bath. The twosome, still in bed, blinked at each other as they heard the maid sing with gusto, "Alouette, gentille alouette, Alouette, je te plu-me-rai!" Both raised their eyebrows and giggled.

Elizabeth whispered, "Next it is the eyes. Do you think she will sing all the way to the legs?"

Georgiana laughed heartily. "I see you are familiar with this nursery song. Oh, Lizzy, however do you think you will manage?"

"I am not sure, but if she plans on waking us at the crack of dawn every morning, singing about the demise of a bird, I am sure Fitzwilliam will not take to it kindly."

Georgiana laughed harder with the vision of her brother awakened from a sound sleep by Yvette's rendition of a lark being slowly plucked to death. "Well, Lizzy, he is the one who wanted a French lady's maid in the first place, and, after all, you cannot speak French, so he will have to deal with her more than he realizes."

These observations from her sister-in-law produced a sparkling smile from Elizabeth. She bit her lip and impishly stated, "I suppose you are right, Georgie. It will be so much fun to see Fitzwilliam having to interact with her more than he had anticipated."

Suddenly, Yvette came into the chamber and began chattering away. Elizabeth saw her sister-in-law's eyes widen in surprise, and asked, "What is she saying, Georgie?"

"Oh, Lizzy, she says it is time for us to be up and about. She will not wait around all day while we loiter in bed. She has many tasks to perform, and she keeps a strict schedule."

Elizabeth's eyes went wide as well, and both ladies erupted in laughter, harder than before. "Oh, Georgie, this is too cruel. I am sure Fitzwilliam has no idea what he has done."

The maid marched over to the bed and spoke in an authoritative air. Sobering right away, Georgiana jumped out of the bed and exclaimed to Elizabeth as she was making her way to the door, "She says I have to leave right now, and you are to take your bath. Good luck, Lizzy, and I do mean that I think luck has everything to do with it." Before her words even registered with Elizabeth, Georgiana was out of the door.

Obediently, Mrs. Darcy arose from her bed and went to her dressing chamber. Yvette efficiently pinned up her mistress' braided hair and grabbed her nightdress by the hem, pulling it hastily over her head. Continuing to rattle on in her native tongue, Elizabeth supposed she was to enter the bath. Breathing in deeply, the mistress stepped in the tub, rested her head on the copper rim and closed her eyes to relax in the steamy water.

She was jolted from her trance, however, as Yvette began to scrub her legs. Elizabeth's eyes flew open. Pitifully, she attempted to communicate, "Please, excuse *moi?*" When the maid did not stop scrubbing, Elizabeth pulled her knees to her chest while shaking her head and gesturing with her hand for the woman to halt.

Yvette eyed her mistress with determination as she placed her wet hands upon her own hips. Next, she lifted her soapy hand, shook a pointed finger at Mrs. Darcy and began chattering away yet again. Elizabeth had no idea what she was saying, although she gathered by the stern tone that the foreign woman was seriously displeased. Again, Yvette stooped to clean her mistress' body, but Elizabeth gripped the maid's hands to stop her. Looking directly into the abigail's eyes, Elizabeth attempted to tell her she would cleanse herself.

Holding her palm forward, she picked up the soap with her free hand and demonstrated to the maid that she would bathe herself. Yvette puckered her lips letting her mistress carry out the little display, but just when Elizabeth thought Yvette understood, the maid plunged her hands into the water and gave Elizabeth Bennet Darcy the most vigorous scrubbing she had ever known.

As the Mistress of Pemberley stood to step out of the tub, she noticed that her arms, legs, and everything else radiated redness. At this point, she did not care how prettily Yvette could interweave ribbons within her hair if she were going to behave like a military officer giving commands, instead of taking them.

Walking out of her room, dressed to meet the day, Elizabeth closed her eyes in indignation as the door shut behind her. She then stomped her foot. The nerve of that woman to think that she could coerce her the way she had. Not only had she prohibited her from bathing herself, she had not allowed her to choose what to wear.

Holding her head high, Mrs. Darcy walked across the hall and knocked on her sister-in-law's door. When Miss Darcy answered, Elizabeth informed her that she was going down to breakfast and enquired if she was ready to join her.

Georgiana could tell that Elizabeth was not happy, and as they descended the stairs, she asked, "Lizzy, I take it that you are no longer pleased with Yvette?"

"Ha! Georgie, I am afraid *that* is an understatement."

"Oh, did she remain demanding after I left?"

"Ah! Demanding does not even begin to express what I have just endured. She is truly a *madwoman*, and I am not at all sure I can keep her unless she begins to comprehend that *she* is the one to take orders, *not* I. Truly, Georgie, I have never met anyone quite like her."

Twisting her lips to the side, the younger woman guiltily claimed in a low voice, "I know a person a lot like Yvette." She waited until she caught Elizabeth's eye. "She, too, is used to getting her way and tries to control the lives of everyone around her."

"Who, Georgie?" asked Elizabeth in curiosity.

Inhaling loudly while squaring her shoulders, the young woman replied, "Aunt Catherine."

Elizabeth grinned widely and nodded. "I must concur with your estimation. I fear Lady Catherine would be a more formidable lady's maid than Yvette."

Bursting out in laughter, Georgiana cried, "Oh, Elizabeth, the images you conjure up are too delicious. First, Fitzwilliam waking up to visions of a bird being plucked to death, and now my aunt as a lady's maid—it is more than I can manage for one day."

"Well, the fancy concerning your aunt is truly only a figment of the imagination, but Yvette waking Fitzwilliam may prove to be a reality." Elizabeth laughed heartily with this declaration.

They ate their breakfast in high spirits, discussing Sally's surprise for Mr. Wilkens. They also spoke about what a blessing it was for her to be engaged to Thomas, and his being offered the opportunity of an overseer apprenticeship.

After breakfast, the pair parted. Elizabeth went searching for Mrs. Reynolds. When she did not find her, she enquired of Mr. Greene. The butler informed Mrs. Darcy that the housekeeper had gone into Lambton on an unexpected errand, yet they did expect her back by early afternoon. She then asked him if he had heard any news about the mining accident. He replied in the negative. Mr. Greene patiently waited for the mistress to take her leave, however, she did not go. Instead, she stood in place chewing her bottom lip while staring at the floor.

The butler noticed her preoccupation. "Mrs. Darcy, is there anything else with which I may help?"

Her head shot up. "Has Mr. Sheldon been here this morning? Do you know if he has gone to the mining camp?"

Again, Mr. Greene gave a negative response.

Elizabeth thanked him and wondered what could have taken Mrs. Reynolds away so suddenly. She began to worry for the welfare of her husband and the others. *Fitzwilliam, why have you not yet sent word or are you not able to do so*? It was all so vexing. She did not know how much longer she could endure the strain.

Knowing she needed to post a missive to Lydia soon did not help matters. She did not feel like dealing with another nerve-racking situation when the current crisis had not been resolved. Thus, Mrs. Darcy went to the library to see if reading would calm her nerves. She chuckled to herself at the thought that at least she had not turned to locking herself in her room and using smelling salts to relieve the anxiety.

As she entered the room, she was surprised to find Georgiana within. "Why, Georgie, I thought you were going to play at the pianoforte?"

"Yes, I was, but I truly do not feel musically inclined," she said in a morose manner, "so I decided to come and read the paper."

"Oh, I did not know the paper held your interest," Elizabeth remarked.

"I must admit, I do not read it with regularity, but I do like keeping up with the movement of our troops."

Raising her brows, Elizabeth offered a hint of a smile, as she made her way to the bookshelves. After several minutes of inspection, she chose a book and sat down at one of the tables to read. Both women continued in this pursuit for over an hour until Elizabeth finally put her book aside. "Georgie, where does Mr. Sheldon reside?"

"His home is midway between Pemberley and Lambton. Why do you ask?"

Elizabeth bit her lower lip in apprehension. "Oh, Georgiana, I was hoping to hear something this morning about Fitzwilliam and the others. I am beginning to worry. I know it is useless, but I asked Mrs. Reynolds yesterday if she had any news, and she told me she did not. She informed me that Mr. Sheldon would leave this morning for the camp if word had not come. Yet, she has gone to Lambton on an errand, and Mr. Greene informed me that he has received no word either. To the best of Mr. Greene's knowledge, Mr. Sheldon has not come to Pemberley this morning. I guess I had my hopes set on knowing something by now. At least I had the hope that Mr. Sheldon could discover the progress of the relief party. Our not hearing anything is truly difficult to bear."

Sighing, Georgiana nodded, but said nothing.

Elizabeth looked at the clock on the mantlepiece. It was past noon. Luncheon would be served later than normal, due to their breakfasting late. "Well, Georgie, I, for one, can no longer sit confined in this library. I must know something soon, even if I have to walk the whole distance to the mines to obtain it."

Georgiana joined her sister as they made their way to the kitchen. Elizabeth hoped that Mrs. Potter or some of the other servants might have heard some news. Both of the lady's faces were awe struck when they saw Richard sitting at one of the kitchen tables speaking with Mr. Manning.

Georgiana could not contain herself and ran over to him, throwing her arms round his neck. "Richard, whenever did you return?"

Elizabeth, still standing inside the kitchen's doorsill, searched for her husband through the bustling crowd of servants busily engaged with the preparations for not only their noon fare, but for dinner as well. In vain she looked, for Fitzwilliam was nowhere in sight. She quickly realized that Richard and Georgiana were now walking towards her.

Clearly reading anxiety upon the face of his cousin's wife, the colonel enquired, "Elizabeth is anything the matter?"

"I am just surprised to see you here. I did not know you had returned. When did you arrive? Did Fitzwilliam accompany you?"

With a slight shrug, Richard countered, "Well, we returned late last night. Have you not yet spoken with Darcy?"

In great haste, without giving Colonel Fitzwilliam a reply, Elizabeth crossed the kitchen and ran up the servants' stairs. *Fitzwilliam must have slept in his own chamber when finding that Georgiana slept with me.* She then ran the length of the hall, until she reached her husband's chamber. Without hesitation, she opened the door and walked quickly inside. Her eyes were immediately drawn to the empty, unmade bed. The door of her husband's dressing room was opened a crack. Boldly she pushed open the door providing a clear view of the back of her husband's curly head as he soaked in the tub.

She was oblivious to Mr. Chaffin's presence in the closet area, and the valet was just as ignorant of her presence while he acquired his master's clothing for the day.

With no thought of the consequences, Elizabeth rushed forward to stand behind her husband and stooped, encircling her arms around his neck and shoulders.

Stunned, Darcy jumped, and by so doing, splashed water all over her arms.

"Lizzy!" he cried as he sat upright, grabbing her hand and pulling her forward and around to the tub's side. She did not pause at the bathtub's side, but instead, she lunged forth into her husband's arms.

Darcy's arms came up and out of the water in anticipation of welcoming his beloved wife. Drawing her to his chest, he captured her mouth, eagerly tasting her. While thus engaged, her torso leaned over towards her husband with her hip supporting the weight of her body on the tub's edge.

Mr. Darcy's cry startled Mr. Chaffin. When the valet turned towards the bathing area to ascertain what his master desired, he perceived his master and Mrs. Darcy in an amorous embrace. He quietly laid the clothing aside and slowly opened the servant's door to take his leave.

~*~

As Mr. Chaffin looked upon his master, his heart eased even as an affectionate smile graced his features. Chaffin had not even been aware that his master had returned in the night, until he set eyes on the murky water in the tub that morning. Upon seeing it, he smiled knowingly. All was well with Mr. Darcy. Straightway, he energetically started to empty the dirty water from the copper drum in order to clean it and have it ready for his master's next bath. While thus engaged, he strove to be as quiet as possible, so as not to disturb his master as he slept. He had been scrubbing for no more than a few moments when he heard a shrill voice singing in French. He was quite taken aback. How on earth could anyone have the bad manners to sing out without thought of the sleeping household?

These remembrances came to Chaffin's mind as he made his way to the kitchen. He considered the new maid. She was extremely attractive, but, in his professional opinion, she had a lot to learn when it came to respectable service. Disdainfully, he thought of the French and their passionate ways. They could learn a thing or two about true propriety from their neighbours across the Channel.

~*~

After some minutes, Darcy broke their kiss yet continued to hold his wife in his arms, their faces pressed close. Finally, Elizabeth spoke. "Fitzwilliam, I had no idea you had come home until Georgie and I saw Richard in the kitchen. I have been beside myself with worry for you and all the others. Why ever did you not send word?" Pulling her head back, she looked at him intently as she waited for his answer.

"Lizzy, I can only say that, with the situation being pressing and somewhat chaotic, I was unable to send word. Truly, I am sorry that I failed to do so, but it could not be helped."

"Well, do not feel badly. If it could not be helped, then it could not be helped. It no longer matters, for you are here now." Then, in concern, Elizabeth asked, "Are all well, Fitzwilliam? Has anyone been seriously injured or even…?"

He came straight to the point, realizing his wife's fear. "No one died, Lizzy."

"I am so grateful. Georgie and I prayed for you and everyone." She placed her hands upon his wet chest and gently pushed herself back into an upright position. Hence, while perched on the tub's rim, Elizabeth was able to look over her husband's appearance. She smiled and reached out her hand to brush her fingertips against his prickly cheek. "Oh, Fitzwilliam, I have never seen your beard so long. You look almost wild!" She laughed spiritedly at his appearance.

Darcy smiled widely, but his dimples were hidden beneath his beard. He looked at his wife and said, unreservedly, "Caroline Bingley said the very same thing about your appearance when you had walked to Netherfield to enquire after your sister. After you left us in the breakfast room, she claimed your hair's appearance was almost wild."

Creasing his brow as he looked at his wife's displeased expression, he quickly added, "She then asked for my opinion with the expectation that it would have been the same as hers. I merely told her that I thought your eyes were brightened by the exercise." Looking intently at his wife, he affirmed, "Lizzy, I love your eyes, especially when they are brightened by exercise." He grinned as he waggled his brows.

Lifting one brow, Elizabeth responded sassily, "Lucky for you to have such a sensible reply to Caroline's unkindness." Smirking mischievously, she stated with feigned severity, "I am sure that, at the time, your complimentary appraisal of me disconcerted her greatly. It was quite cruel of you to abuse her so. I wish I had known you thought so well of me then, because I was certain that you and Miss Bingley always saw eye to eye on everything."

Her words hit their desired target, and Darcy's face darkened with her inference to his character resembling Caroline Bingley's. His lips formed a fine line, and he pointedly glared at his cheeky wife. She defiantly returned his glower, and, for several seconds, they continued in this mode.

Mutinously, he stated with a twinkle in his eye, "I have missed you, my dearest Lizzy. It has been far too long and, remember, I know how you like to profess opinions that are not entirely your own." He gave her a salacious grin. "Do you mean to frighten me, Elizabeth, by coming into my dressing chamber to see me? I will not be alarmed because there is a stubbornness about me that never can bear to be frightened, thus, you know that I always arise with your every attempt to intimidate me." Triumphantly he smirked back to her.

Raising her brows in response to his counter, her face remained fixed as she slowly rose from the edge of the tub. While so doing, she quickly dipped her fingers into the bath, flicking water upon her husband's face. "Such cheek, Mr. Darcy!"

His eyelids fluttered from the wet spray as his jaw tightened. "My dear girl, you are as impertinent as ever. I have a mind to come out of this tub and give you a measure of your own medicine."

Elizabeth flashed a reckless smile at her husband. He adored the challenging look she was giving him, and he wanted nothing more than to immediately take leave of his bath in order to kiss it right off of her pretty little face. Hence, he arose to his full stature and quickly stepped over the side of the tub.

Elizabeth shrieked in delight as she ran into his bedchamber, seeking the farthest point of the room with the bed between her and the dressing chamber door.

Darcy entered his chamber bare, dripping wet, with small amounts of lather slowly trickling down his arms, chest, and legs.

Smiling with confidence, he meandered towards the nearest side of the bed. Reaching the mattress, he gazed at his wife directly across from him. He held his hands out from his sides with his palms opened and cautioned, "Lizzy, if I were you, I would not even attempt to run or hide. It would be pointless to do so. I am sorry to have to cause you so much distress in dressing again, but I believe you are the one who waged this war." He grinned at her in that adorable, roguish manner of his.

Her eyes began to journey across the length of his broad-shouldered physique, then moving downward, taking in the masculinity of the sculpted muscles that graced his leanness. This visual exploration ignited the familiar stirring within the depths of her body and, suddenly, she no longer wanted to spar with him. Instead, she needed to be aware of his arms around her, sense his lips upon her skin, and hear his reassuring whispers of adoration intended for her ears alone.

Darcy watched her eyes wandering over his body, and he was instantly filled with desire. Witnessing Elizabeth's attraction towards him was the very balm he needed to soothe his grievances against his cousin and his uncertainties concerning her affection.

As her eyes made contact with his, she perceived the intense desire therein. He then emotionally petitioned, "I am afraid, Lizzy, you have all the advantage, for I appear before you in a state of vulnerability and defencelessness, but I fear that neither of us has lost the battle, for it looks as if we have mutually agreed to wave the white banner of surrender."

Even though she continued to make sport with the words of war, she no longer jested as she voluntarily conceded, "I will gladly lay down my arms and surrender to you, sir."

His eyes never left hers as he strode around the circumference of the bed swiftly lifting her in his arms and shifting them both onto the bed. Huskily, he murmured, "Lizzy, how I have longed for your kisses and so much more!"

Their union was sweet and satisfying, and each felt cherished beyond measure.

Hours later, long after luncheon had been served, word was sent down to Mrs. Potter to have their meal sent up on trays, and to inform the colonel and mistress Georgiana of their absence until dinner.

~*~

Darcy was famished and ate his meal ravenously. It had been days since he had eaten enough to compensate for the energy he had exerted at the mine.

They sat in his chamber in front of the fire. He wore his robe, and Elizabeth sat wrapped in only a blanket. She smiled faintly while watching him devour the sustenance Mrs. Potter's fare provided. Elizabeth loved every aspect of him and marvelled at her inability to stand firm concerning his high-handedness. She had been convinced that she could resist any intimacy with him until he fully understood his propensity for being too authoritative and, at times, too fastidious regarding what he thought was in her best interest. Yet, she had failed. She craved and needed the physical bonding as much as he did. However, Elizabeth knew all too well that if they had anymore strain placed upon their marriage without open and honest discussion devoid of a resolution, their love might not be enough to carry them through the upset. Implacable resentment could then fester to the point of turning their affectionate marriage into a living nightmare.

"Fitzwilliam, I have forgotten to tell you that I have a new lady's maid."

Dabbing his mouth with his napkin, he turned to look at her with surprise and asked, "Lizzy, what do you mean you have a new maid? I thought I made my sentiments perfectly clear that I do not want one of the scullery maids to attend to you."

With a quick roll of her eyes, she stated, "Yes, my love, you did make yourself quite clear on that point. This maid, however, is of your own choosing. She is the French lady's maid you desired to obtain for me."

"I cannot believe it. How can she be here so soon?"

"Evidently, her mistress had recently died in London, and your solicitor, Mr. Kearns, acquired her and sent her to Pemberley. She arrived yesterday."

His eyes gladdened. "Ah! I see. I had hoped to be here to surprise you. She is an early birthday present, Lizzy. I wanted you to have the best maid possible. She has been especially trained. Were you surprised?"

He had asked his question in so much delight that Elizabeth hardly had the nerve to speak her concerns about the maid.

"Oh, yes, excessively, in more ways than one." Elizabeth's voice held a tinge of irony.

Darcy's face effused satisfaction, and he felt serene as he looked upon his wife wrapped in the blanket, some loosened locks of hair falling over her bare shoulders. With pride, he stared adoringly into her eyes. "Hmmm, has your new maid impressed you thus far with her capabilities?"

Striving hard to squelch the smirk threatening to appear at any moment, she acknowledged, "Why, I would have to say she has," her eyes widened in playfulness, "because Yvette is very adroit in all of her undertakings, and *she* even claims, Fitzwilliam, that *she* will surpass all of *your* expectations concerning her."

"I am glad to hear it. I want the best for you, Lizzy."

Her lips puckered into a playful pout. "Last night, she fashioned my braid with an exquisite ribbon. I felt it most becoming." He smiled at her with pleasure. "She is also very efficient with my toilette. There is one hindrance, however." Darcy looked questioningly at her. "She can only speak French, and I can only speak English. Therefore, you and Georgie may be called upon more oft than not. I am afraid you will tire of such an inconvenience."

Amusement was apparent upon her husband's face. She was a little taken aback with his reaction. Darcy found the situation to be quite to his liking. A lady's maid, who could only speak French, in a household where almost no one else could, met with his wholehearted approval. There would never be any disclosures about their relationship within their private chambers.

Heartily, he replied, "I am glad to hear it, Lizzy, and I will not mind in the least to help in your communications with your maid. Georgie and I can help you to learn French."

Her brows shot up in surprise and then creased just as quickly. "I am not at all sure that I desire to learn the language. It is beautiful to be sure, but I have never had the inclination or patience to practice."

He smiled with assurance. "Then let this be your chance to do so. What better opportunity than with a person with whom you may practice daily. What is your maid's name?"

"Yvette."

His face sobered for an instant. The name sounded too much like "Collette" for his taste. "Ah, well, I shall speak with her and ask her to help you along with the language."

"But, Fitzwilliam, I am not at all sure if I care to master the language. I am willing to learn the phrases required for us to understand one another, but anything further is open to debate."

"Very well, Lizzy, we shall start with only the essential phrases." He thought perhaps this would be best, after all. That way, his wife would not become emotionally attached as she had been with her previous two maids. Yes! This situation was better than anything he could have hoped.

"Oh, Lizzy, before I forget, we are to host an informal dinner tomorrow evening. It will be for all of the mine owners and their wives. It is imperative that we meet and discuss the future of the mine."

"If not a formal dinner, then what do you suggest?"

"I told them a buffet would be spread. You may choose whatever provisions you would like Mrs. Potter to prepare. I am sorry it is such short notice, but it is really nothing to fret over."

"Jane and Charles will be here by then," she said in dejection.

"I am sorry, Lizzy, but this meeting cannot be deferred. The men will separate from the ladies for a time, but, thereafter, we will all assemble in the music room, and I thought we could, perchance, implore whomever so desires to perform at the pianoforte. That is if this meets with your approval?"

Biting her lower lip, she thought about his suggestion and desire for her endorsement. It felt, however, that she truly had no choice in the matter. She decided not to say as much but, as an alternative, determined to support him as a wife should.

"Yes, Fitzwilliam, I think it is a wonderful idea not to worry with formality for the evening. That way, I may spend my time with Jane."

Uneasily, he looked towards his wife. "There is also a hunting party planned for tomorrow morning after breakfast."

"Oh, I see. Will the women come as well?"

"No, only the men will participate in the hunt."

"Then, I shall have Jane all to myself."

His lips formed a pleasant smile at her response, and he reached for her hand. She, likewise, put her hand forward as she clutched the blanket close with her other one. He gazed deeply into her eyes. "I love you, Elizabeth. I love you truly. I love the way you love Georgiana and me. It means the world to me."

She smiled and squeezed his hand. "I love you both, as well. Oh, I have almost forgotten. The day you left to go to the mine, when I came down the stairs," Darcy's eyes shone in enchantment with the memory, "I was coming to tell you some wonderful news. Sally is engaged to Thomas Wilkens, and Mr. Manning has offered him the apprenticeship as overseer." Her eyes were radiant as she related this information.

"Does this please you, Lizzy?" Already aware that it did, he wanted to hear her declare it just the same.

"Oh, yes, I am very pleased and very happy for her. She is a deserving girl, and to win the affections of such a fine young man makes me happy, indeed. But there is something that made me much happier than that." She fixed her gaze upon him.

"Pray, Lizzy, continue."

She sighed deeply, and her eyes widened in wonder. "I was so happy to learn of her engagement and their good fortune that I desired to run outdoors and shout to the whole world about my gladness. Nevertheless, the weather was still dreary outside, so I went up to walk in the picture gallery. I studied the pictures of many generations of Darcys, but the one that always holds my interest is yours. As I gazed upon your likeness, I thought about how pleased you would be for Thomas Wilkens, and that is when I knew."

He chuckled briefly, but then noticed that her face revealed intense emotion. Therefore, he tightened his clasp upon her hand. "Knew what, Elizabeth?"

"I knew you were the one who arranged it all for them: the cottage, the overseer's apprenticeship, and every needed thing." Tears glistened in her eyes as she gazed into his.

He shook his head slightly. "I did not provide their love or Thomas's integrity. He has earned this position. I only conferred with Mr. Manning about the possibility and worked out some minor details. That is all."

His vision cast downward, and then Elizabeth leaned forward and pulled her hand from his grasp. She tilted his chin upward with gentleness and looked directly into his eyes. "When I knew you were the one responsible, my heart was so full that, in my eagerness, I ran the length of the corridor and down the stairs in a very noisy fashion to find you. I desired to tell you how much I love you, Fitzwilliam. You are the best of men."

He searched her eyes and knew she meant what she had just said. But his face appeared weighed down. These were the exact words Chaffin had overheard the maids say. These were the words she had spoken to his cousin. In a great agony of spirit, he took her hand and kissed her palm. He then looked at her once more and fell to his knees before her. For a second time, he picked up her hand and began kissing her palm, again and again.

She was moved beyond words at his tenderness. Repeatedly, she caressed the side of his face, smiling as she felt the prickliness of his whiskers. He then laid his head in her lap while tears welled up in his eyes. He now realized that her exuberance on the stairs had been all for him. He did not want to believe she could share the same sentiment for his cousin as well. Who in the bloody hell heard what, where, and when? He felt as if he were going mad from the uncertainty.

Elizabeth could tell that he had become quite emotional, and she quietly asked, "Fitzwilliam, is anything the matter, my love?"

He shook his head, which still rested upon her knees, and with his face concealed from her view, he whispered, "It is nothing. I am only exhausted from having slept little for the past two days."

She ran her fingers through his hair, over the side of his brow, and down his jaw line. They stayed in this pose for several minutes with neither saying a word. Her caresses seemed to bring him comfort from whatever frustration he was feeling, therefore, she continued to lightly brush his temple and outline his ear with her fingertips.

A loud knock at the chamber door startled Elizabeth and caused Darcy to raise his head while leaning backward to sit upon his heels. Turning his face towards the door, he called out, "What is wanted?"

"Brother," Georgiana related through the closed door, "I am sorry to disturb you, and I am happy that you and Richard are home safe and sound, but I have come to tell you some wonderful news. Mr. Bingley and Elizabeth's sisters are now alighting from their carriage. Richard has stayed below and asked me to come and inform you."

"Ah! Thank you, Georgie. Do tell them we will join them before long."

"Oh, Fitzwilliam," Elizabeth cried. "They have arrived a whole day early. I am not dressed, and my hair is a sight."

He noticed the blanket lying on the floor as his wife frantically tried to locate her clothing. Pressing his hands on his thighs, he swayed upon the balls of his feet and immediately arose. "I will help you to dress first. That way you can go down to greet them."

"No, I will go and call for Yvette. You need to have Chaffin come and shave off your beard." Stopping from gathering her things, she walked over to him, placed her hand upon his jaw, and gave it a quick tug. "I think I could get used to this, Mr Darcy."

He smiled. "Here," he said, removing his robe, "wear this and go, now, to your chamber. I will ring for Chaffin and meet you downstairs in the music room in a quarter of an hour."

Nodding, she donned his robe and walked swiftly towards her own chamber while expressing her gratitude for his kindness.

~*~

Colonel Fitzwilliam and Georgiana greeted and entertained the guests for several minutes before a breathless Mrs. Darcy joined them. Upon entering the music room, Elizabeth instantly looked at Jane, and happiness played upon her countenance as the sisters made eye contact.

Jane quickly arose to embrace her beloved sister. "Oh, Lizzy, I am so happy to see you again!"

Her eyes brimming with tears, Elizabeth replied as they held each other closely, "And, I, you. Jane, it has been far too long."

Bingley had arisen as well when Elizabeth entered the room and now stood beside his wife, anxiously awaiting his chance to greet his sister-in-law. When Elizabeth stepped back, she smiled widely to him and exclaimed, "Charles, it is so good of you to bring my Jane to me."

With great cheerfulness, he made answer, "I am delighted to be obliging, Elizabeth. We are *all* so pleased to be here at Pemberley. You look very well and quite happy. I take it Darcy will join us shortly?"

Contentedly, she answered, "Oh, yes, he has been gone for a few days and just returned this morning. Accordingly, he has slept in, but he will soon be with us."

Bingley smiled in high spirits. "Good, good! I so desire to see him again."

"Well, Charles, here I am," Darcy said as he walked into the room.

Everyone directed their attention towards him, and Caroline stood immediately, smiling. When Miss Bingley rose, Kitty looked a little bewildered and wondered if she, too, should stand. Hesitantly, she did so.

Charles stepped forward and extended his hand to his dear friend and, now, brother. Darcy clasped the proffered hand of his brother-in-law as the former shook it vigorously. Darcy winced slightly from the jerking of his arm due to the muscular strain he had encountered while at the mine.

"Darce, I cannot say enough about how glad I am to see you again."

Chuckling lightly, Darcy looked at Bingley and said, "Yes, you are a day ahead of schedule, Charles."

Sheepishly, Bingley answered, "Ah...that ...well, I did send word that we would be coming a day early, but you must not have received it yet. I suppose I should have sent an express."

"Never mind, it is not important. You are here now, and that is all that matters." Darcy turned to Jane and said cordially, "Jane, I am happy you are all here safe and sound. I hope your trip was not too burdensome. I know coming to Pemberley is a journey to tire the most avid of travellers."

Jane smiled serenely. "The trip was lengthy, to be sure, but it is well worth the price to see your lovely home and to see you and my sister again. I thank you for the invitation, sir."

A quick grin flashed upon Darcy's face as he looked at Jane. Her appearance did seem almost...what was the word for it? Ah, yes, Bingley's oft repeated word of admiration, *angelic*. He truly felt that she glowed and the word was an adequate description of her at this precise moment. Contentedly, he gently nodded and said, "We are honoured to have your company and so glad you could bring Miss Bingley and Miss Catherine, as well."

After this statement, Darcy turned to greet both women. Caroline gave a slight bow of her head, smiled demurely, and held out her hand to the Master of Pemberley as she sweetly declared, "No journey is too far when Pemberley is the destination." He took her hand, pressed it slightly, and then gave a small bow. Likewise, he walked over to Kitty and put forth his hand. She stood in awe for several seconds before raising hers to his. This time, he bent lower and bestowed a quick kiss upon her hand.

Kitty's eyes bulged from his attention. With barely a whisper, she stammered, "I thank you, Mr. Darcy, for the invitation as well. Your home is grander than anything I have ever seen."

Darcy's dimples showed for a few seconds after Kitty's open profession and her gawking at all that surrounded her. "Yes, well, I am glad you like it."

From the corner of his eye, Darcy saw Elizabeth speaking with a young maid in the hall. He realized she must have been informing the maid to contact Mrs. Potter and tell her of the extra guests to be expected for dinner this evening.

Mrs. Darcy came back into the room wearing a radiant smile. She walked over to her husband and in a low tone, informed him all was in order for that evening and for the morrow's as well. His eyes brightened with the knowledge that his wife was beginning to fulfil her role as mistress with poise. Darcy then gestured for all to take a seat. Bingley related the details of their trip and reported how the roads were treacherous in some areas, but by and large, they did not have too much trouble.

Georgiana attempted to make some conversation with Kitty. This pleased the other young woman greatly, and they spoke about projects they had been working on over the last few months. Georgiana noticed that Kitty's eyes kept straying in another direction. Therefore, she quickly glanced over her shoulder to see what was holding the young lady's interest. Immediately, she saw not what, but whom. Richard was in rapt conversation with Bingley and Fitzwilliam. Georgiana bit her lower lip and frowned.

Miss Bingley watched Jane and Elizabeth in conversation. Jane was as calm as ever, and Eliza was her usual animated self. Cynically, she stared at the two of them. However had it come to this? Eliza Bennet was a *nobody* from the uncivilized county of Hertfordshire. Mr. Darcy had to have been taken in by her arts and allurements. She knew that Eliza had the type of figure that most men found desirable, and this must have been the only reason he had yielded to her charm. Caroline had considered this possibility and entertained the notion that Miss Eliza had certainly entrapped the master of Pemberley. He had capitulated to his weaker nature. After all, he had admitted at Netherfield that he preferred to watch their figures as they walked the circumference of the room. Eliza must have realized immediately that Mr. Darcy found her figure pleasing. Thus, she, in the course of events, had lured him in. Maybe it had occurred the previous summer when she and her Cheapside relations had wittingly and impolitely dropped in to tour Pemberley. Yes, that had to have been when it happened. He, being the honourable man that he was, became honour bound. It was the only plausible explanation for the whole affair. After all, he had sided with her and Louisa on the matter of the unacceptability of the Bennet family. Yet, here he was married into such a ridiculous clan, and, therefore, so was her brother.

Caroline moved about the room watching and observing as they all visited for a half-hour longer. Finally Elizabeth suggested that they go and rest from their journey and meet again for dinner. Not at all pleased, Caroline dutifully followed as Mrs. Reynolds showed them to their rooms. Jane and Charles were situated on the same side of the hall, next to the master's chambers while she and Kitty were placed across the hall, Kitty being two doors down from the colonel's room and Caroline's two doors further away. Miss Bingley was not happy with the arrangement but said nothing to the housekeeper, feeling that this visit might tax all of her reserve and perhaps not be as pleasant as she had hoped. Deep down, she had hoped that one of these days, Mr. Darcy would come to regret his impetuous and imprudent decision of marrying so beneath him. Surely, it was only a matter of time before Eliza Bennet's allurements would fade. Instead, his passion would be replaced by embarrassment and regret. Yes, Mr. Darcy would realize his loss, and she, Caroline Bingley, would gladly be there to console him. He would then appreciate her true worth.

~*~

An hour later, Sally went in search of the mistress. She found Mrs. Darcy within her study with her head bent over account books. The young woman knocked softly on the open door. Elizabeth's head shot up, and she smiled immediately upon seeing her former maid standing at the door. "Oh, do, please, come in, Sally. I feel my mind needs the rest from looking at these figures for the past hour. Have you told Mr. Wilkens about the cottage?

The young woman smiled graciously and nodded. "Yes, ma'am, I did. In fact, me and Tommy went over there, and he was pleased as sweet molasses."

Elizabeth raised her brows as her lips spread into a wide smile. "Oh, I am so glad he approves."

"He does, indeed! He is so pleased." Sally smiled broadly standing before the mistress' desk and then continued, "I have come to let you know we have arranged to be married the day after next at the small chapel here on the grounds of Pemberley. Mr. Darcy has given his consent for us to do so, and I would so like it if you could attend, Mrs. Darcy. You have been so wonderful to me. I have never known such kindness as I have from you, besides from me mum."

Elizabeth's brows rose in pleasant surprise. Her heart swelled in pride for her husband's continued goodness.

"Sally, I would love to attend. What time is the wedding?"

"Ten o'clock, ma'am. It will just be Tommy and his family and maybe the Mannings as well."

"May I spend the morning with you and help you prepare for it?"

Sally's face lit up, but she hesitated. "I would like that ever so much. Yet, I do know that you have company right now, and I am sure you won't be havin' the free time."

"Nonsense, Jane is the most understanding sister in the world. If Georgiana is able to come, would you mind if she attends as well?"

"Oh, no, I would like mistress Georgiana to come, if she wishes."

"Good, then it is settled. I will join you a little after breakfast on the morning of your wedding. Is there anything else I can help you with presently?"

"No, ma'am, I think everything has been arranged." Sally smiled and then exited the room.

~*~

That evening after dinner, following Jane's request, the family group decided they would all go on a tour of the house, since Jane and Kitty had never before had the opportunity to see Pemberley. The party started out in the library. Caroline could not contain her praises of the Darcy's extensive collection. Pulling her sister-in-law close, Miss Bingley proclaimed, "Dear, Jane, Pemberley's collection is a generational, literary feat!" Caroline then went into raptures over the rarity of some of the books, many of which were first editions, revealing that some had been inscribed with personal sentiments within the cover by the authors themselves.

Lacing her arm through Jane's, she virtually took over the tour from Elizabeth. Bingley was preoccupied in conversation with the colonel and did not notice his sister's machinations. He and Richard were speaking softly, off to one side of the room. Georgiana, likewise, was talking to Kitty about the latest novel she had been reading and asked Kitty if she also shared the love of a good tome. Miss Catherine Bennet looked dumbfounded and shook her head. She admitted that she had never taken the time to become interested in books. In a quick attempt to remedy such deficiency, mistress Georgiana gently pulled Kitty along by the hand to the far side of the room to search for the book that had first sparked her interest in intellectual pursuits.

Elizabeth's arms were folded across her chest as she watched Caroline's ploys from several feet away. The woman was infuriating. Yet, for the sake of Jane and Bingley, she would try to temper her mounting anger coupled with frustration. Darcy had just picked up a newspaper when Caroline's sickeningly sweet voice elicited his help from clear across the room. Quietly rolling his eyes, he sighed and shrugged his shoulders. Tossing the paper back upon his desk, he dutifully walked across the room to where Caroline was holding Jane hostage.

"Oh there you are Mr. Darcy," she smiled brilliantly towards him, "I was just telling our dear Jane that you have many first editions which have been inscribed by the authors upon the flyleaf."

It was all he could do to force himself to converse with such an insipid and fawning woman. "Well, yes, that book you hold there is a first edition of *Lyrical Ballalds* published by Cottle in 1798. My father, and his father before him, took great delight in collecting the first editions of many books and some do have the autographs and personal sentiments of the authors."

Looking to Jane now, Darcy directed the conversation to her. "Jane, this one here," he moved a few steps over to the bookshelf and pulled out a slender leather bound work, "was given to me when I was a young boy. It is a first edition of *Blake's Songs of Innocence*." Opening the volume to the flyleaf and holding it up for Jane's viewing, Darcy pointed at the inscription and added, "There, you can see, is a message addressed to me, written in Blake's hand. He and my father corresponded some, and my father had visited with him on several occasions. We do have many other books in this section that are very old and some which are, indeed, quite rare."

Jane smiled as she read the message that the poet had written to her brother-in-law when he had been a very small boy. "That is so lovely, Mr. Darcy. Did your mother share your father's enthusiasm for learning?"

A light smile graced his lips at her interest. "Yes, she did. They were both lovers of reading and of the exchanging of ideas. I suppose they passed their enthusiasm on to me."

Mrs. Bingley's face shone brilliantly as she stated, "My father, too, shares a passion for reading, but my mother never has. Yet, Lizzy and Mary do. However, Lizzy," she turned towards her sister, "has more extensive tastes than does Mary. My father and Lizzy love to exchange their views on books and often times their conversations can take a lively turn."

Darcy and Jane exchanged a knowing look, and then he stated, "Yes, Elizabeth is a woman of many talents, and I am impressed with her literary interests."

Jane continued to smile at him with gladness in her eyes. Caroline, however, becoming frustrated that she was not a part of the conversation, reached forth, and snatched the tome from Darcy's hand.

"I have never read anything by Blake. I think I shall start to read this tonight." Darcy's jaw hardened as he gently reached to take the volume back. "Allow me to find a spare, Miss Bingley. These books are never taken out of the library." He swiftly crossed the room to obtain a less precious copy of the said book. "Here, this is a newer edition. It has additional poems which the author added to the original. Hence, Blake renamed the volume *Songs of Innocence AND of Experience*. I am sure you will find something that will please you in your perusal of his fine work."

Caroline feigned interest and forced a smile as she stated, "I feel that a woman must constantly expand her mind through extensive reading. It is a mark of true distinction of an accomplished lady to be sure, and I, for one, am a relentless reader."

Jane smiled a faint smile at her sister-in-law but did not comment upon the falseness of Caroline's assertion. Darcy looked closely at his eldest sister-in-law and could tell that she was fatigued. "Jane," he enquired softly, "would you care to rest? I am sure Elizabeth will not mind resuming the tour of the house tomorrow."

Looking kindly at her new brother, she replied, "I must confess, I am a little weary. If you are sure that it would not offend, I do think I would like to retire a little early."

Darcy offered his arm to her. She immediately took it. He led her over to where Bingley and Richard were in conversation and, now, joined by Elizabeth. When Charles noticed their approach, he immediately stood and anxiously asked, "Janey, are you not well?"

Jane withdrew her arm from Darcy's and imparted whispered words of thanks to him. She then looked at her husband. "I feel a little tired, that is all."

Bingley and Elizabeth were by her side immediately, and Elizabeth asked, "Would you like some water or wine, Jane?"

Lizzy, I thank you. I fear the trip has wearied me more than I realized. If it is all right with you, I think I shall retire."

"Most definitely, Jane. Do let me send up some refreshment for you from the kitchen."

"No, please, do not bother. I am in need of sleep only."

"May I walk with you to your chamber?" Elizabeth appealed to her sister. Then, turning towards her brother, added, "That is, Charles, if it is acceptable to you?"

Bingley stated, enthusiastically, "I could think of nothing that would please me more than to have your company, Elizabeth."

Smiling at her husband, Elizabeth took one of Jane's arms as Bingley laid claim to the other. While they were exiting the room, she saw that Georgiana and Kitty continued their enjoyable discussion in the far corner of the room, and she took note of Caroline sitting at the table with a befuddled expression on her face as she attempted to read a book.

The colonel and Darcy continued to stand as they watched them depart. Then, Darcy turned to go back to his desk to retrieve the paper when Richard called his name. "Darcy, I really must speak with you."

Darcy heaved a sigh and turned back to look at his cousin. "Fitzwilliam, whatever you have to say can surely wait until the morrow. I have not had a chance to sit down and read in quite some time."

Colonel Fitzwilliam's eyes bore into his cousin's. "Darcy, I will no longer wait for a likely opportunity which seems to never happen."

In exasperation, Darcy spit out, "Fine, whatever you want to say, say it quickly, before Elizabeth and Bingley return."

"Really, Darcy, I would rather speak with you in your study."

Slumping down into a chair, Darcy raised a hand, indicating for his cousin to do the same. "Here will be fine, Richard. Just speak quietly."

Richard tightened his lips in frustration but decided to sit, anyway. "Darcy, I do not know what is going on with you. You seem to be avoiding me, and I do have some concerns that I would like to discuss with you."

He waited for a response, but Darcy said not a word. His cousin's eyes stared at the toe of his shoes as he clasped his hands together in his lap. In frustration, Richard continued, "First, what on earth was Elizabeth doing in one of your tenant's homes? She could have had far greater injury than what was inflicted."

The colonel was immediately aware of the flinching of Darcy's jaw. An odd expression, one of shock and alarm, suddenly crossed his features. Nevertheless, Richard realized that his cousin's ire had subsided just as quickly as it had begun. The colonel did not know quite what to make of it. He knew his cousin was distant at times to be sure, but Darcy had always shared most of his concerns with him. Had he overstepped his bounds with such enquiries?

"Darcy, is anything the matter?"

Oblivious to the fact that his cousin had just asked him a question, Darcy's mind was preoccupied with the discovery that his signet ring was no longer on his finger. He had moved to twirl it when Richard had begun the conversation, only to discover that it was no longer there.

Looking up hastily at his cousin's repeated question, Darcy asked tersely, "What?"

Richard shook his head and repeated himself for a third time. "Is there anything the matter?"

Quickly standing, Darcy nodded and stated, "I am sorry, Fitzwilliam. I need to go to my chamber. We will have this discussion at a more convenient time. Please, excuse me." He headed for the door and strode from the room.

The colonel scratched his head and then rubbed his hand over his mouth. He thought that he really should leave, for he had business that needed tending. He determined, however, that he would go immediately after the hunt, since he had promised Mr. Caldecott that he would be in attendance. He was not sure what was wrong with Darcy, but he had an idea that Collette Caldecott might play some part in his cousin's ill humour.

When Elizabeth returned sometime later, she found only Richard within the library. Questioningly, she looked at him, and the colonel stated as he rose, "They have all retired for the night."

Her eyebrows shot up in surprise as she said, "Even Fitzwilliam?"

"Well, I am not sure about his plans. He left abruptly a quarter of an hour ago. Miss Bingley, however, said that reading had given her a sudden headache, and Georgie and your sister, Catherine, wanted to go and look at Georgiana's gowns for the upcoming ball at Matlock."

Elizabeth sighed. She sat down and wearily replied, "Oh."

Colonel Fitzwilliam likewise sat. He then eyed her for some seconds before venturing a comment. "Your nose, Elizabeth, is no longer as swollen as it had been, and the bruise on your cheek has faded quite a lot."

"Oh, I have a new maid now, and she has camouflaged it remarkably well with some wonderful powder."

Indecisively, Richard considered if he dare ask Elizabeth about Darcy's frame of mind and why she had gone to a tenant dwelling alone. He thought the better of it, knowing Darcy would be infuriated that he had spoken to his wife about something so personal. No, he would have to wait out his cousin's foul mood. It would not be the first time and surely not the last.

Leaning forward to be closer to the colonel, Elizabeth enquired, "Colonel, I know this is none of my affair, but have you and Fitzwilliam by chance discussed whether Georgiana will be allowed to dance at your mother and father's ball? I am only curious because, with Kitty here, I feel it may be hard on Georgie not to take part in the festivity with everyone else. I am sure whatever you both decide will be what is best, but I do hope you will both consider her wishes as she has expressed them."

Richard also leaned forward and spoke softly, "Elizabeth, be assured I will do everything in my power to ensure that she is able to dance some dances. If it were left to me alone, I would allow her to dance the whole night away."

"Well," Darcy spoke in a clipped tone, standing several feet away, "maybe we should all decide upon the matter here and now. I suppose I am outvoted on any opinions or reservations that I may have concerning my sister's welfare. But, nonetheless, let us cast our ballots." He stood off to the side, several feet away, glaring at the two of them. Richard and Elizabeth immediately sat upright when they heard his voice. Elizabeth's heart raced, for she knew her husband must be angry with her. She remembered all too clearly his annoyance when she had broached the subject with him earlier in the week at which time she had accused him of being overbearing, and she recalled how their discussion had led to spiteful words between them.

Richard's brow knitted as he looked up to his cousin. "Very well, Darcy, this is one of the issues that I have desired to speak with you about. I think it will do no harm to consider Elizabeth's views as well as Georgiana's."

Darcy's eyes looked piercingly into his wife's as he calmly stated, "I am fully aware of Elizabeth's interests on many issues. I know her sentiments concerning Georgiana's inability to attend a dance before her introduction into society. Pray, Richard, as you just told my wife, you would like Georgiana to participate in the activity the whole of the night, would you not? Moreover, if you cannot acquire my agreement with your opinion, then you desire she would at least dance a number of dances. Is this correct?" The calmness of his voice gave way to slight irritation as he asked his questions.

"Why, I suppose those are my feelings exactly," Richard answered.

"You suppose? Did I not hear you state to my wife that you would convince me to let it be so? I imagine that my domineering disposition is a problematical situation for everyone in this household to contend with." He indignantly threw his hands up in the air. "Far be it from me to stand in the way of my sister's wishes. Therefore, I defer the decision of how many dances she is to dance to you, Richard, with my wife's guidance, of course. Please inform Georgiana of your joint verdict. I am going to retire for the night. Take as long as you need to reach your conclusion, but I assume it will not take too long, since you appear to be of one mind already." Instantly, he turned and left the room.

Flabbergasted, Richard and Elizabeth looked towards each other in apprehension. Neither said a word for some moments, until Richard ventured to speak. "Elizabeth, do not let Darcy's words trouble you too much. He has had a lot on his mind with the mining accident. Many of the other owners are not in agreement with his way of thinking, so there is a division among them. He is under great duress right now."

"Richard, I am astounded."

"Do not be. He has his moods, and they are not usually caused by the matter at hand. He has always taken everything to heart and, overall, contemplates far too much. His greatest virtue seems to lead to his greatest vice."

"I am not sure I follow your meaning?"

The colonel drew in a deep breath. "What I mean is that Darcy is one of the most caring men in the world. He feels for everyone, especially those to whom he is closest, and tries to alleviate their burdens."

"This is the wonderful part of him that I adore, yet I do not understand how this virtue could lead to his vice?" cried Elizabeth.

"He loathes himself concerning his shortcomings. There is no possible way for him to grant every needed thing for every individual. Thus, he deliberates and worries whether he has done the right thing or if he should have done something differently. It will eat away at him for some time if he feels he has been in error."

Understanding dawned in Elizabeth's mind. "Yes, I comprehend your meaning now. He does not forgive himself easily, and I am afraid he does not forgive others so easily, either, especially those for whom he has formed a firm resentment."

Richard nodded. "He will come out of it. He always does. If it is all the same to you, I would like to inform Georgie that she may attend the ball for its entirety?"

Elizabeth frowned. She felt badly for her husband's pain. He must be thinking they were conspiring against him. At this moment, she wanted nothing more than to know what he truly wanted for his sister. After all, it was not her place to make decisions of this nature, and she wished she had not interfered by mentioning the subject to the colonel.

"Do what you think is best," she replied. "I am sure all will be well with whatever conclusion you draw. I think I, too, shall retire for the night. I thank you, Richard, for all you do, for the caring friend you are to my husband, and the caring guardian you are to Georgie. We are truly blest by your considerations." She stood.

He quickly rose as well and bowed his head. She curtseyed, and then made her way to her chamber, fearing that her husband would not be in her bed.

~*~

Just as she dreaded, Darcy was not there. Yvette came to help her change into her nightgown. The maid still talked excessively, and all

Elizabeth could do was to nod every now and then or say *oui*. For the most part, she had no idea what was being said, so she thought it best to simply go along.

After Yvette quit the chamber, Elizabeth went through the adjoining rooms and knocked softly upon her husband's inner chamber door. There was no answer. Regardless of his resentment, she entered uninvited. He was lying on the bed with his back to her. She stepped lightly over to the empty side of the bed and used the stool to climb up onto the high mattress. Pulling back the coverlet, she gingerly snuggled in beside him.

Quietly, she whispered, "Fitzwilliam, my love, are you asleep?"

Darcy did not answer, but his inhaling deeply alerted his wife that he was still awake. Moving closer to him, she reached out to caress his shoulder. He instantly tensed at her touch, inched away and rolled onto his back. Yet, this did not deter her. Elizabeth repositioned herself up against his side and began to glide her fingers through his hair. He lay very still, yet she knew he was awake due to his deep breaths. Thus, her hand travelled delicately from his head unto his chest where she gently and ever so lightly caressed him, teasing the skin between the slits in his shirt. She leaned close and placed a kiss upon his nightshirt-clad shoulder. After several moments of rubbing his chest, her hand inched down to the hem of his shirt, crept underneath it, and rested on his belly. Shortly, her fingers began gently twirling the hair beneath his navel. Next, she laid her hand flat and began to massage his lower torso. She rubbed up and across his rib cage, and then slid her hand back down low, letting it slowly slither crosswise from hip to hip. Elizabeth continued in this tantalizing manner for several minutes. She noticed her husband's breath quickening. He was, indeed, aroused.

Without warning, Darcy seized her movement, and with his free hand, he lifted his nightshirt in order to pull her hand away. "Elizabeth, I am fatigued. Please, cease." Then, he quickly rolled over, turning his back to her.

Feeling as if she had been slapped in the face, Elizabeth was stunned, yet the sting quickly turned to anger.

"I suppose you do not want me in your bed?"

A few seconds passed before he replied, "Sleep where you wish."

"That is not the question I asked. Do you desire me in your bed?"

He made no answer.

Bitterly, she spewed, "I will gladly go if that is what you want."

"Do what pleases you."

"I was doing what pleases me, but you have found it to be repugnant to your sensibilities!"

His face contorted in anguish. "Elizabeth! I have said I am exhausted. I never find your love to be repulsive. I have a long day tomorrow, starting early with a hunt and ending with the night's gathering."

Hurt was apparent in her voice as she cried, "You think only of your wants, Fitzwilliam. I feel that you have struck me just now by your rejection. This is the first time I ventured to be so bold, yet you spurn me!" Then in great pain she declared, "I feel deep humiliation!"

Darcy hastily turned over and looked harshly into her eyes. "You speak of your humiliation. What of my humiliation seeing you sequestered with Richard in the library having a private tête-à-tête? And of all things, your conversation dwelt upon *my* obstinacy concerning *my* sister."

Elizabeth froze. Her husband's expressed indignation pierced her heart like a sharp double edged sword. Their eyes never broke contact.

In scorn, he questioned, "Now, Lizzy, do you not agree that we have both suffered extreme humiliation tonight? Let us say no more about it. I must get some rest."

He then turned over onto his other side. Elizabeth realized that she had been holding her breath, thus she exhaled loudly. The tears soon followed, flooding onto her face, wetting her hair and pillow. She strived to stay quiet. She cupped both hands over her mouth and nose to muffle any noise, but it was all in vain. Within a minute, her body began to shudder violently from the suppressed agony she held within.

Darcy sighed as he swallowed back his pain. He could feel the vibrations of his wife's silent sobs. With great effort to sound calm, even though he, too, felt like weeping, he offered a few words as a token for their shared grief. With all the strength he could muster, he stated understandingly, "Elizabeth, I am sorry you feel badly. Cry if you must. I desire to weep, myself. I am exhausted with everything. You are welcome to sleep with me if you so desire."

Nodding her head vigorously, even though he could not see her, she removed her hands from her mouth and softly wailed aloud. "Very well...Fitzwilliam. I do wish...to sleep by you. I thank you."

Darcy shut his eyes tightly in pain. If he had not still been so very angry, he would have taken her into his arms. He felt betrayed, and he did not know if he could stand to have another quarrel with her. He was too frightened of the words he might say. Her crying finally abated, and he could tell that she, at last, had fallen asleep. He wanted his cousin to leave! In fact, on the morrow, he would remind Richard that Lord and Lady Matlock were awaiting his return. After all, his cousin claimed this to be his desire as well.

~*~

The next morning dawned bright and unseasonably warm. Darcy had arisen earlier than his wife and headed down to breakfast, where he ate very little and drank only one cup of coffee. He went out to the stables to make certain everything was in order and that the horses had been readied for the hunt. He had been out at the stables for a quarter of an hour when Richard joined him. The colonel walked up to his horse, murmuring small endearments to the animal as he petted its muzzle. He then held his hand flat offering lumps of sugar to the beautiful creature. Darcy was busy readjusting the tack when Colonel Fitzwilliam arrived, thus his back was turned. Hearing Richard's docile voice alerted him to his cousin's presence.

"Darcy," Richard commenced, glancing towards his cousin's back while he continued to pet his horse, "I have decided on my own accord to inform Georgiana that she may attend and participate in the ball for the whole of the evening. I know this may not be your exact wishes, but really, Darcy, she is nearly seventeen. She will come out this Season, and this is just a country dance."

Standing with his back to his cousin, Darcy replied sharply, "I know that, Fitzwilliam. I am well aware of my sister's age! I gave you my word that you could choose what you deemed best. So be it. By the way, I presume you will be leaving soon in order to spend *time* with you parents before the ball, and before your regiment is relocated."

Richard chuckled and nodded his head slowly. "Why, yes, Darcy, I will leave at first light tomorrow morning. No pleas will stop me this time, so rest assured that I will no longer be a burden."

Darcy remained silent, his eyes fixed on the bridle within his hands. Swallowing hard, he would not turn around to meet his cousin's gaze. He simply stated, "Very well."

~*~

When Bingley came down for breakfast, he informed Elizabeth that Jane desired none. He explained that Jane had not slept well, and desired to sleep through the morning, begging Elizabeth's pardon.

Elizabeth went straight up to her sister's chamber to enquire after her. She asked if she could stay with her or bring some refreshment. Reaching for her sister's hand and clasping it tightly, Jane implored, "Lizzy, do not concern yourself so. I ate a little toast and drank some juice. I will be fine. Yet, I would feel horrible knowing you sat about worrying over me. I have convinced Charles to go on the hunt with the other men. Therefore," Jane's large eyes looked intently into Elizabeth's, "I hope to convince you, my dear sister, to do the tasks which you deem imperative, instead of sitting by my side as I sleep. I was up and down all night, and I am so very tired. I feel I could sleep the whole day and night put together."

Still gazing earnestly into her sister's eyes as she squeezed Elizabeth's hand tighter than before, Jane pleaded, "Please, Lizzy, do not fret. My maid will look in on me and inform you if there is anything I need. I shall be fine."

Elizabeth finally relented and agreed to her sister's wishes, telling her that she would ramble about the countryside for a while, since it was the finest day they had seen in several weeks. Jane smiled, thankful that Elizabeth would be doing something she dearly loved. The sisters embraced, and then Elizabeth went back down to the breakfast room. Kitty and Georgiana were there now, and so was Caroline. Elizabeth greeted everyone, and asked if anyone desired a morning walk. The younger girls just stared at her blankly but then declined. Caroline rolled her eyes and thought that Eliza Bennet, who was now the Mistress of Pemberley, still persisted in her wild, barbarian ways.

Georgiana and Kitty ate hurriedly, for both girls desired to exchange ideas about hairstyles and look again through each other's gowns and bonnets. Happily, they left the room arm in arm to enjoy the morning together.

"Well, Caroline, that leaves you and me. I do want to take a walk, and I would be happy if you were to accompany me. But, if you do not feel so inclined, then I am sure there is something we could find to occupy our time that will be agreeable to us both." Elizabeth said this with sincerity.

"I thank you, Eliza, for your thoughtful consideration, but I do not feel up to a stroll. I do remember, however, that you are a creature of the open air. Please do not let me detain you from pursuing an activity from which, I know, you derive so much pleasure. I desire to go back into the library and read more of Blake's works. I found him to be so sensitive and full of compassion."

Elizabeth looked at her with what she knew must be an odd expression upon her face. Could Caroline be sincere in expressing a true interest in something that had nothing to do with fashion, status, or wealth?

"Oh, I love Blake, too. I am glad you are finding his works enjoyable."

Caroline smiled cunningly.

Elizabeth then declared, "Well, I, for one, am going to go out to see the men off for their hunt, if they have not already departed. Please, Caroline, feel free to use the library at your leisure."

Caroline's eyes brightened at the mere mention of seeing the men off. She anxiously interposed, "Eliza, I do feel I would benefit by having a little bit of fresh air. Would you mind if I came outdoors with you for the small amount of time it will take to see the hunting party off?"

Elizabeth eyebrows rose in amusement. She chuckled softly to herself and replied good humouredly, "Oh, by all means, Caroline, please, do come."

They both went to the front entrance, where the men were gathering. The extremely fine weather was perfect for a hunt. The sun shone brightly and the air was crisp with only a slight hint of a breeze. Elizabeth recognized some of the same faces that she had seen in the vestibule several days earlier.

Both women descended the steps together. Most of the horses were in high spirits as were their riders. Many of the steeds appeared jittery as they pranced about eagerly awaiting for their owners to give them full rein. The energetic hounds yelped loudly as they darted to and fro, wagging their tails in excitement.

Catching sight of Darcy off to the left, surrounded by Bingley and Mr. Caldecott, Elizabeth made her way over to where he stood tightening up the cinch of his saddle. Caroline was not far behind.

Walking up beside him, Elizabeth enquired, "Did you sleep well?"

He held his leather gloves in his mouth, since his hands were busily engaged. He nodded, but did not look at her. Mrs. Darcy then stated, "I hope you all have an enjoyable hunt. When should I expect you back?"

Finished securing the saddle, her husband took his gloves out of his mouth and looked at her, but his vision was instantly arrested as he noticed Richard keenly observing them from the top of his horse, several feet away. A scowl crossed Darcy's face. With clipped words, he said, "I do not know, Elizabeth. You will see us whenever it is we return."

Her brow creased, and she realized immediately that his anger continued for her having spoken with his cousin concerning Georgiana the night before. Placing her hand upon his upper arm, she gave it a squeeze, and then commented, "Very well, I do hope all will go well. I plan on taking a long walk about this morning."

While her hand still rested on his arm, he took the reins in one hand and placed his foot in the stirrup. He did not look at her even once. In one fluid motion, he mounted his horse, pulling his arm out of his wife's grasp. The coldness of his animosity was obvious to all who witnessed it.

Caroline smiled, overjoyed to have been privy to the little display she had just observed. She thought, in merriment, that all was not so well between the newlyweds after all. Darcy must be tiring of her already. The poor, dear man had to have been so smitten with her figure that he was now paying a high price for his reckless decision in marrying someone who was clearly no lady of culture and graciousness. She felt for him acutely and would do almost anything to help him get out of such a shameful marriage.

Elizabeth and Caroline stepped back and watched the riders gallop away, until they were no longer in sight. They turned together to go into the house, but as they reached the door, a woman's voice called after them. Both women spun around to see who it was. Mrs. Darcy inhaled deeply. It was Miss Caldecott.

Collette dismounted and ran briskly towards the steps to meet them. She wore a very stylish riding habit, and the golden ringlets of her hair were fashioned to one side, which lent a dramatic flair to her appearance. Elizabeth noted that Miss Caldecott looked as radiant as ever.

Breathlessly Collette cried as she ran up the steps, "Eliza, I am so glad to see you. I had hoped to catch the gentlemen first, before they departed, but, alas, I will overtake them soon enough."

Elizabeth's heart began beating wildly as she considered what possible purpose this woman could have in desiring to speak with her. She felt a sensation of foreboding overtake her.

"Ah! Do come in, Miss Caldecott, and enjoy some refreshment," Mrs. Darcy offered.

Collette now stood by Miss Bingley and Mrs. Darcy, smiling brightly. Her teeth were perfectly polished and brilliant.

"Oh, I thank you, Eliza, but I do want to join the hunt. Fitz asked me to try my best to come. Therefore, I shan't be able to stay for long. I saw you going into the house, and since I wanted to return a few items, I decided to stop."

Caroline's eyes were wide in wonder as she appraised such a striking woman. She appeared flawless in her beauty, deportment, and speech.

Suddenly, Elizabeth remembered that Caroline had not been introduced yet, and she hastily began the introductions. "Ah, Caroline, this is Miss Collette Caldecott. Her family has been good friends with the Darcys for many years. She lives here in Derbyshire." She then turned towards Miss Caldecott and continued, "Collette, this is Miss Caroline Bingley. She is a close family friend as well. My sister is now married to her brother, Charles, and they are currently visiting."

Caroline spoke first. "Ah! Miss Caldecott. I am so happy to make your acquaintance. Please, feel free to call me Caroline."

"I shall, indeed, if you shall call me Cole. I prefer it so much to my full name. Just like Elizabeth prefers to be called Eliza."

Caroline raised a brow to this morsel of information. Collette quickly put her riding crop underneath her arm and held it there while she dramatically searched the pockets of her jacket. Elizabeth and Caroline watched her in curiosity. "Oh!" Miss Caldecott exclaimed, "I can't seem to find them." Then with her teeth, she started loosening her leather gloves from her hands and when they were fully removed she cried, "Oh, yes, here they are."

On each of her index fingers, she wore a ring. Miss Bingley's and Elizabeth's eyes widened when they saw Darcy's signet ring on Colette's finger.

"Here, Eliza," Collette said as she removed a ring, "Fitz asked me to guard this ring with my life. He was very concerned about it. I have been meaning to return it to him for a while, but then realized that I could just bring it over this morning for the hunt. In addition, this other ring here," she lifted up a small circlet for them to see, "I have loved and cherished for far too long, however, now that Fitz has done the unthinkable, I really should keep it no longer. It belonged to his grandmother. I am sure he would want you to have it now." Collette flashed a smile and then tossed her head with a quick laugh, before admonishing in an exaggerated tone, "Eliza, *do* make sure you put those rings somewhere safe. Fitz cherishes them both."

Elizabeth was angrier than she thought humanly possible, and at someone she hardly knew. In the same pretentious manner, she replied, "Oh, do not worry your pretty little head over such things, *Cole*."

Smiling as widely a possible at the brazen, blonde haired beauty, Mrs. Darcy contrived a sweet reply. "I will most certainly make sure they are given to their rightful owner. I do hope you will enjoy your ride with the gentlemen."

"Oh, Eliza, my dear, I always do, and they always enjoy their rides *substantially* better with me along." She smiled coquettishly. A small gasp was discerned by Caroline and Collette. The latter smiled gloriously, and waved as she descended the steps. The fingers of her gloves, which she still held in one hand, were liberally flapping about with the gesture, accentuating her spirited farewell.

Comprehension dawned, and Caroline instantly knew that Miss Caldecott was not the lady of refinement that she had initially judged her to be. Yet, she was definitely a thorn in Eliza's side and, therefore, so much the better. Darcy must have been, or still was, captivated with this gorgeous creature. Why else did she have his rings, and when had he given them to her? She could not imagine Mr. Darcy agreeing to let just any woman have the family heirloom of the scion of Pemberley, and she wondered at never having heard of Collette's name before now. Could he already have a mistress? She would have never thought it possible of Mr. Darcy, but then again, she never thought he would marry so far beneath him, either. Her interest was piqued, but one thing was certain, Eliza's days of bliss were past. Caroline Bingley took great delight in this verity.

In agitation, Mrs. Darcy made her excuses to Miss Bingley as soon as they entered the house. Elizabeth hastened to her chamber, opened her jewellery box, and put both rings inside. Her eyes caught sight of her cross necklace that her father had given her. She quickly lifted it out and then rummaged through the jewels, until she came upon her brooch, which had belonged to her grandmother Bennet. She withdrew it as well, and then closed the lid. She walked to her closet and found a pair of fine leather gloves with embroidered trim work at the edges and piping accentuating the fingers. She grabbed a reticule and put the jewellery into it. Next, Elizabeth hurriedly put on her field boots, and then she made her way down to her study. Pulling out her ledger, she calculated the balance of her pin money account, and then pulled out a draft note, adding it to the items in her purse.

She again went out the front door, this time walking vigorously, determined to reach Lambton before noon. That would allow her to conduct her business and be home in plenty of time before the dinner party was due to begin. After all, Lambton was merely two miles further than Netherfield had been, and she had always made that walk easily enough. What was four more miles?

Anger spurred her onward as she contemplated the relationship between Collette and her husband. She could scarcely believe he would leave his ring in her care. To the best of her knowledge, he never took it off his finger. When had this occurred? When had he given Colette the ring? Had he remained at the mine, alone, the whole time he had been gone, or had Collette been there with him? Elizabeth quickly brushed back the tears of anger stinging her eyes. If her husband did not confess all, she knew that she could not live like this any longer. She was experiencing a feeling she had never experienced before, and it frightened her. Even when Wickham had run away with her sister, she had not felt emotions such as these. She feared that she could perform bodily injury to Collette, and, at this moment, the actual desire was for something akin to murder.

~*~

Caroline went to the library as planned and did make an effort to read Blake, but for the life of her, she had no idea why a grown man would write about boys who could not even speak intelligibly, saying *weep* instead of *sweep*. Why on earth would anyone want to think about dirty grimy chimneysweepers, especially ones that went off to play in the water instead of attending to their duties?

She slammed the book shut and tossed it onto the table. With what could she occupy herself? Her face brightened at the idea of going through Elizabeth's chambers. There was still plenty of time before anyone would be back from the hunt or that woman from her ridiculous ramble. Hmm…

Caroline arose, ascended the stairs, and only hesitated a moment before turning the doorknob and then walking into the mistress' chamber. "Oh, pardon me," Miss Bingley stated coolly, "I was looking for Mrs. Darcy." Caroline had forgotten that the chambermaids would be engaged in cleaning the rooms at this time of day.

As she went back downstairs, Miss Bingley thought how surprised she had been to find that Eliza's young maid spoke French. When she stepped off the last stair, she decided to go to the pianoforte, and while doing so, she noticed the slightly opened door to Lady Anne Darcy's private study. Now, heaven forbid, it belonged to such an unworthy occupant. Caroline paused and looked about to see if anyone was watching. Quickly, she entered the study and softly closed the doors behind her.

Inspecting the room closely, Miss Bingley sighed in contempt as she thought about how very unoriginal Eliza Bennet was. She had not changed the décor of a single room so far. Caroline's eyes were riveted on the leather folios, which were on the desk. Instantly, she sat in Elizabeth's chair and opened them. As she studied the figures, her brows furrowed. "Oh my!" she whispered in surprise.

Eliza was actually keeping track of the accounts. Did she not realize that is why she had servants? She closed the first ledger and then opened the next one. Ah, the financial record of her private funds! When she saw the monthly stipend that Mr. Darcy had given to his wife, Caroline's eyes almost bulged out of their sockets as her mouth dropped wide open.

After she recovered from her shock, she started to investigate how Eliza Bennet spent such an enormous sum of money. She well imagined that she would need a completely new wardrobe, and a monthly allowance as large as this could very easily put the country bumpkin into the latest fashions from Paris.

Raising her eyebrows, she was shocked to find that the funds were indeed gone, but not spent in shops, on motifs, or for any other luxury. Instead, the entry that depleted the account, read only charitable contributions to LBW. Who on earth could that be? Caroline thought that Eliza must be truly insane to give all of her money away in such an open-handed fashion. Closing the ledger, Miss Bingley contemplated the initials, repeatedly turning them over in her mind. She then began to examine the rest of the desk. It was a beautiful piece of furniture, but too archaic for her own taste.

Opening a drawer, she saw another ledger and some letters. She picked up the letters and started to shuffle through them, rolling her eyes as she saw the names: Jane Bingley, Charlotte Collins, Frances Bennet and Lydia Wickham. Caroline whispered aloud, "Lydia Wickham, Lydia Bennet Wickham!"

Yes, she was the charity case to whom dear Mr. Darcy's money was being sent and wasted upon. She laid down the other letters, looked back into the drawer, and saw another letter far back in the corner. She hastily pulled the letters out and opened all the missives from Newcastle. Her eyes enlarged as she read about Georgiana's near elopement with George Wickham. Hastily, she opened the other missive and instantly realized that Mr. Wickham had been its author. Caroline's lips slowly formed into a malicious smirk.

Suddenly, Miss Bingley heard the scales of the pianoforte, and quickly gathered the letters and placed them back into the drawer as she had found them. Then, to ascertain the amount of money that had been sent to Mrs. Wickham, she took one last look into Elizabeth's ledger.

Silently, she walked out the opposite door from the music room and worked her way roundabout through the entrance hall to gain access to the pianoforte. As luck would have it, Caroline found Georgiana all alone. It was the perfect time for them to catch up on the latest fashions and the upcoming Season with the ton, and surely, she should disclose her concerns to the poor girl. After all, what were true friends for, if not to lend support through such troubling times?

~*~

Chapter Sixteen

Wretched Deceit

With the snow all but gone, only ice-covered patches remained, dotting the landscape beneath trees and underbrush, or interspersed amid the sloping terrain. The weather had turned agreeable and the countryside beautiful. In order to gain access to the main road more rapidly, Elizabeth decided to cut through the fields of Pemberley. She inhaled the freshness of the crisp air while basking in the brilliance and warmth of the sunshine. Nature had always had a way of calming her anxieties, but today it failed to provide its usual solace. She beheld the promising tokens of spring all around her as she walked. Bits of tender green grass rising from the soil, the songs of sparrows overhead as they built their nests, and the friskiness of foals frolicking about the pastures induced by such a pleasurable morn enticed her senses. Yet, thus far, she could not completely lose herself in the splendour of it all. Her mind was too busily engaged at present to allow her the sweet indulgence of fully enjoying that which nature had so readily supplied.

While crossing the pasture, she hoped to find her way and not become lost. If her memory of the trip she had made to Pemberley last summer with her Aunt and Uncle Gardiner now served her correctly, this field would meet up with the road that led into Lambton.

She walked briskly, knowing that she had a little more than three hours to make her way there, conduct her business, and then walk quickly back home. Certain that she would miss luncheon, Elizabeth began to regret that she had not gone in search of Georgiana to let her know where she was headed, but she was sure that Caroline would inform her that she had indeed slipped out for a walk. She was also certain that her sister-in-law would act the part of a wonderful hostess in her absence. In any case, she refused to worry over missing the noon meal. After all, Fitzwilliam had the privilege of going off when and wherever he wanted, and he was not held accountable for the time of his return.

Making her way up an embankment to reach the road, Elizabeth's head was full of all that had taken place that morning: from her husband's rude departure to Collette's self-importance. That woman was maddening, and so was Fitzwilliam for the way he had cosseted Miss Caldecott on the night of the soirée. The mere memory of it made her blood boil. In fact, she was so angry that as she placed her foot upon the road, she paused and stomped it, exclaiming aloud, "Collette Caldecott, you are...are...*a despicable flirt!*"

Mortified at her expletive, she cried out, "Oh!" and then cupped her hands over her mouth while making sure no one was about. Breathing in relief upon finding she was alone, Elizabeth moved her hand to rest over her heart, sighed, and then began to stride in earnest.

After a quarter of an hour, wagons, carriages, and men on horseback seemed to emerge as if coming out of nowhere. Elizabeth was flabbergasted by all the activity but quickly assumed it must be due to this being the first lovely day of the year. Time and again, she would have to make way for wagons which came from behind by treading over onto the grass to ensure plenty of leeway for them to pass. Then, the pattern seemed to change, and traffic appeared from the opposite direction. Coming from Lambton were the post wagons as well as many carriages, some luxuriously equipped and others scarcely so. The men driving their respective rigs looked shocked at the sight of a lone woman trampling over the grass alongside the road, and after several carriages had gone past, one gentleman stopped and asked in concern, "Mrs. Darcy, may I offer you a ride into Lambton? I presume that is where you are going, and I would most gladly turn my curricle around to take you there."

Elizabeth faltered. Here was a man who clearly knew who she was, yet she had no idea of his identity. "Oh, you are most kind, sir. I am indeed on my way to Lambton, but I prefer to walk on such a fine day. Yet, I thank you for your generous offer."

Still pulling back on the reins of his horses, the man again pressed, "I assure you, it would be no bother at all. I would be happy to wait while you attend to any of your needs while in town and then return you to Pemberley."

Taken aback with the man's persistence, Elizabeth declined once more, "I do thank you, again, but I prefer to walk when the weather is so inviting. Good day to you, sir." She curtseyed and started off once more, noticing the man tip his beaver with a good-humoured grin as he prodded his horses onward with a quick slap of the reins. No one else stopped, but many men would dip their heads forward or tip the rim of their hats and extend a cheery salutation of, "Good morning to you, Mrs. Darcy" or "It is a fine day, is it not, Mrs. Darcy?" She was truly in awe that so many people knew who she was, yet to her knowledge, she had never before laid eyes on any of them. She also noted how some of the ladies would crane their necks in an effort to get a better look at her. She made a point to smile good-naturedly as they strained to examine and dissect every aspect of her person in their passing.

When Elizabeth was but a mile from Lambton, Dr. Lowry pulled along side her and slowed his horse's progress. "Why, Mrs. Darcy, may I offer you a ride? You must be near absolute exhaustion if you have walked all the way from Pemberley?"

Astonished to finally see someone she knew, she cried, "Oh, Dr. Lowry, it is so good to see you. I hope your trip takes you out on a pleasant duty?"

"Why, in fact, it does, Mrs. Darcy. I am going to check on Mrs. Henderson and her twins. They were born three days ago, and both babes and mother are in excellent health."

"Oh, how delightful! That is most definitely a pleasure-bound duty."

"And your excursion, is it for pleasure or duty?" he asked with interest.

"Both, I imagine."

The doctor laughed heartily showing his deep dimples and boyish look. "Well then, may I offer you a ride for the remaining mile into Lambton in hopes of making your outing more pleasurable?"

Smiling broadly, she spiritedly replied, "Walking is the part that I find the most pleasing."

Good naturedly, he responded, "Then, do not let me detain you another moment. I look forward to seeing you again this evening, Mrs. Darcy." He doffed his beaver and with a loud click of his tongue, signalled his horse to advance.

Elizabeth breathed in deeply and then began to walk at an even quicker pace.

When she entered Lambton, she noticed that the town fairly bustled with activity. On her visit last summer, she had not remembered so many people rushing about. Biting her lip, she quickly decided to make the required enquiries at the inn where she had lodged with her aunt and uncle.

The innkeeper and his wife were just as congenial as they had been the past summer. They remembered her and greeted her with the familiar ring of Mrs. Darcy. Likewise, they were just as eager to assist with her needs. The moment she crossed their doorsill, she became their most important patron.

From their directions, Elizabeth wove her way through the crowd as she trod the narrow lanes in search of the pawnbroker's shop. Stopping in front of a building, she pulled open the door. The ring of a small bell fastened to the jamb alerted the proprietor to another potential deal in the making.

Lowering the spectacles upon his nose, he frowned slightly at seeing a lady entering.

"How may I help you, madam?"

Elizabeth was relieved that this particular person had not the faintest idea who she was.

"Well, I must confess, this is my first time in an establishment such as yours. I have some items, and I wish to know how much they might be worth."

Placing her reticule upon the counter, she loosened the drawstrings and brought forth the brooch, gloves, and then, with a moment of hesitation, her beloved necklace, yet, she did not place it alongside the other two items, but retained it, clutching it tightly within her hand.

The shopkeeper held the brooch up to the light of the window and turned it over in his hand several times before bringing it up to his mouth and biting it. "Hmmm, this is indeed authentic." He stopped and thought for a moment. "I imagine it could fetch around ten shillings or a little more." He then picked up the gloves and turned them over a few times, gently stroking the leather with his fingertips. "Um...I will offer for these items, twenty shillings, and if you decide to throw in the cross in your hand, I may be able to add in a guinea or two."

Elizabeth painfully considered the reality that her cross was worth more than the brooch and gloves together, but still fetched so little. In contrast, she felt within her heart that it was priceless. She slowly opened her hand to allow the proprietor to inspect the precious necklace.

"Well, I dare say that I could offer you two guineas." He then lowered his spectacles once more and looked at her neck and declared, "I would rather trade for the cross you are wearing, instead of this one." He held her cherished necklace up high in one hand and continued, "Then I could easily give you twenty pounds in addition to the twenty shillings for the brooch and gloves."

The higher price for the finer necklace that her husband had given her was tempting. It would bring so much more, and she could then keep her heirlooms. However, she knew she could do no such a thing. It was not hers to sell.

"No, I thank you for the offer, but I will take what I can for the necklace you hold there."

The bargain was struck. She took the coins, dropped them into her reticule, and asked the man if he could direct her to the nearest posting house. This he did, and she made her way through the winding streets yet again. As she walked down the crowded lane, a shop window caught her fancy, and so she stopped to inspect its wares. There were many bonnets, gloves, trinkets, and fine Irish linen handkerchiefs with delicate embroidery on display. She thought a moment about going in to purchase something for Sally's special day tomorrow, but then thought of how she needed every extra pence to keep her vile brother-in-law in check.

While gazing into the window, she slowly became aware that another individual stood next to her, apparently preoccupied in the same manner. She was ready to turn and leave when the person spoke. "Lovely, are they not, dear sister?"

Her heart skipped a beat at the familiarity of the man's voice. She turned her head and saw George Wickham standing beside her. She noticed a sinister gleam in his eyes as he took in her frightened expression. Sarcastically, he said, "Now, dear sister, is that any way to greet your dear brother and friend? I thought you would be overjoyed to see me and long to hear all the news about your sister, my wife."

Squaring her shoulders, Elizabeth looked him in the eye and without quailing, said, "Mr. Wickham, I have no idea of what you are speaking. I am just surprised to see you here in Derbyshire when you are supposed to be in Newcastle. Is my sister here with you?"

Smiling lustfully as his eyes swept over her figure and then returned to her challenging glare, he responded, "I do admire the fire in you, Elizabeth. It must be the very reason Darcy married you. Few women are as spirited and principled, to boot. You had the right combination for my priggish friend, for he has enjoyed many fiery wenches, but they lacked what you had in your favour, *wholesomeness and chastity.*"

Elizabeth gasped openly and swiftly lifted her hand with the intention of slapping the smug look off Wickham's vile face. "How dare you!"

Just as she was about to strike him, he grabbed her hand in mid-air, and clasping her arm tightly against his side, as if they were about to stroll down the street together, he leaned in and quietly whispered, "Now, now, my dear girl, we would not want the good citizens of Lambton to see the Mistress of Pemberley in a brawl, would we?" He then propelled her forward and warned her not to make a sound if she wanted to secure the safety of her husband, sister, and soon-to-be niece or nephew.

Manoeuvring them through the crowd, he found a deserted alley. As he began to enter it, Elizabeth attempted to kick her brother-in-law and pull away from his grasp, but he dodged her boot and forced her down the length of the alleyway. His hands pinned her arms against the brick wall. Sneering at her angry countenance, he brought his lips softly up to her ear. Elizabeth's mind reeled in terror as she struggled to break free from his vise-like grip.

Repulsed by his lips brushing against her skin, she spit on the side of his face. "Why, you brazen hussy!" he retorted in response to her vindictive act. "I have a good mind to give you what you deserve, but I need your services for another purpose." He shoved her harder against the wall and then vulgarly enlightened her to his perverse imaginings. His hot breath sent chills down her spine as once again his rancorous words sounded in her ear. "I am sure you would be well worth it though, my dear sister, for I am confident you are *lush...*"

Elizabeth cried, "You are despicable, worthless, and the lowest—"

"Now, now, my dear sister, watch your temper if you value the lives of those you hold dear."

"What is it you want?"

"I have waited patiently for an answer to my missive, but, when an express did not arrive, I had to come all this way in order to petition you in person. I have just arrived in town, and what do I see but *you*, my dear sister. How convenient you have made it for me."

"Yes, well here is the money I have gathered so far. I cannot offer more because the stipend for my account will not be made until the first of the month."

Greedily, Wickham took the bag out of her hand while warning her to stay still. He counted the coins and then chucked them down upon the cobblestones as he disgustedly proclaimed, "This is a mere bobstick! It is not even a tenth of what I need. Your fine husband has trapped me in a marriage and profession I detest. I shall have my just due."

Sick to her stomach, Elizabeth tried to gauge what she should do while she continued to stand motionless. If she ran, Wickham could easily make good on his promises by harming her sister, husband, Georgiana, and—heaven forbid—Lydia's baby. At this moment, more than ever, she truly believed him soulless, especially in light of his lewd innuendos concerning her body.

Suddenly, her brother-in-law noticed the blank bank draft protruding from the bag, and his eyes immediately brightened. "Ah! Why did you not tell me in the first place that you had this?" He waved the piece of paper in front of her face.

In anger, Elizabeth cried, "I told you, I do not have the ability to send you more until Mr. Sheldon replenishes the account. I only have twenty pounds remaining after having sent the rest to Lydia, but I will gladly give it all to you. I cannot procure more right now."

Jeeringly, he belied her claim, "Oh, come now, Mrs. Darcy, you expect me to believe that your husband would deny you anything you asked? What is an extra hundred pounds a month to Fitzwilliam Darcy, one of the wealthiest men in England? He most certainly loves you. Why else would he marry so beneath him?"

His words stung despite her knowledge that they were hurled by a rake, and even though she knew he took delight in insulting her, at this moment, she truly felt undeserving of her husband's affections. How could she have allowed this villain to gain the upper hand?

"Now, you and I shall take a little stroll up to the inn were I am staying, and the keeper will provide us with pen and ink. One hundred pounds will be sufficient for now, but I shall expect more by the end of March. Do make sure that you ask for a permanent increase in your allowance because, thereafter, I will expect two-hundred pounds every month."

"I could never ask for half such a sum. He is already extremely generous with me. I know of no one who receives the amount of pin money that I do."

"Yes, I agree. But, I am sure if you charm him, he will gladly increase it one hundred-fold."

Venomously, she spat out, "I shall not do it—murder me if you will, for I shall not do it!"

"Um, well, perhaps I might change your mind." He tightened his hand around her throat as he leaned the weight of his body upon her own to keep her trapped. He then pulled a pistol from his greatcoat. "Your life will not be the one in danger because if you are not willing to help me with my demands, then I no longer care if Fitzwilliam Darcy lives or dies. He can go to hell for all I care. You are my avenue to obtaining what I need. If you are unwilling, Darcy would be better dead than alive. That way Georgiana would come into her wealth and she would be so much more susceptible and therefore more accessible with her dear brother dead and gone."

Elizabeth trembled in fear. She now understood the depth of Wickham's desperation to have come this far, and she realized that he obviously had devised a plan of action, which he would have no qualms about setting in motion should he not gain her cooperation.

Apprehensively, she volunteered, "I...will go to the inn that I frequented last summer...and...fill in the draft. I will make it for the amount you have indicated. However, I will not promise to ask for an increase in my allowance, at least not as yet. You must wait for me outside the inn. I cannot afford to be seen with you as I enter a lodging establishment."

"Very well, dear sister, I will follow you. Do not do anything rash, and be true to your word, or you may have a funeral to attend in the near future."

Gulping for air, Elizabeth noted her breath quickening. She feared she was having another attack of nerves as she had on the night her husband had lain bleeding on the floor of the ballroom. Instantly, she started to tell herself to calm down. If she went along with this leech, it would buy her another month or maybe give her until the Season was over, and then she could figure a way out. She could not stand the thought of Georgiana's reputation being ruined by this knave, and now her greatest fear was for their lives.

Wickham instructed Elizabeth to walk slowly, several paces ahead of him, and he informed her that he would be watching her most vigilantly from behind. When she left the alley, he quickly bent down to gather up the scattered coins from the pavement, placing them hastily in his pocket.

Within half an hour, the arrangement was completed. Elizabeth walked out of the inn and continued slowly in the direction of the blacksmith's shop. There she stopped by the immense tree her aunt dearly loved and to which her husband had run as a boy in horse chestnut season. At another time, her eyes would have revelled in this wondrous sight, and she would have enjoyed the majestic splendour such rare trees displayed, but for now she only felt gratitude for the refuge it provided to conceal her shameful countenance. She was truly ill. Her legs could barely go forward as she wobbled her way around to the backside of the wooden fortress where she could hide from the inhabitants of Lambton. She leaned against the massive trunk to support her trembling frame.

Wickham walked at a leisurely pace. He, too, went around the horse chestnut, and Elizabeth thought as she looked at his face that he smiled like the devil himself. With hate evident upon her features, she silently held out the draft to him.

"I thank you, my dear sister. You are truly the most intelligent of your father's daughters. Remember, no later than the last of March." He bowed and then was gone.

Resting against the tree's rough bark, her breathing became more laboured. What had she done by writing out a bank draft in the name of George Wickham? What would Mr. Sheldon think of her? Nevertheless, the most important concern was what would Fitzwilliam think? For in her heart she knew the day of reckoning would surely come. The only question that remained was when.

Closing her eyes in despair, she breathed in slowly, taking deep breaths as she strived to banish the thoughts of the unacceptable disgrace in which she found her herself. Taking in one last deep breath, she started for home. Her limbs felt unsteady at first, but she walked slowly, hoping she would be able to increase her speed after a little time had passed. Time was of the essence now, for she had already been detained for far too long.

~*~

"Ah! Georgiana, how I have longed to see you again," Caroline simpered and smiled.

Georgiana startled. She instantly stopped playing and looked up at Miss Bingley with apprehension. "I did not see you come in."

Smiling down upon her, Miss Bingley replied as she gingerly rested her hand on Miss Darcy's shoulder, "Yes, well, I went with Eliza to see the hunting party off. The air was so wonderful. I enjoyed my outing with her extremely. After we stayed out doors for some time, I must admit that I needed to come in. I am not the walker Eliza is. However, she has so much on her shoulders now. I do feel for her with all the responsibilities of such an estate the size of Pemberley, and her not having the proper preparation to handle them. You realize of course, Georgiana, that Longbourn only keeps seven servants. Eliza has admitted to me that she is truly overwhelmed with the enormity of her tasks and confessed that it has been a burden, and at times, more than she can bear."

Hearing Miss Bingley's account of this alleged conversation with her sister-in-law, Georgiana's brows creased. "Well, I know there have been times when she has felt relief when my brother, cousin, and I have helped her. I am sure she will adjust. I think she is doing splendidly."

"Oh," Caroline quickly agreed as she drew a chair close to the pianoforte, "I am sure she is. Yet, she did confess that she had no idea that so much would be placed upon her. She worries for your welfare, excessively."

Concerned, Georgiana looked pointedly to Miss Bingley and cried, "For me?"

Caroline leaned in closer, put her hand over her heart and declared while looking off to one side, "Oh, dear Georgie, I am afraid she needs your cooperation and support more than ever now. As we walked out to say our farewells this morning—mine to my brother and Eliza's to yours—I witnessed their quarrel. It was apparent for any to see. Your brother would not even look at her when she tried to bid him adieu. Eliza was truly mortified, yet I remained by her side. It is unimaginable what could cause your brother to act in such a manner. I am sure you have been privy to this very thing because Eliza told me it is not the first time he has treated her thus."

Alarm registered on Georgiana's face. She knew that her brother and Elizabeth had been at odds in the past, but she thought all was better now. With trepidation, Georgiana enquired, "Why do you feel she needs my help and encouragement now, more than ever?"

Caroline smiled the most pretentious, compassionate smile she could manage. She loved how easy it was to dupe the young woman. Miss Darcy was the most gullible creature she had ever known. Snatching Georgiana's hand, Miss Bingley gazed forlornly into the innocent girl's eyes and in a secretive whisper, expressed, "Oh, dearest Georgiana, Eliza confessed something to me that has me fearing for her marital happiness. Due to her anxiety over your brother's cold dismissal of her in front of the crowd, she could no longer suppress her emotions, thus her woes began tumbling out. I am not sure she would want me to tell you this because she fears that your brother is angrier with her now than he has ever been."

Georgiana's eyes were filled with dread and worry. Caroline paused just long enough to give an added flair of suspense to her yarn. "Please, dear Georgie, do not let this distress you. I promise I will keep your secret, and I am only telling you that I know so we can help Eliza through this trying time." Again, Caroline paused as she clearly read Miss Darcy's face, and Georgiana was indeed beguiled. Caroline's countenance feigned sympathy, "Georgie, Eliza confided in me about your planned elopement with George Wickham."

Georgiana gasped. Her eyes widened in shock.

"Now, Georgie," Miss Bingley murmured while patting the young woman's hand, "that is neither here nor there. We have all made our mistakes. Of course, many have not been as foolish as *yours*, but I do take your age into account where such a shameful endeavour is concerned."

Instantly, Miss Darcy's cheeks were aflame with mortification, an emotion she thought she had conquered and had hoped never to feel again.

Yet, all the humiliation seemed to prick her consciousness for the misdeed and made it appear fresh, as if it had just happened.

Simpering as Georgiana's eyes lowered in embarrassment, Caroline cooed and reached forth her hand, placing it atop Georgiana's to pat it. "Now, Georgie, there…there. This is all behind you. Do not fret over past mistakes. My lips are sealed. I assure you. The issue at hand is not your past indiscretion, but it is Elizabeth's detestable *brother-in-law!*"

Miss Darcy suddenly detected a snort from Caroline and looked up sharply, but Caroline managed to appear benevolent once more.

Looking intently into Georgiana's eyes, Miss Bingley stated contemptuously, "Eliza's brother-in-law, George Wickham, is blackmailing her to keep your secret from the ton. She spends all of her personal money to buy his silence. She has not divulged this information to your brother. In distress, Eliza told me that she has noticed that one of Darcy's old flames has caught his eye again, and that she fears that…well… if he were to know about Wickham, it would throw him into the arms of Miss Caldecott."

Georgiana's expression turned to grief. She could not understand why Elizabeth chose to open up to Caroline Bingley, but she reasoned that it must be so. Caroline knew too much. How else could she have gained such personal information?

Stammering, Georgiana quietly asked, "What…what…is it that I should do?"

"Well, first, please do not let Eliza know that I have told you. It would only distress her more. She worries about you so. We must help her whenever possible and encourage her. I am sure it is only a matter of time before the truth will be out, and then we must stand by her."

"But, maybe my brother will not be angry? I cannot imagine him in the arms of another woman. He could not do something of that nature."

"This may be so, but, Georgie, I witnessed with my own eyes just a short while ago that your brother is not happy with his wife, and he had asked Miss Caldecott to ride with their party this morning. This distressed your sister greatly."

Again, Georgiana was grieved with such a report, and, all of a sudden, she felt angry. How could her brother treat Elizabeth in such a fashion? Yet, Caroline's report must have some validity to it, because she had seen with her own eyes how her brother paid attention to Miss Caldecott the night of their musical performance.

Caroline watched Georgiana's range of emotions pass over her face and felt great satisfaction that her scheme had begun to take shape. "Now, Georgie, promise me you will not breathe a word of this to anyone. We must realize the seriousness of the situation and be supportive of Eliza. Do you promise?"

Slowly, Georgiana nodded. "I…shall not tell. I…want to go to my room now. Please, excuse me."

"Oh yes, do go, Georgie. I am sure you are as distraught as am I. It is understandable. I think that I shall go to my room as well. Let us go together."

~*~

That afternoon upon their return, as Darcy, Bingley, and Richard dismounted their horses, the three men immediately became aware of the approach of Dr. Lowry. Darcy took off his beaver and wiped the sweat from his brow with the back of his hand as he waited for the doctor's carriage to come to a halt. "Why, Harrison," Darcy bowed, "you are here early but welcome as always." Smiling at the doctor, he then exclaimed, "You know my cousin, Colonel Fitzwilliam, but I would like for you to meet my brother-in-law, Mr. Charles Bingley. Bingley, Harrison Lowry is our local doctor." The two men shook hands and then Darcy stated, "Come in and have a drink, Harrison. There is time. We have almost three hours before the other guests arrive. Please, do spend the afternoon with us if you are free to do so."

"I thank you, Darcy, but I am not here this early for your social engagement, but on duty." Dr. Lowry exited his carriage as Darcy's brow furrowed with the good doctor's disclosure.

"Why were you summoned, Harrison? Has someone taken ill?" he asked in concern.

The gentlemen all ascended the steps together while Dr. Lowry related, "The young Wilkens boy came to find me an hour ago and requested my presence. Apparently, a Mrs. Bingley is not feeling well."

Charles became alarmed, and he nervously said, "My Janey is ill? Excuse me, gentlemen. Come with me, Doctor. I will assist you in finding her."

The doctor picked up his pace in order to keep up with Bingley's frantic speed as that gentleman rushed to his wife's side.

Darcy and Richard said not a word to one another as they entered the hall. The servants came rushing forward to take their beavers and gloves. Georgiana ran in breathlessly to meet them. "Oh, Brother, I am so glad you are back. May I please have a word with you?"

Nodding, Darcy begged his cousin's pardon and gestured for her to follow him to a side room. Closing the door behind him, he turned to her and asked, "What is it you wish to speak to me about, Georgie?"

"Elizabeth's sister Jane is ill. She has been sick for the last three hours, so I sent for the doctor."

"You sent for the doctor? Did Elizabeth ask you to do so?"

"This is why I wish to speak with you. Elizabeth is not here. She left right after the hunt commenced. She and Miss Bingley strolled together after the party departed, but Caroline said Elizabeth was in low spirits and desired to walk longer." She watched his reaction to this intelligence, trying to determine if what Caroline had told her about her brother's rude behaviour to his wife were true. She did notice his expression appeared rather sullen.

"And, Fitzwilliam…"

He again focused upon his sister as she attempted to speak further. "Yes, Georgie, please continue."

Tempted beyond measure, she almost disclosed the whole of the conversation that she had had earlier with Miss Bingley, but she could not make herself breach her promise.

"Brother, are you upset with Elizabeth?"

"Georgiana, please do not concern yourself with our misunderstandings as she and I have barely had enough time to speak with one another recently. All will be well with time."

"Yes, but, Fitzwilliam…" She held back the tears, sorely desiring to apologize for her past mistake which had cost him so much then and even more so now, but she again faltered.

Gently resting her hand on her brother's arm, Georgiana then related, "Joseph Wilkens claims to have seen Elizabeth in Lambton." She paused when witnessing the surprise in Darcy's eyes. "She…must…have walked the whole way because…no carriages or horses were taken from the stables…beyond those used for the hunt. It is getting so late in the afternoon…that I am beginning to worry for her welfare."

Darcy's jaw clenched, and he quickly asked, "You mean to tell me, Georgiana, that Elizabeth did not inform anyone that she intended to walk into Lambton?"

Instantly, his sister regretted informing him about the servant's sighting of Elizabeth. She now knew that all of what Miss Bingley had disclosed to her this morning was certainly a fact. Her brother's irate reaction served as a testimonial to Caroline's assertions.

"No, I believe she told no one. She only informed Caroline that she desired to walk longer. That is all."

Inhaling loudly, he opened the door and said, "I will do my best to be back in time to prepare for dinner. Please, Georgie, be the hostess for our guests. I am certain you have been wonderful already. I will go and find Elizabeth." He took a step away from her, ready to leave, when he stopped to add, "Please make certain that Jane has anything that she and Dr. Lowry might deem needful and have Yvette prepare Elizabeth's bath at the usual hour. Hopefully, we will return with time to spare, but, to be on the safe side, instruct Yvette to make all the necessary preparations."

With that, he was gone.

Georgiana felt anguish in knowing that she was the foremost cause for their discord. She would leave for London as soon as possible after her aunt's ball. Quickly, she left the room to go and write a missive to Mrs. Annesley.

~*~

"Well, Mrs. Bingley," Dr. Lowry stated with a smile, "I do believe you should be expecting an addition to your family sometime in the early part of autumn. Would you like to see your husband now, to tell him the good news? He is beside himself with worry."

Beaming, Jane answered softly, "Oh, yes, doctor, please do send him in. Thank you for your kindness."

"You are most welcome. Remember to sleep as much as you can and to take a small dose of this." He handed her a brown glass bottle. "It might help with the nausea you have been experiencing this morning."

"Thank you again."

Dr. Lowry closed his bag, gave a bow, and then opened the chamber door, finding a flustered husband standing outside. Bingley exclaimed as the doctor walked out, "Doctor, is she going to be well? Should I take her to London? I will do whatever you recommend."

Amused, Dr. Lowry's eyes twinkled, knowing the happiness this man would soon experience when his wife revealed the true cause of her malady. "Mr. Bingley, your wife has asked for you to join her. If you have any further questions, feel free to ask me this evening when I return for the dinner party."

"Ah! Most definitely, Doctor. Please, excuse me. My wife awaits me."

Again, Dr. Lowry smiled. Mr. Bingley was a very attentive husband. Oh, how he wished that all of his expectant mothers had such husbands. He sighed at the thought of the many unfortunate women in his care who endured so much grief and affliction in loneliness, with no husband to comfort and share their burden. In fact, in far too many cases, the husband was the direct cause of such misery.

Charles entered Jane's chamber, his eyes wide with trepidation. "Janey, the doctor said you wished to see me? Are you going to be well? Can I get you anything, my dearest?"

Weary, she smiled up at her husband as he hovered over her. "No, Charles. I desire nothing at the moment except for you to sit by me. I have something to tell you."

Bingley sat at once and picked up his wife's hand while his heart beat rapidly in dread. "Yes, Janey, what is it, my angel?"

Jane confidently looked at him and smiled broadly. "Oh, Charles, I never thought I could experience more joy than on the day you asked me to marry you at Longbourn nor on the day of our marriage, but I now find I was wrong. Charles, you are going to be a papa."

Blinking at his wife in astonishment, he asked, "Jane, are you quite certain?" Bingley detected his wife's joy, for it seemed that Jane's lips spread in the widest smile he had ever seen upon her face.

She giggled lightly and with a slight nod, merely said, "Yes."

"Jane, my loveliest Jane, do you know what this means? It means you shall be a mama, as well!"

Laughing heartily while nodding her head all the more and looking deeply into Bingley's eyes, she cried "Yes, my dear husband, we are to have a child by this autumn. Are you pleased?"

He picked up her hand and kissed it adoringly. "I am so very pleased. I feel I want to shout out to the whole world," and then, suddenly, he stood and called out loudly, "Hear all of England and the rest of the inhabitants of the earth—I, Charles Bingley, am going to be a papa!"

Jane smiled dotingly at him and reached out her hand signalling for him to return to her side. "Oh, Charles, I am so very happy."

Leaning in close, he pulled her into an embrace and squeezed Jane tightly. "I love you, my dear, sweet, beautiful wife," he whispered as he continued to place the most ardent of kisses upon his wife's lips for some moments, and then he murmured in awe, "I have given life, Janey."

Jane suppressed her mirth and stated sincerely, "Well, Charles, I do hope you consider that I may have aided in the process."

Fearing he may have given his wife true offence, he quickly rectified his claim. "Oh, yes, Jane, I most certainly could have never done it without you."

Reaching to embrace her husband once more, she quietly soothed, "Yes, Charles, we both needed the other to make our sweet bundle. I do love you so." She pulled him close and hugged him firmly.

~*~

Darcy pulled the cinch forcefully against his horse while saddling the stallion once more. *How dare she!* He thought to himself as he strove to suppress the mounting aggravation he felt regarding his wife's intractable behaviour. Their marriage could not continue in this fashion. He closed his eyes in bitterness of mind and wished to the heavens that he could go back—back before all of the obligations of life had weighed so heavily upon them so soon after their marriage.

Hitting his riding crop hard upon the rump of the animal, he spurred the beast on its flanks as he began to gallop at a breakneck speed across Pemberley's open meadow. In all truthfulness, he was not only striving to keep his frustration in check but was also trying to smother the irrational fear that perchance some mischief may have befallen his dear wife. He imagined her injured, fatigued, or what was worse... No, he would not allow his mind to dwell upon such possibilities. What was Elizabeth thinking to walk to Lambton alone?

Memories of the morning flashed through his head as quickly as the horse's hooves beat against the sod carrying him towards the main road: Lizzy's puffy eyes as she lay sleeping, Richard's intent look, his wife's grip upon his arm, his brusque departure, and then Collette's uncanny appearance.

Darcy had awakened, his memory fresh with the hurt he felt over the meddling of Elizabeth and Richard the night before, and the added insult that his wife and cousin shared the sentiment that he was domineering in regard to his sister's welfare. Well, someone had to be! Richard cared deeply for Georgie, it was true, but he had always been too indulgent, being a friend most of the time rather than a true guardian.

Elizabeth, however, saw his cousin in a different light and felt that Richard's approach was more prudent in dealing with Georgiana. This thought cut him to the quick. It also pained him that this morning he had asked Richard to depart. In all of their years together and the countless times Richard had stayed with him at Pemberley and in London, not once had he asked him to leave.

Heavy-hearted due to his inability to overcome his jealousy concerning his cousin, he also felt shame for the way he had treated Elizabeth on parting before the hunt. He knew his behaviour had resembled that of a spoilt little boy, yet he had wanted to hurt her the way she had hurt him. With a quick shake of his head, he wondered at the insanity of his thinking. Here he was, a man of eight and twenty, reasoning as if he were but seven. To top off the morning, Collette had shown up unexpectedly. She had supposedly fallen from her horse when he had come upon her crying because she had injured her ankle. Trailing behind the others, he had found himself unchaperoned, alone with a woman with whom he never desired to be alone with again. For some seconds, he had deliberated about the wisdom of dismounting his horse in order to help her. Anyone who knew Collette Caldecott well knew she could not be trusted. Yet, he had decided to do what any gentleman would. He thanked the heavens that Richard had shown up when he had, and that it was Richard, and only Richard. Bingley may have suffered a shock to his heart from such a brazen display. He despised Collette, and he despised himself for having once loved her.

~*~

Elizabeth's side ached from walking too briskly. She was almost at the turn-off by the meadow when she needed to stop and catch her breath. She turned off the road and walked unsteadily through the tall grass to find a tree to rest upon. Untying the ribbons of her bonnet and removing it, she employed it as a fan to cool her face. While restoring herself in the shade, she felt as if every nerve in her legs had begun to twitch violently. After fanning herself for several minutes, she closed her eyes and slowly released her tension, allowing tranquillity to overtake her as the trunk supported her weary frame. Elizabeth knew she must not tarry long, because the shadows of the day were fast appearing. The hour was growing late. Tilting her head, she closed her eyes, continuing to ponder possibilities. She shook her head and stated aloud, "Oh that I could vanish! But then again, if am really going to wish, why not wish for Collette and Wickham to disappear from the face of the earth? After all, a granted wish such as that would kill two birds with one stone and, in that way, would take care of most of my problems." Oh, well, she thought wryly as she sighed and continued to exclaim to no one's ears but her own, "If wishes were horses, then beggars would ride."

Breathing in deeply, Elizabeth smiled at her frivolity. Wiping the dampness off her brow, she was ready to proceed when she suddenly became aware of a man on a horse rushing past. It was only a matter of seconds until the brains of Elizabeth and Darcy registered one another simultaneously. However, Elizabeth had the advantage from where she stood, since she was able to observe the immediate reining in of the horse as it recklessly skid to a halt, followed by an abrupt turn. Darcy was a good rock's throw away as he sat rigidly upon his saddle. The animal beneath him tossed its head back and forth in agitation as it dripped sweat. High upon his steed, the Master of Pemberley glared at his wife.

~*~

Chapter Seventeen

Entangled Implications

Instant relief washed over Darcy. There was Elizabeth standing next to the road as he raced past. However, his elation concerning her safety was replaced just as quickly by his former feeling of irritation regarding her foolhardy behaviour. Now, sitting motionless upon his horse, well-nigh several rods away from where she stood, he could only stare at her angrily

Similarly, Elizabeth straightened her shoulders and braved his glowering gaze with a defiant stare all her own. She noticed her husband's jaw tauten as he clicked his tongue and prodded the horse into a trot. Neither husband nor wife broke eye contact as the animal obediently moved forward.

Elizabeth's head tilted backward at her husband's approach. She realized just how formidable he appeared on such a tall horse.

Pulling back on the reins, the animal came to a complete halt as Darcy stated, "I take it that you are well, Elizabeth."

She dipped her chin in a slow, even manner, affirming that his assumption was correct.

Then, in a stern voice, he enquired while glaring down at her, "Lizzy, did you inform anyone of your plans to go into Lambton?"

With an instant arch of her brow, she responded, "I did, sir. I informed you this morning that I would be walking about this fine day."

Elizabeth perceived his mouth opening and detected an audible sigh of disgust escape his lips. Afterward, he quickly pressed them firmly back into a straight line. His eyes seemed to burn straight through her as he threatened in a menacing tone, "Elizabeth, I have a good mind to come off of this horse, bend you over my knee, and spank your derrière for the childish behaviour you have shown—and are still exhibiting."

Holding her chin even higher, she countered with her own warning, "I will remind you, Mr. Darcy, that I am not one of your lively horses, disobedient children, nor one of your *spirited* wenches."

His brow furrowed. What was she saying? "Lizzy, I would never think of you as such and I would never..." He became perplexed by her insinuation. "Elizabeth, pray, explain your meaning."

Arching her brows high, she railed boldly, "Only this, sir: you like spirited animals amongst other things. I suppose the challenge they present to you is thrilling. But I am merely declaring that I refuse to be your challenge. You may regulate all about you, but you will *not* control me! I asked you when you were to return this morning, but you would not offer a time at which I might expect you. Yet, I cannot go into town without accounting for when I shall return without raising your ire? It seems to me, sir, that you have a different standard of exactness for me than for yourself."

Incredulity was written all over Darcy's face. He openly gawked at her. "Elizabeth, I understand that you are angry, yet I fail to comprehend how you can turn the tables when, in all actuality, it is I who am justified in my anger. Horses, children, and, pray tell, whatever you mean by *wenches*— which I may add to find highly offensive—have nothing to do with it. It is pure nonsense." Then, through narrowed vision, he bore down. "I am angry, Elizabeth!"

She began to draw back a few steps. He was livid, angrier than she had ever seen him.

"You know you are being obstinate, and by failing to inform Georgiana of your whereabouts, you have not acted sensibly. Your actions have caused her to fret, and you have distressed me to the point of fear as well." Without warning, Darcy swung his right leg over his horse's neck and leapt to the ground.

Standing next to the stallion, he continued with fortitude, "Elizabeth, your argument is not sound. There was no way to determine the exact hour when the hunt would conclude, so that you might have been informed. You are being ridiculous in your assertions."

She spat out, "Am I? I am to be at your beck and call, wear the jewellery you think I should wear, speak the languages you think I should speak. You try to make all decisions for me, and now, I suppose you will not allow me to walk where I desire. *You were never bothered by my behaviour while in Hertfordshire or Rosings!*"

With slow deliberate stride, Darcy began to advance towards her.

The intimidation Elizabeth now felt was even greater with her husband standing a few feet away than when he sat high above her. For every step he advanced forward, she stepped backward.

Noticing her distress, Darcy halted, slowly shaking his head as he rolled his eyes. "Elizabeth, even though I am angry, I have never laid a hand on a woman. My threat a moment ago was meaningless. I never should have allowed myself to utter such idle words in the heat of anger. Please, do not fear me."

With fiery eyes, she cried, "I do not fear you, sir!"

He inhaled loudly. With a deep sigh, he rubbed his hand over his mouth and chin. Then, with prodigious effort of maintaining his self-possession, he spoke patiently. "I hope you do not. I would never strike you. However, I do insist that you never, and I do mean *never*, walk into Lambton unaccompanied again. If you must walk, you shall have a male escort.

Elizabeth, this is a major thoroughfare—one that goes directly to London. You could have been accosted or…you could have been…"

The tension of worrying about her wellbeing became too much. His emotions had run the gamut. Therefore, he momentarily ceased to speak.

Elizabeth perceived his anxiety regarding her safety and felt extreme guilt for her lack of consideration to Georgiana and for yet another disagreement with her husband. However, she was so angry at him for inviting Collette to ride in the hunt and for his having given that woman his signet ring that her own pride stood in the way of allowing her to feel sympathy for him at such a moment—sympathy she would concede he rightly deserved, but which she could not give.

With a calm she did not feel, Elizabeth asked, "Fitzwilliam, did Collette join your hunt this morning?"

She immediately saw his brow crease in confusion at the abrupt change in topic and the mere mention of Miss Caldecott's name.

He answered calmly, "Yes, Elizabeth, she did. I had understood that only the men were to attend."

Sarcastically, she questioned further, "Oh, did you? And I suppose she was the only woman present?"

"Yes." He wondered where she was leading when, suddenly, she changed the subject again by petitioning, "Fitzwilliam, I…I…" She drew in a deep breath. "I would like to ask your permission to have Mr. Sheldon advance my account tomorrow. I find that some needs have transpired which find me in want of my allowance a little earlier than the usual time. Is this acceptable to you?"

He looked intently into her eyes. Was she trying to strike a bargain? Why was she acting so oddly? A tinge of annoyance was clearly discernable when he snapped back, "Elizabeth, do you not find it abhorrent to grovel at my feet for favours? Remember, you feel that I regulate all about me and, therefore, you have vowed you will not allow me to control you. Why seek my permission? Why do you not merely go and inform Mr. Sheldon of what you want and avoid me altogether? Be free in your undertakings. I will not stop you."

Rolling her eyes at the absurdity of his suggestion, she then just as quickly closed them in shame. She hung her head and was silent for a few moments before stating, "I, as you, have said some hateful remarks in the heat of anger. I do not feel you are an ogre, Fitzwilliam, who makes everyone's life miserable, if that is what you are thinking. It is just that I am so confused right now. I am so tired of our disagreements and harsh words, and I feel so exhausted." Suddenly, her valour crumpled as she began to weep in earnest. Through her cries, she muttered, "I am sorry…for going into Lambton…without informing Georgie. I…truly am!"

Elizabeth began crying harder, and, rushing forward, Darcy enfolded her in his arms. She continued through her sobs, "I am so…sorry that I have…have…frightened you…too…and for the spiteful things I have just said. I promise…that…that…I will never walk…alone into Lambton without an escort…again." Her sobs increased in intensity until her whole frame shook violently within her husband's arms.

Tenderly, Darcy soothed, "Shhh, Lizzy, you are fatigued. I am afraid we both are. Yet, we must return directly. It is twilight, and the guests will be arriving shortly. Come."

He held her close to his side as they walked slowly to his stallion. As they approached, Elizabeth stiffened and looked up at her husband and then once again at the sleek steed. He easily read the unease in her eyes as she stared at his horse. She had told them during their engagement that she had never learnt to ride well and was a little frightened by the beautiful, fierce creatures.

Looking intently into her eyes, Darcy made the introductions, "Elizabeth, allow me the honour of introducing you to Sleipnir. He is as trustworthy as he is beautiful." Darcy then pledged, "I shall sit behind you, Lizzy, and hold you securely in my arms."

She eyed the animal dubiously but nodded. Then placing his hands on each side of her waist, she grasped his shoulders while he easily lifted her up, setting her side-saddle upon the gray, dappled charger. Gracefully, he mounted the lofty animal, sitting directly behind her and then, with the heels of his boots, prodded the stallion into a slow trot. Holding the reins with one hand, he secured Elizabeth with his other, drawing her close to his chest. With her head resting under his chin, he could feel the dampness from her hair. Thus, he shifted the reins to his hand which held her tightly and procured his handkerchief before gently wiping the perspiration from her brow.

Elizabeth's promise abated any anger that remained within him. He did desire to discuss other concerns, but it would be some days before time would allow the address of these issues. For now, they did not matter because, while holding her body next to his, Darcy became overwhelmed with feelings of gratitude for her safety and her contrite promise to never repeat such a heedless act again. She was out of harm's way, and that was all that mattered. It was all he would allow himself to think about while his horse carried them back to the security of their home and loved ones who anxiously awaited their return.

~*~

One of the grooms quickly came out to meet the master as he galloped up to the stables. Darcy threw the reins to him, dismounted, and reached his arms upward to help Elizabeth down.

During the ride, Elizabeth dozed in the security of her husband's embrace and was still drowsy as he lifted her off the horse. Softly he spoke,

"Elizabeth, I can make apologies for you to our guests. I fear you are in need of much rest."

She shook her head. "No, I will be well. I just need a bath to refresh myself."

He stated merely, "Very well." He then suggested that they take the servants' stairs to their chambers. That way, he thought, they could avoid observation by any prying eyes, namely Miss Bingley's. Elizabeth agreed, but was so exhausted from her long day of exercise, that she walked sluggishly. Hence, Darcy lifted her in his arms as he took the stairs two at a time. Placing her down gently before opening the door, he entreated, "Elizabeth, if you feel too weary, it is not necessary for you to attend. I will have Georgiana do the honours with the ladies."

"No, Fitzwilliam, I will be fine. I shall attempt to hurry."

Looking at her dishevelled state, he knew her toilette would take more time than she realized. "I will go, then, and inform Georgiana that we have returned. I shall look in on you soon."

Nodding her head, she opened the door to her dressing area to prepare for dinner.

~*~

After crossing the hall to inform Georgiana of Elizabeth's safe return, he had just made his way back to his chamber door when Caroline's voice called after him. He sighed, but waited as she approached. "Ah, Mr. Darcy, I see you are still dressed in your hunting attire. I do hope Eliza is well. Georgie told me how distressed she has been, not knowing where to find her."

Disgust filled Darcy's breast as he strived to stay calm. "Thank you, Miss Bingley, for your concern. Elizabeth is quite well. Now, if you will excuse me, I must dress for dinner."

Ignoring the dismissal, she droned, "Oh, why yes, please do. I realize you are quite late in your preparations and have been detained for far too long already. Yet, there is no need for undo worry, Mr. Darcy, for I am here and shall help Georgiana when the guests arrive. Together, we shall present the epitome of a perfect hostess."

"Yes, well." He could not bring himself to thank her for the offer but only said, "I am sure Georgiana will manage quite well on her own." He bowed his head, entered his chamber, and rolled his eyes while closing the door behind him. What a pretentious woman he found Caroline Bingley to be.

Chaffin exited the dressing chamber and approached his master, offering his customary assistance in removing his attire.

"Chaffin, how much time do I have?"

"No more than a half-hour, sir."

"Well, I wish to soak at least part of that time."

"Very well, sir."

Closing his eyes while relaxing in the tub, Darcy began to turn over the options concerning the mine. He also pondered all of the different angles of resistance from those who opposed his suggestion to close the particular shaft in question. He knew Mr. Pinkerton would create the greatest clamour. Then, many others would conform themselves to that man's greed instead of caring about the hazardous conditions of the workers. Yet, he knew Sir Henry was behind him as was Chalmers. He hoped that more of the men would follow his lead and reasoning as well, putting aside the need of profit over the threat of human life in such perilous conditions.

Taking the soap into his hands, he lathered his chest and arms as he continued to weigh possible arguments that might arise in the impending discussion. All of a sudden, Darcy became aware of the raised voices of his wife and her maid. Sitting still in the tub, he tried to garner what he could from their muffled cries. He could not understand precisely what they said, but one thing was for certain, the women were not happy with one another. He brought up his hand, water trickling down his arm, to rub his chin and exclaimed aloud, "Bah! Chaffin!"

~*~

In exasperation, Elizabeth strived to communicate for what seemed the hundredth time with her foreign maid, "Yvette, I do not like feathers, please, remove them, and neither will I wear this dress and corset. Non!" She tugged at the offending garment, signifying her wish to have it removed.

As Elizabeth embarked on removing the ostrich feathers from her coiffure, her maid walked over to her vanity and shamelessly started slapping at her mistress' hands with each attempt at removal of the grand creation.

Yvette shrieked, "Non, non, j'insiste aussi sur les plumes!"

The women's eyes met in the mirror, each defying the other. Immediately, Elizabeth stood and made her way to her door. While stepping out into the hall, she called to her maid, "I am going to get Miss Georgiana to help settle this once and for all."

Upon closing the door, she espied Richard standing in the middle of the hall smiling brightly. He had already appraised Elizabeth's appearance, and while he thought she looked truly remarkable, he knew that Elizabeth was not the kind of woman who desired such adornment. His smile was born from the irony of the situation, of a woman such as Elizabeth being dolled up by one of the finest maid's to be had. Amusingly, he praised, "Why, Elizabeth, you are dressed to the nines!"

"Yes, well." She sighed rather loudly and then a decided pout accentuated her pink lips. "Are you by chance, Colonel Fitzwilliam, fluent in French?"

"I am afraid the only language I speak well is Portuguese. I am sorry I cannot be of any assistance, but Georgie is rather fluent. I was preparing to escort her downstairs, so I know she is still here."

"Thank goodness! I was on my way to solicit her help this very moment."

Richard walked over to Georgiana's door and knocked.

His cousin quickly answered and offered him a faint smile. "I am ready, Richard." Her eyes were puffy as if she had been crying. Unbeknownst to her cousin and sister-in-law, she had indeed been shedding tears due to the disturbing disclosures she had heard from Miss Bingley. As she exited her room, she instantly became aware of Elizabeth standing by the door across the hall, and she could clearly read the exasperation on her face. "Why, Elizabeth, is something the matter?"

"Yes, Georgie, if it would not be too much of a bother, would you come and speak with Yvette for me. I do not feel at all comfortable with how she has dressed me tonight."

Georgiana looked at Elizabeth and noted that she appeared as if she were ready to attend a grand ball instead of an informal gathering. Georgiana exclaimed, "Oh, Elizabeth, you do look elegant this evening. I think you are quite beautiful."

"Oh no, Georgie, not you too. I do not feel at all comfortable with these feathers and the adornment from so much jewellery." Wryly, Elizabeth stated, "It is too much, among other things."

Richard smirked. He saw clearly what other things she was referring to.

"I look positively vulgar!" exclaimed Elizabeth. "Georgie, please, say you will speak to Yvette and tell her my feelings."

Georgiana sighed. She sincerely felt for her sister. "Why, of course, Elizabeth, I shall do my best." Yet, the young woman feared that the maid might not listen to anything she had to say.

Richard spoke up, "I shall wait for you where I am, Georgie. Take your time."

Both ladies smiled at him as they entered Elizabeth's chamber.

Georgiana began to tell the maid of her sister-in-law's feelings about the excess of her dress.

Yvette would hear none of it. She turned to look at Elizabeth once more and cried out, excitedly, "Ah, vous êtes parfaite et très séduisante."

Looking to her sister-in-law, Georgie interpreted for Elizabeth. "She says, Lizzy, that you look perfect and quite alluring."

Tugging at her bodice, Elizabeth petitioned, "Georgie, help me out of this dress. This mad woman will not, and I shall not go down looking as if I were being presented to the throne. In fact, I would not even want to be presented to the Queen Charlotte dressed like this."

Richard had placed his ear against the door and loved every moment of what he heard. He understood more French than he had let on, and for the moment, he found the discord quite diverting.

Again, Yvette cried to her mistress, "Non, non, Madame, j'insiste pour que vous portiez ce corset. Cela va amméliorer votre silhouette et faire sourrir les hommes. Ce corset est le meilleur et est fait à Paris par la styliste Madame Dietiker. Votre poitrine sera magnifique en étant réhaussée et séparée."

"Oh, Elizabeth," Georgiana said, "She says no. She insists that you wear this corset, and says..." The younger woman looked away, a light blush rising to her cheeks. "She says that it will enhance your figure and make the men smile." Georgiana took a deep breath before she could continue, a rush of words escaping from her mouth, "She says that this *divorce* corset is the very best, that it is made in Paris by a designer, Madame Dietiker." She paused, uncertain if she should relate the last bit of Yvette's argument. Biting her lip and giving her head a slight nod to bolster her courage, she finished, "Yvette says that your bosom will look..." She coughed "...will look magnificent as it is lifted and separated." Georgiana swallowed hard, relieved that she had made it through the most inappropriate interpretation she had ever given.

The maid saw Elizabeth's hesitation and thinking that she was pleased, cried with more zeal than before, "Madame Darcy, j'insiste pour que vous portiez ceci. Faites moi confiance! Je promets que votre mari sera très satisfait de voir la silhouette de sa femme exposée ainsi." Then turning to Miss Darcy, she said, "Dites-lui, Mademoiselle Georgiana, que je sais ce qui est mieux."

Turning red, Georgiana giggled. "Lizzy, she insists that you wear this, that you trust her." The colour in Georgiana's cheeks intensified. "She...she promises that your husband, Fitzwilliam, will be very pleased to see his wife's figure so displayed." The young woman burst out laughing freely now as she strove to relate the maid's last remark. Finally able to catch her breath, she shed light on the whole situation. "She told me to tell you that she knows what is best." Again, Georgiana laughed hard. "Oh, Lizzy, you might as well give up. She will not believe that she does not know best!"

Elizabeth's face registered shock. "Georgie, this is too much! You may think this funny, but I am sure you would not care to have such a maid."

Shaking his head, Richard attempted all in his power to contain his mirth. He wished they had left the door ajar because he worried that someone would see him with his ear pressed to it. Then, unexpectedly, Richard heard Darcy's voice, and he assumed that Darcy must have entered the chamber. The colonel thought that this would get even better now. He no longer heard his cousin's voice but, instead, heard the maid rattling away in a high pitched voice. The colonel's eyes almost popped out of his head, and he could no longer control himself. The chortle which escaped from his throat echoed down the length of the corridor.

Yvette, upon seeing Darcy walk in, instantly marched over to him and repeatedly jabbed her finger in his chest while shouting, "Non, non, Monsieur Darcy, je n'autorise pas les maris dans mon boudoir. Vous devez partir immédiatement. J'insiste!"

Elizabeth and Georgiana's mouths gaped wide.

Elizabeth whispered, "What is she saying to Fitzwilliam, Georgie?"

"Oh, Lizzy, she told him that she does not allow husbands in her boudoir, and that he must leave. She insists!"

Both Georgiana and Elizabeth giggled excessively. "Lizzy, I never thought I would see the day when anyone would boss my brother around. The only one who might come close would be Aunt Catherine, but even she doesn't hold a candle to Yvette!"

At this statement, the women giggled all the more until a pounding on the door was heard which made them jump. "Oh, Georgie, that must be Richard. Before you leave, I have something to quickly ask you." Elizabeth walked over to her vanity, opened her jewellery box and took out the ruby ring that Collette claimed had belonged to Darcy's grandmother. "Georgie, do you happen to recollect this ring and whether it belonged to your grandmother? Fitzwilliam has given me so many beautiful jewels that belonged to your family. I confess that I am at a loss as to whether I remember this piece's origin correctly?"

Georgiana took the ring from her hand and gazed at it. "Yes, I believe it did belong to her, but I have not seen it in the longest time. I think the last time I recall seeing it was when I was a young girl. It has not been kept with the other jewels." She lifted her eyes to her sister-in-law. "I wonder why? It is lovely, is it not?"

Elizabeth replied half-heartedly, "Oh, why, *yes*, quite lovely." The knock was heard once again and with an even greater intensity. "Go answer it, Georgie. I guess I shall have to go down as I am. I shall be right out."

She then placed the ring back in the box and whispered aloud as she lifted her eyebrows, "Let the performance begin." Before turning to leave, she took one last glimpse at her appearance in the mirror. She raised her eyes to glance upward to the pinnacle of the longest quill above her head, then allowed them to descend and settle upon the diamond earrings that dangled brightly from each lobe before they slowly dropped to rest on the large diamond choker about her neck. It coordinated in dimension and sparkle to the diamond bracelets which graced each wrist. Lastly, she looked at her bosom. She had always been amply endowed, but the divorce corset made it appear doubly so. The buxomness it created in such a low cut dress seemed quite improper to Elizabeth. Even Louisa Hurst's chest never appeared as bosomy and bold as hers did now. Sighing, she exclaimed aloud, "For the time being, it cannot be helped. I shall not think upon it." With these words spoken, she turned to meet the others in the hall.

When she left the room, she found her husband, Georgiana, and Richard awaiting her.

Moments earlier, before either Elizabeth or Georgiana had come out of the chamber, Darcy had exited his room in a huff, strutting towards his wife's door when he spotted his cousin across the hall.

Richard attempted to appear nonchalant as he leaned against the wall near Georgiana's door. The colonel perceived the scowl upon his cousin's countenance, and therefore, he pressed his lips together in an attempt to keep a grin from appearing on his face. He offered a quick nod to his indignant cousin, and when Darcy's back was turned towards him, he smirked freely while his cousin knocked adamantly on his wife's door.

First Georgiana came out and softly said, "Fitzwilliam, I am afraid that Yvette is a very demanding woman and with the language barrier it only makes it all the more difficult. Elizabeth is not happy that Yvette has insisted that she wear feathers and all the other things. Brother, she dislikes what she perceives to be Yvette's partiality for ostentation. Yet, I would not mind it in the least, if it is all the same to you, Brother, to have Yvette as my maid. Lizzy may then have Nancy. Personally, I would welcome Yvette's resourcefulness."

Darcy frowned. He was not sure he wanted to keep this maid in his employ, let alone unleash her upon his defenceless sister. Nettled from the unbelievable incident with the maid, he acquiesced, "Very well, Georgie, I shall speak with Elizabeth about your desire."

When Elizabeth walked out into the hall Darcy's eyes widened in wonder, never had he seen his wife displayed in such grand splendour. She was truly a sight to behold.

The colonel could only imagine what was crossing his cousin's mind but he quickly dismissed such thoughts from his head and turned to his other cousin. "Georgie," said Richard, "shall we?" Georgiana turned to take his arm, and they descended the stairs together.

Likewise, Darcy held out his elbow for his wife. Elizabeth rested her hand on his arm, and they slowly made their way to the stairs when Darcy stopped to say, "Lizzy, I am sorry you feel uncomfortable, but must I say, you look ravishing." She looked up to him sharply. "I mean it as a compliment, for you look truly pulchritudinous tonight. However, I find you so always. In fact, I, too, share your preference for simplicity."

Again, she eyed him. "If this is true, sir, why hire a French maid? I am under the impression that you thought I needed guidance in my unvarying and Philistine sense of country fashion."

Darcy heard the hostility in her tone and knew she was still angry with him. They were half way down the stairs when he hurriedly whispered, "Elizabeth, you are labouring under a misapprehension. My reasons for hiring a French lady's maid have nothing to do with your fashion sense in any way. I shall explain it all to you after our guests leave. Yvette will no longer be your maid. Georgie has requested that Yvette assist her from now on, not you. If this meets with your approval, I shall inform Yvette of the change later tonight."

Elizabeth caught Darcy's expression and felt his sincerity. "Yes, I would find that to be most agreeable if Georgie is certain she wishes to take on such a woman."

He nodded his approval as they stepped off the stairs and noticed that the first guests were being ushered into the reception area.

Introductions were made, and then all were guided into the dinning hall. The sideboard and additional tables were laden with an array of the finest, most scrumptious fare from Pemberley's kitchen. Mrs. Potter was a woman truly gifted in the culinary arts and a great asset to the estate. Many families in the surrounding neighbourhood knew that Pemberley was to be envied for the proficiency of its cook.

The ladies were given the honour of filling their plates first. Many of the women expressed delight for such an unceremonious affair. Elizabeth heard some refer to the buffet as if it were a picnic or as if they were breaking their morning fast. Not all delighted in the evening's lack of formal etiquette, because several, in false, hushed tones, expressed their sentiments unreservedly.

Jane immediately noticed her sister's elaborate dress and her discomfiture with it. She sat next to Elizabeth and said, "Lizzy, this is splendid. Pemberley is truly beautiful, and you, my dear sister, look so lovely tonight. I am truly happy for you." Elizabeth smiled wanly at her sister while all the ladies sat, waiting for the gentlemen to join them before they began to eat. Leaning over to her sister, Jane whispered with a tinge of excitement in her voice, "Lizzy, may I speak with you in private before retiring for the night?"

"Why, yes, Jane, of course. For since you arrived, we have hardly had a chance to see one another, and there is so much I need to discuss with you, but are you feeling well enough?"

"Yes, I feel fine."

Elizabeth smiled and replied cheerfully, "Then come to my chamber before you retire. I shall wait for you."

As the gentlemen were seated, a lull of silence fell upon the great room. All awaited the Mistress of Pemberley to lift her fork to commence, and upon her so doing, the din of voices again filled the air.

After all were satisfied, the men went straightway to the library while the ladies gathered in the music room. Elizabeth had noticed both Collette and Caroline scrutinizing her for most of the evening, their eyes often unwaveringly fixed upon her person. She felt silly for being dressed to the hilt, and she felt that these ladies sensed her uneasiness. Everyone had been seated for several moments but not a word had been spoken aloud. Elizabeth felt at a loss, not knowing what to say to such a large gathering of women. Finally, she remembered the unseasonably warm day. "The weather was exceptionally fine today, was it not? I thoroughly enjoyed it. Were any of you so fortunate to enjoy the sunshine?"

The ladies all stared at her. Caroline smirked. Then Collette spoke, "Oh, yes, Eliza, the weather was grander than I have ever remembered a February's day to have been in Derbyshire. It made the hunt so much more enjoyable. And I dare say, if it had not been warm, I would have been truly uncomfortable when I fell from my horse. I waited for someone, anyone, to come and help me. Is it not sad that I sprained my ankle and could not even stand on my own? Was it not inconvenient that I was so perfectly helpless?"

Mrs. Pinkerton stated, "Well, I hope you did not have to wait too long for some assistance. With all of the men busy trying to find Chalmer's fox, they may have never thought twice about you lagging behind."

"Oh, I was afraid of that myself. But Fitz, I mean Mr. Darcy, noticed straight away that I was missing and came in search of me. I do not know what I would have done if he had not. I tried, but I could not get to my feet. He found me by the hedgerow and gallantly lifted me in his arms, carrying me to safety. Oh and he was ever so graciously kind to stay with me until more help arrived." Collette's eyes shifted to Mrs. Darcy as she spoke each word with confident self assurance.

Mrs. Chalmers looked suspiciously at Collette and stated, "It is a wonder that he had to carry you at all. You looked as if you could walk well enough to grub up some fare upon your plate in the dining hall awhile ago, and you walked in here sure footed enough."

Collette smiled smugly. "Well, yes, I am much better now. There was so much time before anyone else came to our aide that Mr. Darcy helped me bear some of my weight upon it while we waited. And I must say that I am so glad for the support of his strong arms. I am sure I would have fallen if he had not been there to allow me to lean upon him so. He is a most thoughtful gentleman."

Distressed over Collette's rudeness, Georgiana dared a glance at her sister-in-law to see how she managed. Elizabeth seemed pale and withdrawn.

Miss Bingley also took in the expression of all. However, she was not quite sure whether Collette was fabricating a tale or had truly charmed Mr. Darcy. She would have to wait for the men to return in hope of some kind of open display of affection by Mr. Darcy to ascertain Collette's standing with the man.

~*~

In the library, the men were not in any hurry to get down to the business at hand. Darcy poured various wines while Richard, Bingley and Mr. Sheldon handed them to each gentleman. After the dispensing of the beverages was complete, Mr. Pinkerton audaciously declared, "Darcy, I had no idea that you could not afford a carriage to take your wife into town. My wife and I saw her walking into Lambton this morning, unaccompanied." This remark earned a few chuckles.

Richard gauged his cousin's reaction as did Bingley and Dr. Lowry. Darcy chose to ignore the comment, but Bingley piped up in Elizabeth's defence, "Oh, my sister-in-law is an avid walker, and I am sure, with the weather being such an inducement today, she could not help herself. She often walked to town while living in Hertfordshire."

This comment shot up more than a few brows.

Darcy had turned his back to the group while pouring himself a drink. He rolled his eyes upon hearing many of the men's responses to Bingley's explanation about Elizabeth's habits.

Some uttered in unison, "I say!" whilst others exclaimed, "By George!"

With a drink in hand, the Master of Pemberley turned again to face the group of men. "Now, gentleman," Darcy began in all seriousness, "we must speak and open the discussion about the safety and continued operation of the mine, giving consideration to all of the collapses in recent years. I have had Mr. Sheldon hire a Mr. Sumner, who specializes in the appraisal of mining excavation. His report shall detail the economy of continued operation of the mine, and the hazards that might arise from such a venture. He shall also recommend what efforts of conservation we, who have vested interests, must do to ensure the safety of those who work on behalf of our profit. He shall also offer us those changes which must be implemented and will know what things should be retained for that purpose."

"You make it sound as if the miners are doing us the favour," said Mr. Pinkerton, "instead of it being the other way around."

"Hear, hear!" was heard from most of the men in response to Mr. Pinkerton's statement.

Taking a sip of his drink, Darcy merely waited until the uproar died down, "Yes, well, I understand that many of you feel the workers are being paid, and that is their just reward, but I, for one, cannot be a part of working conditions which prove to be unsatisfactory and, quite frankly, shoddy and dangerous. I shall take the necessary legal action to separate myself from this enterprise if we cannot all come to an agreement on what is ethically sound."

At this point, Mr. Chalmers entered into the discussion and voiced his support of Darcy. A few of the other men nodded in agreement, but Pinkerton and the rest shook their heads the more. Pinkerton spoke up. "If we were to do as you suggest, Darcy, there would be no profit at all. All of the revenue would go into wages and materials for maintenance. What you suggest is unsound business and everyone would lose. If we close the mine, the workers have no pay. Face the facts. Mining is a perilous occupation. That is why mine-diggers are paid higher wages than tenant farmers. They are willing to take the risk. Leave it at that!"

"Hear! Hear!" erupted yet again, and then the men all began to speak at once. Darcy rested against his desk while sipping his port. He looked around the noisy room and made eye contact with Richard. They stared at one another for some seconds until Mr. Caldecott animatedly spoke up. "Tell us, Darcy, if it is true, have you gone and hired a French maid for your wife? By the looks of her tonight, I can assume the answer is yes!"

Immediately, laughter erupted.

Darcy's jaw hardened. As he began to rub his hand over his mouth, Richard quickly spoke, "Maybe we should join the ladies now. I, for one, could use the cheer and comfort which we are at all times rewarded from their splendid skill to produce such melodious songs and tunes."

All the gentlemen heartily agreed as they stood, setting their empty glasses aside. Darcy sighed as he watched them leave.

Bingley lingered at the door, and in concern asked, "Are you coming, Darce?"

"Go on, Bingley, I shall be with you shortly. I must speak with Mr. Sheldon before he takes his leave."

Bingley replied, "Ah! But of course. I shall wait for you then in the music room."

Darcy nodded and motioned for Mr. Sheldon to take a seat.

~*~

When Darcy entered the crowded room, he instantly noted Georgiana playing the pianoforte. Elizabeth, he observed, sat in the far corner of the room surrounded by a group of women. He searched for a vacant chair, finding the only nearby place was by none other than Collette. He rolled his eyes and elected to stand for the rest of the evening. If Richard ever gave up his post by the instrument, perhaps he could take his place. Yet, this thought only made him shudder. He hated being the centre of attention. No, he would remain on his feet if needs be. Thus, his eyes searched the room to find the best spot. He saw no seats by his wife or by Bingley and Jane. He imagined the empty chair near Mrs. Chalmers had been saved for Georgiana. On the far side of the room, he discovered an area behind Caroline that seemed spacious enough. He quietly made his way over to where Miss Bingley sat and stationed himself behind her. At this angle, he had an excellent view of the pianoforte and could enjoy observing his wife's profile.

Many of the women desired to exhibit. Caroline showed off her dexterity at the keys by playing with a fury unsurpassed. After her exuberant performance, the room cheered. Collette then hurriedly made her way to the pianoforte with some music in hand and petitioned Miss Bingley to play for her. Putting the music in place, both Caroline and Richard studied it for a few seconds, before Caroline began to play the French air, and Collette's voice wafted about the room. Her song, a tale of misery between two lovers, spoke of passion, betrayal, and ardour that lingers brilliantly, even with the passage of time.

As she sang her song, she shamelessly stared at Darcy. His only desire and thought during the performance was to escape the room. He offered up silent thanks that his wife did not understand French. Yet, Caroline, Richard, and Georgiana most certainly did. He could see the shock on Georgiana's face and an expression of dismay upon that of his cousin's. Caroline seemed perplexed as she concentrated on the notes before her. Darcy's eyes tried to look upon anything or anyone else in order to avoid Collette's penetrating gaze. Many in the room became tempted to look over their shoulder to see at whom Miss Caldecott was staring, because it was obvious that her compelling performance was aimed at someone in particular. Darcy chanced a glance over to his wife. He quickly averted his vision when his eyes met hers. She was watching him with the same intensity as Collette, except Elizabeth's gaze was not conveying the passion of desire which Collette so obviously displayed, but instead, clearly indicated indignation.

Not knowing what else to do, Darcy turned his head to the left and then to the right. Finally, leaning against the wall, he crossed his arms over his chest and lowered his face. He released a sigh and brought one hand up to cover his eyes, slowly rubbing his fingers over his brow. In great agony, he felt as if the song would never finish. He bitterly thought to himself that the evening had turned out to be a complete failure.

At length, the performances came to an end. Darcy and Elizabeth smiled and gave departing words of gratitude to their guests. Many thanked them for such an enjoyable evening. Mr. Caldecott, in particular, told Elizabeth that she looked magnificent and commented on how he would like to find a French maid for his daughter, and then indicated that they were so hard to come by that he had no hope of ever finding one. He congratulated Darcy on his luck to have found one so readily. Elizabeth nodded and offered a gracious smile that never reached her eyes.

After everyone had gone, Darcy asked if any would like some wine. Everyone responded in the affirmative. He and Richard did the honours of pouring and handing out the drinks. Kitty was in awe when her brother-in-law crossed the room to offer her the goblet. He next approached his wife and handed her one as well. Taking the glass from his hand, he noted Elizabeth would not look at him. He sighed in response as he walked back to fill his own glass.

Bingley and Jane were whispering to one another when suddenly that gentleman stood and asked permission of his brother-in-law to offer a toast. A little taken aback, Darcy gladly gave Bingley the floor.

"Well, I dare say that Jane and I want to take advantage of this unforeseen opportunity while we have it."

Darcy smiled bitterly. He knew all too well what Bingley meant. Beaming, Bingley lifted his glass and announced, "I would like to propose a toast to my wife Jane, for she and I would like to share with all of you the information that we are expecting a child come early autumn."

Elizabeth's face brightened amidst the cheers of congratulations. She immediately stood and rushed to her sister, embracing her warmly. "Oh, Jane, I am so happy for you. How long have you known?"

"We only found out this afternoon when Dr. Lowry came to see me."

"Oh!" Elizabeth stated. Again, she felt guilty for not having been present when her sister needed her.

Kitty and Georgiana stood beside the women, each desiring to express their heartfelt happiness over the news.

Elizabeth stepped aside. She stood watching her sister's radiant face as she listened to the others offering their congratulations and well wishes. Bingley remained beside Jane with a huge grin on his face. They looked truly happy. It made Elizabeth feel incredibly melancholy. Suddenly, she noticed Darcy standing beside her.

He leaned over and whispered, "Lizzy, Mr. Sheldon shall advance your account first thing in the morning. If you ever desire anything more, feel free to ask Mr. Sheldon or me. I have told him that you may approach him freely with any of your financial dealings."

With a knot in her throat, she nodded her head without removing her eyes from her sister.

"Georgie and I," Darcy continued in hushed tones, "are going to speak with Yvette in a moment. I shall try to be with you shortly, though I realize that you have not had any time to spend with Jane. If you desire to do so, I shall wait up for you. I need to speak with you, Elizabeth."

Nodding once more, she continued to say nothing, nor would she look at him. When he laid his hand upon her shoulder to squeeze it, she instinctively flinched from his touch. Closing his eyes tightly, he withdrew his hand and made his way over to his sister. She gladly took his arm, and they left the room together as the others were still discussing whether the baby might be a boy or girl and what names should be considered.

Caroline stood near the gathering. Instead of becoming caught up in the mania over becoming an aunt, she had watched Darcy and Elizabeth's cold exchange. Nothing could have given her more pleasure than to witness their animosity towards each other.

~*~

Darcy and Georgiana entered Elizabeth's chamber, where they rang for Yvette and awaited her arrival. "Brother," Georgiana ventured, "I desire to speak with you about Collette."

Darcy stared at her in surprise, "About Collette? Did something happen this evening concerning her?"

"Yes. She told everyone…"

Elizabeth opened the door and walked into the room. Darcy and Georgiana turned simultaneously to look.

Elizabeth could sense that she had interrupted their conversation and was ready to take her leave when Yvette arrived. The petite maid smiled at Elizabeth and again complimented her on her beauty, expressing her delight that the mistress had not changed out of the dress that she, *Yvette*, had selected, and that Mrs. Darcy had allowed the feathers to remain. Elizabeth was able to catch snippets of words but could not be completely certain of Yvette's meaning.

Finally, Darcy addressed the maid, "Yvette, nous sommes reconnaissants pour ce que vous avez fait. C'est juste que ma femme n'est pas à l'aise avec les meilleures parrures. Cependant, ma soeur désire vos services. Par conséquent, ce sera sa femme de chambre, Nancy, qui s'occupera de Madame Darcy alors que vous assisterez Mademoiselle Georgiana à partir de maintenant."

Georgiana whispered to Elizabeth what her brother was saying. "He is telling Yvette that we are grateful for all that she has done. Fitzwilliam is explaining that you, his wife, are not comfortable with all the latest finery, but that I, his sister, desire her services. Therefore, he says, we shall have my maid, Nancy attend to you, while Yvette attends to me from now on."

Yvette's face perked up at the suggested arrangement. She felt that now she would have a lady who would truly appreciate her abilities. Immediately, Yvette walked over to Mrs. Darcy and quickly kissed one cheek and then the other. Then, she took Georgiana by the hand and led her to her chamber. Georgiana informed Nancy about the switch, and upon that notification, Nancy made her way to the mistress' chamber. Elizabeth allowed Nancy to help her out of her gown while Darcy watched from across the room as he sat on the bed.

Elizabeth sighed in relief as Nancy removed the feathers. She now sat in front of her vanity wearing the divorce corset, chemise, and pantalets while Nancy had gone in search of a nightgown.

"You did look quite lovely tonight, Elizabeth," said Darcy, "yet, I think you look just as lovely if not lovelier as you appear now. Your beauty needs no embellishment. Your eyes sparkle finer than the glistening from the jewellery you wear." He then dared, "What was said tonight that has caused you to be so angry with me? Is it still concerning my hiring of Yvette? I only wished for you to have the best, Lizzy."

Nancy walked back in carrying the gown. She unlaced the corset and took off the choker and earrings. She had removed the bracelets earlier, prior to helping Elizabeth out of her dress. When the maid began to remove the first pin from Elizabeth's hair, Darcy stood, walked across the room, and with the wave of his hand, dismissed her. Standing behind his wife, he met her gaze in the mirror. "May I remove your pins, Elizabeth?"

She looked into his eyes and then averted her gaze. "If you desire, you may."

As he pulled a pin from her hair, she stole a glance and saw that he still stared at her. When the last pin had been removed, and the last tress fell upon her shoulder, Darcy leaned forward and kissed the bare skin on her neck. Again, Elizabeth recoiled with his touch.

The hurt was evident as Darcy looked into her eyes. "I suppose, madam, you no longer desire my company?"

With a chilled tone, she cried, "How can you expect me to desire your caresses and kisses when your arms have been around another woman?"

Incredulous, he contradicted, "I have no idea of what you are speaking, Elizabeth. There is no other woman. Why do you make such accusations? Why did you accuse me earlier of something to do with wenches? How can you make such cruel insinuations?

"Insinuations?" cried Elizabeth. "Is it a fact or merely an allusion that you held Collette Caldecott in your arms today?"

His left eyebrow rose in shock, and his cheek twitched as her eyes flashed to meet his in the reflection. He opened his mouth and then closed it again. Elizabeth continued, "Is it reality or imagination on the part of Collette that you let her *lean her body* upon yours as she strove to put some weight on her foot?"

"Elizabeth, I can explain it all."

"Can you, Fitzwilliam? Can you explain why you will never speak of her when I ask? Why you changed seating arrangements so she could be near you? Why you invited her to ride with you?"

"That is a falsehood!" he cried.

"Which one, Fitzwilliam?" queried Elizabeth. "Did you or did you not hold her or allow her to lean her body against yours?"

Nervously, he rubbed the small finger on his left hand between his thumb and index finger of his right. Elizabeth quickly saw his agitation as he reverted to the familiar habit of twirling his ring, only the ring was no longer there. She knew how he hated confrontation.

"Pray, Fitzwilliam, does the cat have your tongue?" She glared.

Looking at her, he stated, "Elizabeth, there is a reasonable explanation for everything."

"I do hope so, Fitzwilliam, because you cannot imagine the humiliation I have endured this evening. Collette made sure that everyone present knew how strong your arms were and how wonderful it was to be within them!"

Rapping was heard, and Elizabeth immediately stood to go and open the door. "Oh, Jane, do come in." Jane tentatively walked into the chamber only to be taken aback at finding her brother-in-law within and the accompanying tension. "Oh, Mr. Darcy," said Jane, "I shall visit with Elizabeth at another time."

"No, no, Jane. I know you and Elizabeth have not had any time whatsoever to really converse with one another." He smiled glumly at the irony. "I am not retiring as of yet and shall speak to Elizabeth after the two of you visit. I insist."

Bowing to Jane and then to his wife, he strode through the dressing chambers to his own room. Pausing in place for a moment, he decided to return downstairs to his study. As Darcy opened his door, he found Bingley standing in the hall with his hand poised in the air. "Ah, Darcy, I say, I did not even knock."

"Yes, Charles, may I help you?"

"Well, I was wondering, if you are not too busy that is, if you would not mind having a visit. I am so elated that I am sure I shall be beside myself until Jane returns."

"Where do you suggest we have *our* visit?"

"Well, I could come into your chamber or, perhaps, you could come over to mine?"

"Charles, I find I am in need of brandy. Do you care to join me?"

"Oh, that is an excellent idea. I shall have wine, however, if it is all the same to you."

"Wine it is, Charles."

"Oh, I would like to find a book to read about childbirth. Perchance does your library have something on the subject?"

With a grin, Darcy remarked, "I shall see what I can find."

After he poured himself a brandy and Bingley wine, Darcy went over to the far wall of the library with candle in hand. He set his drink down and pulled three books from the shelf. Darcy held the books out before him, tilting his head so that he could read the titles to his friend. "Here they are, Charles, they are called: *The Knowledge of Midwifery and Their Suitability for the Task, Abstract Midwifery*, and..." He paused, taking a breath and lifting his eyes to Bingley. "...*The Midwife's Companion*. You need be careful with the last one. It may prove too much for your sensibilities. It has a section which refers to terrors regarding the use of medical instruments." With that warning given, he handed the books to Bingley.

Bingley's eyes widened. While taking the offered books from Darcy's hand, he asked, "Which is the one that may induce nightmares?"

"It is the one on top."

Quickly, Bingley handed the book back to Darcy and said, "I would rather not know."

Taking a sip of his brandy, he nodded in understanding and then walked back to the shelf and replaced the book. As he returned to his brandy, he commented, "Dr. Lowry may know of some more recent publications. The books you hold there are somewhat old, considering modern methods with men now assisting in the birth process."

"Well, I am grateful to have them, and I shall take extremely good care of them. Who knows, Darcy, you may need them soon yourself."

Darcy gave a quick shrug of his shoulders and nodded slowly.

"Darcy, do you not find married life to be exhilarating? Just think, this time last year, I was pining away for my angel and you were battling your attraction for her sister."

Rolling his eyes, Darcy thought dryly, *and a daily battle it is*. There was nothing he wanted more than to go upstairs and have it out once and for all with Elizabeth. Surely, she could not believe that anything improper happened between Collette and himself. He felt a faint headache coming on.

"Darcy, there is one thing I wish to speak with you about."

Bingley had his full attention, "Well, go on, Charles," said Darcy, "I am listening."

"Very well. I have not said a word of this to anyone, so I ask your secrecy. I am thinking of letting my lease on Netherfield go. I think it is truly time that I find an estate and settle down. You know, put down roots and all."

"And you think Netherfield is out of the question as that estate?"

Looking rather sheepish, Bingley skewed his lips and nodded.

Darcy chuckled and asked, "Do you need my assistance? Is there somewhere in particular you would like to purchase an estate?"

"Well, Darce, I would like to settle somewhere close to Pemberley, what with our wives being as close as they are. And before long, our children will then be close enough to know one another." Bingley eyed his friend in expectation, waiting for his response.

Darcy's face lit up as he displayed a heartfelt smile of pleasure. "I would like that, Charles. I know Elizabeth will love it when you are ready to reveal your plans. I shall advise Mr. Sheldon to watch for any estates which may become available."

Bursting with happiness, Bingley shifted from foot to foot and exclaimed, "It does not necessarily have to be in Derbyshire. I was thinking no more than thirty miles though."

Nodding, Darcy finished off his drink, clapped Bingley on the back, he cried, "Congratulations, Charles. I am very happy for you and Jane."

"Thank you, Darcy, and by the way, Louisa and Hurst are expecting a wee one in late summer."

"Really? I am truly surprised. They shall be pleased to have a cousin on the way as well, I imagine."

"Yes, I sent an express off this afternoon."

"Well, Charles, I think I shall call it a night. You are welcome to stay and read or help yourself to another glass of wine."

"No, I shall return with you in the hope that Jane and Elizabeth are talked out."

"Yes." *I hope so as well.* "Well, shall we go and see for ourselves." With his books in hand, Bingley nodded and smiled at his brother-in-law's suggestion and then both men departed in search of their wives.

~*~

Jane and Elizabeth sat upon the enormous bed giggling in delight, enjoying one another's company again. Elizabeth asked her sister about her feelings of being with child. Jane told her that she had been sick only a few times, but that she was sleepier than usual and required long naps during the day. She also mentioned that her breasts seemed fuller.

Then, without warning, Jane announced that they had spoken enough about her. She stated that she wanted to know about all the happenings at Pemberley. Elizabeth considered telling her about Fitzwilliam nearly dying due to the fencing accident, her distress while her husband was gone to help with the mine collapse, and about how frightened she was for his life. She also considered telling her about Collette. Yet, she did not want Jane to worry now that she was expecting. She dearly desired to tell her about Wickham, but this too would cause her sister undue distress. What would she say? *Jane, Wickham is blackmailing me about Georgiana's reputation. He says he shall kill my husband, our sister, and maybe even harm Lydia's baby if I should not cooperate.* It was too much. How could she share a burden such as this with her dear Jane? No, she would shoulder it alone. Yet, she knew it would not be her secret alone. Soon, Mr. Sheldon would realize something odd was transpiring due to her frequent requests for additional funds. Oh, what was to be done?

"Well, Jane," Elizabeth uttered in all seriousness yet with unmistakable merriment in her widened eyes. "I have been through three lady's maids already. They all feel I am too demanding!"

"Oh, Lizzy, do be serious."

"Oh, but I am, Jane."

They giggled, and then Elizabeth detailed her adventures with her maids and even came down from the bed and gave a visual performance for her sister of how Yvette had scrubbed her hide raw. It was during this presentation that she heard her husband's voice.

"Ahem, Elizabeth, I think Charles is missing Jane." Both Jane and Elizabeth absorbed in each other's company had jumped at their sudden appearance, not having heard the light knocking on the door. Darcy smiled within at his wife's spirited display. Bingley stood behind his brother-in-law at the doorway.

Spinning around, Elizabeth replied in surprise, "Oh, yes, it is rather late." She smiled to Bingley and sincerely stated, "I thank you, Charles, for sharing your wife."

"I am delighted to do so, and I shall happily share her in the future as well."

"Goodnight, Lizzy," Jane said as she hugged her sister tightly and kissed her cheek. Then, turning to go, she commented further, "And thank you, Mr. Darcy, for allowing me to have this time with Lizzy."

"You are most welcome, Jane. Please, will you not call me Fitzwilliam?" He smiled warmly before adding, "And, Jane, I am delighted for you and Charles regarding your wonderful news."

"Thank you…Fitz …william, that means a great deal to me."

After Jane and Charles had crossed the hall, Darcy shut the door. He leaned against it and looked at his wife. Neither said a word for some moments. "Elizabeth, would you please sit and let me explain what happened today during the hunt?"

"Why, Fitzwilliam," she stated with flippancy, "does your story differ from *Cole's.*"

A sobering expression crossed his mien. "Elizabeth, what I have to say is not a fabrication. It is fact. No matter what you think or what Miss Caldecott has indicated, I did not ask her to join the hunt. It is true that she fell from her horse, or so she claimed. I was alone with her for a few moments and debated about riding ahead for help, but she cried out so in pain that I felt at a loss to know what to do."

"Ah, so you swept her up in your strong arms and stayed with her for some time, until you were finally discovered by the rest of the party. How convenient it was for you both."

"Elizabeth!" Darcy's voice boomed, "I only helped her. I did not desire to be alone with her, and you may enquire of Fitzwilliam as to how long I had been away from the party. He will attest to the fact that he came in search of me when I was detained."

"Oh, you shall allow me to speak with Richard when it is in your behalf. Do I dare? Are you sure you shall not sulk? If I remember right, last night you found my verbal exchange with your cousin very disturbing!"

Elizabeth saw the anger come over him, but she did not care. Walking speedily over to her jewellery box, she flipped open the lid and procured the rings. "While I am asking Richard to verify your story, maybe he can also tell me the validity of what you will say to these." First she held out the ruby. "Fitzwilliam, does this ring look familiar?"

He looked into her eyes and then peered at the ring. His brow creased and he nodded. "Yes, it belonged to my grandmother. I have not seen it for some time now. Why do you ask, and however did you come upon it?"

"Ah, well, I guess you have forgotten, since it has been so many years ago. Collette gave me the ring this morning after you departed in such a rude manner. Do you remember your behaviour towards me by chance?" He winced at the sarcasm she freely hurled at him and at the fact that her words were just.

Visibly shaken, Elizabeth's voice became strained. "Maybe this shall refresh your memory. Collette claims you gave her this ring several years ago. She says she hated to part with it, but since you have done the *unthinkable*, she feels it is rightfully mine. Yet, I do not desire it." Hotly, she pressed the ring into the palm of his hand. She desired to say more but could not. Instead, her body began to tremble in anguish and tears started to flow down her cheeks.

Darcy quickly came closer to embrace her, but she pushed him back. "No," she cried, "I do not want your arms about me. Here!" She opened her other hand. In her palm lay his signet ring, which for many generations had graced the hand of Pemberley's heir.

Darcy looked upon it and then met Elizabeth's gaze. With a dreadful feeling in his gut, he questioned, "Elizabeth, may I enquire as to where you found my ring?"

Taking in a deep breath she wiped the tears from her face and resolutely stated, "You most certainly may, Fitzwilliam. I did not find it, however. Collette was wearing it upon her finger when she arrived this morning, and she claims that you asked her to guard it with her life." Then, in a chilling manner, Elizabeth posed to Darcy the accusations that her eyes now revealed and to which her lips would soon attest. "So, my question to you, my dear husband, is this: Can Richard also vouch for the innocence of the clandestine meeting between you and your fair seductress as well as its duration? And what of the *earlier* meeting which was evidently held somewhere in the proximity of the coalmine—the *rendezvous* where you entrusted her with one of your most treasured possessions?"

Darcy gravely eyed his wife as he declared, "Elizabeth, I hope your presumption is spoken in anger. For if it is not, you have very little trust in me, and our marriage hangs by a thread. You may as well send me to Newgate in London with Mr. Hibbs or, better yet, ship me off to France. The guillotine would be much quicker."

~*~

Chapter Eighteen

Patience and Limitation

Elizabeth rolled her eyes at her husband's exaggerated words. "Really, Fitzwilliam, do you not think you are being overly dramatic? Men never pay for their dalliances as long as they are accomplished with panache and discretion. I have never heard of a man's reputation being tarnished or even ruined for very long, if at all. On the contrary, society is amused by the faithlessness of the male sex. But for a woman, it is quite a different story. I have never heard of any man being strapped to a dunking stool and submersed until he was proclaimed dead. Far from it!"

Emphatically, Darcy retorted, "No, Elizabeth, my exaggeration, as you call it, has nothing to do with the just punishment that any individual should endure for infidelity! Instead, if you truly believe I am capable of succumbing to Miss Caldecott, if you give credence to your suppositions, thus, in reality, I would rather face prison or the guillotine. There is no hyperbole intended. For your allegation that I must have met Miss Caldecott clandestinely implies that you deem me capable of such treachery, and therefore, your accusation shall serve to annul all of my hopes and desires for our life together. My every happiness would vanish, and my life would be void of all purpose and pleasure. How can we ever find sanctity in our union if you truly believe this possible?"

Elizabeth closed her eyes and hung her head. Neither she nor her husband showed any signs of acting sensibly. When she looked up again with intentions of speaking, she saw Darcy's hand gesture for her to remain silent.

Pacing back and forth, Darcy's face bore the anguish he presently felt. "I want to say this much. I do not know how Miss Caldecott came into possession of these rings. I never asked her to guard my ring with her life, nor did I invite her on the hunt. I removed my ring when working at the coalmine. I then found myself at a loss as to where I had placed it. I thought I had secured it within my satchel. Yet, when I sought to recover it, it was not there."

Stopping abruptly in his trek, he stared openly into his wife's eyes and exclaimed with feeling. "Chaffin has been turning my chamber upside down in an attempt to find it. Now, really, Elizabeth, do you think I would have Chaffin perform such a search if I knew Collette had it in safe keeping all along? I promise you, I shall get to the bottom of this! Until then, I think this discussion only does us more harm than good."

Sighing in frustration, Elizabeth folded her arms over her chest, and with a challenging look, she countered her husband, "Fitzwilliam, I do not know what to think. Your actions do not always conform to your words. Can you deny that you desired for Collette to sit near you the night of the soirée? *Miss Caldecott* came here this morning and had both rings! What am I to think?"

Attempting to regain some level of control, she placed a hand over her heart and breathed in deeply. In a gentler tone, she resumed, "And then, tonight, she claims you had your arms around her." Turning to look pointedly at her husband yet again, Elizabeth questioned further, resentment burning upon her lips. "Fitzwilliam, she claims you gave her your grandmother's ring many years ago. Is this true? She did have the ring. And, furthermore, tonight she sang words of love for *you* alone! Everyone saw it."

Casting a piercing gaze at her husband's exasperated expression, Elizabeth stated in rising agitation, "I may not understand the language, but I have eyes, Fitzwilliam!" Finally, her voice rising, she demanded, "Were you in love with Collette at one time? For I am convinced *she* is in love with you!" She fell silent and continued to observe him closely.

Darcy rolled his eyes and a tossed his head, puffing in derision. "Pfft!" He then inhaled deeply and folded his arms across his chest and shrugged. "Elizabeth, as I stated a moment ago, I am afraid that, if we continue with this conversation, it will cause more damage rather than afford a beneficial conclusion. Doubt and accusations are not conducive to resolution."

"No, Fitzwilliam, they are not, but forthright explanation is!" She stomped her foot. "Oh! Your unwillingness to communicate is the only thing that is damaging!"

"Elizabeth," Darcy sighed, "I love *you*! I do not love Collette. I refuse to have this discussion when you have so many misgivings about me. I cannot bear it. For the time being, I feel we should strive for civility with one another, at least until the misconceptions can be explained. It is evident that you need them clarified."

Wearily, she cried in exasperation, "But, Fitzwilliam, if you would just tell me why she is throwing herself at you. Can you not see how it all appears to me? Have you no compassion…?" Elizabeth stopped herself and realized the words which almost tumbled out of her mouth were: *'for my poor nerves?'* Oh! What would be next, fluttering and trembling all over her body? She was turning into her mother! What was she thinking?

Darcy eyed his wife's shocked expression and feared that she would accuse him of something further. She averted her gaze and twisted her lips to the side. Composing herself, she stated, "Very well, Fitzwilliam. We shall agree to continue this conversation later when you feel you can better validate your assertions. I am not even sure what they are, excluding, of course, your claim that you do not love Collette and did not give her your ring."

Observing her guardedly, he slowly nodded his head. "Very well, Lizzy. I shall attempt to find out how she came to possess my ring, and I shall have Richard tell you his version of the sprained ankle incident. Elizabeth, I need you to look at me."

She lifted her eyes to him, and they stared at one another for several moments.

With a softened expression, Darcy declared earnestly, never breaking eye contact with his wife. "I wish for us to be happy again. I want you to be capable of trusting me. I have not always been wise, and I ask for your patience. Can you grant me that?"

Shaking her head, Elizabeth sighed in displeasure but agreed resignedly. "Very well, Fitzwilliam. Do what you must. However, I never want that woman invited to Pemberley again! I find her despicable and cannot extend the same tolerance to her that you ask for yourself. Is that understood?" She held her breath as she observed his aspect.

Darcy looked to the right for only a second before his eyes swung back to engage his wife's. "Yes, I, too, desire that she never pass over the threshold of *our* home again."

Elizabeth drew in a sharp breath. The hope that his declaration was true allowed her to breathe freely again, and the relief that she felt was plain for her husband to see.

"I shall speak with Mr. Caldecott regarding the ring before we leave for Matlock. However, Elizabeth, I cannot ask others to prohibit Collette's presence in their homes. She will likely be at my aunt and uncle's ball. But, in this home she shall no longer be welcomed, and, first thing in the morning, I shall give instructions to Mrs. Reynolds and Mr. Greene regarding this fact. And, if by chance she should call, she will be told that we are not available and requested to leave her card."

Closing her eyes in gratitude, Elizabeth heaved another sigh of relief. She nodded in acknowledgment and whispered, "I thank you, Fitzwilliam."

For the time being, their successful truce seemed to mollify their frayed emotions. After they wordlessly viewed each other for several, drawn out seconds, Darcy, in awkwardness, gestured with his hands towards the dressing chambers. "I shall go and prepare for bed, and then, if it is all right, Lizzy, I should like to come to your chamber to sleep with you." He clasped his hands together and cast an expectant gaze towards her.

Noticing his discomfort as he rubbed his thumb nervously over his small finger, which still lacked the signet ring, Elizabeth felt compassion for him. How could she not when she saw the child-like anticipation in his eyes as he patiently awaited her encouragement.

"Let me see your hand, Mr. Darcy."

Darcy's brows shot up. "Sorry?"

Smiling good-naturedly, she turned his left hand over. He allowed her to do so. With her right hand, she reached within his vest pocket and took out his signet ring and slid it onto the little finger.

"There," Elizabeth exclaimed as she clasped Darcy's hand tightly and glanced upward to gauge his reaction. "I do not want you chafing your skin."

A muddled grin appeared on his face as he continued to look intently at her. Finally, she nodded. "Yes, Fitzwilliam, you may sleep in my chamber tonight, however," she grew serious once more, "I desire your companionship and nothing more. I hope you understand. I need some time to deal with all that has transpired."

With eagerness, he nodded. "I understand." Then, he gave another quick nod, and rapidly retreated to his own chamber to dress for bed.

Elizabeth wearily raised both brows while puffing her cheeks full of air. Hopefully, she thought, the tide was turning for them. She then went straightway to her dressing area to clean her teeth and complete her own preparations for retiring. Having finished, she returned to the bedchamber, found the stool, and crawled atop the mattress.

Soon, her husband joined her, and after shifting about for a few moments, they both lay in companionable silence until Darcy finally spoke. "Lizzy, may I kiss you goodnight?"

Unequivocally, she replied, "Yes."

Turning on his side, he first kissed her on the cheek, and then, instinctively, she turned her mouth towards his. His lips covered hers, cautiously at first. Pausing in their progress, so he could look into her eyes and express what was in his heart, he whispered, "Lizzy, I love only you!"

Emotionally, she nodded while staring back into his eyes, yet the pain was still so fresh that she quickly averted her gaze.

His hand gingerly cupped her chin, turning her face towards him once more. Instantly, his mouth captured hers. This kiss was unlike the other. It was forceful and demanding. Darcy needed to know that *she* still loved *him*. In a half-hearted fashion, Elizabeth allowed him to bear down firmly upon her lips. He became aware of her languid response, which caused him to remember that she did not wish such intimacy, thus, he reined in his longing. As the intensity of his ardour waned, his lips were no longer insistent. Instead, they lingered lazily, slowly savouring and nibbling intermittently on each of her fair ones.

Consequently, the tantalizing enticement created by his mouth awakened Elizabeth's concupiscence, stirring her as it began to rise within the lowermost recess of her body. Impulsively, she seized the back of his head with her hands, entwining her fingers amongst his curls while pressing her mouth over his. There was no mistaking what kind of kiss she wanted.

Fuelled by his wife's unexpected appeal, Darcy unreservedly joined her in the deepening of their heated, passionate exchange.

It seemed that, by their own accord, his hands roamed freely over her gown, and at first, Elizabeth welcomed his advances, moaning in delight. But when Darcy broke their kiss to turn his enthusiasm elsewhere, she remembered her desire for nothing more than companionship. "Fitzwilliam!"

In smothered preoccupation, he muffled out, "Mmm?"

"Fitzwilliam, if you recall, I only wanted your *company* for now and nothing more. You said you understood."

His head shot up. In a sensual haze, he was momentarily baffled by her reminder. Then, he eyed his wife closely with a knitted brow. "Are you quite certain, Lizzy?"

"Yes."

Out of breath, he rolled over onto his back and reached for her hand, simply to hold it. He inhaled deeply.

"You did agree to understand," Elizabeth reminded him.

Darcy nodded. "Yes...well ...it is just that your response to my overtures allowed me to hope as I had never hoped before."

She smiled. "Oh. I do love you, Fitzwilliam."

He nodded faintly.

"Goodnight," said Elizabeth, rolling onto her side, facing him. She snuggled closely while he continued to hold her hand.

Then giving it a tight squeeze Darcy softly replied, "Good night, my Lizzy."

Elizabeth quickly fell into slumber. Darcy's rest did not come as easily. While waiting for his pent up passion to subside, he pondered on the morrow. He would first have a word with Richard and have him speak to Elizabeth. Then, he would go in search of Mrs. Reynolds and Mr. Greene to inform them that Collette would not be allowed at Pemberley House ever again. It would be an awkward situation to explain to Mr. Caldecott, and he knew that eventually the whole of the neighbourhood would become aware of it. Yet, it could not be helped. He also wanted to speak with Mrs. Reynolds about his grandmother's ring. He felt sure that he remembered something concerning it, but he could not recall exactly what.

Later in the morning, Thomas Wilkens and Sally were to be married in Pemberley's chapel. He also desired to remind Mrs. Potter to send the victuals and wine to the newlyweds' cottage following the wedding. Additionally, in a few days' time, he and Elizabeth would travel alone to Matlock to spend almost a full day before the others joined them. His mind spun with all that this might entail. Did he dare leave Georgiana in the clutches of Yvette? James and Elisha were sure to be at Matlock, and he knew they would very likely snub his wife. Anger welled up inside of him from just thinking about their pompous airs. Elisha was close to his Aunt

Catherine, and in the near future, he would more than likely find himself required to deal with them both when Georgiana had her coming out. His mind kept turning about his every concern in a repetitive cycle. After some time, however, drowsiness began to set in and he bent his head to observe his wife once more before falling asleep. She was beautiful!

~*~

Darcy was up early while Elizabeth still slept soundly. Dressing for the day, he informed his valet that his ring had been found. Mr. Chaffin looked expectantly at his master with raised brows. After all, he had searched Mr. Darcy's chamber most painstakingly, lifting every rug, turning out every drawer, and rummaging through the closet. Darcy met his valet's expectation full-faced. "I thank you, Chaffin. I know you have been diligent in your search, and it has caused you much grief and extra work. I appreciate your dedication to this matter."

Chaffin's disappointment was apparent as he turned to go about his duties. His master was a man of few words.

Darcy felt badly. What could he to say to his valet: *Chaffin, do you by chance remember Miss Caldecott? Well, yes, how could you ever forget? Somehow, she came into possession of my signet ring. I know what you are thinking, man. No, I did not meet her at the shearing house, nor by the pond, nor at the cottage or wherever else you were wont to always stumble upon us. I did not give her the ring!*

What would the man think? Darcy shuddered from the sickening sensations those memories triggered. He marvelled at how tangible the shame and rawness of his behaviour at that time could feel, even now. He remembered the fateful afternoon when he had entered the shearing house without warning, and how the stark discovery of Collette's true character had been exposed to him in full force. Chaffin had purposely sent him on the unusual errand that day. Hence, Darcy surmised that his valet had known exactly what he would likely find there. He did not comprehend, however, how Chaffin knew of it, and he could never bring himself to ask or discuss it with the man. He did not have to. Chaffin's face had said it all upon his return. The valet's demeanour spoke of sympathy and regret. Darcy could not look directly into his valet's face for many days thereafter. Not only could he not meet Chaffin's eye, he could barely tolerate his own reflection. His conduct that summer had been, indeed, reprehensible, and it took him many years to put such indiscretions behind him. Yet, with Collette's return, together with her blatant flirtations and devious ways, he felt that he was doomed to carry this albatross around his neck indefinitely.

When Darcy arrived in the breakfast room that morning, Caroline, Georgiana, and Kitty were within. "Ah! Good morning, ladies," he exclaimed as he began to pour himself a cup of coffee at the sideboard.

"You are all up bright and early." He approached the table and smiled down at his sister and sister-in-law.

Caroline smirked. "Yes, Mr. Darcy, I feel it only proper to do so when you are a guest in someone's home. Pray, is Eliza not with you?"

"Yes, well, Miss Bingley, I hope you will feel comfortable enough while at Pemberley to order a tray if you ever desire doing so. At present, I am having one sent up to my wife. We beg your pardon." He paused, took a sip from his cup and nodded towards his sister, "But, we have a wedding to attend this morning—that is, Georgiana, Elizabeth and I." He drank the last of his coffee and, without looking directly at Caroline, walked back over to the sideboard. "Please, feel free, Miss Bingley, to use the library and pianoforte, and do not hesitate to ask for assistance from the staff if you are in need of anything. We will be back shortly." Looking at his sister after pouring another cup of the warm brew, he enquired, "Georgie, have you seen Richard? He is not in his room, and I thought I would find him here."

"Oh, he has already departed for Matlock."

Instantly, Darcy remembered the conversation they had in the stable and Richard's expressed desire to leave. Due to the current turmoil with Elizabeth over Miss Caldecott, this fact had slipped his mind.

Georgiana added, "At the crack of dawn, he had the groomsmen help to take the sleigh runners off and put the carriage wheels back on." She held up a sealed letter. "He has asked me to give this to you, though."

Nodding briefly, Darcy set his empty cup down. Walking over to where Georgiana was sitting, he reached out, took the letter from her hand and conveyed his gratitude.

Bowing to all the ladies present, he begged to be excused and made his way to his study. As he departed the room, he heard Caroline eagerly ask Georgiana whose wedding they would be attending. Darcy smirked, imagining the utter shock that Miss Bingley would receive when his sister informed her that the ceremony was for a tenant farmer's son and a housemaid.

Upon entering his study, he opened Richard's missive and after reading its contents, a frown overtook his features. He pulled the bell cord for the housekeeper. Then, perusing his cousin's directive for a second time and looking over various correspondences pertaining to the estate for several minutes more, it occurred to him that Mrs. Reynolds had not arrived. He arose to go in search of her. She was not in her office. Thus, Darcy went to enquire of the butler.

"Ah, Greene, by chance have you seen Mrs. Reynolds this morning?"

"No, sir, she is not here. She has gone out of town for a short time and should be back by week's end."

Darcy grimaced. He and Elizabeth were to leave for Matlock by the week's end. He then asked the butler to come to his study, for he wished to have a word with him. Once they were safely ensconced within, he informed Mr. Greene of his desire never to allow admittance of Miss Caldecott through Pemberley's doors again. Instead, if she were to call, he was to ask her to leave her card and say nothing more. Mr. Greene was surprised. This was the second time in the Darcy's service that he had been instructed *not* to admit a guest. The other person who had been banned from the Great House was none other than Mr. George Wickham.

After Mr. Greene departed, Darcy wrote two missives, one to a Mr. Strasner of Lambton and another to his father in law, Mr. Thomas Dennet of Longbourn. Sealing them with wax, he then made his way to the kitchen. When he walked into the spacious room, every servant simultaneously stopped whatever they were doing. All eyes turned and fixed upon their master, and they quickly curtseyed and bowed. Not seeing Pemberley's cook among the staff before him, a flustered Darcy wondered who was in charge. With a quick shrug of his shoulders, he asked of the whereabouts of Mrs. Potter. He prayed that they would not tell him that she, too, had gone till the week's end.

Finally, the scullery maid, Penny, spoke up, "She is busy in the cellar, sir."

"Ah! Yes…well, would you please go and inform her that I wish to speak with her."

The young maid curtseyed and went hastily down the steps. In the meantime, Darcy pulled out a chair and sat by one of the long tables. He hated waiting. Laying the missives aside, he leaned back and briefly relaxed, folding his arms over his chest. Crossing one leg over the other, he again looked about, only to find that the servants all seemed frozen to the spots where they either sat or stood. He wondered glumly, *Am I so terrible that I cause such fear?* Sighing, he raised a hand and waved it about. "Please, go about your business. Do not mind my presence."

They reflected on him for only a moment longer, at which point, their limbs slowly began to function again. Luckily, Darcy did not have to linger long before the cook made her way to the kitchen from below. Mrs. Potter smiled heartily and asked how she might help him. At her appearance, he stood and grinned. He had never known a happier person, apart from Bingley, than Mrs. Potter. She was sunshine personified. "Good morning, Mrs. Potter, I wished only to make sure that you remembered to have a basket prepared for Thomas Wilkens's wedding today."

"Oh yes, sir. Would you like to see it?"

A twinkle shone in Darcy's eyes as he assented to the cook's eagerness. She took him to the larder and pulled a sheet from an enormous basket filled with fruit, sweet breads, dried venison, a variety of cheeses, sweetmeats, and cakes. The master's eyes filled with delight at the array before him. Furthermore, he instructed her to make certain that two bottles of the best wine from their cellar were sent along. Then, in afterthought, he added, "Oh, and send two crystal tumblers with the wine." Mrs. Potter nodded cheerfully and asked if there was anything else he desired. He requested that she dispatch one of the stable boys to town to have his letters posted express. He handed her the missives and then thanked her for the delicious spread she had orchestrated for dinner the previous night and for the preparation of the sumptuous basket. The cook beamed from such praise, told him he was most welcome, and said she would make sure a young footman was sent off to Lambton right away.

As Darcy began to depart, he paused and turned upon remembering one more request. "Mrs. Potter, could you also have the boy locate or leave a message of invitation for Dr. Lowry to dine with us tonight at the usual hour."

She nodded her assent, and merely added, "Yes, sir."

~*~

That morning when Elizabeth arose, she had been informed by Nancy that Mr. Darcy had prearranged for her breakfast to be taken to Sally's chamber, so that she and the young woman could share their morning meal on the bride's special day. Nancy made certain that the master's preface for his proposal was clearly communicated to the mistress. "Mr. Darcy wants me to inform you, Mrs. Darcy," said the maid, "that this plan will only be carried out if it is acceptable to you."

Elizabeth smiled and nodded her assent. She was grateful that her husband was beginning to care foremost for her opinions. She informed the maid that the idea was indeed agreeable. Then, Elizabeth hurriedly dressed for and went straightway to Sally's chamber, carrying the cream-coloured dress and accessories.

In excitement, Sally answered her door and invited Elizabeth into her chamber. She informed the mistress that the breakfast trays had just arrived. Elizabeth suggested that they eat first and then start the dressing preparations. They enjoyed the meal while discussing how Sally wished to fashion her hair. When she completed her meal, Elizabeth arose to show the young woman all of her jewelled hairpins and ribbons that were available to adorn the finished coiffure. Sally chose some of the same rosettes with which Elizabeth had adorned her own hair for the Netherfield ball.

Soon, buckets of steaming water arrived and were poured into the tub standing in the corner of the room. Elizabeth rolled up her sleeves, walked over to the bath, and added a little of her lavender oil to the water. The fragrance filled the air. Sally beamed from such pampering. It was the first time she had ever had the privilege of such attendance, excluding when she had been a wee babe in her mother's arms. After the bath, Elizabeth styled her former maid's hair with the iron curling rods and formed it into an elegant coiffure. She then helped Sally into the dress, stockings, and shoes, and placed the bonnet carefully over her hair.

~*~

The church was overflowing with local well-wishers. Seated in the family section of pews beside Darcy and Georgiana, Elizabeth took great pleasure in Sally's appearance as the bride walked, with her face now veiled, towards Thomas and the reverend. Darcy immediately recognized the gown Miss Hibbs wore, as the same one Elizabeth had dressed in for Bingley's ball at Netherfield. The memory produced a pleasant sensation within him. He turned and gazed at Elizabeth sitting by his side and observed her elated countenance. He was the luckiest man in the world. She was truly the most caring person and unlike any woman he had ever met.

All eyes turned as Sally entered the church. And as it would be, the preparations from the early morning had their desired effect. As Sally walked down the aisle of the chapel on the arm of Mr. Manning, Elizabeth could see the reaction on the groom's face. It was apparent for all that witnessed it. Thomas Wilkens's breath caught in his throat. His soon-to-be bride looked divine, and from the way he stared, Elizabeth knew he had never seen her dressed in such a stunning manner. Mr. Manning surrendered Sally to stand by her betrothed and stepped back. The words of the cleric rang out, *"Dearly beloved, we are gathered here in the sight of God to join this man and this woman in Holy matrimony…"*

As Sally repeated the words of the parson, *'I plight thee my troth,'* Elizabeth concentrated on their meaning. *To pledge in truthfulness.*

Darcy listened attentively as Thomas recited, *"With this Ring I thee wed, with my Body I thee worship, and with all my worldly goods I thee endow: In the Name of the Father, and the Son, and the Holy Ghost. Amen."* He recalled vividly his feelings while vowing these exact words to Elizabeth before the parson of Longbourn Chapel, before those witnessing their marriage, and especially before his Maker. It was the most monumental moment of his life, equal only to the consummation of their marriage. He was pulled from his reverie, however, by the sound of the congregation repeating aloud, "Amen."

Elizabeth raised her eyes to behold her husband, only to find him staring adoringly upon her. Her breast filled with devotion as she took in his look. Her eyes swept over the facial features she had come to admire and in which she took such pleasure: his dark, curly hair, the fullness of his lips, the cleft in his chin, his strong jaw line, the entrancing gaze of his eyes, and his ever–captivating, boyish grin. Oh, how she cherished him. What had she been thinking? She did not need any more time. Tonight, she would show him just how much she loved and desired him.

~*~

That evening, just as those making up the dinner party were descending the stairs, Mr. Greene announced the arrival of Dr. Lowry. Caroline's brow creased. *Not that doctor again*! Was Mr. Darcy taking leave of his senses having a local physician as a constant dinner guest? But, she reasoned with a sneer, he had also taken leave of them while in Hertfordshire.

Dinner provided enjoyment with the usual superb food and excellent wine. For Darcy, just having Dr. Lowry in attendance brought an added measure of interest to the conversation. Thus, he found himself drawn to the man more and more. He liked Harrison Lowry very much. Personally, next to having the physician's good company, Darcy hoped the doctor would not become upset with him over his secret motive in extending the invitation to dine.

After having completed the last course, the women separated from the men. Bingley and Dr. Lowry followed Darcy to his study to have their drinks. It was during this enjoyment of their evening ritual that Darcy broached the topic he dreaded. Nodding at Bingley and at Dr. Lowry respectively, he stated, "Um… Harrison, Bingley, I feel rather sheepish to admit that, in addition to your excellent company at our party, gentlemen, I have an ulterior motive for inviting you."

This admission received a surprised expression from the good doctor. "Please, you have my curiosity. What hidden motive could it be? Pray, Darcy, do not tell me you are an imbiber and have gout in your big toe on your left foot that you wish me to examine."

"No. Actually, Harrison, it is on my right."

Bingley was not quite sure what to make of their friendly banter. He smiled anxiously, wondering for what reason, besides a social or a medical one, Darcy could possibly have wanted the doctor.

"Well…gentlemen, my cousin, Colonel Fitzwilliam, left me a letter this morning informing me that my aunt, Lady Matlock, desires to have the waltz danced at the ball she is throwing in honour of Mrs. Darcy. Thus, if you are so inclined to do a great service, Harrison, I wonder, would it be asking too much for you to help us practice tonight?" In afterthought, Darcy looked to his brother-in-law and stated, "And, of course, you as well, Charles. I mean, with the ladies? Georgiana has never danced the waltz and, therefore, I have commissioned the dance master from Lambton to come and refresh our knowledge of some dances and more especially, to teach the waltz. I suspect that even my wife does not know it. I, however, have danced it a number of times. Some people still feel quite hostile towards the performance. So if you feel this would be an inappropriate favour, please do not hesitate in saying so."

Dr. Lowry smiled and stated most adamantly, "On the contrary, I, too, have danced the waltz, and, for one, love it, especially when accompanied by any of Mozart's tunes. Count me in, man!"

Darcy grinned warmly and then informed them that the dance master would arrive at any moment. They finished off their drinks and headed for the music room.

The ladies were quickly enlightened of the pending plan and were pleased with the prospect of spending an evening engaged in such activity. Before the instructor arrived, the servants had cleared the room of all chairs, sofas, and side tables.

Mr. Strasner, the dancing master, with two men accompanying him, was shown into the music room. Darcy greeted them immediately and then made the introductions. One man went straightway to the pianoforte while the other stationed himself near the instrument with a violin in hand.

First the cotillion and the minuet were practiced, mainly to help refresh Georgiana's memory from her instruction of the previous summer.

All the other ladies in the room were well acquainted with these dances—even Kitty, since she had been attending the assemblies in Meryton for several years. After some forty minutes in this occupation, Mr. Strasner informed the party that he would now teach the waltz. This dance was foreign to Kitty, Georgiana, *and* Elizabeth. They had heard of it and of all the scandalous rumours that were associated with it, but they had never seen it performed first hand. Each lady was giddy in anticipation. Caroline found the whole goings-on to be tedious. The only man she was interested in dancing with would more than likely only dance with his wife or sister. Therefore, she cared little to participate. However, when Jane declined to dance due to her fatigue, Caroline found herself suddenly whirled onto the floor by the dancing master. As predicted, Darcy did pair up with his wife. Georgiana joined with the doctor, and, now, Bingley became the partner of Miss Catherine Bennet. This left Miss Bingley as the chosen one for Mr. Strasner, to help him demonstrate the dance for the other ladies. Caroline found this beyond belief, and it was all she could do to try to remain civil.

Holding Miss Bingley effortlessly in the first position, Mr. Strasner announced with enthusiasm, "The waltz is the dance of romance, with sweeping movements, spiralling turns, and refined poise. It is a dance that commands the attention of the participants each to the other. Now, the basic progression of the waltz is a three-step sequence, going forward and backward." He began to demonstrate with Caroline, pulling her nigh.

Elizabeth smiled at the look of disdain upon Miss Bingley's face, discerning Caroline's perturbation. Watching the demonstration, she could easily see why this dance was so controversial and considered by many as *the forbidden dance*. The legs of the master and the lady were constantly advancing, flirting near the other's, and their upper torsos were fairly close. Mr. Strasner called out to the spectators, "You should concentrate on making sure all steps are smooth and flowing, and with the sway, rise, and fall, very smooth." He then silkily dipped Miss Bingley and brought her upward just as effortlessly. The dance master exclaimed, "Why, madam, I must say you are an extremely elegant and graceful dancer—very light on your feet."

Caroline rolled her eyes and cringed inwardly. *Really, the things I must suffer*!

"Also," Mr. Strasner pronounced, "one more very important point, pull your partner tighter like this." He drew Miss Bingley extremely close to his chest. "Then you will be able to turn more quickly and effectively. Make sure to keep your eyes focused on your partner's face or just off to the side to avoid light-headedness. Now, let us all begin!"

The music hummed anew and the couples commenced to follow the master's example. They began to glide upon the floor with nary a mishap except Georgiana occasionally stepping upon the toes of Dr. Lowry's boots. The good doctor just smiled warmly at her nervous exhibition. However, with all the gentlemen present being previously familiar with the dance, it did not take long for the ladies to become true proficients as well. It was an easy dance to learn and left all the ladies, excluding Caroline, with a feeling of exhilaration.

Georgiana blushed profusely as Dr. Lowry held her tightly in his arms. She had never been this close to any man other than her father, brother, and Richard. Well, there was George, too, but none of those associations was similar to the extended physical proximity this dance afforded over the usual country variety. It was all very new to her, and she found herself looking forward to dancing this dance at her aunt's ball—and with someone in particular.

Dr. Lowry admired Miss Darcy immensely and appreciated dancing with her.

As Darcy twirled his wife about, he could tell she was enjoying herself excessively. When leaning her low, he whispered, "I take it that you do not find this dance so bold."

"Oh, quite the contrary, Mr. Darcy," she whispered in turn, "I find it exceedingly bold and—how shall I say it—evocative of the art of making love." Darcy's eyes widened. He, too, started to feel excitement mounting within him, yet, unlike the ladies, his came from another source entirely. The warmth of Elizabeth in his arms and the pleasing view presented with every gyration and decline of her full-bosomed figure did much to provoke him up and onward.

"Umm...so I take it that your inference bespeaks smiles of pleasure in partaking of the waltz itself, and that the images evoked by this dance are—what shall I say—just as desirable in the participation?"

Elizabeth's face flamed crimson as she averted her gaze, and, with a raised brow, cheekily replied, "Um...why yes, Mr. Darcy, you could say as much." She bit her lower lip.

"Why my dear wife, you know not how you drive me to distraction!" He pulled her closer as they revolved around the room.

Jane took pleasure in watching the rehearsal. She was happy that Charles was so willing to dance with Kitty. She had high hopes for her younger sister, and she knew Elizabeth felt the same, understanding that Kitty would be able to improve her manners now that she was out of Lydia's direct influence. She and Elizabeth desired that Kitty and Mary would someday marry for love, just as she and Elizabeth had been blessed with the privilege of doing.

At the end of the evening, Darcy asked Dr. Lowry if he could return to practice with them one more night, and he assured him that it would be his pleasure. The doctor, instructor, and musicians bid their farewells, giving their word to reappear on the morrow. All looked forward to another night akin to the one just spent. Naturally excluding Miss Bingley, for Caroline vowed to herself that she would make certain to be inconvenienced with a headache.

~*~

As Nancy stood brushing her mistress' hair, Darcy entered the chamber. He leaned his shoulder against the doorframe of Elizabeth's dressing area, mesmerized by his wife's beauty. He loved her hair down and free. The maid hurriedly braided it and then wished Mrs. Darcy goodnight. Elizabeth returned her wishes and thanked her as well.

Immediately upon arising, Elizabeth became aware of her husband standing against the casing of the door. Smiling brightly to him, she asked, "So, in all sincerity, Fitzwilliam, do you approve of the waltz?"

Slyly, he smiled and then answered with a slight waggle of his eyebrows, "I have had my reservations, but with your comparison tonight, I see it from a whole different perspective."

She smiled openly. "But what of your sister and all other ladies who are single? Is it a dance quite fitting?" Elizabeth's queries were made in partial jest, as the uncertainty of her husband's reservation for his sister to dance at the Matlock's ball still lay heavily upon her mind.

Walking forward, he reached for her hand and then led her to the bed, quickly scooping her up into his arms, forgoing the need for the stool. Laying her upon the mattress, he then jounced down beside her. "Elizabeth, these are serious questions."

They turned on their sides towards one another and Darcy continued. "I am not overly happy that Georgie will be dancing for the full length of the ball, but I gave my word to Fitzwilliam, and I also felt you really desired it as well." Elizabeth began to speak, but he shook his head. "No, Lizzy, do not concern yourself. I am no longer angry regarding it. The time is at hand that I must start to let go. She will be seventeen this summer. There are many young women at that age who are betrothed and some even married." They both gave each other knowing looks. Lydia was barely sixteen when she ran off with Wickham. "Ah…well," he sighed, while reaching out to brush an errant wisp of hair from Elizabeth's eyes. Then, looking deeply within them, he stated, "Richard is very much his mother's son. My aunt is bold in having the waltz played, but he received word from her yesterday with a behest that Georgiana learn that dance. Aunt Adeline does not want her feeling out of place. In fact, Lizzy, I think you will like my aunt very much."

Elizabeth noticed that he began to twirl his ring. "I am sure I will," she stated, "after all, if she is like her son, I know I will like her extremely well." Darcy quickly looked away, nodding his head at her last assertion.

"Yes, well, as for the waltz being suitable for single young ladies, I must admit when I first saw the dance, I was alarmed by the level of intimacy required. It can be a very stimulating dance and may cause certain persons to imagine that they are in love. The excitable feelings which this dance may generate from having such close contact could easily mislead a young woman to believe that she is in love without knowing anything of the young man who has ignited those new sensations that she has never before experienced."

"Yes, but, Fitzwilliam, can this same argument not be used for young men as well?"

"Perhaps, for some, but I do not think it as plausible. Men are creatures of sight and touch, Elizabeth." She listened to him carefully. "They certainly desire physical intimacy, but many are not honour-bound if they cross the line of what is deemed proper. The dance may fuel many undisciplined men to seek such familiarity without commitment. Whereas, while women feel the physical sensations, too, they may, however, define it as love, believing the man feels likewise in committing to a marital union."

She understood his reasoning, for this was exactly what she perceived to be Lydia's case. "Yet, for married couples, you do consider the waltz to be quite safe?" This question was asked in a lilted air of playfulness.

He grinned. He loved it when she teased him. "Yes, Lizzy, I do consider the waltz appropriate for those who are married, but as for it being safe, that could be debatable. In the past, the waltz never had any effect upon me. However, tonight, with my beautiful wife in my arms, I was disturbed to distraction. Hence, I conclude that waltzing is not at all safe. It should be danced in the bedchamber instead of a ballroom."

She smiled. "I do not have a dance card, sir, but, if you can overlook the formality, I am available to dance the waltz in this very chamber at this precise moment." Again, she bit her lip while gazing into his eyes.

He smiled and quickly sat up. "Mrs. Darcy, may I have this dance?" He held out his hand as he slid off the bed.

She placed hers within his and arose as well.

Dressed in his nightshirt, with bare legs and feet, he chuckled at the silliness of his appearance, but as he looked deeply into his wife's eyes, the mirth fled. Before allowing him to place his hand on her back, she discarded her robe. She noticed her husband's eyes roaming over her figure, the sheerness of her gown enticing him.

"Now, sir," Elizabeth enquired in an arch manner, "where do I place my hands?"

Darcy smirked. "Why, Mrs. Darcy, do allow me to enlighten you about the waltz." He reached for her hand. "You rest your left hand here," and he placed it in its appointed position upon his shoulder, "and then, like so, you shall hold my left hand with this one." He grasped her right hand within his left.

They began to step, turn, and sway to the three-fourth timing with no instrumental accompaniment. Darcy quickly remedied the deficiency and improvised a tune by humming that which they had heard earlier in the evening.

Elizabeth smiled serenely. She was pleased by the perfect intonation and harmony his a cappella performance created. Their eyes remained locked one upon the other until Darcy tilted her low, and then his vision hastily descended across her lips and neck and seemed to brighten up all the more upon the scope of her voluptuousness.

Each witnessed the growing desire in the other as the rhythm of their bodies fell and rose in unison. Abruptly, Darcy's melodious refrain stopped as his breathing became ragged. Elizabeth hovered in a backward pose, secure within his arms. With a penetrating stare, he whispered, "I adore you, Elizabeth." Then, he gently lifted her towards him and they embraced.

He carried her over to the bed, eased back the counterpane, and placed her upon the mattress. He then pulled the coverlet back further and crawled in beside her. Reaching for her hand as they lay flat on their backs, he squeezed it, and caressed her fingers with his thumb. "Good night, Elizabeth."

"Mmm," she replied, and without warning, she pulled her hand from his and rolled over on top of him. Darcy stared at her in disbelief. "Fitzwilliam, I was wondering—may I kiss you goodnight?"

An instant grin appeared upon his face. He replied with alacrity. "Yes, Mrs. Darcy, I think that would be most agreeable." Tentatively, Elizabeth kissed his lips. He followed her cue and kept the kiss light. Before he knew what was happening, she had begun to shower his face with small kisses, trailing across one cheek, over his nose to the other, from temple to temple, over his brow, and then descending along the side of his face to his jaw line. Faint moans of delight emanated from Darcy's throat and were discernable to Elizabeth as she generously continued in her feathery ministrations. After lavishly kissing the length of his neck and back to the tip of his chin, her lips strayed upward to his ear. Tugging at his lobe with her mouth, she whispered between nibbles, "I love you, Fitzwilliam, and I...do trust you."

Placing his hands on her shoulders, he raised her up and looked her directly in the eye. "But, Elizabeth, I want you to know for certain that I did not give anyone those rings and that I never had a rendezvous of any sort."

"I already know. I was hurt, angry, and humiliated. Therefore, I spoke while in great agitation. Deep in my heart, I felt you could not, would not do such a thing. I do feel your love for me. You show it to me in countless ways."

Uncertainty lined his brow. "Yes, but I still need you to know in surety."

"Fitzwilliam, I need no assurances from you. Your word and sentiment that Collette is not a desired guest—or a welcomed one—in our home has done much to soothe my heart."

He stared at her for some moments.

She smiled beguilingly at him and playfully asked, "Why, Mr. Darcy, does the cat have your tongue again?"

In mischievous aggression, he rolled her over in one swift motion, settling himself on top of her. With a roguish grin, he stated, "Yes, it undoubtedly does, if this feline is confident she desires more than mere companionship tonight." Her brow rose as her eyes mirrored his delight.

Later, lying close with their arms and legs entwined, Darcy construed, "I shall have to invite Mr. Strasner more often to Pemberley. You seem to have enjoyed the evening's activities tremendously."

"Yes, but Mr. Strasner was not the cause of *all my enjoyment*. He, in and of himself, is most definitely an odd sort of individual, do you not think?" She giggled and cast a gleeful look at her husband. "I must admit, however, that seeing Caroline so shocked and displeased did afford me a great sense of pleasure."

Darcy propped himself upon his elbow and gazed freely upon his wife's cheerful countenance. He smiled at her wicked confession, delighting in her animated musings.

"Although, my dear husband, I must say that I do find the waltz to be a very seductive dance, it is hardly so when compared to the seductiveness of your stare towards me after Sally's wedding. When you look at me in that certain way, which I have seen so many times before, I know that you adore me."

This admission caught Darcy off guard, causing his heart to swell. "I do adore you, Elizabeth. I am glad you felt it this morning and fully realize it. I am sorry, again, for my many errors. I still ask for your patience. I am afraid I am set in my ways, and it may take time for me to overcome some of my insensitive habits."

"Oh, but you are coming along quite nicely, Mr. Darcy. I am very grateful for your thoughtfulness in having trays sent to Sally's chamber on her special day. Yet, I am so much more thankful that you had Nancy convey your insistence that trays would *only* be sent to Sally's room pending my acceptance of the plan. You know not how much your consideration for my desires means to me. I thank you, Fitzwilliam. You are too generous. In fact, I, too, need your patience, for I am just as wilful as you are, only in other ways. Take walking to Lambton for example, without informing anyone, just because I was reacting like a spoilt child, angry at you for Collette's duplicity and your cold greeting before the hunt."

Breathing in loudly, Darcy found he was still uncomfortable with the mere mention of that woman's name. He looked intently at his wife and stated with sincerity, "Elizabeth, I love that you enjoy walking and that you adore the outdoors. That is one of the aspects I found so appealing about you when we first met. It is simply because the road to Lambton is busily travelled that I fear for your safety, not only because you are a woman, but you are also the wife of a wealthy man."

Elizabeth pondered his perspective and the possible ramifications of such an incident that, for some reason, had never occurred to her before. She was beginning to realize that his wealth had many far-reaching effects upon her in ways she had never imagined. Having been raised in a small community, within a comfortable, but by no means well-to-do family, she was used to coming and going at her leisure. There was a lot of unexpected responsibility attached to being Mrs. Fitzwilliam Darcy.

"Elizabeth, I want you to know," Darcy whispered, "that I feel you are the most compassionate person I know."

Shaking her head with a quick roll of her eyes, she countered, "Oh, no, I will not have it. It will not do! You are sounding too much like Jane. What about my admission to you just moments ago concerning my malicious pleasure towards Miss Bingley's miserable state tonight? And you call me kind!"

"You are kind. You may not be a saint in every meaning of the word, but you are truly benevolent. I immediately recognized the dress Sally wore today. You are so good, Elizabeth. I think that is why I adore you."

"Ah! And here I thought it was for my impertinence and all of my wild, brazen ways."

Darcy murmured in her ear while snuggling close. "That is what is so delightful and alluring. There is a dualism about you, Lizzy, which has captivated my heart and soul. Given that, I find at times you are, indeed, extremely good and then, again, you can be *very, very naughty*. Grrrr!"

She feigned shock. "I take it back, Mr. Darcy, you are nothing akin to my dear Jane." They smiled knowingly at each other, their passion rekindled once more, and thus, the very naughty Mrs. Darcy materialized right before his eyes.

~*~

Chapter Nineteen

Painful Confessions

In the early morning hours, Darcy and Elizabeth made their way in the landau across Derbyshire to Matlock. The morning held the hint of a chill, causing husband and wife to snuggle close together beneath a throw. As they travelled, Darcy remained silent, resting his head on the back of the seat, pondering all that had transpired over the course of the week. The last few days had been splendid. The night following the first dance lesson, Dr. Lowry had returned to continue the practice. Darcy easily observed the delight that Harrison found in his sister. He wondered if Georgiana could be attracted to the doctor in return. She seemed to enjoy herself very much while in the good doctor's company. Darcy noticed the blush upon her cheeks but could not determine if it was from the exertion of the exercise or the bashfulness of attraction.

Unbeknownst to Elizabeth, Darcy had gone to call on Mr. Caldecott the next morning in an attempt to determine why Collette had had his ring in her possession. He was told, however, that the family had made a hasty trip to London and would not be back until the end of the week. Disheartened by this news, he knew there was nothing he could accomplish on this quest at present. Until another time presented itself, he would just have to wait for the answers he so desired.

Likewise, he mulled over Yvette. Georgiana claimed that all was well with her new lady's maid, but he was not so sure. His sister was not one to assert herself. After Elizabeth had expounded to him in merriment all of the shenanigans she had endured for the short time she had had Yvette as her maid, he truly worried about leaving his sister with such a single-minded woman. Fortunately, Georgiana would not be alone with the woman for too long. She had stayed behind with their guests and would join them the next day at Matlock for the noon meal. This would allow he and Elizabeth to have one day alone with his relations before the influx of guests on the morrow—*an entire day with Lord and Lady Hazelton.* Darcy groaned inwardly at the thought.

Elizabeth noticed her husband's nervous tension as he fidgeted with his ring. "Fitzwilliam, are you looking forward to the ball and the time with your aunt and uncle?

"Hmm…why yes. I am happy that you will have the chance to finally meet them." He wished to apologize to her because, excepting Georgiana and Richard, his family had not shown themselves for their wedding. Yet, he did not want to distress her with the idea that his uncle and aunt were of the same mindset as his Aunt Catherine. In fact, if it had not been for his Aunt Adeline's defending their union before his uncle on their behalf, he was certain that an invitation to visit and give a ball would never have come from the Earl. For this he was grateful, but he remained leery of his uncle's reception of Elizabeth.

When the carriage pulled up in front of the manor, servants came forth to open doors and collect trunks. After Darcy stepped out, he turned to help his wife descend. The Earl, Lady Matlock, Lord and Lady Hazelton, and Colonel Fitzwilliam all stood upon the steps to greet them. Darcy felt encouraged by this gesture of goodwill from his family. When Elizabeth lifted her head and perceived the Fitzwilliams gallantly awaiting them, she smiled radiantly to each one as her eyes quickly danced from face to face. Immediately, she noticed that Lord Hazelton was the perfect likeness of his father.

Darcy guided them up the stairs, pausing just one step below the point where his uncle and aunt stood. "Uncle Selwyn, this is my wife Elizabeth, and, Elizabeth, this in my uncle, the Earl of Matlock."

The Earl bowed as Elizabeth curtseyed, and then, with a regal air, he spoke. "So, this is the fair lady who has captured my sister's dear boy. We welcome you to the family, Mrs. Darcy," The Earl arched his dignified brow as he took note of the vibrancy of Elizabeth's eyes while listening to her reply.

"I am so happy to make your acquaintance, my Lord, and to be honoured with the ball."

Next, Darcy introduced his aunt, Lady Matlock, his cousin, Lord Hazelton, and his cousin's wife, Lady Hazelton. Elizabeth expressed all of the customary niceties, as expected, and, when all formality was complete, Richard exclaimed, "Now that you have met the entire Fitzwilliam clan, Elizabeth, you must disclose your honest opinion. Do you not find that my father and I tend to come across as if we are brothers while Hazel gives the impression of being our father?"

Elizabeth's mouth hung open at the jest, she had no idea how to respond to such a question. By this time, Lord Hazelton stood tall and noisily puffed out in derision at the taunt, whereas his wife, Elisha, clearly suffered, her eyes, shooting daggers at her brother-in-law. To all this, Elizabeth felt it best to counter with a simple, passive smile.

Lady Matlock personally showed them to their rooms, which were directly across from Richard's. She informed them that Georgiana would stay next to them, and that Elizabeth's family would be across the hall, next to her son's chamber. Elizabeth thanked her. Darcy's aunt then suggested that they rest and offered to have a tray sent up, if they preferred.

Darcy met Elizabeth's gaze, as if to say, what do you desire? His countenance softened at the devoted twinkle he read in his wife's eyes in answer to his unspoken query. Lady Matlock took note of the silent communication between the newlyweds and felt it was a reassuring sign that her nephew was not only considerate of his wife but revered her as she did him.

"Oh, I am fine. I would love to join the family for the noon meal, if you feel up to it, Fitzwilliam."

Darcy smiled and turned to his aunt. "Aunt Adie, I do believe that we shall be down promptly after we freshen up."

"Very well, I shall have two extra settings placed. There is no formality. Feel free to come straight to the dining room. Let me say again, Elizabeth, how happy I am that you both have allowed me this opportunity to throw a ball in honour of your marriage. I am quite delighted to finally meet you, and, well, after Georgiana's praises, I knew that my dear nephew had finally found a wife whom he loves and of whom he can be proud."

At first, Elizabeth was a little taken aback with Lady Matlock's candour, but then she quickly remembered what her husband had told her that Richard was very much his mother's son. "Thank you, Lady Matlock. Georgie, I mean, Georgiana is too kind."

"Well, I am certainly pleased to see my niece so content and happy as of late. But enough talk for now. I shall see you both in the dining room in a half hour's time."

When the door closed, Darcy removed his tailcoat and rolled up his sleeves. "So, Lizzy, what think you thus far, of my mother's side of the family?"

"Well, I must admit, your uncle and his elder son bear a striking resemblance to each other and to your mother."

He nodded as he dampened his hands in the washbasin, and then he splashed some water in his hair in an attempt to tame some of his unruly curls tousled about during the ride.

Elizabeth continued her account. "Your aunt is very gracious and considerate in taking the time to escort us to our rooms and by arranging for my family to be close to us. And…"

Darcy noted Elizabeth's hesitation and the pensive look which crossed her face as she bit her lip. By now he knew that expression all too well and realized her mind was in active thought.

"And what, Lizzy?"

"I do not suppose," she looked expectantly at him, "that Lord Hazelton thinks very highly of Richard."

Drying his hands on a towel, Darcy looked back to his wife and asked, "Why do you say so?"

"Oh, nothing really, just the way he exhaled in disgust at Richard's jest. I guess I also sense that Lord Hazelton seems quite serious, not at all charming like his brother."

Darcy's brow furrowed at her continued praises of admiration for his youngest cousin, but he quickly pushed the disturbing thought aside. Walking over to Elizabeth with a small smile upon his face, he stated good-naturedly, "Yes, for the most part, Hazelton *is* serious. Yet I remember you thinking the exact same thing about me if I am not mistaken?"

He put his arms around her waist as he gleefully looked into her eyes.

She met his gaze and replied, "Yes, Fitzwilliam, I did find you to be quite grave at first."

With delight apparent in his expression, he asked, "But you no longer find me as such?"

"Oh, I would not go so far as to imply that. But, upon closer observation, I find that you are a man who is very easy and full of humour when in the company of those with whom you are closest."

"Yes, I thought you had begun to notice that element of my disposition."

He picked her up and plopped her on the bed and then toppled upon her. "Really, Fitzwilliam, you go to all the trouble of wetting down and neatening your hair, just to tumble about on the bed?"

With a low growl, he contended, "I was just showing you how easy and full of humour I am when in the company of the one with whom I am the closest." He grinned widely.

"Please, sir, do get up. You shall wrinkle my dress."

"What, no playful Lizzy today?"

"No, Fitzwilliam. If you wanted a playful Lizzy, as you put it, you should have opted for a tray."

As he rolled over on his back, she added, "Do you suppose Lord Hazelton is as playful with his wife as you are with me?"

Darcy exclaimed disgustedly, "Elizabeth, please, I have no idea about Hazelton's spirited nature with his wife, and I have no desire of knowing."

"My, my, you are testy, Mr. Darcy. I only meant to consider whether he ever gets as frolicsome as you are at times?"

He thought about Hazel for a moment. And then he felt as if it was one moment too much. "He and his wife Elisha, do share, I suppose, a similar humour with each other. So, in their own way I would say yes, Hazelton does have his amusing side." *A cynical one, howbeit*, he pondered glumly, to himself.

~*~

Elisha sneered at her husband as they sat at the table waiting for the rest of the family to join them for luncheon. "Really, James, she looks like a tomboy."

Lord Hazelton was tall and slender, similar to Darcy in build. His hair was blonde and much lighter than was his brother's, with just a hint of a wave about it. His eyes—a deep blue—combined with his defined jaw line, made his facial features more striking. Thus, he appeared quite distinguished and handsome.

Primly, he rejoined, "Elisha, my pet, I am not quite sure of your meaning. Do you mean to infer that our dear cousin's bride is an active sort of girl with a boyish spirit about her, or are you deducing her to be a hoyden in more ways than one?"

"I confess to not knowing your meaning, James."

"I mean, my dear sweet, that if you are of the same mind as am I, I am sure our dear cousin enjoyed romps with her while a single man. Therefore, he made an honest woman of her."

Snickering in delight, Lady Hazelton cried, "Oh, you are monstrous! Yes, I am sure she played her cards right and hoodwinked our poor Darcy. I would wager she is already with his child, and the baby will be said to be born too soon due to complications."

Lord Hazelton considered to himself that his cousin had to have lost his right mind in marrying so far beneath him. He admitted that Darcy's wife was indeed attractive in many ways, but could his cousin not have gotten a grip on the situation and made other arrangements instead? Darcy had always been one to stand on principle far too strongly in comparison to Hazelton's way of thinking. There were acceptable places, many establishments, in fact, that were considered respectable for men of their standing, where they could dabble in the carnal pursuits, but his exacting cousin frowned upon them, and not once did Darcy allow himself to succumb and indulge in the forbidden fruit. Lord Hazelton reasoned that Darcy had to have been tempted out of his wits to yield so low. Yet, he could now see for himself just how hard it must have *been* for his strait-laced cousin to be stuck in the savage county of Hertfordshire with such a carrot dangling before his eyes. Yes, Fitzwilliam Darcy had finally fallen, but to have sunk so low was out of Lord Hazelton's scope of understanding.

Shaken from his reverie, Lord Hazelton immediately stood when the aforesaid *carrot* and his cousin walked into the room. Darcy pulled out the chair for his wife, who was seated directly across from Elisha, who sat beside her husband, the Viscount. Both gentlemen remained standing as Lady Matlock and the Earl breezed in. "Ah," proclaimed the Earl, "I see, Nephew, that you and your wife are already here—most fortunate. However, I see that Richard is the one who obliges us to wait."

"Not for too long, Father, I am sure." Richard hurriedly took the seat beside Darcy.

With the Earl's signal, they all began the meal. "So, pray," said Lord Hazelton, "Tell us, Darcy, all about your meeting our dear, new cousin."

Elizabeth's vision swept to the side to peek at her husband as she tried to imagine how he would begin to answer his cousin's query.

Touching the napkin lightly to his mouth, Darcy looked directly across at Lord Hazelton and replied, "We met at an assembly in Meryton. I think you know that I spent some time there with my friend, Charles Bingley, when he took an estate near that village."

Elisha chimed in, "Was it love at first sight?"

Richard looked at Darcy and saw how his eyes swerved in the direction of Elisha, but just as quickly looked down upon his plate before answering, "Not at first sight, but very much on the second viewing."

Elizabeth smiled sweetly at her husband's open acknowledgement. Then a question was directed at her by the Earl. "So, Elizabeth, tell us, were you smitten by my nephew when you first laid eyes on him?"

"Oh, I feel that I can honestly say I thought him extremely handsome when he walked into the Meryton assembly with his friends."

"Ha, he captivated you then from the start, did he?"

Darcy looked at Elizabeth, and she at him, even as Lord and Lady Hazelton shot each other knowing glances, which Richard observed. The colonel rolled his eyes at the mere sight of his brother and sister-in-law's shared drivel.

"Well, I would have to say no," professed Elizabeth. "I was not totally captivated with Mr. Darcy upon first acquaintance. It took some length of time before I found myself truly smitten by your nephew."

The Earl boomed, "Come, come, after *some* length of time? Surely, it should have never taken so long to have been attracted to such a handsome and *rich* fellow."

Elizabeth's cheeks burned bright at the insinuation of Darcy's uncle. Elisha leaned over and whispered low in her husband's ear, so only he could hear, "Perhaps she confuses the term captivate with *conception?*"

Lord Hazelton smirked. Elizabeth sensed something odd from them and imagined that they felt she had married their cousin for his wealth.

Lady Matlock hastily intervened, "I, for one, am glad you took your time, Elizabeth. Far too many young ladies never think twice when considering marriage, and thus, they rush into commitment without truly considering their future companion's strength of character.

Elizabeth gave Lady Matlock a smile of gratitude for the compliment but said nothing.

Darcy's aunt continued, "I hope you both will forgive me for changing the subject, but I am afraid if I do not mention it now, I may not remember it. My memory is not what it used to be."

Richard ventured, "Mother, you have an amazing memory, but maybe you have forgotten that you have."

Lady Matlock shot her younger child a deadly look, "Richard," she said with warning in her voice and a small frown upon her face, "my addled brain must arise from the distress you love to give your dear mother."

Elizabeth looked at her husband. With a slight shake of his head, raised brows, and a small grin, Darcy tried to alleviate Elizabeth's concern for his aunt's verbal retribution to his youngest cousin's good-humoured taunts.

Lord Hazelton spoke up, "Yes, Richard, you do put our mother through too much. What are you now? Five and thirty, and you *still* have not found a wife?"

Colonel Fitzwilliam snorted, "Hazel, I think you are sadly mistaking your age with mine. Remember I am the younger son of the Earl, not you."

Elizabeth remembered the conversation she and Richard had had about his need to marry for wealth because of his situation in life. Yet, she had no idea why this would be a cause of disagreement between the brothers.

Lady Matlock interceded by offering what she had meant to propose earlier, before her younger son had foolishly sidetracked her, "Fitzwilliam, Elizabeth," she said, inclining her head in their direction, "Richard tells me that Georgiana has agreed to come out this Season instead of next. I think this is splendid. Do allow me make all the arrangements with the court, and, especially, let me throw a ball in her honour."

"Aunt Adeline, that is very considerate of you, and I thank you for the offer, but Elizabeth and I have not decided on a course of action as of yet. We shall let you know as soon as we do so."

"Oh, but, Darcy," cried Elisha, "it is imperative that these details get worked out as soon as possible. With Richard not available, and Elizabeth not experienced with such goings on, I am sure you should leave it entirely in our hands. After all, the Darcys and Fitzwilliams are of the upper order of society, and we cannot leave something as important as Georgiana's introduction into society's most affluent circles to mere chance."

Glaring, Darcy coldly replied, "I am afraid you are labouring under a misapprehension if you think I would leave it to chance."

With an inflated voice, the Earl exclaimed, "Now, now, Nephew. Elisha only wishes to help. We all want what is best for Georgiana."

Again, Elisha ensued further, "Why, yes, that is all I am saying. I mean no offence. We all love Georgiana, and we all desire her to marry well and *within her own sphere.*"

Darcy's hand cupped his mouth as he continued to look down at his plate. He had always disliked James's wife.

Elizabeth felt dreadful for him and quickly established that there were relatives other than Lady Catherine who opposed their union.

Continuing, Elisha submitted, "I know one of the Patronesses of Almack's personally. She is a good friend of my mother's. You do realize, Darcy, that Georgiana must have her consent to be allowed to dance her first waltz?"

In a clipped tone, Darcy set his drink aside and replied, "Yes, I know that, and I also know—"

Richard cleared his throat rather noisily and quipped, "Well, really, Elisha, all these formalities seem pointless when Georgie will dance her first waltz here, at Matlock, tomorrow night." He raised a brow of challenge to his sister-in-law, knowing that she would never dream of saying anything contrary to his mother's wishes.

"Oh!" cried Elisha in feigned injury.

Lord Hazelton's lips tightened as he took in his brother's slight of his wife's generosity. His Lordship declared, "Richard, you have always been rag mannered, and you always have pockets to let."

Colonel Fitzwilliam laughed, "Yes, Hazel, true. A colonel's salary is nothing compared to the heir of an Earl."

"Now, here, here!" The Earl glared at his youngest son. "There will be none of this nonsense at my table, Richard. You shall upset your mother, and what will Fitzwilliam's wife think of you?"

Richard looked off to one side as he took a bite of veal.

"Well," stated Lady Matlock to Darcy, "you and Elizabeth are free to handle it alone if you so desire. I am merely offering to help. I am sure if you desire to plan it all yourselves, you shall manage admirably. I, for one, think Georgiana is an exceptional young lady and such development of talent, affability, and intelligence derives not from mere chance. She has had excellent guardians. Fitzwilliam, you and Richard should be proud of your exemplary guidance in the shaping of her character."

Lord Hazelton gave a quick roll of his eyes, but knew enough not to say a word, so he picked up his knife and continued to eat.

"Thank you, Mother," said Richard. I am sure that Darcy should receive credit for the whole of it."

Darcy spoke up, "No, Richard, I have always felt the influence of your opinion. I revere your instincts greatly where Georgiana is concerned."

After this comment, the conversation flowed easily about benign topics of interest. Everyone waved off the last course, opting for sweet breads with tea later on, so with the meal concluded, the Earl suggested, "Let us all take a turn about the gardens, shall we? It is good for the constitution, and, Elizabeth, I hear from Richard that you are an enthusiastic walker and great lover of the outdoors."

Darcy gazed adoringly at his wife as she smiled and told Lord Matlock that she did, indeed, love to walk and partake of nature. Thus, they all removed to enjoy the warmth of the afternoon. James and Elisha contrived fatigue due to Elisha's condition of being with child.

When the others had vacated the room, Lord Hazelton turned to his wife and stated disdainfully, "Richard's instincts? Ha! To me, it is more a case of the blind leading the blind and poor Georgiana, to have such guardians."

"Yes, well, can you believe Darcy getting all out of sorts by my offering to help Georgiana? I swear, James, if your father and Aunt Catherine do not intervene on behalf of that girl, she shall very likely marry a lawyer, doctor, or pray to the heavens, hopefully not a military officer. Darcy does not take it seriously, and he is certainly no example for his sister to look up to after what he has done."

Mary Sherwood

Lord Hazelton patted her hand, trying to soothe his wife's agitated feelings. "Now, now, my pet, you must think of our little heir, whom you are carrying, and not let my ridiculous brother and cousin upset you so. Come, let me take you to rest."

"Oh, James, you are so good to me. I know you are right. It is just so horrible, knowing what Darcy has done to embarrass us all, and to think what it has done to mar his sister's chances with the ton!"

The afternoon and evening passed away in tolerable leisure. Elisha performed on the harp after dinner. Her profound and stimulating flair entertained everyone. The Earl asked Elizabeth to play and sing. She complied with his wishes in an immediate manner, with Richard's accompanying her, singing, *My Lady*. Lord and Lady Hazelton bestowed insincere approval on their performance, yet Lady Matlock's praises came from her heart as she commended the pleasing effect created by the harmonizing of their voices.

~*~

Because Nancy and Chaffin were to come with the others on the morrow, Darcy helped Elizabeth remove her clothing and prepare for bed. She, in turn, untied his cravat, unbuttoned his waistcoat, and then the top buttons of his shirt as well. As they crawled beneath the counterpane, Elizabeth asserted, "Fitzwilliam, I take it that your cousin and his wife are not happy with your marrying me."

Lying on his back, he closed his eyes while delivering his response. "You are correct, Elizabeth. Richard has told me that they have voiced their opposition quite adamantly. Elisha and Lady Catherine are great comrades in deciding whom or what is proper, noteworthy, and commendable. They thrive on the misfortunes of others and on the unions of those whom they deem to be wise and unwise. In my case, Hazelton and Elisha are, I am sure, incensed at me for not marrying for fortune and connections as they did." He opened his eyes, venturing to look at her.

Turning upon her side, Elizabeth gazed directly at her husband. "Well, you certainly are not holding anything back, Mr. Darcy. Why did you not warn me earlier?"

"Would you have wanted me to warn you, Lizzy?"

"Well, I suppose it would not have mattered if you had told me beforehand."

"I did not say anything for three reasons. First, I had hoped they might have changed their sentiments. Therefore, my second reason was that I did not want to influence your opinion of them. And, thirdly, which I suppose should be first and foremost, I had hoped to spare your feelings. I cannot bear seeing you hurt by my foolish relations."

She smiled, and, with excessive politeness, stated, "That is very sweet of you, Fitzwilliam, but really, you do not need to protect my feelings so. I stood up to your Aunt Catherine, if you care to remember. Lord and Lady Hazelton cannot be any more formidable than she."

This statement earned her a smile from her dear husband. "Yes, Lizzy, so you did. I shall strive to never underestimate your abilities again."

"What did Lord Hazelton mean when he told Richard that he has always been rag mannered and has pockets to let?"

"I take it that Hazel feels that Richard behaves like the masses and is always in want of funds."

"Oh! I gathered that it concerned money, but why does he feel that Richard has bad manners? I find him to be very gentlemanly."

"Elizabeth, I am not sure why Hazelton has animosity towards Fitzwilliam. It is unfortunate, as is the fact that he holds great influence over my uncle."

"Poor Richard. Now I understand why Georgie was so willing to defy all of the relatives on his behalf."

"Yes, well…I am sure Richard will find his way."

"Why does Lord Hazelton harass him so for not being married?"

"Again, I am not certain, but they have introduced Fitzwilliam to many eligible women who possess great dowries. I assume they are resentful that he has never endeavoured further than these introductions. I imagine my uncle will bequeath Fitzwilliam a small sum, and maybe Hazelton and Elisha feel it will take away from their portion. Hence, if they marry him off to an heiress, they would keep more of the pie for themselves."

"If this is what having a fortune can do to people, I am rather glad that my father's estate is entailed away and that he does not have great wealth."

Chuckling lightly, Darcy countered, "But, Lizzy, this is not the case with all families. Georgie and I are not at odds with one another over our allotment."

"Yes, but, Fitzwilliam, Georgie is not a male. If she were, then the situation might be very different, indeed. She has accepted her lot. Poor Richard has had the misfortune of being born a second son."

"Elizabeth, Richard is by far the richer one. Do not feel sorry for him."

"Yes, you are right. I do worry about our children, however."

Darcy's face brightened. "Elizabeth, our children will turn out fine. How could they not with you as a very understanding and capable mother."

She began to cry. Tenderly, Darcy asked, "Lizzy, what is the matter? I do mean what I said. You are the woman I have chosen to be the mother of my children, and it is something I did not leave to chance!"

His last declaration made her laugh through her tears. "Oh, I believe you, Fitzwilliam. I am just so weary. I do not even know why I am crying. I guess I have not had much sleep, and I do worry for Richard. I worry more of late than I realized. I am afraid you have married my mother."

His eyes widened. "Never, Lizzy! You are nothing like your mother. You take after your father's disposition."

She cried in earnest now and whimpered, "I am not so sure, Fitzwilliam, and I do love my mother."

"Of course you do, my love. She does have her virtues."

She looked at him warily through tear-filled eyes. "What sort of virtues do you think she has?"

Placing his hand upon his mouth, he rubbed his fingers over his lips while contemplating his mother-in-law's merits, he wondered how long it would take him to respond when, suddenly, he exclaimed, "She is a very beautiful woman and has passed on her beauty to her daughters."

Elizabeth laughed all the more. "Oh, Fitzwilliam, do not worry. I am well aware of my mother's shortcomings. Yet, I do love her dearly, and, for some reason, I miss her right now."

"I am sorry, Elizabeth. Is there anything I can do to alleviate your loneliness for your family?"

"Hold me, my love. I just want to be held."

Darcy wrapped his arms around her and held her close, scattering tender kisses atop her head and brow. "I love you, Elizabeth Bennet Darcy." She sleepily nodded in response and snuggled against his chest. The last sensations of which she was aware before drifting into a peaceful slumber were warmth, security, and the sense of being cherished while within his tender embrace.

~*~

The morning of the ball dawned with the promise of fair weather. Kitty and Georgiana arrived safely with the Bingleys—the valets and maids in tow—just before the noon meal. Elisha wasted no time in lacing her arm through Georgiana's, claiming it had been far too long since they had last talked. Caroline watched with interest. She delighted in her introduction to Lady Hazelton. The woman was well known and respected by the prominent ladies of the inner circles of the ton. Miss Bingley realized the introduction could advance her own needs.

By late afternoon, great commotion filled the mansion as servants bustled about unloading trunks from the carriages of overnight guests, completing last minute darning and pressing of gowns, and hauling buckets of hot water up the servants' stairs.

Fitzwilliam Darcy lay upon the bed in his wife's chamber, pressing a hand over his brow as Elizabeth entered and noticed his shaven face and black coattails. "Why, Fitzwilliam, my love, are you not feeling well?"

"Um, I have a faint headache. That is all."

Elizabeth had just dried off from her bath. She walked over to the bed and gently sat next to her husband. Leaning down upon her elbow, she began to massage his left temple. He removed his hand, gently relaxing from the calming relief supplied by her delicate fingertips.

After several minutes, she softly asked, "Are you worried about the ball tonight, my love?" With his eyes still closed, he nodded to her query.

"What, pray, is it exactly that worries you?"

"I dislike large crowds, Elizabeth."

"Yes, but it will all be over soon enough. I will be by your side, as will Charles, Richard, and Georgiana."

He took hold of her hand and kissed it. "I know you will be there for me always. I just detest these sorts of occasions where I must be the centre of attention."

"I know." She bent low and kissed his brow. "I must finish dressing."

He nodded.

Nancy came to tighten Elizabeth's corset and help her slip on the shimmering cream gown, its overlay of chiffon lending a rich airy sheen to the pearly silk beneath. The evening dress clung tightly to Elizabeth's form, enhancing her figure quite nicely. Piping decorated the area beneath the bodice, and the rear of the gown had smartly defined pleats just above the small of the back with the skirt having only a hint of a train spilling upon the floor as Elizabeth walked. She decided to wear Lady Anne's emerald and diamond choker and droplet earrings, feeling that they complemented the colour of her eyes. Her wrists remained bare of jewellery, with only the glimmer of silken gloves gracing her hands and forearms.

Next, Nancy styled her hair with specific instruction from the mistress. Elizabeth desired to wear it in the same fashion as she had at the Netherfield ball, excluding the rosettes. Instead of the flowers, jewelled pins were intertwined about her coiffure, creating a sparkling effect every time the gems caught the light, sending subtle, dancing sparkles of vibrant colour about the room.

With all in place, she arose and gingerly made her way to the bed. "Mr. Darcy," she quietly beckoned, "do you feel well enough to join me in the receiving line?"

Rubbing his face with both hands, Darcy sat up. "I am ready, Lizzy." As his eyes took in his wife's dazzling appearance, he smiled broadly. "Why, Elizabeth, you are even more beautiful than on our wedding day, if that is possible. Where did you find a gown made of such an exquisite fabric?"

Her expression shone as much as her dress and jewels combined, due to her husband's elated astonishment. She could not have been more pleased with his reaction. "I take it you approve then, sir?"

"How could I not approve? You are a stunning sight, Elizabeth. I find the effect of your appearance so dizzying, that I do not care to go down and share you. "Instead," Darcy growled, "I would rather disrobe you of your adornments to admire the greater treasures beneath."

"Oh, my, I fear your aunt could never forgive us if we did not show."

With a scowl, he replied, "Yes, I am afraid, my dear girl, you are right."

Elizabeth's brow furrowed, she loathed when he used that form of address with her.

While coming down the staircase, they could see the Earl, Lady Matlock, Lord and Lady Hazelton, and Richard standing about, waiting to form the line. As Darcy and Elizabeth descended, all heads turned to view them. Their eyes swept quickly over Darcy, but arrested upon Elizabeth when observing her loveliness.

Elisha's chin rose high in defiance at the admiration Mrs. Darcy was receiving, but if she had been looking at her husband's face, she would have easily noticed the sparks that flickered within his eyes. Lord Hazelton could definitely understand Darcy's fascination and weakness for Elizabeth, but why marry her? Why not have her for a mistress? That way, the heir of the Earl reasoned, his cousin could have had the best of both worlds. In fact, he would not mind having a woman exactly like his cousin's wife for a mistress or even for a mere tryst. Darcy immediately saw all of their admiring expressions, although he perceived a little too much appreciation from Richard.

The line formed, and the guests began to stream into the large reception hall. Elizabeth recognized many faces, yet there were many others whom she did not know. Her hand ached and felt as if it were about to break when the last four guests made their way through the line. Before them stood the Caldecotts and the only face she had not seen before was their son, Ashton. He was tall, handsome, and two years Collette's junior. Elizabeth made a mental note that his teeth were just as perfect as his sister's. She also noticed how his eyes seemed to linger upon her décolletage, and a sordid feeling washed over her. She held familiarity with the feeling. She had suffered it when in seclusion with George Wickham at Lambton as he spoke to her in his lewd and lascivious manner. Her stomach lurched.

They entered the grand ballroom to the billowing hum of music filling the air and the din of voices from the guests who now crowded the elegant space. Lady Matlock whispered something to her husband, and the Earl made his way to stand before the orchestra. At a gesture of his hands, the musicians ceased to play, and the room fell silent.

"Again, we welcome you and are glad you have come to join with us in the celebration of the marriage of Fitzwilliam Darcy and his lovely bride, Elizabeth Bennet. He is the son of my sister, Lady Anne Fitzwilliam Darcy and her husband, George Darcy. We shall commence the dancing with my nephew and his wife taking the lead on the floor. The Earl bowed, and the ensemble began anew. Darcy proffered his arm to Elizabeth, and they walked out onto the immense dance floor in a stately manner. Without warning, Darcy twirled Elizabeth and then bent her low as if they were performing the waltz. The crowd cheered and many exclamations of

"Ooh!" and "Ah!" were heard as a round of applause erupted. Promptly, many other couples entered the dance and the ball was now in full form.

Most of the older generation milled about, stopping occasionally when finding someone with whom they wished to speak. Several great tables lining one wall were laden with rich hors d'oeuvres, a variety of nuts, fine pastries, and the customary liquors. Servants stood ready to help quench any guest's request.

An older gentleman of about forty years, a man with a bald spot and sporting a bulging girth, appeared at Kitty's side, her first partner for the first dance. To Kitty, it seemed that he drooled as he eagerly eyed her. She was sickened by his disgusting interest and tried to remain pleasant as they met and parted for the duration of the dance. He reminded her of her cousin, Mr. Collins, only with less hair and a larger waistline. For that same dance, Georgiana found herself partnered with Ashton Caldecott. Her card listed James as her partner for the second set, and he would be followed by her uncle. Fitzwilliam had asked for the dance just before dinner. As of yet, Richard had not secured a dance with her, but she had many free sets and, therefore, hoped he would approach her soon. He had barely said two words to her when they had arrived that afternoon, and then, after they had partaken of the noon fare, everyone withdrew to their own chambers in order to rest and prepare for the night's festivities.

The evening progressed splendidly, with everyone enjoying themselves immensely. Somehow, through the pressing throng, Elizabeth had lost her husband. While jostling her way among the crowd in the hopes of finding him, she bumped into Charles and Jane. They both told her how exquisite she looked and expressed their thrill that such a lovely ball was being given in her honour. She thanked them and then asked if they had seen her husband. Bingley informed her that he had observed Darcy standing near the side tables. He added that he trusted Darcy would still be there by the time she might manage to make her way through the crowd. Bingley also informed her that Jane felt drowsy and he planned to accompany her to their chambers to tuck her in for the night, but would return to the festivities once he knew that his angel rested snug and sound.

As Elizabeth made her way to the tables, she looked up just in time to see her husband leaving the ballroom with Mr. Caldecott and Collette. Confused, she stood frozen in place. Why on earth would he leave the ballroom, and why, especially, in the company of Collette? Deciding not to dwell upon it, until she could specifically ask Darcy, she turned in the other direction, only to find herself face to face with the younger brother of the aforementioned woman. Mr. Ashton Caldecott smiled gregariously at her. "Mrs. Darcy, so we meet again. In fact, this is no chance meeting at all."

"Oh?" responded Elizabeth.

"Yes, I purposely came in search of you. I assume you were looking for Fitz?"

"You assume correctly, Mr. Caldecott."

"Oh, please, our families go way back. Call me Ashton, and would you honour me with the next dance?"

"Well, I was hoping to speak with my husband, so…"

"Oh, he will not be back for some time. He and father desire to give Collette a special something to surprise her on her birthday."

"Pardon me?" Elizabeth displayed a pensive brow, and Ashton laughed most heartily at her confusion. "I would rather not say more. It is a surprise that Fitz and my father intend to give her, that is all. I am sure you are aware that my sister and your husband at one time were immensely in love, and if it had not been for a small misunderstanding between them, then most likely you would never have become Mrs. Fitzwilliam Darcy."

She eyed him contemptuously. "I am sorry. I cannot favour you with the next dance, for I find I am in need of a rest. I thank you." With those words spoken, Elizabeth rushed hastily through the crowd only to bump straight into Darcy's cousin, Lord Hazelton. The collision caused her to stumble. This, however, was prevented when the Viscount caught her in his arms. Steadying her with one hand tightly on the side of her waist and the other grasping the side of her breast, he called out to her, "Whoa, my dear girl, we do not want you falling over and hurting yourself, do we?" After securing her on her feet, his one hand slowly slid down her side and then quickly began to tug on the fabric of her dress as he stated, "There, we would not want you waltzing about with your dress out of kilter." She flashed her eyes at him. Was he being in earnest?

After a moment of hesitation, she said, "I…I thank you, Lord Hazelton."

Lord Hazelton smiled engagingly and then remarked, "Please call me James, after all we are now family, and if you really desire to thank me, Elizabeth, please allow me the honour of the next dance."

Her brow furrowed faintly, but then she acquiesced. A new dance was about to begin, and, seizing her hand within his, he led her out onto the centre of the floor. A waltz began to play. Elizabeth felt startled when she realized that she would be in such close proximity to James for the duration of the piece. She tried to figure out the reason as to why she felt so uncomfortable. Was it because of the playful repartee that she and Fitzwilliam had shared earlier in the week about the seductiveness of the dance, or was it the fact that she knew that Lord Hazelton did not approve of Fitzwilliam having married her? Furthermore, she had already formed a dislike of him due to the spiteful way he had spoken to Richard.

"My goodness, Elizabeth, are you always so silent? My brother Richard tells us that you complement my cousin in so many ways, and one way in particular is your effusive manner compared to his reticence."

Elizabeth looked at him in amazement. Was this supposed to be a compliment? She replied, "I am only a little tired, is all. Of what do you wish to speak?"

"Well, for one, why did it take you so long to fall in love with my cousin?"

"Oh, no, I cannot allow myself to speak about love while on the dance floor."

"Why ever not? It is as fitting a place as any other, especially with the atmosphere created by the waltz." He pulled her to him tightly as he manoeuvred them amongst the mass of dancers. Every time Elizabeth tried to look off to the side, she found herself becoming faint from all the whirling and being bent backwards and up again. Yet, when she concentrated on Lord Hazelton's countenance, she found herself experiencing a decided queasiness. When the music ended and he led her away from the dance floor back into the midst of the maddening crowd, she felt genuinely grateful.

Colonel Fitzwilliam stood across the room observing the dancers. He would leave for London the next day and then, after six weeks training there, would be off to Portugal to fight the French. Leaning against the wall, he made out his brother waltzing with Elizabeth. He snorted in scorn as he contemplated the fact that his arrogant brother was actually dancing with the so-called peasant from Hertfordshire. My, my, was not Hazel ever the charlatan? After watching them for a full minute, he noticed Bingley dancing with Kitty. That spurred him to realize that he must shake himself out of his funk in order to go and socialize with the ladies. After all, Kitty seemed to be a fun sort of girl.

Then, his eyes detected Darcy with a beautiful blonde in his arms. Who was she? Adorned in a stunning gown of sapphire blue, the woman's skin resembled the purest cream. They twirled so fast, weaving in and out of the other dancers that Richard had to stand up straight and walk forward, along the outskirts of the bystanders, in order to get a better view. Uttering aloud to himself, he exclaimed, "Oh, my, it cannot be, but it is! It is Georgie!" He suddenly realized that he had not seen her since the ball began, and here she was before him, dressed in a very alluring gown, looking as if she were three and twenty, instead of the mere seventeen years that she was soon to be. He could not believe his eyes. That barmy maid had really known her craft. Yvette had discarded the prim dresses from Georgiana's girlish wardrobe, unshackling his fair cousin's figure and displaying it to its best advantage in a very daring gown. The garment revealed her lovely, lithesome, yet womanly form most favourably. He could not tear his eyes away from his cousins as Georgie's svelte body swayed with the beat and the direction of Darcy's command. Inhaling deeply, Richard felt like her girlhood had now passed in the twinkling of an eye. She had grown up and before him stood a woman.

Dinner was called. The arrangements petitioned for a light affair, serving only three courses. Elizabeth looked for her place card. She found it and, as one of the first ones at the table, quickly discovered the others who would sit with her. Richard's amiable countenance smiled at her from her left while Lord and Lady Hazelton found their seats to her right. Darcy, she discovered, had been placed on the opposite side of the beautiful but rather too tall floral arrangement situated in the middle of the table. She felt somewhat irked that, despite his height, she would have to rise up in her chair in order to see her husband over the blossoms. She frowned.

Everyone was seated when Darcy finally arrived at the table. Elizabeth tried to catch his attention with a forward stare, but Mr. Caldecott, being seated beside Darcy, began to converse with him. She felt total frustration. Elizabeth also took notice that Ashton was assigned on her husband's right, with Georgiana next to him. Collette sat by her father.

When the last course had been served, the opportunity finally presented itself for Darcy to lift his eyes and look carefully across the table at his wife. It was his first chance to give her more than a passing glance. Yet, Collette would have none of it. Therefore, she leaned over her father and called out his name. Darcy's head turned towards her voice.

Elizabeth found herself instantly peeved. She could not believe that she had only been by her husband's side for no more than the amount of time that the first set had afforded. Richard, too, busily engaged with his own quandary, was not aware of her plight. He sat seething as he watched Ashton Caldecott talking excessively to Georgiana.

Gradually the guests and hosts alike began making their way back to the ballroom to continue the dance. Elizabeth arose from the table and gave her husband a meaningful look. He shrugged his shoulders and silently mouthed words to her. She could not make them out, however. A small party of women surrounded her in passing when one called her name and desired to engage her in conversation. By the time she had finished speaking with them, she turned to realize that her husband was no longer anywhere to be seen. She huffed beneath her breath, *Fitzwilliam Darcy, for all of your disappearing acts and dinner conversations, you had better have a good explanation*!

As Elizabeth re-entered the ballroom, couples were already forming a line to dance the Cotillion. She felt at a loss, not knowing any of the people about her. They were all friendly enough, yet she felt very much alone. She saw Lord Hazelton from the corner of her eye, approaching in her direction. Hence, Elizabeth quickly turned to hide behind some older men who enjoyed a discussion on the advantage of certain varieties of barley for a better breeding outcome of their sheep. When Lord Hazelton finally passed by, she sighed in relief. Then, she turned about only to find Richard staring at her with a silly grin upon his face. "I take it, Elizabeth, that you desire to avoid the dance at all costs?"

She replied to the colonel in a light tone, "Most certainly, especially when one finds certain partners undesirable."

They both stood by the other when Bingley happened upon them. "I say, I have never seen so many people dance so soon after having eaten."

Richard and Elizabeth nodded and grinned at his observation. "Yes," replied Elizabeth, "everyone does seem eager to kick up their heels."

All three watched as the couples finished their set and began to leave the floor. In an attempt to locate her husband, Elizabeth stood on her tiptoes, looking over peoples' heads. Richard smiled at her efforts when he noticed a shadow cross her visage. He quickly scanned the crowd to see what had caused her such consternation. It did not take him long to discover Collette loitering by his cousin's side as Darcy participated in a conversation with several men. Colonel Fitzwilliam shook his head in dismay. Strains of music announced that a new dance was beginning. Richard, in astonishment, observed Darcy going out onto the floor with Collette. He thought to himself, *what is the man thinking?*

The colonel quickly glanced to Elizabeth, hoping that she had not noticed. From the sorrow he read in her expression, it was obvious that she had. The music had truly just begun when Richard politely beseeched, "Elizabeth, please allow me this dance. I have not danced once as of yet. Please grant me this honour."

Elizabeth looked up at him and numbly nodded. He led her to the floor and put his hand upon her waist. She realized it was another waltz. Her eyes widened in surprise and she searched the floor to find her husband. Quickly she observed him for he appeared quite near and quite entranced with Miss Caldecott. Richard, on the other hand, lost all concentration on Elizabeth when he discerned Ashton nearly embracing Georgiana. His jaw clenched. Ashton Caldecott was a snake in the grass! He had warned Georgiana about him. Why would she consent to dance with such a rake?

While the colonel's mind became preoccupied with Georgiana, tears began to course down Elizabeth's cheeks. Before Richard knew what had happened, she pulled her hand from his and hastily left the floor. Richard followed at a fast pace.

Darcy was incensed. He had been involved in a conversation regarding the coalmine when Collette suddenly flashed her dance card in front of the faces of all the men. Making certain that they all could see it, she claimed that Mr. Darcy had signed it. She waited for him to accompany her onto the floor for the commencing waltz. Darcy baulked and asked to examine it, but all the men began to rib and censure him for not allowing the fair lady to have her dance. They assured him that they would await his return to continue their discussion.

As he and Collette began the sway about the room, Darcy sputtered to his partner that he had had enough of her baleful malice. She only laughed the harder and tried to pull him to her. However, he kept her at arm length. As he pushed her back, she noticed Elizabeth in Richard's arms and cried,

"Well, Fitz, I see nothing has changed. Your cousin is as much in love with your wife as he was with me when we were all younger."

Darcy's eyes swung over to see his cousin and wife. As he strived to keep them in his field of vision, Collette made her next move. A faint echo of sincerity met the Master of Pemberley's ears as Miss Caldecott purred out his name. "Fitzwilliam, my only love, I shall settle for being your mistress. Please say all is forgiven and that you will love me again as you once did." Right after she had made this provocative offer, Darcy noticed Elizabeth crying and hastily making her way out of the room with Fitzwilliam close behind.

His eyes returned to Collette, and he glared at her, vehemently. As she smiled maliciously at him, Darcy pulled her closely against him and began to speedily twirl about the room. She became a little confused and began to laugh from the excitement of it, closing her eyes in delight as they picked up momentum. Yet, when they abruptly stopped and he bent her low, but did not raise her up, she opened her eyes and stared into his, feeling certain that he intended to kiss her. Instead of a passionate exchange, Darcy stated heatedly, "Never come to Pemberley again, Collette. Never speak to me or my wife again, and I do mean *never*. I am through being a gentleman for someone who is truly *no* lady."

Her eyes widened in fear as she felt the support of his arms slipping away. He firmly deposited her on the balcony floor. "How dare you!" Collette cried, tears of anger stinging her eyes. After that declaration, Darcy heard no more because he began to weave quickly through the crowd in search of his wife. Many of the young men who were standing near the balcony doors witnessed the whole scene and began to laugh. Incensed, Collette began screaming warnings to him as he boldly walked away, causing the young men to chortle all the more.

Richard caught up with his cousin's wife in the entrance hall and grasped her arm. "Elizabeth, it is not what it seems."

"Oh, is it not, Colonel! My husband always seems to find himself in the company of that woman!"

"Yes, but I can assure you he does not desire it to be so. He is only playing the gentleman. She means nothing to him. It was only young, calf love. Please, she is not worth dampening your rosy cheeks."

Shaking her head in wretchedness, Elizabeth tried to free her arm from Richard's clasp, but he held onto it tightly.

As Darcy approached the doorway to exit the ballroom, Bingley caught sight of him and followed quickly upon his heels. "Darcy, where are you going?"

"Not now, Bingley."

Entering the grand hall, Darcy saw his cousin and wife near the passageway that led to the library. He perceived that Elizabeth appeared distraught by how she kept trying to pull her wrist from Richard's grip.

Overcome with indignation Darcy shouted with a deafening volume which was seldom heard from the man. "Fitzwilliam, take your hand off of my wife!"

Bingley's eyes went wide in shock. Colonel Fitzwilliam turned to look behind him as Elizabeth broke his grasp and ran down the length of the corridor. Darcy raced to his cousin and shoved him hard. Richard grimaced at the push but straightway pounced back, pushing Darcy back just as forcefully while saying through gritted teeth, "You are such a Jack in an office!"

"Me? I do believe you are mistaken, Fitzwilliam. You are the one behaving in an audacious manner towards my wife! And you do it just to spite me!"

"What, Darcy?" Colonel Fitzwilliam cried with a look of incredulity. "Do you hear what you are saying? You are acting ludicrously! And why do you suppose I spite you, Darcy? Is it because of Collette? You are, indeed, insane!"

Darcy spewed out, "**FITZWILLIAM!**"

Nervously twisting his hands as his countenance bore a pained expression, Bingley tried to intervene. "Now, Darce, I do think your cousin has a point."

Darcy snapped, "Stay out of this, Bingley!" His brother-in-law's eyes went even wider, and he hurriedly nodded his head in fright as he replied, "As you wish, Darcy. It is just that?"

Raising his voice again, but not as loudly, Darcy barked, "Bingley!"

Charles pressed his lips tightly as he stood there staring wide-eyed at the two men. Darcy and Richard glared at each other in defiance. Just as Richard began to speak, he noticed his mother approaching them with a very stern look upon her face.

With authority, Lady Matlock reprimanded, "Now, you boys know better than to act so foolishly. I have a good mind to take you both by the ears as I did when you were small. I will not have you openly arguing for the whole of the county to hear." Forcefully, she took hold of Darcy's and her son's arms, propelled them forward, and then shoved them into the library. She stated angrily, "Finish your quarrel in here. I am going to find Elizabeth. You should be ashamed of yourselves! Oh, and close the door!"

Both Darcy and Richard were stunned. Bingley quickly shut the door behind Lady Matlock, and then eagerly turned his attention back to his brother-in-law and the colonel.

In the meantime, Darcy had managed to rein in his anger and stated composedly, "Bingley, you had better leave."

"Why, Darcy?" asked Richard bitterly. "I do not see why Bingley cannot hear anything we have to say. I am not the one hiding from my past. I will freely admit to any of my sins!"

Bingley looked awkwardly over to Darcy. Darcy just shook his head and put the back of his hand against his mouth.

There was stillness until Richard embarked upon the subject at hand. "Darcy, it is time to call a spade a spade."

Darcy silently seethed, "Fitzwilliam, do you deny that you are attracted to my wife?"

Snorting, Richard made answer, "I have no wish of denying it, Darcy! But just because I find Elizabeth to be a charming woman does not mean I have designs on her, far from it. I respect and care deeply for *both* of you. I harbour no dishonourable feelings for her at all. I am only acting the gentleman, for it seems that my cousin is acting more of a gentleman to a *biter* than to his wife, who is very much a lady."

Darcy glowered and then spat out, "Collette has nothing to do with this conversation!"

"Darcy, she has everything to do with it, and, until you can come clean, you will continue to be haunted and tortured by your misdeeds."

Immediately, Darcy sat and moved his hand to cover his eyes. Richard continued in full force. "So, Darcy, is it that your name resides in the black book, or do you still feel bobbed from so many years ago?"

Removing his hand quickly, Darcy seethed through clenched teeth, "How dare you, Richard? You know that I no longer care for her!"

"Then that leaves the black book. So what, my little cousin, if you have a stain on your character? Welcome to the rest of the world, Darcy, and quit berating yourself over something that was not even your fault."

Darcy cried out, shaking his head bitterly, "I compromised her, Richard!" Bingley's eyes bulged as he remained deathly silent.

In astonishment, Richard contradicted, "No, little cousin, it was more a case of Collette compromising you! Darcy, do you not see how she flattered us all, each of us thinking we were the favoured one? Oh," Colonel Fitzwilliam added with a sneer, accompanied by a shake of his head, "she was a clever girl." He exhaled noisily, frowning in disgust at the mere memory of Miss Caldecott's duplicity.

"No, Fitzwilliam," Darcy whispered hoarsely, "it is not that simple. I did things that a gentleman should never do. And...I am utterly ashamed to this day."

"Like it or not, Darcy, we all are guilty of past transgressions. At least your sins were only minor indiscretions. Mine were far worse—lucky for you to have gone to the shearing house that fateful day. Oh, that I could have been enlightened so easily!"

Darcy looked up sharply. "How do you know about that?"

"George Wickham told me. He informed me that he and Collette were...um...riding St. George when you opened the door and caught them in the act. He bragged to me that Collette had *sprained* her ankle with him and said that she had planned to seduce you and convince you that you were the child's father. The only thing Wickham failed to comprehend while relating his braggart tale, I presume, is that I, too, had known Collette. Thus, I was a brother starling. She, of course, had healed herself of her sprained ankle when she and I..." Richard looked away in embarrassment. Clearing his throat, he continued with great emotion, "You will never know what that summer did to me, Darcy. You will never know what agony I felt for my irresponsible behaviour. I wondered for many years if I had fathered that child that Collette had so easily terminated. It changed my life. So, do not give me your sob story concerning your ungentlemanly behaviour. Be thankful that George Wickham granted you the best gift possible. Your life would have been a living hell with that woman. She is a brazen-faced hussy and not worth your permissiveness. Get some pluck, man. Tell Elizabeth every detail. She deserves to know all, considering what you and Collette have put her through."

After finishing his discourse, Richard inhaled deeply. He looked over at his cousin, who by now had his head in his hands, and stated, "Well, I have not danced a whole dance through tonight. I am off for London tomorrow, so I think I shall try to catch a set before this ball concludes. Why do you not join me, Bingley? Kitty looks like she could use some rescuing from Mr. Wilson's fanciful eyes."

Richard strode over to the door, opened it, and was gone. Bingley was indecisive. Tentatively, he asked his friend, "Darce, I will gladly stay with you if you like?"

Darcy shook his head while his hands still covered his face. With a choked voice, he stated, "No, go, Bingley, and enjoy yourself. I am sorry for all of this."

Looking miserably at his dear friend and brother, Charles waited for a few seconds, but decided it was best to depart.

A few moments later, Darcy felt a hand squeeze his shoulder. Without looking up, he stated, "Please go, Bingley. I shall be fine."

"Fitzwilliam, my love," said Elizabeth softly, "look at me."

Slowly, Darcy's hands slid down as he turned his head to look up into the face of his wife.

She could tell that he was overcome with emotion. "I love you, Fitzwilliam, but we must return to the ball. It will not do for us to spurn your aunt and uncle's kindness in this manner. Let us go and dance together for the few remaining dances that remain."

"But, Elizabeth," he replied huskily, "I need to speak with you. I need to tell you something."

She leaned over and kissed him on the cheek. "Whatever it is can wait until we are alone in our rooms. I love you, Fitzwilliam. We shall converse later, but now, we shall dance."

Nodding gently, he arose and they made their way back to the ballroom. A dance had just ended when the Earl again stood in front of the orchestra to call one and all to attention. "We wish, again, to thank everyone for coming to Matlock and sharing this special occasion. It has been a most enjoyable evening. My wife, Lady Matlock, has informed me that she wants one more dance before bringing this celebration to completion, and, once more, she desires our honoured couple to take the lead. So, without further adieu, Mr. and Mrs. Darcy, wherever you are in this throng, please, come forth to execute the last waltz of the evening. Thank you."

The stringed instruments commenced to hum while Darcy and Elizabeth made their way forward and out onto the floor. "Oh, my," cried Elizabeth as she met Fitzwilliam's eyes, "your aunt must have a fetish with this dance. I do believe this is the fourth time in the course of the evening that it has been performed."

"Yes," Darcy replied, "it is the fourth time, yet the first time I am honoured to dance it with you, Elizabeth, on the floor of a ballroom." She gave him a slight smile, and they proceeded to graciously sway about.

When Richard had returned to the ballroom awhile earlier, he observed Georgiana over by the side tables sipping on what he presumed to be wine. He quickly wound his way through the crush of onlookers. As he approached, Georgiana noticed him coming towards her. She handed her glass to a servant in order to be ready in case he would ask her to dance. Taking in a deep breath, she hoped that he had finally come to seek her company.

Richard's face beamed as he bowed with gallantry and then complimented his young cousin with a teasing air. "My little duckling is no more, Georgie, or perhaps from now on I should address you as Miss Darcy—for I cannot believe my eyes! Is it truly you, Georgiana?" His voice took on a serious tone as he declared, "You are a vision of loveliness."

"Oh, I was only fair to middling before?" She bit her lip as she delighted in his smile at her jest.

"Oh, you have always been a very pretty girl. But tonight, I find you have grown up right before my very eyes. Your gown, and the way you are wearing your hair—they are exquisite and suit you extremely well."

"So, Richard, am I handsome enough to tempt you to dance with me?"

He chuckled from her inference to Darcy's blunder when first meeting Elizabeth and nodded, while raising his brow. "Most definitely, and I am sure that when you come out next month, all of those Bond Street chaps will not be able to take their eyes off of you."

Quickly, a saddened look crossed over her features as she dropped her eyes to study her slippers. "What is wrong, Georgie?" asked Richard, "I did not mean to upset you, and, yes, you are correct. If you are free for this dance, I would be greatly honoured if you should dance it with me."

Slowly raising her eyes, she smiled but quickly averted her gaze to scrutinize her dance card. Richard smiled at her all the more for her playful jest. Little did he realize that she had deliberately saved the last set for him, warding off enquiring gentlemen with the claim that her card was full.

After Darcy had made a complete round with Elizabeth, the other couples joined them on the floor, Richard and Georgiana leading the way.

Nearly an hour later, all of the guests who had not planned to spend the night departed. The Earl and Lady Matlock turned to Elizabeth and Darcy, and the Earl said with a yawn, "It has been a success, Fitzwilliam. I think the whole of Derbyshire is smitten with your wife's beauty. I am now for *Bedfordshire*. I hope to see you at breakfast before you are off for Pemberley. Goodnight."

Lady Matlock gazed at her nephew, and then turned to Elizabeth with a pleased expression on her face. "You both made me so very proud of you tonight." She smiled wider as she added, "I am delighted with having you in the family, Elizabeth. You have chosen well, Fitzwilliam, and so have you, my dear." She directed her last words to Elizabeth."

The Earl had halted his progress at the bottom of the stairs and called out to his wife, "Are you coming, Adie?"

"Yes, Winnie, I am." Then Lady Matlock stood on her toes to embrace her tall nephew.

Darcy, by reflex, startled at his aunt's unexpected intimacy, but quickly rewarded her attempt by warmly returning the embrace. She whispered in his ear, "I am sure Anne and George would have been proud, for I am." She then kissed his cheek. When their hug ended, she likewise reached for Elizabeth, tightly pulled her to her chest, and whispered, "I am also proud of you, my dear."

With broad smiles, Elizabeth and Darcy wished them a goodnight and stood in place as they watched the elder couple ascend the stairs.

Darcy turned and looked down at his wife. She met his gaze. Both remained silent for several seconds. Finally, Darcy broke the stillness, and asked anxiously, "Elizabeth, I need to speak with you privately and beg, once more, for your forgiveness. Shall we go to the library?"

"Oh, no," she laughingly answered, "forgiveness in a library is not to be borne. There are too many distractions and too great a risk of being overheard by prying ears. I feel the privacy of our bedchamber is best."

Darcy looked at her in a dazed manner. Could she possibly be joking about his need to speak with her? Was she merely being playful, or would the fire and brimstone crumble about them with the closing of the chamber door?

~*~

It was a good thing Elizabeth had chosen to have their discussion in the privacy of their chambers, for the library was already in use by two people who were having their own tête-à-tête. Colonel Fitzwilliam and his fair cousin occupied a settee on the far side of the room. Richard reached for Georgiana's hand. "Georgie, have you heard that my regiment is being called to London?" She shook her head. "I am to leave tomorrow and shall be stationed there for some weeks. It is expected that we will be sent to the Continent very soon."

He noticed her distress and squeezed her hand in an attempt to reassure her. "Georgie, please do not encourage Ashton Caldecott. He is a vile person. I could not bear seeing you in his arms tonight."

Stonily, she looked into Richard's eyes. "What does it matter? My reputation is tarnished. When people find out about what I have done, even Ashton Caldecott might not want me."

"Georgie, what are you saying? You have done nothing to make you unworthy. Many men will find you quite desirable and deserving."

She shook her head with a tremor running through her body. "No, I am quite sure of it, and even if many men could find me worthy, there is only one man's opinion I care to have, besides that of my brother."

Colonel Fitzwilliam's brow creased. *What is she saying?*

Quickly, Georgiana changed the topic by asking, "Please, Richard, let me go to London with you tomorrow? I have written Mrs. Annesley and requested that she meet me there this week. She has responded and said she is in London, already, visiting her son. I have the letter upstairs." Her eyes turned to the door, prepared to prove her point. "She assured me that she would join me if I did return. I planned to ask Fitzwilliam tomorrow if I could go with Mr. and Mrs. Bingley, but I would much rather ride with you. Please say you will take me. It may be the last time I am able to see you for so very long."

"But would you rather not wait and go with your brother and Elizabeth in a few weeks?" he asked.

Shaking her head, she cried, "No, they need time alone. I do not want to burden them with my company any longer."

Richard stared at her, wondering why she felt she was a burden. Nodding slowly, he stated, "Very well, Georgie, I shall take you to London with me if your brother approves." She smiled hesitantly. "Does this not make you happy?" asked he when seeing her unease.

"Oh, yes, I am very happy. It is only that," she reached forth, grasped his hand and squeezed it," I am sad you will not be able to be with me in London when I am presented at court and at my ball. I shall miss you dearly. Will you write to me? I shall worry about you so." She sighed heavily as she cast an imploring gaze at her cousin.

"Georgie, I always write as often as I can. Do not be distressed. I have gone to battle many times."

"Yes, but I have always worried for your welfare. Please promise you will write letters to me instead of Fitzwilliam. Anything you have to say to him, I can relate. Please?"

He smiled at her and brought forth his other hand, taking both of hers in his and holding them tightly. "Yes, Georgiana, I promise to write to you and to no other. If anyone else desires to know of my welfare, they shall have to enquire to you for it."

Hastily, she freed her hands from his grasp and lunged forward, taking him into a tight squeeze. The quaver in her voice was not lost to the colonel as she declared with feeling, "I love you, Richard. I love you more than you know."

He was confused by her heightened emotion, and yet, he returned her embrace with an intensity of his own. While locked therein, he tenderly whispered, "I love you, too, Georgiana. I shall speak with Fitzwilliam tomorrow and beg him to let you go with me. Does this make you happy?" He felt her head nod upon his shoulder.

~*~

When Darcy and Elizabeth entered their chamber, they found Nancy laying out Elizabeth's nightgown. Elizabeth walked over to the young woman and thanked her. She then asked her to retire, saying she would manage with Mr. Darcy's assistance.

Darcy's brows rose at the dismissal, but he acted as if he had not noticed. Elizabeth then walked over to him and began to untie his cravat while saying, "Fitzwilliam, please go and tell Mr. Chaffin that his services are not needed, for I shall take care of your needs."

He swallowed hard, staring at her oddly. "Lizzy, I seldom have Chaffin wait up for me when the hour is this late. I usually deal with my nightly preparations myself, unless there is a problem, and then he knows I shall ring for him."

"You are a most considerate person, Fitzwilliam," she said as she continued to disrobe him, first removing his tailcoat and then his cufflinks.

For a second time Darcy swallowed hard. He had expected Elizabeth to unleash her repressed frustration for his dancing with Collette. Yet, here she stood, as calm as a summer's morning, doffing his waistcoat without so much as a peep over the mortification he had cost her. Just as he was attempting to comprehend her meaning, she suddenly turned and asked him to unfasten her dress. This he did.

She then pulled her arms out of the sleeves, allowing the gown drop to the floor. "Do you mind undoing my corset, also?"

Again, Darcy was taken aback at his wife's easy comportment. His brows rose as his eyes veered off, silently considering what she was about. "No, Elizabeth, I shall be only too happy to oblige."

After he unlaced the feminine garment, Elizabeth discarded it and began stretching her arms high above her head while standing in her chemise and pantalets. "Oh, it feels so refreshing to be free from the constraints of clothing, do you not agree, Fitzwilliam? I feel that I may truly relax now. So, come with me to the bed." She grasped his hand and began to lead him along "Once there, I shall take off your shoes and stockings, and you will tell me all you wish to say and ask for my forgiveness."

Darcy blinked and nodded but remained uncertain of her true feelings. Was she in earnest or was he a lamb about to be led to the slaughter?

Elizabeth took in his stunned expression as she escorted him to the bed and once there, she released her hold and asked if he would be so kind as to lift her up onto the mattress. This he immediately did. She crawled beneath the counterpane and lay facing him, propping her head up on her elbow. Invitingly, she reached forth and gently patted his side of the bed. "Come, Fitzwilliam."

He had just sat down on the edge of the mattress when she quickly popped up, rolling over upon her knees. "I had almost forgotten. Let me have your feet." Lying down on top of the covers, his feet barely hanging off the side, Darcy allowed her to remove his slippers and stockings. She again returned to her former pose and looked at him expectantly.

Turning his face towards hers, he continued to gaze at her in a guarded manner. "Lizzy, I do not know where to begin."

"Begin wherever you wish, Fitzwilliam. Take all the time you need."

Again, he nodded as his throat constricted, and with a deep breath, he commenced. "During the summer when I had turned eighteen, I had more leisure time than I could ever remember having had. My father's health had begun to decline, and I was left to enjoy a summer fairly free of responsibilities and commitments. He desired, I suppose, for me to have one last, relatively carefree summer before taking on all the burdens of Pemberley and of Georgiana upon my shoulders." He swallowed hard, turned his face from her and lifted his eyes to the canopy overhead.

His lips trembled. Taking in another deep breath, he continued. "As was Richard's wont, he spent the duration of that summer at Pemberley. George Wickham was there as well. We passed our time in various activities, such as shooting and fishing, and we had many evenings which were spent with other young people in the vicinity." He paused, inhaling sharply to fortify himself. "Collette was one among that group of many. Of course, I had known Collette and her family for a number of years. She would come with her mother, father, and brother to play cards and participate in other pursuits with my family. I had always been attracted to her. She was a lively girl and always happy. When in her company, everyone seemed to enjoy themselves so much the more. At the time, I was convinced that I was in love with her. She and I began to take many rides, alone, without the others. Sometimes, on these excursions, we would dismount to allow the horses to rest."

Elizabeth reached for his hand, and Darcy anxiously received it. Apparently, she sensed his distress and he was grateful for her comfort. He closed his eyes in shame as the memories from being with Collette began flooding his mind. They were still so vivid. It had been the first time he had ever experienced such an awakening, apart from his dreams, but Miss Collette Caldecott constituted the first time he had dared to act upon those desires.

Clearing his throat, Darcy attempted to speak, but faltered, unable to choose the proper words. "Elizabeth, I..." Squeezing his hand, Elizabeth brushed his knuckles with her thumb. "Hmm... I... I compromised Collette."

Her eyebrows knitted together. "How is it that you compromised her? What do you mean by compromised?"

Pulling his hand from hers, he moved it to cover his eyes, even as his other hand lay upon his chest and formed into a fist. "We would tease and indulge in nonsense. I found myself captivated by her every look and gesture. We would often wrestle on the grass and partake in all sorts of child's play. Eventually it became more than mere play."

Elizabeth tensed as a quiver of fear crept into her heart. She waited, but he remained silent. Warily, she asked, "Do you not wish to speak of this any further, Fitzwilliam?"

He shook his head. "No, Lizzy, I do want to continue." Sighing, he then said, "I compromised Collette in that I kissed her. At first, she did not allow me to do so, but I kept pressing her for a kiss. I kept encouraging the situation."

"Did you force her, Fitzwilliam?"

With a distant look of contemplation, he replied, "Well...no. Yet, there is more than the kiss, Lizzy."

Elizabeth felt queasy. "Please, Fitzwilliam, just say it."

"I had carnal knowledge of her."

"Carnal knowledge, what do you mean by carnal knowledge? Are you saying you made love to Collette, as a husband does with his wife?" She held her breath, but she knew she would have to face it if he told her that he had.

"No, I did not, at least not in that sense of the expression."

"Fitzwilliam, please," Elizabeth cried, "you are torturing me. Just say it and have it over with."

"I felt... I touched her in ways that a man should only fondle his wife."

Elizabeth processed these words in her mind. *...He touched her in a way that a man should only fondle his wife? Was he saying that was all, or was there more?* With a sharp intake of breath, she closed her eyes. Did she truly want to be familiar with all the details? Yet, she felt compelled to know, and thus Elizabeth slowly opened her eyes and forged onward.

"What ways, Fitzwilliam?"

"Lizzy…"

"If you do not wish to say, then I shall accept it."

He pinched his brows between his thumb and forefinger. "My hands became familiar with her body."

With trepidation, she asked, "Did this happen only once?"

He shook his head, bringing his other hand to cover his face. He choked out, "No!"

"What happened that you never married Collette?"

Uncovering his face, Darcy quickly reached for her hand, and she eagerly caught his within hers. Elizabeth sensed that he had relaxed a little. "In mid-August, Chaffin sent me to the shearing house. The building is immense, and there is a razor room in the back of it. You shall see it when we shear the sheep in the spring. Chaffin asked me to go there to retrieve his riding crop. He claimed that he had mislaid it there the week before, and he worried for it. He was most adamant that this mission need be done right away. So I saddled my horse to go on an errand I thought quite bizarre." Darcy turned on his side, still grasping Elizabeth's hand, as he looked intently into her eyes. "Chaffin never misplaces anything."

Darcy again rolled upon his back and stared overhead. "I saw two horses tied up as I came to the house. I recognized that they belonged to the Caldecotts. When I walked onto the shearing floor, I expected to see who was within, but no one was about. I simply made my way to the razor room," he sighed deeply, "and there lay Collette and George Wickham, stark naked, in the act of union."

Darcy turned his head once more, and he and Elizabeth looked deeply into each other's eyes. "What did you do, Fitzwilliam? Did they hear you? Did they see you?"

"Collette did not, she was…well…but Wickham did. He looked at me with gloating triumphant."

Intrigued, Elizabeth asked in full curiosity, "What did you do?"

"I simply shut the door, instinctively walked back to my horse, and returned to the house."

She nodded. "Was Mr. Chaffin angry with you for not bringing his crop back?"

"Elizabeth, there was never a riding crop in that room. He invented that reason to send me on an errand. How he knew, I still do not understand. I could not bear to look at him for some time. I felt he knew my every sin. He had come in search of me on many occasions throughout the summer, and I fear he clearly witnessed many of my transgressions."

"Fitzwilliam, do you regret that you lost Collette? Do you regret that she was not true to you and that she did not become your wife?"

His eyes widened in astonishment. "No, Elizabeth, no. I do not. That day taught me many things. My greatest sin, Lizzy, is that, if I had not discovered Collette with Wickham, I could have very easily been the man on that floor with her. I still cannot bear to think of what I allowed myself to do that summer. I went against the very principles that my father had painstakingly taught me for so many years."

"And what did he teach you, Fitzwilliam?"

"He taught me to honour women, Lizzy, yet I selfishly desired to fulfil my lust. Thus, I did, in essence, compromise Collette."

"Ha! Fitzwilliam, I deny that you were blameworthy at all. No, from what I have seen of the woman, there is little doubt in my mind that she is the one who compromised you!"

He looked at her queerly. "That is exactly what Fitzwilliam said."

"Well, if Richard said it, then it must be so."

"Elizabeth," Darcy said, rising up on his elbow while staring at her, "You think very highly of my cousin?"

"Yes, I do."

He closed his eyes tightly for a brief moment, his mind painfully troubled. He asked in dread, "In all honesty, Elizabeth, if Fitzwilliam had asked you to marry him while you were at Hunsford, and had not let his position as the younger son of an Earl hold him back, would you have said yes?"

Now, she was shocked. "Fitzwilliam Darcy, where are such notions coming from? Why would you entertain such a foolish idea?"

"Please, Elizabeth, answer my foolish question. I have eyes, Elizabeth. I see how Richard admires you, and I see how highly you think of him." Darcy paused and inhaled deeply, mortified by his jealousy and his need to ascertain that his wife did not love his cousin. "I feel... I feel...oh, Elizabeth..."

With one raised brow, she looked piercingly into his eyes. "Fitzwilliam, I am in love with you. I have never been in love with Colonel Fitzwilliam. Yes, I find him charming and engaging company, and I am fond of him, but I can attest to the fact that I have *never* loved him. When you gave me your letter that morning in Rosings Park, I was agitated more than you will ever know."

Darcy averted his gaze for a moment. He remembered all too well the disastrous proposal and thought that he knew just how agitated she could become.

"I was in a very bad temper when I returned to the Parsonage. Charlotte told me that I had missed you when you had come to take your leave, yet you did not wait long. She said, however, that the colonel had waited for the length of an hour, hoping for my return, and he had even announced that he planned to walk out to search for me. Mariah and Charlotte thought I would take the news that I had missed him hard. Yet, I secretly rejoiced in it. I desired only to read your letter, compelled to discover what you had to say."

He smiled and asked, "Truly?"

Nodding merrily, she answered, "Truly, Mr. Darcy. I have often thought back on this, and I have come to the conclusion that I felt a strong attraction from the moment my eyes set upon you at the Meryton Assembly, but you had wounded my pride, and worse, ruined Jane's chances with Bingley." She noticed his face darken. "Oh, no, Fitzwilliam, you will not sulk over that misdeed again. I will not allow it!"

"Lizzy, there is something else I must tell you."

She sobered and looked surprised.

"Lizzy, Mrs. Reynolds told me some weeks ago that Sally saw you and Richard in a compromising embrace, and she said that you had kissed him."

"What? And you are just telling me such a tale? Do you believe it?" Her eyes grew wide in disbelief. "You do believe it!"

"No, at least not completely. That is to say, I do not feel that you are guilty."

"Well, thank you, Fitzwilliam, for your vote of confidence. I have never kissed your cousin except on his cheek and that was the night of the fencing accident?"

"Why ever did you kiss him on the cheek that night?"

"Remember, I told you that I did not act at all composed. In fact, my love, I am sure you would have been shocked and dismayed at my behaviour. Dr. Lowry insisted that I leave the ballroom, yet I would not. Colonel Fitzwilliam had to forcefully remove me and restrain me. I tried in every way I could to return to your side, and I am ashamed to confess that I pinched Richard's arms very hard in an attempt to make him release me. I am sure he had bruises for a week thereafter. Yet, Richard did drag me away from the gawking faces of the servants, physically compelling me along the hallway, until I fainted from such consuming agitation."

Darcy stared at her in surprise. She continued, "Richard picked me up and carried me to your study, where he gave me some wine. He knew how upset and truly frightened for your life I was. Therefore, he began to tell me about how angry you were when I did not accept your marriage proposal at Hunsford."

"He told you *what*?"

"Oh, yes, he said how you were in such a foul mood when you returned to Rosings that you were not fit to be reckoned with. He told me how you did not even pay attention to Lady Catherine's wishes, and how, therefore, she became incensed because of it, lecturing everyone the whole time about punctuality and propriety. You, my love, vexed her extremely."

Darcy smiled. "Yes, and she remains so."

Elizabeth returned his smile. "That night, Richard informed me that I was the only woman who had ever made you get off your high horse, and he told me how I captivated you. Your cousin made me forget, for a few brief moments, that my husband lay near death's door. He treated me so well, offering me such comfort, helping to calm me down. That is why I kissed him on the cheek, and I told him that he was the best of men. And I meant it, Fitzwilliam. At that moment, he was a godsend."

Darcy covered his face with his hands and in a muffled voice, exclaimed, "Oh, Elizabeth, I have been such a fool."

"Yes, Fitzwilliam, you have. Now, is this the part where you wish to ask for my forgiveness?"

He silently nodded beneath the pavilion of his hands.

"You are forgiven!"

Revealing his face, he glanced over to her. "Pray, Lizzy, how can you forgive me so easily? I saw you run away from Richard, crying. I know I hurt you again this evening."

"Yes, I was rather upset. It did hurt me to see how you spent most of the evening with the Caldecotts, but your aunt came in search of me and helped me to understand the situation. She also encouraged me to seek you out and return to the ballroom to dance."

"What did she say to you?"

"She told me..." Elizabeth raised her brows and bit her lip in hesitation. "Lady Matlock told me that Collette Caldecott is a...a *whore* and has always been one. Hence, she convinced me that I had no reason to cry."

Darcy looked at her, utterly shocked. "*My aunt* called her a *whore*?"

"Well, I think her exact wording was *a wealthy whore*. She said the rationale behind Collette getting away with such lewd behaviour, is that, for the gentry, wealth covers a multitude of sins. I do indeed find your aunt to be very similar to Richard. In fact, I like your Aunt Adie very much!"

Raking his hand through his curls, he exclaimed, "Oh, Elizabeth, how can you look at me the same, knowing what you now know of me?"

"Really Fitzwilliam, if you would have only told me this from the start, so much hurt and anger could have been avoided. I feared you were still attracted to Collette. She *is* beautiful."

"I find no beauty in her." He paused for a moment, recollecting a conversation he had had earlier. "Oh, I found out how Collette came to have my ring, yet I still cannot fathom how my grandmother's ring wound up in her possession." Darcy pursed his lips to the side and shook his head. "Her father's satchel was next to mine while at the coalmine. I must have accidentally placed my ring within his bag. He recognized it and asked Collette to ride over to return it."

"Is that why you spent so much time talking to Mr. Caldecott tonight?" Without waiting for an answer, Elizabeth recalled her conversation with Ashton Caldecott and his insinuation about the special gift his father and Darcy had for his sister. Quickly she exclaimed, "And, what about Collette's birthday?"

"I have one more confession, Elizabeth. I have acted high-handed, yet again. I offered to give Yvette to Mr. Caldecott, for him to present her to Collette for a birthday gift. He claimed that he would like to procure such a maid for his daughter. Caldecott and I went to see Collette to present her with the offer. Her father told her you could not speak the language at all. Collette is delighted. She thinks she is taking something away from you. I must admit, Lizzy, I allowed her to think it. In fact, I helped it along."

"Why, Mr. Darcy, I thought disguise of every sort is your abhorrence."

He grinned. "Lizzy, can you imagine the combination of Yvette and Collette? With Collette having such a maid, I am reminded of the game of roulette. Wagering on which one shall win the power struggle is a gamble. I would be hard pressed to know where to place my bet!"

Elizabeth squealed in glee at the thought of Collette having her hide scrubbed raw and cleaned clear off her bones.

After hours of exchanging confidences, husband and wife finally found sleep at four in the morning. Elizabeth had never bothered to put on her nightgown. Her undergarments sufficed. Likewise, Darcy never changed into a fresh nightshirt. He still wore the breeches and shirt in which he had danced. Just before dozing off, Darcy confessed one more act of ungentlemanly conduct to his fair lady. He informed her that during the waltz, he had manoeuvred Miss Caldecott through the multitude of dancers, out into the open air of the terrace, and very firmly sat her bottom upon the hard stone floor, leaving Collette crying in his wake. Elizabeth sleepily revealed a toothy grin and then said in drowsiness, "I am glad to hear it. Someone should have given her a good set down long ago. If they had, maybe she would never have turned into such a wretched creature. I love you, Fitzwilliam Darcy."

Darcy kissed her on her forehead and professed his love as well. He felt better than he had in a very long time. There were no more skeletons to fear in his closet, and his jealousy had fled. His albatross, had indeed, fallen from his neck.

~*~

Chapter Twenty

Discernment and Uncertainties

At seven in the morning, after only three hours of rest, a loud knock awakened Darcy from his deep slumber. Groggily, he peered over at his wife. She slept soundly. The rapid succession of blows persisted. Yawning, he threw back the covers and made his way to the door. Georgiana awaited his discovery.

"Brother, it is imperative that I speak with you. May I come in, or would you rather dress and come to my room."

Wiping the sleep from his eyes, he asked softly, "Pray, Georgie, what is so important that you feel you must wake me?"

"Brother, may I come in? I do not wish to speak in the hall." Gesturing silence with a finger pressed to his lips, he swung open the door to allow her access.

Georgiana took in his appearance, twisting her lips as she suppressed a smirk. She had seldom, if ever, seen him dressed in knee breeches with no stockings. She found it to be quite comical. It was not the fact that she had never witnessed his bare legs before, for she had, on many occasions when he wore his nightshirt and robe in her presence. Yet, beholding the short-legged trousers and his half-tucked in shirttail made him seem, somehow, less fastidious, revealing the informal side of her brother that she rarely observed.

Clasping his sister's hand in his, Darcy led her to the dressing chamber area at the farthest end near the closet. "Please speak softly, Georgie. I do not wish to disturb Elizabeth." Squinting and then widening his eyes sporadically, Darcy tried to awaken in an attempt to focus on her face as she spoke.

Taking extra care to speak in low tones so as not to awaken her sister-in-law, Georgiana whispered, "Brother, Richard is leaving for London today, and I desire to go with him. I have written Mrs. Annesley and have received an express from her in reply the evening before last. She has agreed to come and stay with me as soon as she can. It is acceptable to Richard, and he requests to speak with you before departing, but we must leave soon." She reached forth, placed her hand on her brother's arm, and expressed earnestly, "I am sorry for having awakened you, but it is urgent that you grant your permission now." She abruptly thrust a piece of paper into his hand. "Here is the letter from Mrs. Annesley."

Darcy took the missive and carefully unfolded it. Rubbing his whiskered chin, he strained to read the neatly scribed words in the dim light. Looking up with a gentle sigh, he said, "Georgie, I do not understand why this is so pressing. Jane and Charles leave later this morning. You could very easily go with them and be in their company. Their trip will not be as strenuous as Richard's will. He needs to report upon arrival. What will happen if Mrs. Annesley cannot come immediately? James and Elisha are here. There is no one in London at present, except the servants at Ackerley House. Even Mrs. Averill is visiting with her family up north, so, who is there to cook for you?"

"Really, Brother, I can go to the kitchen just as well as anyone. Food is always to be had at Ackerley."

"Umm," Darcy sighed as he raked his fingers through his dishevelled curls. "Where did you say Fitzwilliam is right now?"

Impatiently, Georgiana replied, "He is in the breakfast room."

"Very well, I shall call for Chaffin to help me dress, and then I shall go down. Please, be quiet as you leave, Georgie. Elizabeth has not been getting enough rest."

She again apologized for disturbing their slumber, thanked Darcy and promised to be as silent as a mouse when leaving. Dolefully, Georgiana felt that she was the cause for Elizabeth's inability to sleep. It must be so, since her sister-in-law spent all of her pin money in order to buy Wickham's silence. She felt horrible as she slipped out of the chamber, fearing that her stained reputation would somehow become public preceding her coming out. She did not feel secure in trusting Caroline Bingley with their secret. Georgiana was not sure she would be able to survive it if it were made public. Elizabeth must have been distraught, indeed, to unburden herself to Miss Bingley, and she worried for her sister-in-law's welfare if her brother were to find out. She had witnessed the strain between them the previous night when Elizabeth, crying, broke free from Richard. She was sure it was due to the fact that Fitzwilliam had Collette in his arms. What was to be done?

~*~

In less than no time, Darcy, properly attired, made his way to the breakfast room. As he entered, the colonel took a last sip of his coffee. Richard grunted upon seeing his cousin's approach. Condescendingly, he stated, "My Darcy, it must be important for you to be up so early to seek me out. Usually it is the other way around, with me always grovelling at your feet, begging for a moment of your *precious time*."

The colonel's words cut Darcy to the quick. He knew he had not treated him well for the last several weeks. Resentment had clouded his judgement, causing him, more often than not, to impart an inhospitable air towards his cousin. Darcy frowned while meeting Richard's stare and then tried to respond. "Yes…well…I have been…well…"

"*Jealous?*"

Darcy looked narrowly at him. "Fitzwilliam, you must admit you have given me cause."

His cousin sniffed derisively as he shook his head and nonchalantly flicked a speck of lint from his trousers. "I suppose what brings you here is Georgiana's wish to accompany me to London. She wishes desperately to go. I am not sure why, exactly, but I think she feels responsible in some way for the friction between you and Elizabeth which, at times, has *oft* been felt by us all." Obviously hurt, Richard continued as he flippantly slung out, "Of course, Georgie need not feel that way at all, because you and I both know that *I* am *entirely* at fault for *your* marital discord."

Wearily, Darcy heaved a deep sigh as he pulled out a chair. Once seated, he strove to rid the sleepiness from his mind by rubbing his face with both hands. Again, he sighed as he noticed Richard watching him from the corner of his eye, waiting for him to speak.

"Fitzwilliam," Darcy began weakly, "can we…I mean…well, could we let it be behind us now? I am sorry for my brooding manner, as Bingley likes to call it, towards you of late. It is unpardonable, but I do ask for your forgiveness. I shall attempt to be a more considerate cousin to you, as you have always been to me."

Slumped in his chair, with his arms folded across his chest and looking pensively at his empty plate, Richard slowly moved his head up and down. He had concluded that this was more than likely all he should anticipate from his cousin—convinced that it was decidedly the best apology Darcy could muster. To his surprise, Darcy unexpectedly went on.

"I have handled things preposterously. You warned me not to let my reservations for society's opinions get the better of me, yet I did just that. Besides Elizabeth, you are my closest friend. You, Elizabeth, and Georgiana mean the world to me. You have never let me down. You understand me like no other. You are the brother I never had."

Unconsciously, Richard pressed his lips together as he turned his head to the side in an attempt to control his emotions. The constriction of his throat nearly overtook his composure. Darcy was changing. This was the second time he had expressed his gratitude. Yet, this time, Richard realized he was not doing it as a token of thanks for saving his life. Instead, Darcy was expressing his remorse with heartfelt sentiments that meant more to him than his cousin would ever know. Richard was moved beyond words.

Silence ensued as each man's heart silently testified to themselves of their love, one for the other. Finally, Richard nodded his acceptance. Shifting about in his chair, he cleared his throat and said, "I…I thank you, Darcy. I care greatly for all…" his voice cracked, "…of you as well."

In a strained voice, Darcy answered, "Yes…well…I am concerned about sending Georgie with you. What is to be done if Mrs. Annesley cannot come right away? You must report for duty, and Georgie will then be at Ackerley with only the servants. Thus, she would become housebound."

Richard saw his point. For what purpose should Georgiana go, only to remain a prisoner in the house, with no companion about? While pondering the possibility that Mrs. Annesley might be detained, a logical solution came to his mind. "Darcy, why not see if Elizabeth and Jane would allow Miss Catherine to go to Ackerley and offer Georgie companionship until her companion can come. That way, if Miss Catherine travels with the Bingleys, Georgie would only have one night and day in the house without company."

Darcy asked, "Could you not take Miss Catherine with you?"

"No, I must leave within the hour. Georgiana is packing now. Besides, I want the privacy to speak with Georgie about her concerns."

"Very well, I shall go and seek permission from Bingley and Jane. I am sure it will be all right with them to take Kitty. I suppose, if need be, we could come to town earlier than we had planned. I shall meet you in the courtyard before you go if I do not see you sooner." Darcy arose, but, before taking leave, he turned to his cousin. "I spoke with Elizabeth last night and told her everything."

Richard looked at him soberly and nodded. "I am glad that you did, Darcy. Does she feel better now?"

"Yes. Your mother did a lot to assuage her concern over Collette."

Lifting an eyebrow, Colonel Fitzwilliam chuckled. "Oh, my mother has made her feelings about Collette known, has she? Then I am sure Elizabeth now knows what kind of a woman Miss Caldecott *truly* is.

"Mother cannot stand Collette. I am not sure if you realize this, Darcy, but Collette and Hazel had a little fling long before *we* came onto the scene." Darcy's surprised expression revealed to the colonel that his cousin had *not* known. Solemnly, Richard resumed, "That autumn, following our *rather* eventful summer, Mother somehow found out about Collette's situation of being with child, and she feared you or I might have been involved—that we might have been the child's father. I suspect Mrs. Chalmers had told her details concerning Collette's pregnancy, since that lady is a good friend to Mrs. Caldecott. I assured her that you had nothing to do with it, and I never mentioned my knowledge about Wickham, either. But mother knows about me. I freely admitted it to her because I desired to do the right thing, even knowing that it might be George's babe as well as mine. Collette refused to marry me. Instead, she went to London and found some help in that quarter. Mother told me it devastated Mrs. Caldecott, but Mr. Caldecott insisted that his daughter would not marry so low when she could have any man in England. I think he held out with high hopes that you were going to marry his daughter, and I think Collette harboured them as well. She has never recovered from your disinterest in her either. She suffers, you know, from an overly-inflated case of egotism. She is a sensualist if there ever were one and is ever self-seeking, self-idolized, and in addition, Miss Caldecott is," the colonel paused and shook his head as a rueful smile played upon his lips before concluding with, "full of self-conceit and self-flattery. Her infatuation with you continues to this day."

Slowly shaking his head, Darcy stared at his cousin in disbelief. "I never knew. Why did you not tell me all of this before now?"

Snorting again with the same rueful expression exposed upon his features, the colonel rejoined, "Why have you not ever told me that you caught Collette and Wickham rendering *the beast with two backs*? I imagine it was for the same reason that neither of us spoke of it. We were too sickened by the whole sordid business. I assumed you knew since you ceased having anything to do with her. We woke up to reality that year, and I, for one, am glad. It was indeed painful, but it has made me a better man because of it. Yet, I must always thank the *King's army* for the development of the other half of my character." He smiled wholeheartedly at his own, awkward jest.

Grinning warmly at Richard's sarcasm, Darcy stated, "Yes...well...I shall see you soon." He arose and strode out of the room, heading off, regretfully, to wake Bingley. Advancing forth, Darcy reflected upon the fact that every bit of money he had ever given to George Wickham was well worth it, as it had saved him from the clutches of such a vile, deceitful woman who was reckless beyond imagination. Thus, it clearly proved that Lydia, and other frivolous girls like her, were quite innocent in comparison to the likes of Miss Caldecott.

~*~

Elizabeth had awakened almost immediately after Darcy had left their chamber. Hurriedly, she washed and dressed for the day. Leaving the chamber, she walked down the massive hall, trying to remember which way she needed to turn after descending the stairs in order to find the breakfast room, when, from behind, Lord Hazelton called her name. Startled by his sudden appearance, she halted her progress.

"Oh, Elizabeth, I am so sorry to have frightened you. Are you going down to break your fast?"

"Yes, I suppose so, but I am also in search of Fitzwilliam."

"Please, allow me to escort you." Holding out his arm in invitation, Lord Hazelton watched her hesitate but then comply. As they began to navigate the stairs, the Viscount brought his other hand over and rested it firmly on top of Elizabeth's as he said, "Let us do be careful. Darcy would never forgive me if anything untoward happened to his bride."

Mary Sherwood

Elizabeth felt a wave of nausea settle in the pit of her stomach. What was it about Lord Hazelton that made her feel this way? She knew he was a snob, but she had had adequate experience around snobbish people all of her life. She felt that perhaps it was because he was being more than just self-important, and that he was patronizing her. She had experienced condescending people before, so she did not think that was the sole reason for her unease. There was Mrs. Long and her daughters, her cousin Mr. Collins, Caroline Bingley, George Wickham, Lady Catherine and most recently, Collette. Of course, she apprehended that next to the others, Wickham and Collette were in a class all their own. Even though these people shared the similarity of arrogant superiority and both displayed continual rudeness through veiled cordiality, there was something markedly different when it came to the heir of Matlock, but she could not put her finger on exactly what it was.

When they entered the breakfast room, they found no one else present. Elizabeth instantly began to turn back, but was forestalled from disengaging her arm from Hazelton's as he kept a tightened hand upon hers. "Whoa there, my dear girl! You are flighty today—akin to a green filly breaking into a mad dash. Did you not desire to eat?"

"Oh," she cried, looking at her husband's oldest cousin. "I would rather wait for Fitzwilliam. I had hoped he would be within. But, alas, he is not. So—"

"So, you shall wait for him and everyone else while sitting here and keeping me company." He removed the firm grip of his hand and pulled out a chair, gesturing that she take the seat.

Dutifully, Elizabeth decided to sit, since she had no idea where her husband might be, and sitting would be preferable to standing next to his Lordship. She walked around in front of the chair and began to lower herself into the seat. Lord Hazelton, unbeknownst to her, had manoeuvred the chair further back with his foot, inching it hind ward ever so slightly. As she felt herself plummeting, Elizabeth shrieked, her arms flailing in the air. "Oh, my!" called out the Viscount as he leaned in close to catch her. "There, my dear girl, I have you!"

Elizabeth flushed with embarrassment. The fall itself had played a part in the tension she currently felt, but not nearly as much as the sensation of James's hands on the sides of her breasts as he slowly lifted her onto the chair. Tension filled her body. He never moved his hands from their position while helping her up. Instead, it seemed as though he pressed them more firmly against her breasts. With his fingers spread wide, he used her chest for the leverage he needed in hoisting her.

"Ups-a-daisy!" he exclaimed in amusement.

Pure mortification flooded through Elizabeth when he settled her in the chair. She froze in place as the Viscount's hands lingered a few seconds, lightly caressing the sides of her womanly figure. Her chest heaved, not only from the fright of the fall, but also from the terror of Lord Hazelton's needless attentions.

Lord Hazelton enjoyed her distress excessively. He found it enticing, delicious, and intoxicating to his senses. And, while leaning over and glimpsing at her profile with his hands securely against the sides of her breasts, he asked good naturedly, "Are you unwell, Elizabeth? May I get you something?"

Just at that pivotal moment, when Elizabeth began to violently twist her body in an attempt to free herself and command him to stop, she heard voices nearing and noticed that Lord Hazelton quickly slid one hand up and over the left side of her torso onto her shoulder while the other hand quickly patted her plumpness before taking it away entirely.

He heard her gasp. A lascivious smile curled upon his lips. Miss Bingley and Elisha came in to see the future Earl of Matlock standing by Elizabeth with his one hand resting on her shoulder. "Ah, ladies, we almost had near disaster. Our dear Elizabeth practically fell to the floor when she misjudged the position of her chair. Luckily, I caught her before any real harm could befall her."

"Oh, Elizabeth," Lady Hazelton professed with feigned solicitude, "fortunate for you that *my sweet* was here, He is always so attentive to the needs of others. You are such a gentleman, my darling." Lord Hazelton smiled at his wife and Miss Bingley.

Visibly upset, Elizabeth arose unsteadily. Quickly composing herself, she said to the others, "If you will excuse me, I find myself no longer hungry." Giving a quick nod and nothing more, she barrelled out of the room.

"Why, Lord Hazelton," asked Elisha, "did our new cousin not even offer her appreciation for your gallantry?"

"No, she did not, my pet, but I am not affronted. The fall truly upset her. She seems a clumsy sort of girl." He moved to the sideboard and began to butter a muffin.

Caroline smiled, feeling that she was finally around people who truly understood the gravity of the situation she had to live with. She felt most fortunate that she had been invited to the ball that Darcy's aunt and uncle had hosted. Her attendance could only advance her connections into the upper circles, bringing new acquaintances and, more importantly, additional gentleman into her life.

Elisha noted Miss Bingley's reaction to her husband's words and thought she might be able to wheedle something worthwhile from the woman. "Oh, Miss Bingley," she purred, "your brother is married to Mrs. Darcy's sister, is that correct?"

Sniffing most profoundly and thrilled by the notice of Lady Hazelton, Caroline answered, "Oh, yes, he is married to Eliza's older sister, Jane."

Lady Hazelton laid her hand lightly upon Caroline's forearm and implored, "So, I suppose you are familiar with Darcy's courtship of his wife. We would be delighted if you would join us when we are back in Town for the Season, so you could relate and expound upon it. Do say you will come. I am sure we shall find the story immensely regaling."

Her ladyship's attentions put Caroline immediately at ease and her heart soared at the invitation. "Oh, I am most grateful, and I am, indeed, familiar with the circumstances of their courtship to some extent," she paused, her voice dropping to a whisper, "but not all."

"Then, it is settled between us. I feel you and I shall become fast friends." Elisha smiled brilliantly to Miss Bingley, yet, in all reality, inside, she shrewishly looked down her nose upon the social climber. What real connections did Caroline Bingley have, after all? Besides Fitzwilliam Darcy's relationship to her brother through such an ill-considered marriage, she had none. She was nothing more than a *nouvea riche* daughter of a *tradesman*.

~*~

Elizabeth raced up the stairs, her heart pounding wildly in her ears. After bolting the door to her chamber, she leaned against it, tilting her head back in despair. Tears of frustration and anger began to trickle down her flushed cheeks as she closed her eyes tightly. Her lips quivering as she bitterly reflected on how smoothly everything had progressed during their visit— until now. She desired to make a good impression for her husband. Lady Catherine already stood as a thorn in their flesh, and she had had great hopes that the honour of the ball would reunite her husband with this side of his family in an effort to calm the Fitzwilliam's familial waters so to speak. Even though Darcy had made excuses to explain why his aunt and uncle could not attend their wedding, Elizabeth had not been fooled. She grasped the importance of this visit with Earl and Countess of Matlock and hoped it would be successful, eventually leading to reconciliation with Lady Catherine as well. If she were to tell her husband of what had just transpired in the breakfast room with Lord Hazelton, it would only complicate their relations further and dissolve all that had been accomplished thus far. Except for Darcy, who would believe her? She knew Lord Hazelton had deliberately moved the chair in order to cause her fall and create an opportunity to touch her in such an intimate manner, or was she mistaken? Was it just a fluke that his hands caught hold of her in such an inappropriate manner? Yet, it could not have been a mere coincidence that they lingered and stroked her the way they did. Could it? It all happened so suddenly, yet it seemed so protracted in her memory. What could she do? She felt violated and soiled, just as she had when Wickham's lips brushed against her ear, and he whispered of how he desired her. She shuddered in revulsion at what Lord Hazelton had done. That, combined with the sordid memories of Wickham, made her jump all the more when a loud thud shook the door. Having no idea how long she had been leaning against it, she feared that Lord Hazelton might have come to enquire after her welfare. The knocking became louder. With her fingertips, she hastily brushed away her tears and, after taking a few deep breaths, enquired, "What is wanted?"

"Lizzy, it is Jane. I wish to know if you desire to go down to breakfast with me and Charles." The door flung open and Elizabeth flew into her sister's arms, burying her head on her sister's shoulder. "Oh, Jane, I love you so dearly!"

Jane and Charles's surprised expression quickly turned to concern when they discerned Elizabeth's tear-stained face and her frantic tone. "Elizabeth," Jane asked, "what is the matter? What has happened?"

Lifting her head, Elizabeth looked deeply into her sister's eyes. Choking back tears, she whispered, "Oh, nothing, it is just that I am so sad that I have had scarcely any time to visit with you, and you are to leave in a few hours. I cannot bear it." Elizabeth began crying anew.

Jane eyed Charles, and he her. Both knew that something else must be amiss besides Elizabeth's sorrow over Jane's departure. Bingley spoke up, "Perhaps I might ask Darcy if we might return to Pemberley for a few days longer before leaving for London."

Elizabeth raised her head and nodded, looking at Charles through her tears. "That would be lovely, if you would."

"Oh, but, Charles!" Jane exclaimed, anxiety etching her features, "Mr. Darcy, I mean Fitzwilliam, desires for us to depart today so we can deliver Kitty to Georgiana by tomorrow evening."

"Oh, my!" Bingley uttered in regret. "I am so sorry, Elizabeth. It simply slipped my mind that Darcy requested that favour of us just an hour previously."

A look of surprise crossed Elizabeth's brow regarding the sudden change of travel plans, but, putting on a brave face, she endeavoured to sound cheerful. "Then we shall have to content ourselves with what little time we have this morning before you leave and then look forward to our time together in London. Fitzwilliam tells me the Season may start late this year due to Easter falling mid-April. So, we shall have almost a month to enjoy ourselves before our agendas become too hectic."

Jane and Charles smiled at her, happy to see her recovering from whatever had upset her. Bingley wondered, silently, if his sister-in-law's misery arose from Darcy having told her of his former love. He felt terrible for them. He lacked knowledge of all the particulars, but he thought it appalling that Elizabeth and Darcy were experiencing grief so early in their marriage. It must have been a blow for Elizabeth to learn of Darcy's former love. Yet, surely, they would be over the worst of whatever had besieged them in a short while. He believed that both his brother-in-law and sister-in-law were truly in love with one another.

Elizabeth accompanied Charles and Jane to the dining room, where they found some of the overnight guests leisurely congregating for the morning meal. Having time to reflect, Elizabeth wondered about Caroline accompanying Elisha into the breakfast room earlier, instead of joining the other company. As far as she knew, Caroline had only met Elisha the day before, so it surprised her when she saw Miss Bingley on Lady Hazelton's arm... invited to partake of the meal with the family in their private breakfast room. Then, she wondered if Darcy would come in search of her in the general dining hall.

Not too many of the guests were about with only a small number sitting at the great table. Elizabeth leaned into Jane and whispered, "Few are in attendance this morning. Perhaps it is still too early, but that is to our benefit as we can have most any seat at the table." After filling their plates at the sideboard, they chose to sit at the far end, off to themselves. Charles pulled out a chair for each woman, waiting until they were comfortably seated before taking his own seat. While eating their meal, he and Jane told Elizabeth more about Darcy arranging for Kitty to join Georgiana and stay with her in town. Evidently, Georgiana had decided to return to London earlier than planned, and Darcy did not wish for her to be alone for too long until her lady's companion could come to join her. Elizabeth considered the arrangement and thought this was in the best interest of both girls. Thus, she was in favour of the proposal, which would grant Kitty an opportunity to further her acquaintance with Georgiana.

As Jane spoke to her sister, Elizabeth perceived Bingley's eyes rise as he hastily stood. Turning to see what had caught her brother-in-law's attention, she observed Miss Caldecott coming towards her. Collette looked radiant, as usual, with some of her golden locks draped to one side, smartly fashioned with a beautiful ribbon. *Another of Yvette's creations*, Elizabeth imagined with a twinkle in her eye.

Emanating confidence, Collette declared, "Eliza darling, you cannot imagine how happy I am to have Yvette. She is a dream and such an expert in her profession. I feel that Father and Fitz have pampered me excessively. I am sure you know that today is my birthday. Fitz says he thinks of it every March. I just wanted you to know," she looked directly at Elizabeth, "I am utterly tickled with his notice and do offer my condolences to you for having never learnt the language of romance. You will never experience how lovely Fitz's voice is when he speaks that language. The memory of his lips upon me while the French words tripped off his tongue, tickling my skin, is ever vivid and still causes my body to quiver. His superb accent captures the passion which is the essence of the French people."

"Ah! I am so glad you find Yvette to your liking, then," exclaimed Elizabeth with raised brows, smiling lips, and a hint of daring in her eyes.

"She arrived as a birthday present for me as well, albeit, an early one. But, alas, you are correct, the language is a barrier, and, as you say, I could not possibly appreciate the passionate spirit of the French. Thus, I will never enjoy my husband's rich voice speaking words of love in that tongue. Yet, I find that when there is a weakness in one area, there usually is strength to offset it in another. The language that *I* find very passionate—one in which my husband is quite fluent and wherewith I am perfectly familiar in comprehending—is the language which requires no words at all." Elizabeth's triumphal rebuttal rendered Collette speechless. As she stood motionless, observing the fiery sparkle in Mrs. Fitzwilliam Darcy's eyes, Elizabeth elaborated further, "Yvette is indeed a conscientious gift from my husband to you and, I dare say, she is a person whom you will come to cherish for her determination, initiative, and uncompromisingly high standards. She is an *all-encompassing* maid. Regrettably, I shall have to have a lesser maid to attend to me. Happy birthday, Collette! I am glad Fitzwilliam remembered your special day. And, *Cole*, are you quite certain it was Mr. Darcy who whispered French endearments to you? If I am not mistaken, I distinctly remember another gentleman, who, after a visit with my family, bid us farewell in the French tongue." She paused for effect, and then moved to reveal the man's identity. "Mr. George Wickham."

Although Elizabeth veiled her words concerning her former maid's attributes, the birthday greeting and smile that now appeared on her face were genuine and communicated in unconcealed honesty. Nevertheless, she had added the snippet of a comment concerning her brother-in-law, George Wickham, for good measure.

Flustered that Elizabeth had the upper hand in their verbal exchange, Collette, in response, merely raised her chin and tossed her head back, shrugging one shoulder forward before taking her leave. Bingley's eyes loomed large with the realization that *this* woman, who had so boldly approached Elizabeth, was none other than the *other woman* Darcy and Colonel Fitzwilliam had spoken of in the library the previous night. She was the woman who had ridden St. George in the razor room within the shearing house! Bingley felt dumbfounded at the shamelessness of Miss Caldecott speaking about Darcy romantically fondling her body with his lips, and he found himself equally flabbergasted by his sister-in-law's explicit response to Collette's taunt. Jane's exasperated voice, however, roused him from his shocked state, and he sat down once more.

"Elizabeth, who is that woman, and what in Heaven's name is she inferring about Mr. Darcy?" Astonishment enveloped Bingley, yet again, when hearing the agitation in his angel's tone and especially with reference to the heavens.

Before Elizabeth had a chance to answer Jane's question, she caught sight of her husband stepping aside within the threshold, allowing Miss Caldecott access in quitting the room. Collette endeavoured to speak with him, but he boldly turned his head, failing to acknowledge her presence. Incensed, Collette gnashed an expletive through her teeth and departed in a huff.

All eyes rose to meet Darcy's countenance when he addressed Elizabeth. They could easily read the ill temper in his demeanour. "Elizabeth, I have been searching everywhere for you. Elisha said you were nearly hurt, something about missing your chair while being seated. May I presume that you are well?"

He asked the question with the warmth of true concern and with no indication of the annoyance that his search for her might have cost him.

Elizabeth's heart gladdened as she realized his apprehension for her safety triumphed over any imposition he endured in finding her. "I am sorry, Fitzwilliam, to have caused you any undue distress. I did fall but, as you can see, I am safe and sound."

Darcy's mind then turned to a concern of a different nature. "Harrumph! What did Miss Caldecott want?"

Elizabeth looked up enchantingly at Darcy's perturbed expression, her mirth quite apparent as she answered, "She only desired to share details about her special gift, her love of the French language, and how happy she is that *you* remembered her birthday. She also mentioned that she pities me for not comprehending *that* language, which made it impossible for me to keep Yvette in my service. I had just wished Miss Caldecott a *most* happy birthday when you arrived." Concluding her reply, Elizabeth saucily raised one brow to her husband. She puckered her lips coquettishly and added, "I do believe she was a bit overcome with emotion by my heartfelt felicitations."

A broad smile spread across Darcy's face as their eyes locked in mutual understanding and delight.

~*~

An elated Georgiana sat on the seat across from Colonel Fitzwilliam. She wanted to pinch herself. She could scarcely believe her good fortune at being alone with him for the lengthy journey to London. For a short time back at Matlock, she feared her brother might insist that Nancy ride with them, and, even though she loved her maid dearly and was thrilled to have her back, she desired to have this time alone with Richard more than ever. She did not regret Yvette's move to Miss Caldecott's employment, as she no longer required that maid's services. The false panels Yvette had applied to her dress the night of the ball had done their trick. She would certainly use them again to help her figure appear fuller in the daring evening gowns she intended to purchase while in London.

Richard smiled at her, and she mirrored his expression. The carriage jostled every so often, causing them to bump their heads against the padded seats or on the sides of the enclosure. As the minutes turned into an hour, Georgiana's hair began to loosen from the quick twirl of a bun she had primed that morning. She had dressed and groomed herself before they had left, since Yvette had already moved to Collette's service, and Nancy had not yet been reassigned to her. So, on her own, she had quickly whipped her golden tresses into a simple coiffure so as to depart by sun up.

As the silky strands fell, one by one, the colonel's eyes followed their progress. Each lock slowly inched its way free from its confinement. Every so often, Georgiana found him stealing fleeting looks in her direction. She wondered if he thought she appeared a sight. Each time her eyes found him gazing upon her, he would casually alter the direction of his vision, looking at anything: the roof, out the window, specks on his clothing, and even inspecting his fingernails several times in succession. He diverted his attention to contemplate anything other than her.

A little over an hour into their journey, Georgiana began to nod off, but each bump in the road awakened her. Finally, Richard held out his hand to her, beckoning her to sit by his side. With alacrity, she crossed over to his seat. The colonel was surprised when she began to speak instead of resting, launching all sorts of questions concerning his regiment. What was its size? How was rank ordered in the chain of command? Would he be made a Brigadier General soon, and how would that come about? He answered these questions and silently marvelled at her interest. After he had finished responding to all that she enquired of him, a hush fell upon them once more, the rattle of the carriage the only audible sound. Just when he thought she had exhausted all of her enquiries, she surprised him with a whole slew of new ones. These questions were of a different nature, however, their content connected directly to the Peninsular wars on the Continent, and her desire for him to elaborate on the battle strategy utilized. He complied with her every query, afterward feeling complete exhaustion at having done so. Again, he wondered at her interest, but he also appreciated her keen insight and comprehension of all the battles they had discussed. He had never known that she held such fascination in the military way of life.

Once again, Georgiana's eyelids became heavy. Richard put an arm around her, pulling her close. She relished the warm sensation of snuggling against his chest. Before she dozed off, she asked him one last question through a yawn. "Richard, do you like being in the army?"

This questioned stumped him further. No one had ever asked it of him, never caring to know. "Well, Georgie, I suppose it is not a question of whether I like it or not. My father purchased a commission for me when I was young, and I have always accepted it as my lot in life."

"If you could do anything you wanted, what would it be?"

Again, he did not know how to answer. After a pause during which he contemplated several possible options, he responded honestly, "I am not sure, duck. Can I think on that one and get back with you at a later time?"

"Do you promise that you will?"

He chuckled. "Yes, my sweet, I promise."

"You have never called me that before. I like it very much."

His brow creased slightly at her words.

Soon, the motion of the carriage and the warmth from Richard's body lulled her to sleep, and, shortly, her cousin also found slumber. When he awoke, he found Georgiana's head resting in his lap, her hair suffused over her face and upon his legs. He smiled and recalled how lovely she had looked in his arms the previous night as they had danced the waltz, and how happy she had been when he told her that she could travel with him. Taking his fingers, he tenderly pulled back her hair to peek at her. She had grown into a very attractive woman. He began to stroke his hand over her hair, gently intertwining his fingers within it, enjoying the feel of it gliding between them, and then lifting one lock to his nose to pleasure in its scent. For some time, his eyes drank in the splendour of her profile adorned in curls while his hands continued to bathe in the silken sensations of her fallen tresses.

Suddenly, something he had never felt before washed over him. In the inner core of his being, he felt complete adoration for her. The feeling overpowered him. He desired to take her up into his arms and hold her—not the way he had previously embraced her. No, he gently shook his head. He wanted something much different. He longed for a distinct embrace, an embrace that meant more than the mere passing of affection. Fear crept into his soul. What was he doing and thinking? Why would she want a *nobody* such as he? No, she deserved so much more than he had to offer.

With her head lying on his lap, Georgiana savoured the sensations that Richard's attentions created. She allowed him to believe she still slept, fearful that he would stop his present occupation if he were aware that she had awakened. No one, except her maid, had ever touched her hair in such an intimate manner, but even Nancy had never engrossed herself with it the way Richard was doing. His attentions felt glorious. It was all she could do to keep a smile from appearing on her face and to keep her hands from tightly encircling his thigh beneath her head. Oh, how she loved and adored him!

~*~

Charles and Jane departed Matlock, with Elizabeth and Darcy promising to come to London soon. The couples freely exchanged hugs, accompanied by wishes for safe journeys. Again, Kitty experienced surprise when Darcy kissed her hand and bid her to fully enjoy Ackerley House. He also thanked her for her willingness to spend time with his sister and assured her that she was welcome to stay with Georgiana as long as she desired. Caroline felt extreme irritation that she had not been the one to whom they applied to stay with Miss Darcy. Earlier, Darcy had proposed of Elizabeth whether she could spare Nancy for Georgiana once more, and she assured him that she could. Therefore, Nancy journeyed ahead with Bingley's valet, Jane's maid, Cassandra, and Miss Bingley's maid, Drusilla.

Back in their rooms, Elizabeth opened her trunk, setting it on the bed in order to begin packing her things so they could return to Pemberley by nightfall. She desired, most anxiously, to be home. Darcy's trunk had already been packed and sent downstairs by Chaffin. Her husband asked if he could assist her, yet she declined, encouraging him, instead, to check on their carriage. She knew how meticulously he prepared when it came to their travel and safety, and she wished to allow him time to do so, for his peace of mind. Then, she halfway laughed to herself, adding to the thought. *He is fastidious for the safety of everyone under his care: be they woman, child, man, or beast.* A fond smile appeared as she contemplated her husband's expressions of compassion for his sister and her sister, Kitty, the coalminers, Sally and Thomas, and for her former maid, Clara, when she had desired him to arrange travel for her. He was truly—an amazing man— the most benevolent one she had ever known. His liberal hand more than made up for his reticent nature.

Just as she folded her last article of clothing, a knock sounded upon the door. She absentmindedly called out, "Come in," assuming that a servant had come for her trunk. "I almost have it ready."

Lord Hazelton opened the door and stepped into the room. Elizabeth had her back turned towards him as she closed the lid of the chest. "Darcy stated that you are nearly ready to leave. He asked me to call a servant to come for your things. I assured him that I would take care of it myself."

A cold chill ran down Elizabeth's spine. Her hands fumbled as they shakily attempted to latch the lid. Swiftly, the Viscount came to her aid, graciously placing his hands next to her trembling ones. With one flip and pull of the straps, the closure was complete.

"There," exclaimed Lord Hazelton, "that should do it." He looked over, smiling engagingly to her. Her breathing became irregular while she remained frozen in place, her eyes fixed upon the trunk. He found the anxiety that his presence produced in her stimulating.

"I hope you have enjoyed your stay at Matlock, Elizabeth. We are happy to have you in the family. I can understand more than ever now, after having met you, why my cousin took such a fancy to you."

She bit her lower lip, deciding right then and there that if he were to lay one hand on her, she would pummel him with both of her fists.

However, to her utter astonishment, he hefted the trunk from off the bed and said, "I shall take this down now. I am sure Darcy wants it loaded before he does his customary final inspection."

She rolled her eyes and heaved a sigh of relief when he left the room. Pondering what had just happened, she considered whether she was being ridiculous where Lord Hazelton was concerned, or whether there really was something there. What had he done, after all, except to offer to come and fetch the trunk? She went over each and every word he had stated, and not one appeared unseemly. He had welcomed her to the family and even extended a compliment to her on her beauty. Was she just imagining the whole of it? Could she be wrong about her husband's cousin?

Whispering aloud to herself, she reasoned, "Lord Hazelton's parents, Earl and Lady Matlock, are very honourable people as is his brother Richard. Lydia and Wickham's letters must just have me on edge and worried about Fitzwilliam's reaction to them." Rationally, she thought this must be the case and, in reaching this conclusion, she immediately felt better about the situation with the Viscount, the future Earl of Matlock. It was all a misconception on her part. In the past, she had read people's characters erroneously enough. True, the man was a snob, but that did not make him a libertine. Elizabeth heaved a sigh of relief as she picked up her bonnet and made her way down to the courtyard to depart *for her beloved home—for Pemberley*.

~*~

Chapter Twenty-one

The Unburdening of Secrets

In the gently rocking carriage, Elizabeth slept soundly during the entire trip from Matlock to Pemberley. Darcy revelled in the feeling of his wife's slender body leaning heavily against his side, and the lingering scent of her perfume pervading his senses. He loved Elizabeth more than he could ever express. It seemed that his love for her grew stronger with each passing day. When the carriage came to a halt, Darcy shook her shoulder gently and spoke her name with tenderness. Dazed, she sat up and grasped his hand, allowing him to help her alight. Leaning upon his arm for further support, she wearily made her way to their chamber to bathe and prepare for dinner.

"Elizabeth," Darcy's rich voice soothed while he held her close to his side, "since you are exhausted, I shall have a tray sent up. I could have one sent up for myself as well, but I shall have to partake quickly, for Mrs. Reynolds has asked to speak with me after dinner and so has Mr. Sheldon. Therefore, as much as I would like for us to have a quiet evening alone, I shall need to go down to meet with them. Um...Mr. Sheldon has requested an audience with you as well, but due to your weariness, I shall have him return on the morrow."

An ominous feeling came over Elizabeth. Why would Mr. Sheldon desire to speak with her? She could think of no reason other than the bank draft to George Wickham. Shaking her head in resolve, she informed her husband that she would be ready to go down in time for supper, but reminded him that she needed his help with her corset and dress fasteners.

Darcy silently wondered at Elizabeth's rationale for going down, as her fatigue was quite apparent. He decided, however, not to question it. Therefore, he complied with alacrity to all her needs.

As they descended the stairs, Elizabeth thought how odd it felt to have the house to themselves once again when compared to the last several weeks of activity with all of the company about. She wondered what they would find to occupy their time. Darcy pulled her chair closer to his and began to partake of the meal, frequently casting a vigilant look towards his wife.

The aroma from the meat, which permeated the air, assaulted Elizabeth's senses, causing a sudden wave of nausea to wash over her. Cupping one hand over her mouth and nose, she placed her fork upon the plate and pushed it forward.

Noticing that she was not eating, Darcy set down his fork and knife and queried, "Lizzy, are you not feeling well? I know you love roasted veal, especially with carrots."

"Oh, I am fine. I am feeling some queasiness, is all."

Immediately, Darcy wiped his hands on his napkin, leaned close, and with the back of his fingers, felt her forehead. "You do not appear feverish. Perhaps taking a sip of wine will settle your stomach?"

"No, I think I shall just drink a little water. I am sure it will pass."

"I should send for Dr. Lowry."

"Oh, no, please. I shall be fine. You will see."

With nary a word more, Darcy rose, lifted Elizabeth's plate, and set it down several feet away. Seated once more, he reached forth and squeezed Elizabeth's hand before once again taking up his knife and fork. While hastily finishing his meal, he periodically glanced over to his wife to ascertain her condition, wrinkling his brow in concern while he observed her. He made mental note of how she waited patiently, alternately sipping water and then holding her napkin in front of her nose in an attempt to smother the smell emanating from the roast.

With the last bite, Darcy wiped his mouth and tossed his napkin upon the table as he arose. He had seen enough to know she was unwell.

"Come, Elizabeth. Let us get you to bed."

"Oh, no, Fitzwilliam, I cannot. Mr. Sheldon will be here soon, and I desire to help resolve whatever concerns he may have. I am certain it will not take too long, and, I promise, I am already feeling much better." To convince her husband of her words, she endeavoured a small smile of reassurance, but failed miserably.

Darcy eyed her warily, but taking her wishes into consideration, he was reluctant to enforce his directive. Elizabeth's past resentment towards him, over what she deemed to be his officious nature, had taught him enough to proceed with caution when regarding her wishes. "I have no idea why Sheldon desires a meeting with you, but if you are set on the interview, I shall go and speak to Mrs. Reynolds while you speak with him. Then, if luck is on our side, I may be able to wind it up with Sheldon, and we shall go to the library or do whatever you desire. I, for one, am anxious to have some time alone with just you, Lizzy."

The light in his eyes took on a softer glow as he stared adoringly at her. Biting her lip, Elizabeth bobbed her head absent-mindedly in acknowledgement of Darcy's thoughtful regard. Convinced that Mr. Sheldon could have no reason to speak to her other than concerning the bank draft, dread started to coil its way through her gut, up to her stomach, and from her stomach all the way to her throat. The fear of showing her sister's letters to her husband was all-encompassing. The time had come!

She realized that she could no longer put off her confession. It was just the two of them now—no intrusions to fear—no loved ones to witness the eruption of his temper that she knew would surely follow her disclosure. She had hoped to wait until the morrow when they would both be fresh, but now, with Mr. Sheldon desiring to speak with her, it could only compound matters. Fitzwilliam would be livid when he found out that she had not only paid off Wickham but that she had handed the note to him, personally. Yet, what was done, was done? She only prayed that her husband would understand her reasons, and that he would not react foolishly in trying to rectify a futile situation. Oh, she felt truly ill! No wonder she could not eat a bite.

~*~

Georgiana and Richard were on the last leg of their journey to London. The colonel desired to press onward for another hour or so before giving the horses an extended rest. They were in the county of Northamptonshire, on the outskirts of the village of Sulgrave, when the unthinkable happened: a horse threw a shoe, making the creature lame and slowing the team to a snail's pace. The driver reined in all four horses. When the carriage came to a standstill, Richard alighted to discover the cause for the stop.

"Aye, Colonel Fitzwilliam," cried the driver, Jerry, as he made his way down. "It looks like our right lead gelding has thrown a shoe and is favouring his left flank." They both went to survey the hooves of the horse having the difficulty. After determining that the animal would, indeed, need to be shod, Richard crouched low by the legs of each horse, inspecting their shoes. He sighed in relief. Those remaining appeared to be close-fitting.

Straightening back up to his full height once the last hoof was inspected, he stood for a moment lost in thought. The driver remembered an inn about a mile up the road and called it to the colonel's attention. He suggested that he could go there to enquire after the blacksmith.

Opening the carriage door, Richard ducked his head inside to inform Georgiana of the situation and instructed her to stay within the carriage until they drove it off to the side of the road. Jerry held the front animals by their bridles as Richard climbed up onto the driver's seat and gathered the reins in his hands, slapping the leather straps upon the horses' backs. The animals trudged to the side up a grassy knoll, stopping next to a small grove of trees. Immediately, Jerry and the colonel began to unhitch the team and tie up the uninjured horses.

Once all was secured, Jerry left with the maimed creature to enquire of a blacksmith while Richard and Georgiana retired to the inn, *The Cross Keys and Crown*. Inspecting the exterior of the establishment, the colonel deemed it a little rough for his liking—he hoped they would be able to get the horse attended to quickly, so they could resume their travel. Richard grasped Georgiana's hand and made his way into the crowded, smoke-filled room. He hated bringing her into such an establishment. As they entered, the colonel's guard went up. The rowdiness ceased for a time as the men of like-minded rabble took note of the young, blonde darling by his side. Richard observed how some of them drooled at their jowls, staring at her, leering with a look he'd seen all too often when a lady entered an establishment such as this. Except for two bar maids, Georgiana was the only woman in the place. Breathing deeply with an air of half-felt confidence, the colonel secured a table for them near the back of the tavern.

After having ordered a meal, Richard desired to take care of the necessities of life but was loath to abandon his cousin's side. He well imagined that Georgiana needed a respite as well. Thus, unwilling to leave her with so many men eyeing the fairness of her countenance and form, he enquired over the clamour, "Georgie, do you need to accommodate yourself?"

Her eyes widened as a blush spread over her cheeks. "Yes—yes I do. I shall go and ask one of the maids to point me in the direction of the... the... a... *chamber pot.*"

"No, you stay put. I shall go enquire, and then, I think, we shall go together."

Shock was apparent on Georgiana's face at the terrifying image of lifting up her skirts in front of her cousin. Richard read her expression and laughed openly. He reached for her hand and gave it a reassuring squeeze. "Not in with you, Georgie. I shall wait for you by the door, and then you shall wait for me. I shall also have one of the maids keep our table for us. Stay put. I am only going over to the bar and shall be right back."

Earlier in the day, they had frequented inns with fewer people swarming about, and the calibre of the individuals had been quite different from the horde that patronized this dwelling. Georgiana closed her eyes and took a deep breath. This place gave her cause for concern. They could not leave soon enough to suit her.

Colonel Fitzwilliam returned through the throng of men and reached out his hand, beckoning her to take it. She arose, gladly taking his offered assistance. "Stay close," he directed as he manoeuvred amongst the crowd. Georgiana's field of vision stayed fixed on Richard's shoulders. Yet, every so often, when it did veer off, she met toothless grins accentuated by tobacco spittle. As her eyes moved from the men's juicy, stained lips and ventured upward, she witnessed the lascivious, darkened looks in the countenances of many. Hence, the prickle of goose bumps spreading upon her skin made Georgiana shiver in repulsion.

At the end of a dirty hall, Richard halted before a door. He pulled it open, letting it swing wide as he stated, "This is it, duck." The room reeked. Georgiana crinkled up her nose and made a face at her cousin. With a shudder, she eked out a determined resolve and replied, "I shall hurry, Richard."

"Do not rush on my account. Take your time." He lied, fully aware that he was about to have worse problems to reckon with than a lame horse.

Embarrassed, she crossed the threshold and shut the door. The room smelled of raw sewage and stale beer, and, in addition, was small and untidy. Georgiana managed to take care of her needs as quickly as possible, but when she went to wash her hands at the basin, her face twisted in disgust from the murky water that issued from the pitcher. She cried, "Blast!"

Opening the door, she sent a commiserating smile to her cousin. He smiled knowingly in return, and then stated most emphatically, his eyes locking with hers, "Georgie, you lean against the wall here." He pointed to the partition directly adjacent to him. "You do not move an inch. I do not care if someone were to yell fire. You stay put. It's imperative. Do you understand me?"

Rolling her eyes, she cast him a quick glance and nodded. Stating with a tinge of annoyance, one eyebrow shot up, "Richard, do I look like a child?"

He heaved a sigh and then responded, "You look...wholesome...that is what you look like, a very beautiful, *wholesome*, young lady, and those men in there," he wagged a firm finger towards the taproom, "are well aware of it."

Her brow creased at his declaration. He stepped into the small room and then backed out just as quickly, stating yet again, "I do mean what I say, Georgie, do you hear me?"

In exasperation, she rolled her eyes once more and assured him, "Yes, I heard you, Richard." Abruptly, Georgiana stood straight, and raising her right hand to the side of her forehead with the palm turned outward, she saluted the colonel as her commanding officer.

He gaped at her gesture, yet a small smile soon crept over his lips, accompanied by a faint chuckle and a slight shake of his head. He pulled the door shut.

Leaning against the wall as she waited, Miss Darcy looked down the darkened corridor. She saw two men pass by. One turned and peered down the passageway. Their eyes locked and then Georgiana's almost popped out of her head as she witnessed them coming down the length of the hall. Like a mouse, she squeaked in fear, "Eek!—Richard!"

The men came up to her, and one in particular enquired, his eyes probing her figure, "You lost your way, lassie? I think this *necessary* here," he pointed to the door of the room Richard occupied," could make you find it again, if you get the gist of my meaning, darling?" He leered, offering Georgiana a big toothless grin of eager anticipation.

Suddenly, the colonel forcefully bolted out of the privy closet, slamming the door into one of the men and knocking him to the floor before levelling a menacing glare to the caterwauling chap who had made the insinuation. The man left standing gawked at him, grinning rather nervously. Cautiously stepping backward, he cried, "I will be having no quarrels with you over the missus. I hadn't known she had a husband." The other man had already scrambled to his feet, racing past his friend trembling in fear, slowly backing up before turning to flee. Richard heaved a sigh of reprieve when he saw the ne'er do well take off in a mad dash.

Colonel Fitzwilliam looked over to Georgiana and asked, "Did they harm you, Georgie?"

"Well, Richard, that all depends on how you look at it."

Anxiously he searched her face and maintained, "I am afraid, Georgiana, that I do not follow your meaning."

Skewing her nose and lips to one side, she redirected her gaze and cried, "I am afraid they have sullied my mind because I have never before seen a man with his...um...his unmentionables undone."

In anger he swore, "I shall kill those bloody..."

"No, Richard," she said, suppressing a giggle, "not them. You! You are the one with his unmentionables undone."

Quickly, he looked down, finding that the flap of his breeches, indeed, hung wide open, putting his personal attire on display. Hastily, he turned to button them and mockingly declared, "Oh, you little tease!"

When he turned to look at her again, she could see his embarrassment. A scarlet blush spread prettily upon his face. She tried hard, but could not keep her lips from forming into a smirk.

Slowly shaking his head, the colonel rolled his eyes and pressed his lips in a firm line staring at her with sternness.

She exclaimed mischievously, "Why, Richard, you look just like Fitzwilliam when you smile like that."

His eyes narrowed, and given the menacing stare she saw him levelling at her, she feared she had gone too far. Suddenly, right before her, she saw the familiar flicker of merriment return to his eyes and witnessed his lips curl up quite attractively.

"Georgiana Darcy, how did I get myself talked into bringing you with me?"

Bluntly, she stated in a serious tone, "You brought me because you love me, Richard."

All jollity ceased as he took in her look. With a scarcely perceivable nod, he reached for her hand and kissed it, then acknowledged in earnestness, "Yes...I do, Georgie...that I do."

They made their way back to their table and ate their stew in companionable silence. Neither looked at the other while eating, but each speculated about the depth of meaning behind the words they had spoken only moments before, and the thoughts of both drifted to the episode in the hallway. Richard felt gratitude for the modesty afforded by the design of men's extended shirttails, whereas, in annoyance, Georgiana begrudged their length.

~*~

The butler had just shown Mr. Sheldon in as Darcy and Elizabeth entered the foyer. The steward tipped the brim of his beaver to the mistress before removing it and handing it to Mr. Greene. Darcy called out in welcome, "Ah, Mr. Sheldon, it is good to see you. Mrs. Reynolds informed me that you wish to speak with Mrs. Darcy and myself. If you will excuse me, however, I must speak with my housekeeper on a pressing matter. I trust that you will not object to speaking with my wife now. Then I shall join you as soon as I am able."

"That is quite agreeable, Mr. Darcy."

"Well then, I shall leave you." Darcy smiled warmly at his wife, before he confidently strode down the hallway to his own study.

With a slight elevation of her chin, Elizabeth raised her brows and gave a half-hearted smile to her husband's steward. "Well, Mr. Sheldon, if you will follow me?" She advanced towards her study, strolling down the entrance hall to the door on the far left. Walking directly to the chair behind her desk, she sank into it and gestured with her hand for the steward to take a seat in one of the comfortable chairs in the room. He eased down into the green tub one that her husband always favoured. The door remained open.

"Mr. Sheldon, I think I can well imagine what has brought you here tonight. But, since I am not certain, I shall let you inform me of your concerns." She sat and pressed her lips together while taking in the steward's nervous countenance. Quickly, she averted her gaze, but realizing she must face whatever he had to say, she again made eye contact.

"Ahem…Mrs. Darcy, I do have a definite concern that brings me here tonight. I suppose that this could have waited till the morrow, but I have suffered great anxiety over the past few days. Therefore, I hope you can alleviate the position in which I find myself."

Elizabeth slumped over her desk, resting both elbows upon the sleek surface and interlocking her fingers to support her chin. The sickening sensation she had felt earlier, returned, but it seemed intensified tenfold. Lifting her head slightly to speak, she urged, "Pray, Mr. Sheldon, continue. I promise to do all in my power to help you."

Her husband's steward inhaled loudly and Elizabeth thought she detected a tremor with his inhalation. "I would not care about your private business, Mrs. Darcy, if it did not affect mine. The arrangements Mr. Darcy has made, allowing you to solicit more funding from me, is very generous indeed, which I am sure you agree. However, I am still responsible for safeguarding the accounts, and I answer directly to Mr. Darcy. Your husband is not an apathetic master. He is very much involved with the affairs of this estate, and it would not be long before he would notice, shall we say, a *discrepancy* of sorts with your accounts."

Sitting erect once more, Elizabeth folded her hands on the desk. Catching his gaze and holding it, she replied, "Yes, I quite agree with your assessment of Mr. Darcy. I can well imagine that he would instantly see any discrepancy in the books upon examining them. I dare say, I would be surprised if he did not. I fully expected this Mr. Sheldon. Please, believe me when I say that I am not trying to deceive you or my husband."

"Oh, ma'am, I am by no means implying that that is your design. I just find it such a delicate situation, one I have never had to deal with before. That is why I must speak to you first. Mrs. Darcy, you are well aware that you wrote a bank draft to Mr. George Wickham for the sum of one thousand pounds, but what you might not be conscious of is the fact that there were insufficient funds in your account to meet that amount?"

Elizabeth's face froze, showing nothing but sheer astonishment. Her mouth dropped open in an unladylike fashion. In extreme agitation, she replied, "Mr. Sheldon, I can assure you that I did no such thing. Yes, I wrote a bank draft to George Wickham, but only for the sum of *one hundred pounds*."

The steward looked relieved with her declaration. "I see. My question to you is no longer necessary, then."

"What question would that be, Mr. Sheldon?" she prompted.

"I came here tonight to ask you if you desired me to advance your account for the monthly sum of one thousand and two hundred pounds." Elizabeth's eyes widened. He continued, "I never desire for the bank to again tell me that they had to extend a courtesy on an overdraft on a Darcy account. I pride myself, Mrs. Darcy, on performing my duty as a steward to the utmost of my ability. This situation with the overdraft has, quite bluntly, put me between a rock and a hard place. I do not wish to be the cause of contention between you and your husband. Your husband authorized me to advance your account with whatever amount you deem fit. I only want to ensure that adequate funds are available to cover any drafts you write. That is all. I shall leave it to you to explain your reasons for the amount to your husband. However, if you did not authorize the note of one thousand pounds, that is, all together, a horse of a different colour and legal redress should be sought. Yet, I again ask you to explain what you have told me to Mr. Darcy. I know he shall see the sum at some point, and I fear it will be sooner rather than later."

Elizabeth cupped her hands over her mouth while tears threatened to spill on her cheeks. Mr. Sheldon felt terrible seeing her thus. He feared he had been too harsh with such a young woman. In an effort to rectify his forthright and what he feared might appear as an unsympathetic, delivery, he commenced to soften his tone and stated supportively, "Mrs. Darcy, I do not know what kind of predicament you are in, but of this I am certain, your husband is one of the best men I know. He will understand."

Nodding her head, with her voice taut, Elizabeth breathlessly expressed, "Yes, I know that. I am only sad that I have allowed it to come to this. What you must think of me!" Her last words were said in a whisper and, afterward, she closed her eyes and bowed her head.

Mr. Sheldon stood, looking upon the young mistress with sympathy. With conviction, he stated, "I think you are a fine woman, Mrs. Darcy. I have never known Mr. Darcy to make any major misjudgements. I think you are a fine woman, indeed!"

She lifted her head, striving to turn her frown into a smile for his kind words. "You are too good." Inhaling deeply, she stood and declared, "Mr. Sheldon, you need not fear that this shall ever happen again. I do not need to have you advance my personal account any further. The original allotment will do, unless you are otherwise informed by my husband to the contrary. I shall speak to Mr. Darcy concerning this matter within the hour. Rest assured that I shall inform him of the situation in the fullest detail. I hope you will forgive me for the embarrassment I have caused you and for the anxiety that my imprudent act created. I thank you for your honesty, kindness, and understanding."

He nodded his head in acknowledgement of her promises. "I thank you, as well, Mrs. Darcy. I think I shall take my leave now. If you would, please tell Mr. Darcy that I shall see him tomorrow afternoon, unless he sends word desiring that I come sooner."

She inclined her head in his direction, indicating her agreement. "Yes, I shall gladly do so. Thank you again, Mr. Sheldon." Elizabeth walked with him to the door. They each bowed their head in parting. Immediately, she crossed the room to her desk to retrieve the detestable letters from Lydia. A deep sigh escaped her lips, but with a renewed sense of purpose and a set to her jaw, she marched to Darcy's study where she patiently waited beside its closed door.

~*~

That same evening, across the miles at Matlock, in the chamber of Lady Hazelton, Darcy's older cousin was in a great stir. Desiring to bed his wife, he felt complete rejection from the usual gauntlet of excuses through which Elisha put him. Her disinterested and insipid attitude drove him to the verge of madness, especially anytime they were visiting the country estate of either of their parents.

"James, I am not up to it. You know how tired I feel. I do love you though, my Earl."

Hard-pressed by his wife's side, Lord Hazelton's face clearly showed the deep dejection he suffered within. Elisha *never* felt like it. She always had excuses at hand: 'my head hurts, you shall wrinkle my gown, it is Sunday, my parents will hear, it will hurt the baby, I feel faint, I shall have to take a bath again, you smell like a horse.' Yet, the one which grated his nerves more than all the rest was: 'It is not a new week.'

"James, you do understand, do you not? The baby truly taxes all my energy."

"Oh, do not distress yourself, my pet," he stated resignedly as he rolled over on his back. "I understand, perfectly." While staring at the bed's canopy overhead, he wondered how they had ever conceived a child in the first place with his wife constantly requiring him to sleep in his own chamber. It usually did not bother him too much when in London. There he had White's, and of course, Drury Lane. His needs met satisfactory relief while in that quarter of town, as did his whims. Yes, the services rendered there quite adequately satisfied any imaginable fancy he craved, whether from those experienced or, more in particular, from those yet untouched and naïve.

He pulled back the counterpane and tumbled from the bed.

Elisha cried, "Will you not even kiss me goodnight?"

Lord Hazelton rolled his eyes and plopped back down to kiss her cheek. He had not attempted to kiss her lips for many months now. When he attempted to, she became vexed with him, and her bad temper could last well over a week. Thus, he no longer ventured.

Again, he began to rise from the bed, when he thought once more about his cousin's wife. "Elisha, we must have Darcy and Elizabeth round to supper when we get back in town."

Elisha lifted her head and stared at him in dismay. "You cannot be serious, James. What shall my friends say? They all know that her mother's people are in trade. Oh, do say you tease me."

He rolled his eyes once again. "No, my pet, I do not jest. Mother expects us to do our part in befriending Elizabeth and helping her to become acquainted in society. We must bear our cross. I know of no other woman, besides you my pet, who understands the true essence of propriety, refinement, and graciousness. What better mentor for her than you and I? We must accept our lot. With Elizabeth under our wing, in little time, almost no one will think of her hoyden ways and low connections ever again. I am sure you could tame it out of her, and then she would very much play the part of a true lady. With my help, of course, I would not leave you to take it on all alone."

Inwardly, Lord Hazelton knew he would love the opportunity to do just that, as he imagined the grooming of Mrs. Darcy to be filled with intoxicating exploration and vigorous animation.

"Therefore, we shall have them round often, and you need to have Georgiana and Elizabeth without Darcy. I shall be there for you, willing to help at every turn. Your direction shall work wonders upon them."

His words hit the bull's eye of Elisha's vain heart. Flattery always provided the best approach with his wife. "I shall think on it," she said. "I must admit she does need my guidance."

"Please do, my pet. I shall forever be in your debt for helping me in this endeavour." She smiled to him, but quickly informed him that he must go because she needed her rest. Reluctantly, he left his wife's side to lie alone in his cold bed, with his fantasies as his only companions. The contemplation of returning to London and the hope of furthering his familiarity with his cousin's wife provided him with some degree of comfort. After all, Mrs. Darcy's younger sister *had* run off in abandonment with George Wickham. He had heard the sordid details from Lady Catherine. The foolish girl surely had been influenced by the examples of her older sisters. For that reason alone, Lord Hazelton assumed that he required only a bit of time and the right opportunity to have his way with Elizabeth. She, without doubt, would not object, not with such passion in her blood. Yes, he could wait, and the wait would only intensify the pleasure he would realize within the arms of his cousin's lively, voluptuous wife.

~*~

When Darcy opened the door of his study for Mrs. Reynolds to take her leave, he most happily found his sweet wife before him, leaning against the opposite wall. He smiled dotingly at her. She returned his greeting with a smile, yet hers was limp by comparison. She and the housekeeper exchanged pleasantries, before the older woman went on her way. Darcy's brows shot up as he enquired, "Where is Mr. Sheldon?"

"Oh, he asked that I relate a message for him…he shall return to Pemberley tomorrow afternoon to speak with you, unless you send word that you require him sooner."

Darcy shrugged and blinked in response, having no idea why his steward had requested an interview with him in the first place. Again, he smiled happily at his wife and asked how she desired to spend the remainder of the evening. He took in Elizabeth's hesitancy in answering while watching her bite down upon her bottom lip.

"Elizabeth, is something the matter?"

Squaring her shoulders, she replied, "Yes, there is, Fitzwilliam, and I wish for you to hear me out before you say a word. May we go into your study?"

Elizabeth discerned the softness in Darcy's eyes as he stepped aside and gestured most willingly for her to enter. Oh, she felt ill. The time was at hand. Walking before him in trepidation, she thanked him and then stopped dead still in front of his desk. He followed her and sat in one of the chairs, reaching for her hand, to entreat her to sit on his lap. Again, he noticed her biting her lower lip while she shook her head, letting him know that she did not want to join him.

Drawing in a deep, long breath, Elizabeth stared at him for some seconds. She glanced between where he sat and the large imposing desk. She sighed and requested in a grave tone, "I would rather that you sit behind your desk, Fitzwilliam."

He chuckled and said, "My, Lizzy, you seem so serious. If you do not mind, before you share whatever it is that you desire to speak about, I should like to tell you of what Mrs. Reynolds has just informed me."

Inhaling loudly, she decided that it did not matter if he did so—what would a mere *five* minutes more add to her painful and appalling procrastination? "No, I do not mind in the least. What had she to say?"

Again, Darcy tried to persuade Elizabeth to sit upon his lap, but she shook her head, continuing to rest casually against the edge of his desk as he began to speak. Contentment exuded from his every word as he related his message.

"As you are well aware, Mrs. Reynolds took leave of Pemberley to go out of town. She just informed me as to the reason she decided to leave so abruptly. Evidently, past gossip deeply concerned her, gossip she had originally thought lay at Sally's door, and she decided to investigate the situation further. She went in search of Mary, the young maid who had once worked at Pemberley, the one who had accused Sally of instigating all the hearsay regarding your encounter with Richard after the fencing accident. The girl's family lives just outside of Lambton on a neighbouring estate, and they told Mrs. Reynolds that after leaving Pemberley, their daughter had secured a position in a tavern in Dovedale. Well, to get to the point, Mrs. Reynolds travelled there and reasoned with the girl to own up to her half-truths. She told her about Sally's circumstances with her mother and father in order to help soften her heart. Hence, Mary freely admitted that Sally had never told the falsehoods in the first place, and the girl readily expressed her sorrow for having caused such havoc. She claimed to have been jealous of Sally and Thomas's regard for one another."

He looked at Elizabeth to gauge her reaction. She stared at him blankly. "Does this not make you happy, Elizabeth?"

"Oh, indeed it does, Fitzwilliam, for your sake. I, however, never needed validation, since I harboured no suspicions in the first place."

His brow creased while he shifted in his chair. She had not presented the response that he had thought she would. "I asked Mrs. Reynolds about my grandmother's ring, also. She informed me that it had been stolen many years ago, which may explain how Collette came to have it, for I am sure Wickham must have been the culprit."

Anxiously, he studied his wife's face to see what effect this information had upon her. "I would not be at all surprised that this is the scenario that took place. George Wickham has long been known to be the perpetrator behind many crimes." Upon hearing his words, Elizabeth gasped for air as a sense of light-headedness overtook her.

Darcy arose immediately when he witnessed her distress and cried, "Elizabeth, please, sit down. You do not look well. In fact, you look very ill." She allowed him to help her to the chair beside the one where he had been seated. "May I go and get you some wine?"

She nodded her acceptance of his offer. Without delay, he strode over to the cabinet and poured a tumbler full of the dark, rich liquid. Returning to her side, he handed it to her. Smiling to him as she received the drink, she guzzled it down in one gulp. Darcy's eyes widened in alarm, for if he had not known her nature as he did, he would fear that she had turned into Hurst. He knew of far too many women in the upper crest of society who drank to escape their failing marriages, a cruel fate that he hoped his Elizabeth would never suffer.

Wiping her lips with the back of her hand, she held out the empty glass towards her husband. Darcy took it, eyeing her in concern, debating whether he should offer another glass. His deliberation, however, was soon forgotten by the miserable, pleading look conveyed within his wife's eyes.

After drawing in a deep breath, Elizabeth commenced, "Fitzwilliam, you must allow me to speak freely and allow me to complete what I have to say before interrupting, or I am afraid I shall not be able to finish."

Alarm overtook him again as he persisted, "Elizabeth, this sounds truly grave. Please, my love, come and sit with me."

Violently shaking her head, Elizabeth declined to join him, and, with an upraised palm, she cried, "No, Fitzwilliam, I cannot." He sat down in the chair next to her and reached for her hand with his free one—his other hand still holding the crystal tumbler. She gladly accepted it, bringing it rapidly to her lips to kiss it lovingly, and then released it just as quickly as she stood and began to pace. He remained poised in the chair, his eyes fixed on her every move.

"Oh!" she cried. "I do not know where or how to begin."

In an attempt to pacify her, Darcy stated, "Elizabeth, I am sure that whatever you have to relate cannot be as terrible as you fear."

Nodding emphatically, she cried, "Oh, yes, it can, Fitzwilliam, and I am certain you shall be saddened, disappointed, and quite angry with me when you hear all."

With incredulity, he merely shook his head at her presupposition, and vowed, "Elizabeth, I love you. I have no idea what alarms you, but I assure you that no matter what it is, I love you, and I shall still love you after you divest yourself of this ominous undertaking. Please, commence wherever you desire, and I shall listen without interruption."

Walking behind her husband's desk, Elizabeth sat in his chair attempting to suppress the overwhelming desire to pace the room from wall to wall. Taking in a deep breath, she began. "Not long after coming to Pemberley, I received some missives from Lydia. I must admit that my perusal of the first one did alarm me exceedingly. I considered informing you regarding them, but then thought the better of it, knowing what suffering you had already endured on behalf of my sister's foolishness."

Elizabeth noticed Darcy start at the mention of her alarm over Lydia's letter, yet he said nothing. He persisted only in watching her in a pensive manner. She sighed as she brought the two letters from the pocket of her skirt and placed them on the desk, sliding them across the gleaming wooden surface towards him.

"I must say, the situation quickly spun out of control, and I was wrong to try to take matters into my own hands. I know that after you read these letters, Fitzwilliam, you shall become infuriated, and rightfully so. I deserve your anger. I have incurred it. I only ask that you hear me out and let me explain my reasoning before you respond."

Darcy arose, lifted the letters off the desk, and then walked over to the mantlepiece where he placed the tumbler down upon the shelf. He unfolded the first missive and began to read:

My Dearest Lizzy,

I suppose you are on your honeymoon now. Mama told me that your dear Mr. Darcy kept the whereabouts all to himself. I can only imagine that he has taken you somewhere truly grand. You now know the pleasure to be had in the marital bed, I'm sure, unless your husband is not as amorous as mine.

Darcy rolled his eyes but kept reading.

It is such a shame that George and I weren't able to attend the wedding, but as we are so far away and so low on funds, you can only imagine how heartbroken we were to have missed the festivities. You will never guess what my dear George told me about your new sister, so I will tell you. He said that he was once engaged to Georgiana, only a year and a half ago. They met at Ramsgate and renewed their acquaintance that summer. They had planned to elope but were forestalled by her ominous brother.

Elizabeth saw her husband's jaw set and realized that he had probably just read the part concerning Georgiana's near ruin at Wickham's hands.

Darcy read on.

Really, Lizzy, I do have a hard time understanding how you could marry such a man, but back to my tale. Anyway, your husband dissolved their engagement and prevented their marriage, so much the better for me. La! So you see, your new sister and I have so much in common. I dare say that she still pines for my George, and I feel some pity for her because he is indeed an exceptional husband. When I come to visit you, I am certain that Georgiana and I will have so much to impart to one another.

One more thing, Lizzy, and I hope this is not too much of a bother, and it should not be so with the amount of money you now have at your disposal, but George wants me to ask if you could not spare a small, monthly allowance for your dear sister and brother, who live on so little here. Honestly, Lizzy, we have only one servant, and she can only come a few hours a week.

I must say that I am dying to hear from you soon and hope to visit your grand estate by summer's end. George sends his sincere congratulations and the love of a brother.

Your most beloved sister,

Lydia

Darcy folded the letter with evident disgust while looking to his wife. Her sorrowful countenance spoke imploringly to his sense of reason. He longed to command Elizabeth to assure him at once that she, in no uncertain terms, had warned Lydia to never divulge such information, but he had given his word to remain silent. Therefore, without comment, he opened the second letter. Upon reading it, a ghastly look traversed over his visage. Elizabeth observed the change in the colouring of his face as it altered from rosy to pale to scarlet.

Darcy's eyes looked as if they were on fire as he recognized Wickham's hand in the content of the missive and in the contemptible suggestion the rake made by inferring how Elizabeth's body was clearly more desirable than Lydia's. The reference to Elizabeth's cleverness in having ensnared a wealthy husband did not bother him in the least, for he knew the truth of that matter. By reading Wickham's plea for money, it enabled him to instantly understand the situation before him. His wife had been blackmailed by her own sister and their slimy brother-in-law. He realized this was why Elizabeth had asked him for additional funds. She had been buying the Wickhams' silence to protect Georgiana. With quick steps, he came back to the desk and tossed the letters upon it.

Elizabeth marked that his expression showed disbelief mingled with bitterness. His scrutinizing gaze seemed to know everything she still held back. Therefore, she resumed her narrative, determined to tell it all so as to leave no detail unspoken. "Please sit, Fitzwilliam. I cannot continue if you keep looking at me in that manner."

Darcy's obvious agitation showed in the way he firmly pressed his lips together. He gestured with a shrug of his shoulders at his impatience in hearing her out, before sitting once more in the chair he had occupied earlier. He began twisting his ring apprehensively while staring directly at her with a contemptuous look.

"The reason Mr. Sheldon wished to see me tonight was to discuss the amount he has advanced to my account. I wrote a bank draft to George Wickham for one hundred pounds." At this point, Elizabeth paused and closed her eyes tightly. She drew a deep breath, praying that she could regather her courage in order to continue. Then, in one swoop, she blurted, "I wrote a bank draft to George Wickham for one hundred pounds." Continuing in a rush, she added, "Nevertheless, the scoundrel somehow managed to forge over my writing of one *hundred*, and replaced it with the sum of one *thousand*, instead." After drawing in another deep breath, Elizabeth resumed her narrative, anxious to have all said and done. "My account would not allow for such a large sum, yet the bank honoured the draft all the same, owing to the fact that I am the wife of Fitzwilliam Darcy. Such a courtesy of good faith they extended and, thus, George Wickham is *nine hundred pounds* the richer. I affirmed all this for Mr. Sheldon and promised him that I would tell you everything."

"Elizabeth!" He looked at her in exasperation, but then remembered his promise and strove to resist the temptation to interrupt. Yet, he no longer knew if he had the fortitude to follow through with such a commitment.

"I am almost finished," she stated softly. Fighting frustration, Darcy closed his eyes and supported his head in his hands. Elizabeth ventured onward. "I trust that you understand that Wickham urged my sister to ask for the money by threatening to disclose Georgiana's attempted elopement with him, and he has also written to me directly, asking for assistance. However, what you do not know, and what concerns me the most, is this fact: the day I walked into Lambton, I knew I needed to send money to my sister for I worried about how desperate her husband might become and what he might do if I did not follow through with his demands. I took a bank draft with me as well as my grandmother's brooch and the cross necklace that my father had given me." She heaved a deep sigh.

Darcy discerned the heightened emotion in Elizabeth's voice concerning the jewels and lifting his head, witnessed the ache to which her countenance bore witness. Again, he lowered his head, but this time in shared grief for his wife's suffering.

"I went to the pawn broker's shop to sell my brooch and cross. I knew that I must raise more money than I had in my account. I was able to get but very little for the jewellery, yet, I knew that it would have to suffice. I did not want you to pay one single pence more for my family's impropriety!"

Once more Darcy's head shot up at hearing the intense strain in Elizabeth's voice. He detected the welled up tears escaping her eyes and trickling down her cheeks. She turned her head to the side and wiped them away, striving to brave what still must be unveiled. "I came forth from the broker's shop with the intention of writing out the bank draft and sending it express to Newcastle, and I also wished to add the money I had just received from the sale of the jewellery to my account. I stopped to admire a shop window when...Oh, Fitzwilliam, please," she swallowed hard attempting to keep her composure, "try to remain as calm as you are now."

Darcy stared at her, his confusion now combined with a sense of foreboding. Instinctively, he brought up the back of his hand to cover his mouth while his eyes remained fixed on hers. He wondered at the greatness of Elizabeth's fear and what more she could tell him that might be worse than what he had already heard.

Elizabeth lowered her gaze and rhythmically, nervously, began to brush her fingertips over the smooth surface of the desk. "As I said, I stopped to admire something in the window of a shop when, low and behold, I discovered George Wickham standing by my side. He spoke to me, telling me that he had come to Lambton with the express purpose of seeking me out." Peeking through her lashes, she saw the intense hatred burning in her husband's eyes, and then, suddenly, he held up his hand, directing her to stop. "Elizabeth, do not torture me so. Say it quickly!"

Closing her eyes briefly, she inhaled deeply before commencing anew. However, fearful of his response to what she was about to reveal, Elizabeth cast her vision downward, focusing her eyes on her trembling hands. "He pulled me by my arm for some way down the street, warning me not to make a scene." Darcy gasped and jumped to his feet, his hands instantly forming into fists. Elizabeth did not look at his face, but she could see his fingers tightly clenched and understood the severity of his upset. Before resuming, she licked her lips. "He pinned me to the wall in the alley and made some rather unpleasant remarks about my person, which I shall not repeat, and demanded the money he had asked for in the missive you just read. He ordered me to request a permanent increase to my pin money, so I could send him a monthly stipend. I told him I could not, I would not ask you to increase it, and informed him that I would rather he kill me then and there."

The sound of quick steps made Elizabeth aware that her husband no longer stood in front of the desk, but had now taken up residence at the mantlepiece, before the fire, with his back towards her.

"Please understand, Fitzwilliam, I did try to approach you before this, on several occasions, but there were always interruptions, or I found you in such an ill temper that I feared telling you. The remarks Wickham made, which trouble me the most, include the fact that he may put your life as well as Lydia's and her unborn child's in danger if I do not cooperate. To emphasize the seriousness of his point, he held a pistol on me. However, he said he needed *me* alive, and if I did not help, then he assured me that I would attend a funeral in the very near future. He reasoned if you were dead, then Georgiana, or more specifically, her money, would become accessible to him. After he rifled through my reticule and found the blank bank draft, he demanded that I fill it out for more than what was in my account. I informed him that there was not enough to cover the draft. I explained that Mr. Sheldon deposits my money at the first of the month, and that if he would wait until then, I could satisfy his needs, but he persisted, contending that I could easily charm you in order to receive more funds. He claims you have trapped him into a marriage and a profession he detests. And thus, you shall pay for it until your dying day."

Darcy snorted while shrugging in disdain. Mockingly, he exclaimed, "What profession would George Wickham not detest, apart from that of a professional gambler and philanderer? Sadly for him, society does not pay *rogues* for these services."

Silence descended between them after his derisive comment and neither said a word for some moments. Darcy gripped the mantlepiece with both hands, leaning his body forward. Elizabeth stared at his posture and wondered what thoughts were going through his mind. She bit her lip.

"Elizabeth, is there anything else you wish to tell me?" His tone was menacing.

"Only that I am sorry, Fitzwilliam, for not having told you sooner, but I feared what you would think and do. I fear for Georgiana's reputation, especially with her coming out, and I am so sorry for Wickham's insult, for his forging the amount of the bank draft, and for it costing you a thousand pounds."

"Elizabeth, the money is inconsequential, but your keeping this from me is **not**!"

She gasped. Quickly she moved her hand over her mouth in an effort to mute her despair, grateful that he had his back turned so that he could not see her silent tears.

In a stern voice, he enquired, "Elizabeth, what unpleasant remarks did Wickham make about your person?"

A tremulous sob escaped her throat, and she quickly covered the whole of her face with her hands. Through the snuffling, she pleaded, "Please, Fitzwilliam, do not make me say."

"No, Elizabeth, I feel I must know."

"Oh, but what good shall come of it? It is nothing! Please!"

Unmoved, he petitioned again, "*Elizabeth*, I must know!"

She cried harder now, yet nodded and replied, "He...he...said he admired the...the...fire within me, and he...he...assumed it was...was...for this aspect of my character that you...you...mar...married me. He said if...if...he did not need my assistance to...to...help him acquire the mo...mo...money, he would rather do...." she paused and gulped in some air and then cried out, "other things to me."

Darcy felt a painful stab in his throat. He opened his eyes from having held them clenched tight as she spoke. Blindly, he stared upon the exquisite woodcarving, etching the mantlepiece before him. Then, licking his dried lips, in a strained manner, he uttered, "Elizabeth, did he touch you? Please, tell me exactly what he said and did to you."

In fury, she spat out, "He had me pinned against the wall and pressed his lips to my ear and said he wanted to touch my body. He said he wanted to kiss me, and he thought that my body would be lush!"

The shattering of glass caused Elizabeth to startle. Engulfed with seething anger, Darcy had lifted the tumbler from its location on the mantlepiece, and hurled it into the grate. He then turned and briskly vacated the room, vanishing from before her eyes. In misery, she laid her head and arms upon the desk's cold surface and wept freely. Her world, her marriage, had come to an end.

Every muscle in Darcy's body tensed as he strode down the corridor. He wanted to kill Wickham, and kill him he would. Abruptly, he stopped and stood still for a few seconds, a bewildered expression upon his mien. What was he doing? For the time being, he could do nothing to resolve such a dilemma. Quickly, he turned, hastening back to his study.

Upon entering, he observed the tremors of Elizabeth's shoulders as she attempted to control her weeping. Crouching beside her, he lovingly placed an arm around her waist, gently pulling her torso towards him while pressing his head against her side. She flinched at his sudden touch but calmed quickly when hearing the compassion and love in his address.

"Elizabeth, I apologize for my thoughtlessness in leaving you just now. I do not hold you accountable for this. I am out of my mind with anger. I desire to run Wickham through and at this moment, if the opportunity presented itself, I am certain that I would." Raising his head and reaching forth, Darcy gently brushed back Elizabeth's fallen tresses which had concealed the side of her face and exclaimed, "I love you greatly, and I cannot stand to think what he might have done to you and what he might still do to you and to Georgie. I cannot bear it!" Tears sprang to his eyes and he buried his head within her lap.

His words of tenderness soothed her, and Elizabeth's sobs soon ceased. Then, muffled words of contrition met his ears as she spoke with her face still upon the desk.

"Fitzwilliam, I am so sorry. Can you forgive me?"

Lifting his head and turning towards her, Darcy responded with passion, "Forgive you, Elizabeth? Forgive you for *what*? I have been a pompous fool. *I* am the one who has acted so high-handed with you, the woman I adore and cherish as no other, and *you* ask *me* to forgive *you*?"

Sitting up straight now, she bent her head and gazed into his eyes. "Oh, *yes*, Fitzwilliam, I have been just as foolish. I should never have walked into Lambton, and I should have told you all that has happened, immediately. I *beg* your forgiveness!"

Darcy pulled out his handkerchief and handed it to her as he declared, "Elizabeth, I *forgive* you. Will you forgive me for being so insensitive, and for walking away just now?"

While blowing her nose, she vigorously nodded, "I *do* forgive you, Fitzwilliam."

He stared into her eyes while she peeked at him periodically amidst her constant folding of the hankie and blowing of her nose. Then, observing her befuddled expression when the cloth was thoroughly saturated, Darcy smiled adoringly to her. Arising, he held out his hand to her, and she, too, stood. He encircled her in his arms, drawing her close to his body while whispering in an aching, fervent voice, "I love you, Lizzy. I do not know what I would do if something were ever to happen to you."

Darcy pulled his head back to bestow a kiss on Elizabeth's lips when he became aware of the unsightly, decidedly wet substance that besmeared her face. He twisted his head and noticed her desperately trying to dry up the dripping of her red swollen nose with the drenched handkerchief. Hastily, he reached into his pockets in search of a dry one when he heard her exclaim in nasal voice, "Oh, Fitzwilliam, I have ruined your beautiful desk!" He immediately turned to look to where her head had lain. There, on the surface of his cherished mahogany escritoire rested a puddle of his wife's shed tears. She lifted up her dress in an attempt to dry the wooden surface.

"No, Lizzy, here." She saw him fumbling to untie his cravat. "Use this instead," he implored as he handed it to her, "but first," his face grimaced in commiseration, "use it to dry your face."

Her face broke into a smile at the sweet thoughtfulness of her husband. Quickly, she blew her nose, and wiped her face clean. Folding the long cloth several times over, she then mopped the desk almost dry. In haste, she lifted her dress high and exclaimed, "It needs one more swab." Pleased with the finishing touch that her skirt afforded, she proclaimed with satisfaction, "There!"

Turning her head to look at Darcy, Elizabeth found him staring at her dotingly, a small smile tugging at the corners of his mouth. "What, sir, makes you so happy?"

"That I find my beautiful wife rescuing my desk from utter ruin. Is this not a just cause for happiness?"

She smiled broadly and inclined her head as she stated with a sparkle in her eyes, "Yes, I suppose it is. But, I should not have succeeded if it were not for my husband gallantly sacrificing his cravat."

"A sacrifice, do you call it? I fear you are mistaken, for I must inform you, my sweet, sweet wife, it is *no* sacrifice at all. I had ulterior motives. I desired your face free of impediments, so I could take you in my arms thus." Darcy gathered Elizabeth close as an admiring glint shone from his eyes. "And kiss you much like this." He lowered his head and captured her lips with his own, and each hungrily participated in the shared display of affection. The kiss began quite ardently, but soon gave way to frivolity. For several moments longer, they each delighted in the playful parrying of their tongues and the nibbling of their lips before parting.

Breathless, they took a step back, one from the other, and Elizabeth said while attempting to inhale, "I must say, Fitzwilliam, if this is how I shall be rewarded every time I have blubbered all over my face and over your lovely desk, then I shall cry more often, for I love seeing your exposed neck." She turned her head, moving in closer, and began nibbling at his Adam's apple.

"I must say, Lizzy, I shall inform Mrs. Reynolds that you are solely in charge of cleaning my study, and, in particular, this desk." He removed his arm from around her waist and pointed at the massive piece of furniture. "However, you are to clean it only when I am present, and only with your skirts, because the vantage point from here," releasing her further, he took a step away and slung his body into the master's chair, "shall be perfect for viewing my wife's pantalets and the pretty shape of her derrière."

In feigned shock, she cried, "Why, Mr. Darcy, *you* are incorrigible!"

He arose swiftly to embrace her once more and, while holding her close, he whispered, "Yes, Lizzy I am hopeless…hopelessly in love with you!"

She tightened her arms about him, returning his embrace with increasing intensity when she felt a sudden sting upon her buttocks. Speedily, Darcy backed away, smiling roguishly. He challenged, "Now, Lizzy, there is no need for such fire in your eyes, my dear girl. After all, you started this only moments ago with your teasing tongue during my heartfelt kiss."

"Then I shall repay such an atrocity with an act of violence all my own!" She picked up the soiled cravat, but before she was able to deploy her weapon of choice, Darcy called to her as his long legs crossed the room in haste, informing her that her response was too slow. The glare she gave him made him smile all the more. "Catch me, Lizzy!"

Quickly he swung the door open, and then, in a full run, he departed, dashing down the length of the corridor and all the way up the stairs, taking them two at a time. Elizabeth did not lag far behind. Mr. Greene, who had been lighting the candles in the hall, looked shocked as both the master and mistress rounded the corner from the passage that led into the foyer. Likewise, Mrs. Reynolds stood just around the corner at the top of the stairs, instructing a young maid in an unfamiliar task, when Darcy reached the landing and shocked the women when he nearly ran them down. As he raced by, he panted out, "Please, ladies, I beg your pardon."

Elizabeth could hear her husband's laughter, which only fuelled her desire to overtake him. However, upon reaching the landing, she instantly became aware of Mrs. Reynolds and the new girl. Abruptly stopping her chase and nodding to them in a friendly manner, she, very decorously, walked the remaining distance to her chamber. The housekeeper and young maid stood in astonishment. Not only did the sight of their master racing down the hallway in reckless abandon cause them to experience great bewilderment, but upon seeing the backside of the mistress' dress and noting her skirts gathered about her waist, exposing her pantalets to full view, their mouths gaped opened wide. Elizabeth paused at her chamber door, and contrived a stoic smile, which she threw at the servants, and then entered therein. Mrs. Reynolds and the young maid cast a wide eye look at one another, both struck speechless.

In Mrs. Reynolds's heart, however, she rejoiced to see her master and mistress acting in the same, easy manner as when they had first arrived, shortly after marrying. She smiled knowingly that, *ere too long*, the halls of Pemberley would echo with the laughter of children…something she truly desired and anticipated.

After Elizabeth closed the door, Darcy pounced upon her and carefully grabbed the offending item out of her hand, before she knew what had happened. He tossed it on the floor near her dressing chamber. Swiftly, he picked up his wife, who by now, due to her sense of propriety, had calmed down, and carried her over to their bed. Elizabeth made no attempt to tease, kick, or scream in retaliation for his offence, only a small shriek of delight escaped her lips. Instead, they settled down to luxuriate in each other's arms, knowing that they had reached a milestone in their marriage. Each now felt secure in their trust of the other. Hence, they expressed their confidence quite vigorously, in a language in which they were both becoming truly proficient.

~*~

Elizabeth had fallen asleep within her husband's arms. However, sleep did not come so easily to Darcy. Worries for his sister's reputation and safety filled his mind. Lying awake for some time, he decided that he and Elizabeth would need to leave for London much sooner than they had planned. Knowing what he now knew about the blackmail, Darcy could not bear the thought of Georgiana without them. The intelligence that George Wickham had swindled a thousand pounds made him worry that he had not returned to Newcastle, but that he had gone instead to the gambling tables of London.

Once deciding on a plan for their return, he gazed at his wife's pretty face until a soft somnolence finally overtook his sensibilities. He slept deeply for many hours, not even awakening when the bright, morning light streamed into the room. Without warning, a stinging slap upon his bare derrière aroused him from his slumber. His eyelids flew open as he attempted to discern the origin of the curious assault. At first, disoriented, Darcy had no idea what had happened, but then, he heard his wife's uncontrollable laughter, followed by her smug exclamation of, "Touché!"

~*~

Later that morning, after the master and mistress had dressed and gone downstairs, Chaffin began his daily duties by collecting Mr. Darcy's clothing, which had been scattered about Mrs. Darcy's chamber. When reaching down to pick up the gentleman's discarded cravat, he marvelled at its condition. Hence, with caution and a grimace upon his brow, the valet pinched the offending item between his forefinger and thumb and lifted it, keeping it at a distance from his person. He wondered what had caused the cloth to suffer such pollution, but then thought the better of it. Mr. Darcy's private interactions with his wife were just that. To Mr. Chaffin…where his master and Mrs. Darcy were concerned…expecting the unexpected had become the standing order of the day.

~*~

Chapter Twenty-two

Taken by Surprise

The next morning, after their breakfast was complete, Darcy informed his wife of his need to attend to the correspondence that had arrived while they were away. Since Elizabeth had her own tasks to look after, they agreed to meet in one hour to discuss their departure for London.

At his desk, the master burrowed resolutely into the stack of missives before him. One by one, he perused the appellation of each sender and then designated the letter into one of three piles. He stopped short when noticing the name of Mr. Thomas Bennet of Longbourn, Hertfordshire. Laying the remainder of the posts aside, he turned his full attention to his father-in-law's communication.

Dear Mr. Darcy,

I hope that you and my daughter are in excellent health upon the reading of this missive. The matter that prompted you to contact me previously has been given serious consideration and intense discussion has occurred in the Bennet household. I am happy to report that within a few days after you have read this, the subject of your petition shall arrive. Mrs. Bennet was only too happy to oblige her favourite son-in-law's wish, and I concurred most heartily. How could I deny anything to a man such as you, particularly when the appeal is exclusively for the welfare of my dear Lizzy? Or should I say our Lizzy? Thank you for inviting us to visit in the early summer. I can assure you that I look forward to seeing your estate, and, principally, your library. I shall, of course, enjoy Lizzy's company as well as yours at that time.

Well, until then,

Your devoted Father-in-law,

Thomas Bennet

Smiling as he laid the letter aside, Darcy quickly took pen in hand to express his gratitude for his father-in-law's kindness.

After sealing his message, he returned his attention to the mail upon his desk and continued to sort through each communication in order to complete all necessary business before their departure.

~*~

While Mr. Darcy coped with a great deal of correspondence, Mrs. Darcy discovered only one lonely missive awaiting her and that from Mrs. Chalmers. Elizabeth was relieved to find this to be the case, since she felt exhausted and wished to attend to her letter writing. She had been such a poor correspondent as of late and felt the need to reply to Charlotte, Jane, her mother, and Mary.

Poor Mary, thought Elizabeth as she sat down at her desk. To be confined at Longbourn with their mother as her only female companion seemed an injustice. Mary had never had much attention from either parent, and with the constant reminder from their mother that Jane was by far the fairest, Mary somehow faded into the background. Sorrowfully, Elizabeth contemplated her sister's lack of social grace. Sometime during their informal upbringing, Mary devised her own little world of existence where she strove to excel with the reading of *Fordyce's Sermons to Young Women*. Often, Elizabeth and Jane tried to involve her in their various conversations, but Mary never seemed to feel comfortable with these discussions. The comments offered by their younger sister usually followed along the lines of what did and did not constitute a proper topic upon which young women should converse. Elizabeth smiled, tilting her head to one side, and admitted to herself that she and Jane did not feel comfortable with Mary censuring them when they spoke of all the parties, assemblies, and balls that they attended.

Here, again, Elizabeth caught herself and smiled knowingly. It was not Jane who felt uneasy with Mary. Jane always accepted people for who they were, looking favourably on the whole world. No, most of the sisterly intolerance and vexation of spirit towards Mary came from her alone. She was the one who would grin and bear Mary's moralizing, rolling her eyes and scarcely offering a comment in return, impatiently waiting for her younger sister's philosophical denunciations to end. Jane, in contrast, would always pay rapt attention to Mary and showed unfailing consideration to all her sister's words. Whereas when Elizabeth wanted her eldest sister's sole attention, she would give Mary only a fragment of her time and then speedily whisk Jane away, leaving the girl all alone to indulge in the moral scrutiny of her fellow creatures. In fact, Elizabeth realized that this might comprise Jane's only failing, for she knew that, much to her younger sister's censure, her elder sister truly enjoyed the wicked commentaries regarding human foibles that she would often describe in such a lively and free manner.

Elizabeth thought it odd that she had never before considered this selfish aspect of her own character. A pang of shame welled up inside of her. She, not unlike her father and mother, had been just as neglectful of Mary, who reached out for love and recognition in the only way she knew how. Whispering aloud, Elizabeth cried, "Oh, Mary! I shall try harder—may you now find me not so judgmental." Instantly, she shook her head, smiling, knowing that this would never be the case. She would always find the follies of others entertaining, just as she now discovered her own to be. No, she would never cease to find diversion in the absurdity of human nature, but she would begin to execute a genuine interest in her sister's welfare. Mary must come and spend the whole of the summer with them. Surely, Fitzwilliam would not object. It would benefit her sister greatly. After all, Jane and Charles hosted Kitty for the Season. Mary needed to feel just as wanted, and it would make her mother happy for she also wished Mary to spend the summer at Pemberley. Elizabeth felt certain that her mother's wish came accompanied by great hope that her middle daughter would find some rich man lying in wait for her, fair maiden that she was, tempting him to swoop down, that he may clasp her into his arms and lead her off onto the glorious path of matrimony.

Absentmindedly, Elizabeth broke the seal on Mrs. Chalmer's letter and smiled at the image of a romantic Mary. Somehow, she found it oxymoronic. For the man would require a strong constitution or completely agree with Mary's first and only true love, the Reverend Fordyce. Nevertheless, that would change. She and Georgiana together would see to that, and she hoped that, in time, Mary would find a man to love for his own merits and one who would love her for hers in return.

~*~

Leaning against the threshold of the mistress' study with his arms folded over his chest, Darcy observed his wife reading a missive. "Ahem," he called out as he knocked upon the open door.

Elizabeth startled a little and then looked up in pleasure. *Oh! How handsome he is*, she declared to herself for the hundredth time that morning.

"I wonder if now would be a convenient time to speak with the lovely mistress of this estate?"

Raising one brow high, she smiled enchantingly and replied in a conspiratorial air. "Yes, it is. Please, do come in, sir. I am privy to her perspective, and in her eyes, you are a priority at all times. She has informed me that if ever the master of this estate were to request an audience with her, she would yield most readily."

"But, I must know before entering," said Darcy in light-hearted jousting, "does she yield with conviction? If my memory serves me correctly, when

Mrs. Darcy, formerly known as Miss Bennet, stayed at Netherfield while attending to her ill sister, she felt that yielding readily to the persuasion of a friend was a true sign of friendship. In contrast, the master of this estate feels that to yield readily without conviction, is no compliment to the understanding of either party."

Elizabeth rose from her chair, wearing a seductive smile. She came around the desk in order to approach her husband. In merriment, she sashayed her way to where he stood and, while putting her arms around his neck, saucily stated, "I guess we must first determine the degree of intimacy existing between the two parties." She again raised one brow and looked up into his darkened eyes.

"Yes," Darcy growled low. Gazing into his wife's brilliant eyes, he encircled his arms about her waist. "I dare say, before we resume discussing the underlying principle of a subject, which we were never permitted to debate further while at Netherfield as Bingley feared it might have lead to an argument. Therefore, I must know your position, dear lady, if you are certain that you shall not become quarrelsome?"

Standing on tiptoe while running her fingers through Darcy's curls, Elizabeth batted her eyelashes coquettishly and conceded, "Oh, well, I must admit that Charles was mistaken when he forbade us to argue, but he was correct about your being a *great tall fellow*, especially in comparison with myself, therefore, I must pay you deference as does he."

Tightening his grasp around her, he quipped, "Ah, cowering in the guise of reverence? That sounds not at all reminiscent of *my Lizzy*."

Taking delight in his repartee, her eyes drank in his every gesture: the lifting of his brows, the twinkle in his eyes, and the movement of his lips as they pronounced each word. She loved his voice, so dignified and melodious. How had she ever thought he mocked her all those times when they were in Hertfordshire and Kent?

"Now, the first issue for us to ascertain is whether the mistress should put down her missive?"

"Yes," cried Elizabeth, "but before we can answer *that* question, the degree of intimacy existing between the parties must still be established?"

"Ah, you are correct. So, what is the level of familiarity between the mistress and the man who desires this interview with her?"

"Oh, I can assure you, sir, the mistress does succumb most readily to this man, and she does so with fervent conviction. If truth be told, she yields to him and to no other."

"I am glad to hear it! In fact, if this were not the case, I am afraid the master of this estate would be sorely disappointed, and as Bingley so kindly pointed out, he should, perchance, repine every Sunday evening while he sojourns on this earthly sphere."

Stroking his chin with her fingertips, her index finger dallying in the cleft thereof, she whispered, "I adore you, Fitzwilliam!"

He tenderly stated, his breath brushing her cheek, "As I do you, Elizabeth."

They embraced for several moments, each savouring the depth of their love. Sorely tempted to lock both doors and proceed to have his way with her, Darcy, in his mind, weighed the wisdom of taking advantage of such an opportunity, but thought the better of it. So much still required their attention, and, moreover, Elizabeth deserved the comfort of their bed. She was too good to him.

Backing slightly away from her, he gestured towards the letter and enquired, "From whom is your missive?"

"Mrs. Chalmers. She writes to invite me to a literary gathering at her home in London on the third of April. Should I accept, do you think?"

"That decision rests entirely with you, Lizzy. Mrs. Chalmers is a very astute woman and one of noble character. Some might consider her eccentric, but I suppose it all depends upon whether you feel comfortable with her forthrightness and her tireless tendency to speak about Pope, Donne and Dryden. I am sure that most of those present will be older than you are, so if you feel that it would not be something to your liking, feel free to make your excuses. She will not take offence. I well imagine it would take a great deal to offend the woman."

"No, I think I would rather like to venture to one of her get-togethers. I am sure it would prove entertaining, and I think older women have more insights for the offering. Besides, on the night of the buffet, she put Collette in her place concerning her sprained ankle, and I feel she is a kindred spirit for doing so."

"Oh! I see. And, pray, what did she say to Miss Caldecott that you found diverting?"

Impishly, she smiled. "She told Collette that her ankle could not be hurt too badly, because she was able to walk about in our dining hall with no trouble while she," Elizabeth paused and stood up straight, then, pulling her chin down and puffing out her cheeks and chest, she perfectly mimicked Mrs. Chalmers's gruff brogue, "*grubbed up* the food upon her plate."

Caught up in a feeling of fascination, Darcy grinned and inhaled deeply as he stared into his wife's eyes. "Elizabeth, you bewitch me daily."

"Well, I am happy to know you feel so. Now, come over here." She led him to the green tub chair and bid him to sit and then she nestled herself in his lap. "In all seriousness, now, tell me what you plan to do about Wickham."

"Oh, Elizabeth!" he moaned as he tilted his head against the wall above the back of the chair. "I need Fitzwilliam more than ever, yet I shall have to search for that villain without his aid. My cousin is on the Crown's time, now, and I fear his freedom shall be limited. Wickham more than likely has stolen away to London to take his chances at the gaming tables there."

The sudden mention of their brother-in-law's name brought back the familiar anger that had burned in Darcy's eyes the night before. But before Elizabeth could make a comment, he continued. "I want to meet with Mr. Sheldon when he comes today after our noon meal, and then, I think, I shall accompany him into Lambton to meet with Mr. Hines, the proprietor of the local bank, and inspect the forged draft. The clerk should have surely been leery to accept it. Never again will the bank accept any draft made out to George Wickham unless my steward or I send personal word otherwise. Wickham has his dastardly connections everywhere and with Georgiana's safety and reputation paramount in my mind, I wish I had never allowed her to go to Town without us."

Elizabeth observed his anxiety and felt terrible.

He continued, "I must also rearrange my meeting with Mr. Sumner concerning the coalmine. I was to meet with him on Friday, but I hope to reschedule a meeting for a later time during our residence in London. I also want to see Harrison before we depart. So much demands my attention, yet, if I had my way, I would be on the road post-haste." He smiled glumly at her concerned expression and apologized for his rambling.

"Oh, no, there is no need for apology, Mr. Darcy. I only wish there were some way that I could share your burdens."

A look of astonishment overcame his features. "You are sharing them, Elizabeth, by allowing me to hold you in my arms as I vocally strip myself of my frustrations over our forestalled departure."

"Yes, but I desire to do more."

He glimpsed at her in an odd way. "I assure you, Lizzy, I must tie up these loose ends myself. You may ride with Mr. Sheldon and me into Lambton, if you so desire. I would love to have your company."

Elizabeth rose off his lap and made her way to the door. Darcy called after her, asking if he had offended her in some way. She closed the door and bolted it while shaking her head. Then she crossed the room to repeat the same procedure with the other one. Darcy's eyes widened. He realized she had plans which included him.

Leaning against the door that she had just locked, she exclaimed in all seriousness, "I find that I desire you, Fitzwilliam, and I shall be distraught should I discover that you do not desire me as well. Am I being too forward?" She raised an assertive brow.

He gulped and shook his head. "No, Elizabeth, I have always admired you for the liveliness of your mind, and I hold in equal estimation, the dynamism of your body. I shall gladly yield most readily and with conviction to your persuasion. However, my love, I feel that the softness of our bed may be more to your preference."

"Oh, no, Fitzwilliam. I find this very room to hold many charming memories for me already. Memories I hope to continue creating over the course of our marriage."

In alacrity, Darcy rose from the chair and gathered his wife in his arms. "I love you, Elizabeth Darcy." He smiled, looking deeply into her eyes. "Have I ever told you just how much I love you?"

"Oh, yes, but I never tire of hearing of it."

Thus, the Master of Pemberley held his private audience with the mistress, stripping himself of other things besides his frustrations as he showered his wife with tender expressions coming straight from his heart. Their loving was not rushed, but lingering, with each not wishing to leave the other's arms even when they knew the time was at hand for Mr. Sheldon's arrival. However, part they did, but, after Darcy helped to fasten his wife's dress and then handed her pins to her while she conformed her fallen tresses back into an elegant coiffure, he softly stated, "Thank you my sweet wife for sharing my burden in the way that only you can. I love you completely." The only reply Elizabeth gave to this declaration was a gentle, "Yes, I know," followed by a quick peck on his cheek.

~*~

When Darcy left for Lambton with his steward, Elizabeth decided to take a long nap. She found it a difficult decision to make, however, for the weather appeared breathtaking. Her desire to ramble through the woods by the pond nearly won out, but she feared the temptation to take her desired rest underneath an oak too great. Her husband would be distressed if he returned home and did not find her within the house. Instead, she made her way to her chamber, climbed up upon the massive bed, and then snuggled underneath the coverlet. She pulled Darcy's pillow close to her chest and envisioned the time they had just shared in her study. Warmth filled her bosom with thoughts of how her husband had pleased her with his fine attentions. Her Aunt Gardiner had been correct. The marital bed was divine. Oh, she had neglected to write to her aunt. No need to worry. Before long she would be in London, and then she could surprise that relation with an unexpected visit. She smiled at the vision of her aunt's elated face. This daydream quickly gave way to envisioning her husband's lips upon her skin, the look of desire as he had gazed into her eyes, and the words of endearment he had uttered as they expressed their love. Elizabeth's insides quivered anew, educed by the enticing recollections of her husband's enthusiasm for her body. Warmth enveloped her conscious thought as it gave way to a pleasant stupor, and there, the Mistress of Pemberley slept soundly for several hours.

~*~

At midnight in the west side of London, Jerry reined in the horses, halting the Matlock carriage in front of Ackerley House. Richard had been wide awake for a number of hours, having napped for the whole of the afternoon. Thus, he was alert at the moment of their arrival with his emotions astir. Georgiana dozed beside him on the seat. Gently, he brushed her hair from her face and quietly spoke. "Georgie, you are home."

The young woman's eyelids fluttered open as she slowly sat upright, stretching her arms and then quickly covering her mouth to stifle a yawn. It had been two gruelling days on the road for them, but, even in her dishevelled condition, Richard thought her gorgeous, and he was absorbed by her every move. For the past hours, his head had been filled with meditations about this fair-haired beauty by his side. She would soon be presented at court, and the suitors would form long queues for a chance to vie for her hand. Soirées, parties, balls, theatre engagements, opera attendance, carriage rides, and shopping were sure to fill her days during this Season. He believed that she would flit from one activity to another, and sadly, his absence would prevent him from witnessing it and having his minute share in the whole of it. But, this realization did not cause him to feel wounded, for wounded aptly described what he felt at present. No, he surprisingly grasped that *he* desired to be *the one* to take her on pleasant afternoon rides, *the one* to hold her in his arms as they swirled around the ballroom floor, *the one* to watch her delight in the plays of the Season, and *the one* to entwine his hand with hers as she peered in the shop windows of Bond Street. Suddenly his attention was arrested from these thoughts by the sound of his cousin's voice.

"Oh, Richard, I am so glad to be here!"

Stepping down, the colonel quickly turned back to assist Georgiana, but instead of reaching for her fingers, he impulsively put his hands on her waist, lifted her from the carriage, and affectionately placed her feet upon the pavement.

Georgiana became breathless from the intimacy of this simple act and the thrill that the mere pressure of his touch created within her body. His hands lingered only briefly as she gazed smilingly into his eyes, and then offered her thanks for his assistance.

In the meantime, Jerry unloaded Miss Darcy's lone trunk, carried it to the front door and stood there awaiting further instruction from the colonel.

Coughing awkwardly, Richard instructed Jerry to ring the bell since the door was locked. After several moments, Mr. Coates, the butler, answered. Surprise easily overtook the servant's sleepy expression upon seeing the young mistress standing on the front stoop in the middle of the night, accompanied by two men. Yet, his distress evaporated with the recognition that one of the men was none other than Colonel Fitzwilliam.

Georgiana and Richard entered the foyer, followed by Jerry hauling the trunk. The butler exclaimed, "Why, Mistress Darcy, we had no idea!"

"Yes, well, I am sorry for not having informed you sooner, but our plans changed at the last minute. I hope my coming early will not cause any great disturbance to the household."

"Oh, no," cried Mr. Coates, "I can assure you that I am overjoyed to see you, and please rest assured that the rest of the staff and servants will feel the same. Does your maid accompany you?"

"No, she and Mrs. Darcy's sister, Catherine, will join me tomorrow. I hope that will not be a problem."

Richard smiled at Georgiana's unnecessary concern, yet realized that her humanity towards others had always been a part of her gentle nature.

"No, I shall ring for one of the maids to prepare your room, straight away." He bowed before leaving to make the arrangements.

Jerry spoke up, "Well, Colonel, I shall wait for you outside."

Richard nodded to the driver and told him that he would only be a moment longer. He then turned his eyes upon Georgiana. "Well, duck, I guess I shall see you whenever I am granted a leave of absence. However," he sighed, "I am almost certain I shall not receive too many, yet, I do hope to see you some during the Season." His eyes then looked steadily into hers. "I shall miss you, Georgie."

Georgiana detected the tightness in his voice, and when gazing into his eyes, she witnessed the sadness therein, and became conscious that he seemed solemn in their parting. She feared that he felt a premonition that he would not survive the war.

The thought that he might die seized her heart, and tears quickly sprang into her eyes.

"Oh, Richard, please do not leave me. Stay here. Depart from here in the morning. Stay with me tonight!"

"Ah! Georgie, I cannot do such a thing. It would be completely inappropriate."

"Why do you say that? I have ridden in a carriage alone with you with only Jerry as my chaperone. Are you saying this has been improper, too?"

"No, not so much that as…I just feel that circumstances being as they are, now, well…I feel it no longer proper."

"What circumstances? You have spent the night at Ackerley many times when I have been the only family present. Why is it any different now?"

"You are alone and your maid is not with you, Georgie, and neither is your lady's companion."

"Truly, Richard, these are just excuses. You have always been forthright with me. Will you not continue that way now?"

Richard broke eye contact with her. "I feel it is different. That is all I can offer."

"Why will you not say more?"

Looking up sharply, he met her imploring gaze. "Georgie, what do you wish to hear?"

She closed her eyes firmly as a few tears escaped and trickled downward, and then looking deeply within his eyes once more, she implored in a strained voice, "I want you to say you will keep safe, that you will not take any undue risks in battle, and that you will come back to me!"

The strain of the moment overpowered him. Thus, he reached out and pulled Georgiana to his chest, and, closing his eyes tightly as he embraced her, he offered a faint laugh in an attempt to diffuse the tension. "Oh, Georgie, do not worry about me. I am too ornery for our dear Lord to take me home just yet. He needs better men than me."

In anger, she backed out of his arms and spat out, "Stop it, Richard! You are a *good man*. You are *the best man* I know. I never want to hear you, either in seriousness or in jest, refer to yourself as someone who is not worthy."

"Georgie, please, calm down. I did not mean anything by it. I shall do as you ask, and I shall be back before you know I have gone. Besides, I have many weeks of drills and exercises before my company faces war. And there is the slim possibility that we shall not go at all. They may choose not to deploy us."

"No, you will go. I feel it." She began crying harder while covering her face with her hands. Anguished by her fear for his safety and for his inability to proclaim his love for her, she cried out, "Just go, I cannot bear this a moment longer."

"Georgiana, I cannot leave you in such a state. It pulls at my heartstrings to see you so distraught."

Her body began to tremble as she fought to gain control of her emotions, but to little avail. She could not contain her weeping, and thus, she bent over and softly wailed. The burden of knowing that she was the direct cause behind Elizabeth and her brother's discord was almost too much to bear. And additionally, the fear that her past transgression would precede her come-out distressed her greatly, but not nearly as much as the thought of losing the only man she cared for, the only one with whom she could act at ease within his company. That possibility was devastating.

Immediately picking her up in his arms, Richard made his way into the morning room and with the kick of his boot heel, he closed the door, and then sat down in a chair with Georgiana cradled upon his lap. Her body shook from her sobbing, but the comfort of being in the arms of the man she loved soon seeped in to calm her unravelled emotions, and the wails heard only moments before, were replaced by tiny sniffles and the nestling of her brow underneath his chin. The pressure of her head against his neck made Richard painfully aware of how his every swallow felt pronounced, accentuated by the smarting from the constriction within his throat.

Striving to hold back his desire to caress her hair, to smother her with kisses, and to vow that he loved her, Colonel Fitzwilliam remained silent and held her tightly. In spite of this, when Georgiana reached her arms around his neck and pressed her cheek next to his, it became his undoing.

With energy, they both began to pull each other closer and their breathing became erratic as the intensity of their embraces built, soon giving way to one drawn out clench of force. Richard crushed her to his chest and, before he realized it, he began to shower her hair with kisses. When she tilted back her head and raised her eyes to look into his, he stopped only a fraction of a second, before placing his hand on the back of her head and pulling her forehead to his lips. In a frenzy, he placed kisses on her brows, eyelids, and cheeks, and just as Georgiana raised her face upward, yet again, desiring that he capture her lips with his own, Richard perceived the longing in her eyes and somehow came to his senses. He quickly pressed her against his chest, once more, holding her fast while groaning aloud.

The very thing he knew he needed to avoid, he had done. He could not believe that he had practically kissed her lips as well.

"Oh, my, with the witness of the Heavens, Georgie, please forgive me!"

"I love you, Richard, there is nothing to forgive."

She felt his head turn from side to side and then he croaked out, "Oh, I cannot believe I have done this. I am truly ill!"

Georgiana froze. Did he not want her? Was she now compromised that much more with another man that did not love her? She felt ashamed. Thus, she began to arise from Richard's lap when he caught hold of her wrist and pulled her back down, sensing that she had misunderstood his meaning. "Georgie," he cried while embracing her anew, "I feel ill that I have taken advantage of you in this fashion. I feel you deserve so much more. I have nothing to offer you, my dear, sweet girl, nothing at all."

In silence, Georgiana considered his words. Was he saying he wanted her? Finally, she managed to pluck up the fortitude to speak as her head rested on his chest. "Richard, I said I love you. I do not mean as a cousin, a friend, or a brother. I love you in the way a woman loves a man." Not certain that she should go further, she felt that she must, for the chance might never come again. Her tremulous voiced pronounced his name, "Richard…"

In all sincerity, he replied before allowing her to enquire, "Yes, Georgiana, I do love you. I have only recently discovered how much."

Again, she backed out of his arms to look into his face. Their eyes locked. "You love me the way a man loves a woman? The way a husband desires to love his wife?"

"Oh, Georgie," Richard soothed while brushing back a stray lock of hair from off her brow, "a thousand times yes, but I have nothing to offer you and you deserve so much more. I fear I am an old man, Georgie, whereas you are so young—not even out. You have so much of life ahead of you—

you do not want a man such as I. At the Season's end, you will feel differently towards me."

"Well, I hope that I am not *that fickle*! I have desired you for a long time. I shall come out, but, please, Richard, I have no desire to accept any other suitors, for I only want *you*."

Colonel Fitzwilliam could not believe all that was happening. How had he allowed it to transpire? Darcy would kill him. "No, Georgie, I cannot marry you. I only have a salary of two thousand a year. The quality of your customary manner of living would diminish drastically."

"Yes, but, Richard, I have thirty thousand. That will surely help us to live better than you imagine."

Colonel Fitzwilliam inhaled deeply, while cupping his hand over his mouth, searching for a way—endeavouring to make her understand his rationale. His hand slipped downward upon his chin before stating, "Georgie, I am almost thirty years of age. You are not yet seventeen. I am destined to serve in the army for the whole of my life. I cannot ask you to follow me from assignment to assignment. It is too much to ask of any woman, but I especially could not ask it of you."

"Why, not me, Richard? Why, am I better than any other colonel's wife or a general's wife? I am a woman, just as they are."

"But, Georgie, you have the ability to marry for so much more. You could have a husband who would offer you security and stability, which I could never do."

"Richard, are you saying that Fitzwilliam should never have married Elizabeth?"

"Oh, of course not, but his situation is far different! Your brother would not have been deprived of his means of living, whereas, if you were to marry me, that is exactly the situation you shall face. And, Georgie," his voice caught in emotion as a look of pain overtook his features, "you would have to give up so much if you married me. I do not know how I could bear depriving you so."

"Do you not think that I should have a right to make that decision for myself? Or is it that you do not desire me for your wife?"

With a catch in his voice, he made his answer, "Oh…I do desire you, Georgie. It is just that I know that you deserve the best, and I am certain that I am not the zenith that you can obtain."

"I told you, Richard, I never want to hear you say such things again! I only desire you, and I shall always desire you! I do not wish to wallow through the *ton's* prescribed display." She rolled her eyes in emphasis, and Richard smiled at the adorable, exasperated look that crossed over her features. "What do you find so amusing?" she queried.

"I find *you* amusing."

"Oh!" she replied in charmed surprise. "And do you find it in your heart to consider my feelings concerning us, Richard?"

"Very well, Georgiana. I do love you, and I do wish to marry you. However..." He lifted a finger to stop her interruption. She closed her mouth and patiently listened. "As I said, I shall not be here for your coming out. I shall miss seeing you dressed in your finery, surrounded by so many admirers, and I can honestly admit that I am, quite frankly glad of it. I am afraid I would not be able to contain my jealousy." Georgiana's eyes sparkled in delight at his confession. She could not believe he had actually admitted that he was madly in love with her. He observed her expression and shook his head in amusement at her unreservedly gleeful expression. "Yes, I am besotted with you, Georgie. You knew exactly what you were doing when dancing with Ashton Caldecott." She smirked and tried to avert her gaze, but Richard caught hold of her chin and made her look at him. "How shall I survive with such a sly wife?"

Her heart nearly leapt into her throat. He had truly declared himself!

Taking in her anticipation, he quickly came back to his point. "I shall not ask to court you until you have gone to all the parties that you can, until you have mingled with all the young men with whom you shall be introduced, and until you truly know if the whirl of London society sickens you to the very core of your being. Then, and only then, shall I make my addresses known. If, however, you discover that you love the thrills that all the assemblies have to offer, adore men's admiring smiles, and if by chance, a young man other than me captures your heart, then I shall understand. The only thing I promise at this moment is that we have an understanding of what *you* need to do. Do I make myself absolutely clear?"

A smile diffused across her face. "Yes, I understand you perfectly."

"Well then, I must go now."

He continued to sit, and she did not move a muscle either. They stared affectionately at one another for several moments, each overcome by their declaration of love to the other. At length, Georgiana quietly said, "I love you, Richard. Do not forget about me."

Nodding, he pulled her to him, enfolding her close to his chest while drawing in air through his parted lips before stating, "Oh, this will not do. We cannot keep expressing our feelings in this fashion. I do love you, but I truly want you to enjoy this time. It is your *special* time. I shall always love you, even if you choose another. I shall not forget you! I love you, Georgiana. Do you hear me, for I am saying it freely? But, we have an agreement, do we not?"

Inhaling deeply, she nodded. "Yes, we do." Then, with one last squeeze, she arose from his lap and stood. He likewise followed suit.

"Will you still write to me?"

"Yes, I shall write to you as often as I am able. And I remember, I will write only to you."

She smiled happily with his renewed conviction. Taking him by the hand, she led him to the door and asked, "Will you not kiss me, Richard?"

"No, Georgiana, my lips shall not touch yours until you become my betrothed. Then and only then shall we taste each other's kisses."

She nodded and reluctantly replied, "Very well."

Opening the door, he made his way to the entrance and pulled at his watch fob. Poor Jerry he thought. It was now one-thirty. They stood transfixed. He wanted nothing more than to grab her up into his arms and tell her how much he desired her yet again, but, he could not. Thus, he whispered hoarsely, "I shall write to you, Georgie."

"I shall write to you, too." He nodded and lifted her hand to his lips, bestowing a loving kiss thereon. Then, looking deeply into her eyes one last time, he turned to quickly open the door and quit the house.

The silent elation Georgiana felt within her breast was enough. She knew he loved and needed her. His actions confirmed that more than his words ever could. Her body, while surrounded by his arms, awakened to something it had never felt before. Resolute in keeping her word, she climbed the stairs to her chamber, making a mental commitment that she would be the most engaging woman of the Season, proving to Richard and her brother that she could be socially adept. Yet, for herself, she need not make such a show because she knew and felt certain in her own heart that she would become Mrs. Richard Fitzwilliam.

~*~

With a satisfied air, Darcy returned from Lambton. All was in place for them to depart for London on the morrow. Walking into the house through the courtyard entrance, he asked a servant to inform Mrs. Reynolds of his return and to have her meet him in his study. The young maid bobbed her head and scurried away to do her master's bidding.

As Darcy rounded the corner of the front entrance hall, he became aware of Mr. Greene approaching him. Hence, he stopped in his tracks and waited for the elderly gentleman to join him. "Mr. Darcy, a young woman from Longbourn has arrived within the past hour. She and Mrs. Reynolds are awaiting you in the library."

"Ah! This is wonderful news, Greene. I shall go and join them. Thank you."

Darcy felt true and complete satisfaction. Sarah had been the only remaining loose end. He could not believe that she had arrived. Earlier, he had decided that they would leave for London without her and that he would arrange a carriage to deliver her to Ackerley at a later time.

But now, all was falling into place. In his mind, Darcy felt he could not leave too soon.

Mrs. Reynolds immediately stood with a smile upon her face as the master entered the room. He smiled at her in return, and then his eyes focused upon Sarah. He noticed that the girl appeared quite young and seemed a little nervous as she glanced up at him, and then quickly averted her gaze. When she stood, Darcy's suspicion was confirmed by the apprehensive, unsteady manner in which she arose.

He stepped forward and promptly offered his hand to the girl, his eyes smiling with warmth. Her eyes widened, but she shook his hand with a quick firm grasp. "Sarah, I am happy that you are here. I hope your journey was not too strenuous, for we shall leave for London early in the morning. Our plans have been altered, and we must depart sooner than intended." She nodded her understanding in a blank fashion. Darcy then asked with delight, "Have you seen Mrs. Darcy, yet?"

She shook her head.

"Ah, well, we shall remedy that situation post-haste." But then, lowering his head, he paused and commented further, "Hmmm, on second thought, she has no idea you are coming." His head shot up and a bright light gleamed from his eyes as he eagerly asked, "Do you mind if we surprise her with your presence?"

Amazed that this tall, formidable gentleman would suggest such a thing, Sarah nodded hesitantly, a little uncertain of the idea but game all the same. Mr. Darcy seemed happier than ever in witnessing her agreement. The evident joy in his countenance proved contagious, and Sarah Hill soon found herself just as excited at the thought of Elizabeth's shock upon seeing her. Thus, she returned the master's boyish grin with a silly one all her own.

"Splendid!" he exclaimed with a clap of his hands. Darcy then realized that he sounded similar to Bingley and chuckled at himself all the more. "Mrs. Reynolds, please take Sarah to her quarters and offer her something to eat. I am sure she is famished." He looked at the maid, yet again, with gladness in his eyes. "I shall ring for Sarah to come when I have all ready. In the meantime, introduce her to Chaffin, show her the servants' stairway to reach our chambers, and, please, accompany her to my dressing chamber when I ring. Then, we shall surprise the mistress." His eyes twinkled at the thought of Elizabeth's delight. "Oh, and Mrs. Reynolds?" The elderly woman paused to see what else he desired. "Please send some maids up with buckets of hot water as soon as possible." The housekeeper nodded, and then directed Sarah towards the kitchen.

Ecstatic, Darcy took the steps of the grand staircase two at a time, eager to see his wife.

Quietly opening her chamber door, he espied her asleep. Softly, he stepped over to the bed and, for a moment, indulged his fancy, observing her snuggled up with his pillow to her chest. His brow creased at the realization that Elizabeth slept soundly. He wondered if she had just lain down or whether she had been resting for the entire time he had been away.

Delicately, he sat upon the mattress and, owing to the rosy hue of her complexion, felt her forehead to determine if she were feverish. No, she was not with fever.

"Lizzy, my love, I have returned from Lambton. Are you unwell? How long have you been resting?"

"Hmm?" she muttered while opening her eyes and yawning wide, "I have been asleep since you left with Mr. Sheldon. Is there something wrong?" Rubbing her eyes while rising upon her elbow, attempting to discern the hands on the clock, she queried, "What time is it?"

"It is almost time to dress for dinner, my love. Would a hot bath sound agreeable to you?"

Elizabeth suppressed another yawn with the back of her hand before replying. "Oh, yes, that would be lovely. A hot soak sounds heavenly."

"The water is on its way."

"Oh, Fitzwilliam, you are too good to me. I think you have been the best lady's maid that I have ever had."

He frowned suddenly, followed by a quick roll of his eyes. "Oh my, Fitzwilliam, such a look, and it is not even Sunday," she cried.

"Lucky for you, Elizabeth, I shall overlook such remarks and shall aid you despite your ridicule."

Sitting up, she tried to ascertain if he were truly offended. He seemed to become most solemn. "Oh, Fitzwilliam, I *am* only teasing. I love your consideration and attentiveness. I shall miss your attentions when I obtain another maid."

"Yes, well, when you do acquire another maid, I shall, indeed, have time to myself again."

A little taken aback by his comment, Elizabeth stared at him in wonder, trying to determine if what he had said were in jest. Suddenly, the sound of the maids in the dressing chamber could be discerned.

Reaching out his hand to her, Darcy bid, "Come, Lizzy, let us get you ready for dinner."

Willingly, she began to undress with her husband's assistance and soon found herself relaxing in the tub.

The warm water felt wonderful to Elizabeth's fatigued body. Upon entering the bath, she felt instantly rejuvenated. Leisurely, Darcy hung about, having gone to his own chambers only moments before, just long enough to ring for Mrs. Reynolds and Sarah. When he returned to her boudoir, he began to pursue idle conversation, contriving an interest in her gowns and asking which fabrics she favoured the most. As a barrage of remarks continued to roll from Darcy's lips, a tiny sense of annoyance began to assail Elizabeth's nerves at her husband's odd behaviour. She could not begin to relax with him offering constant comments and questions such as: "I find you look best in the colour of white with a faint yellowish tinge to it. Do you not agree?"

Abruptly, he walked over to the tub, fixing his eyes on her lovely form. In a smitten trance, he stated, "I think you will need more towels. I shall be right back."

Elizabeth hastily called after him, "Oh, please *do* take your time, Fitzwilliam. I am in no hurry."

He turned and looked into her eyes, nodding with a faint smile on his face, then his eyes momentarily slipped lower and became mesmerized by her womanly form once more. Sighing, he again mumbled a few words and was gone.

Elizabeth laid her head back upon the tub's rim and closed her eyes. "Ah! This feels divine, so peaceful."

Hearing the adjoining door open, she lifted her eyes heavenward, waiting for another onslaught of observations, yet silence ensued. "Fitzwilliam, are you there? I know I heard you come in. Are you there, my love?" Lifting her brows, she wondered if she were imagining things.

Darcy stood behind the door, peeping around it. With his eyes, he encouraged Sarah, who kept looking over her shoulder in a hesitant fashion, to walk forward and, from behind, offer Elizabeth the towel.

"Oh, Fitzwilliam," Elizabeth cried, "why ever did you not answer me?" She took the proffered linen and began to stand up. Sarah stood ready, holding open Elizabeth's robe in her raised hands. Again, she waited behind the mistress to offer her the wrap, and Elizabeth teasingly stated, while drying off her body, "My, Fitzwilliam, you are so very quiet compared to earlier. I presume, after having noticed the transfixed manner in which you were staring at my breasts, that you desire to *rest* before dinner?"

Sarah turned red as a beetroot as did Darcy. Mrs. Reynolds, situated behind the master, only raised her eyebrows. Elizabeth turned, expecting to see her husband's amused smile at her provocative suggestion, but instead, she was thunderstruck and screamed in fright. Happily distinguishing Sarah's face, she called out her name, and quickly stepped out of the tub to hug the young woman, taking no thought that she held only a towel to her bare chest. Sarah did not mind a bit, howbeit, a bright blush still graced her cheeks. After returning a quick embrace, she helped to put the robe around Elizabeth's shoulders.

Mrs. Reynolds, still standing to the rear of her master, who nimbly poked his head around the door, smiled at the mistress' response and the master's eager interest, and then silently showed herself out through the servants' passage.

"Sarah, I cannot believe you are here!" Elizabeth exclaimed as she tied the sash of her robe. "When did you arrive?"

"Oh, your husband, Mr. Darcy, sent a missive to your father, asking if your mother and sister could spare me. Mr. Bennet asked Mrs. Bennet, and she asked my mamma. They were all willing to let me come to you if I wanted, and I did, I mean, I do."

Giggling in delight, Elizabeth just shook her head, her eyes glistening. Pulling Sarah to her again, she held her closely and passionately related,

"Oh, Sarah, I am so glad you have come and that you desired to come of your own accord. I have missed you all so dearly."

The young maid smiled meekly and nodded.

"Ahem," Darcy cleared his throat. Whirling around, Elizabeth became aware of him standing in the doorway. Levelling a feigned look of anger towards her husband, she cried, "Oh, you are a devious man, you are!"

"I take it you are pleased, Lizzy?"

A bright smile beamed from Elizabeth's countenance as she replied wholeheartedly, "Yes, I am."

"I am glad to hear it. I shall leave you two then and go and dress for dinner."

Elizabeth gazed lovingly into his eyes, silently communicating her heartfelt gratitude for his thoughtfulness on her behalf.

"Thank you, Fitzwilliam."

Darcy smiled, pleased that the surprise had thrilled his wife to such an extent and, after a quick, responsive blink of his eyes to offer his heartfelt acceptance of her appreciation, he retreated into his own chamber, closing the door behind him.

~*~

After dinner, Darcy and Elizabeth retired to the library to spend the remainder of their evening in the leisure activities of reading and letter writing. The hour found Mr. Chaffin and Sarah busily engaged in Mr. and Mrs. Darcy's respective chambers, gathering, folding, and packing their master's and mistress' trunks for London. Elizabeth sat at a table attempting to catch up on her overdue correspondence. Thus, she was quite happy to have concluded one letter to Charlotte and another to Sally, but most importantly, before having penned either missive, she had written a letter of thanks to her parents for their generosity in sending Sarah. She told them that having Sarah with her made her feel as if she had a part of them also.

Darcy sat at the desk reading the newspaper. He noted that Parliament planned to convene in two weeks time. Thus, they must plan for Georgiana's Season immediately when arriving in London. Laying the paper aside, he glanced at his wife and realized that she had just capped the ink bottle, indicating that she had finished for the evening. He observed her as she sat lost in thought for some moments and noticed a blush spread on her cheeks.

"Elizabeth, are you feeling well?"

"Oh, yes, quite so."

"But I see that you are flushed. Are you sure you are well?"

Sighing loudly, she acknowledged, "I only suffer from a delayed reaction. That is all."

"A delayed reaction to what, my love?"

"Ah, I feel embarrassment for having thought Sarah was you, for I made a reference to your gazing upon my…umm…bosom."

Smiling knowingly at her, he stated, "Yes, I am afraid it was my fault for staring at you so, but when I find such beauty before me, I am at a loss."

"Well, you are forgiven. This is only the first time for such embarrassment in front of Sarah, though I am sure there shall be many more in the course of our marriage. Since I have a lady's maid once more, what do you plan on doing, now having your time to yourself again?"

"Gaze freely upon my wife as her maid unpins her hair and readies her for bed."

"Oh, Fitzwilliam, I am afraid that I shall blush profusely if you do so, and so shall Sarah."

"Blush, if you will. In fact, my dear wife, according to Fordyce, it pleases a man. 'When a girl ceases to blush, she has lost the most powerful charm of beauty.'"

"Oh, no, Fitzwilliam, this will not do. *You* quoting *Fordyce*? I fear for our daughters."

Darcy smiled engagingly to her. "Come now, Lizzy, Fordyce has some merit to his views."

"Ha! I am glad you think so because—"

"Yes, I think having Mary for the summer is a wonderful idea."

"Fitzwilliam, however did you know that I was prepared to ask that very thing of you?"

"There is no great mystery there, Lizzy. We were discussing Fordyce. I only presumed that you should desire your sister to stay on with us after your parents' visit. After all, Kitty is with Jane and Charles. I am sure Mary's time with us will do her good. I think that when we are in London, I shall purchase a special book for her."

Darcy arose and walked over to his wife. "Come, Lizzy, we have a long day tomorrow."

"It is rather early to retire, Fitzwilliam. What shall we do to occupy our time? Shall you quote more from Fordyce?" She smirked.

"Yes, I suppose I could. Obedience of womankind is definitely one of Fordyce's fortes, and one I am rather fond of myself."

Fervently, Elizabeth said, "Ha! I would desire that we discuss anything besides Fordyce. Believe me when I say that I am *rather* familiar with all of his sentiments."

Darcy chuckled and then stated, "Francis Bacon agrees with you, my dear. He says: 'some books are to be tasted, others to be swallowed, and some few to be chewed and digested.'"

"I should like to add another category, some books—Fordyce's in particular—are to be gagged upon and then heaved."

Darcy smiled and put his arm around her shoulders, squeezing her close as he exclaimed, "Enough of books. I cannot think about them when I am in my bedchamber. I am sure we can find more agreeable topics of interest to discuss there.”

“Pray, sir, such as?”

“I could recite poetry to you, if you think our love is stout and healthy enough to bear it. I could even help you memorize some passages in preparation for Mrs. Chalmers’s gathering.”

They reached the landing of the stairs when Elizabeth granted her husband permission to proceed with his recitation, which prompted him to enquire, “Are you familiar with the works of Robert Herrick?”

“No, but his name sounds familiar.”

“Well, he was born in Cheapside and became a vicar. He never married and died as a bachelor at the age of three and eighty. I came upon his poetry in my youth, and I must say, Lizzy, there was a time I read him as much as Mary reads Fordyce. There is one poem in particular that I feel you should share with the bluestockings.”

“Oh?”

They stood in the hallway and Elizabeth watched her husband close his eyes trying to recall from memory the particular verse.”

When opening them again, he said, “Ah, I think it goes something like this:

> HAVE ye beheld (with much delight)
> A red rose peeping through a white?
> Or else a cherry, double grac’d,
> Within a lily centre plac’d?
> Or ever mark’d the pretty beam
> A strawberry shows half-drown’d in cream?
> Or seen rich rubies blushing through
> A pure smooth pearl and orient too?
> So like to this, nay all the rest,
> Is each neat niplet of her breast.”

“Fitzwilliam Darcy, you are appalling! You are a teasing man! You have contrived that verse yourself!”

His eyes bespoke humour at seeing Elizabeth’s shock. “I assure you, my sweet wife, I did no such thing.”

“That cannot be a true poem, Fitzwilliam.”

“Oh, yes, I have the book in the library to prove it.”

“Pray then, what is the name of the poem?”

“I am afraid the title is more shocking than the actual poem, ‘Upon the Nipples of Julia’s Breast’.”

Cupping her hands over her mouth, an unmistakable, flabbergasted look took up residence in Elizabeth’s eyes. They, however, soon danced in merriment as she narrowed them upon her husband and exclaimed, “Yes, I can well imagine you reading such poetry without end.”

"Well, Lizzy, after all, I am a man."

Raising one brow to him, she saucily agreed, "Oh, yes, Fitzwilliam, I am well aware of that fact. I can assure you, it has not escaped my notice."

"Yes, well," he stated while smiling naughtily. "Shall we retire now, or should I fetch Herrick's book of poetry from the library and read to you? There is one poem in particular that describes how I felt on my second observation of you, Lizzy, and on every observation thereafter."

"Oh, and the poem that you have just recited does not remind you of me?"

With his mellow voice, he made a significant declaration as he looked deeply into Elizabeth's eyes, "Oh, most certainly, but I now find a great discrepancy between the poet's expressive words and the exquisite beauty that I find in your voluptuousness. No words can begin to give credit to your beauty, Elizabeth... none whatsoever."

Elizabeth gazed into his eyes, reflecting the deep love that she, too, felt. Her pulse quickened, and then, with unadulterated feeling, she whispered, "I think we shall retire now, William."

Darcy's eyes widened slightly as he stared at her in amazement. She had only called him by that name during their heightened moments of intimacy. A small smile began to steal over his features.

Notwithstanding the master and mistress retiring early for the night, they found ample inspiration to occupy their hours to the agreeability of both, before collapsing into blissful oblivion.

~*~

Chapter Twenty-three

The Epitome of Discretion

The brilliant weather exhibited only a hint of a mild breeze for the long ride out to Sandhurst Park. Darcy affectionately pulled his wife close to his side, inhaling the lavender scent from her skin. Elizabeth tilted her head upward in reaction to his gesture and rewarded her husband with a radiant smile. She loved riding in the open carriage, taking pleasure in the clean fresh air. It reminded her of the trip she had taken last year with her Aunt and Uncle Gardiner, and yet, now, as a married woman with her doting husband by her side, she experienced a new dimension of happiness she had never imagined possible. The contentment that she presently felt in their marriage permeated her soul.

Upon leaving Pemberley for London, Darcy and Elizabeth had first discussed their dilemma, and then decided that it was best not to enlighten Georgiana about George Wickham's threat of blackmail. They both felt that the knowledge of Wickham's intimidation to divulge his and Georgiana's secret engagement at Ramsgate would only alarm Georgie, causing her undue fear at a time when she already endured so much anxiety regarding the upcoming Season and her debut into society. Darcy also consulted with Elizabeth concerning the generous offer from his aunt, Lady Matlock, to assist in presenting Georgiana for her coming-out. Elizabeth listened to all the advantages and disadvantages. After weighing each one, they both agreed that acceptance would offer the best course, especially considering that they would need all of their energy to tackle the current situation regarding Wickham. Elizabeth felt that allowing Aunt Adie, and even Lady Hazelton, to assist would only strengthen the familial bond between the relations. Therefore, they would gladly accept Lady Matlock's proposal to throw a ball and consent to Elisha's offer to orchestrate Georgiana's acceptance to Almack's. Hopefully, they could also petition on behalf of Kitty, that she might be granted a voucher into that establishment for the one evening as a guest of the Darcy family.

The morning after they had arrived in London, Darcy sent missives to his aunt and his cousin's wife, accepting their kind offers if they still stood. Immediately, both women responded that they were only too happy to oblige. Lady Matlock's sentiments read as genuine. She delighted in the thought of participating in her niece's special Season. Within her heart, she knew that Georgiana's mother, Lady Anne, would have been happy to know that the Fitzwilliam family rallied around her children.

In contrast, Lady Hazelton's expressed views to Darcy were not sincere in the least. She suffered anger at the knowledge that he would dare ask her for the favour of Catherine Bennet joining her and Georgiana for their interview with the patroness of Almack's. What was Darcy thinking? Elisha felt mortified and, in no uncertain terms, told Lord Hazelton that it was an outrage and a vulgar presumption on Darcy's part. Despite her husband's attempt to calm her with gushing admiration of her abilities and indulgent promises for anything she desired, infuriation with the Fitzwilliam family surged through her, and she voiced them quite openly. They expected too much from her and did not appreciate the fact that their son had married into one of the most illustrious families in England. The Viscount inwardly rolled his eyes at his wife's oft-repeated grievances while silently questioning. *What on earth do the Fitzwilliams have to do with a request that came from the Darcys?*

~*~

As the carriage proceeded down the Exeter Coaching Road, Darcy began to relax a bit. Reflecting upon his arrival at Ackerley, where he found his sister safe in the company of Miss Catherine, he had felt instant relief. However, Georgiana and Kitty informed him that they had planned a shopping expedition for the following day, yet his desire to seek out Colonel Fitzwilliam at Sandhurst, to consult with him about Wickham's threats and a legal concern, took precedence and since they could not go without male escort, he had suspended their happy plans. His refusal caused Georgiana to become frustrated with him, but she said nothing. Kitty, on the other hand, as they all relaxed within the library, made such a mournful expression and moped about so shamelessly that Darcy truly felt like a cad. Elizabeth, observing her younger sister's rude behaviour, had taken her off to one side of the room and whispered softly to her, trying to talk some sense into the girl's head. She spoke firmly but with affection, telling Kitty that her new brother had urgent matters to which he must attend and then promising her that they would plan another shopping trip upon their return. When her counsel seemed to take hold, Elizabeth felt significant gratitude, for Kitty no longer frowned nor openly lamented the unforeseen delay in their plans.

Then, as luck would have it, the unexpected happened. Mr. Coates came into the room to inform his master that Mr. Charles Bingley had arrived to look in on the ladies. Darcy informed his butler to have Mr. Bingley come to the library straight away. Bingley was a little taken aback to find Elizabeth and Darcy within, since he still thought them at Pemberley.

Darcy thanked his brother-in-law for his kindness, apologized for not having contacted him sooner regarding their early arrival, and requested that Kitty stay on a while longer. They agreed upon this, and then Bingley happened to mention that he and Jane would be out shopping on the morrow. Georgiana piped up and asked if it were possible for her and Kitty to accompany them. She noticed that her brother seemed somewhat annoyed at her forward manner, but, when Bingley's face lit up, thinking it a splendid idea, Fitzwilliam's countenance seemed to soften.

Darcy walked with his brother-in-law to the door, thanked him yet again, and then paused. Bingley noticed the pensive look on his friend's face and the uptight deportment of his stance, and sensed that he seemed troubled. So, he waited, in silence. He knew Darcy required time to mull over everything on his mind before ever saying a word. Finally, Darcy looked into Charles Bingley's eyes and charged, "I need you to promise me, Bingley, that you will keep an eagle's eye upon the girls tomorrow. They require a male escort at *all* times while in London."

In concern, Bingley assured him, "Of course, Darce, you can count on me. Is something amiss? I mean, I know it is none of my affair, but has something happened?"

Averting his gaze, Darcy replied unevenly, "Well...yes...and no." He then lifted his eyes to meet Bingley's and stated, "I promise, however, that I shall tell you all when the time is right. I do not wish to worry Georgiana, but I am concerned that Wickham may have taken up residence in London. I know you do not know the whole history about him, but you do know that he cannot be trusted. Please, look after them, Charles."

"On my honour, Darcy, I will. I hope your fears are unwarranted. I shall make sure the girls remain in my company."

"Thank you, Charles. I feel I can depart for Sandhurst tomorrow with barely a worry, knowing that you will accompany them."

~*~

Hence, at present, Fitzwilliam Darcy's concerns had lessened as the miles took them further from London and further from his sister's side. When the carriage began to enter a wooded area, Darcy began to expound to Elizabeth on historical details of interest for the remainder of their journey.

"This, Elizabeth, is the Windsor Forest. It served as the royal hunting grounds for many centuries. Sandhurst was originally a farming community that thrived on the abundance of deer and swine that freely roamed here. The River Blackwater was a favourite with the sovereigns. It is known that King Henry VIII would hunt and fish from sunup to dusk."

Elizabeth stated impertinently, "Truly, it is a wonder that the king found any time to hunt for venison amongst his chase for so many *wives*."

Darcy smiled wryly and then continued. "Yes, well, Sandhurst became an estate which was purchased by a retired army officer. He sold it to his wife's uncle, Prime Minister William Pitt, who, in turn, sold it a few months later to the War Ministry. It is thought to be a perfect location for the training of cadets in that it is an adequate distance from the distraction of London's amusements. The park takes in the union of three counties: Surry, Berkshire, and Hampshire. The Royal Military College was completed just last year, taking a total of eleven years to build. The first six years were devoted to the manufacture of the bricks alone. It is a stately building, one that I think you shall find impressive."

Elizabeth smiled. "Fitzwilliam, I stand amazed at your breadth of knowledge. I always find it fascinating when you share it with me."

"Well, Lizzy, you once told me I was a man of sense and education, and as such, it is my pleasure to share what I know with a woman who can appreciate it." He gave her a roguish grin with a twinkle in his eyes. Turning to the left, he said, "Ah, it looks as if we have arrived."

As the Darcy carriage pulled up to the central portico, known as the Grand Entrance in front of the white elongated edifice, Elizabeth gazed at the building, taking in all she saw as she admired the eight massive pillars in the Doric style of Greece. It seemed to her that the pillars stood as sentinels to the two flights of steps. As they ascended, Elizabeth noticed and admired the ironwork of the lantern holders adorned with lions' heads and claws. The brass door handles and foot scrapers at the entrance bore the same lion ornamentation.

The Darcys were shown into the waiting area of the Major-General's office. They did not wait long, however, for as soon as General Kirkham heard who desired to speak with him, the Darcys were ushered into his office without delay.

"Mr. Darcy, I am happy to make your acquaintance, for your generosity to the college is greatly appreciated." Elizabeth's eyebrows rose in surprise as her husband smiled modestly in acceptance of General Kirkham's words of acknowledgement regarding his monetary support. Darcy then reciprocated the General's compliments, and, in turn, introduced his wife to him. After all greetings were complete, the commander asked them to have a seat and offered them some wine. They seated themselves in the chairs but graciously declined any refreshment. General Kirkham asked how he might assist them and volunteered to conduct them on a personal tour of the building. Again, Darcy declined the honour but stated that they would enjoy such a privilege at a future time. A tour would then be most welcome. After expressing his gratitude for the General's kindness, he finally came to his point and requested special permission to seek out his cousin, Colonel Fitzwilliam. He explained to General Kirkham that he and his cousin held joint guardianship over his sister, and owing to pressing legal issues, he needed to obtain his cousin's advice before having some documents officially authorized by his attorney in London.

The general quickly called for a cadet to come with fresh horses and a carriage to take the Darcys out to the North section of the Barrosa Training

Area. After dismissing the young man, General Kirkham turned to Darcy to expound on his cousin's military service.

"Mr. Darcy, your cousin, Colonel Fitzwilliam, is an exceptional officer. He performs his duties with discretion and his men admire him greatly. He has a natural knack and the ability to discipline with such diplomacy and composure that he succeeds where other leaders are rarely successful."

The general smiled at his guests and continued, "Forasmuch as he holds high expectations for his men to excel and exhibit complete obedience, he leads them with not only a firm hand, but with a sense of humour, which makes the men honour him all the more. He asks no more of them than he does of himself. His troops are among the finest, best trained soldiers I have ever seen, and also the happiest."

Darcy smiled at the compliments that the general offered on behalf of his cousin. He knew of Richard's talent in humouring his men, but he found the added insight, that Richard demanded excellence in his soldiers, enlightening.

While walking out to the carriage, General Kirkham again thanked Mr. Darcy for his generous endowments to the college. He told him that they were welcome to return at anytime, and again offered a tour of the establishment at their convenience.

A young cadet, Daniel Higgins, drove them out to the fields. Darcy asked him how the area received the name Barrosa and why the troops drilled in this locale. The youth explained that the sandy terrain resembled that found over on the Continent at the site of a Peninsular War battle, the Battle of Barrosa, and the Royal Military College staff named it thus since the War Ministry was anxious to have this area designated exclusively for combat training given all the British casualties suffered at the beginning of the campaigns.

The carriage turned off the main road and onto the fields. Thus, the ride became bumpy. Cadet Higgins reined in the horses and leaned down to ask a lieutenant to direct them to the location of Colonel Fitzwilliam. The officer pointed him in the right direction, and they resumed crossing the training ground.

When the horses came to a halt, the young man jumped down and tied the steeds to a nearby tree. He then excused himself to the couple to go and enquire after the colonel's whereabouts. Gazing across the expanse of the field, Darcy and Elizabeth observed young men traversing felled tree trunks strategically positioned over a large stream. After a few moments, they detected Richard on the other side of the water with his arm draped around a young man who appeared no more than fifteen years of age. They stood with their backs turned away from the remaining company who attempted to retain their balance as they relentlessly scurried back and forth across the logs. Dripping wet, the lad appeared distraught, and Richard stood there for some time speaking with him.

As they descended the steps of the carriage, Darcy and Elizabeth took note of how the young man's head nodded every so often while the colonel leaned in close to his ear. They then observed Richard offering the youth an encouraging squeeze on the shoulder and a slap on the lad's back before turning around to inspect the activity of the rest of his men.

Colonel Fitzwilliam bellowed out for his band of soldiers to speed up their progress, emphasizing his point with a loud clap of his hands, "*Grandmamma* moved slowly boys, but she was an old woman. Let's hoof it up!"

Suddenly, the colonel became aware that some of his men across the stream dallied about, looking at something in the distance. Richard quickly scanned the field before him to see what had distracted them. He smirked when seeing his cousin and Elizabeth standing by the carriage. Chuckling low, he realized the lads were admiring Darcy's wife.

Imparting an enthusiastic wave overhead towards the Darcys to acknowledge their presence, the colonel hurriedly stepped in line with his men as they advanced in the direction of his relations. Darcy marvelled at his cousin's dexterity, balance, and speed in negotiating the long section of trunk without faltering. While crossing, the colonel called to his men to quit gawking and get back to their drills, assuring them that he would return presently to scrutinize their progress.

Smiling brightly as he approached Darcy and Elizabeth, he pulled off his gloves and slipped them over his belt. Sweating profusely, he pulled out a handkerchief to wipe the moisture from his face. He walked up to Darcy, and the cousins clasped arms and hands. He then bowed to Elizabeth. She nodded her head and curtseyed in return.

Breathlessly, he exclaimed, "Why Darcy...Elizabeth...I am at a loss to see you so soon and here of all places. I hope all is well. I can see that Georgie does not accompany you. She is well I presume?" Elizabeth could hear the apprehension in Richard's enquiry.

With a disgruntled air, Darcy stated, "She is well for now. I need to speak with you, Fitzwilliam, and I know that you are busy with your training, but General Kirkham assured me I could speak with you if necessary while you are here at Sandhurst. I hesitate to interfere with your duties, but I urgently need your opinion on a matter of great import. It is about Wickham. I have written a letter describing everything in detail, and I ask that you read it and then burn it when you have finished." Darcy reached into the inside pocket of his greatcoat to retrieve the missive. Richard accepted it and immediately placed it securely within his own coat pocket. He noticed a blush spread upon Elizabeth's cheeks and realized with confusion that something had embarrassed her.

Darcy looked pointedly at his cousin. "Wickham is attempting to blackmail Elizabeth if we do not send him a monthly allowance. He threatens to inform London society of his engagement and near elopement with Georgiana, and I am sure he would embellish his tale quite grotesquely. However, as my letter will explain, he has also threatened my life and the lives of others if his demands are not met."

Richard's eyes bulged, balking at the very thought. But then he drew in a decisive breath as his jaw clenched and his vision narrowed.

Elizabeth caught her breath at the sight of the instant anger that flared up in Colonel Fitzwilliam's expression and deportment, his hands forming into tightened fists and his eyes blazing with fury. She had never witnessed the colonel in such a state as this. He seemed quite fierce. He swore loudly and then turned quickly around when realizing he had done so in front of her. Darcy cast an apologetic look to his wife and whispered, "Elizabeth, we will just walk a short distance, but I shall return promptly. Please remain next to the carriage."

She smiled slightly and nodded her head reassuringly at her husband.

When the cousins had moved several paces away, Darcy implored Richard to read his missive if he could perhaps spare some additional time away from his troop. Colonel Fitzwilliam pulled it from his pocket and began to read the particulars. His younger cousin had painstakingly given an account of all the details gathered from the letters written to Elizabeth by her youngest sister and new brother and from all that Elizabeth had told him personally. He did not omit a single point. Thus, Richard learned about Wickham accosting his wife in Lambton, and the lascivious references he had made to her. The communication also enlightened him regarding the forgery of the bank draft and the threat to kill Darcy in order to have free access to Georgiana should Elizabeth not cooperate.

Darcy monitored Richard's expressions as he followed the events unfolding in the letter, waiting patiently for him to finish before stating, "I fear he has taken the money and now stays in London at the gaming tables. I fear for Georgiana and her reputation. I do not think she shall be able to bear it if anything untoward manages to get out and starts to circulate around the rumour mill of the *ton*. I worry she may retreat into that silent creature she became after Ramsgate. Yet, what I fear most is that he may try to harm her. I cannot believe he has sunk so low. He holds such anger because I made him marry Lydia."

Shaking his head repeatedly, Richard struggled to keep his emotions in check. At the moment, he wanted nothing more than to retrieve his gun, take the carriage, track Wickham down, and put a bullet through the bastard's skull.

Standing there in silence for several moments, Darcy waited for his cousin to respond. Richard had dropped his head and held the letter wadded up in his right hand. His anger showed clearly, as it had when he had heard about the attempted elopement. No, it seemed greater, for Darcy had never seen him remain this silent for so long.

Finally, Darcy could wait no longer and exclaimed, "Elizabeth and I felt it best not to inform Georgiana of any of this. We do not wish to spoil her Season in London."

This logic elicited a small response from the colonel and he began to nod periodically while his eyes remained focused on the ground.

Darcy continued, "I need to know what you think, Fitzwilliam. Should I search for Wickham? I could start with Mrs. Younge, but with the amount of money at his disposal, he may seek finer establishments and accommodations."

Again, the colonel merely nodded.

"I also desire your permission to safeguard Georgiana's inheritance in a special holding, not allowing her or her future husband to have access to it, until she is much older—something I should have done long ago. I have given this considerable thought for the past few days, and I am of the mind that it may discourage predators who seek to marry her solely for her fortune. Of course, I do realize it is not foolproof. She shall always be welcome to live at Pemberley should I die before she obtains her inheritance. I thought to put the age of receipt at thirty. What do you think? Is it too much to ask?"

Richard's head shot up. He looked Darcy squarely in the eyes. "She may need that money if she does not marry into wealth. It would help her continue to have a lady's maid and insure that she does not want for luxuries."

Darcy's brow creased. "I know this, but I cannot imagine that this will be the case with her. She is beautiful and talented, and I am sure there shall be many men of means who think so. I feel it adds a measure of protection. That is all."

Quickly, Richard averted his gaze and heaved a sigh. "Yes, I well imagine you are right, Darcy. She will not have any problem finding a *wealthy* husband. I agree with your plan as long as you speak frankly to Georgie about your concerns for taking such legal action. She must approve, or I shall not. Tell her that. Do you understand? I only agree if she does."

"Very well, Richard. I know how you feel about informing her concerning everything, so yes, I shall tell her, and I shall tell her that you think it *wise* also?"

He choked out, "Yes, tell her I think it wise. And, Darcy, do not seek Wickham out. He may not be in London and even if he were, he may have a winning streak at the tables and, therefore, not feel a need for retaliation. Just insure that Georgie remains with someone responsible at all times. Please, I beg you to make sure. Where is she as we speak? Is Mrs. Annesley with her?"

"No, because of Kitty's companionship, Georgie wrote to Mrs. Annesley that her services were no longer needed at this time. She and Kitty are shopping today with Bingley and Jane. I had Bingley promise not to leave the girls alone, and he assured me that he would stay with them."

Staring at Darcy, Richard nodded calmly at the proffered information. "I am glad to hear this. You need to tell Bingley all that has transpired, so he understands."

"Yes, when the time is right, I shall."

"Darcy you amaze me. When shall the time ever be right?" Richard saw Darcy's wounded look and instantly said, "Never mind, Darcy, do as you feel best. I find myself frustrated about this, out of my mind with worry, annoyed that my hands are tied, and aggravated that I am not at liberty to do anything."

"You have listened to me, and that is all the help I need right now. My father knew he could trust you, Richard. I needed your counsel to know how to proceed. I know this is hard on you, too, and I am sorry to interrupt your training. I cannot promise, however, that I will not return here again."

Huffing loudly and waving his hand at his cousin's last statement, Richard exclaimed, "You had better keep me informed. I do not care if you wake me at the crack of dawn. Well, in fact that is when I do awake. Wake me at midnight if need be. I shall find a way to come if an urgent situation arises. Even if I am court-marshalled in the process, I shall find a way."

A small smile broke on Darcy's face. He nodded. "You know I shall, Fitzwilliam."

"Yes…well…here, take this offensive letter and burn it yourself. I do not want to take the risk of losing it before I have the opportunity to dispose of it properly." Darcy took the crinkled mass from him, flattened it against his leg, and refolded it, then put it back in his pocket. Inhaling loudly, Richard looked glumly at his cousin and said, "Well, I best get back to my band of soldiers before they desert the premises to find fair ladies all their own." Then, teasingly, he remarked, "Whatever were you thinking of, little cousin, by bringing Elizabeth with you to taunt my men and make them dissatisfied with their lot?"

Darcy looked over to the youthful lads and saw that many of them were still goggling in the direction of the carriage. He shook his head and laughed lightly. As they walked back to where Elizabeth waited for them, he informed Richard that Parliament was set to convene earlier than expected due to Easter arriving so late in the Season. Therefore, Georgiana's presentation at court would occur in two weeks. Darcy promised to write soon with all the specifics and briefly mentioned that Aunt Adeline and Elisha had offered their help. The colonel's brows rose at the thought of what Georgiana would suffer under his sister-in-law's meticulous attentions.

Richard approached his cousin's wife and softly stated, "I am sorry, Elizabeth, for being so insensitive with my language just now. I hope you shall find it in your heart to forgive me."

She smiled and replied, "Most certainly, Colonel. I fear that while I have never voiced such oaths, I sadly admit to having thought them, especially when I find myself forced to recall *that despicable man*. I find him a scoundrel, a fiend, and… well…" Elizabeth paused, remembering her manners, and then smirked before concluding, "I am sure you grasp the *general* idea, Colonel."

Richard smiled at her and then laughed heartily.

Darcy stared expressionlessly at his wife. He thought, bizarrely to himself that, if she had been a man, her temperament would have resembled Richard's. The similarities of their minds and natures truly astonished him at times. Such insight made him feel as if he had been granted a glimpse into how she would raise their children. She would treat them much as Richard had Georgiana—allowing all of their daughters to dance before officially coming out. This realization startled Darcy, and he did not know quite what to make of such a notion.

Despite all the assurances that Elizabeth had expressed to him regarding her feelings about his cousin's particular attentions towards her at Kent, a small, insecure sensation still niggled deep down inside of him. He wondered if Richard had offered courtship to her before or after his own disastrous proposal, whether Elizabeth might have accepted his cousin's hand in marriage, and then, instead of now bearing the name of Darcy, she might be recognized as a colonel's wife and graced with the title of Mrs. Richard Fitzwilliam. He shuddered at the thought.

~*~

Caroline Bingley was a very dissatisfied woman. The past three days had been odious. First, having to travel to London with Kitty Bennet and her brother's expecting wife, Jane, was almost more than she could bear. They had to stop so often to accommodate *dear Jane*, the angel, that Caroline thought she would go mad from all the delays. But today, all was forgotten, because upon awakening at noon, her maid handed her a missive from Blackwell House. When Caroline's eyes lit upon the name *Hazelton*, she anxiously ripped opened the seal. A look of triumph crossed her face. Lady Hazelton was inviting her to dine with them tomorrow evening.

Throwing back the covers, Caroline swiftly made her way to her closet to establish something suitable to wear. She considered dress after dress, until she suddenly realized that she must quickly bathe and attire herself. She had absolutely nothing to boast of. Hence, she must go shopping to find the perfect frock. This was her good fortune to gain access into one of the highest circles of the *ton*, and she had to make the best impression possible. Calling out to Drusilla in a strident voice, she requested that the maid inform her brother of her need for the carriage.

When the maid informed Mr. Bingley of his sister's behest, he marvelled at it. Caroline seldom stirred from her rooms till way past two. He asked the maid to inform his sister that she was welcome to join him and Mrs. Bingley along with Miss Kitty and Miss Darcy, or he would allow her to hire a hackney.

Drusilla knew instantly that this information would not go over well with her mistress, and as expected, Caroline's eyes squinted in disgust when informed of her brother's edict. She would rather be hung than stuffed in a carriage of five. No, she would hire a hackney, instead.

~*~

Miss Catherine Bennet and Miss Darcy waited in the parlour at Ackerley for the Bingley carriage to arrive. Kitty thrilled at the opportunity to spend time with Georgiana and to experience the grandeur London had to offer. This was her first chance to spend any amount of time in the celebrated city besides the occasional visits with her aunt and uncle in Cheapside. Yet those stays never afforded her with the opportunity to experience society at large. This afternoon, however, she and Miss Darcy were actually going to shop on Bond Street and Kitty found the anticipation for their departure hard to bear.

Thus, when the carriage pulled up to the entrance, the girls hurriedly made their way out the door, not waiting on propriety for Bingley to ring first. Georgiana merrily thought to herself...if her brother had witnessed her brazen behaviour, he might have died on the spot. He would surely be appalled by the loutishness she displayed.

Charles Bingley, on the other hand, did not mind in the least. Cheerful as usual, he helped the young ladies into the carriage and they were off. Jane smiled serenely at them and explained the necessities for which she planned to shop. She then enquired what their desires were. Georgiana and Kitty looked at one another and then at Jane. Suddenly, they both began giggling.

With a grin, Bingley asked what they found so humorous. The girls told him that they were so excited to go to town that they had given no thought to what they hoped to accomplish.

Jane smiled and told Kitty that she would manage to make her purchases quickly to allow them adequate time to admire the wares in many stores.

They stopped first at the textile sellers. The enormity of the shop and the grand arrangement of the bolts of cloth astonished Kitty. She took in the details of the eye-catching textiles, which draped from rods near the ceiling, showing each texture and colour to be had in a wide array of fabrics. The shop in Meryton held nothing in comparison to this vibrant display. Jane requested that her sister look over the selections and pick out material for two ball gowns. Thus, while Jane searched the assortment for her own frocks, Georgiana helped an excited Kitty inspect the many fabrics she felt were most suitable for evening attire.

With Georgiana's suggestions, Kitty was able to make her choices rather quickly, since the essential aspect of the gown that held her interest was the colour of the cloth. The girls then waited patiently while Jane spent some additional time admiring the various shades of the materials for her own dresses. Georgiana and Kitty watched in complete astonishment as Bingley assisted his wife by holding a number of silks against his face and asking, "How does this look, Janey?" Jane would bashfully smile with a sparkle in her eyes at each thoughtful demonstration from her husband. When Mrs. Bingley finally made her choices, she instructed the proprietor on the yardage she desired from each bolt, and, after handing him her card, asked that her purchases be delivered to the address thereon.

The foursome then made their way down the crowded avenue, moving amongst the streams of people who had recently returned to London in anticipation of the upcoming Season. The grandeur of all the shop windows with their alluring exhibits caught Kitty's eye. She felt as if everything glistened behind each pane they passed.

They next stopped at a fan store. Georgiana told Kitty that this store was one of her favourites because when she was young girl, her brother and cousin would bring her here while they all awaited her father as he tended to business. The young men would open the folds of different styles of fans, which had been set out for inspection, and flutter them back and forth before her face. She and Kitty admired the devices, whipping them open with the mere flick of their wrists and enjoying the breeze of cool air created by the waving of their hands.

After Jane had purchased all she set out to acquire, they strolled down the street and decided to enter a small tea shop. Bingley wanted to purchase a special blend he had tasted while at Pemberley. Georgiana informed him of its name, and he commenced to tell the owner to wrap up two pounds when Kitty noticed that Jane had begun to have another bout of morning sickness. She approached her elder sister and asked, "Jane, would you like me to accompany you out into the fresh air to wait for Charles?"

Jane nodded and asked Kitty to inform the others of their plans.

Kitty followed her orders and quickly informed Georgiana. As she turned to rejoin her eldest sister, she charged Georgiana with the task of passing the information on to Bingley. Georgiana quickly moved to relate the message and watched with concern as a flustered husband anxiously attempted to hurry the completion of his purchase. Grabbing up his package and exiting, he rushed to his wife's side and asked, "Janey, are you not feeling well? We can go home this instant."

Jane wanted to do just that, but she could see the downcast expressions on the girls' faces. "No, Charles, I feel the fresh air has helped. I think I can carry on." He eyed her suspiciously, knowing that, if she were not careful, she might very well begin to heave at the slightest onslaught of any offensive aroma. He assumed that the scent from the various teas might have brought on the nausea, and felt badly that he had unintentionally triggered his wife's latest spell of queasiness.

Making their way through the throng, Bingley kept a close eye on his angel, and, when he saw her hands fly upward and cup her mouth, he insisted that they end their excursion earlier than planned. It was at this precise moment that a familiar voice rang out. "Why Miss Darcy, I am happy to see you this afternoon. I gather that you and your friends are enjoying the fine weather." Dr. Harrison Lowry smiled engagingly at Georgiana, his deep dimples making him appear handsomer than ever.

"Dr. Lowry!" she replied warmly. "I am surprised to see you here. Whatever are you doing in London?"

Before answering her, he doffed the brim of his hat to Jane, Kitty and Bingley. They likewise nodded their greeting. "I arrived yesterday to attend a medical conference at St. Thomas and Guys'. I shall spend almost the whole of the month here. Dr. Stafford watches my post for me in Derbyshire, and I shall do the same for him come autumn." The doctor then looked at Jane and asked, "How are you feeling, Mrs. Bingley?"

Charles spoke up, "Oh, Dr. Lowry, she has such bouts with odours. Will this ailment last the whole of her confinement?"

Harrison Lowry shook his head, smiled indulgently at Bingley's enthusiastic concern. "That is not usually the case. In another month, the episodes should lessen."

"Well," Bingley exclaimed, "I dare say, despite our disappointment, we must cut our outing short today because she is feeling unwell."

Harrison took in the unhappy looks from Miss Darcy and Miss Bennet and quickly made a decision. "Mr. Bingley, I have the rest of the afternoon free. Would you allow me the honour of escorting the young ladies for a few more hours? I shall gladly bring them home."

Kitty and Georgiana instantly looked at Bingley with hopeful anticipation. He seemed perplexed, uncertain whether he should allow the girls out of his sight, remembering his promise to Darcy. Looking to Jane, he widened his eyes to her in a silent plea for direction. She smiled and nodded. "Well, Dr. Lowry," Bingley exclaimed with energy, "If you are quite sure this is how you wish to spend your free afternoon, then I shall heartily concur with your choice."

Dr. Lowry's face showed his pleasure at Bingley's acceptance of his application. He pledged, "I shall take prodigiously good care of them, for I can think of no better way to spend an afternoon than in the company of such fair damsels."

Georgiana and Kitty giggled in delight, pleased that the gallant doctor had come to their rescue. Charles handed Dr. Lowry a card and asked that he escort the girls back to his townhouse no later than five o'clock. The doctor assured him that he would see to their safe return. Bingley then enquired as to whether he might be free to join them for dinner. Dr. Lowry accepted most readily, and then Bingley guided his dear wife back to their carriage.

Harrison Lowry looked down into Georgiana's eyes smilingly and asked, "Where shall we go from here, Miss Darcy?"

Georgiana bit her lip and felt a little nervous under the doctor's intense gaze. "Oh, we shall let Kitty lead the way? This is her first time to shop in London."

"Ah!" the doctor exclaimed as his eyes turned to Kitty, "that is special. Why, Miss Bennet, we await your command."

Kitty's heart fluttered as the doctor's deep blue eyes looked happily into hers. Before she made an answer, the doctor addressed both ladies once more. He asked them to excuse him for a few moments, so he might to inform his colleagues that his plans had changed, and he would not join them for the afternoon. He gestured towards a group of men occupied in rapt discussion some way down the expansive avenue.

Miss Darcy assured him that she and Kitty would patiently wait for him where they stood. In a flash, he crossed the busy thoroughfare.

Kitty commented that she thought the doctor quite handsome. In fact, she thought him the handsomest man not dressed in regimentals that she had ever seen. Georgiana's heart skipped a beat, and she smiled absentmindedly.

As they waited, Georgiana observed the spirit booth close by. Crystal flasks, sat in a straight line, each filled with different, colourful liquors, sparkled brilliantly, their glimmer enhanced by the glow of candles lit behind them. Georgiana stepped up to the booth and looked at the wide variety of rums, wines, and brandies. She turned to Kitty and enquired if she had ever tasted brandy. Kitty shook her head, and, with a lack of interest in appraising strong drinks, indicated her desire to go into the lace shop located directly behind the booth and asked Georgiana if she would care to join her. Miss Darcy declined, devising an obligation to wait for Dr. Lowry as the reason for not accompanying Miss Bennet, yet she encouraged her friend to go ahead. Before departing, Kitty promised to return quickly.

Georgiana continued to stare at the different liquors. The man attending the booth noticed her fascination and asked if she would like to sample some of his ware. She looked surprised by his offer. He noticed the artful appearance on the young miss' face as she peered far off into the crowd of people and then briefly observed the lace shop window behind her. Suddenly, she grinned and nodded. "I think I should like to try that one. It is a brandy, is it not?"

"Why, yes, ma'am, one of my finest." He handed her the tumbler and she took a swallow, quickly crinkling up her nose. "Oh, my, that is *horrible*!" She wondered what Fitzwilliam and Richard found so alluring in the disgusting drink.

The vendor chuckled. "I recommend this instead. It's Irish whiskey." He handed her another glass, and she again brought the spirit to her lips to take a sip."

"My, my, my, Georgiana Darcy, could it be my dear little Georgie? Becoming an imbiber, are we?"

Georgiana's insides ran cold as she slowly put the glass back down. The merchant who had helped her had shifted his attention to assisting someone else. Slowly, she turned and looked straight into the face of George Wickham. She paled.

"My, Georgie, you are even lovelier than at Ramsgate. Do you remember, my dear?"

He reached for her hand, only to catch hold of the tips of her fingers as she quickly pulled it away, his tightened grasp yanking off her glove. He stated with a devious glint in his eyes, "So much the better, I always loved kissing your bare skin."

Her eyes widened as fear gripped her throat. He again reached for her hand. "Come, come, Georgie, is this any way to greet the man with whom you wanted to spend your life and whose children you wished to bear?"

In an attempt to repudiate his claims, she stammered, "I...I..."

Relief instantaneously washed over her when Dr. Lowry suddenly stood by her side. She witnessed Wickham's expression as his eyes oscillated between her face and the doctor's, before again putting on the façade of a gentleman. He lifted the rim of his beaver to her and said, "It was lovely to see you again, Miss Darcy. I am off to Newcastle, so I must bid you adieu."

Georgiana sighed deeply. Relived, she began to breath freely again.

Dr. Lowry asked in concern, "Do you know that man, Miss Darcy?"

"Yes, he is the son of my father's late steward. He grew up at Pemberley."

"Did he say something to upset you?"

"No, I only experienced surprise at seeing him. That is all."

Kitty quickly came out and joined them, and they spent the remainder of the afternoon looking into the shop windows and visiting the book and music sellers. Dr. Lowry treated them to some sweets at the chocolatier, and they made their way back to the Bingley home in Mayfair to enjoy the evening together.

Afterward, Dr. Lowry took Miss Darcy to her own house without her friend. Kitty had decided to stay with the Bingley's to meet with the seamstress whose arrival on the morrow they anticipated, so she could take her measurements in the preparation of fashioning her ball gowns.

~*~

Mary Sherwood

On her way to Lord and Lady Hazelton's townhouse, Caroline Bingley kept meditating on what she had seen the day before while shopping. Mr. Wickham and Georgiana Darcy were having a private conversation while standing, in broad daylight, on Bond Street. She could tell from where she had been positioned that Miss Darcy did not welcome the encounter. She even noticed that Wickham kept Georgiana's glove in his hand when he hurried away. What would Mr. Darcy think of such a rendezvous? She speculated on the probability that Wickham would leak the Darcy secret to polite society. Something had to be done to ensure that *dear* Georgiana did not lose her standing in the upper circles. The unsuitable manner in which Elizabeth Bennet dealt with Georgiana's come-out only reinforced the fact that that woman did not deserve to be given any notice by the fashionable elite let alone *be* Mistress of Pemberley or sister-in-law to Miss Darcy. It made her ill to think that, due to Mr. Darcy's unrestrained, lustful impulses, his sister had been made to suffer so. Yet time would tell all, and she knew within her heart that Fitzwilliam Darcy would soon rue the day that he had succumbed to the alluring wiles of Elizabeth Bennet.

As the butler ushered Miss Bingley into the entrance hall of Blackwell, she noticed that it was an elegant townhouse, richly furnished and decorated with an Oriental flair. Within the drawing room, Caroline's sense of taste found a well-appointed home with the opulence presented by strings of pearls interspersed with rubies which mingled within the folds of the silken drapes, producing an exotic effect.

In her greeting of her new found friend, Lady Hazelton congratulated herself on her artistic eye, openly telling Miss Bingley that she directly conceived and orchestrated the decorative composition of her home. She felt it was a sign of a truly proficient woman.

Only four were in attendance for the dinner. Lord and Lady Hazelton had invited Mr. Ashton Caldecott to join their small party. Caroline did not mind, but entertained no expectation in the focus of that young man, comprehending that Mr. Caldecott was some years her junior. But, there was always a faint hope that the connection might lead to other introductions.

Making friendly overtures to Elisha, Caroline sang the praises of the heavenly cuisine their divine hostess had granted them. Elisha smiled with self-satisfaction. Quickly, Lord Hazelton and Mr. Caldecott arose to leave, in order to partake of their brandies at their club. His Lordship leaned over and kissed his wife's hand, telling her to not wait up for him. Elisha smiled and waved them away. She then invited Miss Bingley to join her in the parlour, insisting that Caroline take her arm as they made their way to that room.

Not too many minutes after Elisha and Caroline had settled down in comfortable conversation, the former brought up Darcy and Elizabeth's courtship and asked Miss Bingley how it came about.

Caroline commenced to tell her how Mr. Darcy, in the beginning, had been as resolute as she had where it concerned the unsuitability of the Bennet family. He had even thought that Elizabeth appeared as no great beauty, but somewhere along the way, he came to mention that he found her eyes to be very fine. Yet, despite that observation, he had desired to remove himself from Netherfield as soon as possible after her brother's ball, where the whole Bennet family had acted disgracefully, showing their ill-breeding quite openly. She related that the mere memory of that night still made her skin crawl.

Elisha listened, enthralled by Caroline's revelations. Miss Bingley continued to tell Lady Hazelton how Darcy had even persuaded Mr. Bingley not to seek the elder Miss Bennet's hand. He had also helped to conceal from her brother that Jane Bennet had come to London last winter, and Caroline then added her opinion that Miss Bennet had come with the sole purpose of ensnaring her brother. Elisha nodded sympathetically to all of Miss Bingley's assertions. She then gave an account of how Elizabeth had toured Pemberley with her *Cheapside* relations. Elisha, in astonishment, covered her mouth with her hand.

At length, after Caroline had spoken of all the mortifications and frustrations that she had endured because of her brother's connections with the Bennet family, Elisha put forward, "Caroline, my dear, I can well imagine your great suffering. My husband and I, likewise, are still suffering from Darcy's abominable choice of a wife. We are convinced that our dear Darcy was seduced by his wandering waif. Richard has informed us as to how she dearly loves to ramble alone in the woods, and we are certain that something improper must have occurred during one of those jaunts. Certainly, if not while in Hertfordshire, then perhaps while she visited at Rosings, for I hold no doubt that she endeavoured to trap him. Yet, now you tell me that she also pursued Mr. Darcy at Pemberley. Evidently, she and her elder sister have been taught all the artful ways of seduction."

Caroline nodded most empathically to all of Elisha's opinions, happy to have found someone who truly understood and shared in her anguish. "And, I must say, Caroline, Lord Hazelton and I fear greatly for young Georgiana. My husband's aunt, Lady Catherine, is beside herself with dread, as well. My father-in-law tends to agree with us for the most part, but Lady Matlock has dissuaded him as of late, and that is why she threw a ball in honour of the Darcys at Matlock."

Shaking her head in pity, Caroline stated, "I fear for dear Georgiana, too. On my way over to Blackwell tonight, I kept thinking about her, and I worry for her reputation."

"Yes, Lord Hazelton and I concur. We fear that a really suitable bachelor may be reluctant to seek her out when he realizes she has connections to such a family, especially with the former son of George Darcy's steward as a brother-in-law to Mr. Darcy!"

This sentiment expressed by Elisha pressed heavily upon Caroline's feeble mind. Miss Bingley could not conceal a look of indecision mingled with one of caution from flitting across her countenance, and Elisha read it well. Smiling inwardly, Lady Hazelton asked, "Caroline, what troubles you? You seem distressed."

Bringing the back of her fingers beneath her nose, Caroline sniffed loudly and nodded in misery. She shook her head as she exclaimed, "Oh, it is indeed dreadful, but I cannot say."

Lady Hazelton immediately placed a hand atop Miss Bingley's free hand which lay resting on her lap. "Caroline," she said beseechingly, "you can confide in me with whatever ails you. I am the epitome of discretion."

Eyeing the room against prying ears, Caroline nodded and then heaved a sigh before she related in a solemn whisper, "Dear Elisha, what I tell you must never leave this room…yet perhaps you can help in some way." Lady Hazelton patted Caroline's hand reassuringly, urging her to continue.

"While at Pemberley, Elizabeth confided in me that her horrid brother-in-law has attempted to blackmail her over a past indiscretion which involves Georgiana." Elisha's brows furrowed, yet she remained silent. "Apparently, sometime in the past, George Wickham and Georgiana attempted to elope. They were secretly engaged, but Mr. Darcy discovered their plan and put a stop to it."

Lady Hazelton's eyes widened while her heart smirked in delight at such intelligence. *My, my, so dear Brother Richard and Cousin Darcy are not the best guardians after all.*

"Mrs. Darcy's dreadful sister, the one married to Mr. Wickham, has been writing to Elizabeth and begging for money. Even Wickham has written to her to the same purpose. He even insinuated how he thought…well…oh, it is too ghastly to repeat."

"There now…" Lady Hazelton squeezed Caroline's hand in encouragement "but you must tell me."

"Well…I believe in his letter, Mr. Wickham declared his preference for Elizabeth's body over that of her sister's."

Elisha exclaimed, "No!"

"Yes, yes he did. He also congratulated her for ensnaring a wealthy husband and claimed that Darcy had forced him into a marriage and a profession he despises. Please, I beg of you, Elisha, never breathe a word of this to anyone." Caroline's eyes began to glisten with affected tears as she insisted, "I fear for Georgiana. Thus, I felt I must tell you. You may be able to help."

Grasping Miss Bingley's hand tightly, she assured, "I promise that the information shall not leave this family circle. You have done the right thing in telling me. We must be vigilant in finding Georgiana a husband. A stain on her character such as this could substantially diminish her chances for a successful match and would only pull down the Darcy name even further."

Looking straight into Caroline's face, Elisha queried, "Now, you say that Elizabeth told this to you personally?"

Squirming for just a second, Caroline raised her chin and gave a quick nod of her head. Miss Bingley felt a pang of guilt for a mere moment. In any case, what did it matter if she contrived how she attained the information as long as the essentials were true?

"Poor Eliza was distraught at the time. Apparently, she and Mr. Darcy have been experiencing, what shall I say, *marital discord*. He knows nothing concerning the blackmail."

Dryly, Lady Hazelton commented, "Yes, I imagine not."

Caroline took a deep breath. "There is one more thing." Elisha raised her eyebrows in curiosity, her eyes beckoning for further elaboration.

Poising the back of her hand over her brow, Caroline ingratiated herself. "My dear, Elisha, it is the most dreadful thing. When I was out shopping yesterday afternoon, I had not been about for an hour or more, when I discerned through the crowd, George Wickham and our Georgiana in a tête-à-tête."

Overcome with shock, the mistress of the house did not keep in check how very unladylike she appeared with her jaw gaping wide. Elisha asked, "Are you quite certain it was *our* Georgiana with Mr. Wickham?"

"Yes, quite certain!"

"Was she not accompanied by *anyone*?"

"No, not at the time of her meeting with Wickham, but soon thereafter, she was joined by the local doctor of Lambton, a frequent guest in the Darcy home."

"Oh! I feel a headache coming on. I am afraid I must retire, dear Caroline. I do hope you understand."

"Most certainly. I only ask, again, that you please keep my confidence."

Elisha reassured her that she would never divulge from whence her knowledge had come, and that, hopefully, only the immediate family would ever know of Georgiana's near ruin. Afresh, she told Miss Bingley that she had done the noble thing in sharing the information with her, reasoning that she could not help Georgiana had she not known.

Swiftly, Lady Hazelton led Caroline to the door and bid her goodnight, promising to visit her very soon. Upon the door's closing, Elisha's mind began racing. *Good Lord*, she thought, *the situation has become desperate.* She had to do something, and quickly. Her name and the name of her unborn child were at stake. They must marry Georgiana off to someone this Season, and it did not matter to whom as long as the gentleman could be prevailed upon to have the foolish girl. Waiting another year posed far too great a risk. It was imperative that she make a visit to Rosings Park. Yes, she would do just that, for Lady Catherine would know exactly how to proceed with such a volatile matter. Elisha's beady eyes tapered as she whispered out loud, "Perhaps the girl's *noble* guardians shall be forced to consign sweet Georgiana to the Fitzwilliams, sans Richard of course." Yes, Lady Catherine, without a doubt, would concur, and that grand lady, in turn, would persuade her brother, the Earl, to do likewise.

~*~

Chapter Twenty-four

Malicious Schemes

The next morning at Ackerley, Darcy was up early and in his study trying to catch up with the correspondence that had accumulated while he had been at Pemberley. The pile was enormous. As he embarked upon this task, he felt at ease. Speaking with Richard the day before had mollified his concerns greatly. After breakfast, he planned to go to his club to seek out his father's good friend, Mr. Samuelson. The man owned a lovely estate just outside of London, which was perfect for the pursuit of horseback riding. As a boy and youth, Darcy had spent many afternoons in leisure activity there. Just the thought of teaching Elizabeth to ride caused him to abandon his business affairs and return to his wife's chamber to assess her new equestrian attire. Anything looked lovely upon his wife, but he ached to see her dressed in what he considered one of the most eye-catching apparels fashioned for women—the female riding habit.

~*~

Elizabeth knew of Darcy's desire that she and Georgiana learn to ride. He had often told her how much he had always desired for his sister to master equestrian skills, but that she had been too frightened due to a fall from a horse when she was very young. He felt certain that, with Elizabeth by her side endeavouring to learn the exercise as well, Georgiana would brave another attempt.

When they had honeymooned in London before their departure for Pemberley, Mrs. Darcy had been fitted for a riding habit with Darcy's personal tailor in Bond Street. The outfit—including boots, hat, and gloves—awaited her upon their return to Ackerley. After trying on the ensemble, Elizabeth was quite pleased with the precision of the fit. The habit was of an emerald hue with a high waistline and a full-trained skirt. The jacket sported a masculine look, possessing a stiff collar and brass buttons down the front. The trimming also had a military effect from the soutache, frogs, and braid which adorned it. In the back, the jacket showed smart pleats, revealing Elizabeth's tiny waist. Even the habit shirt beneath the jacket was reminiscent of a man's, except for the feminine touch of a green ribbon tied in a bow where a cravat would have been displayed.

Walking up behind her as she examined her reflection in the mirror, Darcy exclaimed boldly as his eyes soaked up the mesmerizing proportions of her womanliness, "It shows off your figure quite handsomely, Lizzy."

Flashing a radiant smile when meeting his reflection in the glass, Elizabeth agreed that the outfit did indeed look striking on her. She witnessed, however, more than his admiration of her appearance in the riding habit. Elizabeth watched the fluid movement of her husband's eyes as they re-examined her curves. His hands quickly followed suit, freely roaming over the plush fabric of the garb, luxuriating in the tangibility of her form that lay beneath, a generous, concrete delight, which his mind's eye vividly and enthusiastically recalled.

As Darcy pulled the ruffled collar aside and began to kiss the hollow of her neck, Elizabeth rolled her head to one side, closing her eyes to savour the maddening sensation his lips created in her body. Intermittently, he paused, looking into the mirror, until her heavy lids fluttered open to meet his fiery gaze.

"Elizabeth, you are so enticing, my love. I have a good mind to disrobe you and reside in our bed for the remainder of the day."

Snapping out of the trance he had produced within her, she smile brightly and rejoined, "Yes, I gathered that, Fitzwilliam, but I have not tried on my hat as of yet." She raised her brow with an amused smile and gestured for him to fetch it from the bed.

"Oh, you teasing woman!" he growled as he good-humouredly met her eyes. "Yes, I shall go and do your bidding." Darcy turned and took quick steps over to the bed to retrieve her bonnet. "I think you will love riding, Lizzy. You have the disposition for it, you know."

She bit down upon her lip at hearing his assumption. The last several days had been so breathtaking between them. No more secrets and no more jealousies remained. Their world seemed harmonious beyond measure. The pleasure Elizabeth had derived within Darcy's arms during their lovemaking had been indescribable, and she truly felt that nothing would ever again threaten the loving bond they now experienced. In spite of his assurance, the mere thought of mounting a horse and learning to ride filled her breast with uncertainty. However, taking in her husband's hopeful expression as he walked towards her, she inwardly pledged diligence in the enterprise of equestrianism. She felt she could master anything, if only to please him.

Darcy handed her the hat, which was mannish in its design. It was not tall like his beaver, but stout, sporting a green band around the circumference of the crown. Carefully, she donned it, holding it by the front and back of the brim. Skewing her lips to the right as she slanted the hat to the left, she raised her eyebrows and then glanced at her husband's face. "I prefer it tilted, Lizzy. It lends a more feminine flair."

"Then, dear husband, tilted it shall be." They looked at each other's reflections a moment longer, before she turned to face him. Darcy held his arms out wide, welcoming her into his embrace. Bestowing an eager kiss upon his wife's sweet lips, he informed her that he needed to attend to his correspondence, after which he would join her and Georgiana for breakfast to discuss the various plans and activities for the week. Smiling in agreement, she assured him that she was looking forward to it and would meet him in an hour's time.

Thus, Darcy returned to his study and presently worked with diligence through the stack before him. Detecting a missive from the magistrate's court, he swiftly opened the seal. "Hmm!" he exclaimed aloud upon reading the missive. Releasing a deep breath, he laid it aside to continue his burdensome task while a disgruntled expression overspread his features. Dismay continued to line his brow from the many invitations that had already arrived for the Season. Again, he quickly selected the ones he desired to attend and set the others to one side.

~*~

Georgiana smiled brightly when Elizabeth walked into the breakfast room. "Lizzy, you look sleepy still. Did you not rest well?"

"Oh, no, Georgie, I assure you, I slept like a log. I so often seem to be fatigued these days. I suspect all the travelling of late—first to Matlock, then back to Pemberley, next to London, and then, yesterday, to Sandhurst and back—has exhausted any energy which remains within me."

Taking her seat after filling her plate, Elizabeth mused drolly to herself, *Apart from the many other taxing, yet pleasurable activities which have been consuming a good portion of my nights and mornings.*

In shock, Georgiana asked energetically, "You went to Sandhurst yesterday? You went to see Richard? Why? What did he have to say?"

Good gracious! Elizabeth thought wearily. What reason could she give her sister-in-law? Happily, for her, Darcy entered at that precise moment to join them for their morning meal. They noticed that he carried a large stack of letters, which he placed next to his table setting. "Ah! I see that both of my dear girls are here. Did you sleep well, Georgiana?"

"Yes, I did, Brother. What did you go to see Richard about yesterday?"

Darcy looked up suddenly as he placed his napkin upon his lap and stared at Elizabeth. She raised her eyebrows to him in an overwhelming manner as if to say that she had accidentally let *that* particular detail slip out.

With a loving smile and a quick shake of his head, Darcy let her know that he was not upset in the least.

"Yes, Georgie, I did go to see Fitzwilliam yesterday. I went to discuss some legal matters about your inheritance with him."

In rapid succession, Georgiana fired off: "How did he look? What was he doing? Did he ask anything about me? Did he say if he will be sent off to the war soon?"

"My, my, are we not full of questions this morning? No, he did not mention war. However, he did ask about your welfare, and he looked the same as he did when you last saw him.

"But, he is well?"

"Yes, Georgie, he is quite well and the same Richard we have always known."

Darcy gauged his wife's amused air to his and Georgiana's exchange and wondered why she seemed so charmed by it.

Just as he took in a mouthful of eggs, his sister asked, "What sort of legal matters did you discuss with him, and what did you say about how *I* was doing?"

Bringing his napkin to his mouth, Darcy hurriedly swallowed. "I told him that you were in good health and were shopping with Kitty and the Bingleys. I also informed him that Elisha planned to take you to Almack's, that you shall make your curtsey to court soon, and that Aunt Adie is throwing the ball for your coming out. The legal matters we discussed, I shall discuss with you after we have eaten our meal. So, if you can hold off any other questions until then, I shall endeavour to finish as quickly as possible." They smiled lovingly at each other. All ate rather hurriedly. Elizabeth and Georgiana finished first and waited patiently as Darcy buttered one last scone, devouring it quickly before leaning back and placing his napkin upon the plate.

"Very well, before discussing legal matters, shall we discuss the activities scheduled for the remainder of this week and into the next?"

Georgiana and Elizabeth eyed one another knowingly and then turned to Darcy, nodding their heads. Incredulously, he stated, "If you dear ladies would rather discuss judicial matters first, I assure you that we can."

"Oh, no, Fitzwilliam, I think Georgie and I agree with your suggestion. Save the more arduous issues for later."

He shrugged his shoulders, looking attentively at his wife and sister. "Very well, as I was saying, there are many activities we must accomplish this week. Some are of necessity, yet others, I believe, we shall find more to our liking. "Tomorrow," Darcy turned his attention towards Georgiana, "Elisha will take you and Kitty for your interview with the Patroness at Almack's. I had hoped to accompany you, but I now find that I have pressing business at the Magistrate's court. Elizabeth and I must confer with the magistrate concerning Mr. Hibbs's crimes."

He noticed Elizabeth's frown. "Yes, well, Georgie, I have a stack of invitations from many young women who have been informed that this is your coming out year. They request your presence at quite a few teas and outings." I shall allow you to look through them and choose those you would prefer. You must make your replies this morning, since some of the occasions are scheduled for later this week. Accept only those you truly desire to attend."

Remembering her inner conviction to strive to be as assertive as possible, Georgiana swallowed her fear and cried somewhat forcefully, "Oh! I...I...I am most anxious to partake of as many as possible."

A startled Darcy replied, "You are?"

She nodded her head vigorously while looking steadily at him.

His brow creased for a brief second, and then he smiled. "I am glad to hear it. This leads me to my next venture." He grinned before going on, "I desire that you and Elizabeth learn to ride. I have already spoken to Elizabeth, and she has agreed wholeheartedly. After I finish up here, I am off to my club to seek out Mr. Samuelson to accept his open offer for the use of his stables and grounds. He has a beautiful estate that I am sure you will both enjoy. I trust by the week's end, we shall be able to partake of equestrian training there."

The light in Darcy's eyes could not have been mistaken. He looked at Georgiana with an intense hope and determination. She clearly understood the tenacity of his resolve. It had been sometime since he had last tried to engage her in the sport. To be exact, his last attempt had been on her fourteenth birthday. He had bought her a beautiful horse and all the tack to outfit the animal. To please him, she tried to appear brave, but when he put her upon the beast, she burst into tears and froze in place. Consequently, Darcy had lovingly reached up and helped her down. He never again pressed her on the matter, until now.

His sister remained silent as he closely observed her face and Darcy ventured to ask, "Are you game for another go, Georgie, if Elizabeth is by your side learning to ride as well? I desire for you to be capable of participating in the many parties in the country where there shall be shooting and riding. I want you to gain confidence in the exercise and derive enjoyment from it. The sense of freedom one feels while galloping across an open field is inexpressible. I find few experiences comparable to the exhilarating sensation one achieves from riding."

Impishly, Elizabeth raised her brow and gave him a knowing look, as if to defend that she knew of *one* experience in particular which held the same *exhilaration* and sense of *inexpressible freedom* for him.

Darcy returned her gaze in befuddlement, until he comprehended her innuendo, and then a small smirk crept onto his lips. His silent reply to her mischievous implication was accompanied with a quick shake of his head and a playful narrowing of his eyes.

"Yes," Georgiana blurted out, jarring her brother and sister-in-law out of their private communication. "I do want to learn the sport! I think I am ready to take it on again. I desire to be able to ride, someday, at my future husband's side."

Darcy marvelled at his sister. *First she desires to go to as many gatherings as possible, and now she has no qualms about horses, but is, instead, eager to ride.* Smiling handsomely, he said, "I am glad of it, Georgie! I shall be off then." He arose quickly, but hesitated.

Walking around the table to where Georgiana still sat, Darcy crouched down beside her and gently took her one hand in his. "Georgie, one of the concerns I spoke of with Fitzwilliam yesterday was your inheritance. Everywhere you go, the amount of thirty thousand pounds will precede your coming. Some gentlemen, if you can call them by that title, size women up exclusively by the size of their dowries. Therefore, Fitzwilliam and I feel it best to safeguard Father's bequest to you in a special holding which will neither allow you, nor your husband, to acquire it until you are, say, thirty?"

Georgiana's eyes widened. "Is that possible? Can you rework Father's bequest?"

"I am not certain, but I had to receive Fitzwilliam's permission before I even attempted to do so."

"Richard does not care?"

"Well, at first he was concerned that you would need the money if you did not marry into wealth, but I assured him that I found that a very unlikely possibility."

Georgiana looked at her brother with a tinge of horror on her face.

He continued, "I told him I know that this is not a fool-proof proposal, but I do hope that it will keep men who are disguised as gentlemen from your door."

"Like George Wickham?"

"Well, not exactly. Wickham posed as a gentleman in manners, but I am referring to a man who is a gentleman in means, also—one who truly has the wealth he professes to have when entering into your marriage."

"You expect me to marry someone truly wealthy—wealthy as in owning an estate?"

"Foremost, I expect you to marry for love, but yes, I desire you to continue to have the means to which you are accustomed."

With apparent anxiety, she asked, "Richard thinks I need to marry into wealth as well?"

Squeezing her hand and smiling indulgently, Darcy replied, "No, dearest, he merely agreed with me that, more than likely, you shall have the prospect of doing so."

Georgiana cast an uneasy expression at her sister-in-law, and Elizabeth gave her a compassionate look in return. Again, she observed her brother's countenance. He reached for her other hand and held it tightly. "Fitzwilliam had me promise to explain this safeguard to you clearly, and he told me, quite plainly, to let you know that he only approves of such an action if you do. He said it at least three times."

Once more, her eyes searched Elizabeth's face. This time Elizabeth smiled to her. "May I think it over, Brother? I am not quite certain it is for the best."

"Yes, you may, but Fitzwilliam did say he thinks it is for the best if you approve."

"Yet, if I do not approve, he does not either?"

Darcy drew in a deep breath and nodded as he expressed, "That is correct. And if this shall be the case, Georgiana, then I shall not endeavour to proceed."

In a low tone, Georgiana replied, "I shall let you know in a while, after I have given it some thought. I do not wish to rush into anything of this magnitude."

"Yes, but Georgie, I desire for it to be known that this is the state of affairs with you."

Firmly, she stated, "I understand, Fitzwilliam. I simply need a month or so to think it over. That is all."

Taken aback that his sister not only questioned his prerogative as her guardian but also felt compelled to dwell upon his wish for such a length of time, Darcy gazed at her in complete surprise. "Very well. I can wait for a month."

"Yes," Georgiana rejoined with suppressed agitation, "now go and make arrangements with Mr. Samuelson, and I shall send replies 'round to all my *new-found friends.*" Georgiana said the last part with mild sarcasm, but it escaped her brother's notice. He only felt jubilation at her desire to undertake equestrian instruction again.

Darcy came to his feet, lifted Georgiana's hands to his lips and bestowed a loving kiss upon them. Then, before his leave-taking, he came around the table and leaned over to kiss his wife goodbye. After his departure, Elizabeth arose immediately and walked over to her sister-in-law.

"I would like to help you with your invitations and replies. Please allow me to do so, Georgie."

"I would love it if you would assist me, Elizabeth, if you are quite certain that you wish to do so."

"Yes, I am."

Elizabeth reached out and picked up the invitations. She and Georgiana linked arms and then walked side-by-side to the library. Each thoroughly enjoyed reading the summonses to teas, parties, outings and soirées. Georgiana claimed that she had never heard of half the young women inviting her and scarcely knew the other half.

Yet, out of the multitude, she did manage to pick three offers and wrote her acceptances to them. Elizabeth then petitioned Georgiana to play for her on the pianoforte which she agreed readily to do. As they made their way to the music room, the younger woman asked, "Elizabeth, when you were growing up, was it difficult sharing a maid with your sisters? I mean, was it hard to manage on your own?"

"Oh, I suppose one gets used to it. I must admit that being without a personal maid is not so bad when your husband is around to help with the fasteners on your dress. Such help is essential. I find that I can take care of most of my other needs, other than the fasteners or my corset when it laces from behind."

"Lizzy, do you think a housemaid could also serve as a lady's maid for such instances?"

"Oh my, yes!" Elizabeth exclaimed as a fond look of remembrance lit up her countenance. "Mrs. Hill, Sarah's mother, has been our housekeeper, cook, and lady's companion to my mother and, many times, to the rest of us."

Georgiana smiled at her sister-in-law's positive outlook upon such insufficiency of help, and after she had made herself comfortable at the pianoforte, she played to her heart's content while Elizabeth drifted to sleep on the sofa.

~*~

The Darcys' first week in London passed by quickly. All the family members of Ackerley had much to occupy their time. As previously planned, Elisha arrived the following morning and had taken Georgiana and Kitty to meet with Lady Sefton, who was currently one of the acting Patronesses of Almack's. The interview went well, notwithstanding Elisha's chagrin at including Catherine Bennet. Yet, Lady Sefton happened to have been a dear friend to Lady Anne Fitzwilliam when they were young debutantes. She told Miss Darcy how she and Lady Anne had become fast friends when they met at various activities during their coming out year, and about how they corresponded quite regularly after their marriages. Thus, Lady Sefton looked kindly on Georgiana's request for Kitty to attend one evening at Almack's. Her verdict was quick as she wrote out the "Stranger's Ticket" for Miss Bennet to present at the doors of the grand establishment.

When Elisha dropped the girls back at Ackerley, she asked Georgiana to allow her to host a special tea for her after her coming out ball. She desired that Georgiana stay over at Blackwell to help make out the invitations. Georgiana agreed and thanked her cousin for the offer and for helping with the interview at Almack's. Elisha smiled insincerely and assured her that it was nothing at all. She had been most happy to assist. After the girls went inside, Elisha informed her driver to head in the direction of Kent. She was off to pay an important visit to Rosings Park to extend a special invitation for Lady Catherine to stay over at Blackwell during Georgiana's coming out. More importantly, she had to disclose Georgiana's terrible predicament regarding her secret engagement and near elopement with George Wickham being revealed to the *ton* with the hopes that the grand lady would sanction her conspiracy for dear Miss Darcy's future.

While Kitty and Georgiana were gone with Elisha, Darcy and Elizabeth had made their way to the heart of London to answer the magistrate's summons they had received.

Both husband and wife were questioned at length about the incident that had taken place on the fifteenth of February past. After listening and considering the testimonies of the Darcys, the attorneys decided to send Mr. Hibbs's case to the Old Bailey, where a judge and jury heard all felony cases. Before having heard Mr. Darcy's added testimony about his tenant's attempted assault against him with a gun, the officers feared that they could only charge the farmer with manslaughter for killing his wife while physically disciplining her. However, the "Lord Ellenborough's Act" stated that the attempt to violently inflict bodily injury upon a person with a firearm could be considered a felony, and therefore, if Mr. Hibbs was found guilty, he could be sentenced to death. Thus, Mrs. Darcy need not testify in person, but Mr. Darcy would need to remain available for the next three weeks in order to appear in court.

Shopping and dining with the Bingleys, and they in turn dining with the Darcys, filled the remainder of the week. During this time, Dr. Lowry joined them for dinner twice, much to Darcy's delight. Throughout the rest of the seven-day period, Georgiana attended two teas and one outing at the park, and enjoyed making the acquaintance of other young ladies who were also to be presented at court the following week.

While her sister-in-law was thus engaged, Elizabeth made a trip to Gracechurch Street to surprise her aunt and uncle, and Darcy accompanied her. Mrs. Gardiner was, indeed, pleased to see them, and she quickly sent a note informing Mr. Gardiner of their visit. Hence, that gentleman rushed home from his business in order to see one of his favourite nieces and her husband. They spent the whole of the afternoon discussing a myriad of subjects to the enjoyment of all. Before Darcy and Elizabeth departed, the Gardiners insisted that they must arrange a date for dinner when they could establish a free night.

~*~

It was not until two days before Georgiana's presentation at St. James's that the Darcys finally made their way to Mr. Samuelson's estate outside of London. Miss Darcy was in high spirits this beautiful spring morning because a certain letter, addressed from Sandhurst, had arrived ten minutes before their departure. Dashing up the stairs with the missive in her hand, she had called back to her brother that she must fetch an extra pair of gloves. She did desire to obtain the gloves, but foremost, she wished for the privacy of her chamber when perusing Richard's letter.

My Dearest Georgie,

I hear you have been rather busy of late. Mother tells me you have been attending many social engagements with your new acquaintances. She says you have even made a friend with another young lady who will be presented this year as well. I am glad to know you are enjoying yourself. I have been busy likewise.

My men and I have been industrious in the felling of trees and constructing of bridges. I enjoy the work. It helps the time to pass by quickly. We will be allowed to come into London on furlough, but my superiors have not informed us when that might be.

Darcy spoke with me about his desire to safeguard your inheritance. I do think it wise. I have seen too many marriages where a woman is left destitute because her rake of a husband married her solely for her dowry only to gamble it away at the tables. Thus, I too, think your brother's concern is well justified. I am sure he told you, however, that the final decision lies with you. As for me, Georgie, I am used to living without the finer things in life. Now, you must decide if you can.

Servants, carriages, estates, and all the finery that goes with them help one to enjoy living in comfort. And, certainly, it is no great sin to possess them. Yet, I have seen too many individuals who do not know how to manage such privileges. Instead, they put on a façade of happiness, while in all actuality, they are wallowing in misery amongst the innumerable parties, fancied friends, and mass fortunes they endeavour to acquire. They can never get beyond themselves.

Wealth does not bring happiness. Yet, the attainment of riches seems to be the hub around which our universe revolves. Happiness is such an elusive thing. For many it is not easily obtained, yet once painstakingly discovered, it can elude one just as quickly as it came. I believe this is because many assume that happiness is found in the pleasures of the moment, the acquisition of more possessions, or the ability to shine above all others. Over time, however, they find that it is never enough. Pleasures wane, property shackles them with burdening responsibilities, and the passing moment of vainglory leads to emptiness. Instead, I feel true happiness is something we must foster from within. To me, it is found in honesty, service, and love. You are my happiness, Georgie, and I want you to enjoy yourself and be brave. I am so proud that you have been out and about, socializing with the other young ladies. You know not how I love you, duck. Follow your heart to whichever road it takes you. Foremost, that is what I desire for you—the liberty to follow your heart's desires. I feel I can say this freely, because I know you are a wise, virtuous woman, who would never wilfully do a foolish thing. You are my sweet Georgie! I trust your judgments.

I hope to see you before too long. I wish I could attend and watch as you are presented at court. Ah! Remember to tell Elizabeth, Darcy, and my parents that I am well. They must now totally rely on you for reports about my well-being.

Your devoted confidante and admirer,

Richard Fitzwilliam

Swiftly, Georgiana pressed the letter to her heart. Closing her eyes tightly, she willed the remembrance of Richard's lips upon her face, the pleasure she derived while in his arms, and the essence of being cherished therein. Holding the parchment out once more, she read: "You know not how I love you, Georgie." Softly whispering, she said, "I love you, too, my dearest Richard!"

Folding the missive, she quickly placed it in her jewellery box. Next, she acquired an extra pair of gloves before hastening out the door and down the stairs.

~*~

At the Samuelson estate, the driver directed the carriage to the front of the stables. A young groom had readied three of the master's best horses for Mr. Darcy's use.

Alighting from the carriage with eagerness, Darcy sized up the three saddled horses tied to the hitching post nearby. They were beautiful creatures—two chestnut thoroughbreds that Darcy had never before seen, and one pale Peruvian gelding, imported from South America. Happily, he turned to help his wife and sister descend. He asked the youth to go and fetch a mounting block. The lad went straightway into the stable and returned quickly with the block.

Elizabeth's heart did an acrobatic flip. The towering steeds seemed daunting. Nellie, her family's riding mare, was at least two full hands shorter than these creatures appeared to be. Taking in a deep breath, she willed herself forward. Darcy was by her side extolling the glorious day that greeted them for riding, the beauty of the horses, and the delight he gathered at finally having the opportunity to coach his dearest girls. The timbre of his melodious voice was evidence of the passion within his heart. They moved closer to the animals until they stood several feet away, and she watched her husband methodically take each horse by the bit, look into its eyes, and then, firmly run one hand downward over the breast of the animal before inspecting the cinching of the saddle. She noticed that he examined the Peruvian a little longer than the other two.

A pleased expression materialized upon his face after his assessment was complete. He turned to the lad and asked if the horses were truly trustworthy. The youth assured him that they were the best horses to be had in their stables.

Nodding in satisfaction, Darcy turned to look at his sister and wife and thus began to expound upon the parts of the saddle. Next, he instructed the ladies how to position their legs to achieve balance. "Remember, when riding side-saddle, one must sit squarely in the seat. Your right hip and shoulders should be back. When riding in the correct posture, from behind, it is difficult to tell a side-saddle rider from one who rides astride."

With pleasure, he again turned towards Georgiana and Elizabeth, and asked who wanted to give it a go first. He suggested that he would initially lead them around on the animal before advancing out to the fields. Georgiana eagerly approached her brother. Elizabeth read the delight in Darcy's eyes as the lad placed the block beside the horse where her husband had directed.

Taking his sister's hand as she ascended the step, Darcy advised, "Remember to breathe. We shall take this slowly."

Georgiana nodded as her brother's hands encircled her waist, hoisting her into the saddle atop the animal. He then adjusted her skirt and the stirrup length, encouraging her to sit up straight. Inhaling deeply, she did as he said. Darcy held the reins with his hand and asked if she was ready. Again, Georgiana nodded. He informed her that he planned to walk only a short distance within the paddock before handing the reins over to her. Additionally, he instructed that she place her hand on the top pommel of the saddle, and that if she felt insecure at any time during their first jaunt, she could also gather the horse's mane for support.

Leaning slightly downward, Georgiana held on tightly to the pommel with her right hand, and gripped the mane of the animal with her left. "I am ready," she exclaimed bravely.

Advancing forward, Darcy led the horse around the stable yard several times. He constantly peered over his shoulder to determine that his sister was not frightened. Each time he did so, he contentedly noticed that she appeared poised, since she had let go of the mane and was courageously sitting erect.

"My, Georgiana, you have a perfect seat," he called out. "I do believe you are ready to try this on your own, just around the yard, of course." Enthusiastically, she nodded, and after his explanation on how to steer and halt the animal, she took the proffered reins from his hands.

"Now, use your riding crop to spur the horse onward, and remember when moving out from a halted position, it is best to do so towards the right."

With a light tap from the crop, the horse began to walk forward. Elizabeth looked on in amazement. Georgiana did not appear anxious or reluctant at all. If truth were told, it seemed to Elizabeth as if her sister-in-law was a natural born horsewoman. As she watched Georgiana nudge the horse into a trot, Elizabeth was alerted to the sound of thundering, horse's hooves quickly approaching from behind her. Turning, she immediately perceived Lord Hazelton and Ashton Caldecott rapidly descending upon the stables. With a quick roll of her eyes, she turned back to watch her sister-in-law once more.

The two gentlemen rode up and speedily dismounted. They then walked up alongside Elizabeth and wished her a good morning. She nodded, but did not make eye contact with either. Lord Hazelton moved closer to her side, brushing his shoulder against hers while he asked, "So, is Darcy teaching my little cousin to ride?"

"As you see," replied Elizabeth in a clipped tone.

"Why, Elizabeth, have I done something to offend you?"

Pursing her lips to the right, she wished that she could scream out that she found his mere presence beside her to be offensive, but instead she answered, "No, not at all."

"I am glad to hear it. Do you plan to ride today as well?"

"Yes. Fitzwilliam desires that we learn."

By now, Ashton Caldecott had walked over to the fence and leaned upon it as Georgiana made her rounds. He appraised her delicate form in deep contemplation.

"I, for one, Elizabeth," said James, "think women should never ride in such a ridiculous manner. Riding *astride* is much safer."

Elizabeth looked sharply at him but made no answer. Then, in a presuming air, the Viscount asserted, "I bet a woman as active as you, Elizabeth, would prefer *straddling* the horse."

James heard the quick intake of air from his cousin's wife, and he chuckled within.

With vehemence, Elizabeth exclaimed, "You know nothing of my preferences!"

Hazelton smirked at her spirited response, but pretentiously acted wounded as he professed, "I only mean to infer that you seem to be a no-nonsense woman. That is all." He walked away to join his friend who still drank in Georgiana's every move.

Darcy cried out when his sister reined in the horse, "Wonderful, Georgie, you were simply superb!" He then looked back as he heard applause break forth from behind. Upon seeing his cousin and Ashton, he murmured under his breath, "Humph!"

"Darcy," Lord Hazelton beckoned, "Mr. Caldecott and I would be happy to assist you with the instruction."

Holding his countenance to an amiable demeanour, Darcy replied as he walked towards his wife, "I thank you, Hazel, but I think I can manage quite well on my own. We are not venturing very far today as it is."

"Well, have it as you will. Ashton and I have come to do a little shooting, but if you are in need of our assistance, we would gladly forgo the pursuit."

"I thank you again," Darcy responded, "but I think we shall manage. Please, go about your activity. Do not concern yourselves with our welfare. My supervision will suffice."

"Very well, have it your way, Cousin." James next looked towards his younger cousin and said, "You are a natural rider, Georgiana. Keep up the good work."

Ashton then spoke up, "Yes, Miss Darcy, you were exceptionally graceful as you rode about the yard just now. I enjoyed witnessing your accomplishment."

Georgiana smiled and thanked both gentlemen for their praise.

They then walked back to their horses and tipped the rims of their hats to both Georgiana and Elizabeth before speedily riding away.

Darcy let out an exasperated sigh as he watched them go. "Elizabeth, are you ready to give it a try?"

"Oh, y-yes, I am ready." She inhaled deeply, fortifying herself and steadying her nerves for the intimidating challenge at hand.

Leading her to the Peruvian, Darcy elaborated on the many attributes of such a horse. "This horse can make an inexperienced rider appear quite accomplished, Lizzy."

"Ah! So you think I need a horse that shall make me exhibit well, no matter how haphazard my performance truly is," cried Elizabeth.

He smiled, understanding that she knew he thought no such thing, and then he began to expound upon how this particular breed's gait was exceptionally graceful, even adding that the author, Miguel de Cervantes Saavedra's character, Don Quixote, spoke of the Peruvian stallion's attributes. Darcy's rich voice cited: "...that he costs not a farthing in keeping: for he neither eats nor sleeps, neither needs he any shoeing. Besides, without having wings, he ambles so very easily thro' the air, that you may carry in your hand a cup of water a thousand leagues, and not spill a drop..."

Smiling at her husband, Elizabeth marvelled at the capacity of his memory and the depth of his intelligence. He seemed always full of interesting details and extracts to fit perfectly every occasion that they pursued. Briefly, she thought back to their conversation at Netherfield where she had practically accused him of being vain and prideful. His answer to her accusation was, *But pride—where there is a real superiority of mind, pride will be always under good regulation.* At the time, she had to turn away to hide her smile at his bold assertion, but now that she knew him, she viewed his answer in a different light. He never made others feel inferior in their lack of understanding or aptitude when compared to his own. Instead, he was ever patient and willing to help assist and direct others in the improvement of themselves. She now felt that he was *not* conceited in the superiority of his mind, even though she knew that he was well aware of it. No, she had never witnessed him deliberately show off or directly belittle anyone. In fact, he was quite the opposite, for he solemnly bore the stupidity found in others, like her mother, sisters and, pray tell, even in *Mr. Collins*. Yet, she had also learned that if on occasion he did inwardly demean another and acknowledged it to himself or to someone else, he would severely chastise himself at great length for such heartlessness. Oh, how he had berated himself over his ill-conceived proposal at Hunsford. Yes, he did keep his pride under good regulation.

Georgiana patiently waited as Fitzwilliam went over all points of instruction with Elizabeth. The interval allowed her to imagine Richard's delight upon discovering that she could and would ride. She was sure that the news would come as a shock to him, since he was the one who had taken her on that fateful ride. It happened while visiting at her aunt and uncle's estate where Richard invited her to ride with him on his horse. Halfway through their outing, he had coaxed her into attempting to handle the charger on her own, telling her that he had confidence in her success. She had fallen from his towering steed, spraining her arm in the process, and causing such ugly bruises that it was at least two weeks before they faded. Due to the fright caused by the fall, she would not allow Richard to put her back on the animal for the return trip to Matlock. In spite of the pain, she insisted that they walk the lengthy distance. The incident left her emotionally scarred. She never tried to mount a horse again, except for the one time on her fourteenth birthday, when she did so to please her brother, but even that proved disastrous. The catastrophic venture with Richard caused him to feel terrible, and he blamed himself for her reluctance to try again. Many times throughout the intervening years, he apologized for his unremitting persistence that day and tried to convince her that she could indeed master the exercise if she would only take it on again.

Coming out of her trance, she observed Fitzwilliam leading Elizabeth around the stable yard. She could sense her sister-in-law's unease by the strained smile that appeared on her face. After sometime, Darcy again explained how to command a horse and then asked his wife if she were ready to try it alone. Warily, she nodded, and he handed her the reins. She rounded the yard several times at a slow pace and then halted beside Georgiana.

Happily, Darcy strode over to where his wife and sister awaited. Looking up to them he asked, "Are you both ready to vary the scenery and venture forth into the park?"

Georgie immediately nodded, and then glanced towards Elizabeth, noting the surprised expression on her sister-in-law's face. With raised brows, Elizabeth stated in masked dread, "Oh, most certainly."

Satisfaction suffused Darcy's countenance as he gazed adoringly at his wife. Subsequently, he dashed over to where the third horse waited, quickly freeing it from the restraint of the rope, and in one seemingly effortless movement, he vaulted onto the majestic animal's back. Elizabeth managed a grin at his boyish zeal and only hoped she would not disappoint him.

They were off, albeit, slowly at first. The smoothness of her horse's gait amazed Elizabeth. Nellie had always jarred her to the bones.

Darcy peered over to them and asked, "How do you like it thus far?"

"Fitzwilliam," Georgiana cried, "I love it!" Please, allow me to be the one to inform Richard. I mean if it is all the same to you?"

"Yes, Georgie, you may inform him of your major feat. I am so pleased for you, and I know he will be as well."

"Thank you, Brother. I am only able to accomplish it because of your kind patience. And, I do not need to wait to give you my answer. You may safeguard my inheritance if you wish. I am sure that my husband and I shall get along splendidly without it for the first several years of our marriage."

Darcy's heart warmed from her generous words of appreciation but felt complete relief at her willingness to allow him to safeguard her dowry. Then, full of intense enthusiasm, he asked, "Do you think we should speed things up a little?"

Georgiana smiled and took her crop, slapping her horse into a trot.

His vision then took in Elizabeth's demeanour, and he readily grasped her anxiety, for she held her horse's mane in a death grip. He manoeuvred his horse next to hers.

"Elizabeth, use your crop to cue your horse to pick up speed."

Nervously, Elizabeth shook her head and stated, "I have tried that already. No, I think I shall walk for now because my horse keeps snorting and violently shaking her head to and fro. I think she does not care for me, Fitzwilliam."

Darcy leaned his head back and laughed heartily at his wife's misleading notion. "Elizabeth, she has formed no opinions concerning you and does not dislike you, but I suspect that she senses that you are nervous. Therefore, you must take charge by letting her know that you are the master."

"Oh, no, I feel that she and I both know that *she* is indeed the one in charge," she exclaimed good humouredly.

Pulling his mount to a halt, Darcy alighted and kept the reins in his hands. While walking towards Elizabeth, he asked her to pull in on the reins of her horse. "I shall take my crop and strike her, and at my command, you shall use the spur on your boot to prod her at the same time."

Elizabeth nodded in understanding.

~*~

Off in the copse of trees, not too far away, Lord Hazelton and Ashton watched the riders advance. James glanced at his friend and sardonically queried, "Are you up to having a little fun, Ash?"

Ashton posed, "Will anyone get hurt?"

"No," Lord Hazelton grinned cunningly. "I do not think so, unless they forget to hold on for dear life."

The conspirators chortled in malevolent amusement and commenced to layout their scheme. A minute later, both men raised their rifles in the air. First, one shot rang out, loud and clear, followed by a second deafening blast.

The exact second that the first shot cut through the air, Darcy struck the Peruvian as his wife jabbed its side with the spur on her boot. Instantaneously, the horse jerked its head downward, ripping the reins from Elizabeth's hands. She felt every muscle of the horse tighten and begin to quiver beneath her as her own body stiffened in fear. Darcy witnessed the shocked expression on his wife's face, and he swiftly darted forward to collect the fallen reins when another gunshot boomed. Pandemonium broke loose. Darcy's horse reared, yanking its reins from his grasp as his wife's mount jolted and darted forth at a furious pace. Shrieking her husband's name, Elizabeth hunkered low over the saddle, clutching the horse's hair as she clenched her eyes shut.

The runaway mare shot past, rousing Georgiana's mount to enter into the chase as well. In disbelief, Darcy beheld the two women he cherished most being swept away at breakneck speed. He quickly ran to his horse, only to find that the creature was in no mood to be mounted. It chaotically sidestepped and circled several times before Darcy could catch hold of the reins and scale the saddle.

Mr. Caldecott and Lord Hazelton observed the scene in fiendish pleasure. They faced each other smirking. James nodded to his astute friend and pointed to the left, the direction opposite to the one Elizabeth's horse had taken. He desired Ashton Caldecott to lead his priggish cousin on a wild goose chase.

~*~

Chapter Twenty-five

Difficult Uncertainties

Ashton Caldecott came barrelling down the hill, preventing Darcy's pursuit of his wife by misdirecting him. He called out to Lord Hazelton's cousin just as that gentleman mounted his cagey horse.

"Darcy! Mrs. Darcy's horse is headed for the south field towards the grove, and Miss Darcy went in the direction of the lake. I shall see after your sister's welfare, so go, man, **GO!**"

Underneath his breath, Darcy murmured something unintelligible, took his crop, and thrashed his horse into a full run, heading straight for the orchard.

Ashton, just as quickly, turned in the direction in which he had last spotted Miss Darcy's horse careening onward.

~*~

Elizabeth's heart pounded wildly. The air swished loudly in her ears as the spooked mare beneath her rushed pell-mell across the meadow. However, she mustered up a degree of courage and peeked through her lashes in an attempt to determine the landscape around her and the direction in which she was heading. Not only did the jouncing terrify her greatly, but the brisk ride and blurred greenness of the passing scenery made her queasy, so much so that she opted to, yet again, grit her teeth and clench her eyes shut. It was just as well that she had chosen to do so. The vision that would have soon greeted her may have rendered a sudden attack on her nerves that all the smelling salts on earth could not revive. Mr. Samuelson's Peruvian mare on which she rode rushed uninhibited towards a fenced hedge of immense elevation.

Elizabeth's brain did not have adequate time to grasp the reality that her mount had stopped abruptly. Forcefully, her body flew over the creature's head, somersaulting through the air and landing hard. She would never remember the harrowing event because the forceful blow, which her head sustained when she collided with the railing, consigned her to oblivion.

~*~

The hooves of Miss Darcy's steed moved rapidly over the pasture, kicking up clods of dirt in its wake. Instead of feeling panic, amazingly, Georgiana felt at ease, allowing the animal full rein. After all, was this not the indescribable sense of freedom that her brother professed one feels while galloping on a horse across an open field? It was true. She found the rush of air upon her face and the power of the beast beneath her truly invigorating.

Unexpectedly, she detected Mr. Ashton Caldecott riding beside her. He smiled broadly to her and shouted, "Why, Miss Darcy, if I did not know better, I would think you had been riding all your life! I came to rescue you, yet I can see that there is no need."

"Oh," Georgiana called back, "I may need your help if my horse never tires and decides to run into the lake. I cannot swim! I am counting on the fact that maybe he cannot either and shall, therefore, call a halt to his adventurous excursion."

She grinned over to Mr. Caldecott, and his pulse quickened from the sudden baptism of fire coursing through his veins. He found the flushed look of Miss Darcy's face very stimulating. She was so wholesome. He had never before been as captivated by a girl as he was by her. He wanted her, even if it meant he had to abandon his wild ways in winning her hand. Yes, he was almost certain that, for Georgiana Darcy, he could become an honourable man.

Anxiously, she enquired, "Is my sister-in-law out of harm's way?"

Mr. Caldecott assured her that her cousin and brother were in pursuit of Mrs. Darcy, just as he had come to seek after her safety.

The chestnut gelding did weary before reaching the water's edge. It was drenched in foam and Georgiana let the reins fall so the animal could lap up the cool water. Ashton quickly reined in his horse and jumped down, straightway going to support Miss Darcy who was attempting to alight with one boot in the stirrup. Suspended on the iron support, she hesitated. The distance between her and the ground seemed like a great chasm.

"If you would allow me, Miss Darcy," he proposed with a tip of his head as he stood behind her, "I shall be happy to assist." At this distance, he determined that she held onto the saddle with both hands as her right leg dangled freely.

Nodding, she assented, "I thank you. I fear, in the end, I need rescuing after all!"

Ashton put forth his hands, placing them upon her tiny waist. He felt a spine-tingling sensation as he did so. She was so slender and frail. The tips of his fingers nearly met as his hands easily spanned her middle. Lifting her gently away from the horse, he deposited her safely on the ground.

In the process of turning to thank Mr. Caldecott, Georgiana lost her balance and teetered forward, causing her to fall against his chest and into his sturdy arms.

Tilting her head backward, they stood frozen in the moment, staring deeply into each other's eyes. Georgiana felt the heat of embarrassment burn upon her cheeks for her clumsiness and for the intent way Ashton scrutinized her countenance.

He loved the way she felt in his arms and the beauty of her innocence. Yet, he knew he must remedy the incident immediately. He did not want her to feel that he had compromised her in any form or fashion.

Ashton spoke with a reassuring smile. "Here, let me help to steady you. I am sure that, after the spree you just experienced, you are feeling quite wobbly." He helped to balance her as his hands slid from her back to her shoulders, resting upon them until her equilibrium returned.

"There, are you all right now?"

Grateful for his good manners, she nodded while looking down at the toes of her boots, still immensely horrified at the awkwardness and precariousness of the situation.

Stammering, she apologized, "I...I am...sor-sorry! Please... forgive me, Mr. Caldecott."

"Nonsense, Miss Darcy, there is no reason to forgive you. You have done nothing wrong. It is a natural after-effect of your frightful ride. I am not affronted in the least. Please, do not give it another thought."

Blinking timidly, she softly made answer, "I thank you, sir."

"Come, let us sit over there upon the clover while our horses rest a bit, and then, I shall help you onto your saddle so we may return. I am sure your brother will be anxious if we stay too long."

"Oh, yes, I do not want him to worry."

Mr. Caldecott removed his coat and laid it on the ground for Georgiana to sit upon. She again thanked him. They sat in companionable silence until Ashton began enquiring about her. She was a little surprised by his interest. Never before had anyone asked so many questions concerning her activities in such a way. He wanted to know what she did in her spare time. What kind of books did she read? Why had she waited so long to pursue riding? And, he desired to know if she longed to travel. His interest in her likes and dislikes took her off guard, and she wondered why Richard thought this man could not be trusted. He seemed nothing like his sister, Collette. He seemed neither boisterous nor conceited. Truly, it appeared that he acted as a gentleman. Maybe he took after his mother's disposition.

~*~

The Peruvian stood rider less, complacently grazing in a clearing, when Lord Hazelton caught up with it. His brow furrowed. *Where was Elizabeth?* He took note that her hat lay on the ground beside the animal. Riding up next to the bonnet, his eyes quickly discovered his cousin's wife sprawled against the fence, seemingly lifeless. Slowly, he dismounted and cautiously walked over to the hedge.

The bushes had cushioned the fall of her body, but with only a glance, he could tell that her head had taken the brunt of the impact. Blood trickled from her mouth as well as from the left side of her forehead, which showed deep-purple bruising. Her cheek had been scratched by the underbrush.

Was she alive?

Kneeling down beside her form, his Lordship stared at her for some time before touching her neck. He felt for her pulse. It was faint, but beating.

Resting upon his heels, he looked intently upon Elizabeth's countenance. She was a very alluring woman. Reaching forth, he pulled back the fringe of hair that wreathed her face in order to examine her wound. It looked like a nasty gash. "Hmm…" He then looked closely at her features. Her dark eyebrows were striking upon her high brow line, and the vivid contrast of her milky, smooth skin glowed beneath the framing of her brunette coiffure.

Cautiously, he put forth his fingertips, running them lightly over each brow and downward upon the cheekbone that was not spoiled, and then continued along her jaw line. The silky sensation of her skin felt exquisite. He could only imagine the ecstasy of having such a woman as Elizabeth for a mistress. Bending his face low, alongside her neck, he briefly breathed in her scent. Ah, lavender. He loved it!

The green ribbon around her collar caught his attention. Momentarily, he lifted his head and became extremely still, listening intently. He could hear no sound indicating a rider's approach. Hence, his full attention was drawn to Elizabeth's attire and what lay beneath it. With precision, he unbuttoned the jacket of her habit only to become frustrated when discovering that she wore a full shirt instead of a dickey. In aggravation, he exclaimed, "Damn!"

Elizabeth began to moan. Fear gripped the Viscount's heart. Instantly, he laid his head upon her chest. When Elizabeth's eyelids fluttered opened in a daze, and she felt what she thought to be her husband's head upon her, she asked, "Where are we, Fitzwilliam?"

Realizing that she was confused, Lord Hazelton made no answer. Then shock overtook his senses as Elizabeth ran her fingers through his hair and tenderly began to caress the side of his face. The shock soon gave way to a momentary indulgence and the notion that her caresses were indeed intended for him alone. Having been lovelorn and deprived of affection for so long caused suppressed cravings for fondling, being desired and truly loved to emerge.

Trying to focus her vision, Elizabeth became alarmed when she realized that the hair colour of the head that lay upon her was not dark and curly, but flaxen.

Stiffening in fright, she exclaimed, "Richard!"

Smirking to himself, Lord Hazelton lifted his head and looked at her. "Elizabeth, you have taken a rather nasty spill, and I was trying to determine if your heart were beating."

Fearfully, she cried, "Who are you? Where am I, and where is my husband?"

"You do not remember who I am?" Hazelton asked in amazement.

She shook her head and then winced from the sudden movement.

Blast it all, Hazelton thought. If he had not needed to worry about Darcy finding them, this would have been his perfect opportunity *to know her.* She would not have the temerity to tell, for she would be utterly ruined in Darcy's eyes. No—what was he thinking—he had to stop this infatuation. It was going too far!

While buttoning up her jacket, Lord Hazelton stated, "I am Darcy's cousin, Richard's brother, James. You met me at Matlock some weeks ago. Come, let me help you stand."

Unbelievingly, she asked, "I have been introduced to you?"

Pulling her upward, he assured her that, indeed, she did know him. When on her feet, Elizabeth stood a little unsteadily and, quickly losing her footing, fell into Lord Hazelton's waiting arms. He gazed upon her bewildered features and noted that she began looking about her in a vague and uneasy manner. He could clearly read her uncertainty.

Still confused, and somewhat sceptical of his earlier answer, she asked, "Who are you?"

Lord Hazelton laughed and said, "I am Darcy's cousin James, better known as Hazelton or just Hazel. Colonel Fitzwilliam's brother."

"Where are we?"

"Come, Elizabeth, you are bleeding, and you must see a doctor. Come with me. I shall take you to Darcy."

She obediently allowed him to take her by the hand and lead her to his horse. Picking her up by her waist, he lifted her up onto the saddle, and then ascended behind her.

"I have fallen, you say?"

"Yes, Elizabeth, you fell," he gestured with his head to the other horse, "from that animal over there." Elizabeth could not imagine that she had ridden the horse that Darcy's cousin indicated. She never rode alone for she was no horsewoman.

Prompting his mount into a canter, James held onto the reins with one hand while his other arm snugly secured Elizabeth against his body. She smelled divine, and he realized how temptation had overtaken Darcy's resolve, effortlessly drawing him into an imprudent and inferior marriage. Her hair had loosened from its confinement, and Lord Hazelton noticed how shiny and silky it appeared. *Having Elizabeth at my disposal, whenever I wanted, would be utter heaven. I would gladly lose myself in her arms every morning, noon, and night.*

Not able to focus upon or differentiate anything that the gentleman told her for any length of time, Elizabeth felt completely at this stranger's mercy and hoped that he was who he claimed to be. In panic, she turned to him and pitifully announced, "I fear I am ill. I feel very dizzy."

Lord Hazelton slid his hand up her arm onto her shoulder. "Here rest your head against me and close your eyes."

Extremely grateful for his offer, she did rest upon his shoulder, hoping that her light-headedness would shortly pass.

Guiding his horse into the clearing, Hazelton immediately perceived Darcy frantically calling out his wife's name as his cousin emerged from the grove. "Darcy! Darcy!" James shouted importunately, "I have found her! We are in need of a doctor!" Elizabeth raised her head from his chest to look for her husband, but the wooziness persisted. Thus, she clutched Lord Hazelton's lapels for support and again closed her eyes, burying her head once more against him.

Whipping his horse into a full run upon catching sight of his wife, Darcy rushed to meet them. Instantly, he dismounted to inspect her. "Elizabeth!" he cried. She turned away from the Viscount's embrace, anxiously holding out her arms to her husband. Helping her down, Darcy pressed her to him and then held her back to look at her bleeding face. "Oh, Good Heavens! Elizabeth! We must get you to a doctor." He pulled out a handkerchief from his vest pocket and began to dab gently at the blood by her mouth. He then quickly moved the cloth and applied pressure to the gash on her forehead. James pulled out his own handkerchief and began wiping the sweat off his brow. While doing so, he looked down and saw blood upon his lapel. Frowning, he tried to wipe it away the best he could.

Wretchedly, Elizabeth stated, "I do not feel well, Fitzwilliam. I want to go home to Pemberley."

Lord Hazelton offered, "I am so sorry, Darcy. Ashton and I did not realize that you were riding in the park when we shot our rifles at that hare."

Darcy looked stonily at him, but made no answer. James volunteered, "I shall send someone to fetch the local doctor if you like."

~*~

Gathering the reins in his hands, Ashton handed them to Georgiana, and then picked up her slender frame and set her upon the horse. She blushed most becomingly and thanked him. "I am glad to be of help to you, Miss Darcy." They rode back together at a rapid pace. He looked over to her and saw that she truly enjoyed equestrian exercise. "It is splendid, is it not?"

"Oh, yes," Georgiana interjected, "I think I have found my new love!"

Ashton Caldecott's heart leapt. Dare he hope that her words held a double meaning?

~*~

Lord Hazelton and Darcy turned at once towards the sound of riders approaching. Gratitude welled up in Darcy's breast when seeing that Georgiana was whole and well. Pulling closer to the trio, Ashton observed Mrs. Darcy's bleeding and called out, "I shall fetch a doctor."

"No, I desire to take her back to Town and call upon my friend, Dr. Harrison Lowry, but I would accept your assistance aiding my driver in raising the landau's hoods."

"I shall immediately go and help your man." Ashton quickly made his way to the stables, where Darcy's driver waited by the carriage.

Hastily, Lord Hazelton informed his cousin that he would go and retrieve the mare and return it to the stables. Darcy remained silent and only offered a slight nod of agreement to his cousin's proposition.

Soon they were on the road back to Town. Elizabeth clung to her husband, resting her head upon his shoulder and nodding off every so often, only to be awakened by occasional ruts in the roadway.

Darcy had given Dr. Lowry's address to Mr. Caldecott, asking him to go ahead on horseback to request that the doctor meet them at Ackerley.

Ashton rode foolhardily through the streets of London to seek out the physician, hoping that the doctor would be at home when he arrived. What Mr. Caldecott desired, more than anything at that moment, was to gain Fitzwilliam Darcy's favour. He knew that he would need it in his personal quest to win the hand of that man's sister.

~*~

When Dr. Lowry arrived at Ackerley, Mr. Coates ushered him in without delay to Mrs. Darcy's chambers. Sarah had already helped Elizabeth remove her riding habit and change into a clean gown. Darcy sat on the bed by her side, patiently reiterating the events of the day in an attempt to help her remember. Not only did Elizabeth have trouble recalling the happenings of the day, neither could she recollect travelling to London or account for many other activities that had taken place in the recent past.

As the butler led the doctor upstairs, Georgiana saw Mr. Caldecott to the door and thanked him most emphatically for his kind consideration in helping her sister and herself. He assured her that he was only too glad to offer assistance and expressed his wishes for Mrs. Darcy's speedy recovery. Before taking his leave, Ashton stated, "I do hope to have the pleasure of dancing with you this Season, Miss Darcy. Please allow me that honour."

"I would be happy to, Mr. Caldecott. I anticipate seeing you often among the countless activities I shall attend." Georgiana smiled openly.

"I do hope so. Well, until then, I bid you goodbye." He made a start to go, but then stopped and looked imploringly into Georgiana's eyes. "I am truly sorry for the mishap which occurred today. I do hope all will be well with Mrs. Darcy."

"You have nothing for which to be sorry. It is not your fault. No one is to blame."

For a brief moment, a faint frown graced Ashton's lips before he tipped his beaver and was gone.

~*~

Relief washed over Darcy as he witnessed Dr. Lowry entering the chamber.

The doctor stood by the bed, looking at Elizabeth in concern. Gesturing with his hand at her fringe of hair, he asked, "May I?"

Elizabeth nodded slowly and grimaced from the exertion. As Dr. Lowry pulled her hair away from the side of her forehead, Darcy told him about the accident, about how his wife could not remember it, and that she appeared to have lost not all, but most of her memory of the previous weeks.

Dr. Lowry acknowledged his friend's words with a faint nod, and then asked, "Mrs. Darcy, do you mind if I examine you more fully?"

Elizabeth looked to her husband with a questioning expression and noted him bow his head in approval. Reluctantly, she met the doctor's gaze and nodded her permission. Dr. Lowry then stated, "If you will just wait out in the hall, Darcy, I shall inform you when you may re-enter."

Darcy's brow creased at his friend's command, but he complied. Before exiting, he looked lovingly to his wife and smiled.

She smiled weakly in return.

Sarah, who had been standing in the corner of the room, immediately came forward and handed the doctor a clean cloth and a bowl of hot water she had ordered to be brought up from the kitchen. He cleaned Elizabeth's wound and inspected it closer. "I think you may need a few stitches to close the gash. I warn you, Mrs. Darcy, that it will smart some."

"I assure you, Dr. Lowry, it cannot hurt any more than the headache I am enduring at present."

He smiled and began his handiwork.

Elizabeth grimaced every time the needle entered her flesh, but she did not make a sound or move.

"There, now, you are as good as new. The cut on your mouth is superficial and shall heal well on its own. Now, if I can have you lie flat, I would like to make certain that you did not suffer any internal injuries. Let me know if anything feels exceptionally tender."

The doctor gently proceeded to press the back of her head and neck before following suit down the rest of her body. After examining Elizabeth's rib cage, he pulled the covers back farther to probe her abdomen. Upon doing so, he noticed blood on her nightgown.

When the examination was complete, he again covered her and asked, "Mrs. Darcy, are you having your courses right now?"

Elizabeth blushed with embarrassment. "I am not sure."

He looked towards her maid, "Is your mistress having her courses at this time?"

Sarah reddened brightly as well but quickly answered, "No, sir. I have attended her these past weeks, and they have not come. She was not bleeding when I helped to change her into her nightdress." The doctor could see the young maid's concern.

"Is it time for your courses, Mrs. Darcy?"

Elizabeth hated discussing such an issue with this man. He did not feel like a doctor to her. He seemed more like her husband's personal friend. She knew she was being unreasonable in her way of thinking, but she could not help it. "I do not know. I have never been able to predict when my courses would come as many of my sisters have."

Dr. Lowry could tell she felt mortified, but knew he must forge onward in his questioning. "Do you recall when your last monthly flow transpired?"

Brightening a little with the realization that she did indeed remember this particular detail about her past, she gratefully stated, "Yes, I believe it was the last of January."

"Do you usually skip months without bleeding?"

"Occasionally, I have."

"Do you have any recollection of how you have been feeling of late? Are you hungrier than usual? Have you felt nauseous at times? Have you felt the need to relieve yourself more often? Are you sleepier than usual?"

The doctor's last question hit Elizabeth like a ton of bricks. She remembered feeling sleepy and, suddenly, the very conversation she had had that morning with Georgiana was at the forefront of her mind. Instantly, she understood, and fear seized her heart.

Dreading the truth, Elizabeth asked, "Dr. Lowry, do you think I am with child and losing my baby?"

She observed his face closely to read what his expression would reveal.

Dr. Harrison Lowry did not mince his words. "Mrs. Darcy, I fear that this may be the case. Yet, we cannot be certain due to the irregularity of your courses."

In misgiving, she cried, "I *have* felt extremely fatigued for weeks now. Does that mean I am with child? I should have known!" Distressed,

Elizabeth grasped the reality that she may have conceived, and in all probability, she was losing the baby she had longed for ever since she knew she would marry Fitzwilliam Darcy.

The physician took her hand as tears began to fall upon her cheeks. She welcomed his gesture of kindness, and grasped his hand tightly, sensing the compassion in his eyes. Candidly, Dr. Lowry acknowledged, "I imagine you are with child, but you may not lose the babe if the bleeding ceases. I want you to remain in bed for the next twenty four hours. Only get out of it to take care of your personal needs and then return straight away. Likewise, you should not have relations with your husband while the bleeding persists."

She nodded in acceptance, blushing even more than before.

He then asked, "I would like to examine you once again, if you do not mind."

"I understand," she rejoined.

Again, Dr. Lowry lowered the sheets, feeling her lower abdomen and checking to see how much blood was lost.

Having completed his task, he queried, "Are you experiencing any cramps?"

"No. Is that a good sign?"

"Yes, Mrs. Darcy that is a very good sign."

While he washed his hands at the water basin, Elizabeth pleaded, "Please, Dr. Lowry, may we put off telling my husband about this possibility? I do not wish him to feel as if he were at fault, for he desired that I learn to ride, and I fear that if he thought this accident cost us the life of our child, he would find it hard to forgive himself."

Nodding, Dr. Lowry answered, "I shall inform him that I want you to rest due to your head injury. You may inform him about the pregnancy when you desire. Hopefully, the next four and twenty hours will tell us what to expect. May I allow him to return now?"

With a saddened expression, she nodded and quickly wiped away any remaining tears.

Upon opening the chamber door, Dr. Lowry saw Darcy pacing up and down the corridor. He informed the anxious husband that his wife seemed well but to be on the safe side, he wanted her to have plenty of bed rest for the next day and, maybe, for the one thereafter.

Darcy thanked him for coming so quickly. The doctor stepped over to shake his hand and told him he would be by in the morning unless they required him sooner.

Closing the door behind him, Darcy turned to look at his wife. "May I join you, Lizzy?"

Elizabeth held out her hand to him. Carefully, he crawled next to her and clasped her fingers within his own. He asked, "Can I get you anything, perhaps some wine? Is there anything you need or desire?"

Softly she replied, "I thank you, but no. I only want you here by my side."

Remembering his sister, Darcy exclaimed, "Before I join you, I should go and enlighten Georgiana. I fear she must be fretting."

Squeezing his hand tightly, Elizabeth entreated, "Please, stay a little longer or send word with Sarah." Hearing the tension in her voice, Darcy easily agreed to her suggestion and pulled the bell cord. Sarah was readily dispatched to explain the doctor's orders to Miss Darcy.

~*~

The maid hurried down the stairs to deliver the communication, but as she entered the vestibule, she noticed the master's sister engrossed in conversation with Dr. Lowry. Hence, Sarah decided to wait until they concluded their discourse. She worried that if she strayed from Miss Darcy's vicinity, she might have to go in search of her, and, although she felt odd doing so, she sat on a step where she could keep an eye on her objective and tried hard not to listen. This she did by keeping her mind occupied with the many tasks which she needed to complete before bedtime. Occasionally, her eyes would wander to the faces of the two, still deep in conversation, and Sarah could tell how captivated the doctor was with Miss Georgiana. She wondered if Miss Darcy returned his admiration. To her, the doctor was a very striking man, much like Mr. Darcy and his friend, Mr. Bingley. Sarah thought they were the handsomest men she had ever seen in all of her born days.

Finally, Dr. Lowry donned his beaver and bowed to the young woman before him prior to quitting the house. Georgiana turned to leave and saw Sarah walking towards her. The maid offered a brief curtsey and quickly began to deliver her message. "Miss Darcy, Mr. Darcy wants me to inform you that Mrs. Darcy has been ordered to stay abed. They shall have their dinner brought up on trays, and he desires for you to join them, if you wish."

Pleased, Georgiana thanked Sarah and told her that she did, indeed, desire to join them.

Hastily, Miss Darcy darted up the stairs and entered her own bedchamber to change out of her riding habit and prepare for dinner. Nancy came to assist her and informed her mistress that hot water was already on the way. Georgiana thanked her and then slipped on her robe, asking the maid to notify her when the bath was fully prepared.

Nancy curtseyed and retreated. Finally alone with her own thoughts, Georgiana pondered the events of the day. Instant gratitude swelled within her breast that Elizabeth, though somewhat injured, was safe, and just as quickly, a stunned awe filled her mind that she too was alive and well and what was more, she no longer feared riding. Anxious to see her brother and sister, she chose to pass away the time until she could join them by reading her letter from that morning. Thus, she went to her jewellery box and retrieved Richard's communication. She lay on her bed, reading each line repeatedly, and after perusing a particular section several times, she laid it aside and reached for her pillow. Hugging it closely to her chest, she envisioned Richard's arms around her and the merriment in his eyes as he gazed upon her. She summoned forth the aroma of his cologne from memory and this mingled with her recollection of the warmth of his lips and hands upon her skin, caused her to breathe in deeply.

These thoughts evoked pleasing, pleasant sensations within her body and mind. The stimulating contentment lingered for a quarter of an hour, until Georgiana became aware of Nancy's attendance. The interruption of her reverie caused Miss Darcy to sigh heavily as she arose and then, lovingly, she folded the treasured missive and returned it to its box for safekeeping.

~*~

Darcy called for the servants to bring many pillows to Elizabeth's room, which, upon their arrival, he personally plumped up and placed behind her back.

On entering the room, Georgiana ran to her sister-in-law, reached for her hand and squeezed it tightly. "Lizzy, I am so happy that you will be well."

Elizabeth thanked her, and then the small party of three settled down and shared their meal in satisfaction. Darcy and Georgiana spoke of the ride and accident at great length, among other topics, since Elizabeth pressed for more details. Some memories of the day had begun to return, but she felt greatly frustrated by the many blank spots that remained. She had no recollection of the ball at Matlock, riding out to Sandhurst, nor appearing at the magistrate's for questioning.

Darcy and Georgiana were surprised, indeed, when Elizabeth told them that she could not remember having ever been introduced to Lord Hazelton. She indicated how dreadfully helpless she felt when she came to, not knowing where she was or whom the person helping her might be.

Darcy asked, "What did my cousin say when he realized you did not know him?"

"He assured me that we knew each other and explained that he was Richard's brother and your cousin. When I asked about his identity a second time, he found it humorous. Yet, he took very good care of me, for I was quite disoriented and off-balance for some time. There was even one moment when I feared I might retch. Therefore, he had me close my eyes and lean against his shoulder. He was truly the gentleman, much like his brother."

"Humph!" was the only response Darcy made. He wondered what Elizabeth would think of her current assessment regarding his conceited cousin if she could remember her former opinion and compare the two estimations. Overall, he deemed that her memory would come back almost in full just as his had after the fencing accident the past winter. He now remembered almost everything in its entirety, except for the accident itself. Darcy even remembered accusing Richard of wanting his wife. He still burned with embarrassment from that particular recollection. Periodically, when he thought upon it, he wondered what Harrison Lowry must have thought of him at the time when he had hurled such a hideous accusation towards his cousin. What an introduction to the Darcy family that must have been for the good doctor!

After the trays were cleared away, Georgiana began to give an account concerning her runaway experience. Her gaze was fixed upon her brother as she told him that she was not terribly frightened by the incident. In fact, the only aspect she did find daunting was dismounting. "Luckily," she said with gratitude, "Mr. Caldecott arrived just in time and helped me down, or I do not know what I would have done." Next, she enumerated on Mr. Caldecott's considerations for her welfare. She, too, expressed her opinion that she found him to be very much the gentleman. Regarding her brother to ascertain his feelings, she detected an indefinable expression upon his countenance.

Lost in thought at the mere mention of Ashton Caldecott, Darcy was taken by surprise when Georgiana unexpectedly leaned down to kiss him good night. Awkwardly, he acknowledged her gesture by quickly clasping her shoulder, kissing her cheek in turn, and muttering goodnight. Georgiana looked at him pensively and wondered what had caused him so much preoccupation. She then walked over to the bed and squeezed Elizabeth's hand tightly, wishing her a speedy recovery.

Elizabeth had noticed her husband's absentmindedness as well, and as soon as the door closed behind her sister-in-law, she asked, "Fitzwilliam, is there something troubling you, my love?"

He quietly rose to strip off his robe, extinguish the candle, and climb into bed. "No, Elizabeth, nothing troubles me per se. I am only grateful that the dreadful affair of today has not caused any more harm than what has occurred. I know I have expressed my sorrow for what you have endured due to my lack of judgment, and you have chided me for it, but I find it difficult to forgive myself. And realizing that Georgiana was alone with Ashton Caldecott makes me feel twice as guilt-ridden."

"I do not understand. It is not as if he compromised her. Even you were alone with me many times before you asked me to marry you at the parsonage and at Rosings. Have you forgotten all those times that you just *happened* to meet me when walking about the park?"

She smiled at him, but could immediately perceive that he was in no mood to be humoured. "Fitzwilliam, really, is it that horrible that Georgie was alone with the man for such a short time?"

"Yes, Lizzy, it is. I have failed her again."

"Really, you take too much upon yourself."

"I suppose you do not remember Ashton Caldecott, either?"

"Oh, but I do. He came to Pemberley with his parents and Collette." She frowned at the mere thought of Miss Caldecott.

Darcy merely shook his and asked, "Do you remember anything about the ball at Matlock?"

For a moment, Elizabeth tried to will any memory to come forth, but gave it up as soon as the pounding in her head intensified and became unbearable. "I am sorry, Fitzwilliam, at this moment I do not recall much of anything beyond little bits and pieces of today and yesterday. Some memories are simply there while others are not. Remember, I was surprised to see Sarah here as well. But I can honestly say that my memory does not fail me so greatly that I am unhappy to discover that Yvette is no longer my maid, for I do have vivid memories of that woman!" She shuddered.

Darcy smiled in the darkness before turning over on his side and reaching gently across his wife's chest to pull her close. "I am also glad you no longer have her for a maid. I am sorry for imposing so many things upon you, Elizabeth. For now, we need not speak of what you can and cannot remember. I know you are weary. Your memory will come back soon enough. Of that, I am certain."

Lovingly, he softly kissed her cheek and asked, "Is there anything you desire before we surrender to sleep?"

Desperately, Elizabeth wanted to confide in him that she might be carrying his child. The temptation was great. She desired and needed his consolation regarding the possibility of losing their baby. Yet, she knew at present the guilt of the loss would be too much for him to bear. Moreover, she was unsure if she could bear it herself. The strain of her voice became unequivocal as she choked back the tears and requested, "Fitzwilliam, could you just hold me?"

"Oh, Elizabeth!" He shifted, soothingly encompassing her within his arms and then said, "I am so sorry, Lizzy."

"I know. Let us speak no more of it. My head hurts. Would you mind rubbing it for me?"

"Not in the least. I have some Dover's powder left. It will help you to sleep. Let me make it up for you."

He started to rise when she adamantly stated, "No, Fitzwilliam, I will not take that. For I hate how it makes me feel.

"But, Lizzy, it will help with your head."

"No, I only desire for you to stay by my side, please!"

Lying back down, Darcy again held her close and began to stroke her head with his fingertips. His gentle ministrations did much to soothe her fears as she fervently prayed for the life of their unborn child.

He continued to gently and lovingly massage Elizabeth's scalp and smooth back her hair for the length of an hour, ever mindful of her sutured wound, until he was certain that she had fallen into a deep sleep.

Afterward, he rolled upon his back and gave free rein to his thoughts. Ruminating on his cousin and the firing of the gunshots, Darcy instinctively felt that Hazelton had done it maliciously. It had to have been. But he knew he could not prove it. Without a doubt, the shots came from the woods, the woods sloping upward by the clearing. From the hill, Hazel had to have seen them enter the park. Furthermore, Ashton was there in a matter of moments to inform him that Elizabeth's horse had headed in the direction of the grove. Yet, after several minutes of searching, he quickly came to realize that she was nowhere to be found. In contrast, James had found her most readily. Darcy's anger began to boil. What was his cousin up to? Was it just a negligent prank, or was there something more?

Over the years, Darcy had come to realize that Ashton Caldecott associated closely with Hazelton. He considered them partners in idle dissipation. With certainty, he did not care for Ashton, but he felt utter contempt for James. Ever since Darcy could remember, Hazel had been a thorn in his flesh, and he suspected that he would ever remain thus.

Yet, when all was said and done, Darcy felt that, ultimately, he was the one responsible for the accident. In the still of the night, he stared into the darkness and, for the millionth time, berated himself for having been so enthusiastic and foolhardy in having Elizabeth and Georgie take on too much in one lesson, bringing injury to his wife and risking his sister's reputation. Grimacing in humiliation, he admitted that his damnable, high-handed officiousness had once again been his demise. He sighed, thinking with remorseful resignation, *I alone am responsible for Elizabeth's fall and for jeopardizing Georgiana's good name.*

Rolling onto his side, Darcy watched Elizabeth sleeping peacefully, and gratitude welled up within him. Whispering softly, he affirmed, "I am so sorry, Lizzy, yet, again. I fear I may never learn, but I shall keep trying with all my heart. I shall always try for you, my love. You are truly a woman *worth* the earning." Lightly brushing his lips upon her hair, he lay there for a time, silently offering up a prayer of indebtedness to his Creator for preserving his dear wife's life, and then, he reverently petitioned for her to be completely healed. As the minutes of solitude ticked away, his soul filled with peace, and rest finally claimed him.

~*~

Chapter Twenty-six

A Time to Rejoice

The orange streaked horizon revealed morning breaking over the metropolis of London. Some inhabitants still slept, at least those wealthy enough not to work for a living and the luxury of lying about for the first half of the day. But for those not so fortunate, the day had begun long before sunrise. Those souls were occupied well before dawn, greeting the capital and hard at work at their various jobs: extinguishing street lamps, sweeping walkways, filling food carts, and shovelling manure from the avenues.

Few carriages traversed the streets at this time of morning. However, Dr. Harrison Lowry was up and about early, making his way to the west side of the city to check on Mrs. Darcy. This he needed to do before attending to the other pressing duties on his daily agenda. The doctor's skin tingled in the fresh air, and he felt certain that the prospect for a fine day was upon him. Suddenly, an exquisite equipage bearing an intricate crest speedily rounded the corner towards him. Detecting no one in his path, he quickly prompted his horse onto the walkway to avoid a collision. Breathing erratically in disbelief, Harrison Lowry observed that neither the driver nor the passengers had the foggiest notion of the imminent accident. Instead, they were oblivious to his presence. If he had been familiar with the carriage's occupant and could have made out the insignia borne upon its door, he would have realized that the owner was none other than the great Lady Catherine de Bourgh.

~*~

The first rays of morning light began to filter into the mistress' chamber at Ackerley. Elizabeth had lain awake for over an hour, fearing that she might have bled too heavily during the night. Thus, she waited to arise. The time afforded her a period of quiet contemplation. Memories began to flood her mind, albeit, bits and pieces at a time. Flashing images assaulted her consciousness: Richard's agility in crossing a log, the trees of Windsor forest, attorneys grilling her husband by throwing questions at him faster than he could answer, and Georgiana's brilliant smile when receiving a missive yesterday morning. These random thoughts pressed upon her as she desperately tried to connect them all together. Her efforts were well worth it, for in an instant, the trip she and Darcy had made to Sandhurst flitted clearly before her, each and every detail remembered with clarity. Cheerfully, she turned on her side, anxious to share this mental triumph with her husband.

His face was ever so handsome, notwithstanding the coarse beard that darkened his rugged jaw. She found his facial hair quite appealing, as she loved to brush her hand over it, feeling the stubby prickles upon her fingertips. As she did so, she thought it was further evidence of his masculine virility. These feelings induced an intense longing within her, causing her to nuzzle close to his side while drinking in every feature of his countenance. Continuing to gaze at her sleeping husband, Elizabeth felt her love for him intensify more than ever before. He was the father of her child—she was carrying his child!

When Fitzwilliam Darcy opened his dark brown eyes, he saw a pair of radiant green ones staring directly into his. His lips curled into a smile. "Good morning, Lizzy. Did you sleep well?"

Elizabeth nodded.

Darcy smiled and asked, "Does your head still ache?"

She shook her head slightly.

"So, you are feeling much better?"

Again, she nodded. Darcy huffed out a small chuckle at her silence and said with a yawn, "How long have you been awake, my love? You seem bright-eyed and game!" Raising his brows, he thought to himself, *At least I hope you are.*

Even though her silence persisted, the intensity of her gaze was all the answer a husband smitten with his wife needed. Bolstered by the passion he witnessed in Elizabeth's eyes, Darcy reached forth his hand to touch her ear and began to tenderly wind his fingertip along its contours. Their heads remained level, their noses nearly touching, when he forthrightly stated, "I love you, Elizabeth. I am so honoured to have you in my life. I am the most fortunate of men."

Pursing her lips and tilting her face upward, Elizabeth kissed the tip of his nose and then lowered her head as it had been before. Again, their eyes locked. Moved by his wife's simple act of adoration, Darcy quickly gathered her into his arms, hungrily capturing her mouth with his own.

No longer did Elizabeth look upon her husband. Once his mouth took possession of hers, she instantly closed her eyes. The kiss was long and hard, and when she thought it was at an end, Darcy increased what was an already heated kiss by probing further and demanding more. Gasping for air as they parted, Elizabeth once more looked deeply into Darcy's darkened eyes and breathlessly acknowledged, "I love you so much." Without giving her adequate time to take in a proper breath, Darcy lunged in again, but this time, his hands simultaneously accompanied his lips in seeking domination of his wife's exquisite body.

Similarly, Elizabeth's hands spontaneously began roaming across her husband's back, sides, neck, and arms as well as through his hair. Both husband and wife found themselves lost in an escalating whirlwind of fervour.

Immediately after her momentary suspension in blissful ecstasy, Elizabeth remembered Dr. Lowry's instruction and blurted out, "Fitzwilliam, we must stop!"

Numb with surprise at his wife's outburst, Darcy blinked in wide-eyed shock. The crease between his brows revealed his bafflement. "We what?"

With a matter-of-act air, she again stated, "We must stop."

Darcy tossed his head, shrugging his shoulders in disbelief at her taking pleasure while his remained wanting.

Darcy scathingly snorted, "Phfft! Pray, Lizzy, why must *we* stop?"

"I am experiencing my courses right now."

As his wife took in his exasperated look, she observed beads of perspiration dotting his temple, and the reproach in his tone was not lost on her. "Elizabeth, we have already been over this. Blood does not bother me in the least." His eyes seemed ominous as they bore into hers.

Light-heartedly she chided, "That is debatable, sir. The night of the fencing accident, you swooned, reminiscent of a woman, when seeing your shirt crimsoned with your own blood."

Elizabeth heard him exhale loudly. His eyes again widened as his jaw set, a contemptuous bobbing of his head accompanying it. Wincing at his contempt, she bit her lip and averted her gaze.

Striving to contain his mounting frustration for what he perceived to be an irrational excuse on his wife's part, he attempted to control his sarcasm before saying another word, but his effort was paltry. "Elizabeth! You have just claimed that you feel better, and I witnessed for myself just *how much better* you now feel, and so—"

Suddenly, a loud knock from the door jarred their attention away from each other.

The fates are against me. I am not allowed to make love to my own wife! Conceding defeat, Darcy swung his body over, plopped on his back and bitingly snapped, "What?"

Mr. Coates's eyebrows shot up upon hearing the irritation in his master's voice. Did he dare enter? Choosing to remain in the hallway, the elderly gentleman squealed out, "Mr. Darcy, sir, Dr. Lowry has come to see Mrs. Darcy. What shall you have me to do, sir?"

Darcy looked over to Elizabeth and asked, "Are you ready to see him, or shall I have him wait?"

"No, send him up. I shall go change into a fresh shift." Elizabeth arose and made her way to her dressing chamber, knowing the inevitable could no longer wait.

Also arising, Darcy went to open the door to speak to his servant in a civil tone, desiring not to repeat their shouting, and therefore, risk waking the rest of the household. The butler took in Mr. Darcy's tousled hair and heightened colour. "Ah! Coates, please escort the doctor without delay and, um, thank you."

"Yes sir, straightaway." Mr. Coates turned and wobbled his way to the staircase. Darcy watched him go, bemused by the man's perseverance. Though his servant was old and not able to move as readily as he once had, he was still stalwart, and his mind remained just as keen as it had been in his younger years.

Closing the door, he turned to see his wife dressed in a clean gown, brushing her hair. Laying the brush on the vanity top, Elizabeth braided her long tresses and then returned to bed, pulling the coverlet around her.

Retrieving his robe from off the chair, Darcy donned it and then sat down to observe his wife. He noted that she seemed pleased about something.

Catching her husband's gaze, Elizabeth smiled at him. She was full of optimism and full of life, for she had nothing but good news to tell the doctor.

Dr. Lowry hailed a cheerful good morning to the master and mistress as he entered the room, after which he immediately turned his full attention to his patient. "How did you fare last night, Mrs. Darcy?"

"I slept well."

Placing his black bag upon a side table, he then walked over to the bed and asked, "Has your headache subsided?"

Barely able to contain her exuberance, she nodded. "Yes—yes it has!"

Gesturing with his hand, Dr. Lowry asked, "May I?" Again Elizabeth nodded and only winced slightly as he lifted her fringe to inspect her laceration.

Darcy anxiously awaited the esteemed doctor's words, hoping he would pronounce that all was well. However, instead of being informed about his wife's condition, the doctor without so much as turning to look at him, directed, "Darcy would you please step outside into the hall? It will only be for a moment."

The scowl materializing upon her husband's countenance was endearing. It was all Elizabeth could do to hide her delight over Darcy's childish petulance, and she had to bite back an impish grin when her husband annoyingly asked, "*Why?*"

Harrison Lowry walked over to his bag without looking at his friend. "It will only be for a moment. I shall call for you when you may return."

Slowly, Darcy arose and stood unmoving. Harrison Lowry returned to Elizabeth's side before he turned to look fixedly at his friend who stared at him defiantly. Darcy became a little unnerved by the physician's scrutiny, and therefore, with a slight shrug of his shoulders, often displayed before doing anything he deemed disagreeable, he obeyed and exited the room, howbeit, reluctantly.

"Now, Mrs. Darcy, you seem to be in happy spirits this morning. I hope I have not misconstrued your expression."

"Oh no, Dr. Lowry. I mean yes, Dr. Lowry, I am happy, very happy, indeed. I have not bled a single drop. Is this not reason for happiness?"

The doctor's dimples shown brilliantly and his blue eyes shared the joyous lustre of his patient's smiling ones. "Yes, Mrs. Darcy, that is excellent news. Has there been any sign of cramping?"

The sparkle of Elizabeth's eyes seemed brighter than before, if that were possible, as she confidently shook her head while not breaking eye contact with the doctor. Dr. Lowry had never seen a woman as joyous as Elizabeth Darcy. Her happiness was not containable. She was bursting at the seams.

Her enthusiasm was contagious, and in intervals, Dr. Lowry shook his head and then nodded, sharing in her joy. "Shall I call your husband back in?"

"Oh, yes, I mean, should you check me first?"

"I see no need. I feel assured you are expecting when considering the weariness you have been experiencing of late."

"Oh, and I remember feeling ill at the smell of my favourite meats."

Dr. Lowry laughed. "Yes, that is common. Still, I want to caution you to stay in bed for the remainder of this day, and I also want you to have no relations with your husband for another day or two. Just as a precaution. That is all." He closed up his bag and bowed. "I shall see you in a few days, then."

"Yes, thank you, Dr. Lowry. Thank you so much."

Upon stepping out, the doctor espied his friend leaning against the opposite wall with his eyes closed and arms folded over his chest. Hearing the opening of the door quickly brought him to attention.

"Will she be well?" Darcy asked.

"Yes, she will be fine. She has a strong constitution. I think all will be well with your wife. I do want her to have bed rest for one more day though."

"But my sister is to be presented at court tonight and—"

"Yes, see that Mrs. Darcy does not attend. She truly should stay down for another day."

"But Harrison, is she in some danger from her head injury? I do not understand what the problem is. Would you please explain it?"

"I must go, Darcy, but your wife will fill you in on all the details. Just rest assured, she is healthy and on the mend. Her cut is healing nicely, and there is no sign of infection."

Dr. Lowry commenced to depart, but quickly turned back and humorously stated, "You and your wife have had quite the misfortune, both experiencing concussions in such a brief period of time. If you were to ask me, it is a rather drastic measure to escape marital woes. I shall have to reconsider my position on the notion of matrimony." He smiled broadly to his friend and swiftly turned, gallantly taking his leave.

Incredulously, Darcy stared after him and silently questioned, *was the man being facetious?*

Anxiously, Elizabeth desired her husband's return. She was giddy with anticipation, trying to imagine his response when he knew that she was with child.

Entering the room, Darcy rolled his eyes. "Elizabeth, I think something is wrong with Harrison. He is behaving oddly. Did you notice?"

"Oh, Fitzwilliam, do not worry about that. Come here. I have something to tell you."

With his hands in the pockets of his robe, he walked sulkily to the bed and stood by its edge, looking at his wife. She patted the mattress, yet he remained standing.

"Fitzwilliam, really, you are going to have a permanent wrinkle between your brows."

"Why did I have to leave, Lizzy?"

"Oh, surely, Fitzwilliam, you are not sulking about that still? This is a happy time, a time for rejoicing."

With a shrug, he sat next to her. He picked up her hand and stared at it. "I am happy. I am very grateful you are safe and well." One by one, he began to caress each finger with his thumb, lingering on each trimmed nail as he swirled circular patterns over them. "Harrison says you must remain in bed. I am sorry that you will not be there for Georgiana's presentation. We could wait until next year."

"No, that would be too cruel for Georgie. She is doing splendidly, and I am sure she will understand my situation."

Still looking down at her hands, he softly stated, "Yes, but *I* will miss you. I do not want to leave you, but I must be there for Georgiana. If Fitzwilliam were here, he could go with my aunt as she presents her."

"Nonsense, even if he were here, you must go. You are her brother. You are like a father to her, and she needs you there. You will dance the first dance with her."

His head was still downcast when she said, "Just as you will with our daughter in seventeen years."

Darcy's head shot up, and he looked at her quizzically. "What are you saying, Lizzy? Are you saying what I think you are saying?"

"That all depends on what it is you think I am saying."

A serene euphoria overtook his senses, and he stared in wonder at his wife. Each silently drank in one another's love and elation. "Say it, Elizabeth. Tell me." He held his breath, and his eyes took in his wife's every movement, from the curl of her lips to the rise of her brows.

"I am with child."

Instantly, Darcy's face lit up and a boyish grin spread over his countenance, the very one that made Elizabeth's heart skip a beat. He inhaled deeply and kept gazing into her eyes. "I love you, Elizabeth Bennet Darcy."

"I know."

Snatching up her hands, he brought them to his lips and kissed each one repeatedly. He then turned them over and softly bestowed a loving kiss upon her open palms. "I am a blessed man, my love, twice blessed."

"I hope you feel so when I tell you the doctor's orders." Elizabeth then related all the details of her pregnancy to Darcy. She told him that it was for that reason alone that she needed to rest and not have relations with him.

"Lizzy, you should have told me. I felt spurned—first by you and then by Harrison—but *your* rejection cut to the quick."

Impishly she cried, "Yes, I imagine abstinence will be a trial for you, umm…us."

"No amount of teasing from you can upset me at this moment. I am too elated. You mentioned a daughter. So you think the baby is a girl?

"I have no idea what the babe may be. Will you be upset if it is a girl and not the desired heir?"

"Elizabeth, if you presented me with seven daughters in succession, I could never be disappointed, particularly if they were the image of their mother."

Studying his countenance, she felt he truly meant it.

Comprehending the amazed look in her eyes, he added, "Elizabeth, I, like any man, want a son, but never at the expense of the child given. Each child is precious, male or female. I shall never regret the sex of any child we are blessed with. If the tables were turned, would you pine for a daughter?"

"I think the odds are in my favour."

"How so?" he baited.

She stated with a sparkle in her eyes, "Lest, I need remind you, Mr. Darcy, my mother has *five* daughters."

He chortled merrily, and his response brought forth an open smile from his wife. The sound of his laughter was music to Elizabeth. She felt completely at ease with his sentiments regarding the expectant heir. Deep inside, she desired to give him a son, but she also knew that he spoke the truth—with open arms, he would gladly cherish whatever the heavens chose to bestow upon them regardless of its sex.

~*~

In the early hours of the following morning, after returning home from the court of St. James, Darcy quietly entered his wife's chamber and gingerly edged his way onto the bed, settling himself beside her. He had considered sleeping in his own chamber for fear of awaking her, but his desire to be by her side became too great.

Her soft breaths imparted a hypnotic effect, and he soon felt himself unwinding from the energetic evening of his aunt introducing Georgiana to society. Just as his eyelids became heavy, Elizabeth sleepily asked, "Did all go well, my love?"

"Hmm, yes, it went very well."

A few more minutes ensued before Elizabeth enquired further. "Did Georgiana enjoy herself?"

No response.

"Fitzwilliam, did you hear me, my love?"

"Shh, Lizzy, go back to sleep."

"But I cannot. You have awakened me, and now I am anxious to know how everything turned out. Please, do not leave me in suspense."

He exhaled noisily, but turned on his side, complying with her wish. Thus, his discourse began. He told of the tediousness for his sister and aunt while waiting in the long lines and of Georgiana's nervousness in enduring the gradual progression. In his opinion, she had no reason to be anxious. He thought she was the epitome of all loveliness, and others opined similarly, since after her presentation, she danced nearly every dance. He also elaborated on his introduction to many of the young women with whom she had been associating of late. He knew most of their parents, but was glad to actually meet the young ladies of his sister's acquaintance face to face. One young woman, in particular, Lady Lillian Pierson, daughter of the Earl of Milbank, was designated by Georgiana as her dearest favourite. Upon hearing this, Elizabeth proposed that they invite Lady Lillian to spend time at Pemberley either in the late spring or during the summer. Darcy nodded in agreement with the idea and commented that he thought Georgiana would be pleased with the suggestion.

All in all, Darcy expressed his satisfaction that the event went well, excluding his aggravation at seeing Lady Catherine in attendance, yet on this point, he said no more. Elizabeth's curiosity was fully piqued, and she insisted he go on. Her demand for details made him wish he had not mentioned the blasted encounter at all as the taste of its bitter ashes still remained fresh upon his tongue. "Suffice it to say, Elizabeth, that my aunt is still in opposition to our marriage."

In open awe, Elizabeth asked, "Fitzwilliam, what on earth did she say to you?"

"Believe me, Lizzy, when I say, nothing that we have not heard before."

"Oh, but, Fitzwilliam, did she say this in front of others, and whatever did you say in return?"

"Elizabeth, if you must know, yes, she spoke out quite openly. When has my aunt ever considered propriety when saying anything? Furthermore, I did not respond to her poisonous venom."

"I suppose you merely looked at her and walked away."

Nodding in the darkness, he smiled dryly. "Yes, Lizzy, your deduction is correct. Now that you are awake, may I ask for a kiss?"

Replying aggressively with her whole body, Elizabeth rolled atop her unsuspecting husband and clasped his face between her hands, planting a passionate kiss on his lips.

"Lizzy, I shall never find sleep now. How can you be so cruel?"

Smiling at his words, yet sorry for his predicament, she offered, "Roll over, and I will rub your back. Thus, you can quickly forget about my body and be lulled into rest by the gentle caresses of my fingers."

"Harrumph! I am quite certain that I shall not forget so easily."

Yet with each subsequent stroke upon his flesh, his mind and yearnings started to settle. Elizabeth's touch did much to placate his longings and snuff out the vicious attack from his aunt. That woman's harsh words kept ringing in his ears. ...*So, Fitzwilliam, you were wise enough not to bring that chit here where she will never belong, at least some sense remains in you. Keep her far away for Georgiana's sake. Your sister should not be made to suffer because of Richard's mistake and yours...* Darcy wondered at her words. What did she mean by his and Richard's mistakes? He clearly understood that he had married someone his aunt considered beneath him and, more to the point, had not married Anne. In spite of that, how was Richard involved? What mistake had he made? Of what was Lady Catherine implying?

~*~

The morning of Miss Darcy's coming out ball finally arrived. At Georgiana's request, Kitty had spent the night at Ackerley helping with all last minute decisions. As they ate, the girls chatted amicably through the course of their breakfast. They discussed the particulars of the many choices before them—those delicate details that young women find so essential and enthralling to sort out before any major event. How should they style their hair? Should their tresses be adorned with ribbons, jewels or nothing at all? Dare they wear the cosmetic powder that Yvette, the French lady's maid, had introduced to Georgiana? She had showed her, after all, how to apply it subtly to enhance her features and allure men. Although she wore the reddish powder the night of the ball at Matlock without Yvette, Georgiana was not as confident in its application. She felt certain that if her brother knew, he would never allow it, so the idea was set aside for the time being.

Darcy ate his breakfast quickly. He had business to attend to in town with his attorney and Mr. Sumner concerning the mine. As he drank down the last of his coffee, he observed his sister with fascination. She was truly blossoming into a beautiful, confident woman—one who was willing to be adventuresome yet polished. Observing her outgoing attitude of late, especially under Elizabeth's tutelage, he felt certain that Georgiana would find an acceptable marriage, one in which she would be cared for in the luxury she deserved and in which she would esteem her companion. In his mind, his sister was sure to be one of the most sought after young women of the Season. Therefore, he must exert exceptional care regarding with whom she might associate and wherewith she might venture. He and Fitzwilliam, along with Elizabeth, could not be too vigilant where Georgiana's welfare was concerned.

Elizabeth kissed her sister and sister-in-law on the cheek before departing with her husband. Today was Mrs. Chalmers's literary gathering. It was also the first day that Dr. Lowry allowed Elizabeth out of bed. She and Darcy had decided not to inform another soul about the pregnancy until more time had passed. Elizabeth preferred it that way. She felt it gave the two of them the opportunity to enjoy their intimate secret a little longer. The world would intrude upon their idyllic interlude soon enough, and she understood that the eventual intrusion was as it should be. Yet, she relished this interval that only she and her husband now shared.

Alighting from the carriage first, Darcy turned back to aid his wife, and, once her feet were safely upon the ground, he openly embraced her. He then walked her to the Chalmers's entryway and remained by her side until the door was answered. While they waited, he reminded her of where she could find him if she were to become ill, and he also advised her not to tire herself. If she desired to come home earlier than planned, Mrs. Chalmers, he assured her, would be most accommodating to her needs. All Elizabeth need do was ask.

In an effort to reassure her husband, Elizabeth smiled lovingly to him, squeezing his hand tightly before allowing the butler to usher her away.

The Chalmers's townhouse was richly furnished, and like Pemberley and Ackerley, Elizabeth found the decorations not overly ornate, but functional and dignified. Not knowing what to expect at such a meeting, Elizabeth found herself a little surprised to discover such a large number of women in attendance and to find other women her own age.

The ladies gathered in the drawing room. Mrs. Chalmers had already given everyone an individual welcome as they entered her home. Standing in front of the whirr of animated, feminine voices, the hostess held up her hands to attract the attention of the gathering.

"I am happy to welcome everyone to my seventeenth annual assembly. Many of you have been in attendance from the start, but for some it is your maiden voyage, and we hope you will continue to journey with us in the years to come. We are an open-minded lot and desire everyone to be comfortable and feel free to let your voice be heard. All opinions are taken into account and never belittled. So please, feel free to participate. As I always say: the more the merrier. Now, it is customary that introductions be made. I, for one, throw propriety to the wind and dispense with that formality and let each individual tell a little something about themselves. I shall start, and then we shall go around the room in a clockwise fashion."

Elizabeth listened attentively as each lady stated such details as her name, marital status, county of residence when not in Town, number of children or grandchildren, and any special literary interests she may hold. She was surprised to find that these ladies did not seem as condescending as many of the other ladies who had met from London's high ranking circles. Rather, they were grounded and down to earth. One woman, in particular, caught Elizabeth's interest, a Lady Abigail Hatherton. When this woman introduced herself, the elderly lady sitting next to Elizabeth whispered that that young woman had been recently widowed, not a year ago. Her husband had been in line to become an earl, and they had had one son, who was not yet three years of age. Immediately, Elizabeth's heart went out to the woman. She could only imagine how she might feel if Darcy were to die, leaving her to raise their child all alone. She shuddered at the thought.

The first hour passed quickly with several readings of John Donne. After the last poem was discussed, the ladies were then invited to the dining hall for refreshments and conversation. It was during this interval that Elizabeth found herself seated next to Lady Hatherton. The two women reintroduced themselves to each other. Each listened with interest as they shared their points of view regarding Donne's works. Finally, Elizabeth asked Lady Hatherton if this were her first time to attend Mrs. Chalmers, and she said it was.

Emboldened by Lady Hatherton's open manner, Elizabeth ventured further. "Did you know very much about Donne's works before today?"

Lady Hatherton revealed a sly smile, "No, I admit that I am not at all familiar with the man."

"And... did you find him to your liking, then?" Elizabeth asked candidly with a look of scepticism.

Lady Hatherton found Mrs. Darcy's light heartedness delightful. "I fear I found some of the passages difficult to understand. However, I own that I did not spend any amount of time with his works and would need to earnestly study them before I can pass off a knowledgeable judgment."

Nodding in understanding, Elizabeth interjected, "I, likewise, am not familiar enough with his works to offer any rational assessment, but I can truly say that after hearing a full hour of his writings, I am relieved we are done with Donne."

Lady Hatherton laughed lightly at Elizabeth's witticism. She could easily understand what had attracted Fitzwilliam Darcy to his wife. Elizabeth Darcy's vivacity was exactly what the man needed in his life. She liked Mrs. Darcy very much and found her own spirits elevated by merely being in the younger woman's company. Lady Hatherton silently considered, *I wonder if Darcy has told her? After all, he is my son's godfather. Dare I mention it?*

When the ladies reconvened in the drawing room for the last hour of reading which covered various works of other authors, Elizabeth and Lady Hatherton chose to sit together. They remained quiet during the dynamic discussions that followed each reading, though both women dearly wondered what the other was thinking. Despite the muteness of their tongues, their eyes radiantly revealed their thoughts to each other, in fact, more so than their words could have done. Each woman took pleasure in her unspoken camaraderie and each felt as if she had known the other for a long time. Elizabeth hoped this simple encounter had presented her with a lifelong friend.

At the conclusion of the gathering, Mrs. Chalmers arose and thanked everyone for their participation and attendance. Then she did something out of character and called attention to the fact that for the first time in seventeen years, she had a request from someone's *husband* that a poem be dedicated and read for his wife. This caused a stir among many of the ladies, and they sat up in excited interest. Mrs. Chalmers chuckled at the hush that fell over the room as she unfolded the parchment that bore a broken seal.

"All right ladies our esteemed gentleman petitioned me a week ago, stating that today was a special day for him and his wife. He did not mention why it was special, but he said she would know. This poem is written by Robert Herrick."

There were some "ahs" and "ohs" heard here and there amongst the crowd.

At the mere mention of the poet, Robert Herrick, Elizabeth's heart froze. Surely her husband would not dare. Surely, this could not be happening to her. *Oh, please dear Lord, do not let it be the one about the niplets!*

Lady Hatherton immediately sensed her new friend's distress and realized that the poem must be for Elizabeth. She smiled reassuringly to Mrs. Darcy, trying to bring some solace to her.

Every person paid rapt attention as Mrs. Chalmers's stately voice bellowed out the title of the poem. "The name of the poem is, ***Delight in Disorder***. Here we go ladies." Mrs. Chalmers's clear tenor enunciated every word perfectly.

> A sweet disorder in the dress
> Kindles in clothes a wantonness:
> A lawn about the shoulders thrown
> Into a fine distraction;
> An erring lace, which here and there
> Enthralls the crimson stomacher;
> A cuff neglectful, and thereby

Ribbons to flow confusedly;
A winning wave, deserving note,
In the tempestuous petticoat;
A careless shoe-string, in whose tie
I see a wild civility;
Do more bewitch me, than when art
Is too precise in every part.

Elizabeth blushed, bit her lip, and looked down at the toes of her shoes. She heard many women sigh dreamily. Others inhaled loudly, while the remaining exclaimed, "How romantic!" They all seemed to speak at once, demanding to know who had the doting husband who was so affectionate. Elizabeth was positive that it had to be Fitzwilliam. This was the poem that he had spoken of, the one that had reminded him of her in the early stages of their acquaintance. A sigh escaped her lips and then a smile spread across her features as she thought, *And all along I thought he judged me harshly for my muddied petticoat when, in all actuality, he had been bewitched by it*. The memory made her grin all the more.

Despite all the pleas, Mrs. Chalmers would not relent and reveal which husband had made the request. Instead, she diffused the situation by thanking them once more and reminding them that next year's event would concentrate on the compositions of Sir Thomas More and the sonnets of Shakespeare.

As Elizabeth and Lady Hatherton queued up, waiting in the entrance hall for their carriages to be brought forth, they exchanged cards and promised to call on one another before the Season ended. Lady Hatherton then braved to ask her newborn friend, "Was the poem from *your* husband, Mrs. Darcy?"

Elizabeth's bright eyes were all the answer she needed, but she enjoyed what the young bride had to say just the same. "Yes, I imagine it was. He told me weeks ago that there was a particular poem by that poet which reminded him of me when we first became acquainted."

"Your husband must be a very romantic man to discover a sonnet which he feels depicts his feelings for you. It was delightful to hear something so private revealed at this special time. He must love you very much. You are a most fortunate woman to have a husband so in love with you."

Laughing nervously, Elizabeth replied, "Yes, he does have his moments. Perhaps it would be best to keep them a little *less* public." She quickly averted her gaze, uncomfortable speaking about such a personal subject with Lady Hatherton, fully mindful of the fact that this lady was newly widowed and would never again hear romantic words from her deceased husband's lips.

"Oh, Mrs. Darcy, do not let that point make you uneasy. All the ladies enjoyed it so. Why else do we turn to poetry and novels? My dear, they help us to escape into a world other than our own, if only for a little while, momentarily allowing us to forget the burdens which weigh so heavily upon us in reality. They refresh us!"

The truthfulness of her words earned an acknowledging smile from Elizabeth, and she felt that besides speaking in a straightforward manner, Lady Hatherton, for such a young woman, was immensely sophisticated and wise. Elizabeth found that she liked her very much.

~*~

Having been delayed in his meeting, Darcy was unable to personally retrieve his wife from her outing. Therefore, Elizabeth was assisted into the carriage by a footman. He informed her that her husband had, unfortunately, been detained by his business, but that the gentleman would meet her at the planned destination. He and the driver then whisked her off to an unknown location to await Mr. Darcy's arrival.

On the seat across from the one on which she sat, Elizabeth noted Darcy's cane and a picnic basket that had not been there when he dropped her off at Mrs. Chalmers's home. A small smile graced her lips. When the carriage came to a halt, she anxiously looked out the window, observing an elegant building, instantly realizing it to be one of London's famous pleasure gardens, and her small smile grew to greater proportions. Yet, as the hour waned, so did Elizabeth's spirits. The desire for fresh air and a stretch of her legs became paramount in her mind, and she knew she could not attain it while waiting in the carriage. Thus, with the knob of her husband's cane, she tapped on the ceiling of the compartment.

The footman opened the door to discover a woman with a design all her own. As he helped his master's mistress to alight with a questioning look upon his face, Elizabeth assured him. "I shall stay right over there," she pointed towards the paved walkway beside the carriage, "so you need not worry that I will get lost."

The servant eyed her warily, knowing that Mr. Darcy would have his head if any harm were to befall his wife. Then, suddenly, at the exclamation, "Mrs. Darcy!" both servant and mistress turned.

Lord Hazelton, having caught sight of his cousin's wife from across the thoroughfare, quickly made his way through the throng, calling after her.

Upon hearing her name, Elizabeth looked up and recognized her husband's cousin from her recent riding mishap. She paused and smiled.

"Why, Elizabeth, I could not have imagined seeing you here. You are well, I presume, having recovered from your trauma?"

Smiling brilliantly, Elizabeth answered that, indeed, she was well. Lord Hazelton gallantly offered his arm to her, and she accepted it, cheerfully. He accompanied her over to the walkway and asked, "Are you all alone?"

"Fitzwilliam is to meet me here, but he has been detained with some sort of business, and our footman, Grearly, waits with me until he arrives."

James glanced over at the simple Grecian entrance and stated, "Then, do allow me the honour of escorting you inside for a small walk around the front gardens. The weather is delightful, and there is no way of discerning how long you might need to wait. I shall be glad to accompany you until Darcy arrives."

"Oh, I would not think of inconveniencing you in such a fashion."

"Truly, Elizabeth, it is such a fine day. I have already concluded *my* business, and I would find it a pleasure to escort you. I can inform your servant to direct Darcy, upon his arrival, along the central avenues, where he shall find us without difficulty."

Elizabeth was sorely tempted. As of late, she had spent very little time outdoors, and the weather was indeed exceptional. Besides, she had been seated for the whole of the morning, and she did not relish the thought of sitting even longer while waiting all alone. Additionally, she feared to offend her husband's cousin. Thus, she could not bear to disoblige Lord Hazelton's suggestion.

James smiled at her concession and quickly told the footman in which direction they could be found.

The servant frowned. He did not like the interference and hoped that his master would not be angry that he had not followed through with the itinerary given him.

Elizabeth took the Viscount's proffered arm, and the two made their way along the wide forecourt. Hazelton loved the way it felt to have Elizabeth's arm upon his. She seemed so agreeable that it made him wonder if she might be softening towards him. Might there be a chance she would consider entering into a tryst? He knew many couples who had open marriages as long as they were carried forth discreetly. The mere thought of her as his served as an aphrodisiac, filling him with instant desire. It was all he could do not to caress her hand or pull her close. He would have to be patient until he was certain. If she kept this easy manner in his company, he might be able to win her over. Yet, there were other ways if need be, for he was certain that she could be blackmailed into it. This notion had overshadowed his thoughts of late. If Wickham had managed to blackmail her, could he not do the same with his acquired knowledge of her nasty predicament regarding the matter, keeping the information from her prudish husband? However, he would not require her pin money for his silence. This might upset the plan that Elisha had in place, but if he could manage to acquire Elizabeth, plans could very easily be altered.

They walked along agreeably with him pointing out areas of interest. Elizabeth enjoyed the novel sights and Lord Hazelton's light-hearted banter. It reminded her of Richard. Yet, she was fully aware that the older brother had been endowed with a very handsome mien, and in his physique, he was much taller than his younger brother with fine broad shoulders akin to her husband's.

Conscious that they had been walking for a little over a quarter of an hour, Elizabeth expressed a desire to return to the entrance in case Darcy might be in search of her. Before turning to go, James stated that he was happy to know that she had recovered and expressed his concern for her continued welfare. He revealed that seeing her lying there in the hedge on the day of the accident had frightened him. He truly feared for her life. Elizabeth took this opportunity to properly thank him wholeheartedly for assisting her and being so kind during the mishap. She even went so far as to suggest that she thought he was very much like his brother, the colonel.

Silently, Lord Hazelton scoffed at the comparison, but he assured her that there was no need for her gratitude. He only did what any gentleman would. He then suggested that if she *truly* wished to thank him, she might allow him to dance the first dance with her that night at Georgiana's coming out, since Darcy would naturally be escorting his sister. Immediately, he added that his wife would not be attending due to her confinement. Elizabeth gladly responded that she would happily save the dance for him.

Rounding the corner to the front quarter of the gardens, James perceived a very disgruntled gentleman rushing towards them, and he smirked quite gleefully at his cousin's annoyance.

Similarly, Elizabeth became cognizant of the fact that Darcy did not look pleased, and despite witnessing his apparent displeasure, she wondered at it, reasoning that not only was she with a male escort, but her attendant was none other than his trusted cousin.

Darcy became livid the moment the footman informed him that Lord Hazelton had arrived on the scene and was presently escorting Mrs. Darcy around the gardens. Hence, when seeing Elizabeth and James drawing near, her arm resting on Hazelton's, he instantly halted and stood as still as stone, discharging a menacing glare, first at his cousin and then at his wife. Silently, he questioned in anger, *"How could she?"*

~*~

Chapter Twenty-seven

Georgiana's Gala

The afternoon was bright and mild. Many had taken advantage of such a fine day to enjoy a stroll in the pleasure gardens. Thus, there were numerous individuals swarming about the pathways. Nevertheless, Fitzwilliam Darcy was oblivious to their presence. He had eyes only for his wife.

Beholding Elizabeth arm in arm with his loathed cousin, in seemingly cheerful spirits, momentarily rendered him speechless. The repercussions they had endured from the accident instantly tumbled to the forefront of his mind and resurrected the accusation which had lain buried within his heart: that Hazel had been the perpetrator behind it all. They had nearly lost their child because of his repugnant cousin's, heartless prank!

Suddenly propelled into action by his righteous indignation, Darcy's long legs boldly stalked forward. He strode directly to Elizabeth and Lord Hazelton and abruptly disengaged her arm, whirling her to his side, and gruffly exclaiming, "Your services are no longer required, Hazel. We shall bid you a good day!"

Flabbergasted at her husband's rudeness, Elizabeth gawked at him before she cried, "How dare you, Fitzwilliam! I have never been so humiliated as I am at this moment!"

Lord Hazelton took great pleasure in hearing the backlash Elizabeth delivered in apparent ire to his priggish cousin. Darcy's puffed-up air would only facilitate his sordid plans all the more.

With a firm hand around his wife's waist, Darcy whisked her speedily towards their waiting carriage. Elizabeth was seething at his despicable, public display—certain everyone in the garden had taken in the whole scene.

Once within the confines of the carriage, she let her anger spill forth. Hotly she cried, "What is wrong with you, Fitzwilliam? Why have you disgraced me in front of your cousin and heaven knows who else?"

He rolled his eyes and countered, "*I* have disgraced *you*? I think *not*! Can you not recollect any of your former opinions concerning my cousin?"

"No," Elizabeth intoned while sitting up straighter than before. "I only remember he was very kind to me after the accident. He was truly considerate of my situation—and this is how you repay him?"

Darcy's jaw hardened. Expelling a huff of air, he turned his head and glanced out the window.

"Oh my, Mr. Darcy, you have let jealousy interfere again! Am I never so much as to speak to another gentleman without your disapproval? I was merely sauntering about the grounds."

Disbelievingly, Darcy met her gaze and narrowed his eyes, staring at her for a full minute before speaking. "I know not how you can feel he is a gentleman. Believe me when I say, Elizabeth, that I feel certain that he is responsible for your accident. I cannot prove it, but madam, as well as I know my own name, I know he is responsible."

"I do not understand how he can be responsible for my misfortune. I may not remember everything about Lord Hazelton, but I do remember not wishing to ride. But, due to your constant hounding, I felt that I must! Thus, sir, *you* are the one responsible!" *Oh, no! I have said it aloud, and to him. How could I?*

"Elizabeth, hold your tongue. You know not of what you speak. I did not *force* you to ride," Darcy hissed through clenched teeth. "Were you not informed to wait for me in the carriage until my arrival this afternoon? If you had done as you were told, we would not be having this disagreement."

"For the life of me, I cannot believe you, Fitzwilliam Darcy! Pray, why is it that we are not now strolling the avenues together? Is it because you have not gotten your way, and now, like a spoilt child, you must sulk?"

"I will not discuss this any further with you, madam. I am afraid that anything said by either of us would reflect poorly on us both."

Holding her chin high, Elizabeth spiritedly exclaimed, "Fine!" With a sharp snap, she averted her gaze out the window, feigning interest at the passing scenery while in actuality she desired to burst into tears. Why could he not see his overbearing behaviour? Then again, she realized that her reaction to his authority was just as contemptible. How had they arrived at this point again? Her bottom lip began to quiver slightly. She turned her face completely to the side. She would not give him the satisfaction of seeing her cry.

Darcy sat in silence, sickened by the thought that Elizabeth felt he had forced her into riding the horse. She had never before stated that she had felt forced. She had never said that she did not want to ride. Why had she hurled such accusations at him? Did she truly hold him responsible for what happened to her? *Was* he responsible? He began to twist his ring and then stole a glance in Elizabeth's direction. He immediately observed her hands tightened into fists, informing him that she was still angry. He lifted his eyes to her face and noticed it was completely turned aside. Freely he looked upon her. She was so beautiful when angry. He huffed aloud, closing his eyes and barely shaking his head at the irony of it all.

Here he sat with Elizabeth, in the same carriage, a thing he would have never dreamt possible a year ago, this day. Yet, time and fate had been on his side and now she sat on the seat directly across from him, as his wife. *What is wrong with me? She does not remember her previous opinions about my abominable cousin. It is not her fault. How could I have been so insensitive? I must be patient. It is just that I cannot bear seeing her taken in by such a libertine. I cannot bear to have him touch her!*

Darcy reached forth his hand to take hold of hers and tenderly, regretfully, said, "I am sorry, Lizzy, and you are correct. My behaviour towards you in the park was extremely rude." Elizabeth started to withdraw her hand, but, hearing the contrition in his tone, she allowed him to retain it within his own.

"I am also sorry," his voice became hoarse with emotion, "that you feel I forced you to ride."

She turned to look at him.

He observed the tears brimming and threatening to spill forth from her eyes. "I assure you it was unintentionally done. I never wish for you to do anything against your will. I love you, Elizabeth. I am sorry for what you have borne due to my officiousness. I know that I can be overbearing in my opinions, and therefore, as my wife, I ask you to tell me freely when you feel I am acting so towards you. Please know, Lizzy, that I would never intentionally have you do *anything* against your will."

Relief washed over her countenance as the tears trickled downward. Elizabeth turned to face him directly and quietly stated, "I am just as much at fault. I should have told you of my fear of horses. I am sorry for saying such cruel things to you. You did not force me. I rode out of my desire to please you. I want you to be proud of me." The tears came in earnest now and her body shook.

Instantly, Darcy crossed over and sat next to her, taking her into his arms. She sobbed hard upon his shoulder. "Please forgive me, Fitzwilliam. I do not blame you for the accident. I blame no one!"

Striving to quiet her anxiety, he lovingly caressed her back and handed her his handkerchief. He watched her wipe away her tears and then blow her nose several times. With the last sniffle, Elizabeth became aware of her husband observing her with an intent look of adoration. Embarrassed, she casually asked, "Pray sir, what do you find so captivating about a woman blowing her nose?"

"I find that I cannot take my eyes off of your face, Elizabeth, be it contorted in anger, swollen from tears, or lit up in joy. You are the most handsome woman of my acquaintance. Your beauty captivates me."

With a raised brow and a lopsided grin, she replied wryly, "Oh, yes, I forgot, *disorder* is to your liking, it bewitches you!"

Realizing she was referring to the poem that he had asked Mrs. Chalmers to read, Darcy anxiously questioned, "So, I take it you liked the poem and realized it was from me?"

Tossing her head and shoulder forward, she playfully answered, "Yes, when I heard the name Robert Herrick, I instantly remembered your citation and immediately knew that you were the enigmatic husband whom every female in that room was dying to fathom. You gave me quite a fright, however. My heart skipped a beat for fear that it was going to be the poem about Julia's breast. You teasing man!"

Oh, how he loved her facial expressions when she became animated! Darcy wholeheartedly chuckled at the image of Elizabeth sitting in fearful mortification surrounded by a roomful of women. "No, Lizzy, I would never be so cruel, but did you like the poem?"

Sincerity settled across her features as she looked directly into her husband's eyes. "Yes, Fitzwilliam, I did like the poem. I am still amazed, yet honoured, that you found delight in me so early in our acquaintance. I had no idea at the time that you found me attractive in my muddied petticoat, or," she raised her brows and widened her eyes for effect, before saucily saying further, "as the poet states," 'the tempestuous petticoat.' "Had I known it was so easy to acquire your affections, I should have gladly let my hair go wild and pranced about in sullied petticoats all the day long. I would even have allowed my bonnet to hang askew!"

Pulling her to him, he squeezed her tightly. "I love seeing you out of kilter, for you are quite tempting as such. It has been three days, Lizzy."

Looking knowingly into his eyes, she softly stated, "Yes, it has."

He gazed at her tenderly. Then, his voice, soft and inviting, said, "Shall I have the carriage turn around to take us back to the gardens for our picnic? I am sorry for reacting with anger and inconsideration."

With a slight blush on her alabaster cheeks, she lifted her eyes to his. "No, I am not at all hungry." Dropping her gaze demurely, she added, "At least, I do not possess *that* kind of hunger." She smirked.

His lips curled into an impetuous smile. "Then, shall we have luncheon in our chamber?"

Biting her lip as she raised a brow, Elizabeth replied, "*Yesss*! I would find that quite satisfactory, Mr. Darcy."

As soon as the chamber door shut, both husband and wife began to discard their clothing with frenzy: tailcoat, waistcoat, dress, shoes and cravat were hurled through the air. During the disrobement, Darcy asked, "How did you find Donne? Mrs. Chalmers had mentioned that his works were the topic of interest."

"Oh, I must confess," Elizabeth exclaimed breathily while removing her silk stockings, "that I am not at all familiar with his works. The ones we considered were not that captivating. Yet, many of the ladies were quite enthusiastic in their discussion. I wished I would have taken the time to read more of his writings before going."

Darcy froze in place as Elizabeth lifted her foot to remove her stocking. He could do nothing more than gaze upon her beauty. His clothing forgotten, he watched her as she crawled onto the bed, freely admiring her voluptuous figure. Shaking himself from his scrutiny, he reached for the tail of his shirt, pulling the garment up and over his head before tossing it to the floor.

From her vantage point atop the bed, Elizabeth viewed Darcy's activity. Unconsciously, while her eyes followed her husband's fluid movements, she bit her lip, twirled a loose lock of hair, scrunched her toes, and inhaled deeply. She found his sculpted physique very pleasing.

Nearly tripping with the removal of his trousers, he asked, "What particular works did you discuss?"

"Oh, *An Anatomy of the World*—it was very long! And a *Hymn to God My God, in My Sickness* and *A Hymn to God the Father*. I enjoyed those much better, and I must admit I prefer his meditations compared to Fordyce's notions.

Darcy gave a slight smile, but pulling his trousers back on, he quickly added, "Let me go down to the library and retrieve a poem of Donne's that I am quite sure will please you. He can be like Herrick."

Surprised at seeing her husband don his trousers once more, she rolled her eyes and said with a trace of exasperation, "Surely, Fitzwilliam this can wait?"

"No, I assure you, madam, the wait will only heighten your anticipation and the reward will serve to gratify." Before she had a chance to say another word, he was out the door, clad only in his trousers, and a robe and slippers.

Hurriedly, Darcy made his way to the library and crossed the room directly to the shelf to claim a slender leather volume. Without delay, he re-entered the hall and spotted his butler. Mr. Coates, pretending not to take notice of his master's bizarre attire for the middle of the day, averted his gaze in their passing and merely stated, "Good afternoon to you, Mr. Darcy"

"Um, why yes, thank you, and one to you as well, Coates."

The sheet was tucked up around Elizabeth with only her unclothed shoulders visible when Darcy entered the room. Yet, so intent was her husband on sharing one of his favourite poems by Donne, that he did not even take notice. Elizabeth mused that he most likely would not have been aware if she had not been covered at all.

Sitting on the bed, he quickly opened the tome and instantly turned to the desired sonnet. "Ah, here it is, Lizzy. Donne's satire and wit is to be greatly admired. I am sure you will enjoy it immensely. The title of the poem is *The Flea*.

"Truly, Fitzwilliam, it is about a flea?"

He looked roguishly at his wife and replied in the affirmative, but before his eyes reverted back to the verse, his vision was momentarily impeded when taking in his wife's creamy, bare shoulders. Suddenly his lips felt dry. He breathed deeply and licked them before reciting the poem.

Elizabeth took great pleasure in noticing the effect she had on him.

> MARK but this flea, and mark in this,
> How little that which thou deniest me is;
> It suck'd me first, and now sucks thee,
> And in this flea our two bloods mingled be.
> Thou know'st that this cannot be said
> A sin, nor shame, nor loss of maidenhead;
>
> Yet this enjoys before it woo,
> And pamper'd swells with one blood made of two;
> And this, alas! is more than we would do.
>
> O stay, three lives in one flea spare,
> Where we almost, yea, more than married are.
> This flea is you and I, and this
> Our marriage bed, and marriage temple is.
> Though parents grudge, and you, we're met,
> And cloister'd in these living walls of jet.
>
> Though use make you apt to kill me,
> Let not to that self-murder added be,
> And sacrilege, three sins in killing three.

Elizabeth smirked.

With great zest, Darcy read the last stanza:

> Cruel and sudden, hast thou since
> Purpled thy nail in blood of innocence?
> Wherein could this flea guilty be,
> Except in that drop which it suck'd from thee?
> Yet thou triumph'st, and say'st that thou
> Find'st not thyself nor me the weaker now.
> 'Tis true ; then learn how false fears be;
> Just so much honour, when thou yield'st to me,
> Will waste, as this flea's death took life from thee.

Darcy looked up from the book. "Did you like *this* reading from Donne?"

"Yes! I found it to be quite naughty—comparable to the Herrick poem. Oh my, Mr. Darcy, how you must have devoured such poems as these in your youth." Elizabeth smiled. She could see the pleasure shining in his eyes, and it warmed her inner being.

Laying the book aside, Darcy again disrobed and joined his wife under the covers. Grinning, he stated, "Yes, Lizzy, I suppose I did take much delight in them at that time, yet, I also had interests in weightier subjects, but now… now my delight is centred utterly and completely in you. We have created from us two," he placed his hand upon her abdomen, caressed it and then gave it a gentle squeeze, "our own pampered swell."

She smiled at his words. "Oh how I adore you, Fitzwilliam!" No more verbal exchange was needed. The cadence created from the harmony of their pulsating hearts and rapid breaths, measured as the perfect couplet for their loving expression.

~*~

The design of the gown Georgiana had chosen for her *'coming out'* was, indeed, fetching upon her. It showed off her slender frame most becomingly, and the false panels helped to bolster her bosom. Such a low cut décolletage revealed that this young lady was quite womanly in her own right. Again, she had chosen a silk taffeta, the colour of sapphires. Kitty's dress was the finest gown she had ever owned. The pale blue of the silk did much to show off her finest attributes. It pleased her tremendously.

In addition to fashioning her mistress' hair, Nancy had also fashioned the young Miss Bennet's. Both ladies' coiffures suited them and highlighted their loveliness. Kitty had jewelled pins interspersed throughout her tresses while Georgiana had chosen no embellishments, but had opted to let a generous lock of her golden hair hang off centre from the nape of her neck. The plump ringlet dangled freely away from the confinement of her bun, draping around one side of her neck, and with the slightest movement, it bounced most alluringly upon the bare skin of her collar bone.

While the two young misses where making their preparations, Sarah laced up Mrs. Darcy's corset and then began to arrange her mistress' hair in a style reminiscent of the coiffure fashioned for the Netherfield ball. As Sarah held up the cream gown with the interlaced-chiffon overlay—the very one Elizabeth had worn at Matlock—another vivid flashback came to the mistress. She suddenly remembered Mr. Ashton Caldecott in line with his parents and sister. It had not been at Pemberley where she had seen that perfect smile, but at Matlock. Accompanying that memory was another of the manner in which Mr. Caldecott had regarded her cleavage and the rude insinuation he had made to her that had Collette and Fitz not had a disagreement, she would never have become Mrs. Darcy. Her aversion towards the young man returned in full force, and she quickly understood her husband's unease over the fact that Georgiana had been left alone with him.

The lateness of the hour afforded no time for Elizabeth to have an intimate conversation with her husband. It would prevent her from communicating her realization to him. Therefore, at the first possible moment during the course of the evening, she determined to tell him her most recent recollections.

~*~

The Earl of Matlock's London townhouse was enormous, twice the size of Ackerley. The lavish richness and splendour was above anything Elizabeth had seen before. In her opinion, the decor rivalled Rosings and Matlock, itself.

Darcy's aunt, Lady Adeline, on detecting their entrance, swiftly came forth to greet them. Eagerly, she hugged Darcy, Elizabeth, and then Georgiana. After which, she stepped back and examined her niece's appearance. "Oh, Georgiana!" she exclaimed, "You look simply stunning!" She then cast an attentive gaze at Kitty. "I can tell you girls helped each other in your preparations, for you, my dear Miss Bennet, are just as beautiful in appearance as my niece." Kitty smiled widely at the compliment and then graciously thanked her.

The Earl, upon seeing his niece, called out, his voice booming, "Aw! Georgiana! I see you have made it in the nick of time, and you look absolutely radiant. I am sure you will be asked to dance every dance." He reached forth and stroked her ringlet before. "Yet, you must remember to take time to rest." He embraced her quickly and then gave a curt nod towards Elizabeth, Darcy, and Miss Catherine. Darcy felt the sting in his uncle's cool salutation and wondered at it. Had something happened to cause such a rebuff, or was it merely the lateness of the hour?

Darcy had little time to contemplate his uncle's dismissive air for the Earl commanded everyone to form the line post-haste seeing as the first guests were ascending the steps even as he spoke. Kitty was escorted into the ballroom by a servant and offered a glass of wine while she waited for the impending crowd. Two other guests had arrived earlier and had been seated. Kitty thought the elderly woman resembled Mr. Darcy's aunt, the one who had visited Longbourn the previous autumn. The woman's countenance looked quite severe, and the young woman seated next to her appeared rather pale and sullen. A few minutes had passed when Miss Bennet noticed a group of guests entering, and upon seeing the grand lady, they eagerly approached her with their felicitations.

It was not long, however, before Kitty received the reward of seeing a familiar face. The seventh person to walk through the entry of the ballroom was none other than Dr. Harrison Lowry. Kitty smiled brightly at him, thinking that he looked very handsome in his formal attire as he made his way to where she sat. Instantly, she realized she was gawking and looked down.

Laughing lightly, Dr. Lowry bowed and then asked, "Why, Miss Bennet, you looked momentarily disturbed. I hope my coming this way to greet you has not caused you any undue distress."

"Oh," Kitty stammered, "No-no, not at all." Nervously, she quickly rose to greet him properly, when, unwittingly, she stepped on the hem of her gown, causing her to fall backward into the chair, landing in a sprawled out manner.

"Oh, Miss Bennet, please allow me to help you." She could hear the concern in the doctor's voice, but it was too late. The sting of embarrassment burned hotly upon her cheeks. Despite her humiliation, Kitty took his offered hand when attempting to arise for a second time. Dr. Lowry smiled warm-heartedly to her and asked, "If you do not mind my asking, Miss Bennet, may I secure a set with you?"

Softly she replied, while looking down at her slippers, "All of my dances are available. Do you have a preference?"

"May I have the first set then?"

Looking up in surprise, she noticed the bluest eyes she had ever seen staring directly back into hers. She hesitated for the briefest moment and then answered, quickly, "Yes."

They began to converse over general topics. Kitty's skill in advancing a conversation was wanting, but Dr. Lowry's easy manner lessened her awkwardness, his ability adequate to keep their exchange afloat. She marvelled at his intellect, but was indeed grateful for his kindness and patience in encouraging her to participate. She felt surprisingly comfortable in his presence.

More people began to stream into the room. Among them were Mr. and Mrs. Bingley, accompanied by his sister, Caroline, and an unknown young man. Kitty instantly realized that this must be her brother-in-law's cousin, the one from Scarborough who was to come for a visit. He was tall and rather handsome.

Swiftly, the small party made their way over to where Kitty and Dr. Lowry stood.

"Why, Dr. Lowry," Bingley cried, "it is so good to see you again. I do hope you are in good health. You look as though you are in excellent health! And, of course, I am happy to see you too, Miss Catherine."

Kitty smiled at her brother-in-law and then stole a glance at the new gentleman. Unfortunately, to her utter mortification, he was openly gazing upon her. She blushed profusely and quickly turned away.

Harrison Lowry smiled, thanking Mr. Bingley and assuring him that he was indeed well.

"Good, good! It would not do having the doctor become the patient." Again Dr. Lowry nodded in amusement at Bingley's infectious enthusiasm.

"Ah, let me introduce my cousin to you both. Dr. Lowry, may I present to you my cousin from Scarborough, Mr. Iain Burns, who has just completed his ordination. Turning to his cousin, he continued, "Iain, allow me to present Dr. Lowry, from Derbyshire. Both gentleman shook hands and exchanged words of greeting.

Next, Bingley moved to complete the introductions. "Miss Catherine Bennet, my cousin, Mr. Burns. Iain, this is my lovely sister-in-law, of whom we have told you a great deal, Miss Catherine Bennet." Kitty noted the cousins were of similar height and build and that Mr. Burns's eyes were of the same blue hue as Bingley's. In contrast, his hair was not as curly and was the darker shade of Caroline's.

Mr. Burns bowed as Kitty curtseyed. "I am pleased to have finally met you, Miss Bennet. I have heard much of you and feel as if I know you already." He smiled warmly.

Kitty was in shock. What had they told him? Bashfully, she nodded, thanked him, and acknowledged that she, also, was happy to make his acquaintance.

While all the introductions and greetings were being performed, Caroline Bingley stood off to one side of the group, watching the proceedings with disgust. What on earth was that *country doctor* doing at Georgiana's ball? Surely, Darcy had lost all sense of convention. In vain, Miss Bingley hoped that tonight would present some form of interest for her. Elisha had sent word that she could not attend the ball due to her confinement, but added she would be in the house and wished to speak with her. Hence, she would send for her sometime before supper.

The ballroom seemed filled beyond capacity. The orchestra had been playing light melodies for the last quarter of an hour as the guests waited for the dance to officially begin. Redolent of the occasion when the Earl had stood at Matlock, welcoming all in the celebration of the marriage of his nephew and his nephew's new wife, he stood anew this evening and hailed all in attendance on behalf of his niece, Miss Georgiana Darcy.

When the dance commenced, Darcy and Georgiana lead off the first set, a minuet. Lord Hazelton immediately approached Elizabeth for her hand. She smiled, openly. However, she remained cautious in her mind. She reminded herself that there must be something about him, some basis for Fitzwilliam's notion that his cousin had caused the accident. Again, she reminded herself to ask Darcy about her former opinions of the Viscount.

~*~

Looming breathtakingly in the night sky, the full moon shone down with brilliance. The cool air imparted sweetness from the fragrant blossoms that grew along the roadside. In the stillness of the night on the Exeter coaching road, the pounding of a horse's hooves could be easily discerned. Yet, no other soul was present to hear them. The rider's ears alone took in the rhythmic beat of each hoof in the relentless percussion of the steed's hammering flight.

Colonel Richard Fitzwilliam recklessly impelled his mount onward towards the lights of London. He was determined and hard-pressed for time to make it to his parents' townhouse before the ball concluded so as to dance at least one dance with his sweet Georgiana. His mother had written to him, telling him that she would secure the last set for him if, perchance, he could attend.

General Kirkham had given him leave, which would have afforded him plenty of time to arrive and still be present for the entire gala *if* a certain incident had not occurred, an incident which deferred his departure. Early that afternoon, nearing the time for dismissal of his men from their drills, a young cadet had become over-wrought with his commanding officer. Heated words were exchanged between them. Richard had been busily engaged a half mile away with the younger soldiers and in the process of resetting the rifle targets for the morrow.

The vociferous verbal exchange between the student and sergeant which began as a minor skirmish, quickly escalated into fisticuffs, and the men, awaiting discharge, gathered round, hollering and whooping at the excitement of it all. It was not until gunfire rang out that Richard knew something had run amuck with the other company of men. Upon hearing the shots, he and his men immediately ran the length of the field to determine why there had been any discharges when all drills had been completed for the day. The group of men that had formed the circle around the brawl instinctively parted upon the colonel's approach to allow him access. As the hubbub died down, each face turned sombre and every eye fell upon him.

When Colonel Fitzwilliam reached the centre of the excitement, he found an alarming spectacle before him. The young cadet lay on the ground cold dead. The sergeant, also lying upon the soil, had been wounded by what appeared to be a self-inflicted rifle ball. He, however, was not dead, but remained conscious, slowly choking on his own blood. Richard knelt beside him, grasping his hand and looking directly in the young man's eyes. Gurgling out his last words, the officer strangled the more to say, "Tell my...mo...ther...I'm...sorr—" He was gone. Inhaling deeply, Richard closed his eyes and shook his head in despair.

Thus, after drawing down the officer's eyelids, the colonel questioned all the men regarding the dispute. He received several conflicting stories about how the incident had transpired. In return, he found himself being questioned at great length by *his* commanding officer. Before leaving for London, he had to write and submit a detailed report of all that he had witnessed as well as provide a comprehensive account of each version of the tragedy that had been told to him. Richard realized they would never know the whole truth of the matter, yet one thing was certain: the quarrel, which had taken the lives of two men, had begun over a gambling debt amounting to a measly five shillings…a mere five shillings…two men's lives for such a paltry sum.

The sad task of writing to the families of both men still remained. Yet, his letter would not inform them of their loved ones' deaths, for that would come from the officiating general. No, his letter would be more personal— one that would describe each man's achievements and contributions to the King's Army. It would also express condolences for the passing of such fine men.

It was all Richard could do to clear his mind of the tragic event as he rode on through the night at breakneck speed. He greatly desired, for the time being, to have his thoughts focused on only one event, and more to the point, on one person—Miss Georgiana Darcy.

~*~

The evening progressed splendidly. After the first twelve dances, Lord Matlock called supper to order. Immediately prior to the summons, Mr. Ashton Caldecott had danced with Georgiana. Accordingly, he gladly escorted her to the dining hall. Upon finding her place card, he was delighted to discover his card next to hers. He felt that he could not get enough of her company. As soon as they took their seats, Lady Matlock came in search of her niece. Upon her approach, Ashton immediately stood. She smiled to Ashton and then asked if she might borrow Miss Darcy for a moment. All too happy to comply with her request, Mr. Caldecott smiled and held Georgiana's chair.

After they had achieved privacy, Lady Matlock asked, "I just wished to make sure that you are leaving the last set open?"

"Yes, Aunt Adie, I am. Will you not tell me with whom you intend me to dance?" Deep down, Georgiana knew it must be for Richard, but with the hour growing late, she imagined that her aunt may have someone else in mind.

"It is a surprise, my dear, one that I think will please you. However, my dear, I must speak with you about something of great import. I have seen the interest Mr. Caldecott has been paying you. You do realize, Georgiana, that you have already danced two sets with him. People will get the notion of an attachment if you continue to show such preference. I am not scolding you. I only wish you to be aware."

"I appreciate your concern, Aunt Adie. I shall attempt to refuse him if, perchance, he asks again. He will understand."

Lady Matlock's brows rose slightly at her niece's certainty of Ashton Caldecott's way of thinking. She hoped it was just a presumption on Georgiana's part, instead of a growing attachment.

~*~

Darcy had been in a bad humour ever since taking notice of his Aunt Catherine's attendance. Furthermore, his anger rose upon finding that he was not seated anywhere even remotely near his wife during the meal. Elizabeth had been assigned two tables over, but he was happy to know that she was at least in the company of her sisters and Bingley. He, on the other hand, was seated between his uncle and Mr. Pinkerton. Darcy also observed Lady Catherine seated several settings down from him. Hence, his mind filled with gratitude for not having to suffer direct discourse with his aunt, considering how it grated on his nerves every time he heard her abruptly interject, "I must have my share in the conversation," interspersed throughout the conversational hum that wafted down the length of the table. These loud outbursts forced him to exert every ounce of control he possessed in order to command his tongue.

Yet, after everyone had dined, the dancing resumed and Darcy quickly found his wife. In a stately manner, he asked, "Madam, may I have the honour of this waltz?"

Elizabeth smiled brilliantly and answered, "With pleasure, sir,"

Thus, he escorted her to the floor, and they began to glide across the ballroom. Elizabeth took advantage of this opportunity to speak with him concerning her recollections. She told him how looking upon her gown had shaken her memory about Ashton Caldecott. She had been in error thinking she had met him at Pemberley, for instead, it had been in the receiving line at Matlock. She could not remember the entire visit there, but she felt certain it would come to her. As of late, so many snippets had emerged that she was sure her ability to remember all would soon come to pass.

Her words gladdened Darcy, and he listened attentively as she related her accord with him in concern for Georgiana's reputation. She told him of the indecent feeling she had experienced when meeting Mr. Caldecott and the keen interest that man displayed while looking upon her. Careful not to give her husband too much detail for fear that he would become angered, Elizabeth chose to neglect the particulars about Mr. Caldecott's roaming eyes. Even without such specifics, she could tell that Darcy was incensed, therefore, they danced the remainder of the waltz in relative silence, each lost in their own thoughts.

She began to wish that she had not told him of her impression, fearing that he might do something rash, but her fears were alleviated when Darcy half-whispered, "I am glad you have told me, Elizabeth. Never fear telling me such things. You need not substantiate your feelings with fact. I trust your instincts. I know you feel that you have judged erroneously in the past, but you were wounded by your pride at the time. You are an excellent judge of character, my dear. Always listen to your sixth sense, as Richard would say. Society is full of base individuals, and most do not live in squalor. Many are, instead, found amongst the noble ranks—especially within the *peerage*. I shall not call for a duel if that is what you think. But, let us be on our guard, and believe me when I tell you that my cousin, Hazel, is no gentleman, either."

Elizabeth's brows furrowed. A cold chill ran up her spine. She had no idea why her husband insisted on saying such things about his cousin, especially his calling specific attention to rank and file. Lord Hazelton, whom she felt was just as much of a gentleman as was Richard, had yet to give her cause to doubt him. Yet, one thing Elizabeth did know—she would trust her husband. He was the most honourable man she had ever known. Quickly, she whispered to reassure him, "I believe you, Fitzwilliam. Even though my present opinions concerning Lord Hazelton have been favourable, I shall be ever vigilant when in his presence."

He nodded in satisfaction, and at the conclusion of the dance, dipped her low and whispered, "I love you, my sweet, beautiful, wife."

While making their way to the perimeter of the dance floor, they each noticed Georgiana surrounded by several young men, and Ashton Caldecott stood in the middle of them. Darcy and Elizabeth shared a look of dismay. They would need to keep a cautious eye on this situation, for it appeared as if Mr. Caldecott had developed a preference for their Georgie.

~*~

A solitary rider entered the alley behind the Matlock residence. He and his horse were exhausted and both were completely drenched in sweat. Before entering the house through the kitchen, he had handed the reins to a stable boy and asked him to offer the animal plenty of water and a full measure of oats.

Edie, the head cook, was sitting at a table resting her weary bones as she drank a cup of tea amongst the clatter. The kitchen was full, with many of the staff and servants hustling to and fro in order to provide for the needs of the guests. Young maids, carrying baskets full of dirty dishes from the dining hall, continued to pour into the bustling room. They would be up for many hours to come, until every plate was washed, dried, and put properly away. No one minded that the cook was resting. They knew she deserved it. She had been laying the groundwork for the current festivity for the past ten days, regulating all the culinary courses which had come to fruition earlier that evening. In addition, she had tended to the everyday meal preparations whilst overseeing all to readiness. Edith Barnes was her given name, but everyone, including the family, called her Edie. She had begun working for the Fitzwilliams when she was but a young woman, hired as a scullery maid. However, their former cook had taken note of the lass's propensity for adding a little of this or a little of that to the food, making it delectable to the palate. Thus, Edith became the cook's special aide. Her natural talent, along with the skill she developed throughout the years, made her the fitting choice for head cook when the former had retired. Some members in the household considered Miss Barnes as if she were part of the Fitzwilliam family. Everyone knew that the Countess adored her, and in return, Edie adored the mistress. When the family removed from London for Matlock, Edie came along, too.

Consequently, when Edie saw Colonel Fitzwilliam walk through the kitchen door looking drenched like a cat just in from the rain, it was no wonder that she quickly arose, aching muscles and all, to greet her favourite darling.

She hastened to help him with his cap and cape, but in the process, she always hoped for something a little more personal when finished. Richard, never one to fail, tonight hesitated, due to his pitiful state of appearance. However, when seeing the disappointment in the stout woman's eyes, he exclaimed, "I would gladly hug you, Edie, but I am soaked to the skin and smell far worse than a sweaty horse."

The cook laughed heartily. "Ah, you know that Edie don't mind that none, Master Fitzwilliam. I need to hug me boy!" Thus, she encircled her big arms around the grown man and embraced him tightly.

Richard freely allowed her to squeeze him with all her might to her heart's content. He could smell ground cinnamon upon her neck, and as they parted, his coat bore evidence of the encounter with a generous dusting of the excess flour from her apron. Fond were the memories he had of this woman. As a youngster, she had always held him on her lap on baking days, feeding him cookies, tarts, and sponge cake in excess. He marvelled that he had not become fat by the way she had doted on him throughout his childhood and youth. Being a man now, the colonel comprehended that Edie fancied him for the child she never had, and he considered her akin to the grandmother he had never known. It mattered not that she was a little younger than his own mother, and though he was not blood-related to this jovial woman, her pampering was the closest display of motherly affection Richard had ever received while growing up. The colonel knew in his heart that his mother did love him, but only recently had she striven to show it. He was not sure why his mother had become more affectionate of late. He surmised that she probably feared for his life in the war.

In a flash, Edie had Colonel Fitzwilliam's needs attended to. He was whisked up to a warm bath, and the cook, herself, opened his satchel and removed his uniform. She took great care in brushing it down and then polished the brass buttons until they gleamed. Likewise, she polished his boots just as smartly.

~*~

Mary Sherwood

As Colonel Fitzwilliam entered the crowded ballroom, he looked gallant in his regimentals. The thick, unyielding throng made it difficult for him to have a good look at the dancers out in the centre of the room. Just as the dance ended, he caught sight of Georgiana being led off the floor by Dr. Lowry. She stole his breath away! He began to make his way through the crowd, keeping his eyes fixed upon her, when he abruptly stopped in his tracks. Ashton Caldecott had instantaneously approached Georgiana and now, grasping her elbow with his fingers, escorted her back onto the dance floor. Richard stood there transfixed, gaping after the couple. After a moment or two, he turned and made his way back through the mass to wait in the shadows. He would not subject himself to the torture of watching her with *that* man. Returning to the entrance to take a seat, he quickly discovered his other cousin sitting all alone.

"Why, Anne, I am surprised to see you here. I hope you are feeling well. Does your mother accompany you?"

She barely nodded. He spied her mouth turned downwards, as if in a frown, but Richard knew this was Anne's normal expression. Sitting down beside her, he tried to coax her into a conversation, a task not easily achieved. She did look upon the colonel full–faced, her eyes withdrawn and complexion pallid, and he felt great pity for her. He never knew if she were truly ill, or whether, due to Lady Catherine's having kept her pent up for all of her short life, she languished for want of the outdoors and the freedom to partake of life as she might wish.

The colonel was grateful that she made an attempt to exert herself, even if only slightly, telling him that she and her mother would soon be going to Bath. If he was not mistaken, Anne's eyes took on a wee lustre just speaking about the imminent trip. He was happy she had something to look forward to. In turn, he told her that the army had been giving his troop a good work-over at Sandhurst. Thus, they would be prepared to embark for the Continent and face battle upon the order's issue. He then asked if she would allow him the honour of dancing with him. This Anne declined, feigning that she did not feel up to it.

Truthfully, she felt too fearful to step onto the floor and become the centre of attention, nor did she have the nerve to try. Richard sensed that she wished to give it a go. Hence, he asked if he could take her into the fresh air and dance a little on the balcony. A grin appeared upon her lips for just an instant. She thought the idea terribly wicked and took pleasure in thinking about the possibility of shocking her mother. But the moment soon passed, and she again thanked him, however, begged to be excused all the same. At first, Richard patted her on the hand and gave it a quick squeeze, but then, on impulse, he brought his cousin's frail hand to his lips and tenderly kissed it. Before taking his leave, he said in true compassion, "I am glad to see you, Anne. I shall look forward to visiting you again when I return from abroad. Enjoy your time in Bath. I shall be thinking of you."

Anne offered him a small smile, and he bowed in return. She watched her cousin's pleasing physique wend through the crowd and inwardly smiled at the fetching figure he cut. Oh, how she dearly loved a man in uniform!

Halting at the edge of the bystanders, Richard observed Georgiana and Ashton Caldecott weave in and out while going down the line of the dance. Their hands would barely touch followed by their bodies circling around each other. He witnessed the look in Ashton's eyes every time the man came face to face with his fair cousin. Richard knew that look and recognized it for what it was. He could feel his jaw hardening, and the suffusion of anger rising to warm his breast as he fastened his eyes on their every movement. Suddenly, he became aware that Georgiana had lost her timing and Ashton attempted to hasten their steps.

Unbeknownst to the dark, handsome young man of four and twenty, his partner had become distracted by a gentleman who stood on the outskirts of the crowd, wearing a uniform. A uniform that looked very much like the one in which she had dressed a particular snowman the previous winter. Her heart leapt at the thought that it might be Colonel Fitzwilliam—*her* colonel!

When the music ceased, Mr. Caldecott led Georgiana back to the gathering of people along the edge of the dance floor. Richard made a beeline in the same direction. As the colonel approached, he could hear Ashton pressing her for the last set. Georgiana had not seen Richard moving in their direction and did not realize he now stood only a few feet away. She tried politely to tell Mr. Caldecott that she had already promised the set. Finally, after realizing that his petitions were in vain, Mr. Caldecott bowed and thanked her for the dances with which she had already graced him with. He then proclaimed that he looked forward to seeing her at the Millbank's outing, later in the week.

Georgiana acknowledged his gratitude and assured him that she, too, would look forward to his company in a few days' time. Lifting her hand, he almost kissed it but, reconsidering, pressed it affectionately instead and then departed. Richard rolled his eyes at their exchange, but instead of rushing to Georgiana's side, he waited to see what his fair cousin would do next. A grin materialized upon his face as he witnessed her upon tiptoes, frantically searching the crowd in the direction in which he had been standing. A downcast expression overcame her features as she slowly lowered upon her heels and surrendered her quest, only to look up in astonishment at finding the very man she sought standing by her side.

She cried with exasperation as she swatted his arm, "Richard Fitzwilliam, you devil!"

"Now, Georgie, is that any way to greet your favourite cousin?"

Her eyes were full of delight in taking in his appearance. "I had hoped you would come, and I feared it all the same."

"You feared it?" His heart stilled. Had she already lost her feelings for him? And what was worse, were her feelings now set on Mr. Caldecott?

"Yes, I longed for you, and I feared to do so, knowing I would be devastated if you did not appear. So, you see, I feared to hope."

"Oh, Georgie! You can always bring a smile to my face, you sweet, sweet girl!"

"Well, Richard, are you not going to ask me something?"

She took in his confused expression and laughed. "For such a wise man, my love, you can be so dim at times." Again, she giggled because his confusion turned to utter astonishment.

Did she just refer to me as her love?

"You are supposed to ask me to dance. Is that not why you came all of this way from Sandhurst, to dance with me, or was it for the fine wine in your parents' cellar?"

"You are a cheeky girl! I have a good mind to walk away and let you wallow in your puckish ways!"

"But you will not, for you cannot live without me. I know it, and you know it. So, you will have to dance with me. After all, I have saved the last set for you, and one of the dances is a waltz. I want nothing more on this, my special night, than for you to hold me in your arms."

Richard inhaled loudly, lost in the emotion of being very much in love—a feeling he never thought he would feel again. Yet, this time, it was beyond anything he had ever imagined possible. He did not know what he had ever done to deserve this. She was the epitome of pureness, beauty, and life. He feared that if she found someone else while he served his country, he might not have the capacity to carry on with his life. He did not know what he would do without her.

~*~

Lost in the swarm of people, Elizabeth, upon her tiptoes, tried unsuccessfully to look above the heads of all those who obstructed her view in the hope of finding someone familiar. The room was stifling, and she had begun to feel light-headed. She realized that she required some fresh air and attempted to make her way to the door. Turning to squeeze out of the crush, she came face to face with Lord Hazelton.

"Elizabeth, I have come to ask for the next dance. Yet, I can see you do not feel well. May I help you?"

The room had begun to spin, and before she could make answer to the Viscount's offer, she fainted into his all too willing arms.

Pulling her close to his chest, he held her steady, lifting her into his embrace. Then, in a dash, he headed for the entrance hall and down the corridor.

Bingley had seen the incident from where he stood. Turning to his wife, he implored, "Janey, your sister has fainted. Go and find Darcy or Dr. Lowry. But please, be careful my angel. I shall go to help."

A look of alarm overtook her visage. Nodding, she commenced to make her way carefully to the other side of the room, where Darcy and his uncle stood in conversation.

Quickly, Bingley began pressing his way towards the entrance, hoping to locate the Viscount and Elizabeth.

Entering the library, James kicked the door closed with his heel, then laid Elizabeth on the divan with her knees bent in an upward position. Gazing upon her, he noted that she looked so lovely in that dress—the same one that had enticed him at Matlock.

In an instant, his hands roamed over Elizabeth's sides, and he quickly began to lift her hem, pulling her dress up over her knees. His hands boldly entered within the sides of her pantalets, caressing the softness of her flesh and gliding over the silhouette of each leg, oblivious to anything or anyone.

Bingley methodically searched for his sister-in-law and Lord Hazelton, but so far all had been in vain. Then, from the corner of his eye, he noticed the library door barely cracked open. Unthinkingly, he began to pass it by, but for some reason, he stopped and decided to peek in, since he had not been able to locate them in any other room near the entrance hall. As he ducked his head in for a quick look, instant repulsion assailed the core of his being. *Good God! How **dare** he!*

Before Bingley could hurl an accusation, he saw Lord Hazelton quickly pulling down Elizabeth's dress and smoothing her skirts. Elizabeth began to moan, her eyelids fluttering open as she came to. Bingley boldly swung the door wide and strode over to the divan. With apparent ire, his face flushed and his jaw clenched, he addressed the Viscount, "I say, your Lordship, you need to go and find the doctor. I shall stay with my sister. You must go, *now*!"

"Have I fainted?" Elizabeth questioned weakly as she tried to focus her eyes.

Lord Hazelton attempted to answer her when Bingley again insisted, "Go, **now**, man!"

Both Lord Hazelton and Elizabeth appeared horrified at Bingley's intonation. He did not care. Elizabeth had never seen her brother-in-law act so forcefully.

The Viscount rose to his feet, looking smugly at Mr. Bingley. "I do not know your country friend. I suggest you go find him yourself. I am not accustomed to being spoken to in this tone, Mr. Bingley."

"I rather wonder at what you are accustomed to, but at this moment, I do not give a—" The swift entrance of Dr. Lowry, Darcy, Jane, Kitty, and his cousin, Iain, cut off Bingley's retort. Thus, he backed away from Elizabeth's side to allow room for the doctor. Yet, Charles Bingley's heart continued to beat violently. His whole frame trembled from the righteous indignation he strove to rein in.

~*~

Lady Matlock took great pleasure in watching her youngest son dance with her niece. She knew that Georgiana adored Richard a great deal more than a mere friend or cousin. Moreover, she had great hopes that her son would reciprocate Georgiana's sentiments. She greatly desired to see him find someone he could love and esteem, someone with whom he could build a happy home. Observing them as they waltzed, taking in their intense, shared gaze, she confidently determined that they were in love. Oh, how she prayed he would live to come back to her niece.

The Mistress of Matlock was not the only one who noticed how the couple seemed to lose themselves in each other's eyes. The other individual with an intense sense of awareness: Ashton Caldecott. He had startled upon seeing Miss Darcy with Colonel Fitzwilliam and whispered beneath his breath, "When the devil did *he* show up?" With great interest, he scrutinized their every move as they sailed around the room and felt that the colonel held Miss Darcy a little too closely than propriety allowed. Georgiana seemed to beam at the man, and by the way they grinned and smirked as their eyes remained fastened upon the other, he felt they shared some private joke between them. Ashton's hand gripped the glass he held, wondering what, exactly, the colonel was up to.

~*~

As the evening grew to an end, the Earl thanked everyone, and then called for one more dance. Richard and Georgiana, however, stole off to the balcony for a breath of fresh air and the chance to spend a few precious moments alone. Pulling Richard by the hand, Georgiana led him to the far side of the terrace where an overhang from the branches of a large tree would conceal their presence from prying eyes.

Once ensconced amongst the greenery, Georgiana threw her arms around Richard's neck, leaving him at a loss as to what to do. He had promised himself that he would not let their relationship progress any further than it already had. Yet, his rationale did not win out over his passion. When Georgiana pressed her body against his, he instinctively reacted to her advance by encircling her petite figure within his firm arms and pulling her close to his chest.

"Oh! How I love you, Richard!"

The intensity of his voice bore witness to his fervour as he exclaimed, "Oh, my Georgie, you are making it hard for me to keep my resolve! I adore you, Georgie! I think about you every moment of the day, and many times my thoughts centre on you when they should be elsewhere. You have muddled my brain. I am hopelessly, madly, and completely in love with you!"

The side of Georgiana's face pressed against the fasteners of his uniform, yet she did not mind the slight discomfort from it. Her whole being filled with elation. His passionate declaration had been exactly what she needed and had longed to hear. His words, she committed to memory. *'You have muddled my brain. I am hopelessly, madly, and completely in love with you!'* The smell of his cologne intoxicated her. Oh, how she loved his heady scent! She did not want this moment to end, ever.

Richard's head nestled carefully atop hers, but mindfully, taking heed not to spoil her coiffure, knowing they must soon return indoors. He, too, allowed himself to revel in the moment. She felt so delicate within his arms, and the sensation of her hair, so silky smooth against his lips as he gently pressed a kiss upon it, caused any reason or logic he might have possessed to vanish.

They spoke no words for several minutes. Neither Richard nor Georgiana wished to part. If they had interrupted their silent embrace and confided in one another what they each imagined, their collective thoughts of Gretna Green may have, at present, proved too much of a temptation for the couple.

Finally, breaking from their embrace, Richard picked up Georgiana's lone curl which bobbed freely upon her collar bone and began to twirl it around his fingers. "Your hair looks lovely, Georgie. Was this style your idea or Nancy's?"

"Mine." She smiled at how he admired it.

"I find it very alluring, you know?"

"Yes."

"Ahem..." She took in the perplexed look upon his brow as he continued to finger the curl.

"I had it prepared for you. I remembered how much you enjoyed playing with my hair in the carriage on our way to Town. Thus, I thought," she flashed him a coquettish smile, "I would leave some of it down for you. I want to charm you, Richard, and only you."

Instantly, Richard's eyes met hers, and a shocking thought flew into his mind. *She was awake all that time that I dallied with her tresses?* Continuing to gaze deeply into her eyes, he earnestly declared, "I love you, Georgiana Darcy!" Again, he pulled her to him for one, last embrace.

Returning to the ballroom, the couple made their way to the Earl and his lady. Many of the guests had begun to file into the entrance hall to await their carriages. Richard's father was a little surprised to see him but was pleased all the same. The great man did not take notice of his niece's cheek, but his wife did. The Countess perceived the outline of an imprint upon Georgiana's face, an imprint which looked akin to the fasteners on her son's coat. Thoughtfully, she raised her brow while smiling knowingly, silently hoping this dear girl would someday be her daughter-in-law.

~*~

The Bingley carriage rolled along in the darkness. All the occupants remained silent during the trip back to their residence—each lost in thought, pondering their own quandary. Distraught with the information that Elisha had imparted to her, Caroline clasped her hands together and brooded over what she would do if it came out that *she* had been the one who told them about the blackmail? She only hoped that she could depend on Lady Hazelton's discretion. Doubtlessly, Charles would be furious, but really, Elisha needed to take Georgiana under her wing. After all, Darcy had brought this on himself. She could continue to say that Elizabeth had disclosed the matter to her. How would anyone ever know otherwise? Louisa would be home by the week's end. Yes, her sister would offer her appropriate counsel.

Mr. Iain Burns sat across from Miss Catherine Bennet, twisting at his hat while staring at her through the darkness. Already smitten with her, the thought of living under the same roof as this lovely creature for a whole month made his heart beat rapidly, and he shifted about in discomfort. Such an unforeseen temptation for the young clergyman did present a problem, for he greatly desired a wife, yet, he had no living presented to him at the time to enable him to secure an attachment.

Kitty felt equally apprehensive to be thrown into the company of Mr. Bingley's cousin. She found him extremely handsome and so gentlemanly. The magnetism seemed exceedingly great, for she could barely keep her eyes from wandering to his face. Yet, she detested the thought of a collar over a sabre and a red coat. Additionally, the image of her cousin, Mr. Collins, kept popping into her head. Was there a remote chance that Mr. Burns could be as idiotic as he? She shuddered at the thought of reading sermons by firelight and being fawned over. Well, at least Mr. Burns proved pleasing on the eyes. However, could she be the wife of a parson, an exemplar of piety for the congregation in the parish in which she was to live? Could she deny herself of all frivolities and entertainments that she enjoyed so much? Could she live in some remote village, where her position would require her to tend to the sick and dying? These were questions of the heart for which she did not yet have an answer. Her brow furrowed. *Why must life be so cruel?*

Jane sat meekly and wondered what had happened to her husband. He was acting so strangely. When she had tried to engage him in conversation, he would not even look her in the eye. Could he be angry with her? To this point of their marriage, they had not had a quarrel.

Bingley looked out into the darkness not knowing what to do. How do you tell your best friend... your brother, that his cousin is...a...a...? He could not bear to finish the ghastly thought! Would Darcy demand a duel? He might be killed! Then, in added horror, Bingley considered: what if Darcy did not believe him? Anxiously, Charles turned his head to look at his wife. Jane eagerly met his gaze. They stared at each other in silence.

Jane could tell her husband was still not himself, but she no longer feared that she was the reason for his despondency. Smiling reassuringly at him, she reached for his hand, and holding it firmly, whispered, "All will be well, Charles."

He likewise squeezed her hand and turned back to look out the window. *Jane will know how to advise me. She will know what to do, for, as the sun shines, and I take in breath, something must be done!*

~*~

Chapter Twenty-eight

Severing Ties

The week following Georgiana's coming out progressed at a hectic pace for Fitzwilliam Darcy. Mr. Sheldon arrived from Pemberley to conduct business requiring the master's immediate attention. In addition, the magistrate's mandatory meetings, held before the trial forthcoming in three days, required a great deal of his time. He also met with his solicitor concerning Georgiana's inheritance and the drawing up of all legal papers pertaining to the sale of Pemberley's share in the coalmines. The days were gruelling. Darcy would leave his townhouse first thing after breakfast, and on many evenings, would return with barely enough time to properly prepare himself for dinner.

With his agenda full, Darcy had little occasion for socializing. Furthermore, while away from Ackerley House, he constantly worried for Elizabeth's wellbeing. After her fainting spell on the night of the ball, he felt a small amount of fear that she might swoon again, and pray, what if this time not a soul were there to catch her? The mere thought of such a possibility caused considerable unease. Dr. Lowry, however, strove to convince him that such bouts were only natural for a woman in Elizabeth's condition, and standing still in an extremely warm room, could cause anyone to faint. Therefore, the physician had hoped to conciliate Darcy to the unlikely probability of such an incident happening again. And even though Dr. Lowry's confident reassurance certainly helped, Darcy still worried nonetheless, for there were many pressing matters upon him.

Not only did the strain of his exacting schedule and the concern for his wife cause him a certain amount of anxiety, equally, Darcy had not seen his sister since the night of the ball, and he had begun to grow anxious regarding her absence. He had allowed Georgiana to visit Blackwell House to help Elisha plan a tea to be given in his sister's honour, but that was five days ago. Despite Elisha sending messages that Georgiana was doing splendidly and having the time of her life, she had failed to mention when she would be returning to Ackerley. Yesterday, the fourth day of Georgiana's absence, Darcy had sent word to Lady Hazelton that he desired his sister's return, insisting that he would send his carriage round after the breakfast hour on the morrow. Those at Blackwell immediately sent a response, informing him that his plan would be impossible, for Georgiana had gone to spend a few days with her friend, Lady Lillian, at that young lady's father's country estate outside of London.

The missive arrived while he and Elizabeth were partaking of dinner. When Coates put the silver salver beside his master's place setting, Darcy instantly laid aside his cutlery to read the communication. Elizabeth watched him eagerly break the seal and unfold the letter. She knew he had been apprehensive about his sister, but the words she heard escape her husband's lips were revelatory. He cursed under his breath as he threw down the parcel. Next, his eyes met hers as he informed her of the objectionable situation.

Elizabeth's vision rose upward after Darcy hastily threw his napkin upon the table and stood to his full height. He looked down to her and made his apologies for interrupting their meal, but explained that he felt it urgent to reply to the Viscountess and demand that she arrange to send Georgiana home immediately upon her return to London. Thus, a message was dispatched with the behest and a query as to when he should expect his sister.

In a short amount of time, the answer to his request arrived, informing him that he might expect Georgiana sometime on Tuesday, yet Elisha was not certain of the precise time. Therefore, she invited Darcy and Elizabeth to join them at Blackwell for dinner that evening. Her communication commented further that Georgiana would have surely returned by that time, and then Darcy could collect her himself and take her home. The missive ended with Elisha's flattering accolades of appreciation for allowing Georgiana's visit, claiming that she and her husband had truly enjoyed the girl's company.

In frustration, Darcy sent word, again, that Mr. and Mrs. Bingley had been invited to dine at Ackerley on the same evening as her invitation. Charles Bingley had come to Ackerley twice during the time Darcy had been away, desiring to confer with him. On these occasions, Elizabeth informed her brother-in-law of her husband's need to attend to pressing business, she then would invite him to return in the evening in order to speak with Darcy. Bingley, however, had fixed engagements for each evening during the week and plans to be away for the weekend. Thus, everything combined, increased his apparent frustration.

Hence, Elizabeth asked if he and Jane might dine with them on Tuesday of the following week. After dinner, he would be free to meet with Darcy for as long as he needed. He readily accepted this arrangement. For this reason, the Darcys were loath to cancel their engagement with the Bingleys in order to enable them to attend Lord and Lady Hazelton's invitation.

With alacrity, Elisha sent back an additional invitation for Mr. and Mrs. Bingley to join them at Blackwell. She also indicated that she would take great pleasure in Miss Bingley's joining their small party. Darcy and Elizabeth thought over her proposal, and due to Darcy's anxious feelings for his sister, they agreed to it and petitioned Bingley for his thoughts regarding this slight change of plans. In the note which Darcy wrote, he assured his brother-in-law that after their evening at Blackwell, he and Jane would be welcome to return to Ackerley. The men, he said, would enjoy a nightcap and discuss whatever he desired. After Darcy sealed his letter, he arranged to send it post-haste.

~*~

The footman handed a missive from the master of number 7 Brooke Street to the master of number 20 Park Street in Mayfair. Bingley instantly tore it open and began to read. A contemplative air rapidly overtook his features as he pondered the impending invitation of dinner at Blackwell House. He did not like the idea of dining in the home of the Viscount, when his Lordship's dishonourable behaviour was the very reason why he needed to speak with his brother-in-law in the first place. The prospect of spending several hours at the table of the offending party only heightened his agitation over his need to deliver such an unpleasant allegation, one to which he felt sure would have far-reaching ramifications for all concerned. Bingley knew there could be no positive outcome to such a dilemma. In fact, many dreadful scenarios played out continuously in his imagination. Nevertheless, he put these worries aside when recalling Jane's counsel to him from the night of the ball.

After they had reached the privacy of their chamber, he made certain Jane felt well enough to bear intelligence of such a disconcerting nature. When she assured him she could, he had related to her all that he had witnessed in the library. Jane's shock was all that Bingley had expected from such an angel, and he professed to her his abhorrence for the need to report such sordid details to one so pure.

Once the initial shock abated, however, Jane assured her husband that he had done the right thing in telling her. Yet, she did question Lord Hazelton's actions, asking her husband if he was certain that the Viscount did not attempt to help her sister by reviving her with some means foreign to them? She suggested that they could speak to Dr. Lowry and ask his knowledge about such a method. If the doctor could verify this means of revival, then Darcy's cousin might not be as contemptible as they were imagining.

Bingley stared at his precious wife for a full minute as he considered her naive outlook, waiting just long enough before refuting her suggestion. No, he adamantly assured her that he had no doubts about what he had witnessed. In his opinion, Lord Hazelton used no new fangled method of progressive medicine. Confidently, he told her that he had observed a lasciviousness in the Viscount's look seldom seen in a true gentleman.

Jane considered her husband's words carefully. In her sweet spirit which Charles so loved, she hated to condemn anyone of such a vile crime. Yet, she seemed to have exhausted all avenues of redemption for the Viscount's guilt, and therefore, she could do little but concede to her husband's assertions. Mr. Darcy must be told, she calmly stated to her husband, and so must her sister as well. Thus, with her support, Bingley's enjoyed comfort in knowing that he, indeed, travelled along the right course of action.

Consequently, upon reading the prospective invitation to dine at Blackwell, he once again sought out his wife's prudent counsel while inwardly hoping she would desire to decline the request. But at last, the application of their company to dine with the Darcys at Blackwell had the opposite effect on Mrs. Charles Bingley.

Suddenly, Jane expressed her belief that one more ray of hope shone through this supposed darkness. An aura of angelic splendour seemed to increase around her as she made the declaration that they must attend the dinner to clarify whether Mr. Darcy's cousin truly was the villain they feared. It afforded them an opportunity to discern his covetousness of her sister in small company. The information they held would prepare them to pay special heed to all of the man's gestures and looks. If they perceived anything that warranted even a flicker of hoped for innocence in Lord Hazelton's behaviour, then they would reconsider informing Mr. Darcy.

Bingley heaved a big sigh, certain that regardless of the desired flicker of hope, he would, nevertheless, impart the ruthless facts to Darcy. However, his wife's viewpoint did present a different perspective for him. Instead of looking for a ray of hope, he was certain that he would find a flame of lust, for he had seen it, and he knew that a blaze of that magnitude, left out of control for too long, would surely reduce to ashes all within its path. Emboldened by his inner conviction, he looked forward to breaking bread with the scoundrel, and fuelled with renewed resentment, Charles Bingley no longer feared the encounter. Instead, he determined to leave no stone unturned in the disclosure of his Lordship's dastardly deed, and were a confrontation to transpire, so be it. Tuesday could not come soon enough!

Therefore, he sent his acceptance to number 7 Brooke Street, gladly consenting to the Darcys' change in plans, and very much desiring to accept the nightcap at Ackerley before bringing the evening to its conclusion.

~*~

Lady Lillian Pierson enveloped everything charming for a young woman of seventeen years. She held talent at the pianoforte and harp, and her voice rang clear and true with the melody of a nightingale. Although she could not be called a handsome woman by any stretch of the imagination, nevertheless, her appearance was attractive in its own right.

Her dark blonde hair curled about her face, framing her fair and bright complexion and expressing her youth while her eyes shown a brilliant hue of green seldom seen, giving the outward show of a keen intellect. And to supplement her looks, she possessed a sensible mien that complemented her composed temperament.

Both her parents came from noble families, with her father, Lord Millbank, being a dignified member of the House of Lords. Despite the family's superior rank within the aristocracy, they presented themselves as gracious people who, in all respects, sought to bring relief to the poor and to elevate their possibilities of advancement within society. Lord Millbank constantly fought for reforms in providing education for the children of the underprivileged, and he strongly supported Robert Owen's school of reasoning, where people corrupted by the harsh ways of life, with the right environment and rationale, learned to become good and humane because people were inherently good. Hence, Lord Millbank lent financial support to Owen's personal project of building institutions for the community of New Lanark, thus providing for the textile workers' children to attend nursery and infant schools.

Consequently, they raised their daughter, Lillian to be conscious of the plight of the disadvantaged—with her sensitive and gentle nature, eager to help every living creature in any possible way that her abilities enabled her.

Lord and Lady Millbank were hosting a weekend party for many of the eligible male and female members of the ton. Lady Lillian desired Miss Darcy's presence, and so invited her to come a day earlier before the beginning of the festivities. Activities would include: croquet, strolls, picnics, charades, and equestrian exercise, along with the execution of musical performances in the evenings.

When Georgiana received the invitation, she fairly bubbled with excitement, at least until Elisha, James, her Uncle Selwyn and Aunt Catherine enlightened her to the fact that they knew all about her terrible, secret indiscretion. The memory of it still made her burn with shame as she sat at Lady Lillian's side in the open carriage, the cool breeze of the April morning kissing a blush upon her cheeks.

The dreadful incubus began right after breakfast on the third morning of her stay at Blackwell when Lord Hazelton's butler had come to inform her that the Earl of Matlock desired an audience with her in his Lordship's study. Startled at the request, but nonetheless anxious to comply, she had quickly departed the breakfast room and made her way to where her uncle waited. Upon entering the study, she immediately sensed something was amiss and her stomach lurched. Silently, she questioned the presence of her Aunt Catherine and the austere glares from everyone in the room. She did not have too long to wait for the forthcoming answers.

When the butler closed the door, the Earl stood like the perfect gentleman he perceived himself to be as the authoritative patriarch of the family. He invited her to sit in the chair directly before him. Her uncle then moved behind his son's desk with Lady Catherine by his side. Georgiana quickly complied, and her world instantly began to spin out of control.

"Georgiana, you can have no doubt as to why we have requested a conference with you."

She paled, fearing it had finally happened—Wickham's loose tongue had begun to wag and they all knew!

The Earl taking note of her embarrassment, determined to do what he could to save the Fitzwilliam name and what remained to salvage for the name of Darcy. Thus, leaning over the desk and peering down upon his niece like a falcon about to snatch a timid field mouse, he said, "We have learned from a reliable source that you and George Wickham were engaged just shy of two years ago, when you were but fifteen, and that you were attempting to elope with him when, luckily, your brother unexpectedly happened upon your tryst and thwarted your clandestine carryings-on."

Georgiana sat extremely still and her eyes remained wide open as she focused on her clasped hands within her lap while her uncle continued with his diatribe.

"Your youth at the time accounts for much of the weakness on your part. But several points concern us, points for which we know you are not directly responsible. Firstly, we are outraged that your brother and my younger son have kept this alarming occurrence from the Fitzwilliam clan. You are our niece, and as such, we should have been informed. Secondly, Darcy and Richard should have taken better care in your upbringing. They have been careless, imprudent guardians—"

Georgiana's mouth hung open as her hands formed into fists.

"—and I shall never understand why George asked them to oversee your care in the first place. What was the man thinking of to have *two single men* taking charge of a *little* girl?"

Her uncle had gone too far. Defiantly, Georgiana jumped to her feet and boldly declared, "I shall tell you what my father was thinking. He was thinking about having me cared for by two people, two people who had always shown the greatest concern and consideration for my feelings and welfare, and who would care for me, and love me always. That is what he was thinking!" she screamed. "And, maybe such cold and unfeeling people, such as yourselves, cannot recognize love, even when it appears right before your very eyes!"

"Insolent girl! Lady Catherine roared. "I warn you to stop this instant!" She pounded her cane against the floorboards. "Do you see, Selwyn? Do you see the effects that little chit has had upon our niece? I warned you!"

Georgiana froze with her aunt's explosion. The mortification still burned in her breast.

The Earl commanded her to sit, which she did at once. He then reprimanded her for her outburst and advised her that she should not speak until they deemed it necessary.

"Thirdly," he continued. His stare was cold and stoic. "Not only have Richard and Darcy been grossly negligent about informing the family, but they have also been remiss in their handling of this whole sad affair. Your reputation remains at stake, my dear girl. No respectable man will ever attempt to court you if this makes it to the rumour mill. He could not be certain that you have remained virtuous for him. Thus, your dowry will act as the sole temptation to scoundrels of the worst kind in applying for your hand. However, where your brother and cousin have failed you, we shall not. It is our familial duty to take matters into our own hands, and we have."

Georgiana felt as if a bucket of cold water had been thrown in her face. How could her uncle behave so cruelly and with so little feeling?

"Therefore, before it becomes too late to curtail the consequences of your past, we shall arrange a marriage for you with a respectable gentleman, one who shall understand this sort of fallibility in a girl so young. Two gentlemen of our acquaintance have expressed an interest for your hand. One knows of your past while the other gentleman does not. The latter gentleman's wife died two years ago, and he saw you at the ball the other night and took a fancy to you. This man came to me and enquired after your qualifications. He wished to know whether you played, if you could sing, and if you were of hearty frame, and of course, the size of your dowry. At forty-five years he still has no heir and desires to marry a youthful woman with health enough to raise the son he hopes to sire. His credentials are impeccable, and you will never want for anything."

Nausea began filling Georgiana's stomach all the way up into her throat. How could this be happening? How could her uncle speak of her as if she were mere chattel? She wanted to scream, to run away, but what she wanted more than anything else, at that moment, was to be held within the safety of her brother's arms. She hung her head in shame, striving to hold back the tears.

"The other gentleman under consideration is a young man who has asked to court you. Yet, we have informed him there is a blemish on your character. He does not yet know the specifics but stated he did not care. You are familiar with this man. He is Mr. Ashton Caldecott. He is not as rich as the former gentleman whom I have mentioned, but he is young and has expressed an uncommon feeling of attachment to you. He states that he is in love with you." Georgiana's eyes went wide as her head remained cast down while she stared at the floor. "We shall let you choose, but it must be a swift courtship. That way when the sordid rumour makes its way into the heart of London, you shall be well on your way to the altar."

Shock replaced the nausea. Out of irrational fear, they were forcing her to marry, forcing her to sacrifice herself to protect her reputation and that of their own! The rest of the conversation became a blur. Georgiana did recall, however, her Aunt Catherine announcing that she would accompany her and Anne to Bath to be introduced to and spend time with the older gentleman, so as to make a knowledgeable choice. Their assistance would allow her to take her proper position in society and avail herself of all the benefits connected with marrying a true gentleman within her exclusive sphere. In addition, they insisted she should receive their timely intervention with gratitude!

When they finally allowed Georgiana to speak, she had but one question. "When shall I be allowed to go home to Fitzwilliam and Elizabeth?"

"Never!" the Earl responded, a scowl darkening his features. After a moment, however, he relented by adding, "At least not until we have rescued your future by securing your hand in marriage. Then, and only then, as a married woman, may you return your brother's house."

Covering her face with her hands, Georgiana broke down and bitterly wept.

Lady Hazelton and Lady Catherine watched with great satisfaction as Georgiana's slender frame shook in wretchedness, both women feeling the sweet reward of retribution.

The latter deemed it Darcy's just due for wilfully going against the aspirations held by his mother and herself for him to marry Anne, while the former felt overjoyed that she had single-handedly preserved the Fitzwilliam-Darcy name from sheer ruin. Likewise, Lady Hazelton smiled at the accompanying benefit of bringing spite to her bother-in-law, a small incentive in its own right. She never cared for Colonel Fitzwilliam's lack of respect for the precedence and convention of the peerage and was certain that he was green with envy of his brother's position and title. In her mind Richard treated them with a contempt—contempt that one with such inferior rank should never display. He had spurned her offers of helping him raise his advantages far too often, slapping the very hand that could guarantee the prestige and affluence of which he so desperately needed.

Lord Hazelton's only motivation in the dismal scene before him was to help his friend obtain his cousin's hand in marriage, for Ashton would then become his cousin-in-law.

Georgiana was warned that she should not try to escape while visiting at the Millbank's estate. The woods between there and London were full of gypsies, and she would very likely be injured, murdered, or possibly *far worse*! The social gathering would present a time for her to become better acquainted with Ashton Caldecott. Following this, Mr. Caldecott would accompany her back to London with a servant, and she would then be whisked off to Bath.

~*~

Tuesday night had finally arrived. The Darcys and Bingleys rode together to call upon Lord and Lady Hazelton. Darcy was most anxious to see his sister again and Elizabeth noted that her husband's anticipation left him in high spirits despite the prospect of spending an evening with his cousin, whom he detested. She also observed that her brother-in-law did not seem his usual jovial self. Instead, Bingley appeared more subdued and serious, and yet, he was very attentive to every word spoken to him.

The party entered Blackwell House only to discover an unexpected dinner guest: Ashton Caldecott. Georgiana had not yet arrived, but Elisha informed them that she was, indeed, on her way. Darcy's disappointment at not finding his sister was palpable to all.

Dinner progressed with little conversation, apart from Caroline's occasional utterances of overt flattery for the host and hostess. At the conclusion of the meal, the sexes did not follow the usual custom to separate. Lady Hazelton insisted as an alternative that the entire party convene in the drawing room to await Georgiana's arrival. All agreed with her wishes.

Darcy, however, became increasingly irritated that his sister had still not made her appearance. Every time he asked Elisha for specifics concerning Georgiana's activities, his cousin's wife replied with vague answers. It was all that Darcy could do to contain his anger. He felt certain that something gravely wrong had occurred.

Unbeknownst to him, his wife easily read his mounting frustration by the way he intermittently shifted about in his chair, and then placed the back of one hand over his mouth, only to take it down again moments later to allow him to fidget with the ring on his left hand.

The group sat in uncomfortable silence for the first few minutes until Lady Hazelton suggested that they could bring out the whist tables. No one answered.

Elizabeth glanced at her sister and was aware that Jane felt the ripples of ill ease in the uncomfortable atmosphere, too. It seemed to be awkward for everyone involved. Throughout the meal, Elizabeth had noticed how Jane appeared to be attentively scrutinizing Lord Hazelton as they all sat staring blandly at each other.

And the Viscount, too, was on edge. He looked queerly at Mrs. Bingley every so often, as if wondering at her gawking at him. In addition, when his eyes paused upon Bingley, Elizabeth believed that she witnessed a threatening gaze from her brother-in-law directed towards Lord Hazelton and wondered why. Ashton Caldecott also seemed to acknowledge a sense of nervous expectation.

Elizabeth could no longer take the escalating tension of the situation for fear that her husband's patience might not endure waiting one minute more. Nervously, she stood, and all eyes followed her progress. "I suggest we discuss poetry while we wait. I have had the opportunity of attending a very interesting assembly of late, where we discussed John Donne. Are any of you familiar with his works and might you wish to comment?"

Ashton Caldecott immediately spoke up. "Yes, I am familiar with his work. My favourite is *A Valediction: Forbidding Mourning*. Elizabeth's brow furrowed, she was not familiar with that particular composition but was grateful that Mr. Caldecott seemed willing to take to the floor. At once, Darcy stopped his fidgeting and raised his brow at Ashton while Lord Hazelton simply rolled his eyes.

The young man stood and began to relate how the poem centred on the image of a compass. He turned to the Viscount and asked if he had Donne's book in his library. James snorted at the comical figure Ashton presented and imagined his friend's chivalry was all in pursuit of his cousin's favour. Before the Viscount could answer, however, the butler entered and informed Mr. Darcy that his uncle, the Earl of Matlock, requested his presence. This time all eyes swerved towards Darcy. He looked surprised but immediately rose. He turned to Elizabeth and whispered that he hoped he would not to be too long. She smiled her assurance and watched him as he quitted the room.

Elizabeth then took her seat as Ashton began to relate the particulars of the poem. Suddenly, Lord Hazelton interrupted and suggested that they play a game. Caroline and Elisha displayed a sudden enthusiasm for such a pastime in order to forgo the drudgery of the poetry. Thus, James speedily left the room to gather the needed items to play blind man's buff.

~*~

While walking to his cousin's study, Darcy pulled out his watch fob. It was half past eight. What could be detaining his sister at this hour? He paused abruptly mid-stride and tilted his head to the side as he blinked several times at the sudden realization for the queerness of his uncle appearing at Blackwell at such an hour to speak with him. *Good God! It must concern Georgiana. That explains Elisha's evasiveness for the whole of the evening.* With quick strides, he hastened to the study, passing the butler in his pursuit.

Upon reaching the room, Darcy paused within its doorway, surprise besieging him as his eyes met Lady Catherine's. That grand lady sat close to his uncle who held his position behind the desk. Next, he observed his Aunt Adie, sitting off to one side of the room, looking quite distraught. Suddenly he felt a tightening in his chest as dread swept over him. *Had something dreadful happened to Georgie?*

"Come in, Nephew," the Earl said and then turned to address the butler, "Sigmund, do close the door."

Walking a little farther into the room, Darcy stood motionless, staring at his uncle.

"Please be seated. I do not like looking up to you. Make yourself comfortable."

The Earl arched a brow at the brief shrug of Darcy's shoulders. Darcy canvassed the room as he moved to the seat off to one side of the desk. Darcy deliberately did not choose the chair positioned in his uncle's direct field of vision. Raising his coattails, he sat down in a ceremonious fashion, unreservedly staring at his uncle with a dour expression.

From the look in his eyes, Darcy knew this subtle defiance was not wasted on the Earl, and Darcy also knew something was amiss as the Earl cleared his throat and spoke.

"Yes, well," Lord Matlock began rather nervously, "I must admit this meeting is most difficult, and I do hope, Fitzwilliam, that you will not make it any more difficult than needed."

A small shiver of fear crawled up Darcy's spine. "That is contingent, Uncle," Darcy stated coolly, his eyes piercing his uncle's, "on what the motivation for the meeting might be. I am here. Do not beat about the bush any farther. Where is *Georgiana*?"

"I do not want to shock you, Nephew, but I must be blunt. A most alarming report has come to our notice. A very reliable and respectable source has informed us of circumstances concerning Georgiana's disreputable business at Ramsgate in connection with George Wickham."

Darcy started to rise from his seat, but then, thinking the better of it, sank back into the chair. He glanced over at his Aunt Adie as she silently wept. Then his eyes briefly veered over to Lady Catherine. She gloated openly. His jaw tightened, and he brought the back of his knuckles over his mouth while his other hand grasped his one thigh. Breathing deeply, he averted his gaze to the other side of the room, but not before he caught the smug look upon his uncle's countenance. The Earl smiled as if he had his nephew exactly where he wanted him.

"Yes, well," his uncle continued, "it seems that your wife is in a scrape because George Wickham is blackmailing her to keep your delicate secret safe in the family. Or, perhaps, I should restate: within your private circle of family, for you evidently do not consider *us* as family. Why else have you and Richard kept this secret between the two of you, or does Richard even know?" He waved his hand dismissively at his own comment and quickly resumed, "I am sure he does. You two have both been as brothers all your lives."

Darcy's head shot up. His jaw twitched as he rolled his eyes before returning to his previous pose.

"Well, as I have mentioned, your wife told a very reputable person all about the blackmail over the incident. She also mentioned that your marriage suffers a great deal of tension."

Darcy cried out as he jumped from the chair, "I beg you, sir, to leave my wife out of this discussion, or I shall quit the room immediately. I shall not sit here another moment and hear you say one more word concerning her. Do you understand me?"

Lady Catherine rolled her eyes and huffed aloud. Darcy did his best to ignore her presence.

"I imagine," Darcy continued, "that this meeting is the reason my sister has not appeared tonight?"

"Yes." The Earl answered.

Darcy sat down and again sank back into his chair as he closed his eyes in overwhelming gratitude that his sister had not been hurt in a carriage accident after all. He then took in a deep breath and thought additionally, *At least my uncle has the decency to spare her this.*

"Darcy, as you requested, I shall not beat about the bush. You are well aware that, when situations such as Georgiana's arise, families do all in their power to find a suitable match for the young woman whose reputation has been compromised."

Darcy sat up straight and moved to the edge of his seat, listening intently, but before the Earl said another word, Lady Matlock burst into tears and arose exclaiming, "I must go, Selwyn. I cannot bear this a moment longer. I oppose this—do you hear *me*? I am in *opposition*!" Hastily, she ran out of the room, slamming the door behind her as she left.

Darcy sat in shock. His vision swung back to his uncle as he glared at the man. With a slow steady voice that belied his building alarm, he said, "Tell me at once, Uncle, why you have reduced Aunt Adie to tears?"

"*I* shall tell you, Nephew!" Lady Catherine spoke venomously.

Darcy stood immediately upon hearing his aunt's shrill voice and began to pace back and forth before the desk.

"You and Fitzwilliam have failed! *You*, who have always prided yourself on familial duty, have failed! You *have failed **me***, your mother, Anne, and now your own *sister*! For that reason, we must pick up the pieces and salvage what we can for Georgiana."

Lord Matlock had taken note of his nephew's rising anger with every word Lady Catherine uttered. Therefore, he held up a hand, gesturing for his sister to cease.

Abruptly, Darcy halted his pacing upon hearing Lady Catherine's declaration that *they would salvage what they could for his sister*. Staring at her, he blinked with indignation. Lividly he turned to those assembled in tribunal. "Pray, I demand that you tell me at once where I may find Georgiana!"

"I am sorry to inform you, Darcy, that you and Richard must relinquish the guardianship you possess concerning my niece. Lady Catherine and I shall now take over as her guardians. She shall be wed, if all goes according to plan, in two months' time. This is the only way to safeguard her reputation before this knowledge of her past enters every home of London's elite."

Darcy turned and stared with a look meant to kill as he glared first at his uncle and then at his aunt. At the top of his lungs, he shouted, "This shall not be borne! I shall go to the authorities to reclaim her!"

"If you do," Lord Matlock cried with a challenging glare, "then you shall personally take responsibility for sharing her misfortune with the whole world, for such a course of action will surely appear in the papers."

~*~

When Lord Hazelton re-entered the drawing room, he was taken aback yet delighted to find Mr. and Mrs. Bingley absent. *Good riddance. I have no interest in your participation. In fact, the game will be much better **without** your company!* He smirked.

Elisha informed her husband that Mrs. Bingley felt faint and had retired to rest in the library. Mr. Bingley stated that he would return shortly. The Viscount rolled his eyes and then began to explain the game he wished to play. He pulled a chair to the centre of the room and asked who wanted to go first. Elisha spoke up and requested Elizabeth.

"Oh, no!" Elizabeth exclaimed, "I am certain I should much rather prefer watching over participating." She smiled as she begged to be excused, offering her thanks for their kindness.

Yet, Elisha would not allow it. "Oh, but I insist. You shall go first, and Caroline may follow you." Miss Bingley raised a brow at Elisha's insistence and then looked to Elizabeth, wondering what she would do.

Somewhat disconcerted, Elizabeth replied, "I thank you, no. I would rather not."

"Nonsense!" Lady Hazelton said sweetly. "You must oblige us in our home."

She then quickly stood and walked over to where Elizabeth sat. James handed his wife the blindfold, and she proceeded to tie it around Elizabeth's eyes.

Greatly agitated, Elizabeth spat out, "I do not wish to play. Stop this instant."

James seized her hands as she tried to take the cloth away from her eyes. "Ah, Mrs. Darcy but you *do* wish to play."

Elizabeth began to raise her voice, crying out in no uncertain terms, "No, I said *no*. I will not participate!"

James gestured with his eyes for Ashton to come and assist him.

Caroline looked on the scene with alarm. With Ashton holding Elizabeth's hands, Lord Hazelton rapidly put a gag around her mouth and then tied her hands behind the chair where she sat. Elizabeth fought the Viscount, but to no avail.

"There!" he exclaimed when finished.

Caroline swallowed hard and stood involuntarily but found herself unable to move a muscle, dumbfounded at the scene playing out before her.

Elisha walked over to her, threading her arm around Miss Dingley's. "Come, Caroline. I desire to show you the nursery. We have only recently had it painted." And, with that said, Lady Hazelton led the apprehensive Miss Bingley out of the room, nearly dragging her along the corridor.

As they progressed down the hall, Caroline could not dismiss Elizabeth's angry aspect, nor could she put out of her mind the passionate struggle that Mrs. Darcy attempted in the hope of freeing herself from the constraints.

As Ashton looked upon the struggling woman, he felt truly ill and nervous. He desired to have no part in this prank. Did Hazelton not realize the danger involved?

Placing his one hand upon the bare flesh of Elizabeth's collarbone, Lord Hazelton bent low and whispered in her ear, "Now calm yourself, Mrs. Darcy, and guess which one of us puts our cheek against yours."

Elizabeth could feel James's breath brush against her skin, and she continued to struggle, shaking her head back and forth vigorously, as Lord Hazelton tried to place his face next to hers. Her face was becoming red and swollen and the Viscount appeared to revel in her spirited plight.

"Very well, since you will not stop turning your head, then you will guess which one of us sits upon your lap."

He then sat down upon her.

Ashton had seen this game performed many times, and he had even participated in it, but never in this fashion or against anyone's wishes. Elizabeth's muffled cries disturbed him greatly, and he worried that Darcy would enter at any given moment. His reluctance to intervene lost to his sense of right and wrong, and thus, Mr. Caldecott began to beg his friend, "Hazel, stop! Do you hear me? Stop! She does not wish to play. It is that simple. Now, I insist, you must stop!"

With all the strength he could muster, Ashton's shaking hands began to untie the knots which bound Elizabeth's wrists. "Please, Mrs. Darcy, do be still. I am trying to help you!"

Yet, Lord Hazelton stilled his friend's motions, disrupting his ability to complete the task. Ashton looked up sharply, only to discover another pair of eyes shooting daggers at them both. Silently, both the Viscount and Ashton stepped away from the chair.

With alacrity, the gag around Elizabeth's mouth was removed, and she cried out, "Charles!"

In a fraction of a second, her hands were also freed, and she automatically reached up and pulled off the blindfold. Instantly she stood and threw herself into her brother's arms. Bingley held her close as he continued to glare at Lord Hazelton who stood several feet away, boldly glaring back at the younger gentleman.

During the humiliating ordeal, Elizabeth's mind recalled every encounter endured at the hands of her husband's cousin. Hotly, she turned away from Charles and marched over to Lord Hazelton and cried, "I remember you! I know who you are! At Matlock, you deliberately moved my chair!"

James laughed at her full-faced. Swiftly, she raised her hand to forcefully slap the scorn off the Viscount's countenance, and James, just as forcefully, grabbed her wrist thereby deflecting her attempt.

So absorbed was his Lordship in foiling Elizabeth's endeavour that he did not become aware of Charles Bingley's advancing to where they stood until Bingley's strong hand took hold of the Viscount's and gripped it mercilessly, forcing the older gentleman to shriek and wince in pain. He loosened his hold on Elizabeth's wrist and begging Mr. Bingley to cease. Bingley obliged his wish most readily only to replace his death grip with the loudest smack that Elizabeth had ever heard.

The younger gentleman had taken his open palm and applied it, most energetically, to deliver Elizabeth's desired strike to Lord Hazelton's cheek. The blow literally made the man stumble backwards. Bingley's action elicited great admiration from his sister-in-law. She fell back into the safety of his embrace, inclined her head upward, and smiled at him with glowing appreciation.

~*~

In another area of the house, Jane continued to lie on the settee as her husband went to inform her sister of their desire to depart. She felt ill at observing Lord Hazelton's desirous looks towards her sister. She could not begin to grasp how any man could covet another man's wife. When the library door opened, she thought it her husband returning to collect her. Yet, much to Mrs. Bingley's surprise, her eyes met those of Mr. Darcy's aunt, Lady Matlock.

Urgently, the lady approached Jane and whispered, "Mrs. Bingley, forgive me for disturbing you, but I need your help."

Jane sat up immediately.

"Please tell my nephew after you depart tonight where no servant of Blackwell can hear to send for my son at Sandhurst. Instruct him to have Richard come to our townhouse at midnight the night after next. Tell Richard to go to Edie. Can you remember?"

Despite her puzzlement at the request, Jane replied with confidence, "Yes. Tell Mr. Darcy to send for Colonel Fitzwilliam and send him to your home at midnight the night after next. Have the Colonel go to Edie."

"God Bless you, Mrs. Bingley."

The Countess squeezed Jane's hand and quickly departed. Jane wondered about the information and could not even begin to speculate about the need for secrecy.

~*~

Darcy stormed into the drawing room. Elizabeth and Bingley's heads turned at his entrance, each noticing his anger. "Bingley, I have ordered our carriage. We are leaving at once!" Instantly, Darcy took in the scene before his eyes. Hazelton's face bore the imprint of a hand, and Bingley held Elizabeth in his arms. Darcy exhaled loudly.

Sternly, he requested, "Bingley, take Elizabeth and leave the room."

Elizabeth looked pleadingly at her husband, silently requesting that he come with them, but, brusquely, he shook his head. She then looked up into Charles's eyes, imploring him to do something.

Menacingly, Darcy stared at his cousin.

Placing his hands upon Elizabeth's shoulders, Bingley gently turned her about, prodding her towards the entrance of the room. As they crossed the threshold, Elizabeth quickly looked back over her shoulder just in time to witness her husband, without forewarning, forcibly and backhandedly strike Lord Hazelton in the face. James's fleeting cry of agony filled the entrance hall.

They heard Darcy utter contemptuously in a fit of rage, "If you do not return my sister, I shall find you and beat you to death! Do you hear me, Hazel! I *shall* kill you!"

Lord Hazelton called to his cousin as that man strode out of the room, "It was not my idea to abduct Georgiana. It was Aunt Catherine's and Father's! I had nothing to do with it!"

Abruptly, Darcy stopped at the threshold and stood stock-still with his back facing his cousin. Icily, he exclaimed, "You have everything to do with it, James! I shall hold you completely accountable."

Without as much as a backward glance, Darcy quitted the room.

~*~

Once ensconced in the carriage, Darcy instantly asked about Caroline's whereabouts. Bingley answered that he had no idea. He only hoped that Elisha would send his sister home. Darcy sighed in exasperation, debating whether they should go back to retrieve her. Elizabeth spoke up at once and told them that Miss Bingley had accompanied Elisha to view the nursery.

All four occupants eyed one another for a moment, silently deliberating their course of action. Darcy took his fist and hit the roof of the carriage, signalling the driver to proceed. He then drew in a deep breath and related to the others the horrible fate to befall his sister.

As he began to speak, so did Bingley and Elizabeth. The three spoke over each other for a moment, until Darcy took control of the situation and raised his palm to silence the others "My uncle," he began, "has moved to confiscate my sister, to remove her from my custody and that of my cousin's. My uncle, along with my aunt, Lady Catherine, feels that we have failed Georgiana. Therefore, they have taken matters into their own hands. They will not tell me where she is nor will they allow me to see her!"

"But why?" Bingley cried, while Elizabeth exclaimed simultaneously, "This is appalling!"

Jane sat pensively, listening to their verbal exchange. Every so often, she would try to enter the conversation by mildly saying, "Mr. Darcy." However, due to the heated emotion, he did not hear her soft interjection.

Candidly, Darcy commenced relating his sister's near elopement with George Wickham. Only Bingley felt surprise at the revelation, since Jane and Elizabeth already knew of it. Charles wondered, but did not say a word. Darcy bitterly told them every word that had transpired between himself, the Earl, and Lady Catherine. He even related their claim that Elizabeth was responsible for revealing the whole incident concerning her blackmail to a very reliable source.

Elizabeth reacted to this with shock. In anger, she spoke up. "I have done no such thing, Fitzwilliam! You believe me, do you not?"

"Of course I do, Lizzy. I just cannot imagine who informed them."

Elizabeth, however, did not believe he told the truth. She eyed him suspiciously and endeavoured to figure out who could have said such a thing. The only other person that knew of the blackmail was Mr. Sheldon. Yet, she knew he would never breathe a word to another soul.

Darcy shook his head and stated, "It is of little consequence, Elizabeth. Do not let this point concern you. It could be Wickham, for all we know."

Looking steadily at him, Elizabeth thought, *that may be, my dear husband, but do you truly believe it? Or, is there a remote possibility that you doubt my word?* She felt ill.

In anguish, Darcy then related that his aunt and uncle planned to marry off Georgiana within two months' time, in order to prevent the possibility of her chances for a desirable connection being dashed, if the tale were to reach the *ton*.

When he stopped to take a breath, Jane's soft voice, yet again, tried to intervene. "Mr. Darcy, I have something important I *must* tell you."

The others sharing the carriage did not hear her because her husband immediately spoke promptly on top his wife's words, "Darcy, I really must speak to you tonight about another matter, just as pressing. I am sorry to have to do so when you are under so much duress with your sister, but it is urgent."

"Charles, I am sorry, but if you must, do so at once, for when I return to Ackerley, I must contact my attorney."

Bingley looked aghast. "Well, Darce, I would rather wait for the privacy of your study."

Elizabeth's pulse began to race. She instinctively understood the purpose behind Bingley's desire to speak to her husband. It could only concern Lord Hazelton. Yet, he had only witnessed what had happened to her this evening. Suddenly, she remembered her brother-in-law's forthrightness in the library the night she had fainted. Had something else occurred at that time?

Turning to face Bingley, Elizabeth boldly asked, "Charles, tell me at once. Why were you angry with the Viscount the night I fainted at the ball? I remember that you raised your voice to him and commanded that he leave to find the doctor."

Darcy's eyes widened as he looked from his wife to Bingley.

Gulping down his embarrassment, the man nervously replied, "My dear sister, please allow me to tell your husband in the privacy of his study. Then, he, in turn, can answer your query."

"Why, Charles? Is it that dreadful?" Elizabeth glanced over to Jane, and she realized that her sister knew. "Charles, does Jane know the answer to the question which I asked?"

"Oh, dear Elizabeth, please do not force me to speak of this to you."

Darcy impatiently commanded, "Bingley, say it at once and have done with!"

Bingley sat up and quickly rattled off, "I had come in search of you because I saw you faint, and then the Viscount carried you out of the ballroom. When I found you in the library, um, well..." his mouth suddenly went dry, and he began to stumble over his words.

"Finish it man!" Darcy cried.

Bingley startled even as his words began racing out of his mouth, "You were still unconscious, and he had raised your dress to your...um...knees and he was touching your, um... umm... legs, um knees and calves in an intimate manner."

Darcy's mien grew dark with intense anger. "As God is my witness, I shall kill *him*! I **shall**," Darcy swore and then opened the carriage door in an attempt to jump. Jane screamed while Bingley caught hold of his arm and Elizabeth held on to his coattails with all her might.

"You are insane, man! Get back in this carriage this instant!" Bingley screamed as he pulled his brother-in-law back inside. "We have already gone more than *three* miles. It would take you half of the night to cover that distance."

Elizabeth looked sceptically at her brother-in-law, not believing that it could take half the night to walk back a mere three miles, but she became distracted from such reasoning by her husband's next words.

In anger, Darcy's chest heaved while he exclaimed, "I *shall* kill him!"

"Fitzwilliam, you will do no such thing. I want my child to have a father. You are upsetting me, and you are upsetting my sister. Do you have no compassion on our nerves?" *Oh, there it is again. This time I actually said it. I **am** turning into my mother!*

Closing his eyes tightly, as tears of anger ran down his cheeks, Darcy felt powerless. He had no idea how to find his sister, and now his wife accused him of causing two expectant women distress. He covered his face with his hands.

Reaching over gingerly, Elizabeth touched one of his hands and caressed it. "I am fine, Fitzwilliam. Your cousin took vile liberties, but I remain unharmed. There shall be no thoughts of a duel and no talk of one either. I shall not allow it. My child's father shall never be involved in a duel. We shall find another way to deal with your cousin, but first we must think of Georgie."

With his face still covered by his hands, he nodded, imperceptibly, in acknowledgement to her words, but he did not agree with them. He silently swore an oath. If he had the opportunity to kill James, he would take it.

After several minutes of silence ensued, Jane raised her voice in an attempt to be heard once more, although, amongst such turmoil, she did so with a degree of apprehension. "Fitzwilliam?"

Uncovering his face, Darcy's head shot up, and he looked at his sister-in-law. She smiled commiseratively at him and stated, "My dear brother, your aunt, Lady Matlock, asked that I relate an important message to you. She wishes you to send for her son, the colonel, and requests that he arrive at her home at midnight, the night after next, and seek out a person named Edie."

Sudden relief washed over Darcy's visage. He dropped his head and wept freely.

~*~

Chapter Twenty-nine

Bittersweet Attachments

It was ten o'clock when the Darcy's carriage rolled to a halt in front of Ackerley. Jane and Charles had been invited to come inside for the promised nightcap, but due to the urgent situation involving Georgiana, they declined. Then again, after Darcy petitioned one more time for their reconsideration to stay on a while longer, they agreed most readily. Darcy was happy that they accepted his appeal, certain that Elizabeth would benefit from their company while he went straightaway to his study to compose an express to be dispatched without delay to his solicitor.

The threesome waited for Darcy in the music room, and it was there that Jane offered her heartfelt felicitations to her sister.

"Lizzy, am I being presumptuous in offering my congratulations on your impending arrival?"

For the first time during the evening, Jane and Charles discerned that Elizabeth's countenance took on a true lustre, especially as she turned to acknowledge her sister's regard.

"No, Jane, you are not being presumptuous in the least. I am indeed expecting as you were both forthrightly informed in the carriage." She half laughed and rolled her eyes. "We ourselves have only recently discovered the joyous news."

Both Bingley and Jane expressed their happiness with the communication. The three then discussed the delights of having their children so close in age, and it was at this time that Jane chose to reveal her revered communication. "I am to have a boy, Lizzy, for I have seen him in a dream. I shall be blessed with a son! There shall be no complications with the birth, and he shall be a very healthy boy. He shall have his father's hair." Jane smiled radiantly.

No matter how hard she tried, Elizabeth could not keep the look of amazement and uncertainty from her face. She had never heard of such a phenomenon beyond anything biblical.

"I know what you must be thinking, dear sister, but it is true, and I am most certain of its occurrence."

"No, Jane, I am sure you are. I am truly surprised, is all." Elizabeth then looked at Charles. She could tell by his admiring gaze upon her sister that he unreservedly believed his wife's divination.

In afterthought, Jane cried, "I even know what his name shall be!"

Bingley interjected most happily, "Yes, he shall be named Crispin Charles! He shall be a saint even as his mother is an angel!"

Jane gazed deeply into her husband's eyes. For a moment, the pair became absorbed in a world of their own.

Elizabeth's brows rose and her lips curled somewhat upward, wondering if she would ever cease to be amazed at the unbending adoration and felicity that her sister and brother-in-law shared one for the other—they seemed to be perfectly suited. If they were certain that their babe was a boy, who was she to question it? In fact, she inwardly envied their conviction. Not in the sense that she wanted to rob her sister and brother-in-law of any part of their inner tranquillity, but more for the fact that she had just endured the anxiety of nearly losing her baby, and also, for the inner fear that she might still lose it.

No, she could never begrudge her dear sister any happiness. She could only hope that she too might come to feel an inner peace with the hopeful expectation of her own child. Would all go well? So many women had complications during childbirth, and so many children did not survive. Oh, how she longed to have the serenity which she was now witnessing in her dear sister and Bingley's eyes!

Her silent meditations came to an end, however, with the entrance of her husband. Darcy immediately went to the sideboard and lifted the carafe to pour some wine for all. Jane indicated that she desired very little, while Elizabeth desired to forgo the liquor, and, as an alternative, requested water.

After dispensing the drinks, Darcy propped his elbow atop the mantlepiece and looked gravely upon them. "Depending on the advice which I hope to receive tonight from my attorney, I will be off for Sandhurst before dawn. If you could find it in your hearts, I would feel at peace if I knew that Elizabeth were not alone. Thus, what I am asking is for you both," he looked first to Bingley and then to Jane, "to come and stay with her tomorrow in my absence."

Elizabeth opened her mouth to object, but soon closed it when her husband raised a hand. "No, Elizabeth, I cannot leave you unattended knowing what I now know about my cousin. I could not attempt to leave you here, with the fear that he may try to come to Ackerley and find you all alone. I cannot bear it!" He cradled his head in his hand, covering his brow.

Bingley, Jane, and Elizabeth felt great compassion for him. They heard the strain in his voice as he spoke. Swiftly, Bingley rose and stated, "We shall gladly come to stay, Darcy! Do not let that point worry you one bit!" Startled by his own eagerness, Charles turned to look at his wife who serenely smiled her assurances to him. He heaved a sigh of relief realizing that he had not upset her by his oversight in first consulting with her wishes.

Raising his head, Darcy's eyes veered over to them with gratitude. The carriage was then summoned to take the Bingleys home. In the vestibule, Jane and Elizabeth embraced warmly.

While they women said their farewells, Darcy took the opportunity to take Bingley off to one side and express his gratitude for his assistance and devoted friendship.

"I am most grateful to you, Charles. I feel at a loss to express my mortification for my family's...well..."

"No need, Darce. You need not say it. Your unfailing friendship has meant the world to me. Besides, you have put up with some of my rather, how shall I say it, less than desirable relations?" Bingley smiled sheepishly. His concession earned a rare smile from Darcy. They both smiled openly to the other and shook hands, with Bingley promising to return to Ackerley first thing in the morning.

~*~

After Darcy had prepared for bed, he joined his wife in her chamber. She was sitting in the chair beside her bed writing in a book. Darcy creased his brow at her activity and asked, "What are you writing, Lizzy?"

"Oh, I suppose a diary of sorts."

"A diary, I had not known that you recorded your musings into a diary."

"Oh, this is the first night that I have attempted to do so. With the loss of my memory, I decided that I never wanted to forget anything again. It is a dreadful feeling not to be able to remember."

He smiled, fully aware for himself just how dreadful it was.

"Come, Lizzy. Chaffin has been informed to wake me early, so please come and let me hold you, for I must rest in order to have the energy I will need to ride out to Sandhurst at dawn."

"Could you not send an express?" She already knew the answer.

"No, I fear I must speak to Richard personally."

Climbing up and nestling beside her husband, Elizabeth understood his need to personally meet with his cousin. Richard had a steadying approach with sharing the burdens in regard to Georgiana, which she herself, could never attempt. Darcy not only needed to devise a plan with his cousin in recovering his sister, but he needed the healing balm which only the colonel's level-headedness could provide. Elizabeth knew of no other soul whom her husband looked to for guidance and counsel other than his cousin, Richard Fitzwilliam.

While holding Elizabeth securely within his arms, shamefacedly, Darcy stated, "I am sorry for all that you have endured at the hands of my family, Lizzy, particularly...from the...hands..." With laboured breath, he choked back a sob as his face contorted in repugnance by the realization of the irony behind his poor choice of words. The simple figure of speech was literal in Hazelton's case, for his libertine cousin had plainly violated his wife with his *very hands*.

Elizabeth observed the lump in her husband's throat as he attempted to speak, and she also sensed the renewal of his anger. She wished to offset any further distress from the emotional upheaval that he had already endured through the course of the evening, and as she plainly saw, was still enduring. In spite of this, she knew that she must tell him all concerning Lord Hazelton's flagrant overtures towards her. She shook her head and nuzzled closer.

"Fitzwilliam, I need to tell you something which I know shall cause you greater misery, and I have even considered not telling you for fear that you might do something extremely foolish."

Darcy became still, directing his full attention upon her, silently encouraging her to continue. His arms slacken and a sudden dread overshadowed his features.

"Tonight, while you were gone to speak with your uncle, Lord Hazelton suggested that we play blind man's buff." Elizabeth noticed his eyes widen and she quickly resumed. "Jane and Bingley had vacated the room when James returned with the needed items. He asked who wanted to volunteer first. Oh, to make a dreadful long story short, I was chosen against my will. James proceeded to blindfold me with Elisha's help. He held my hands so I could not take off the blindfold." Darcy's jaw clenched and she noted the narrowing of his eyes.

"While I continued to plead, he solicited Ashton Caldecott's help, enabling him to gag my mouth and tie my hands behind the chair. I think by this time Elisha had taken Caroline from the room."

Instantly, Darcy bolted to an upright position. He sat in the bed no longer looking at her, enraged at such malice from his cousin.

"Please, Fitzwilliam, your anger is understandable, but it will accomplish very little at the moment."

He made no response.

"Nevertheless, James began to play the hideous game. I cannot believe people play such games. Fitzwilliam, have you played that game, for I have never heard of it before tonight?"

Darcy turned his face towards her and rolled his eyes. In a steely voice he clipped out, "No Lizzy, I have never taken part in such a game. I have seen it played, yet, I find it vulgar."

Elizabeth puckered her lips to the side and nodded, lost in thought.

"Pray Elizabeth, finish!"

His exclamation earned a small huff of irritation from his wife as she came back to the moment.

"There really is not much to say except James tried to press his face next to mine, but I kept moving my head about. Thus, he sat on my lap. Oh yes,

Mr. Caldecott began to implore your cousin to stop, even going so far as to untie my hands. He was very nervous." She smiled at the thought.

"Lizzy, this is no laughing matter. I find no humour in it at all."

"Fitzwilliam, at the time I found none either. Yet, now it seems comical to me how Ashton fretfully begged your cousin in fear as his hands trembled while trying to undo the knot."

Darcy's expression bore no humour whatsoever. Elizabeth rolled her eyes and quickly stated, "When Charles came in they stopped the game. He untied my hands and removed the cloth from my mouth. That is when I remembered all my former opinions about your cousin. I attempted to slap him, but he offset my hand. Nonetheless, Bingley slapped him for me, harder than I could ever hope to have done. James literally stumbled back several steps." She smiled at the memory and then bit her lip in an attempt to curtail her impending mirth. Glancing over to her husband, she noticed that he too was smiling, therefore, she smiled openly.

"Elizabeth, you should have told me immediately."

"Pray sir, if you will remember correctly, you entered the room with the fury of hell!"

Nodding slowly, Darcy said, "You are correct. I entered the drawing room on the loose, decisively taking my cousin to task. You had no occasion, none whatsoever, to tell me what had just occurred. I even noticed Hazelton's reddened cheek. Yet, I was too absorbed with my own plight and that of my sister's, to stop and question why. Lizzy, how you must detest me."

"Fitzwilliam, truly your inobservance at the time is explicable when taken into consideration the appalling confrontation you had just endured with your aunt and uncle. Although your blow to James was executed in behalf of Georgiana, I felt it was mine all the same."

He smiled at her and shook his head in disbelief.

"Yet, I fear, dear husband, that there is one more incident regarding your cousin, Lord Hazelton, which I must relate. I have no proof, yet after what happen tonight in conjunction with Charles's disclosure, I feel assured that I did not imagine it."

Closing his eyes tightly, trying to repress his anger yet again, Darcy finally nodded for her to begin afresh.

"The morning after the ball at Matlock, I went down to the breakfast room to find you. James pulled out the chair for me, and as I began to sit down, I felt that he purposely pulled it back further causing me to fall. He, of course, caught me before I completely plummeted to the floor. Yet, Oh! Fitzwilliam, please remain calm." Elizabeth clearly read the abhorrence mingled with shock appearing on Darcy's face. She shook her head and continued, "Your cousin's hands lingered a little too long while supporting me back to my feet. I felt he," Elizabeth's face crimsoned, "took pleasure in the plumpness of the sides of my...um...bosom."

Her husband's incredulity was unmistakable as his mouth gaped open and his eyes bespoke injury. "Lizzy, how could you keep this from me? How could you not tell me such a thing until now?"

"Fitzwilliam, I pray that you will believe me when I say that at first I too was mortified by his insult. Even so, I rationalized his behaviour away, thinking that it must be in my head. Your family had been so wonderful to us, and you had already been through so much with Lady Catherine that I could not bear to make an allegation that I could in nowise prove. I chose instead to hope it was all in my imagination and nothing more. Due to the injury to my head, I did not even remember the incident until tonight. Please forgive my foolish decision. I cannot bear it if you do not."

Quickly, Darcy covered his mouth with his hand, rubbing his palm over his lips and chin several times while he contemplated the crime of his pathetic cousin. How he detested the man! Hearing his name called softly brought him to his senses, and he sought to console his wife.

Reaching for her hand, he croaked out, "I am so sorry for how he has violated you, my love. I fully understand your hesitation in telling me. But, please, trust me in the future. If Bingley had not enlightened me, I do believe my cousin capable of... forcing his way with you. I do not want to think so, but the facts are plainly before us. I never should have allowed Georgiana to go to Blackwell." He closed his eyes in frustration. "I was kissing the proffered hand for the sake of familial ties, but, no more! I know you do not want me to speak of a duel, yet I see no alternative. You cannot expect me to make nothing of it and act like it is neither here nor there! Your honour has been assaulted!"

Elizabeth raised her voice in alarm. "Please, Fitzwilliam let us speak no more of this for now. I too know that something must be done. Your cousin's transgressions are inexcusable. However, you cannot decide on the course of action all alone. You now have a wife and child to think of. If our marriage is to unite us, you cannot wilfully divide us by doing whatever you please. You must consider my sentiments and see reason. You cannot seal our fate with a duel. You must refrain from such thinking. The risks are far too great, death if you lose or prison if you do not."

She watched to see what effect, if any, her words had upon him. He sat staring into the nothingness. She wondered if he had even heard her, when he finally spoke. "Very well, Elizabeth, we shall decide jointly. First we shall find Georgiana and then we shall deal with Hazelton. Let us speak no more of it until that time. It is too painful."

Lying back down, Darcy gathered Elizabeth within his arms, holding her close. She began running her fingers through his curls. Attempting to rid the offences from their minds, she stated, "Have I ever told you, Fitzwilliam, that I love your hair? I love your curls. I especially love it after you bathe, or after you have exercised. The dampness draws up your locks into tight ringlets."

The touch of Elizabeth's fingers upon his head was soothing. Drowsily, Darcy basked by his wife's side, enjoying the affection which she showered upon him. Her words only intensified the love he felt for her. Thus, he tenderly stated, "I love your loosened, silky tresses," he began winding his fingers through her hair, "your creamy soft skin," softly, he kissed her neck while inhaling the lavender scent which she wore, "and your sparkling fine eyes!" Taking his index finger, he gently tapped the tip of her nose, emphasizing his exclamation. Next, he gently kissed her lips and then murmured against them, "I cannot forget to mention your luscious mouth." Quickly, he drew in her bottom lip between his and nibbled upon it.

When their kiss ended, Elizabeth exclaimed, "I adore you, Fitzwilliam!"

Sleepily, he replied, "And I you, Lizzy. Never underestimate your worth. You mean the world to me. No one else can bring me the comfort and love that you most willingly bestow. You understand me like no other." He yawned and squeezed her tightly just before he fell into a deep sleep.

Darcy's affirmation of her significance generated a small smile of contentment upon her lips, and with an arched brow, she thought, *'tis true, I suppose I do have a mode of succouring you, my dear husband, where none other can.* His soft snore informed Elizabeth that he slept. Thus, she discontinued her occupation of stroking his hair so as to gaze upon his handsome features. After several minutes of this indulgence, she wearily closed her eyes in hopes of dreaming dreams for better days to come.

~*~

His bruised face, not to mention the acute soreness of his nose, had left Lord Hazelton in a rather foul mood the following morning as he dressed for the day. He stared at his visage for some time, taking in his swollen red nose and the huge purple streaked discoloration—a result of Mr. Bingley's hand. He would not be able to appear in public for days, if not weeks! As he angrily gazed upon his features, Darcy's threat reverberated in his mind. *'If you do not return my sister, I shall find you and beat you to death. Do you hear me, Hazel? I shall kill you!'*

In the reflection of the mirror, Lord Hazelton stared into his own eyes and bitterly spat out for no one's ears but his own, "The audacity of that prig in making such a threat. My dear cousin, even though you own half of Derbyshire, you do not own the whole world! I am a Lord of the Realm. You are ***nothing***!"

His Lordship's valet entered carrying his waistcoat and cravat. As he helped his master don the garments, the Viscount asked, "Has Miss Darcy gone down to breakfast?"

"I am not sure, sir. Would you have me enquire?"

The valet could easily detect the bitter severity in his master's tone as he stated, "Oh yes, most certainly. I need to see my little cousin right away. Do not send her to me, I shall go to her. Locate where she is."

His man nodded and exited the chamber, bent on accomplishing his assigned task.

Again, Lord Hazelton stared in the glass, irritably scrutinizing his figure. He knew he appeared quite dashing in his tailored suit and fine knotted cravat. He was well aware of the fact that he was extremely handsome. Whenever he walked into a room, all the females could never bear to tear their eyes away from him, even if they were standing next to their husbands, they could not help themselves. Yet, now this, his expression twisted into a sneer. Now, his face was spoilt! Sinisterly, he contemplated, *well, an eye for an eye, I say. Very well, dear cousin, if you want your sister back you shall have her, and she will be just as marred as my face. Only it will not be visible for the naked eye to behold. Oh no, but she shall be blemished all the same*! Smiling to himself, he snickered merrily at the image of Darcy's rage when he discovered his precious sister's irretrievable loss of innocence.

~*~

It was late in the afternoon when Darcy returned from Sandhurst. Despite his grimy appearance, he met with the Bingleys before he took his leave to bathe. It was his heartfelt desire to offer his appreciation for their visiting with Elizabeth in his absence. An enquiry for Caroline's welfare was also made. Instantly, Charles spoke up to assure him that a carriage from Blackwell had been dispatched for his sister's safe deliverance. Then, both Jane and Charles happily assured him that it was their pleasure to spend the day with Elizabeth in response to their brother-in-law's expression of gratitude.

Darcy pressed them to stay and have supper with them and to spend the evening as well. They declined, however, stating that they had made prior arrangements to take Caroline, Kitty and Bingley's cousin, Mr. Burns, to the theatre. Darcy and Elizabeth saw them to the door and gave their adieus.

Elizabeth observed her husband as soon as the door was closed. She noticed his plaintive look and feared that Colonel Fitzwilliam might not have been given leave for the morrow. "Oh dear Fitzwilliam, why so subdued? You seemed well enough when wishing Jane and Charles off. Please tell me at once. Is Richard unable to come?"

He shook his head and stated, "No, nothing of the sort. He is here already. I had Chaffin attend to him while I came to speak with your sister and Bingley. I suppose the reason I appear subdued is that I am worried that our plan will not work or that we might be too late. Fitzwilliam informed me that our cousin Anne told him at the ball that she and Lady Catherine are going to Bath. I fear they might take Georgie with them."

"Yet, we at least know this information. Surely that is something." She wrapped her arms about him.

He squeezed her quickly and then backed away. "Lizzy, I must first change before I cover you in filth."

"Very well, I shall go and prepare for supper as well. We have, however, two hours before the meal is to be served. If you want to join me, please feel free." She gave him a knowing look and he smiled. Yet, she could tell he was weary and imagined he desired a much needed rest. She longed to question him further about Colonel Fitzwilliam's reaction to the trying situation, but knew that his early departure and the tiring ride he had just endured must have rendered him completely exhausted. Consequently, they parted ways at their chamber doors.

~*~

Georgiana had been reposing on her bed for some time, clad in her nightgown and robe. She had no desire to dress for the day. Nancy had unsuccessfully tried to coax her mistress to eat some of the food upon her breakfast tray, yet Georgiana had lost all appetite. She had managed to eat a little, but not enough to satisfy her maid. Nancy had not the least idea what caused her mistress to become so gloomy as of late. She could not begin to fathom the reason behind Miss Darcy's melancholy. Not more than a week ago, her young mistress was in seventh heaven, exhilarated by the swirl of activity of the Season. It broke the maid's heart to see her mistress so distraught and listless. There was one aspect, Nancy noticed, that brought some degree of solace to Miss Darcy, and that was a letter which the miss continually either read or held to her chest.

Nancy picked up the tray and tried one last time to persuade Miss Darcy to eat. Georgiana scrunched up her nose and shook her head while thanking her maid for her service. Acceptingly, Nancy turned to take the tray from the room when the chamber door swung open. The maid stopped in shock that someone had the nerve to enter without first knocking and then her shock increased twofold. Not only did the uninvited guest not knock, but he was a man who was now boldly entering the chamber of a lady.

"What? Is my baby cousin not feeling well?" Lord Hazelton examined the uneaten breakfast upon the tray and stated with sarcasm, "Tsk, tsk. My, my, Georgie, no wonder you stay so lithesome. You really should try to eat more you know."

Suddenly, Lord Hazelton's eyes bore into Nancy's and the maid quickly understood his meaning, yet she felt she could not leave her mistress. She had never encountered a situation such as this before. Her vision veered to Georgiana. She could tell that Miss Darcy was in as much shock as she found herself to be, for her mistress was clutching her robe about her, striving to hide her nightgown. Nancy jumped when she heard the boom of the Viscount's order, "Leave us immediately!" While looking at Lord Hazelton's angry face, Nancy took in the bruise he wore upon his cheek and his swollen nose.

Again, Nancy turned to seek direction from her mistress. Miss Darcy appeared doe-eyed but nonetheless, nodded to her maid, granting her departure. Nervously, Nancy strived to carry a rattling tray while she quit the room.

After the maid closed the door behind her, Lord Hazelton quickly approached the bed and loomed over his cousin. Heatedly he cried, "Do you see this, my dear girl?" Georgiana looked upon his features, but the enraged gesticulations of her cousin's hands were more fearsome than the sneer and colourful swell that showed on his face.

At the top of his lungs, Lord Hazelton shouted. "This, my dear girl, is the work of your brother!"

Georgiana shrank back within the pillows still grasping her robe with one hand and her letter with the other. Even though she cowered backwards, her eyes remained fastened on her cousin's.

Taking in Georgiana's fear, Lord Hazelton felt a twinge of satisfaction. Inhaling deeply, he stood unmoving and began to closely inspect his cousin's fair face. Considering her beauty, he calmly acknowledged, "You have become very pretty, Georgiana, and quite grownup."

Georgiana felt alarmed by her cousin's quick change of attitude. It sickened her as she watched his eyes roaming over her figure. His lecherous gaze somehow made her feel naked. He had never before looked at her in this manner. She was not quite sure what to make of it. If she had felt alarmed from his roving eyes, she felt a deathly chill when she heard his next observation.

After taking in her long blonde hair, fair complexion, and slight pleasing form, Lord Hazelton's eyes searched hers deeply and then in a self-possessed air, he stated, "Why Georgie, you are just as pure as when you were born. I do believe that dear Mr. Wickham did not lay one finger upon you while you were at Ramsgate—for you have not yet been plucked. My, my, I cannot believe it!"

Georgiana's blood ran cold as her eyes widened and her face flushed. Yet, unable to meet his penetrating gaze a moment longer, she shunned his face and hastily turning away. Never in a million years would she have ever expected her eldest cousin to be so vulgar. She could not believe her ears.

While she was contemplating James's ill-mannered observation about her virtue, that man boldly reached forth and snatched the cherished letter from her hand. Frantically, Georgiana bound off the bed, lunging forward with her outstretched arms to reclaim what was rightfully hers.

Holding the missive high above his head, Lord Hazelton snickered in delight. "Here," he cried as he waved the missive in front of her nose, "is this what you want?" Every time she reached forth her hand to take it, he pulled it away just as quickly.

Finally, Georgiana in one last effort managed to grab it. Lord Hazelton, however, put a halt to her victory by twisting the arm that held the letter until she whimpered in pain. Even so, she would not drop the missive. Thus, he briskly manoeuvred her over to the bed, pushing her upon it and laying atop her. The weight of his body pinned her down, making ineffectual any movement she attempted. Cunningly, with only one of his hands, he seized both of hers, therefore, allowing him to freely take hold of the letter and read it while Georgiana squirmed frantically beneath him.

"What is this, my dear girl, a letter from Sandhurst Park? My, my, and what does my dear brother have to say to you?"

Flicking the letter open with the movement of his wrist, James began to read the missive silently. Tears of anguish streamed down Georgiana's cheeks, her cries stifled by the pressure of her cousin's chest.

My Dearest Georgie, Mother tells me... My men and I have been industrious in the felling of trees and constructing bridges, Lord Hazelton rolled his eyes as he read and inwardly thought, 'Child's play!' *Darcy spoke with me about his desire to safeguard your inheritance. I do think it wise. I have seen too many marriages where a woman is left destitute because her rake of a husband married for her dowry in order to gamble it away at the tables.* Lord Hazelton's eyebrows rose at the content of the letter. Yet, when reading the next line, the Viscount's brow crumpled. What was his brother saying? *As for me Georgie, I am used to living without the finer things in life. You must decide if you can be also.* The next lines seemed just as puzzling. *Wealth does not bring happiness. Yet, the attainment of riches seems to be the hub which our universe revolves around. Happiness is such an elusive thing. For many it is not easily obtained. Yet, once painstakingly discovered, it can elude one just as quickly as it came. I think this is because many think happiness is found in the pleasures of the moment, the possessing of more possessions, or the ability to shine above all others. Yet, in time, it is never enough, pleasures wane, property shackles, and the passing moment of vainglory leads to emptiness. Instead, I feel true happiness is something we must foster from within. To me, it is found in honesty, service, and love. I feel that you are my happiness, Georgie.* Lord Hazelton momentarily looked up and then read the last line again.

I feel that you are my happiness, Georgie.

Still holding the letter within his hand, he rolled off of his cousin unto his back and continued to read the missive. Georgiana lay unmoving beside him, completely humiliated and drained. She no longer cared if he read it. If it were left up to her, she would shout her love for Colonel Fitzwilliam from the roof tops.

...You know not how I love you, Georgie... Your devoted confidant and admirer, Richard Fitzwilliam.

Turning his head back towards her, Lord Hazelton asked, "Is Richard in love with you? He asks you to decide if you can live without the finer things in life. Why is he asking you this? Has he sought your hand in marriage?" Lord Hazelton then snorted with a laugh, "And dear Darcy knows nothing of it. Why else would your brother safeguard your inheritance if he did? Ah! This is rich!"

Indignantly, Georgiana spat out, "Richard has not asked for my hand!"

"Oh, do you suppose I cannot read between the lines, my dear girl, with all this rubbish of fine carriages, estates, and vainglory." Lord Hazelton gaily scoffed at her and jeeringly asked, "What does my brother have to offer you? Nothing! Do not fall for his pathetic appeal to take the higher, nobler road. Fancy words—that is all he can offer you, because he has nothing more to give. Just empty words, mind you. The advantage of your marriage to my brother would be all in his favour and not advantageous to you by any means." Lord Hazelton suddenly realized that his plan would now kill two birds with one... um stone. His brother would become livid that his intended, pure bride would no longer be pure nor his.

Turning back upon his side, Lord Hazelton firmly cupped Georgiana's chin in his hand. "I am sorry to disappoint you, my dear, fresh flower, but you shall never marry my brother, for I shall make certain of it." After one firm tug, he quickly let go of her chin and stood.

He then turned to leave the room when Georgiana sat up and spiritedly exclaimed, "Richard's words are not empty! They are full of meaning! He is a living exemplar of them! Why do you detest him so? Why do you treat him as if he is nobody, a subaltern, an insignificant person?"

Halting at her words, the Viscount merely shrugged and replied smugly, "Because, my dear cousin, he is."

"He is twice the man you will ever be and more!"

Lord Hazelton narrowed his eyes, inched closer, and said in a low, tight voice, "My Georgie, you have it bad! Let me enlighten you about your wonderful colonel. Before you go and immortalize my pathetic brother as a god, let me inform you that he is not unlike any other man. He has blood that runs through his manly veins. All of his noble gibberish is just that. He is just as familiar with the ways of London the same as any other man. Sir Galahad he is not! He pays for his harlots as other men and enjoys their services just the same. In fact... well... we shall leave *that* for another time. Get your rest my dear girl. You are going to need it!"

Georgiana looked queerly at him. He turned to go but spun around to face her yet again. "Here," he tossed the letter towards her, "you had better keep it, for I imagine your new husband will never allow clandestine affairs with our dear honourable colonel." Taking in her tear stained face with a scathing glance, Lord Hazelton gleefully deferred his departure to offer one more insight. "Not to worry my dear girl, your dear colonel will more than likely die on some barren plain in Portugal." On that note, the Viscount quit the room.

Clutching her letter to her heart, Georgiana turned over and wept bitterly. Her small frame shook violently with each sob. She had already attempted several times to escape Blackwell, but servants had been stationed outside her door to hinder such an undertaking.

~*~

Richard had lain down upon the bed in the accustomed chamber he had always occupied when at Ackerley. He had hoped to find some measure of rest before the evening began, but banishing the animosity from his mind was pointless. He was not even aware of how tightly his jaw was clenched or how his hands lay by his side balled up into fists. The resentments he felt towards his father, aunt, and brother were mounting inside of him with each thought of their interference, and as the seconds passed, he began to detect the pounding pulsation surging through every vein in his body.

Up until now, Colonel Fitzwilliam had never experienced so much hostility towards his family. Usually, his jovial good nature would allow him to easily shake off their aristocratic superciliousness. His ability to bear their arrogance in a congenial manner was his way of accomplishing an armistice of sorts. He seldom agreed with their narrow-minded perspective concerning the world about them and more particularly, their censure concerning him. Thus, humour was the only acceptable means that Richard could resort to so as to tolerate such unfavourable circumstances with his overbearing relations, circumstances which in all reality would very likely never change.

This time, however, they had gone too far. He could no longer turn a blind eye to their officious opinions and manipulation and simply go along as if nothing had happened. What were they thinking in forcing Georgiana to marry against her will?

Richard's head throbbed as tears of anger stung at his eyes, and he immediately tweaked the flesh between his brows in an effort to offset the pain. Abruptly, he rose from the bed and went directly to the writing desk. With pen in hand and the inkwell and blank parchment before him, he industriously began to write three letters. The first two being the most poignant in consequence, with the latter being the most cold and apocalyptic. Dipping the metal tip into the black ink, he touched it to paper and began to inscribe in his strong hand, *Miss Georgiana Darcy*. The next missive would be to his mother and the last, to his brother James. He hated to break the promise which he had made to Georgie to not correspond with another except her, but it could not be helped. Besides, it was not as if he were writing while away on duty, and most significantly, the unforeseen quandary warranted it.

~*~

In the dining hall, Elizabeth and Darcy sat at the grand table waiting for Colonel Fitzwilliam to join them. He had sent word by a servant expressing his apologies that he was detained, but would join them as soon as possible, and thus, he begged for them to begin without him. Both husband and wife decided to decline his suggestion and wait just the same. It was during this interval the subject of a duel resurfaced.

Mr. Kearns, Darcy's solicitor, had sent word that he would be ready to accompany Mr. Darcy early in the morning to call at the Earl of Matlock's townhouse a little before the customary acceptable hour for such visits.

Earlier in the evening, just before Darcy bathed, Chaffin had given him Mr. Kearns's missive. Darcy was now sharing this intelligence with his wife as they waited for Richard. Darcy had asked the servants to vacate the room and come back when the colonel arrived.

He began to explain to his wife the legality involved in the reclamation of Georgiana. Tomorrow, he and Mr. Kearns would appear before his uncle just as a preliminary threat in the hopes that his uncle would see reason and capitulate to the law without further address. However, Darcy also related his doubts that the stratagem would have any effect upon his uncle at all, because the Earl had previously challenged him with the upper hand of allowing his nephew to use the law. It was his uncle's trump card. The Earl knew that Darcy would want to avoid scandal at all costs. So if tomorrow's engagement proved ineffectual, then the move was decidedly in Darcy's making, and he would have to determine if he were truly willing to take legal action against his uncle and publicly drag their families' names through every gutter, street, house, and wagging tongue of London and beyond. At this moment, Fitzwilliam Darcy was almost certain that he would do whatever was deemed necessary to retrieve his sister.

After enlightening Elizabeth to the crux of the situation before them, Darcy then offhandedly mentioned, with heated words, that he would also take advantage of the interview with his uncle by informing the Earl about his eldest son's unforgivable, immoral offences to his wife. If his uncle chose to ignore his demand by renouncing his son, then he would call his cousin out.

Elizabeth's mouth hung open for a full ten seconds before she hissed, "How dare you, Fitzwilliam Darcy, flagrantly take matters into your own hands, and of all things to call for a duel in front of an attorney of law!"

Quickly, but not repentantly, Darcy interjected, "I had planned to have Mr. Kearns wait in the carriage."

"Oh!" Elizabeth cried, "And that is supposed to make it permissible! You are insufferable! Just last night you promised me that there would be no more thought and talk of a duel. Really Fitzwilliam, I shall not stand for it!" Immediately, Elizabeth stood and glowered down at her husband.

Darcy unwaveringly met her scowl.

"I see, Mr. Darcy, that we have a stand off all our own, and I suppose you shall want to call me out as well?"

His eyes remained fixed to hers. "No, Lizzy, my spars with you are strictly verbal, well, in a sense they do often conclude in aggressive, corporal encounters." He gave her a roguish smile. Yet, Elizabeth was not amused.

Narrowing her eyes, she cried boldly, "How dare you, Fitzwilliam! I am not of a mind to find any room for humour. I am most seriously displeased!"

Darcy looked at her vaguely. The absurdity of his wife using the same expression that he had heard so often at Rosings was too much and Darcy chortled merrily. His laughter only infuriated Elizabeth further and her eyes widened at her husband's insensitivity to her feelings. Thus, she held her chin high and pushed her chair in place before attempting to leave the room. Quickly, Darcy caught hold of her hand and pulled his unwilling wife into his lap.

"Elizabeth, calm yourself, or the whole staff will soon know of our discord."

"And it is of your making! How can you laugh at me so?"

Squeezing her tightly, he conceded openly, "I was not laughing at you per se, just your choice of words. Do you know how often I have heard, '*I am most seriously displeased*,' from Lady Catherine?"

Elizabeth looked into his eyes and shook her head with a frown. "No, I do not, but I can well imagine over a million." She rolled her eyes for added emphasis to her exaggeration.

"I am sorry for laughing, Elizabeth, but you cannot think that I will allow my cousin to continue on in his guilt. If my uncle will not disinherit him, then I shall do it for him. Please try to understand the seriousness of the situation."

"Fitzwilliam, do you think I do not realize it? Yet, you would have me believe there is no other solution but murder. You would have me believe that James's only rightful and just punishment can come solely from your hands alone. Why not have him stoned to death? That way I can be party to his demise as well? Or better yet, I shall be the one to challenge him to a duel!"

"Lizzy, do be serious."

"Oh, but I am..."

It was at this precise moment that Richard chose to enter the room. He had heard almost their whole exchange and felt a renewed sickening in his gut. He was not in the habit of eavesdropping, but the shame of his family had rendered him immobile when hearing their discussion. Thus, he froze and could not seem to will himself forward. But, when hearing Elizabeth's exaggerated suggestion to take party in his brother's death, he felt he could fall back on his familiar façade of wit.

Upon seeing his entry, Elizabeth instantly attempted to arise from her husband's knee, but remained firmly held in place. In amazement, she turned to look into Darcy's determined eyes with her bulging ones.

"Oh, so you waited for me?" The colonel cheerily questioned. "And since we are on the subject of Hazel's demise, I think that I shall be the one to cast the first stone!"

Darcy smiled widely at his cousin while Elizabeth's face bore her mortification.

"I am so sorry, Richard. I should not have said that just now," she said solemnly.

"Elizabeth, you need not concern yourself in sparing my feelings for my brother. After all, who better is there to be my brother's keeper than myself? Neither of you should worry about Hazelton's fate. I have it sealed. I shall be the one to handle it in due time."

The colonel inhaled deeply and looked charmingly upon the happy couple who were still within each other's arms. Richard rather liked that his cousin felt easy in front of him. He hoped in the future, that Darcy would be just as comfortable when it came his turn to hold Georgiana within his own arms. Outside of rescuing Georgiana, that was the one other real concern the colonel had. Would Darcy accept his suit for his sister's hand?

With the sound of the servants' approach, Darcy finally relinquished his grasp upon his wife, but only before bestowing her with one last embrace.

The trio ate their meal in relative good spirits. Afterward, all three went to Darcy's study to speak of the morrow's agenda and to plan out their attempted rescue. When all factors were calculated and decided upon, the small group retired. But before departing, Darcy asked Richard to wait a moment because he and Elizabeth had something they wished to share with him.

Richard looked on with great expectation while Darcy and Elizabeth stared undecidedly to each other, not knowing who should do the honours. Elizabeth nudged her husband's shoulder with a slight push from her own and Darcy proudly stated, "Fitzwilliam, Elizabeth and I are expecting a child this autumn. We wanted you to know. It is not general knowledge as of yet, even Georgiana does not know."

Immediately, Richard observed Darcy's elation smothered in anguish, and it broke his heart. Taking Elizabeth's hand, the colonel gallantly kissed it and offered his heartfelt congratulations. Elizabeth thanked him and then did the unexpected. She reached forth and embraced him tightly. He responded in kind. Their encirclement was neither swift nor too long. When they parted, Richard peered over to his cousin, gauging his reaction. Darcy smiled openly and in like manner, he too embraced his cousin, but their clench was of longer duration, with each man lost in the emotion of the moment.

As they parted, they both noticed Elizabeth wiping the tears from her eyes. Richard exclaimed, "News such as this helps to buoy us up during such trying times. I am very delighted for you both. I am looking forward to seeing a little one at Pemberley again."

His genuine sentiment instantly reminded him of Georgiana and a sudden pang seized his heart. Tomorrow night would not come soon enough.

~*~

The anticipated night emerged fresh and chilly. Earlier in the afternoon, black clouds had overshadowed London, threatening a tempest. The downpour did come. For several hours rain pelted angrily against Ackerley's windowpanes. The storm merely served as a metaphor for the turmoil which lay in the hearts of three individuals within that dwelling.

Earlier that morning, the meeting between the Earl, Darcy and his solicitor had ended in heated words and exacting promises. Darcy's uncle turned up his nose to the attorney's warnings. He showed no sign of concern that he was out of boundaries of the law. In fact, the Earl's face displayed an egotistical confidence. He felt certain that his nephew was bluffing in the use of legal redress. Consequently, Darcy had asked his solicitor to wait for him in the carriage while he had a few more words with his uncle.

It was at this time that Darcy informed his uncle about his eldest son's shameful offences towards his wife and himself. He demanded a confession from James and disinheritance from his uncle. The Earl scoffed at Darcy's accusations, claiming that his wife must have used the same arts and allurements on his eldest as she had used on him. Darcy became livid and promised to never speak with him again if he chose to ignore his charge. His uncle waved his hand with indifference, claiming that Darcy was overreacting. Consequently, Darcy swore that he would never set foot in his uncle's homes, and in kind, his uncle, James, and Lady Catherine were to never set foot in Pemberley or Ackerley again. Making his indignation perfectly clear, Darcy vowed that he would thrash Lord Hazelton if he ever came close to his wife or any other member of his family. But if the Earl would hand over his sister, he might find it in his heart to forgive the offences of his cousin, to some degree, if the Viscount would plead guilty, make a written apology to him, and agree to stay away from his wife. Darcy's oaths, however, were merely shrugged off as idle threats. The nephew hastily departed, fully intending to carry out his every word.

Subsequently, that day at Ackerley following the supper hour, Darcy, Elizabeth and Colonel Fitzwilliam reposed in the music room during the thunderstorm. Servants had lit the candles when the clouds overshadowed the rays of the day. The colonel had asked specifically to spend their remaining hours before his departure in this particular room. He desired Elizabeth to play for him, to help soothe his mind and refresh his spirit. He had another motive for asking. To him, this room represented the essence of Georgiana. It was in this very room where he and his dear cousin had spent countless hours frolicking about the piano, challenging each other to speedily contend in silly duets. She had always bested him, but he dearly loved giving it a go just the same, if only to witness the delight that appeared on Georgiana's face as their fingers frantically raced upon the keys.

Darcy had brought a stack of papers from his study to peruse. Richard reclined upon the sofa, stretched out with his arms behind his head, acting as a pillow and one leg extended, resting upon the cushion. His other leg bent lazily over the front of the settee, with his foot tapping lightly against the floor, keeping time with the music that was drifting from the pianoforte which Elizabeth played.

While playing the instrument, Elizabeth would periodically look up. She took note of her husband's handsome, pensive face, as he sat by the fire absorbed in the correspondence of his estate. Earlier, the colonel had made some pretence in perusing *The Times*. Yet, as the minutes ticked away, and melody after melody was performed, Elizabeth observed that he had reclined with the paper haphazardly strewn across his chest. He appeared asleep, save for the faint drumming of his heel.

After having played for more than an hour, Elizabeth again took in the scene before her.

The colonel's foot had stilled, and he now slept soundly. She had no way of knowing that he had fallen into a peaceful slumber with sweet images of Georgiana sitting upon the very bench where she now sat. Elizabeth's vision for the umpteenth time took in her husband's deportment. He studiously continued to open, read, and arrange each communication in an assigned stack. Closing the instrument, Elizabeth quietly rose and stretched her arms to relieve the tension from remaining in the same posture for so long. Turning towards the window, she watched as the rain came down violently in sheets.

Suddenly, from behind, Darcy's arm's encircled her waist, and he softly whispered into her ear, "You have lulled Fitzwilliam to sleep."

Turning to look upon his face, she met his affectionate smile. Then in a low voice he entreated, "Come, we shall let him rest."

They crept from the room and waited together in the privacy of their chamber for the sluggish hour of departure to arrive. They sought solace from one another as their arms and limbs were intertwined, generating warmth and security, momentarily easing the anxiety from their hearts and minds.

~*~

The rain had stopped before nine, turning the air quite cold. Colonel Fitzwilliam's small satchel was filled with a few belongings for Georgiana since the shrouded night sky foreshadowed another squall. Darcy had Elizabeth's maid, Sarah, prepare a dress, stockings, nightgown, and a few other necessities for his sister.

While Sarah prepared the items to be bundled inside an oilcloth, Mrs. Darcy entered her sister-in-law's chamber carrying a starched nightshirt belonging to Mr. Darcy. "Here Sarah," Elizabeth motioned for her maid to take the folded shirt, "add this to the bundle."

After the items were wrapped, Elizabeth took the package downstairs to the courtyard. Darcy and Richard were by the west gate next to the stables. It was a half hour before midnight.

Due to the detainment of the trial of Mr. Hibbs at the Old Bailey, Darcy was not able to go and collect his sister himself. Immediately on the morrow, he had to testify in front of judge and jury. Furthermore, Darcy had been fearful to leave Elizabeth alone knowing that his relatives would more than likely pounce on Ackerley with their discovery of Georgiana's escape. Therefore, Colonel Fitzwilliam and Darcy had enlisted the Dr. Lowry's help.

Darcy felt if Richard was able to rescue Georgiana, it would be best for them to leave London on horseback, reasoning that this was the quickest means of removal, and thus the plans were made. Dr. Lowry was to meet Colonel Fitzwilliam at the cottage on Mr. Samuelson's estate in two hours' time. The doctor, personally, would then transport Miss Darcy with the escort of Mrs. Annesley to his grandparents' home in Derbyshire. Darcy and Elizabeth would hopefully follow them in one day's time.

Richard took the parcel from Elizabeth, placed it into his saddlebag, and then bowed to her and tipped his hat. He was dressed in uniform. Afterward, the two cousins walked to the gate and clasped one another with Richard promising to return to Ackerley as soon as possible. A carriage was also to be deployed a block away from Blackwell, in case some unforeseen needs were to arise during the endeavour.

Attaching the satchel he carried to his saddle, Richard swung up upon his horse and made his way to the back alley and through the streets of Mayfair.

~*~

As Nancy brushed her mistress' hair, Miss Darcy's countenance appeared overcast. She was to leave early in the morning for Bath with her Aunt Catherine and Cousin Anne. When the maid completed her task, she told Miss Darcy that all was prepared for their departure. Georgiana thanked her and then dismissed her services.

Staring at her reflection in the mirror, Georgiana nervously mused about her future. *Surely, Fitzwilliam will come for me. Why has he not come? He must come!*

She knew she needed rest, but ever since her cousin had barged in on her the day before, she felt frightened and had been unable to sleep. With James's sinister words still ringing in her head, every noise during the night had awakened her in a fright.

Due to the ghastly bruise Lord Hazelton wore, Georgiana imagined that her brother had come for her, and when James refused to oblige him, Fitzwilliam must have struck him. She had never seen her brother do such a thing before, but she felt it was very possible that he would do so in connection to her safety and future. He had always been unwavering in her care and protection. *Surely, he will come!*

The crinkled letter lay on the vanity-top. She began to pick it up to take with her to bed when she decided to don her robe once more, and before retiring for the night, take one last peek outside her door. Slowly, she opened it. To her utter amazement, for the first time in days, no servant was stationed across the hall. Instantly, she dashed back over to the vanity and picked up the letter, placing it in her pocket and then grabbed her slippers. Even in the darkness of the night, she was positive that she could make her way from Blackwell to Ackerley.

Anxiously, Georgiana once more opened the door only to find Lord Hazelton standing in front of her. Fear gripped her throat while her heart raced wildly. "Now, now Georgie, where are you off to in such a hurry?"

"Get out of my way. I want to go home!"

"We have been over this before, dear cousin. Now turn around and be a good girl."

With all her might, Georgiana attempted to squeeze beyond her cousin, yet he pinned her against the threshold, immuring her back within her chamber.

Once the door was shut, both cousins stared at the other. Georgiana's eyes confronted James's with reproach. Within his, she witnessed a burning flame of malice—a hatred so deep she could not fathom it.

Unexpectedly, Lord Hazelton took Georgiana's arm and twisted it behind her back. She cried out only to have her wail silenced. Gruffly, he gagged her mouth and tied her hands behind her back in a matter of seconds and then forcefully shoved her upon the bed. Georgiana's chest heaved violently in anger as she lay there in a prone position. Lying down beside her, he whispered balefully into her ear, "Calm thyself, my dear, dear cousin. I want no harm to come to you. You will thank me someday, for I am certain that you do not want to be leg shackled to the portly gentleman that Aunt Catherine has in mind for you."

Georgiana's face remained flushed and her breathing was laboured as she continued to struggle in an effort to free her hands. Pressing his lips against her ear, he stated, "Just cooperate my dear girl. Do not fight it. It will be over soon enough and in the morning Ashton will be found with you. Therefore, your marriage to him will be secured. Lady Catherine may even take you straightaway to Rosings to have her clergyman perform the honours! They would not want you living in sin for too long."

Georgiana's eyes dilated in horror from the lewd implication of her cousin's words. The Viscount read the terrified look upon her face. Slowly, his lips curled into a sensuous smile.

Leisurely, he got off the bed and walked to the door. With one backward glance, he took in his cousin's dishevelled state and smiled all the more before leaving the room.

In no time, the door opened again and Ashton Caldecott entered the chamber most reluctantly.

~*~

At the stroke of midnight, the colonel approached the exterior window of his parents' townhouse which belonged to their cook Edie. Resting against the wall which faced the courtyard, Richard leaned sideways to gently tap upon the glass. No sooner had he commenced to rap, when a soft voice caught his attention from the shrubs along the trellis. Quickly, the colonel dashed across the lawn to the shrubbery. There Edie stood awaiting him.

"I would hug you, my boy, but there is no time to waste. My sister, Doris, who is a cook for your brother, is waiting for you outside of Blackwell by the cellar. She has a key, and she will take you up the servants' stairs to Miss Darcy's chamber. Tie your horse in the alley. Please be careful and fleeting, for there is a footman at that residence that makes the rounds every thirty minutes till the wee hours of the morning. Here, take this." She handed him a small bundle.

Instantly, the colonel retrieved two letters from his breast pocket and handed them to the woman. "Edie, please send these as soon as possible. One is to Mother. Please make sure she receives it personally from your hand when she is alone. And by George, Edie, there is time for a hug!" Wrapping his strong arms around the stout woman, Richard lifted her in the air, squeezing her tightly while exclaiming, "I love you, Edie!" When he placed her feet back upon the ground he recognized that she was pleasantly flustered as she shooed him away with her hand. On the wings of a prayer, she watched her favourite darling go with a heavy heart.

~*~

As the door shut behind Ashton, the young man took in Miss Darcy's tousled appearance.

The side of her face was turned towards him. He easily perceived the anger that raged in her eyes.

After a moment's hesitation, Ashton crossed the room and began to untie her hands. "Georgiana, um, I mean, Miss Darcy, believe me when I tell you that I want nothing to do with this. I shall not carry out your cousin's plan. I have no desire to harm you in any fashion. You know I care too much for you."

Immediately when her hands were free, Georgiana began to tug at the gag around her mouth. When she could not manage to undo the knot, Ashton again reached forth and untied it for her.

Breathlessly, she spit out, "How dare you, Mr. Caldecott!"

"Miss Darcy, I will leave this moment, but your cousin is determined. He has his valet watching the hall as we speak and another servant in the kitchen to man the servants' passages. I do not want you this way, Georgiana. I wish you to *want* to marry me, and you know that. I thought I made that perfectly clear to you at the Millbank's gathering. I love you!"

As she sat up, she cried, "Well, if this is love, you have a fine way of exhibiting it!"

He knelt down by the bed and said, "Truly, I have striven to reason with Hazelton. Yet, he insists that Lady Catherine is determined to have you married off to that repellent and decrepit Mr. Delbert Puttfarken."

Georgiana eyed Ashton suspiciously before asking, "Is that truly his name?"

Looking her straight in the eye, Ashton nodded as he said, "Most assuredly!"

He noticed a twinkle of sorts in Miss Darcy's eyes, and he witnessed her struggle while she attempted to bite back the grin beginning to overtake her lips. With a slight giggle she cried, "Oh! That is a dreadful name!"

Ashton likewise smiled in agreement. When their mirth departed, their gazes locked, and for some seconds they stared deeply at each other.

When Georgiana became self-conscious of their intimacy, she blushed hotly. Instantly, she averted her gaze and began to pull at her hair.

Mesmerized, Ashton watched her as she ran her fingers through her golden tresses, trying to brush it away from her heated face. She stopped her actions when she discerned his absorbed look. At that moment she instinctively knew he was telling the truth. He did love her.

Exasperated, she asked, "Ashton, why are you friends with James if he abuses you so?"

His eyes looked imploringly into hers, hoping that she would understand and find it in her heart to forgive him. "I will be honest with you, Georgiana. I have not always been the gentleman that I should be. Yet, I have had a change of heart due to you. You have given me the desire to better myself. I love and need you! Cannot you find it in your heart to allow me to prove myself to you? I will wait for however long you need."

As he put forth his petition, Georgiana's eyes were drawn to his, and her heart ached

Mr. Caldecott thought Miss Darcy's eyes were celestial! He could not believe that she continued to gaze upon him as he knelt before her. He greatly desired to take her hand in his and kiss it, yet he was loath to do so, fearful that she might reject him.

Unbeknownst to the couple, Mr. Caldecott had more to fear than Georgiana's adverse reaction to having her hand fondled and kissed. Suddenly, something pointed pressed towards the inside of his back. The pain was intense. Automatically, the young man slowly lifted his arms and held them outward into the air.

Georgiana's eyes lifted concurrently with the peculiar movement of Ashton's arms. Pure, unadulterated joy overtook her senses and radiated from her face as her eyes raised and set upon a well-known face, yet she did not make a sound. With a firm finger upon his lips, Colonel Fitzwilliam silently indicated for her to remain mute while he levelled the tip of his sabre between Ashton Caldecott's shoulder blades.

~*~

Chapter Thirty

Temptation's Embrace

Colonel Fitzwilliam had no time to waste. Instantly, he commanded in a steely, yet low voice, for Mr. Caldecott to rise. Without a moment's hesitation, Ashton did as he was told. He kept his hands away from his body as he ascended slowly from his knees. He was acutely aware of the pointed tip of the colonel's sword which had cut through his clothing and punctured his flesh.

"Turn to look at me!" the colonel stated resolutely to Mr. Caldecott. "I want you to see what is coming. Though stealth aided my advance, there shall be none in my execution."

When confronting the colonel directly, Ashton's face drained of all colour. He swallowed hard, but remained speechless as Colonel Fitzwilliam redirected the tip of his sabre upon the younger man's chest. The colonel and Mr. Caldecott stared upon one another, the former narrowly and the latter openly.

Richard stated evenly, "I would take great pleasure, Mr. Caldecott, to first vivisect you, then disembowel you, and finally, sever you limb from limb. But seeing that I am hard-pressed for time, I shall have to be merely satisfied in running you through."

Wide-eyed by her cousin's threat, Georgiana instantly cried out as she sprung from the bed, boldly standing in front of Ashton, and determinedly gripping the blade of the sword before challenging her cousin. "If you kill him, you shall gash open my palm while doing so. I shall not flinch! I mean it, Richard. I shall not allow you to steep your hands in his blood. If you do, you shall contend with the drenching of my own as well."

She beheld the flaring of Richard's nostrils and felt his burning anger. He did not look at her, but he was mindful of her interference all the same. The colonel's piercing vision was levelled at the worthless young man before him.

"Move your hand, Georgie."

"No! I shall not! Ashton has not come to harm me. Your brother is the culprit. James sent him to... to... but he has not touched me whatsoever. Instead, Ashton has freed me from James's binding. Look on the bed, and you shall see the swathes of cloth."

For only an instant did the colonel avert his gaze to the bed, beholding the loosened bindings before glaring at Ashton once again.

Imploringly, Georgiana cried, "I beg of you, Richard, cease! Let us go now while there is time!"

Richard knew her reasoning to be sound. Time was of the essence. Yet, he could not for the life of him, abide Ashton's perfidious ways.

"Very well, Georgie," Richard stated coolly as he continued to stare at Mr. Caldecott, "we shall go without shedding blood, but first, I must tie and gag this man if we are to flee successfully."

Ashton finally spoke. "Colonel Fitzwilliam, I assure you I will tell no one of your getaway. I want Miss Darcy to return to her brother as much as you do."

"Do remain silent! Now, Georgie, go and retrieve the rags and bring them to me."

Her brow creased. "How shall I know that you will not kill him when I step away?"

Continuing to look at Ashton, Richard replied to her query. "You shall know the way you have always known. Have I ever told you a falsehood?"

"No." She immediately removed her hand while gazing into her cousin's face and then quickly did his bidding.

With alacrity, Richard withdrew his sword from Mr. Caldecott's chest and put the weapon back in the sheath by his side.

Ashton closed his eyes and gasped for air at the colonel's retreat. He willingly brought his hands together and held them forward, in expectation for the colonel's binding.

Richard rolled his eyes derisively at Ashton's gestured gaffe, and gruffly spun him around to tie his hands behind his back. He then gagged and pushed him upon the bed to likewise bind his feet. Georgiana felt sympathy for Mr. Caldecott. Therefore, she whispered her apologies to him before turning her full attention to her cousin.

A sudden wave of relief came over Ashton as he watched them go through the dressing room to the servants' passage. He was hopeful for the success of their attempted escape and grateful for the colonel's coup. Lord Hazelton could in nowise blame him for his brother's victory, and therefore, his friend need never know of his refusal to compromise Miss Darcy's virtue.

~*~

An unexpected gush of cold air assaulted Georgiana when she stepped outside of the townhouse, shocking her at the sudden turn of weather. The blustery breeze penetrated through her thin robe and gown causing tiny goose bumps to quicken and multiply upon her flesh. Lightning flashed above in the blackened sky, brightly displaying a boiling cauldron of dark clouds which threatened a downpour at any given moment, while intermittent rumblings attested to the fact that a storm was indeed nigh. The pair ran with all their might through the courtyard towards the back alley where the colonel's mount waited, tied to the wrought iron fence. Anxiety etched Richard's brow. He held firmly to Georgiana's arm as they rushed forth, slipping into the night through the dark alleyways.

Edie's sister had arranged for Nancy to be taken to the Darcy's carriage which waited a block away. The maid would then be immediately transported back to Ackerley. He was certain that the carriage had already departed due to the alarming scene which greeted them in the kitchen as he and Georgiana made their getaway. The colonel looked to the left and then to the right. Doris and Nancy were nowhere in sight.

With the approach of such violent weather, Colonel Fitzwilliam debated whether he should abandon the original plan of going to Mr. Samuelson's cottage, and instead go straight to Ackerley? Yet, Richard knew Darcy wanted Georgiana out of London and well on her way to Pemberley as soon as possible. He and Darcy had anticipated rainfall, but nothing like the magnitude of the looming storm. The wind increased in intensity. It heaved sighs in low, steady moans, generating an ambiance of eeriness to their already terrifying flight.

When the colonel and Georgiana reached his horse, he shouted breathlessly over the clamorous gales, "I assure you, Georgie, I shall not let you fall."

"I am not afraid," she cried through chattering teeth. Her hair waved wildly about her head as she stood still, looking into the colonel's eyes. "I am fine!" In anticipation of being lifted, she placed her hands upon Richard's shoulders. He held up his hands, indicating for her to wait. Thus, she withdrew her hands from him. Quickly, he took off his cape, and wrapped it around her. Then effortlessly, he raised her onto the charger, swung up behind her and decisively spurred the animal onward to the darkening outskirts of London.

~*~

On Oxford Street, at Holborn, in the northern section of London, Dr. Lowry, accompanied by Mrs. Annesley, had just begun their journey when the most fearsome downpour either had ever experienced broke loose. The shower blinded the horses, causing the doctor to immediately abandon their pursuit and turn back for safety. He assured Georgiana's former lady's companion that they would set out again as soon as the weather became permissible. The older woman nodded eagerly in agreement. A storm such as this was not to be reckoned with. What good could they do for her young miss if they were killed on the streets of London?

~*~

A few miles away from Mr. Samuelson's cottage, the rain unleashed without mercy. At the first sign of droplets, Georgiana cried out that she needed Richard's headdress. He willingly gave it to her. She reached into the cloak to the depths of her robe's pocket and retrieved her precious letter. She put the folded paper within the crown and placed the cap upon her head, keeping one hand firmly upon it. Satisfied, she snuggled close to Richard, content that her letter was safe.

The colonel imagined it was his missive she had preserved from the rain, but at that moment his anger returned full force, robbing him of any delight that he might have taken in Georgiana's sentimental act.

When the rain began to relentlessly sting their faces, Richard was able to offset the mounting frustration he felt by unconsciously replacing it with a true concern for their health and wellbeing. They were becoming drenched, and he estimated that they had at least a mile to go before coming to the cottage. Once more, he kicked the horse to hurry forward.

Were it not for the colonel's expertise in military logistics, he and Georgiana would have likely strayed aimlessly in the onslaught of the storm. Richard was gifted with a keen sense of direction, and despite the decreased visibility from the heavy rainfall, he mentally calculated the exact location of the cottage.

With alacrity, he dismounted, secured the horse, reached for Georgiana, and then carried her into the lodging. The wind continued to howl fiercely while thunder boomed in the distance and lightening intermittently flashed.

Once inside, Richard placed Georgiana upon her feet and silently began to search for candles. She patiently waited, neither said a word. In no time, a fire was started and the tapers were lit, illuminating the tidy room.

Georgiana inspected the expanse before her. There was a full bed neatly prepared with abundant blankets, sheets and pillows. She then saw a small table off to one side with a pitcher set in the centre and three chairs surrounding it. The mantlepiece was empty apart from the burning candles within their holders. Below, to the side of the hearth, there was adequate kindling in a box and an empty pail beside the pile. Without any adornments except for the ewer, the room appeared sparse but clean.

After her eyes had inspected the room, they fell back upon Richard's figure as he crouched in front of the small blaze adding more fuel to the hungry flames. She noticed the puddle on the floor caused by the excess from his waterlogged uniform. Instinctively she looked down at her own feet, and in like manner, water had pooled around her saturated slippers.

Her head shot up when Richard spoke. He was now standing, and in a decisive manner, he stated, "We must get you out of your wet clothing and into something dry as soon as possible. Come and stand by the fire while I go to retrieve my satchel."

Georgiana did not move a muscle but just looked at him. Both stood motionless staring at the other for several moments. Even though both were dripping wet, resembling drowned sewer rats, neither cared. In those few minutes, more was communicated than the immediate concern for their precarious state. The firelight cast a glow upon Georgiana's face, allowing the colonel to see her every feature, from her blonde brows beneath the rim of his shako to her full, cherry lips. Similarly, Georgiana took in Richard's physique while in his sodden regimentals. The dampness only enhanced his appeal as the droplets rolled off his hair, onto his flesh, and continued to trickle downward upon the length of his jaw line and neck before perishing within the confines of his clothing. Each felt an undeniable magnetism for the other, and both were well aware that they were feeling it jointly.

It was all Richard could do to tear his eyes away from her, but he noticed the quivering of her lips and came back to reason. "Come. Let us get you out of that wet cape."

The trembling of her mouth should have been in direct relation to the fact that until now, she was standing in the middle of a frigid room in wet clothing. On the contrary, Georgiana had ample heat from other sources warming her to the very core and affecting her shivering orifice. As Georgiana drew near him, Richard noticed her pink tongue moisten her bottom lip before her teeth raked over its plumpness. The colonel inhaled deeply and then heaved a sigh. If the rain did not let up, he and Georgiana were destined to spend the remainder of the night unchaperoned, and quite alone in close quarters. Richard had fought many battles and endured many deprivations connected to war, but hours all alone in the company of the woman whom he desired was a conflict he was afraid to confront. He would rather face Napoleon's army with a contingent of only ten men.

~*~

Exactly one hour following midnight, the Darcy carriage pulled into the back alley behind Ackerley. The footmen helped two women emerge, and then provided the protection of umbrellas as the ladies made their way to the front of the house, past the fence, through the wrought-iron gate, and down the steep flight of steps into the service entrance on the right. They made their way upon the flagstone floor and down the narrow hall to the kitchen, passing the wine cellar, washing room, china pantry, servants' stairs, meat larder, and pantry as they advanced.

When entering the kitchen they were met by the butler, Mr. Coates, who sat at one of the long tables with a cup of tea in front of him. He instantly arose as the women entered. He was surprised, especially at this hour in the morning, to see the young Miss' maid, Nancy, with another woman whom he did not recognize. "Why, Miss Erikson," the butler exclaimed, "has Miss Darcy returned?"

Breathlessly, Nancy answered, "No, Mr. Coates. Is Mr. Darcy awake perchance? I feel I must speak with him immediately."

The elderly gentleman started at the urgency in the maid's voice. "Why, I do believe he is. Shall I go and tell him you are here?"

"Yes, please do. Ask if I may have a moment of his time."

The man nodded and tottered away as quickly as his legs could carry him. He headed for the master's study.

In no time, Nancy and her companion were being ushered into the study. In a tense manner, the master stood whilst the women walked through the threshold and Mr. Coates closed the door behind them. Elizabeth witnessed the worry upon her husband's brow. Moments before, when the butler had informed them about Nancy's return and her desire to speak with him, Darcy had become elated with the news, but while waiting for the maid to appear, his elation soon turned to anxiety.

Gesturing with his hand for the ladies to sit, Darcy said, "Ah, Miss Barnes, I am glad to see you again, and I am happy that you have both arrived safely. Elizabeth, this is Miss Doris Barnes. She is the sister to Miss Edie Barnes, who is the cook for my aunt and uncle. Miss Barnes, this is my wife Mrs. Darcy."

Elizabeth, who was also standing, smiled to the woman and expressed her happiness in making her acquaintance. The ladies then sat, but, Darcy chose to remain standing.

He looked earnestly at both women before him. "Please, can you tell me if my sister has been removed from the house?"

Doris spoke first. "Colonel Fitzwilliam came through the gate and met me in the area by the servants' entrance as my sister had informed him to do. I then took him down the hall to the servants' staircase and told him precisely which way to go before we climbed it together. Previously, he had told me a carriage from Ackerley waited a block away on Margaret Street, and he felt I should try to get Nancy out while he retrieved the young miss. We had planned to meet in the kitchen and leave the house together through the back door, around the mews, and then through the alley. But, when Nancy and I came down, Jack, the footman making the rounds, asked what we were about. I told him that Miss Darcy was hungry and wanted something to eat, so I was preparing a little something for her maid to take to the Miss. He then sat himself down, saying he would wait for us to gather up the fare. I'm fearful I may have killed him, Mr. Darcy, for he just sat there while I feigned to make up a tray. I knew we had no time for his interference, and if the colonel were to come down with Miss Darcy, we would be done for. I don't know what came over me. I whacked him from behind with a heavy skillet. He went out cold. Neither Nancy nor I checked to see if he were dead. That is why I am here. I don't know what I will do if he's dead. I know Lord Hazelton will be furious when all is discovered, and I shall more than likely be hung in the gallows. Nancy and I didn't wait around after that. We were too frightened."

Darcy sensed that the woman was distraught and her account only heightened his own anxiety. He looked to Nancy, and she began to speak.

"I wish I were able to tell you more, Mr. Darcy, but I had been roused from a sound sleep by Doris. The last I saw your sister was in her chamber before retiring. She has been unhappy lately, and I presumed it was because we were to leave with Lady Catherine for Bath. Miss Darcy had not confided in me concerning any of the strange circumstances of late, and I have never been one to pry. I love her dearly, but I would never dream of interfering with her privacy."

"Strange circumstances?" Darcy questioned.

"Yes sir, your cousin, the Viscount, has had your sister and me followed by a servant at all times with the exception of when we were in our chambers. Miss Georgiana would not dress for the day since she had no desire to venture from her room. Servants had been stationed in the hall and servants' passages. I was not sure why, but I had reasoned we were under house arrest. I had been informed that we were leaving for Bath soon, and then this morning, I was given orders to have our trunks packed before going to bed, since we would commence our journey early in the morning. Furthermore, I am concerned for Miss Darcy's health. She has eaten very little for the past few days."

"I am sorry for all you have endured, Nancy. I assure you that you shall never again have to go to Blackwell. So neither of you saw Colonel Fitzwilliam leave with my sister?"

The women shook their heads glumly.

"Ah, well the night is still young!" Darcy exclaimed. Doris and Nancy exchanged sidelong glances. Both women sensed Mr. Darcy's disappointment despite his attempt to sound optimistic.

Mr. Darcy gave Miss Barnes his assurance of protection and offered her employment either at Pemberley or at Ackerley, if she desired it. With the fear that she had just murdered a man, she opted for the former. Therefore, she would accompany Sarah, Nancy and Mr. Chaffin to Pemberley on the morrow. Doris wanted to be removed as far away from London as she possibly could.

After Nancy and Doris departed, Darcy turned to Elizabeth.

"I suppose we shall have to wait for Fitzwilliam's arrival, but I fear he shall be forestalled due to the inclement weather. Lizzy, have I judged unwisely by pressing him to take Georgiana out of town?"

Elizabeth could hear the strain in his voice as he questioned his reasoning. "Fitzwilliam, your plan was sound. You felt that having the carriage come here and the colonel go elsewhere might give them the advantage. The colonel even agreed that it was a good strategy. I am sure Richard has everything in control. Surely in the army he has dealt with covert undertakings in tempestuous conditions. All will be well, my love."

Darcy fixed his eyes upon her face, wanting to believe her affirmation and thereby take comfort in her conviction. It was true. His cousin was a skilled officer. Even when they were mere lads running the fields of Pemberley and Matlock, Richard had the edge in many of their pursuits. Memories of their boyhood days began to flood his mind and a small smile started to materialize upon his lips.

After several minutes, Elizabeth softly asked, "Fitzwilliam, you seem worlds away. I gather that you are thinking happy thoughts?"

Affectionately, he made eye contact with her once more and stated, "Yes, I was recalling when Richard and I would fish in the stream at Pemberley in our youth. His favourite mode of catching a fish was with his bare hands." Darcy chuckled and then continued. "He would stand very still for what seemed forever, patiently waiting for the precise moment to launch his attack upon the scaly prey. Inevitably, he would catch more in an hour's time, than I could angle with my hook and line."

Elizabeth smiled warmly and then stood and held out her hand to her husband. "I think I shall retire now. Please join me. You really do need some rest before the trial in the morning. Mr. Coates can awake us when Richard returns."

Arising from his chair, Darcy took her hand in his, grasping it tightly. "You are right, Lizzy. It will not do having the witness fall asleep while in the witness box."

For the time being, Darcy's reflections had brought him some comfort and relieved his troubled mind. Moreover, basking in the warm refuge of his wife's arms, he drifted off to sleep, completely banishing any restlessness which remained.

~*~

Standing directly in front of Richard, Georgiana looked downward and observed the slight shaking of his gloveless hands as they unfastened the clasp of the cape and she noticed that he swallowed hard while taking it from her shoulders. Expressively, her eyes met his and she whispered, "Thank you for coming for me."

Richard looked intently into her eyes and merely nodded. Georgiana could tell that something was not right. He seemed troubled. "Richard, what is wrong?"

His lips parted as if he were about to speak, but before saying a word, he closed them just as rapidly. Georgiana's brow furrowed.

Hastily, Richard looked away and called out while walking towards the table, "I shall put your wet things in front of the fire on these chairs." He carried two chairs in one arm and one in the other. Placing them by the fire, he situated them and then draped his cape over the back of one of them. "I shall be back in a flash."

"Richard?"

Before she had an opportunity to say another word, he was out the door. She was not certain if he had heard her, or if he desired to even speak at all. *He is acting so oddly.*

She did not have long to wait. True to his word, he re-entered the cottage, advanced to the fire and with the corner of the cape, wiped off the water from the leather bag. Not once did the colonel look at his cousin. She, in contrast, continually watched his every movement.

With quick steps, Richard strode over to the bed, opened the satchel, and unfolded the oilcloth. His eyes went wide in astonishment when holding up a man's shirt. Immediately, his vision reverted back to the stack that lay on the bed. Carefully, he examined the remaining items. There was a comb, the small bundle Edie had given him, some stockings, a blue dress and corset, and a lady's nightgown. Before turning around, his vision swung back to the comb and lingered upon it. Suddenly, his face crumbled in pain, and he closed his eyes tightly.

Georgiana waited patiently by the fire, wondering what was taking her cousin so long.

"Richard, is everything well?"

Nodding, with his back still turned, he replied in a husky voice, "Yes."

Spinning about on his heel, he moved to where she stood and placed her nightgown upon the seat of the chair.

He looked at her and stated in a detached manner, "I shall go outside to fill up the pitcher and wait for you to change. There is not another robe or slippers, only a dress, stockings, corset, and comb."

"Richard, what is the matter? You are not your usual self. Have I done something to upset you?"

"The only thing that will upset me at this moment is any further delay in getting you out of your wet gown." Again, he spun around to fetch the container from the table. After that, he hurriedly departed.

Georgiana expelled a small huff of air in irritation as she began to remove her robe and nightgown. They fell heavily to the floor. Before donning the dry gown, she tilted her head to the side, away from her body and wrung out the moisture from her hair. Her body was still damp, so she crossed over to the bed to retrieve a slip-cover from one of the pillows and hurriedly patted herself dry the best she could. Then she went back in front of the fire and slipped her gown over her head. The door opened as she was bending over to pick up the wet articles remaining on the floor.

The illumination generated from the fire shone through the fabric of Georgiana's thin gown. It radiated a silhouette of her shapely legs that instantly greeted the colonel on his re-emergence.

Richard literally stopped in his tracks and silently groaned while gripping the pitcher tighter than before. *Heavens! How shall I last through the night?*

Hearing his return, Georgiana quickly turned and exclaimed, "I have hung up my things. Now you need to remove your wet clothing as well, or you shall catch your death."

Instantly she realized Richard was blushing as he averted his gaze. Without saying a word, he crossed the room and set the pitcher on the table. Georgiana stared at him in deliberation. She too crossed the room and sat on the bed. Looking down, she noticed her clothing. Gingerly, she gathered up the items and placed them upon the floor. She also set the satchel beside her own belongings. While doing so, she noticed the shirt on top of the stack. "Richard, here is a shirt for you to wear."

Turning to look at her once more, Richard shook his head and stated as he leaned against the table, "I shall sleep by the fire and dry out there."

"Richard Fitzwilliam, you shall do no such thing. I insist that you change out of your uniform, and if you do not, then I shall take off my gown at once and don my wet one!"

He glared at her. "My goodness, Georgiana, you have become quite forthright as of late."

The sound of his voice alarmed her. It was not his customary, playful tone. Pensively, she gazed upon his face.

They were at an impasse.

"Very well," Georgiana cried as she stood, "I shall be true to my word."

Boldly, she walked over to the chairs and turned her back while she began to reach for the hem of her gown. "You had better turn away...." Suddenly, from behind, she felt two strong hands grip her shoulders.

"Stop it this instant! I shall not kowtow to your every whim, Georgiana."

She froze in place. Richard had never before spoken so harshly to her or touched her in such a way. Both silently stood for what seemed an eternity to Georgiana. Richard's hands remained on her shoulders, but his fingertips no longer pressed into her flesh. Instead, they rested without a single finger moving a muscle.

Finally, still facing her back, he stated mulishly, "Georgie, go to bed at once!"

Georgiana gulped and willed herself to hold back the tears which threatened to spill at any given moment. With a quivering voice, she begged, "What have I done to deserve your cold heartedness? Do you no longer love or desire me?"

Her question cut Richard to the bone. He gasped aloud and immediately removed his hands as he backed away.

"Please!" he cried, "we must rest before Dr. Lowry arrives."

Georgiana turned to look towards him.

Richard witnessed the tears streaming down her cheeks, but he felt torn. One part of him desired to scoop her up within his arms and lovingly reassure her of his undying devotion, but the other part wanted to lash out at her and berate her blossoming friendship with Ashton Caldecott.

"Richard, you have never spoken to me thus. Pray, I beg you, tell me what is wrong. You have always been frank and honest with me. It is one of your many attributes that I cherish. Please do not spurn me. We have little time. Do not part from me in this cold manner."

The colonel's chest heaved with emotion. He looked intently into her saddened eyes and said, "Georgie, you may not fancy what I have to say."

She squinted in scrutiny and exclaimed stoutly, "The hellish experience I have just endured has enabled me to face anything. It is the unknown concerning you that I cannot bear."

"Very well, I shall tell you what is wrong with me. For the first time in my life I am very disconcerted with you. I warned you not to have anything to do with Mr. Caldecott and before I know it, you dance with him incessantly, dine with him engagingly, smile to him warmly, and now, you are on a first name basis with that fiend. By chance, are you engaged to him?"

Georgiana's mouth hung open wide. "Richard, this is preposterous. You are jealous for nothing. I should be insulted that you would even think I have entered into an engagement when you know I have pledged my heart to you. *No*, I am not engaged to him."

"Then why did you call him by his first name?"

In frustration, she gasped. "I cannot believe this, and from you of all people. I have no idea why I called him by his given name, perhaps because he was calling me by mine." *Oh, that was not the wisest thing to say.* "Truly, this cannot be the only reason you are this disturbed?"

"No, the other reason is because you stopped me from rightfully killing him."

"Richard Fitzwilliam! I cannot believe my ears. I told you that Ashton, um…, Mr. Caldecott is not to blame. How can you be so cruel to me?"

An interval of silence followed her question.

With all his might, Richard strove to regain some composure. This was not like him. He hated what he was doing to her and to himself.

Georgiana conveyed coolly, "Uncle Selwyn and Aunt Catherine informed me that due to my damaged reputation from Ramsgate, no reputable man would wish for my hand in marriage. Therefore, they maintained that a marriage should be arranged post haste, with Mr. Delbert Puttfarken and Mr. Ashton Caldecott the prime candidates for my hand. Mr. Puttfarken's wife died without producing his required heir. Apparently, at my ball he took a fancy to me and spoke with your father about my suitability in bearing children and the size of my dowry."

Richard's mouth became dry. What a fool he had been.

"On the other hand," Georgiana continued while staring directly into the colonel's face, "Ashton Caldecott declared to your brother that he is in love with me and desires to marry me. It is true, you did warn me to stay away from him, but he has been at all times affable and kind towards me, never crossing the bounds of propriety."

In sincerity, Richard gently asked, "Georgie, do you not feel that he has crossed those boundaries tonight?"

"Richard, he was forced by your brother to enter my chamber. I never knew that James could be so cruel. I have never really known James until recently. I pity his poor soul."

Surprise marked Richard's face. "You pity him?"

"Yes, he is a miserable creature who possesses neither heart nor soul."

He nodded with her assessment, but not with her compassion. No, he could not grant pity to Hazelton. Retribution was the only sensation which surged through the chambers of the colonel's unforgiving heart. Mercy had long since departed.

Tenderly, he entreated, "Please continue, Georgie."

"I shall if you will please remove your soaked clothing and change into the nightshirt."

"Georgiana, it would not be proper."

"Richard, I am beyond worrying over what does and does not appear proper. Propriety be damned!"

"Well, I for one do, and I know deep down that you do also. Your brother cares too. We need not help George Wickham's vicious rumours along."

"George? Oh, I am sure it was Caroline Bingley that let it out. George Wickham was going back to Newcastle."

"Newcastle? You have seen George Wickham?" Richard's shock was apparent.

Rolling her eyes at his reaction, she stated, "There is a simple explanation."

"I do hope so, Georgiana, for you are full of surprises of late."

"Richard, please do not start up in that tone again." She then proceeded to tell him every detail concerning her fortuitous meeting with Mr. Wickham on Bond Street.

At the end of her account, the colonel threw up his hands in exasperation. "Georgie, you amaze me! Why were you sampling brandy? Never mind, I already know. One aspect, however, which I am not certain, is how Caroline Bingley knows about Ramsgate and why you suspect that she is the snitch?"

Thus, Georgiana gave another lengthy narration to her cousin, detailing Elizabeth's disclosure to Miss Bingley. She also informed him that Caroline had asked her to never divulge the communication since Fitzwilliam and Elizabeth's marriage was in grave danger.

The colonel gave out a low steady whistle at the end of her account and then his cousin added, "I am not angry with Elizabeth. I remember the time well. Fitzwilliam was acting abominably rude and seemed more concerned over Miss Caldecott than his own wife. I was saddened by the fact that Elizabeth shared something so private, but considering the pressure she was feeling from the blackmail, I suppose she broke down in a moment of weakness and chose not to alarm me. I must confess, I would have never dreamt that Lizzy would confide in Caroline Bingley, of all people!"

"Yes... I find it hard to believe myself, in fact, so much so, that I do not believe Miss Bingley's account at all. I am positive she acquired the information from some other source. Additionally, you are more than likely correct in your assumption that Miss Bingley divulged it, and it would not take a fool to guess to whom she bleated."

"At first, I was not sure how it had leaked out. I assumed it was Wickham, but since then, I have had much time for reflection, and I am certain Miss Bingley must have told Elisha."

"You shot the arrow in the mark!"

"But Richard, if Elizabeth did not tell Miss Bingley, then who did?"

"I am not sure, but I am certain it will not take too much to convince that woman what is in her best interest."

Georgiana's lips twisted in merriment as she slowly rose from the bed.

Richard chuckled at her delight, and then just as suddenly his mind became thoughtful. She had been through so much, he could hardly imagine that she had any smiles remaining. Ramsgate had almost crippled her, but somewhere along the way, Georgiana had gained a fortitude unsurpassed. He marvelled at her resilience. *Oh, how I love you, my sweet Georgie!*

All of Georgiana's imaginings pertaining to Caroline's imminent scolding vanished as she perceived Richard's intense gaze. They were standing several paces apart. Yet the reply to her previous, heartfelt question was now being answered within the colonel's eyes. She could feel the depth of his adoration. Yes, he still loved and desired her.

Their eyes were transfixed on each other. Then instinctively, Richard's sight began to slowly take in the length of her neck and the bareness of her collarbone before arresting upon her pleasing form beneath the delicate fabric of her close-fitting gown.

Georgiana flushed furiously under his inspection, but she welcomed it all the same. When the colonel came out of his trance, his eyes instantly met a reddened face staring back at him. Quickly averting his gaze, he ducked his head, coughed, and then shifted from foot to foot even as his complexion adopted its own rosy hue. *Good, gracious heavens! Control yourself, man!*

As the colonel studied the floor-boards, he observed the appearance of dainty, bare feet facing the toes of his boots. His eyes went wide. The opponent had just entered within the boundaries of his territory.

"Richard," Georgiana stated softly, "you are dripping wet. Please take off your coat." She reached forth and began to work upon the fasteners.

"Georg... I..." Richard's hands were atop hers in a flash. Notwithstanding the coldness of his hands as they suppressed her activity, Georgiana thrilled at their touch.

Pressing her hands to his breast, the colonel negotiated, "If I change into the shirt, do you promise to keep your distance?"

He heard her answer in the affirmative, for his head remained downward with his vision fastened on their hands.

Nodding his head, he removed her hands and said, "Go over to the bed, turn to the wall, and I shall change. When he looked up into her face, she smiled gratefully to him and exclaimed, "I promise not to peek."

He stared glumly to her. "Oh, I am sure it will test your fortitude to the extreme, but I imagine you shall prevail."

Happily, Georgiana made her way to the bed and removed the remaining slip-cover from the other pillow. "Here, Richard, use this. It is not as absorbent as a towel, but it helps."

Taking the broadcloth casing from her hand, he nodded, picked up the shirt and made his way to the fire.

"You can start now. I am not looking."

"Georgiana, I shall tell you when I have completed my task."

"Oh! Very well."

What am I doing? One clasp became undone, *I am only flirting with disaster.* Another clasp parted. *What will Dr. Lowry think if he perchance finds us in this state?* Another clasp. *Better yet, how can I face Darcy?* And then another one. *Propriety be damned, my foot!*

Pulling his arms out of the coat, Richard hung it over the chair. The clank of something heavy alerted Georgiana that her cousin was now discarding his sword. Next, the colonel sat and began to remove each boot. She first heard one thud, quickly followed by another. She bit her lip and contemplated the situation behind her and thought, *His breeches will soon follow.*

There was no time to lose. Instantly, she crooked her neck over her shoulder to see Richard rising from the seat, clad only in his trousers. In rapture, she gazed upon his bare back. *He is a god!* In a matter of seconds her eyes roamed freely over the breadth of his shoulders, the slight narrowing beneath his ribs, the length of his spine, and the chiseled outline of his arms. His muscles appeared rock-solid.

Modesty made claim to Georgiana's scruples the moment she became conscious of Richard's hands gliding separately on each side of his trousers to further their removal. Without hesitation, she turned away, bit her lip, and inhaled deeply.

"Very well, Georgie, you may turn around."

She feigned indifference when turning her face towards his and acted as though nothing unusual had occurred. It took all of her strength to not gape openly at him.

Richard looked at her and debated, should he or should he not approach her. *Surely, I shall not succumb to temptation if I just sit next to her and talk.*

In an effort to keep up the pretence, Georgiana bent over and retrieved her comb to begin to untangle her tresses in the hope of gaining some semblance of composure. She was fearful, however, that the shivers of excitement which tantalized her insides would be easily discerned by Richard, thereby revealing her heightened anticipation and longing to be within his arms.

Sitting at the foot of the bed, Richard observed her begin to rake the teeth of the comb through her damp hair. The process was slow going, with intermittent starts and stops due to all the tangles which had amassed during their blustery ride.

After witnessing her struggle, the colonel asked, "I shall be happy to comb your hair for you, if you find it agreeable?"

"Oh!" Georgiana softly exclaimed. "I would find that very agreeable." Again she tried to the best of her ability to remain calm so as to not appear too forward. She handed the comb to him, and while turning around, pondered, *What would Richard think if he knew that I wished to forgo my hair altogether, and move on to loftier endeavours? Would he be scandalized to know of my secret yearnings?*

The sensations from the comb's movement felt soothing as Richard's hands accompanied the ivory teeth in its occupation. His right hand clasped the comb as his left hand held the gathered strands in place. Then, when each section was untangled, he would lovingly glide his hand over the silky path he had just smoothed.

During this activity, Richard broached the topic he was dreading. "Georgie, we have been given our orders. I shall leave for the Continent by next week's end."

She said nothing in response. His communication did not come as a shock, for she knew that his deployment was inevitable. But the reality of it brought the sting of quick tears attended by a painful constriction in her throat.

Richard was not sure she had heard, so he enquired, "Georgie, did you hear me?"

She merely nodded in answer to his query, because she knew at that moment she was incapable of speech.

The minutes then ticked away in silence, and when the aforementioned task was complete, the colonel softly exclaimed, "Voilà!" as he held the comb over her shoulder.

Georgiana expressed her gratitude while reaching for it. Suddenly, Richard asked, "Do you mind Georgie, if I use it?"

She shook her head and snatched the item from his hand. "I am sorry to say that I do mind."

Richard's brows rose until he quickly perceived her meaning. "I shall now return the favour and straighten yours."

"Um...I am not so sure..."

"I shall not take no for an answer." Bounding from the bed, Georgiana stood behind him and commenced the relaxing ministrations that he had just performed for her. The comb's repetitive movement upon his scalp was heavenly and the service that his sweet lady was imparting became too much when she spoke. "I love your hair, Richard. I love the curly wave of it and the manner in which it flips up when against your collar. I love your eyes. They are so full of life. I love your smile too, especially when you smile at me. I find your figure quite extraordinary. You are so muscular. I still want you for my husband, and I hope you still desire me for your wife."

Richard was staring in a blank fashion at the wall as she declared her sentiments. He stopped breathing. No woman had ever told him that she found him physically attractive.

Without warning, Georgiana put the comb down and began to rake her fingers through his hair. Disarmed by her declaration of attraction accompanied by the loving sensations created by her fingers, Richard was filled with unmitigated admiration for the woman whom he loved so dearly. No longer did he stop and weigh out the danger of the situation. On impulse, he reached for her hand and brought it forward to his lips. Gently at first, he bestowed the sweetest of kisses upon its palm, and then in a raspy voice he proclaimed, "I love you, Georgiana Darcy. I love you with every fibre of my being. My feelings and desires have not changed. I desire deeply to honour and cherish you to the end of my days."

Regardless of the minute detail that they were not yet married, Georgiana came around and flung herself into Richard's arms. She lay atop him and held his face betwixt her hands and cried, "Look at me when you say it, Richard. I need to know that you still want me and that you still love me. I need to see you say it."

Staring deeply into her eyes while lying beneath her, he stated, "I desire and love you, Georgie. Your love is the best thing that has ever happened to me. I adore you and shall prove it to you for the remainder of our lives. Your every desire shall be mine, your every heartache I shall feel, and your every need, I shall fulfil. My happiness is swallowed up into yours."

"Oh Richard!" she cried. "Thank you!" Her body became limp upon his as she rested her head on his neck and wept. Through her tears of joy she exclaimed, "I was so frightened that no one would come, but you came, you came!"

Richard began to stroke her head as he whispered words of endearment to her. Her pent up fears were finally released and she lifted her head once more and asked, "Would you please kiss me Richard?"

His arms were still around her as he rolled them onto their side. Looking earnestly at her he stated, "No, Georgiana, I cannot. Please realize that I have compromised you too far already."

"Then what will one kiss hurt?"

"Georgiana, your kisses should be saved for your husband. I shall not take them from you, or him."

"But you are to be my husband!"

"When I am engaged to you, then I shall kiss you so much you will cry for mercy."

"At this moment, I doubt that shall ever be a possibility."

Their noses were almost touching as they lay facing one another.

"Richard, I want to ask you something which I am afraid may hurt you or make you ashamed. I feel, however, I must ask."

He smiled and nodded for her to continue.

Looking directly into his eyes she set forth her enquiry. "Why is it you cannot kiss me in fear of damaging my reputation, but you can kiss other women, and have no regard for them whatsoever?"

His brow creased. "What has Hazel told you Georgie?"

She bit her lip but continued. "He said that you are akin to all men, that you pay for your harlots and enjoy their services. He found my letter from you and read it. He thinks you have asked for my hand in marriage, but I told him you had not."

He observed the hurt in her eyes and began to formulate his reply to the allegation placed at his door, but before he could begin, she asked one more question.

"Do you kiss women of ill repute?"

"No, I no longer take liberties with women. But yes, in my past, I have kissed women of ill repute. In fact, the only women I have ever kissed have been considered as such."

Observing him closely, as she waited for him to resume, she noticed the emotion that was welling up inside of him.

Richard's hand began to stroke Georgiana's shoulder as he commenced his narration.

"When a young man, my brother introduced me to the ways of life. He took me to establishments in London, and I did participate. He told me that all gentlemen partake of such activity and that my Grandfather Fitzwilliam was the one who had introduced him.

Then a year later, I thought I was in love at the age of eighteen to a young lady, who was younger than you are now, and I thought the lady loved me in return. I was mistaken, however, and was quite frankly crestfallen. I discovered that she had other lovers at the same time and had had many lovers before me."

Georgiana's eyes went wide. "This lady was from one of the houses of ill-repute?"

The colonel shook his head and replied, "No, she was a noble member of the gentry… a gentleman's daughter."

"Richard, you had relations with a woman who was not a paid harlot?"

"Yes, Georgie, I did most foolhardily. She became with child. I offered to marry her, but she and her father refused, claiming she could find someone of higher standing with title and fortune. I only had connections to offer."

"What about her baby? Was her reputation not ruined?"

"She terminated her confinement, and as for her reputation, I think she is known for being a loose woman, and she has yet to marry."

Georgiana appeared perplexed. "What do you mean by 'terminating her confinement'?"

"Georgie, she found someone to abort her baby, stopped it from developing within her womb."

"Oh, Richard! That is abominable!"

"Yes, I agree. At the time, Hazel scoffed at my remorse, telling me that I did not cry for the babies that were discarded by the ladies of the evening. Believe it or not Georgie, I was stunned. I had never once before considered the women with whom I associated in those establishments capable of having my child. I was that callow. After that experience, I would never again accompany my brother or other men to those houses. I never would go alone either. I have not been with another woman since."

She stared at him. He stopped his preoccupation of caressing her arm and waited for her to say something. Yet, she remained speechless.

"I suppose I have fallen in your estimation?"

"Oh never! You have risen. I fear, however, that I will have fallen from yours when I tell you that…"

Richard's heart stopped beating. He froze. *Oh please, Georgie, do not tell me my brother has harmed you!*

"Oh, Richard, I allowed George Wickham to kiss me. I was such a fool."

The colonel closed his eyes in instant relief before opening them again to look into Georgiana's once more. "No, you are not to blame. Your motives were pure. You were inexperienced, and might I add, though secretively, you were engaged."

"Yet, you will not kiss me?"

"Georgie, I have learned through sad experience that it is far better to marry than to burn. Kissing can speedily lead to union, and I, for one, will never again suffer for inappropriate passions. They will be for my wife alone. I desire to kiss you more than you can imagine, but I have given my word. I am already racked with guilt for enjoying you within my arms. I feel I have taken advantage of you far too much already."

"No, Richard, it is I who has taken advantage of you. I fear you may not come back to me, and I so want to be your wife in word and deed. If you were willing, I would gladly go to Gretna Green with you this night."

"I too have been tempted to elope, but you deserve more than that. I promise, I shall return to you, but Georgie, if you feel differently during our separation, I shall respect your wishes with no strings attached. When I come home, if you no longer feel the same, stay your distance. I shall perceive your meaning, and I shall wish you complete happiness with whomever you choose to marry."

"You would wish me happiness, even if I chose to marry Mr. Caldecott?"

Georgiana noticed the range of emotions that swept across Richard's face. At that moment, she realized he was not merely jealous over Ashton, he was deeply hurt and frightened that she might return the man's attraction.

"Oh Richard, I am so sorry. I was only teasing you. I love you. I do not love him in that way at all. He is only a friend. Will you hold me until I fall asleep?"

She read the hesitation within his eyes, but he nodded in spite of his reluctance.

He pulled back the covers and tucked her within. Then lying on top of the blanket beside her, he encircled her within his arms.

Georgiana asked emphatically, "Why must women uphold their reputations and be on constant guard when men can sally forth to indulge with women who do not worry about society's scrutiny? Why are men not branded by society for their lack of moral restraint? We must have chaperones wherever we go. If not, we are then responsible for being too forward, and therefore society condemns us and our virtue is tarnished. Why do we assume the entire burden and men none?"

Richard could detect the bitterness in her tone and he felt she had every right to feel it. He kissed her forehead and stated, "I do not know, Georgie, but one thing is certain, it should not be so. Men should strive to stay as virtuous as they expect women to be. There should not be a moral standard applied more to the one sex than the other, but probity should govern them both. In my estimation, if ever a time does come when this is the case, then this world shall be a better dwelling and shall be akin to Heaven."

Following their theoretical analysis about the dissipated ethics of the human male, the professed lovers turned their topic of conversation to themselves. Word for word, Georgiana related her experience in learning to ride again which had enabled her to no longer fear the activity. The colonel was genuinely pleased with her narrative until she expounded on Elizabeth's accident. Richard was indeed grateful that Georgie enjoyed galloping across the field, yet the additional information regarding his brother and Ashton Caldecott rubbed him the wrong way. He chose, nevertheless, to remain silent about that aspect. Instead, he rejoiced in Georgiana's success by telling her how proud he was that she had finally gained her courage in attempting to ride again. More specifically, he praised her for her bravery while riding on his horse as they had made their escape from Blackwell. Richard's expressed approval made Georgiana's happiness soar as she hugged him with all her might.

Finally parting, she enquired in earnest, "Richard, why does James despise you so?"

"I am not certain why my brother dislikes me. He has been the golden boy all of his life. Father and Grandfather Fitzwilliam have always doted on him. In fact, he seemed to be everybody's favourite while we were growing up. Hazel is an extremely competitive individual. He cannot stand to be bested by anyone, and he has never had to work or do anything against his will. One example was when he loathed his music instructor. My mother insisted that Hazel continue his lessons despite his complaints, but my father allowed him to quit and as an alternative, he made me take the lessons. Hazel thought it was a grand joke that I had to spend tedious hours practicing while he was free to hunt, ride or do whatever pastime he desired. At the time I resented it greatly, but now I can see the benefits that one derives from diligent preparation and commitment.

"The only preferential treatment I seemed to garner while growing up was from our cook Edie and from my Grandfather James when he would come for a visit. Everyone professed that I was the spitting image of my mother's father. As you know, he too was an Earl. Since I looked like him and I made him laugh with tales about my boyish adventures, he would praise me quite openly, sit me upon his knee, and go so far as to nickname me the little Earl. My mother's father likewise, doted on Darcy whenever he was at Matlock. I am sure Hazel resented the attention we received from Grandfather, but I do believe what my brother resented the most was the bond that I shared with Darcy.

"Hazel always felt your brother was too virtuous for his own good. Hence, I imagine your brother's integrity made my brother feel threatened, and when I would no longer accompany Hazel to those districts of London which cater to wealthy men, my brother, likewise, scorned me as prudish."

They talked until they were too tired to say another word, and then, when Richard was certain that Georgiana slept, he carefully removed her arms from around him and slid off the bed. Before turning to go, he picked up the pillow where his head had lain and gazed upon Georgiana's sleeping form. *Please dear Lord, let me return to her.*

The rain still beat heavily upon the roof as Richard walked over to the fire and added more wood. Next, he checked his watch. It was a quarter to four. Inspecting his cape, he determined it was sufficiently dry. Thus, with pillow and cloak, he sprawled out upon the hard floor in front of the blaze.

Despite the hardness of the floor, Colonel Fitzwilliam slept more soundly than he had in weeks. Perhaps it was his proximity to the warmth of the fire, or it could have been the warmth of a conscience void of offence, or better yet, it may have been the warmth provided from the petite shape that joined him beneath his mantle, bringing all the bed coverings in her wake. Whatever the case may have been, both Richard and Georgiana, slept soundly for the several hours before Dr. Lowry's arrival.

Each would look back at this time given them, in this one night, and would reflect frequently upon it, as they began to endure their separation and face the trials that awaited them in the prolonged months to come.

~*~

Chapter Thirty-one

Just Deserts

It was not yet seven in the morning when a carriage advanced on Brook Street, halting in front of the seventh townhouse. Mr. Charles Bingley stepped out and then turned to help his wife descend. Mr. Bingley's deportment gave the impression as he lifted the knocker on the slate-blue door that he was uncomfortable. Seconds after the loud clunks sounded, the door was answered by Mr. Coates.

At the butler's enquiry, Bingley winced slightly before requesting an audience with Mr. Darcy. The couple was immediately shown in and asked to wait in the morning room.

"Janey, I know I have asked this numerous times already, but are you quite certain?"

Jane Bingley smiled warmly at her husband and patiently reassured him yet again, "Yes, Charles, I know it."

Overwrought with worry, Darcy hastily made his way out of his wife's chamber and down the flight of steps to attend to his brother and sister-in-law. He wondered what might be the reason for Bingley's presence at such an early hour. Inwardly he feared that it might have some correlation to his sister. Colonel Fitzwilliam had not yet returned. Thus, Darcy's fears were running rampant.

"Ah! Charles and Jane, I am happy to see you this morning. To what do I owe this honour?"

Again Bingley gave a cautious expression. "I say, Darcy, we have come for a visit."

Darcy's brows lifted and a look of befuddlement soon shown upon his face.

"Um, Charles, Jane, I wish I could visit, but I must be off to court. In fact, I must leave in ten minutes' time. Was there something in particular you wish to discuss?"

Scarcely perceptible, Bingley squirmed in his chair with a lopsided expression on his face. He dreaded revealing what he knew his wife wanted him to say. "Um..."

Reaching over with her hand, Jane gave her husband a reassuring pat and then looked directly at her brother-in-law.

She stated, "Mr. Darcy... Fitzwilliam, we are here because I knew we were wanted."

Darcy blinked. What was Jane saying? "I am afraid I do not have the privilege of understanding you?"

"I am only saying that I know you need me."

"Has Elizabeth sent a note?"

"No," Jane replied with a demure smile enhancing her countenance. "This morning when I awoke, I knew you wanted me."

Darcy's vision instantly averted from Jane to Bingley. He could tell that his brother-in-law was ill at ease with his wife's conjecture.

"Jane," Darcy replied, "I am afraid I am not following you. If Elizabeth has not sent for you, I am afraid..."

Instantly, understanding dawned in Darcy's brain. "Jane, are you offering to stay with Elizabeth while I go to trial?"

"Yes, I felt you needed us."

Darcy inhaled and nodded. "I do indeed. In fact, I have been loath to depart. Colonel Fitzwilliam has not yet returned, and I feared leaving Elizabeth without his protection. My family will be undoubtedly furious when they find that Georgiana is no longer within their influence."

"Then you do wish for us to stay with Lizzy until your return?"

Staring at his sister-in-law in amazement, Darcy nodded in appreciation. "Oh yes, I thank you, Jane." *She is truly amazing!*

Bingley sat erect, smiled and then exclaimed, "Yes, we were quite certain that we were needed, and this is the reason we are here upon your doorstep at such a ghastly hour."

Jane smiled adoringly to her husband.

Darcy smiled at his friend as well. "I am indeed grateful to you both. Please do not mind the hour. I feel I can now go to the Old Bailey and not worry for Elizabeth's welfare. I find that I am in your debt, yet again. Please, make yourselves at home. You are welcome to use the library, the music room, and I shall inform Mrs. Averill that we will have guests for breakfast and luncheon. Jane, you know not what this means to me..., oh, and of course, you, too, Charles."

Bingley smiled in confidence at his friend's approval and appreciation.

"Well, I shall go and inform Elizabeth that you are here, and again, please make yourselves comfortable." Darcy stared at Jane once more before quitting the room. Both brother and sister-in-law silently communicated their shared love for the woman that each held most dear.

~*~

"Lizzy." Darcy whispered into his wife's ear.

Elizabeth began to stir from her slumber. "Hmm?" Suddenly she remembered the situation with Georgiana and her husband's court appearance and with the remembrance, a string of questions followed: "Are you leaving now? Has Richard returned? Is Georgiana safe? Is she on her way to Pemberley?"

"I am not sure. Richard has not yet returned, but the rain has stopped and the wind is strong. Therefore the roads will be in better condition for travelling. I need to leave, and I came to tell you that Jane and Bingley are here to stay with you. Evidently, your sister had a premonition that we needed her. Jane is truly amazing. I now feel at ease concerning your wellbeing while I am away."

Elizabeth sat up and stretched her arms. "Yes, Jane is amazing. I forgot to tell you she has also been given a prophetic dream that all would be well with her child. She even claims the baby is a boy and that he will look like Charles."

Darcy smiled. "Well, I would not be surprised if the child should resemble Charles, but Jane also has fair hair and blue eyes."

"So, are you saying you think my sister embellished her dream?"

"No, on the contrary, I am sure what she dreamt left her feeling joyous. But is it not the same for all of us? We all have dreams that leave us feeling happy, sad, or frightened, and yet, they never come to pass. If Jane feels that she is to have a son because of her dream, I shall not refute her belief. Yet, I would not be surprised if she gave birth to a girl either. I must be off."

"Yes, but she knew to come this morning."

Darcy leaned over and kissed Elizabeth soundly and then stated, "She is worried about you, as am I. She logically feared for your welfare, knowing that I have court and that Colonel Fitzwilliam was to rescue Georgie. I am sure she was guided by her concern, and that is what I find amazing about her. She loves you so very much. She is the best of sisters."

Elizabeth nodded thoughtfully and embraced her husband before he departed. She then rang for Sarah to prepare her bath.

~*~

Scarcely shy of thirty minutes after Darcy's departure for Old Bailey, Colonel Fitzwilliam did advance through the back alley to the stable house.

He entered Ackerley using the kitchen entrance and took the servants' stairs with the intention of going straight to his room, but not prior to asking the cook to send up hot water for his bath.

Upon reaching his chamber, the colonel divested himself of his cape, gloves, shako, and sword. Next, he took off his boots and unfastened his jacket. He knew that he would have to wait at least another ten minutes before the water was sent up. He wished that he could forsake the bath altogether and instead climb into bed and sleep the remainder of the day. The past few restless nights had ultimately caught up with him. Nevertheless, he knew that Elizabeth and Darcy would want to know about Georgiana, so he willed himself to stay awake.

While waiting, he recalled that prior to Dr. Lowry's arrival, Georgiana had asked him to retrieve from her room a letter she had written over a week ago. Quickly, he refastened his uniform and then headed for his cousin's chamber. Peeking round the door, the colonel observed that no one was about, thus, in his stocking feet, he dashed across the hall and entered Georgiana's chamber.

The colonel's agile gait led him to her vanity where the ornate jewellery box was situated. Just as Georgiana had told him, the sealed letter lay on top of her jewels and it was simply addressed to *Richard Fitzwilliam*. As he lifted it out of the box, Richard noticed that it appeared somewhat bulky and heavier than a normal missive. Letter in hand, he turned to quit the room.

Just as the colonel stepped out of Georgiana's chamber, he nearly ploughed into Elizabeth who had just exited her chamber to make her way down the corridor.

Both Richard and Elizabeth were taken aback at the other's sudden appearance.

"Oh, I am so sorry, Elizabeth. I did not mean to frighten you."

Elizabeth held her hand over her heart as she cried, "Oh, you did give me a fright, but I am so happy to see you all the same. Has everything gone according to plan? Is Georgie safe?"

The colonel could read the anxiety in Elizabeth's eyes. "Yes, Georgie is now safe. The storm forestalled Dr. Lowry and Mrs. Annesley's travel and that is why I have not returned sooner, but they are all now on their way to Derbyshire."

Richard noted an odd expression crossing Elizabeth's face before she made a reply. Her vision was fixed on the letter he held in his hand. He realized instantly that she observed his name written in Georgiana's script. Their eyes met as soon as she averted her gaze from the letter. They stared at one another for some seconds till she finally exclaimed, "Oh Richard, I am so glad to hear that Georgiana is well. Fitzwilliam has been beside himself. I shall go down immediately and send him a message to let him know of her being out of harm's way. Please join us for breakfast as soon as you can."

"Us?"

"Yes, my sister and Mr. Bingley are here."

"I see," said Richard. "I need to bathe first, and then I shall be down."

Smiling impishly at the colonel, Elizabeth nodded and turned with the intent to pen a short letter to her husband. Richard watched his cousin's wife go in contentment, receptive of her relief and the relief Darcy would soon feel. The colonel also suspected that Mrs. Fitzwilliam Darcy was intuitively aware of his and Georgiana's burgeoning romance.

~*~

Two brief lines communicated the knowledge Elizabeth was certain Darcy longed to hear: *"My love, your sister is safe and Richard is now with us. All is well."* Elizabeth signed her affection before sealing the message. She handed it to the butler and instructed him to have a footman dispatch it without delay. Then, in cheerfulness, she vacated her husband's study in search of her sister and brother-in-law.

~*~

Once again in the confines of his own chamber, Richard stripped off his jacket and went to lie on the bed to open Georgiana's letter. Upon breaking the seal, the aroma of her perfume invaded his senses bringing pleasant remembrances of holding his dear lady within his arms and smelling the exact fragrance upon her hair and skin. It was this precise scent which had greeted him just hours ago while awakening upon the floor in the cottage, encircled within his love's arms.

When unfolding the missive, a locket fell down upon his chest. He picked it up and examined it closely. It had a gold backing and hinges, covered with a glass front. A pleased smile materialized upon his face while peering into the glass and then in an instant, he opened the ornament. Georgiana had cut a lock of her golden hair and had the strands on one end plated with gold to hold them secure. Directly beneath the metal plating, her hair was plaited until bound by a thin, silken, blue ribbon. The rest of the tresses dangled loosely in a ringlet. Richard thought it was quite feminine and very appealing.

The colonel fingered the coiled strands and pressed it to his nose to take in its scent. Suddenly he recalled the missive which he swiftly unfolded.

Dear Richard,

Thank you so much for your letter. I am elated by it. It sounds as if you have been working hard. I wish I could see you while doing your drills with your men. I am sure that you are the most handsome and strongest man in our King's army!

Richard shook his head in amusement.

Well, even if you are not, you are to me! I long for the day when we are engaged, so you will kiss me till I am breathless, and I long for the day that we are wed so I can show you just how much I love you and how I desire to drive you to distraction.

Instantly, Richard's brow shot up. These sentiments, stated so bravely, surprised him to the extreme. When had Georgie gotten so... so... bold, so marked by an attractive sauciness? He was not certain of the exact moment that her explicit manner towards him began, but he knew one thing for sure, he was quite keen on it!

~*~

Bingley stood quickly when he noticed Elizabeth's entrance.

Elizabeth smiled broadly to them and stated, "I am so sorry for keeping you waiting. Colonel Fitzwilliam has just returned and he tells me all is well with Georgiana, so I have sent Fitzwilliam a missive post-haste to alleviate his concern."

Jane and Charles were delighted with the news. Elizabeth informed them that the colonel would be down shortly, but she saw no reason to delay the meal since Mrs. Averill had the meal arranged on the sideboard.

Suddenly, before they could put food upon their plates, clamorous knocking was heard coming from the vestibule. Jane, Charles, and Elizabeth eyed each other as they considered the apparent urgency of the caller. The trio blanched when they heard an explosive, familiar voice cry out, "Where is my niece? I demand that she come with me this instant! Where is my nephew? Darcy, deliver her at once or else!"

Bingley's eyes widened, as did Elizabeth's. Both brother and sister-in-law froze where they stood alongside the court cupboard with plates in hand. Jane, however, was not shocked at all. She quietly placed her china down and quit the room in search of Mr. Darcy's aunt.

Charles and Elizabeth's astonishment to the grand dame's outburst was nothing in comparison to their realization that dear Jane was walking into the lion's den. They surmised her intent was to soothe the fierce creature. After all, angels always strive to redeem every demon.

In a fluster, both brother and sister-in-law hurriedly put back their plates, anxious to save their precious Jane. As they did so, the fragile porcelain collided, shattering into pieces. Bingley immediately began to apologize.

"Ah, dear Elizabeth, I say, I am so sorry..."

"Never mind, Charles, we must see to Jane!"

Bingley grimaced and then followed his sister-in-law resolutely out of the room. His long legs pressed forward upon Elizabeth's heels towards the din of the clashing forces where the gnashing teeth of hell were being thwarted by the harmonious tones of heaven.

"Who are you? I insist that you tell me at once!"

Jane replied in calmness, "I am Mr. Darcy's sister-in-law, Mrs. Charles Bingley."

"Oh you, you are sister to that woman whom my nephew now calls his wife!"

Charles and Elizabeth rounded the corner in time to see Lady Catherine pointing her finger in Jane's face.

"Bring me my niece at once! Do you hear me girl!"

"Would you not like to come and sit down, and I shall ..."

"Jane," cried Elizabeth, "I thank you, but I am now here."

Lady Catherine peered over to Elizabeth as she came forward. She hissed through her teeth, "I demand to see my nephew this instant! I have no desire to see you or hear anything you have to say. You are a deceiving woman, a Delilah!"

"In that case, Lady Catherine, you have no reason to stay a moment longer because my husband is not here."

Lady Catherine's eyes shut tightly as her whole frame shook with wrath. Striving to appear calm, she stated in a low, sugary sweet voice, "Just send Georgiana down, and I shall gladly depart. We have been detained long enough already."

"I am indeed sorry for your ladyship's delay, but I cannot help. Your niece is not here."

"You cannot or you will not?" Lady Catherine de Bourgh's eyes were squinted while she raised her cane with the full intention of striking Elizabeth as she cried, "Send her immediately. Mr. Puttfarken awaits her in Bath!"

Just as the staff speedily descended to deliver the grand dame's striking blow, Colonel Fitzwilliam beat Bingley in shielding his cousin's wife. Narrowly sprinting in front of Elizabeth in time to deflect the stick, Richard absorbed the wallop intended for her.

When Lady Catherine perceived her nephew standing before her, she became even more enraged. She swiftly lifted the walking stick to thrash him for a second time as she screeched, "Nephew, you...you are the one!" This time, however, Richard grabbed firmly onto her cane, not allowing her to move it another inch.

"Unhand my cane, you buffoon! How dare you, Fitzwilliam! You— you who have destroyed your cousin's chances of marrying well, and have brought this misfortune upon her and ruin upon our families' names. How dare you!"

"Yes, well, Aunt Catherine, it is nice to see you too. I shall now escort you to your carriage."

Twisting the cane from her hand, Colonel Fitzwilliam then took his aunt by her arm, but she would not have it. Standing in a rigid, stubborn pose, she cried, "Unhand me you fool! I shall not leave without Georgiana! We know you have taken her. Bring her to me this instant!"

Richard slanted his head to the side, and in a matter-of-fact air, replied, "I am sorry to say she is not here. But if she were, I would never allow her to be in your company again unless you come to your senses." After his pronouncement, he began to swiftly drag her forward to the egress. Bingley rushed ahead of the colonel to open the door in grateful anticipation of the dreadful woman's exodus. The colonel thanked him in their passing.

From the open door, Elizabeth, Jane, and Charles watched the colonel lift his screaming aunt into his arms and hastily manoeuvre the steps as he carried her to the carriage. She was kicking, hitting, and screaming for the whole of the short distance. Lady Catherine's footman had opened the carriage door expecting that his mistress would not be a welcome guest. Anne sat timidly on the seat observing the scene before her in secret delight. Even though her lips betrayed no such emotion, Miss de Bourgh's eyes twinkled in merriment when they met the colonel's gaze as he deposited her distraught mother within the compartment. Before shutting the door, Richard threw the cane upon the floor.

With the door securely shut, the colonel called out while the carriage lurched forward, "Have an enjoyable stay in Bath." He then turned to re-enter the house. Elizabeth rolled her eyes as she observed the parting and closing of many curtains in the windows across the street. *Well, at least Fitzwilliam has been spared all of this. Yet, facing Mr. Hibbs could not be much better.*

~*~

Several blocks away in Grosvenor Square, Lady Matlock's maid applied the finishing touches to her mistress' coiffure when a knock was heard from the servants' door. "Come," summoned Lady Matlock.

Edie opened the door and stepped into the room. "Lady Matlock, when it is convenient, I was wondering whether I might have a word with you."

Waving her hand to dismiss her maid, the mistress replied, "Now is a good time, Edie. Maureen has just finished. Thank you, Maureen."

The maid curtseyed and quit the room.

"Oh, Edie, I am so glad you have come. I was ready to come in search of you. Has all gone well, do you know?"

"I don't rightly know right yet, ma'am, but your son, the colonel, has asked me to give you this here." The cook held out the sealed missive. "He told me to make certain you were alone when I gave it to you and that you received it by my hand."

Lady Matlock took the letter. "Edie, please tell me as soon as you hear from Doris. I am beside myself with worry. I suppose we shall find out from Lord Matlock though, before we hear from Doris. I am sure Lord Hazelton and Lady Catherine will be at our doorstep before too long if all has gone according to plan."

"Now, Lady Matlock, you know I will. Don't you worry none. Our Richard has been successful. I just feel it! He is the best of men."

Edie's praise for her youngest son brought an immediate smile upon the mistress' lips, and she reached for her dear friend's hand to squeeze it in gratitude. The two women fell into an emotional embrace before the cook lifted the hem of her apron to dry the tears from the corner of her eyes. "Well, I must be going now." Her mistress nodded as the stout woman strode from the room.

The seal was broken and the letter unfolded.

Mother,

I do not wish to alarm you with the words that I am about to pen. I will be embarking for the Continent in less than a fortnight, and while I have gone to war many times, not once have I told you how much you mean to me. I am sure in my early life, that my infant tongue has expressed the three words every mother must long to hear from their offspring. But in my maturity, I have failed to express this to you in a proper manner. I have teased you amply with my loving sentimentality and you have borne it admirably. Yet, know now that the words I write are not fraught with humour's air. I love you, Mother! I love you for carrying me in your womb and for teaching me upon your knee. I love you for directing me in the path that I was destined to follow as a second son. You have always lent me support through your gracious and sometimes stern words of encouragement, howbeit embedded in veiled humour.

You must know how grateful I am for your support at this moment of time, and I am aware of the risk you are taking with Father. You have always had my best interest at heart, and I thank you profusely. I could not wish for a better mother. My childhood eyes perceived you as the very vision of loveliness and beauty. And now, nearing my thirtieth year, my eyes still find you as such.

Before I close this communication, I would be remiss if I did not convey to you just how much you have meant to me when I have been found in the error of my ways. If not for you, I am not sure how I would have endured my failings.

Your devoted son,

Richard

Tears trickled down Lady Matlock's cheeks as a myriad of feelings coursed through her breast. She whispered aloud in the silence of her chamber, "I love you too, my son… I love you, too."

A loud knock on her chamber door roused her from her reflections. She wiped away the tears with her fingertips then hurriedly put away her son's letter before answering.

"Come in."

The door swung open wide and the Earl entered with a pained expression upon his face.

"Adeline, how could you?"

"That is the same question which I have been respectively asking myself about you, Winnie. How could you?"

~*~

Fitzwilliam Darcy strode into his London residence in high spirits. The trial had been successful in finding Mr. Hibbs guilty and his cousin had been successful in rescuing his sister.

When entering his home, Mr. Darcy was greeted by his butler. The master asked him where he could find Mrs. Darcy. Mr. Coates pointed him in the direction of the music room.

Upon entering the room, Darcy paused on the threshold when he noticed that every single occupant was taking a midday sleep except for Colonel Fitzwilliam, whom by the looks of it, had scarcely arisen from his own catnap. While Richard was silently stretching his arms in the air, he too noted that Bingley, Elizabeth and Jane were still resting. Suddenly, from the corner of his eye, the colonel observed Darcy's presence, and when turning to look fully upon him, he became conscious, by the way his cousin motioned with his hand, that Darcy wanted him to quit the room. This he instantly did as quietly as possible.

Both men walked the length of the corridor to the study, and when the door was shut, Darcy immediately barraged Richard with questions.

His cousin answered each and every one to Darcy's entire satisfaction except for the possibility of the footman being dead. Richard shrugged his shoulders and admitted that he did not stop to find out if that were the case. Darcy responded with a glum frown, shrugging his shoulders and shaking his head with understanding.

After Darcy had exhausted all of queries, he asked Richard to give a full account of their escape. Whilst the colonel rendered each detail, he comprehended the flush appearing on Darcy's face due to his cousin's mounting anger.

"Why did you not kill him?"

"Georgie would not allow it. She stood in front of the scoundrel and held her hand upon my sword, swearing that I would have to slice her palm if I chose to do so."

Darcy rolled his eyes and shook his head in disbelief.

"Another detail you might find interesting is some enlightening information about the identity of the reliable source." Darcy's brows rose in expectation.

Richard then revealed to Darcy what Georgiana had told him concerning Caroline Bingley's assertions.

"Richard, you know that is a damnable lie! Elizabeth would never tell Miss Bingley about Georgiana's near elopement."

"Yes, I know, and I told Georgie the same thing sans the expletive. Yet, that woman had to have gotten her information somewhere, and I think it best you find out where before you leave for Pemberley."

"Blast!" Darcy cried as he threw his hands in the air. "Just when I felt everything was wrapping up quite nicely, then there is this! I detest speaking with Caroline Bingley, and I am certain I shall not be able to maintain my composure. If she is the one who went to Elisha, she shall be banned from Ackerley and Pemberley for as long as I live, and I shall specifically declare in my last will and testament that she shall not be allowed even after my death."

"Well Darce," Richard said with mild sarcasm, "that is indeed a very long time, to be sure." A flippant smile graced the colonel's lips.

"Ah! This may be a laughing matter to you, Fitzwilliam, but not to me."

Becoming serious once more, Richard stated, "No cousin, I too want to see Miss Bingley brought to justice. Her mischief has unquestionably cost us all dearly."

"Well, there is no time like the present. I shall go to the only other person whom I know is aware of this and may have, for some unforeseeable reason, told Miss Bingley about Georgiana."

"Darcy, may I ask of whom you speak?"

"Mrs. Jane Bingley."

~*~

The two cousins walked back into the music room to find all three of its occupants awake and in cheerful spirits. Darcy hated himself for what he felt he must do.

Elizabeth's face brightened when she realized that her husband had returned. "Fitzwilliam, how did the proceedings go at court?"

Darcy answered her in a nonchalant attitude. "Mr. Hibbs has been found guilty of attempted murder and in a fortnight the man will hang with eleven others from the platform of Newgate's 'new drop'."

Elizabeth gasped.

"What Lizzy, are you not pleased?"

"Why, I am not sure. I suppose I am thinking about Sally and how she will feel."

"Yes, well, it is a sad affair, to be sure."

Just when Darcy was to embark on questioning Jane, Richard piped up, "This is my last free evening. I would very much like to go to the theatre. Would anyone else be partial to passing away the evening in such a fashion?"

Darcy frowned while Bingley nodded eagerly and spiritedly expressed, "I say, that sounds splendid!"

"Yes," Elizabeth cried, "since we leave tomorrow, I too would enjoy such an evening. Jane, what is your opinion?"

"Well, I think that would be very agreeable if Mr. Dar...Fitzwilliam is in accord, for I fear he is somewhat troubled."

All eyes instantly turned to Darcy. Elizabeth could now see that her husband was indeed uneasy, for he now wore a surprised expression upon his face. Without a moment's hesitation, he crossed the room to where Jane sat on a divan and crouched before her. Taking her hand in his, he asked in all gentleness, "Jane, I am troubled. I have been informed that Miss Bingley has told my sister some disturbing facts with which only certain people are familiar. I need to know, Jane, if you have ever divulged to Caroline that Georgiana had nearly eloped with George Wickham at Ramsgate and if you were privy to Elizabeth being blackmailed by Wickham? Do not fear, I shall not be angry if you have. I know you would only divulge such a thing if you had found it truly necessary."

"Oh, dear brother, know that I have never told a soul, not even Charles."

"Good Gracious Heavens!" Bingley exclaimed, "Darcy, what has my sister done?"

Darcy then asked Richard to provide all the particulars of his conversation with Georgiana. After hearing the colonel's remarks, Elizabeth exclaimed forthrightly, "Fitzwilliam, I have never told Miss Bingley such a thing. You do believe me, do you not?"

"Yes Lizzy," Darcy stated wearily, "that element of the story was never in question."

"Darcy, I promise I shall get to the bottom of this!"

"Thank you, Bingley, but I fear that I need to speak with your sister myself, of course, in your presence."

"Most certainly, just name when you desire it to be, and I shall arrange the meeting."

"I hate to ask this of you, Charles, but now is when I desire to speak with her."

"We can leave straightaway."

Richard spoke up. "Darcy, do you desire my assistance as well?"

"Yes, I should like you to come if you feel up to it."

"If Bingley does not mind, I shall be glad to be of help in any way that I can."

"You are most welcome, Colonel Fitzwilliam."

Richard nodded in acknowledgment to Bingley's offer.

"I shall come as well." cried Elizabeth.

"I, too, shall come," cried Jane. The rest of the party gawked in disbelief as she continued. "I feel if Caroline is at fault, she will more than likely be grateful for the occasion to confess her wrongs to all and thereby become a better person in so doing. In fact, she might inwardly desire this precise opportunity."

Elizabeth and Darcy initially shared knowing glances with each other and instantly reciprocated the same look in Richard's and Bingley's eyes. Jane was ever the guardian angel for the whole of humanity.

~*~

The party of five convened in the Bingley's drawing room. Mr. Bingley had requested his butler to inform his sister to join them as soon as possible.

When Drusilla told her mistress she was wanted, Caroline rolled her eyes. What could her brother desire now that could not wait? Miss Bingley was not made privy, however, to the other guests in attendance. She asked her maid to tell her brother that she would be down directly.

Darcy was pacing back and forth in front of the room's windows while the others chatted genially about the production they were venturing to see that evening at the theatre. While walking to and fro, Darcy noticed a carriage stop in front of his brother-in-law's townhouse. He stopped his nervous preoccupation and stood still to regard who would emerge from it.

Turning to look upon the group, he stated dryly, "Bingley, Mr. and Mrs. Hurst are upon your doorstep." Everyone's attention was drawn in by the intelligence of the new addition to their party, but before the butler announced the Hursts, Kitty and Mr. Burns strolled into the room. Colonel Fitzwilliam and Bingley stood immediately.

Elizabeth's eyes widened, for she could clearly see from her younger sister's dreamy look just how smitten she was with Mr. Bingley's handsome cousin. Quickly, Lizzy looked at Jane who returned her sister's surprised look with one of pleasure. Once again, Elizabeth peered over to the couple now speaking to the colonel. Yes, she could tell that Mr. Burns was just as besotted with her sister as Kitty was with him. A large smile materialized as Elizabeth considered, *oh my, will our mother's nerves be able to manage another daughter being wed within the same year?*

"Mr. Bingley," stated the butler, "Mr. and Mrs. Hurst are here."

"Oh," cried Bingley, "by all means send them in."

In a matter of seconds, Darcy crossed the room to where Charles was sitting. He bent over his brother-in-law's shoulder and whispered in his ear. Instantly, Bingley nodded his head and then leaned over to his wife and in a low voice informed her that he, Darcy, and Colonel Fitzwilliam would speak to Caroline alone with Louisa being the only other person present. Jane nodded in understanding.

Elizabeth watched them in curiosity, longing to know what they were saying. When she was able to catch her husband's eye, he gave her a reassuring look by smiling at her in that special way that only he could.

As Louisa and Hurst entered the room, Mr. Hurst exclaimed, "Ah, you have a whole house full."

"Yes," Bingley cried as he stood along with Mr. Burns and Colonel Fitzwilliam.

This was the first time that Elizabeth had seen Louisa since her wedding. Her expectant girth was not completely concealed by the fashion of her dress, and Lizzy noted that she appeared radiant and seemed genuinely happy. While observing her, Bingley stepped into her line of vision to say something in his sister's ear. Whatever he said had an immediate effect upon his sister. Her happy expression turned into one of dismay, yet she nodded to Bingley and then said a few words in her brother's ear. Elizabeth witnessed a glum expression crossing Charles's features.

Colonel Fitzwilliam spoke up and asked the Hursts if they would like to attend the theatre this evening. He indicated they were all going and even Mr. Burns and Miss Bennet had just decided to attend as well. They accepted the offer, stating they had gone the previous evening, but would be glad to review it again. They raved about the superior performing of the actors and vowed that they were sure everyone would enjoy it. Mr. Burns began to tell when he had seen the same play performed in Scarborough. It was during this juncture that Darcy inclined his head towards Colonel Fitzwilliam's and Elizabeth noticed that he too nodded in sobriety.

Bingley took the opportunity to speak at the first break in conversation. "Jane has ordered tea, and if you will please excuse me, I have some matters to discuss with my sister, Darcy, and the colonel. We shall be back directly."

From across the room, Elizabeth questioned Jane with her eyes. Jane stood and made her way to where her sister sat.

"Before you go, Bingley," cried Hurst, "do you mind if I forgo tea for something a little stronger?"

Charles turned, before crossing the threshold, and stated, "Oh please, have whatever you wish."

Louisa said something to her husband as he poured himself some port. The only acknowledgement or reply that Mr. Hurst gave to his wife was a grunt accompanied by a shrug. She then followed her brother and the other gentlemen out of the room.

If Mr. Burns and Kitty considered the behaviour of the party odd, they did not show it. Instead, they were sequestered in a corner of the room, each quite content to be in the exclusive company of the other.

~*~

Bingley suggested that they would wait in the entrance hall for his sister to descend. This was agreed upon by all. Bingley, Louisa, and the colonel preferred to sit on the divans against the wall, but Darcy was too tense. Therefore, he chose to stand. Richard witnessed his cousin's restlessness. One moment Darcy would lean against the wall with his arms folded and the next he would shift his stance by unfolding them and fidgeting with his ring.

It was not too long before they heard Miss Bingley's footsteps upon the stairs. All heads turned as she descended. She likewise detected her brother, sister, Colonel Fitzwilliam, and Darcy staring at her while she proceeded. A paralyzing chill ran up her spine. Caroline knew something was amiss. Her eyes flew directly to Louisa's as if to ask the meaning of their collective presence, yet Louisa avoided her sister's penetrating gaze.

Charles walked forward to meet her as she stepped onto the floor. "Caroline," he stated gently, "We wish to speak to you in my study."

Bingley could see the flash of fear in her eyes, but she raised her chin high and remained speechless, nodding her acquiescence.

Silently, all individuals marched down the corridor to Bingley's study. To Colonel Fitzwilliam, the grave expressions their faces bore while they advanced, combined with the laborious comportment of their gaits, reminded him of the ceremonial protocol akin to a military tribunal of execution. The mournful, reverberating roll of drums was the only missing component.

Gesturing for everyone to sit, Bingley shut the door and turned to look at the lot of them. "Caroline," he stated softly, "some rather serious incriminating information has been imparted to Colonel Fitzwilliam concerning your involvement in instigating a sad affair for Miss Darcy. I am sure you know to what I am referring?"

With her chin held high, Caroline feigned ignorance. Charles sighed, fearful that this would indeed be her response. Thus, he began to present the particulars when Darcy cut him off.

"Miss Bingley, did you or did you not tell my sister that Elizabeth informed you about her near elopement with George Wickham?"

Caroline's one eye twitched ever so slightly. Darcy's tone unnerved her, yet she strived to maintain her composure. "Yes, I did. The morning of the hunt at Pemberley, Eliza became distraught over your preferential treatment of Miss Caldecott. In a moment of great anxiety, she broke down and wept to me how she could not mange as Mistress of Pemberley. She confessed that it was beyond her scope and that you were not happy with her."

Colonel Fitzwilliam's eyes almost popped from his head. He could not believe that this woman would think that anyone in their right mind could entertain any veracity to her outlandish claims. Peering at his cousin, Richard surmised that Darcy was doing all in his power to remain calm.

"Miss Bingley, what have I ever done to deserve such a treacherous assault from you? You have made my wife and sister, whom I hold most dear, open to ridicule from my family, and fairly likely, by the ton. Even if you hate Elizabeth, you have thought nothing of my defenceless sister, for whom at one time you had sworn an undying affection."

Every soul in the room was silent. No one looked at the other. All eyes were fastened downward except Darcy's and Caroline's.

In a choked voice, Darcy asked once more, "Pray, tell me, what I have done to deserve this from you? Have I not always been a most attentive and an amenable host in my home and elsewhere?"

Caroline could no longer meet his intense gaze. Instead, she declined her head and whispered, "I was doing what was in the best interest of Georgiana."

"What!" cried Darcy. "Have you gone insane? Since when have you the right to take on my sister's concerns?"

"Well, someone had to think of her best interest since you had lost the ability to do so."

"Caroline," entreated Louisa, "Tell them now, or I will."

Miss Bingley looked up sharply at her sister and shot daggers towards her.

"Very well," Louisa stated, "I shall do it for you."

"I swear, Louisa, if you do, I shall never have anything to do with you again."

"My dear sister, those are strong words from a woman who will soon be friendless."

Lifting her chin even higher, Caroline stated in triumph, "Elisha and I had Georgiana's best interest at heart, and if you cannot see that, then you are completely selfish."

A loud snort of derision was heard from Colonel Fitzwilliam across the room.

"Mr. Darcy," cried Mrs. Hurst, "Your wife has never divulged any personal information to my sister..."

Caroline quickly stood and screamed for her sister to be quiet, yet Louisa continued in haste.

"While Elizabeth walked into Lambton, Caroline entered her study and went through your wife's private accounts and read her personal missives."

Through her teeth, Caroline hissed her sister's name even as Bingley exclaimed, "Caroline, have you gone stark raving mad!"

Darcy arose from his chair. "I shall see myself out, Bingley. Please dine with us tonight before we depart for the theatre. I trust you shall impart my request of restriction to Miss Bingley."

Bingley's expression was pained when he made his reply. "I most certainly will, Darcy. We shall see you 'tis even."

Quickly, Darcy and Colonel Fitzwilliam quit the room. Louisa and Charles then turned their full attention towards their sister. Defiantly, Caroline announced that she would be gone for the evening visiting a friend. As she opened the door to leave, Bingley called after her, "Caroline,

Darcy wishes you to never again darken the threshold of Ackerley or Pemberley."

Caroline stopped momentarily when hearing her brother utter Mr. Darcy's repudiation, but she contrived an apathetic posture, squaring her shoulders and keeping her head high. As she stepped into the hall, her brother declared further, "This shall not be the only consequence, for you are mistaken if you think that I shall sit tight. Your true colours have been revealed. Thus, I shall sleep on it tonight, but tomorrow I shall indeed settle your hash."

For the second time in Caroline Bingley's life she felt a sinking feeling within the pit of her gut. The former instance was when Fitzwilliam Darcy had unreservedly announced his engagement to Miss Elizabeth Bennet.

~*~

The group enjoyed the light hearted performance of Shakespeare's *A Midsummer Night's Dream.* The Hursts, with Miss Bennet and Mr. Burns, departed in the Bingley's carriage while the remainder of the party waited for the Darcy's carriage to be brought forth. Darcy helped Elizabeth and Jane ascend the step. Bingley followed his wife, then Richard, and lastly Darcy entered.

The streets were overflowing with the horde of people who were still pouring out of the theatre's lobby. As the driver guided the horses forward, he used caution. It would be slow going for the next quarter of an hour. Elizabeth began to regale some of her favourite lines from the play, making Charles laugh and Jane smile brightly. Darcy looked upon his wife with pleasure and observed her eyes sparkling in gaiety.

Sitting across from his cousin, Colonel Fitzwilliam vaguely took in their laughter since he was absentmindedly peering out the window, mentally calculating all that needed to done before leaving for the Continent. While thus preoccupied, he suddenly detected his brother and Ashton Caldecott cavorting in the alley with two women. In an instant, the colonel reached for Darcy's cane and rapped it vigorously upon the roof. When hearing the thuds, Darcy turned to look at his cousin, who by now was exiting the carriage. Both Darcy and Elizabeth beheld simultaneously the Viscount's arm draped around the shoulders of a very scantily clad woman. In an effort to take hold of her husband's coat, Elizabeth strained but failed. She called after him, but it was too late. Over her voice, Darcy gave the directive for Bingley to stay put and then they heard him mumble some instructions to the driver.

Bingley witnessed the look of terror in his sister-in-law's eyes as the horses pulled forward, yet he knew he was of no use to her. Jane, however, crossed over and sat beside Elizabeth and gathered her within her embrace. "Oh, Jane!" cried Elizabeth.

Richard and Darcy waited a few seconds until their view was concealed from the back window of the carriage. Then the cousins merely nodded to one another remaining silent. Each strode purposefully towards the darkened alley.

Both men cautiously rounded the corner of the alleyway. Providentially for the cousins, Lord Hazelton and Ashton's backs were turned away from them as they entered. Instinctively, Darcy approached James while Richard singled out Mr. Caldecott. In a trice, the colonel tackled Ashton from behind and speedily slammed him against the brick wall. The woman who was walking beside him let out a blood curdling scream. Given that James was a few paces ahead of his friend, at the sound of the cry, he whirled himself and the lady he was escorting just in time to detect Darcy's advance.

Reaching quickly inside his breast pocket, Lord Hazelton retrieved a flick knife, flung open its blade, and then grabbed the harlot beside him by the neck. "I warn you Darcy if you come closer I shall kill her." The woman screamed, but when the Viscount pressed the blade to her throat, terror smothered her cries.

"Pfft!" Darcy spit out. "I should have known you would revert to cowardice."

"I am not afraid of you. It is *you* who should be frightened of me."

Rolling his eyes, he retorted, "Hazel, you are the last person in the world of whom I would ever be frightened. Now, let the lady go, and we shall handle this between ourselves."

"I warn you Darcy, if I do let her go, the odds are against you. You already have one foot in the grave. Better for me then, that way I may finish having my way with your *country hoyden*." The Viscount's expression manifested his depraved triumph.

No longer did Darcy care about the dangerous situation before him. Lord Hazelton's taunt had only added fuel to what was already a raging fire. Thus, the scuffle began. In uncontainable anger, Darcy lunged forth in an effort to seize his cousin's arm that held the knife. Lord Hazelton thwarted the assault by hurling the prostitute into Darcy's chest, sending them both sprawling upon the ground. The Viscount, however, did not stay around to witness his priggish cousin lying on his backside with the lady of the night atop of him. Instead, he fled in haste, hell-bent to depart.

The fall had momentarily knocked the breath out of Darcy, but when he was able to take in air, he became conscious of the woman lying on him and blubbering in fright. He could also discern Ashton Caldecott's voice begging Richard to stop.

Ever so gently, did Darcy say, "I am sorry about this, ma'am, um...if you will just allow me to shift us this way." Putting his arms around her with embarrassment, he attempted to roll on his side, yet she wailed. The Master of Pemberley groaned from within, *Oh, dear Heavens!*

"Why Darcy, I see you have your hands full." Darcy looked up to see Richard's smiling face bent over his. He frowned at his cousin. Colonel Fitzwilliam chuckled and began to help the distressed woman.

"Very well, come my dear lady," soothed the colonel as he helped the woman off of his cousin. "There you are, Miss, are you at all harmed?" The woman shook her head and then ran from their presence. Richard offered his hand to Darcy and pulled him to his feet. He then noticed the knife lying on the ground. He picked it up and turned to look at Ashton Caldecott who was still crouched in a withdrawn position against the wall. His face had been bloodied and his eyes quite swollen, yet the younger man met Colonel Fitzwilliam's darkened gaze.

Waving the knife in the air, Richard exclaimed as his eyes bore into Mr. Caldecott's, "It is your blessed day, Mr. Caldecott, for I am feeling generous. I shall give you exactly three seconds to get out of my sight or I will happily change you from a stud to gelding with one slash of the blade."

Darcy witnessed Ashton's eyes widen despite the swelling as he watched him scramble to his feet and limp hastily away.

Darcy then looked to Richard and stated, "It seems you have fared much better than I."

"Not really, Cousin. Not once did he strike me back. I should have stopped after I bloodied his nose, but I could not help myself."

Wearily, the cousins began to walk out of the alley to catch up to their carriage which was waiting two blocks away as Darcy had instructed the driver.

When they entered, not a single word was spoken by anyone. Bingley, Jane and Elizabeth eyed them closely. Darcy appeared unscathed, for which Elizabeth was grateful, but the colonel's hands showed signs of his blood-spattered encounter.

~*~

The Viscount entered his chamber in irritableness. Tonight was the first time he had left his house since his face had been injured. His valet came to disrobe him. The man knew that something was amiss with his master since he had returned earlier than expected, and he was not his usually jovial self from having spent an evening with the ladies about town.

Before the valet quit the room, he informed his Lordship that a missive had arrived earlier in the evening and he had placed it on the side table by his bed. Lord Hazelton nodded. His servant handed him a warm brandy.

While sipping the fiery liquid, Hazelton momentarily thought about going in to Elisha, but then he thought again. She had been so angry over Elizabeth that she swore to never allow him in her bed again. Besides, he was fed up with begging. Thus, he nursed his drink as he sat on his bed contemplating his pitiful existence. His eyes fell on the parchment and a sudden chill ran through his burning chest. It was Richard's handwriting. Hazelton glared when reading the letter's appellative: *The Dishonourable Lord Hazelton.*

He swallowed the remaining liquor, set the glass down, and stared at the letter for some time. Drawing in a deep breath, he reached for it and then broke the seal. The message was short, but to the point.

Hazel,

You had better hope that I die in the war, for if I do not, I shall surely come back and kill you!

____th Foot, Lieut.-Col. The Honourable Richard Fitzwilliam

Lord Hazelton dropped the offending communication upon the bed, then hastily stood and crossed the room to pour another brandy. He knew his brother was not bluffing. Instantly, he marched to the bed, picked up the aberrant letter and threw it into the fire. He desired to completely banish it and his brother from his thoughts. Then, in a split second, he realized the missive might be vital evidence which could be used in a court of law. Thus, in haste he squatted in front of the blaze to remove it. Several times in rapid succession did the Viscount put forth his hand to snatch the parchment from the flames only to have his fingers scorched during his last attempt.

Instantly, he pulled back his burned hand and shouted, "**Damn!**" The missive rapidly reduced to ashes before his eyes, but the sworn threat from his brother was seared deeply into Lord Hazelton's terrified heart, and the disquieting dread produced therein would linger for countless months to come.

~*~

Coming in 2010

A Marriage Worth

the

Earning

Volume II

~~For Better for Worse~~

Chapter One

Hopeful Prospects

A noble equipage bearing no crest had just entered the park and began to make its way through Pemberley's beautiful woods. Enclosed within, were the master and mistress of the estate. It was an hour before sunset. Thus, the evening rays filtered through the branches of the trees making divergent patterns of light and dark upon the road leading to the Great House. Even though Elizabeth's eyes were closed as she rested her head against the plush upholstered panel within the compartment, she was not entirely asleep.

Darcy sat across from his sweet wife, scrutinizing her every feature. She was lovely beyond compare, yet the master was anything but content with their present circumstances. He and his dear wife were again experiencing marital discord. The coldness of their bed was a testimonial to the fact that his wife was indeed angry. She had kept a cold back to him for the past two nights.

Mrs. Darcy had, in no uncertain terms, related her displeasure to her husband for what she considered reckless behaviour on his part, when two nights prior, he and Colonel Fitzwilliam barrelled out of the carriage in pursuit of Mr. Caldecott and Lord Hazelton. She had clearly stated that his actions were selfish and insensible. He had given his word, and she had reminded him most emphatically that their decisions in dealing with the Viscount were to be joint ones. What was he thinking by being so impulsive, by taking matters into his own volition without any thought about their previous agreement and her feelings in the matter? He could have been killed, and for what, the mere sweetness of retribution? With all her might, she strived to sway him to admit he was in error's way and exact a promise that he would never again act so injudiciously.

Darcy would not capitulate to Elizabeth's reasoning or demands. He allowed her to have her full say, even listening with rapt attention to all of her assertions amidst her vexations, but he begged to differ in opinion, stating in a matter-of-fact manner, that as the patriarch of their home, he had inherent rights to protect and to safeguard his family. Hence, he maintained that in all likelihood, he would continue to do all within his power to defend both her and his sister to his utmost. In this, he was determined. Darcy released a sigh and leaned back and closed his eyes.

He knew Elizabeth was aware of his discontent for she had told him repeatedly in their many arguments that ensued. She was exasperated with his tenacity in their quarrels, or so she had said. She held private reservations concerning his method in his dealing with Caroline Bingley. Again, she felt he should have consulted her before his pronunciation of Miss Bingley's fate. She was not of the opinion that Caroline should *not* be chastised. Quite the contrary, but she was frustrated to the extreme that he had chosen to confer about the matter with Richard instead of herself, a matter which involved her directly. But his discord with his wife was not all that plagued the master. There was another matter of great import.

At the inn, where they had stayed the evening before, an express had arrived from Dr. Lowry. The doctor related that Miss Darcy and Mrs. Annesley were safe within the confines of Pemberley. His sister wished to go straight to her home instead of staying with his grandparents, Sir Henry and Lady Newedgate. When reading the communication, Darcy bristled at his sister's insolence in not following the original plan, but his irritation was soon laid to rest when considering her safety and the success of everyone who had been drawn into the whole affair. They had ascertained in a short missive from Edie to her sister Doris, that the footman at Blackwell was not dead. Instead, the substantial blow he received from Miss Doris Barnes's hand had not brought on rigour mortis as they had feared, but had only rendered him with a concussion and a rather nasty bump on the back of his head.

Darcy noted that the carriage had just begun to make the gradual ascent which led to the top of the eminence where the woods ceased and Pemberley House could then be seen in all of her glory. It was the customary habit for the driver to rein in the horses and pause on this location until the master signalled for him to continue. He debated in awakening his wife to enjoy the view with him. Considering the emotional strain of their journey, he was not exactly sure if Elizabeth even desired to be married to him let alone view their ancestral home together. Despite Darcy's reservations about awakening his wife, in his keenness for their shared delight to be home once more, he crossed over to the opposite seat and whispered into her ear, "Lizzy, my love, we are home. Do you wish to look upon the house before I have Crockett continue?"

Elizabeth's eyelids fluttered opened from her slumber and momentarily forgetting the animosity which she had coddled towards her husband for the previous two days, she exclaimed radiantly, "Oh yes, I love seeing Pemberley from this spot." Anxiously, she inclined her head to peer out the window.

The pure delight which shone in Elizabeth's eyes as she pored over the grand edifice and the surrounding grounds was easily perceived by Darcy. His vision fleetingly took in the handsome stone edifice which had greeted him from this perspective far too many times to number. Now, however, the image that arrested his delight was not the viewing of the structure which tied him to generations of his forebears, but in its place was the appreciation of Elizabeth's countenance that moved and captivated him. The pleasure that he derived from bringing her so much pleasure was immeasurable.

While she continued to observe the vista before her, he in turn looked intently upon her. He loved her more than any mere words could do justice, more even than his body was able to convey during their lovemaking. She was now the essence of his world and all was contingent upon her happiness.

After having gazed upon the house and grounds to her entire satisfaction, Elizabeth averted her vision, meeting her husband's stare of admiration. She suddenly became self-conscious of the paradox before them. She was now joyful despite the remembrance that she had been out of spirits with him. Her doze had left her feeling refreshed and the mere sight that they were finally home from the confinement of London did much to lighten her mood. Besides, she could never stay angry for too long. It was not in her nature. After all, she reasoned, maybe being away from town and all of the family dissension would help to bring alleviation from her current grievances towards her wonderful husband. She loved him dearly.

They stared at one another for some moments before Darcy rapped his cane upon the roof. He risked bringing on her ire again by asking, "Am I forgiven, Lizzy?"

She pursed her lips to the side and rolled her eyes. "I suppose I must, seeing that we are now home. Georgiana awaits us, and the servants are about, so I suppose I must. But..."

Darcy's face effused with delight in taking in her playful manner. He raised his brow and asked roguishly, "But what?"

In an instant, Elizabeth's merriment drained from her face and with a quivering voice she stated, "You must promise me that you will think about my sentiments in all your undertakings. Truly Fitzwilliam, I am beside myself with worry that you shall be killed while..." Her voice broke and she began to weep in earnest.

Quickly, Darcy pulled her into his arms. His heart was torn as he whispered, "Oh, Lizzy, I love you, and I am so sorry that my rashness has caused you such fear and torment. I have acted abominably."

Elizabeth blubbered, "Then you admit that you are in the wrong and acted impetuously?"

"I admit that I was unthinking by not taking into account your feelings when I exited the carriage, but Elizabeth, I cannot guarantee that I would not do so again if another such incident occurred. I cannot promise something which I know in all reality that I cannot keep. Would you have me be a man who says what you want to hear and then go along my merry way, never considering my professed convictions?"

Elizabeth's crying had lessened as she stated in a subdued tone, "No, I would not. I suppose we shall forever be at odds in our opinions."

"On some perhaps, but on many others we see eye to eye." He tilted her chin up to look into her tearful countenance and smiled lovingly upon her.

Meeting his gaze, her face crinkled in submission and she choked out, "I love you so much, Fitzwilliam."

His brow furrowed as he took into her pitiful expression and gently wiped away her tears with his fingertips. Instantly, Darcy's lips made claim to his wife's. Their kiss was fuelled by the desire to reaffirm their love one to the other.

The carriage had stopped, but its occupants were oblivious to the fact. Georgiana waited patiently on the steps, as did the footman positioned beside the door, ever ready if the master so desired.

The minutes ticked away.

Periodically, Miss Darcy would look at the toes of her shoes, then to the sky, then down the road before arresting her vision back upon the carriage door. Shifting from foot to foot, she was restless for her brother and sister-in-law to emerge. What was taking so long? Abruptly, she met the footman's eyes and then and there, she squared her shoulders and advanced.

Reaching to take the handle of the door, she glanced at the servant once more. His eyes widened at the young miss's audacity, yet he remained speechless. Who was he to tell a Darcy what they should or should not do?

Miss Darcy took in his look of surprise. Thus, she deliberated. Looking back at the man, she bit her lip and then grasped the latch. The footman's eyes went even wider while he instinctively shook his head. But alas, it was too late. The door was opened and Miss Darcy's eyes enlarged from the passionate exchange before her.

To be continued...

Mary L. Sherwood is an ardent admirer of Jane Austen. She was born in Lynwood, California. Her family later moved to Conway, Arkansas where she has lived since the age of four. She attended the University of Central Arkansas, earning a BA degree in English. She currently resides on her family farm in rural Arkansas with her husband and two of their four children.

3208856

Made in the USA